A MONUMENTAL NOVEL ABOUT AN ORDINARY MAN FOR WHOM DESTINY CHOSE AN EXTRAORDINARY LIFE

"He was a figure of truly heroic proportions, a man of great energy and intellect with the moral as well as the physical courage to try to change all our worlds."

THE VICAR OF CHRIST

"A BRILLIANT NOVEL, THOUGHT-PROVOKING AND COMPELLING FROM FIRST TO LAST."

—*King Features Syndicate*

"One of the most engrossing, eye-opening achievements in fiction in recent years . . . brilliantly written and spell-binding as a story . . . an old-fashioned novel in the best sense, blessed with a hero larger than life."

—*Yonkers Herald Statesman*

"DISTINCTIVE, AMBITIOUS IN SCOPE AND ENTERTAINING."

—*Library Journal*

THE VICAR OF CHRIST

"NO READER CAN FAIL TO BE STIRRED BY ITS CONTEMPORANEITY, ITS INTELLECTUAL POWER . . . THE MOST FORMIDABLE ENTRY I HAVE READ IN YEARS."

—*John Barkham Reviews*

THE VICAR OF CHRIST

"An astonishing and provocative novel . . . about power and its relationship to justice in three areas: war, government, and religion . . . full of ideas, arguments, events, mysteries that shape Walsh and those around him. Murphy's characters are impressively realized; his style is sophisticated. Critics will be arguing this one, as will readers. It's not easy going, but the rewards are deep and heady."

—*Publishers Weekly*

THE VICAR OF CHRIST

"Most courageous of all is Mr. Murphy's determination to re–state in modern, indeed, sophisticated terms, without sentimentality or doctrinal emphasis, the most ancient of evangels: that if we are to save ourselves, love and justice must be held out to all men."

—*The Book-of-the-Month Club News*

THE VICAR OF CHRIST

"HATS OFF TO WALTER MURPHY . . . A TOUR DE FORCE OF EPIC LENGTH . . . A BOOK OF IDEAS AS WELL AS FICTION, OF INFORMATION, TEACHING. IT DEMANDS PATIENCE AND ENDURANCE . . . BUT THOSE WHO LAST THE DISTANCE WILL FIND IT VERY MUCH WORTH THE TRIP."

—*The Critic,* Chicago

Walter F. Murphy won a Distinguished Service Cross for his service as a Marine in Korea. Now the McCormick Professor of Jurisprudence at Princeton, he is the author or co–author of nine books on politics. In THE VICAR OF CHRIST, his first novel, Mr. Murphy fashions his vast knowledge of contemporary institutions into a modern novel of great magnitude. It is the story of Declan Walsh whose driving ambition and quiet love for humanity set in motion a quest for justice that reaches the highest circles of human society. Breathtaking in scope, here is a novel that cannot fail to touch the heart—and make a lasting impact.

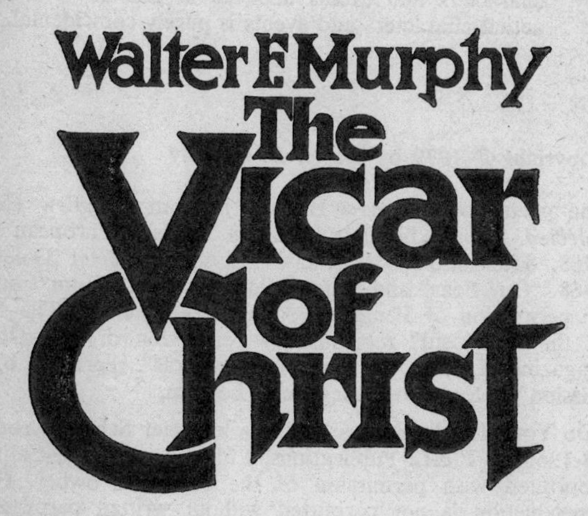

BALLANTINE BOOKS • NEW YORK

This is a work of fiction. Any similarity between characters and events depicted in this novel and actual characters and events is purely coincidental.

The poetry of Zbigniew Herbert is from *Zbigniew Herbert: Selected Poems,* London: Penguin Modern European Poets, 1968. Translation © Czeslaw Milosz and Peter Dale Scott 1968. "Our Fear" and "King Midas Does Not Hunt" reprinted by permission of Penguin Books, Ltd., London. "The Return of the Proconsul" reprinted by permission of *The Observer* magazine, London. "Elegy of Fortinbras" reprinted by permission of *Encounter* magazine, London.

"Do You Hear," music and words by Peter Scholtes, copyright © 1966 by F.E.L. Publications, Ltd., Los Angeles, California. Reprinted with permission of the copyright owner. Further reproduction is not permitted without written permission of the copyright owner.

 Published in the United States by Ballantine Books, a division of Random House, Inc., New York, and simultaneously in Canada by Random House of Canada, Limited, Toronto, Canada.

Library of Congress Catalog Card Number: 78-26478

ISBN 0-345-28371-6

This edition published by arrangement with Macmillan Publishing Co., Inc.

Manufactured in the United States of America

First Ballantine Books Edition: April 1980

The author wishes to express his gratitude to the John Simon Guggenheim Foundation for a fellowship which aided him in the writing of this novel.

PROLOGUE

PAPA FRANCESCO was dead. I could do no more than pick out those few words from the Greek but the church bells and chanting monks dolefully confirmed what little I could translate from the radio. For the second time in twelve months, the Roman Catholic church had lost its ruler. How he had died was drowned in a garble of words that flowed as softly and swiftly as ouzo from a tipped bottle. I would not know any more until the next afternoon when the boat brought the *Daily American* from Rome or the *International Herald Tribune* from Geneva.

I can still remember exactly the thoughts that flashed across my mind when I understood what the radio was saying. It was a vivid recollection of the remark of a woman I had known in Torino, in the north of Italy. Now an ardent Communist, she marked her descent from centuries of Lombard Protestants, proud survivors of the holocaust of the Albigensian crusade. I can still hear her tell her young son the news of Papa Francesco's election: "See, *Bambino,* how sly those priests are! Now they even choose a good man to be *il Papa!* They will kill him, you watch."

How she or most people outside of the United States knew that Papa Francesco was a good man, escaped me. RAI, the state-owned television network to which we had been listening that noon, offered precious few details other than that he had been a simple monk. "They will kill him," she had said.

"They" had now fulfilled her prophecy, whoever "they" were.

I walked down among the small whitewashed cottages toward the beach. I have always thought most clearly at the water's edge. I wanted to absorb the news there, in the cool breeze of late afternoon. Before I had gone a hundred paces, however, I knew that I had already decided what I had to do—what I *must* do. Nevertheless, I walked for a half hour, occasionally looking up at the mountain that held the cave where John the Apostle, possibly mad from thirst, had received his visions of the Apocalypse.

John's nightmares had been horrible fantasies; mine had

been less horrible but real, as I suspected Papa Francesco's had been. During the last few months I had found here in the simple life of Patmos some of the same sort of peace that must have once nourished Francesco when he was a monk. And yet, one recalls Aristotle: "Happiness is for pigs." Eventually, Francesco's conscience—or perhaps his personal devil—had compelled him to return to the world that had created his nightmares. I, too, now felt obliged, compelled, to return and resume my trade (for a writer a sabbatical becomes, after a while, a dry rot) to reenter a universe of psychoanalyzing, belittling, trivializing cynics who, for generations before Papa Francesco, had not seen (or perhaps had not recognized) a figure of truly heroic proportions, a man of great energy and intellect with the moral as well as the physical courage to try to change all our worlds. The compulsive need to learn, to understand, and to explain was once more riding my shoulders, dominating my life, as if it were the spirit of Papa Francesco himself, gasping out its last earthly commands.

ONE

I KNOW, you want to talk to me about those two articles I did for *Leatherneck*. I don't mind. I got time I ain't never used yet. And sitting around a frigging old soldiers' home doesn't give me a lot of jollies. I don't like talking into those tape gismos, but if it's for the colonel I'll go along.

Okay, from the top: I'm Master Gunnery Sergeant Giuseppe Michelangelo Guicciardini, Jr., USMC retired. My father was born in Florence—Firenze, he always called it, like he always made me pronounce my middle name *Mee*kelangelo. He was proud to become an American citizen, but he was proud of Florence, too, and of Michelangelo, and of the Italian language. I guess I was a disappointment to the old guy. He was a gardener, really a frustrated architect, and he wanted me to go to college and study art or architecture or something. But how the hell could a poor, skinny wop kid in Boston go to college in 1936? Especially a kid who had four little sisters and two little brothers? So I enlisted in the Marine Corps. Hell, there weren't many other ways I could get chow, clothes, a bunk, spending money, and even a few bucks to send home.

I don't mean the old man wasn't happy when I got my promotions or when I won the Navy Cross on Guadalcanal. Maybe he blamed me just a little because Raffaello enlisted in the corps after Pearl Harbor and bought it trying to get ashore at Tarawa, or because I never got married and gave him grandchildren. But the old man got his grandchildren from the girls. Christ, he got the little bastards up the Yingyang, seventeen of the little turds, and a college son in Niccolo, though not until after the war. Niccolo is a lawyer now and in politics; he's good but he's never gone far, not with him having to fight both those snotty Back Bay bastards and the Irish Mafia.

But you don't want me to bang your ear about myself. You want to know about the colonel, Declan Walsh. Everybody does. That's why I could peddle those articles in *Leatherneck*. Well, I knew him since Christ was a corporal. We were in the *Old* Crotch together. First time I met him was back in 1944 when he was a fresh-faced lieutenant, a second lieutenant at that. He'd been to law school for a year or two so he was a little older than most of the lieutenants. But twenty-two is young, especially for guys who are just about to die. I was part of the permanent—so I thought—personnel at the replacement command at Camp Pendleton. He was just another piece of gold-barred Jap bait waiting to be shipped out for the Fifth Division. We didn't have a shitpot full of captains and first lieutenants then—too few made it past second lieutenant, for one thing—so we just picked every seventh or eighth second lieutenant and made him a company commander for a couple of hundred replacements. Walsh was one of those poor bastards. I don't know who got the rawer deal, the lieutenants or the snuffies.

Just before this replacement draft left, my name got tacked on the list. I never found out exactly why, but I knew the official reason. Maybe the real reason was because the Old Man had warned me a couple of times about playing cards with officers. I knew all the official crap about officers and enlisted men—even senior NCO's—getting too close socially, and I generally respected the rule. But, shit, when an officer, especially a bachelor second lieutenant, makes up his mind to lose his wad, I've always felt it was my duty to help. After all, part of a senior NCO's job is training young officers, and you can learn a hell of a lot about military tactics from poker and cribbage.

I didn't bitch about being shipped out. I'd been wounded on Bougainville, bounced around by a mortar shell and slipped a frigging disc in my back. After an operation in Australia I'd been shipped back to the States in the fall of '43. The list of dead friends that got longer every few months had me ready to go back and nail a few more Japs' asses to the barn. I was a bachelor, and the corps was all I had except for an occasional broad, if you know what I mean.

The official reason I was shipped out in '44 was that Walsh's first sergeant had appendicitis. So I replaced a replacement. I liked Walsh. Sure, I used to kid him then about hating second lieutenants and that the Crotch ought to abolish the rank. I've kidded all my lieutenants that way, but I really respect those guys. Some of them are wise little turds, but they're the first to get clobbered. The casualty rates show that—better than nine out of ten of the poor bastards who were rifle platoon leaders in combat got killed or wounded in World War II. The figures were a little lower in Korea. I don't know about Vietnam. I'd retired by then.

Walsh was something different. He was a tall kid, well built and sort of blondish—not straw but kind of light brown and the short GI haircut made it look lighter. I remember his eyes, real cool grey eyes. He smiled a lot and his eyes sort of, you know, sparkled, but there wasn't the kind of warmth there that you'd expect from his voice or his smile. I don't mean they were cruel eyes, or mean, or anything like that, just sort of cool, like he was always sizing you up or something.

I liked him, right off. I suppose it was because he could speak Italian better than I could, and liked to talk about Italy. His father had been with the American embassy, and Walsh had grown up in Rome and Dublin. I guess that's why he spoke English funny—not with a foreign accent exactly, but with a different cadence, kind of like one of those light Irish brogues, going up at the end of sentences.

I liked him but I didn't quite trust him, at least not for a long time. I can't explain it exactly. He was always square with me and the troops, you know. He spent a good chunk of his time on that twenty-two-day boat ride trying to make life more bearable for the poor snuffies up in the bow. That damned liberty ship went after every wave in the Pacific. Up in the air, then *kerchunk,* slapping down again. The troops were stacked five high in canvas bunks, the frigging hatches closed most of the night—and during the day whenever there was a sub or air alert—hotter than a camel's ass in the Sahara, with kids puking their guts out plus the smell of garbage cooking in the galleys and perfume from shit-filled toilets that wouldn't flush. It was a dirty, stinking hole, like being locked up on a hot day in a room with Elizabeth—Elizabeth, New Jersey, that is.

You couldn't do much with more than 200 men crowded together in that rolling shithouse. But Walsh tried, and he did a little good. For instance, there was that business of the water. A day out of Diego Town, the ship put the troops on water hours. Piss, shit, wash, and drink at set hours, morning, noon, and night. Too bad about the rest of the time, just cross your legs. The frigging ship's crew had water all the time—the pog navy takes care of its own bastards, but they screw anybody else within range. Well, Walsh spent a lot of time up in the wardroom looking over diagrams of the ship and found a water line that ran behind a bulkhead in our area. After a little hacksaw surgery on the ship, we had water for three full days before the frigging anchorheads found out.

That was good sign, but there was bad sign, too, like the kid who got hold of some booze the morning we were set to leave Camp Pendleton for the boat ride. This snuffy—I don't even remember what the shitbird looked like, now—came staggering into the company office, and one of the NCO's tried to steer him back out. Well, the kid hauls off with a roundhouse right that starts back somewhere around the Mississippi River. The NCO has no trouble slipping under the punch, and two of his buddies grab the kid and start to haul him back to the barracks.

But the door to the CO's office is open, and the lieutenant sees the whole bit. He walks out slow and calm, never raises his frigging voice or anything. But when we march through a piece of San Diego on the way to the ship, with everybody watching, there's the poor snuffy, marching between two MP's, obviously under arrest.

That was a rough way to handle it. Striking an officer or an NCO is serious business, but the kid missed; and he was too shit-faced drunk to know what he was doing. War is mostly head down, ass up, picking crap up off the deck; but to march off to war with your head high and crowds cheering takes a little of the sting out of it. The kid missed that. I hope he isn't buried on one of those frigging islands out there.

Sure, I know, a tough streak's no bad thing in an officer. Without it he'd be psycho the first time he'd have to order somebody to move out and get his ass blown off. But, you know, you got to ease off just a little bit, maybe look the other way once in a while. Tough ain't mean.

Well, I said there was good sign and bad sign. There was also some sign I couldn't read at all. Like, that tub didn't have a Catholic chaplain, so Walsh read prayers for the Catholics on the three Sundays we were on board; I went each time. I usually didn't go to church in those days, but I went then because I've always gone to the curious—what's the word?—exotic things, like a little exhibition in Cuba and China and the Med. Now don't get me wrong. I'm a Catholic—sort of—and I respect religion and all that stuff. Besides, most of the stories you hear about marines and wild living are a crock of shit; just put it down to too much beer talking. Hell, what got me there was that I'd never seen a Holy Joe with a marine's gold bars on his collar.

The first time I went I was thinking of the time a couple of days before when we had to show the troops a VD movie. Now that was a frigging waste of time. Those poor kids weren't likely to see a woman of screwing age for a couple of years, unless they got wounded and shipped back. But the brass had a schedule of such stuff, and the CO was supposed to follow up the movie with a heart-to-heart talk with the boys—just the sort of thing some frigging Back Bay lady in Boston would dream up when she was playing with herself in the bathtub. Can you imagine a heart-to-heart talk about sex with a pack of horny nineteen-year-old kids who know the odds are damned high they're going to get their balls blown off in a few weeks? Well, the movie was a pretty gory show, full color with cruddy whores, crabs, chancres, and dorks getting reamed out—we hadn't found out about penicillin curing syph yet; or if we had, nobody was telling the troops about it. After that movie, what with the rocking of the frigging ship, and the heat below decks, everybody's stomach was ripe and rolling. A lot of CO's went out for fresh air and let the company pecker checker—I mean corpsman—give that stupid talk. But Walsh got up in front of the troops himself. "The message is simple: Flies carry disease. Keep yours closed."

Some days he was like that. Everything was a joke, even on him. You couldn't get a sentence out without him twisting your words around so it sounded like you were propositioning the master-at-arms or one of the corpsmen. He was funny, I guess, but sometimes that got on my nerves. He could do it in Italian, too, and that really got to me because I'd have to stop and figure it out. But it wasn't a "come closer" kind of humor; it was more a put-off, a put-off in a nice way, but you knew he was saying, "Don't get close to me."

There's more to it, but you haven't got all your life to listen to me shoot the shit. I just had an itchy feeling about that guy. I can't explain it, you know. Part of it, I guess, was the natural fear any NCO, especially one who's already had his ass half shot off, has about how an officer will turn out when the shooting starts. It bugs you worse when you can't put the guy in a neat little slot, when you know he's as likely to turn into a wild, frigging gung ho madman as a yellow belly or a psycho case. But—shit, I guess I ought to say it—more than that I had this gut feeling that he wanted to go some place, and that he might sacrifice the whole damned world to get there. Then again he might turn into a conscientious objector and not fight at all. Most guys I could figure the odds on, like picking up a fifth heart in seven-card stud or hitting sixteen in blackjack. But the sign on Walsh pointed in cross-assed ways.

Any worry about his guts was wasted. When we reached our staging area, both of us went as replacements to the same battalion in the Fifth Division. I went as a battalion sergeant major, Walsh as a rifle platoon leader. We went ashore at Iwo Jima four days later, the first battalion on that frigging black beach. Walsh did a bang-up job getting his boys inland. It's funny; you train men for months, drill it into their frigging heads that when they get ashore they've got to get their asses off that beach if they want to live. You hammer it the Christ into them to the point where if you shake them awake at night they'll spout off about getting inland. But then as soon as those mortars start whooshing in—and on Iwo those mammy-jamming buggers really whooshed—those same snuffies will burrow in the sand like frigging turtles laying eggs, just waiting to be slaughtered. And it was awful tempting to dig in on Iwo. The area we hit was soft volcanic ash. The tanks and amtracs bogged down, and us poor grunts sunk in to our ankles, sometimes right up to our rusty dorks. Just moving was hard work.

Walsh pushed and pulled and kicked ass and shoved and led and begged and bullied so that his boys moved inland faster than most—right into machine guns, grenades, and small arms. But they moved off that beach, and most of them lived. Walsh got hit twice, once just a pinkie in the leg. I don't think he even knew about it at the time. The second was more serious. Just as he flipped a grenade into a bunker, a machine gun in the next bunker back caught him with a tracer in his left side under the ribs. It missed anything vital, but you can bet your sweet ass it burned like hell—literally, I mean—and it did tear out part of one rib. He lay there a few minutes and then told one of his troops to throw him a Willie Peter grenade—that's white phosphorous, and that and napalm are the two things that scared me most—and, I shit you not, a lot of things in war scared me. He lobbed that Willie Peter right into the second bunker. He didn't say anything about being hit until after the Japs came running out coughing and smoking. He got written up for a Bronze Star that day. He earned it; but, if every gyrene got what he earned those first few days on Iwo, half the Fourth and Fifth divisions would've got Congo medals.

Walsh, the lucky bastard, went back to a hospital ship. I didn't see him again for six years, not until January 1951. I'd hear a bit now and then. You know how old soldiers gossip, and the Crotch is a small outfit. He'd been discharged after V-J Day, gone back to law school, and then, somebody told me, got himself one of those fancy Ph.D.'s to go along with his law degree and was teaching at the University of Chicago. Well that fit, especially that shit about him teaching international law. I guess he was still leading the boys in prayer, sort of. Maybe I shouldn't make fun of his rice bowl, but the only international law I ever saw was survival—and by any way at all, *any* frigging way *a-tall*.

Like I say, the next time I see Walsh is in January 1951, during the first year of the Korean War. The two of us were assigned to the same replacement draft again. I'd been at the Swamp—Camp LeJeune, I mean—and he'd just finished a refresher course at Quantico for reserve officers who'd been recalled to active duty. We met at the motel in Oceanside, just outside Camp Pendleton. He had his wife with him. Now there was some lady. She had a pretty face, but, man, she was built like a brick shithouse with both doors open.

I don't mean any disrespect, it's the honest to God truth and the first thing anybody noticed. She knew it, too, and could live with it. But I meant it when I said she was a great lady. The three of us lived in the motel. I didn't feel like mixing with the troops too much before going back into a war; and I had a lot more freedom than the colonel. Everybody figures that a reserve light colonel who's been called back needs a lot of instruction; on the other hand, nobody figures he can teach a master gunnery sergeant with fifteen plus years of regular Marine Corps much about soldiering. So I got to know Kate pretty well—I say Kate because she insisted I call her that. None of that Mrs. Colonel crap. We spent a lot of time walking the beach or sitting in a local bistro waiting for the colonel to finish playing soldier boy for the day.

They had a real thing, a lot of passion—I had the room next to theirs and the walls were pretty thin, and so I know what I'm talking about—wall-shaking passion. Of course, they'd only been married about six months. But they had a lot more going between them than the hots. There was tenderness there, too, and you don't see much of that in the corps—or the world, for that matter. She was a bright gal, not just some bubble-headed sexpot, and she understood the colonel. If she'd been my woman, I'd have been the most careful gyrene in that whole war. I'd have worn a sandbag as a jock and never stood straight up unless I was in a hole deeper than I was tall. Well, he was a lucky man there. I don't know that he ever realized how lucky.

Okay, so the colonel and me and a couple of dozen other people, including a guy named Keller I'll tell you about in a minute, get flown out to Korea on a special draft at the end of January, just in time to start Operation Ripper. We'd reached another one of those turning points, as the reporters say, in the war. You remember that the North Koreans just about drove the South Koreans and the dogfaces off the peninsula in the summer of 1950. Then in September, the First Marine Division made a landing behind the enemy at Inchon, and we drove the NK's the hell out of the south, captured their capital, and some doggies even got to the Yalu. Old Dunghead Doug MacArthur was bragging about how the Chinese wouldn't come into the war and he'd have the boys home for Christmas. Then the Chinks came in and, with MacArthur's having divided his command, took us on sorta one at a time. The marines got hit at the Chosin Reservoir, where it was forty below zero, and the Chinks made the mistake of surrounding one marine division with only six of theirs.

Well, we beat the shit out of those gooks, but we still had to get to the coast and sail south, because the Chinese were rolling below the 38th parallel. By Christmas, however, Old Man Winter had taken a bite out of their steam, and we were reorganizing to push north again. Operation Ripper was part of that drive. Walsh got assigned as the commanding officer of the Second Battalion, First Marines. (That means, First Marine Regiment, if you're not familiar with our lingo.) I tailed along as the battalion sergeant major, and Walsh pulled a string or two to get this Captain Keller to come with us as the Three—operations officer, the guy who does the tactical planning—for the battalion. He's supposed to be a major, but in a war you can't keep stockpiles of officers around. A captain'll do, if it pleases the battalion CO, and it did.

Now Keller I got to tell you a little bit about—Sidney Michael Keller, to be exact. He was a kook, but the kind I could understand. There's a lot of prejudice in this world but I've always liked Jews, especially rich Jews who want to play poker and aren't very good at it. Keller—he liked to call himself the Smart Money—may not have been rich by your standards, but by mine he was rolling in dough. And he loved to gamble—poker, blackjack, cribbage, anything. We'd even bet on whether we'd be attacked at night and what time. When I got back to the States I bought a big, maroon Buick Super from Keller's losings—tax-free, too. I've heard since that the Smart Money was a real lover. Classy bimbos all over the place, and a new one every night. Well, he had to be lucky at something.

He and the colonel were old friends. Walsh had stayed in the reserves—how else would he have gotten an all-expenses-paid trip to that frigging mass of hills? He'd been in the Ninth Infantry Battalion that used to meet in Chicago. Keller was a student at the university and joined the marine reserves. He went to law school and met Walsh when he was teaching there. Walsh got Keller—a second lieutenant then—to come into the Ninth Battalion. Actually, Walsh was only three years older than the Smart Money, but those few years in World War II had made him a light colonel and a battalion CO at thirty-one—not unusually young, either. The oldest light colonel we had in the regiment was thirty-six and the youngest thirty. You got to remember how many marine officers are buried on those cruddy little islands across the western Pacific.

Walsh had changed a little. His humor was nastier and he was less patient, too. I had the feeling that he was really more on the make now, like maybe he had a pile driver up his ass. I guess my problem was I couldn't dope out the kinds of dreams he had, and I still couldn't figure out the price he was willing to pay—or get others to pay—to get those dreams.

The troops didn't especially cotton to him at first, and they never did in the way they worshipped old Chesty Puller or Big Foot Johnson. But they respected Walsh and they'd do any frigging thing he said, when he said it. That ain't bad, not *a-tall*. You tell me you're interested in leadership. Well, from what I saw in thirty years in the Old Crotch, three things were key. First, Walsh was just so damned good at his job. It was beautiful to watch him maneuver a battalion, weaving in air strikes, mortars, artillery, and tanks. He kept a couple of hundred things in his head all at the same time. He burned up a lot of taxpayers' money shooting off ammunition; but I shit you not when I tell you there weren't no snuffy who could meet him outside the pearly gates and tell him, "Man, if it hadn't been for you, I'd have got here a lot later." But there would be a line of gooks from here to Richmond with that word. So, what I'm saying is that the troops can't help but respect an officer who's a tactical genius. They may not like his ass, but they'll play follow the leader with him all day—and night—long. When the bullets are coming in, that's no little thing. (Of course, I'd seen how shrewd he was when he was a second lieutenant; he'd never play poker with me.)

I'll tell you something real interesting, too. He enjoyed himself planning that war. Now wait, I don't mean that he liked killing people or almost being killed. I'd say he was as shit-scared as the next guy when we were getting incoming mail, and a lot more pissed off than most at being in *Kohrhea* in the first place. But he was good at tactics, and he liked grabbing old Mousey Dung's boys by the short hairs and twisting. The colonel had a lot of brains, but he didn't run the battalion at a distance like some guru, the way a lot of CO's do. In fact, he worked more like a coolie. He'd be up half the night going over maps—and when we had 'em, aerial photographs. He'd go over them again and again. We usually had a piece of clear plastic over the battalion's operation map so we could mark our lines of attack and defense; the colonel'd drive the poor

Smart Money up the frigging tent flaps the way he was always wiping the Smart Money's marks off the plastic and putting fresh ones on to eyeball different ideas.

When his plans worked out—which for him was taking a hill with no casualties at all or with less than we'd had any good reason to expect—he was like a little kid the way he'd get excited. He sweated blood on those plans, and it showed in the way our kids didn't bleed when they carried them out.

The second thing that made him a good leader was he really seemed to care about the troops. More important even, they thought he cared. It was part of the business of knowing his job and doing it better than anybody else. He wouldn't just break his ass to find the way that'd save kids' lives; he'd stand up on his hind legs and say "go fuck yourself" to the regimental CO when he told us to do something that was likely to get somebody killed for no good reason. The snuffies knew that, and they appreciated it; and they showed their appreciation the best way a snuffy can—by fighting like a wildcat with a burr up his ass.

There was also the funny business about Walsh and our dead. The troops noticed it, too, but I don't think he ever knew that they did. After a firefight, he always went over to where we'd stacked our dead for the trucks or helicopters. He wouldn't move the ponchos, but he'd stare at the pile. You could see he was all torn inside. I heard one of the troops say one day that he thought the colonel might try to bring them back to life. There's always a smart ass or two in every marine outfit.

Now, wait, I don't mean he seemed like a saint or anything crazy like that. I told you about his humor. It was always kind of down to earth. He had a great collection of dirty jokes, like the queer bear who laid his paw on the table. I think he probably enjoyed a little nookie as much as any man, maybe more. From what I heard through the motel wall in Oceanside, there couldn't be any doubt there, none *a-tall*.

Well, anyway, like I was saying, the colonel never talked about his personal life. He wouldn't even play the game "What's the second thing you're going to do when you get home?" He'd laugh when somebody would say "Take off my hat" or "Let go of the doorknob," but he never said anything himself. And he never let off steam by talking about how scared he was. Most of us found that helped, but he'd just pick up his map board and draw arrows or look for places artillery could fire on.

Oh yeah, I said three things were key. The third was training and learning. Now when an officer or NCO comes into an outfit as a replacement, he hasn't had a thing to do with the people he takes over. Some other bastards, maybe a lot of them, have trained them and led them until the minute the replacement takes over. So whether they're sharp or shitty, he can't take any credit or blame for it. But, if he's good, really good I mean, he can pretty frigging-A-well soon shape those guys the way he wants. But he's got to know what he wants them to look like; and he's got to be tough and stubborn, because chances are with marines they think they're already hot shit.

Well, the colonel knew what he wanted, and he was tough and he was stubborn. He'd tell his staff and his company commanders what he wanted, and they knew their asses'd be in a five-foot sling if they didn't deliver. He didn't shout or scream or throw temper tantrums. No kid shit like that. He just laid it straight on the line what they had to do—and straight up the old Yingyang if they didn't deliver, but a lot of praise and maybe a citation for a medal if they did an A–1 job.

That much'll get a replacement CO pretty far pretty quick, but the colonel didn't stop there. In Operation Ripper—which, like I say, was where he comes into my war—we didn't have it too rough, if you don't count it rough getting your hairy cajunes frozen off and having some gook trying to put a bullet between your horns once or twice a day. What I mean is we never had a big, pitched, bloody battle like Iwo, or Tarawa, or the Tenaru Ridge on the 'Canal. The Chinks were trying to hurt us as bad as they could without committing big chunks of their army to full battle. They'd retreat slow. Their rear guard'd stand and make us pay a few casualties for a hill, bug out quick and set up on the next hill, and then play the same little game all over again.

For each day's operations, Regiment would give us an area to clean out and assign an objective for us to occupy, usually a hill mass a few miles north. How we did it was pretty much up to us. Like I say, that's where Walsh was great, using air and artillery and mortars to sting the Chinks before they could sting us and at the same time maneuvering the battalion so we hit them where they weren't expecting us. They don't pass out medals for that sort of thing, but you get lots of brownie points from the grunts whose lives you save.

We'd go through that routine every day for three weeks or so, then we'd get a week in reserve. That's when the colonel turned the big screw. First off, he'd give everybody twenty-four hours to crap out. Man, you needed it, because we'd been running every day all the Christ up and down those frigging mountains, and the gooks'd be probing us at night—not trying to wipe us out or anything, but keeping us awake and tiring us out.

Well, after we'd flaked out for twenty-four hours, the colonel'd start us on a training schedule. Exercises before breakfast, hikes to keep the legs going, and war games ranging from squads up to the full battalion. But only for five or six hours a day. We'd still need lots of rest, and the colonel didn't try to kill us.

The big thing when we were resting up was those morning meetings with the officers and senior NCO's. The colonel would take our unit diaries—the records every outfit keeps of each day's operations—and we'd sit in the mess tent, freezing our asses off looking at maps and rerunning every step of some firefight we'd been in a week or two before. We'd cry-tique that battle, and when I say cry-tique, I mean cry-fucking-tique. And I shit you not. The colonel'd have every officer or NCO whose troops had been in the fight explain what he did exactly when and exactly why he did it that way. Man, you damned well better have a good reason why you'd done it your way and not some other. The colonel was just as likely to push hard if the fight had come out okay as if it had gone sour. Like one of the senior NCO's said, "That man ain't satisfied with nothing less than per-fucking-fection." And that was gospel, and you'd better give it to him—or at least do a hell of a lot better the next time.

I don't say that the company CO's were more afraid of having to explain in front of the rest of us—with the colonel popping questions—than they were of getting shot; nobody's that scared by somebody on his side. But you can bet your Sunday-go-to-meeting douche bag that knowing they were going to have to explain every frigging decision they made kept those guys on their toes when the shit was hitting the fan—and it made them think what they would do even before the crap started to fly. Maybe that was more important. Our troops just never got surprised or bushwhacked.

The last part of it was the best, I think. When we were resting in the same area as a fight we'd had, the colonel'd run us through the map drill a couple of times. Then he'd move out the whole battalion if we'd all been involved, or only one or two companies if that was all that had been in the firefight—but always every frigging officer in the battalion—and we'd walk through the whole battle all over again, this time the right way, and do it slow so everybody'd learn. If we had time, we'd fight it a third time, with the colonel on the radio throwing in new wrinkles to make his officers think and the troops react.

We learned, we all did, and I didn't think after fifteen, sixteen years of crunching gravel I had anything left to learn about infantry tactics. "Learn from your mistakes, gentlemen; live and learn and live," was what he'd tell them. And he'd help. He'd explain, nice and clear, all the big things and most of the little ones you'd have to keep in mind: like whether artillery could reach a place or whether it was so steep you need mortars with their high angles of fire; or like, when the gooks'd have their heads down, how to coordinate air strikes with troop movements so you could surprise the little bastards; and like how to feel for the enemy's flank so you slip around him rather than bang ass up the middle where he was strongest.

You'd better frigging-A-well learn. He'd help, he'd explain, nice and patient and all clear, but make the same mistake twice and it hurt marines or meant gooks got away unhurt, and you'd lose a good hunk of your ass, or maybe even your command. The colonel relieved one company commander and two platoon leaders that I remember. That's a rough thing to do, relieve an officer of his command in combat. He's got no career in the service after that, none *a-tall*. But he was still alive, and a screw-up cost his snuffies a lot more than a career and a pension. The officers bitched, but they respected the colonel for what he was teaching them about tactics and discipline. And so did the troops. They could appreciate that tactical training most of all. They knew whose balls got thrown into the meat grinder when some mammy-jammer screwed up.

That's why we were the best battalion in the Marine Corps. From the colonel right on down to the lowest-assed snuffy, we knew our jobs better'n any son of a bitch in this mammy-jamming world—and what's more we knew we knew it better.

TWO

I WON'T BANG your ear anymore about Operation Ripper in February and March of 1951. We did pretty good, not much hero crap, just a lot of firepower, a lot of smarts, a lot of frigging agony, and we were back in North Korea again, a little north of the 38th parallel. The thing that I remember most was moving north of Hoengsong, recapturing Massacre Valley. Earlier in that winter the gooks had ambushed a convoy from the Dutch Battalion attached to the Second Army Division. It must have been an honest to God massacre. The valley was narrow and it was still covered with wrecked trucks and dead Dutchmen. At the rear of one truck we found a paymaster, frozen solid, killed while paying his frozen troops.

Sorry, I'm off again. Old soldiers love to talk. Like the man says, we don't die; we just bore everybody else to death. What you're interested in happened in April, just after Ripper ended. The other day I read in a travel section of the *Post* that April is a lovely month in Korea. Lovely, shit! Maybe there was something pretty there. I didn't notice a mammy-jamming thing worth seeing. By then it wasn't so cold compared to the Chosin Reservoir or even Ripper, except occasionally at night when that frigging wind would whip down out of Siberia. But you didn't mind so much, because you knew it was getting better. You could see the snow sort of crawling back up to the tops of the mountains, and the scrub pines on the slopes had more life in them. There was even some green spackled along the floors of the paddied valleys.

But I need peace to appreciate things like that, and April 1951 was not a peaceful month in Korea. We heard —the senior NCO's usually hear these things just before the commanding general—that there were peace feelers out all around the world. Those diplomatic jerks in New Delhi, Peking, Moscow, London, and Washington were supposedly having little secret talks mixed in with their boozing and fagging; and even Dunghead Doug said he was willing to "meet on the field of honor" with the gooks and talk about peace. That was A-okay with me. It wasn't *his* honor, because it damned well hadn't been *his* war, but it might be *my* peace.

We had another goodie that took a lot of joy out of life. This one wasn't rumor. It was TSNS—top secret, no shit. Intelligence had the hot, hard cock. The Chinese wanted to go to any peace talks with a big victory tucked away in their jocks. They were going to ram down the middle of the peninsula, beat the bejesus out of us, and agree to talk before we could recover. Then they could dictate the terms. I don't know if Harry Truman or General Ridgeway liked that idea, but we sure didn't.

I guess the best place to begin is at Oran-ni, the little town where we bivouacked one night in the rain and woke up in the morning in a sea of tiny, hopping, frigging frogs —I mean it. Those frogs were hopping on each other like all they ate was Spanish fly. Well, anyway, there was this big staff conference that Colonel "Big Foot" Johnson, our regimental CO, was holding for his battalion commanders. James was the colonel's first name, but everybody called him Big Foot—when he wasn't around, that is. He knew it and I don't think he liked it, but a man who wears size thirteen boots can't do much about a nickname like that. It fit his feet, but not him, really. He was a tall guy, just a little taller than Walsh, about six three, with a neat silver mustache—like mine is now, although mine was black then, you know. So was my hair. Well, I think the guys would have called Big Foot handsome, not one of those pretty Hollywood fags, but a real man type. You know what I mean? He looked like a movie British brigadier in India fighting for the queen. He was a real dude, the way he dressed. His green utilities were always shiny, and he wore a red silk scarf around his neck like one of those British things—yeah, ascots. It wasn't regulation, but neither were those Corcoran paratrooper boots. Still, a lot of the officers wore them. Walsh did. They were better than the frigging GI stuff except when you had to walk a lot in the snow.

I remember hearing that when Big Foot was an NCO—he was a mustang, you know—he had twenty-six changes of uniform in his locker. I believe it. I had a reputation about being a dude, too, even in the field—especially in the field. That's where it really counts—when there's no showers, no hot water, and no laundry. Then you got to be clean-shaven and have a fresh uniform on. It's a trick I learned from the old guys who were in Nicaragua—some of them with Big Foot. Being dirty is bad for morale. There's nothing that makes you want to drag ass more than getting up before dawn and pulling on clothes that're still stinking wet from yesterday's sweat.

Like I was saying, the troops called me a dude and I was happy about that, but I didn't like it when they used to kid me about my suede liberty shoes. What a man wears on liberty is his business. Anyway, Big Foot was a nattier dresser even than I was. He was a bachelor, too. The corps was his life, just like it was mine. He'd put in thirty-five years—Mexico, World War I, Haiti, Nicaragua, long dull stretches during the Depression, World War II, and now Korea. He wasn't a thinking man's marine; his tactics were strictly "Fix bayonets and banzai." But he had a shitpot more sense than he seemed to. Most of the gung ho crap was for the kids. He was a tin god to them. If there was fighting anywhere in the regimental sector, Big Foot would be there, like a cheering section. The snuffies loved to tell the story about his looking at an 81-mm mortar and asking how the hell you could hook a bayonet on it. I think the story's true. It's the kind of thing Big Foot would say.

I don't think he was very happy listening to the briefing at Oran-ni that day. I was there because I always went to CO's briefings with Walsh and the Smart Money. When you've been around the corps as long as I have you learn that the main trick to being a top-notch sergeant major is to find a couple of bright young clerks and look over their shoulders just enough to know what's going on—and boot them in the ass often enough so they'll think they can't fool you. It gave me a lot of free time. Colonel Walsh liked me to come along because he valued my opinion. I liked to come along because I wanted to be near Captain Keller. When a man owes me as much hard cash as the Smart Money did, I get nervous when I can't eyeball him.

I was getting more nervous looking at Big Foot. He was

pretending to be listening to the briefing, but I could tell by the way his mouth was twitching that he had the rag on. The war didn't usually upset him, but he had plenty of reason to be worried that day. Major Charles Stambert, the regimental three—that's the operations officer, I told you—was outlining our battle plan.

"It's a classic hammer and anvil technique, gentlemen," Stambert is saying. "We're to be the anvil; the rest of the division, the Korean Marine Regiment, the army's 187th Regimental Combat Team and Seventh Division will be the hammer. Look here," Stambert points to the large map that took up most of one side of the tent, "Intelligence says the main push is going to come almost straight down the middle of the peninsula. They estimate the Chinese will head right for where we are now, near Chunchon, then turn west and run down the valley of the Pukhan-Gang to where it flows into the Han, cross the river and swing south of Seoul, cutting off that city and with it most of the American and British forces.

"You know from the reports you've been getting that the rest of the First Marine Division has been shifting east. The Chinese have apparently been shifting with them—or we with them. They want to launch their attack against a South Korean unit. It's been a cat and mouse game, but it's just about over. We're running out of peninsula. There's only one more valley east of the Pukhan that would give them a decent route back to the west, and that's the Soyang-Gang. If they take that one, they'll have to cross a steep pass to get back west or else attack on a much broader front than they like to. . . ."

"The point, please, Major," Walsh cuts in. "Anyone who can read a map can see how the terrain constrains the Chinese." That was the way he talked—words like "terrain" and "constrain," and his grammar was always good.

Walsh didn't win any points with Colonel Johnson on that one. The Old Man snapped the twig he'd been playing with. It made a loud crack that caused everybody but Walsh and Major Stambert to turn around. Big Foot and Walsh never got along. Walsh thought Big Foot was dumb—which was wrong—and had no other interest in life but the corps—which was right. Johnson was a gruff but friendly old bear. To him the corps was a band of brothers. They had their faults but like all soul brothers they should love one another, and Big Foot could see that, with Walsh, the Crotch just didn't come first. He was the best of the battalion commanders because he was the smartest and the toughest, and because of Walsh the Second Batt was the best in the regiment. When they were sober even the people from the First and Third Batts would admit it, but as far as Big Foot was concerned Walsh was never "in." He just didn't have the loyalty to the Crotch that for us old regulars came before every-frigging-thing else in life. Big Foot could respect him, but he couldn't ever like him, even though Walsh was a reserve officer and there was no special reason why the corps should be his life like it was ours. You could please me a hell of a lot easier. Christ, I'd even follow a dogface if he was any good, and I suppose a few of them must be.

"Our missions," Stambert didn't even break stride, "are to help channelize the advance of the Chinese and then move down and cut off their avenue of retreat when the rest of the Tenth Corps smacks into them with a counterattack. To accomplish these missions we'll have to be isolated from the rest of the division. The nearest marines will be about four miles south and west of us. The nearest UN unit will be the South Korean division just south of Inje."

"Does this caper have a name?" Walsh asks.

"Yes, sir. Operation Rat Trap. Now if you'll look at the map again, you'll see that the Pukhan River flows out of the Hwachon Reservoir up here west of the Town of Yanggu. The brunt of the Chinese offensive should fall a couple of miles west of us. We can't try and stop that. All we're supposed to do is to stop them from taking this east ridge. And we don't want to deny them use of the valley or the Hwachon flats—at least not immediately.

"We want them to move down the valley toward Chunchon. We'll sting them a bit and air and artillery will pound the living shit out of them. When they hit our main line, they'll have lost a lot of steam. When the counterattack comes, it'll push them back toward the Hwachon Reservoir. We'll squeeze them from the east, the Army's 187th Regimental Combat Team will make an air drop west of the Hwachon, and the rest of the Tenth Corps will come straight ahead."

For a couple of minutes nobody said anything because

nobody believed a frigging word they'd heard. "How large will the counterattack be?" Walsh finally asked.

"As I said, sir, the rest of the First Marine Division, the Korean Marine Regiment, the 187th RCT, the Seventh Division, and of course us."

"And of course, us. About 40,000 men all told?"

"Yes, sir."

"About how many Chinese?"

"Intelligence estimates that the Chinese will commit 280,000 men to this attack. They'll probably use half, more or less, in this sector."

"We hold them, channel them, and then eat them up," Walsh sneered, "before breakfast, I suppose."

"Colonel," Big Foot broke in, "if I say with breakfast then your battalion will eat all 280,000 Chinese with their C rations."

"Yes, sir, but we may have to shit a regiment or two."

"If I tell you to shit," Johnson snapped, "you'll squat and strain and by God gooks better come flowing out."

"Once the Chinese are fully committed between Yanggu and Chunchon," Stambert droned on, "they'll heavily outnumber us, but we'll be several thousand feet above them. Artillery and air will be killing gooks by the ton, and the ground is open enough in some places that the counterattack can make effective use of tanks.

"If you look at the map again, I'll point out the exact positions we'll occupy. We have responsibility for the ridge starting about three miles south of the road that crosses the mountains east and west, and links Yanggu and Inje. Obviously there's a better position just north of the road, but the laundrymen won't move south unless they control a main road that leads straight into their rear. Our lines will be shaped like a large V, with the closed end pointing north here at Hill 915. One leg runs off south and east, and the other south and just a little west."

Big Foot stood up. "Gentlemen, a hill 915 meters tall gives us 3,000 feet of altitude. The valley floor is only 600 feet above sea level. We'll have direct observation of every ant that tries to piss in that valley. We'll hold that ridge until the counterattack comes and then we'll close off that valley like a vise. We don't want to spoil it by calling any fire against the Chinese in the valley, so that area is indexed. It'll take my personal order to fire there. We just watch and tell the division about any movement. They can decide whether to take it under fire. We want to look pretty harmless.

"As Stambert said, we'll be in a V opening to the south. As you can see from the map, the ground is highest at the point, Hill 915 in the north, and runs down on both sides to the opening of the V. But even at the opening, we've still got a thousand feet of altitude above the valley floor. The Second Batt will be at the point, right on the peak of Hill 915. Walsh, you'll bear the brunt of any attempt to push us off that ridge; and if I were a Chinaman, I'd do my best to get us off that ridge."

"So would I, Colonel," Walsh nodded. "Let me play the devil's advocate and ask what makes anybody think one regiment—even a regiment of marines—" that slight lilt to Walsh's voice grated on Johnson—"can stop a Route Army?"

"Several things, Colonel, several," Colonel Johnson answered. "One of the most important is time. The Chinese know that they have to punch through our main line quickly. The longer they have to lock assholes with us on a set battlefield, the less chance they have. Like Stambert says, in a small area air and artillery can kill gooks by the ton. They'll hit us hard, but if we let them have what they really need—use of the valley—they're likely to head south and leave us to be mopped up later."

"You mentioned several factors, Colonel."

"Several thousand, Colonel—3,800 to be exact. Since we came ashore at Inchon seven months ago, this regiment has never lost a hill it's been ordered to hold, or failed to take a hill it's been ordered to capture. We're not going to start anything different now.

"As I said," Johnson went on, "the Second Batt will hold 915, and the First Batt will assume responsibility for the east leg of the V, Third for the west. Chances are the First won't get engaged in any serious fight and can also act as regimental reserve. We'll have our five regimental tanks with us—they'll help us seal off the opening of the V where the ground is lower and flatter—and we'll have two batteries of self-propelled 105-mm howitzers from Tenth Corps. That'll give us eight howitzers, plus my eight 4.2-inch mortars, and each of you has six 81-mm mortars. We'll have plenty of firepower, but we're going to have a real ammunition problem. Once the fighting starts, there'll be no trucks or even pack trains getting through to us, and an airdrop will be difficult with all the artillery that'll be shooting. So don't call for any heavy support unless you absolutely need it. We can get a little help from the 196th Army Field Artillery and their Long Toms, but they'll have lots of other business. We'll have our own Forward Air Control Teams with us from the First Marine Air Wing, but when the big attack starts they'll have other calls, too. We have to remember that stopping the Chinese around Chunchon will be given a higher priority than holding our ridge.

"As I see it," Big Foot added, "the operation depends on three factors: us stopping the Chinese at Hill 915; the rest of the division stopping them near Chunchon; and Tenth Corps mounting a quick counterattack. Three if's, gentlemen, and we risk our lives on all three coming out right."

"There's a fourth if, Colonel," Walsh said.

"Yes?" Big Foot's voice was cold. He had reached the dramatic point of the briefing, when he was going to talk about blood and guts and fixed bayonets, and he was pissed at being interrupted.

"The fourth factor is a Chinese decision not to make a serious effort to hit down the Soyang River in the next valley to the east of us around Inje and cut us and the whole division off. That's a ROK division around Inje. They wouldn't do anything more aggressive than try to choke the Chinese to death with heel dust. If the Chinese move that way, we'll be caught as flat-footed as a pregnant kangaroo."

"That's a possibility," Johnson admitted, "but Intelligence doesn't think the Chinks will hit that far east. It's a risk we have to take. We can't put American divisions everywhere.

"Gentlemen," Big Foot concluded, "I'll want to look at your preliminary defense plans this evening. We'll move out at 0800 in the morning. My command post will be in the ravine in the middle of the V. You'll have a formal operations order in two hours. Is there anything I've forgotten, Stambert?"

"No, sir, but communications has something, I believe."

Major Harold Wilkinson, a fifty-two-year-old mustang, stood up. "We'll put in as much telephone wire as we can, but I expect we'll get hit with a lot of artillery and mortars, so make sure your radios are in good shape. Supply has some extra batteries for the SCR–300's. The call sign for the regiment is Topper. The first battalion is Fedora, the second is Silk Hat, and the third is Toque. . . ."

"Toque?" the CO of the Third Battalion asked.

"Yes, sir, Toque. I don't know why, Colonel," Wilkinson answered.

"A toque," Walsh offered, "is a kind of hat popular in the Renaissance. It's similar to the hat the Swiss Guards at the Vatican wear. It has the double advantage of being a piece of headgear and also starting with T for third."

"Yes, sir. The artillery batteries," Wilkinson went on without blinking—he never wanted to know anything he couldn't use—"will be Bowler 1 and Bowler 2."

"If there's nothing else, gentlemen," Big Foot said, "Stambert and I will see each of you about dinnertime tonight. Keep in mind that in the next few days, the only thing that's really going to stop the Chinks is the guts and cold steel of a lot of gravel-crunching marines. Those kids have got to be ready for a fight, ready to punch cold steel into warm bellies. You've got to get them up for this one."

THREE

Big Foot and Major Stambert had said that the regiment's defensive positions were going to be shaped like a V. But it wasn't like that at all. Map makers put straight lines on things, but there are bad twists and curves on hills and ridges. Once the battalion commanders had checked out the ground and put their troops in, the regimental lines looked more like Caspar, the Friendly Ghost. His head circled Hill 915, and his hands and body flowed out to the southeast and southwest, curving around key peaks and closing off the two ravines—the maps said one, but two were there—leading into the regimental area from the south. Big Foot put his command post in the bigger ravine, between the 105 howitzer batteries pointing north and the tanks pointing south. That sure as shit wasn't the school solution, but in that kind of geography we didn't waste time with what the pogs in Quantico said was the right way.

The picture of the Friendly Ghost sort of hit anyone who looked at a sketch of the regiment's lines, and all of us in the regiment—even at Division, I heard—started calling it Operation Caspar instead of Operation Rat Trap. Big Foot wasn't happy about the switch. His days in the corps were about over. He wanted—shit, he deserved it—to go out on a big victory. The fickle finger of fate had frigged him again. Rat Trap wasn't a dramatic name for an operation, but it did have a kind of brute honesty. It would have looked good in print. But who could think of Operation Caspar, the Friendly Ghost, without smiling?

But we had other problems, and Colonel Johnson didn't have any time for nomenclature. Bulldozers, those big, noisy beasts, were scraping flat places out of the hillsides for a field hospital, for firing pits for the 105's and 4.2 mortars, and for storage areas for ammunition. Two-and-a-half-ton trucks were shitting out food, water, fuel, and medical supplies, but most of all ammunition—piles of metal cans filled with bandoliers of rifle clips or belts for machine guns, cases of hand grenades, and stacks of wooden boxes, each with a pair of artillery shells or mortar rounds. Even in a short firefight a single battalion can eat up big piles of bullets, and at night you don't see the enemy. You sort of feel him; then you can use up tons of crap in a few minutes.

You know, civilians never understand that. A soldier can only carry enough ammunition to keep him going about three minutes if he fires as fast as he can. That's why the Crotch stresses fire discipline so much, and why we clobber trigger-happy clowns. A guy on defense has a big advantage. He doesn't have to pack his ammo on his back. He can stack a half dozen extra bandoliers in his foxhole, along with a case of grenades—if anybody has a case of grenades. This was the only time I ever saw the troops get that many.

The turf in the ravine near the command post had been firm earlier in the morning, but soon that frigging flow of traffic was churning up the ground, and before noon trucks were getting stuck in greasy shit. From up on the hill you could hear the burning whirr of spinning wheels, shouts from angry drivers, and grunting curses from tired marines and Korean workers straining to push the trucks onto harder ground.

The Smart Money and I were glad to leave all that crap, even for the long climb from the regimental command post back up to the rear of Hill 915. It may have been only April 20, but climbing up 400 meters in less than two miles is warm work, and we went slow. Even so, we were puffing before we got one-third of the way. Marines like to talk about being in good physical condition, but after a few weeks in combat, nobody is in shape. You miss too many meals and too much sleep, and have the screaming shits too often (man, one day I crapped nineteen times). There's no fat left on you, that's for sure, but there's not much energy either. I used to keep five or six bars of pogey bait in my pack and gulp them down whenever the shooting started so I'd have a jolt of chocolate energy.

We decided (we didn't have to say anything to each other—after you've been shot at a few times you don't apologize for being human) to rest for a few minutes on the shady side of the ridge, near an unmelted patch of snow. We could look down from there into the ravine; from a half mile, all that wild Mickey Mouse activity in the regimental area seemed to make more sense, like those people and trucks and bulldozers knew what the Christ they were doing. We knew better.

While we were sitting there, the Smart Money told me about how he met Walsh in the Ninth Batt on the Navy Pier in Chicago and went to law school and studied with him, and once even had a crush on Kate when she was a student. Then Keller got a job with a big Washington law firm and moved East in the winter of 1950. From what he said, it sounded like he peddled more politics than law, but I've never cared much about that sort of stuff. Anyway, he'd made lots of money, and if he didn't get tired of poker it was going to do the old Gunny's bank account a lot of good, too.

I'd heard most of Keller's story before and from Kate a lot about her and the colonel. I knew she and Keller had been in law school together, but I hadn't realized until Keller was talking that he'd had a crush on her. Now don't get me wrong. Remember that was a time when a nice girl—and she was one hell of a fine woman—didn't jump in bed with a guy as soon as she shook his hand. I could see why Keller would be attracted to her. I sure as hell had been.

Well, she took the colonel's course and that was the end of one romance and the beginning of another. Kate, Keller said, thought Walsh was a tin god or something. (I've always wondered about those college professors—some of them look pretty horny to me—getting a little bit of all that young stuff in their classes. With Kate it would have been one hell of a temptation. But with her looks and brains, she'd probably recognize any line going and just knee you in the nuts.)

Keller didn't tell me much about what happened between Walsh and Kate, but pretty soon she drops out of law school and marries him. Keller said that raised a lot of snooty eyebrows at the university, even though Kate was twenty-three. Professors just didn't marry their students, not in those days anyway. So Walsh had been looking around for a new job after that and had finally found one at Michigan (where they've got football teams). But that summer, before he could move, Old Harry the Haberdasher sent us into *Koh-rhea,* and there we were sitting on a hill in the middle of a dinky little war, happy just to have our arms and legs still attached and a few more pretty sure days of life.

The whole romance bit was interesting. It wasn't a side of the colonel I'd seen much of. Just from the little I'd seen of Kate I liked her, and when I got to know her better I could understand how someone could want to get married. She was damned near as smart as Walsh and a lot quicker with her tongue. If she liked you, there wasn't a warmer, better friend in the world. If she didn't, that tongue could slice like a shiv. And she didn't give a rat's ass for rank. It's a damn good thing the colonel wasn't a regular officer. She'd have had half the generals' wives in the corps trying to shoot down his career.

Well, Keller and I sat there on the hillside for about fifteen minutes or so chewing the fat. Neither of us was in a hurry to get back and tell Colonel Walsh that we'd busted out on him. He'd sent us down—not really, just hinted and so we volunteered—to try to play a little changie-changie with Big Foot. There was no point in Walsh trying it himself, you know. I've already told you those two just didn't get along, and the more they saw of each other the more they were sure they were right. It's too bad the way they missed each other, you know. Walsh sneered at Big Foot, and when Walsh was around, old Big Foot got downright spooked. He wasn't like a Texas steer; when Big Foot got spooked he didn't run, he just dug his heels in and got stubborner than usual. And that's pretty frigging stubborn, I shit you not.

We were supposed to blow a little smoke up Big Foot's ass and talk him and Major Stambert into a smaller defensive area for the Second Batt. That made sense. Hill 915 was the biggest hill for miles. It was what we call the key terrain feature in the sector. Any military man moving through there would look at a map, put his finger on 915, and say, "I got to have that mammy-jamming hill." Worse, it had three separate ridges leading into it from the north, making it as vulnerable as a white man in Harlem at midnight. The First Batt was on our right, facing generally east along a set of cliffs that only specially trained troops could scale at night, and they'd set up rock slides you could hear back in Pusan. We wanted the First Batt to take over responsibility for about 200 yards of our area; that would mean we'd have just two avenues of approach to worry about, only twice as many as a battalion should have in a situation like this.

Well, we got nowhere, no where *a-tall.* Colonel Johnson was in Stambert's operations tent when we got there. I knew we'd lost as soon as I saw him. He'd put his foot down, and that's saying a peepot full. The Smart Money did most of the talking. They listened and agreed that we were going to have hell to pay one night soon, like maybe tomorrow. Big Foot explained very carefully that with the regiment several miles in front of friendly lines, he wanted his troops in a tight circle with every foxhole within a few yards of that on either side.

Stambert was good people, but the cheese was binding him pretty tight. Two things, really, or maybe three. The big ravine leading up to the CP and the 105 howitzers was a problem, but the tanks could seal it off like a mummy's tomb. Now, the smaller ravine was a different breed of pussy cat. It was all kinds of vulnerable. We wouldn't put any tanks in there, and the Chinks would throw a shitpot full of people against it. With their shock power it was pretty likely they were going to pop through someplace there in the smaller ravine or even at the point of the V at Hill 915. Now the ravines Stambert could talk to Big Foot about, but a breakthrough was something else again. In one way Walsh was right about Big Foot. You just didn't talk to Colonel James McLaughlin Johnson about the possibility of anybody, not even 280,000 Chinese, let alone half of them, breaking through his regiment.

So Stambert had persuaded him to detach one of the First Batt's three rifle companies and put it on the shoulder of the big ravine to "reinforce" the people from H and S and Weapons companies who were supporting the tanks. What the major really wanted was a reserve force that could counterattack either toward the ravine or up 915. I think Big Foot knew it, but Stambert was playing the game Big Foot's way, so that was all right.

Anyway, we got a polite sermon from Stambert, a pep talk from Big Foot about using cold steel, and a few goodies from Uncle Sugar's big larder. But it wasn't what he went after. So I sat in the shade and I listened to the Smart Money talk about how Walsh had "a greater breadth of knowledge"—whatever the Christ that means—than any professor he'd had in law school. Then it was time to go tell the Man we'd bilged out. I knew what he was going to say: "A wagon train mentality means wagon train tactics." We'd been down this trail before.

Standing outside Walsh's tent I could hear my Zenith Transoceanic radio. Jo Stafford was wailing "On Top of Old Smoky": "Oh the grave will detain you and turn you to dust." That wasn't a good sign. The colonel was going to be moody.

"Yoposeho, Mein Colonel," Keller shouted as we went into the tent. "The Smart Money and his faithful Eyetalian companion Taranto have returned, bringing light and joy back into your otherwise miserable life. We bear tidings from our glorious Obergruppenfuehrer."

Walsh was sitting on a camp chair softening up some of the wax he'd stolen from the waterproofing on the SCR-300 radio. He needed it more than the radio did, what with that big walrus mustache he had. He looked older than on the ship out to Iwo, which was natural, seeing as it was more than six years and two purple hearts later. But you got to remember he was still a young man, just thirty-one. His hair was still sort of light brownish, but the mustache had come out a mixture of yellow and copper red—and it came out wild and bushy, making almost a complete circle. It got in his eyes and in his chow. While he was fiddling with his mustache—sorry, I didn't mean that; that's the sort of thing the colonel would have said. Anyway, while he was sitting there he was soaking his feet in a helmet full of hot water. Man, that's real luxury. You know a grunt did a lot of walking in that man's Marine Corps, and sometimes in combat we'd go a couple of days without even being able to take our boots off. When he's not fighting, the first thing a gravel cruncher does is to soak his feet. If you can use hot water, boysan, you're living high off the frigging hog.

Johnny Kasten, CO of Easy Company, was in the tent with Walsh. Johnny and I first met back on the *Ranger* in 1939, long before the war. Johnny'd been a raw farm boy out of the clay hills of Georgia, about as big a hick as you'll find outside of your television set. Later, we were on the 'Canal together in '42. He got his on the Tenaru Ridge and went back to the States about nine months before I did. When I saw him again, he was an instructor at Quantico and had a temporary commission. Man, he was proud of that, I shit you not. 'Course he wasn't too proud to have an occasional vino with old friends, but still proud.

Walsh had been one of Johnny's students at Quantico. Later, the three of us had been on the same replacement draft going out to the Fifth Division and Iwo. The two of them were close, like Johnny was Walsh's pop or something. They'd come back home on the same hospital ship, Johnny with a broken leg from a sniper's bullet. After the war Kasten had fought like a bitch kitty in heat to keep those silver bars. He'd even accepted an LDO commission —that means Limited Duty Only, limited, that is, to his MOS or Military Occupational Specialty. In his case it sounded pretty silly because his MOS was 0302—Oh-Three-O-bituary, or Oh Three, Oh shit! as we used to call it. Anyway the whole drill meant that he could only be an infantry officer, which in the Marine Corps is like saying that a painter can only work with colors. What it really meant was that an eighth-grade dropout wasn't going to get very high up, even though he had a pair of railroad tracks on his collar now.

Walsh looked up. "What's the word from hindquarters?"

"Havva no, Mein Colonel," Keller said. "We have outenbeengestrucken, almost."

Walsh kicked over the helmet. "Nothing's too good for the front line troops, and nothing is what they'll get! A wagon train mind—what the hell can you expect but wagon train tactics. 'Circle the wagons, men. We'll pick them off one by one.' Did that simpleminded turdbrain send up any extra feathers for our arrows?"

"Havva no, Mein Colonel."

"I'm surprised. He and Stambert should have been baptized Wedge and Lever, the two simplest tools known to man. No wonder Big Foot never got married. What woman would want the title of Wedgess?"

"Despairest thou not, Mein Leader. The Smart Money does not return empty-handed, especially when he goes questing with the Wily Wop."

Now usually I'd deck an NCO for a crack like that or chew out an officer or enlisted man so he couldn't sit down for a month. But with Keller, you just had to laugh. He called it a double ploy, whatever that means. All I know is that when he said it, it was funny; with anybody else it would have been a frigging insult.

Well, anyway, Keller didn't stop talking; he had more shit with him than a herd of constipated elephants: "We wrung tocsan loot from our masters. First, a 50-caliber machine gun for our friend Johnny Kasten here to compensate for the feelings of masculine inferiority southern whites usually have. The Yobo Choo-Choo will bring it up this evening with the food and ammo delivery." (You look confused. The Yobo Choo-Choo was a nickname we had for a nickname. Every marine unit had Koreans, mostly deserters from the ROK army, who worked for us as laborers, hauling shit up and down the mountains. They were called the Gook Train or the Yobo Choo-Choo. Not good, I know, but you'll do damned near anything for a smile in a war.)

"And for the common good," Keller went on, "the Smart Money also liberated a bottle of Scotch from our glorious leader's private stock—when he was outside his tent, of course. We know enough about the problems of command not to bother such a busy man with petty details. And, not least, the Ginny Gunny here sold your assorted souls—if any—for a slab of bacon and a dozen real, live eggs, American style. There's a small problem: they've been laid by a rooster but then so have a lot of chickens. Many, many chop chop, havva yes."

"Grand, just grand. At least we won't have to die sober or hungry. Well, Johnny," Walsh turned to Kasten, "our plans don't change much. Have a drink. Do what you want with that extra machine gun." Then to Keller: "Mike, I want sandbags around every machine gun in the battalion by nightfall, and by tomorrow night I want overhead cover for those guns. Supply gave each company three axes. Intelligence expects the big hit to come off tomorrow night, but we'll probably get probed tonight. Tell the companies that starting at 2200 tonight I want a fifty percent watch. One man awake in each foxhole until an hour after dawn."

"Yes, sir. Will do. What happened to your patrol this morning, Johnny?"

"Nothing. They went out about a half mile north of the Inje-Yanggu road. Saw a few sign, but no contact."

"What kind of sign?"

"A bush moving the wrong way in the wind, a bed of ashes still hot, and some rice grains scattered around. Usual scout stuff. They're watching us pretty close."

"You bet your sweet ass they are," Walsh put it. "They've probably spotted our main line four miles back and are wondering what the hell we're doing out here by ourselves. Maybe they'll think it's a trap and leave us alone. They'd never believe that anyone seriously thinks we're going to stop them."

"Don't worry, Dec," Johnny said softly.

"You're telling me not to worry? You've got Hill 915." Walsh smiled as he looked at the way Kasten's blue eyes were sunk way back in his head. The steady strain of seven months of combat had dug deep furrows of worry that ran out from below his eyes like a frigging trench system. His usually pale skin was now a dark grey, like meat going bad.

"You know what I mean, Dec." Keller and Kasten were the only officers in the battalion who dared call Walsh anything but colonel. Johnny was five years older than Walsh; he looked ten. With luck and four more years of life he could retire a major and go back to his wife and children in Augusta.

"You know what I mean, Dec," Kasten said again. "I'm only worrying about East Company's hide—and my own.

You're worrying about the battalion, and worse, about the war."

"I'm worried about my hide, too," was all the colonel said, but I knew he was thinking about the kids who were going to die in that stinking little war.

"I reckon it's a shitty war," Johnny muttered. "But I never heard of a good war, except maybe in Central America. Remember what the Old Gunny here says, 'Those banana wars were tough, but at least we had all the bananas we could eat.' "

I smiled. I liked being quoted, even though I'd never been in the banana wars. Big Foot had, and I'd stolen that from him back in '42.

"That's not much help. I have to send these kids to their deaths for this slimy country. There's no difference between Syngman Rhee and Kim Il Sung, at least none that's worth fighting about. As my academic colleagues would say, there's no variance to explain, much less to die for. Christ!" Walsh sipped the Scotch from the canteen cup, then spat it out on the ground. "Damned alcohol acts on the metal and tastes like rusty iodine."

Kasten nodded and swallowed his drink in a neat gulp. He had 285 men on Hill 915. Each one of them thought Johnny Little Kasten, the toughest company commander in the best battalion in the whole frigging Moreen Crotch, was going to get him home alive and in one piece. By tomorrow night they could all be wrong; and you could bet your douche bag that a lot of them were going to be.

FOUR

IN THE FOXHOLES along the crest of Hill 915, the kids of the Second Battalion were hunkered up in their sleeping bags against the cold rain, waiting for the night—or their lives—to end. I've been through it on the 'Canal and on Bougainville. It's not what you do for kicks, unless you're a frigging kinko or something. Most of the guys were sitting up, with their sleeping bags unzipped, just loosely wrapped around them. Their M–1 rifles were loaded with a round in the chamber and the safety catches were off. It was only 2230 but I don't think anybody was sleeping.

The bitter, metallic taste of fear was souring mouths and stomachs. I still get it every once in a while—though never when I watch a Hollywood movie. It's like getting heartburn and then having a dentist drop a piece of silver filling on your tongue. It's sharp and nasty tasting. You don't know whether to puke or spit.

That morning it had been Dog Company's turn to send out a patrol. They got only 2,000 meters out when the Chinese opened up. Their fire had been lazy, almost as if the frigging slopeheads were saying that they were coming soon and would appreciate it if we waited for them. The patrol had orders to look and not to fight, so the lieutenant had to bring his men right back. There weren't any casualties, but his pride was smarting. Gyrenes just don't go that running shit, except when it's after somebody.

Tonight, out ahead in that big black dark, you could hear sounds of shuffling feet and the groans of men moving supplies and equipment. Before, whenever the Chinese had attacked they had come up real soft. Those shitbirds had a talent for that a professional second-story man would turn green over. That often gave them a lot of tactical surprise, but tonight they didn't give a shit if we knew they were coming. They were pretty frigging cocksure of themselves.

Back at the battalion command post, I was sitting with Walsh and Keller. The three of us were staring at the map board. There wasn't anything else to do. I don't play cards unless I can concentrate one hundred frigging percent. The four-foot-high parapet of sandbags around the tent gave a phony feeling of safety, just like the canvas overhead did, even though the canvas couldn't keep out all of the rain, much less any shrapnel. It's funny. I can remember when I'd get so scared back on the 'Canal that I thought I'd go apeshit, I'd wrap myself up in my poncho for an hour or so. With all that dark I felt all safe and hidden, but it's a quick way to die if any hostiles find you. The danger back here was from mortars; the only real protection would be an overhead cover of logs and sandbags, and we didn't have that.

A Coleman lantern—*my* Coleman lantern; Walsh had taken it over, saying something about the commonweal, whatever he meant—flickered near the map board, and in a corner of the tent two grunts were sharing what little dryness they could get out of an empty ammunition box.

One of them had two telephones—one on each ear. One line ran to the rifle companies and the other to the regimental CP. The second marine was coddling an SCR–300 radio, our other line of communications.

"I'm still worried," Walsh was saying. "If they see we're doing the wagon train act, they'll play Indian and circle around looking for a weak spot. They're sure to see we've got two ravines leading right up our ass. The big one with the artillery is packed with people and those tanks will clean house. The smaller one's going to be trouble; it runs right up behind us. If they get into that draw they can ram straight into our anal aperture."

"That doesn't sound kosher," Keller commented. "I may be a homosexual, but I don't practice. And besides I've got a Korean as my washy-washy boy; I don't need any Chinese. Can we swing back in the morning along the middle ridge? We could make that ravine a death trap."

"No. Stambert's convinced Old Numb Nuts that we need to give the artillery and mortars a little more breathing room. They couldn't cover troops so close to them. Stambert's really afraid that if the Chinks break through anywhere they can put the artillery and mortars under small arms fire, but he can't say that directly to Big Foot. At least Stambert's put the reserve company on the ridge behind the ravine. I still wish. . . ."

Walsh's sentence was cut short by a loud hiss, followed almost instantly by a crunching bang. It's a noise that makes the frigging bile rise from my stomach right up to the back of my mouth. That hiss and bang came five times, one right after the other. All of us in the tent hugged the muddy deck.

"The laundryman cometh," the Smart Money cracked as he groped along the soggy deck for his steel helmet.

"Regiment wants to know if we're being shelled, Colonel," the telephone operator called out.

"Tell them," Walsh said more calmly than I'd expected, "that they must have a sixth sense to perceive our difficulties so swiftly."

"Is that affirmative or negative, sir?"

"A-fucking-firmative, son." Then to Keller: "Note the time, please, Mike: 2135. What kind of stuff do you think that was?"

"120-millimeter mortars, Mein Leader. Have no fret, by

now my people in the operations tent will have a report already typed up in triplicate."

The first rounds were a teaser—and I guessed an accidental one at that. The mortar's target had probably been the crest of Hill 915, but like most of us early in a firefight, they were scared shitless and missed. They'd get better as the night wore on. By the way, I know a lot about what went on on the Chinese side. About a year ago, when I was doing those two articles for *Leatherneck*, I took a taxi over to Headquarters Marine Corps every day for two weeks and went through this stuff on April 1951. It's all in the historical section. I never liked history in school, but it's different when you've lived through it. And that shit they got is great. In May we captured the unit diaries of the Ninetieth Chinese Division, the one that did most of the attacking. Somebody translated them, and now you can tell exactly what each company was doing at what time. I've got to go back and read their Jap stuff on the Tenaru Ridge. I don't have much else to do. I'm sort of keeping it as something to look forward to.

But you're interested in Korea, not the 'Canal. I waited a half hour, and went outside the tent. I knew it would happen. Just as soon as I started to pump ship, the shelling started again. This time there was a shitpot full of 50-mm and 82-mm mortars along with the 120's, and now you could hear screams from wounded marines. Christ, that sound chills me. You hear a kid scream because a mortar has torn a piece of him off, and you think about joining a monastery. After eight minutes of terror, the crump of the mortars stopped, and some frigging slopehead started tooting a bugle. The poor bastard was so shit-scared, you couldn't tell whether he had the horn in his mouth or up his ass. Anyway, in a few seconds, a full Chink company, 150 men, came jogging up the trail along the ridge that led from the east to the crest of Hill 915, straight into Easy Company's position. Two more rifle companies followed at a dog trot, ready to make the most of what they thought was going to be a breakthrough.

At the first sound of the bugle, Johnny Kasten had shouted to his artillery forward observer, "Normal barrage!!! Normal barrage!!!" But church was out. An 82-mm shell had landed right in the frigging middle of the FO's foxhole, splattering him, his two assistants, and their communications gear all to Christ around the hole. The 4.2 mortar observer heard Kasten's order and sent it to his battery. In three seconds their first shells had left the tubes, headed for the western ridge. Too bad the Chinese weren't using that approach.

Just as the lead Chink company got within a hundred yards of our positions, their commander fired a green flare. His men stopped jogging and started running at a wild frigging gallop; they easily leaped over the single-strand barbed-wire fence and came straight at Easy, firing their burp guns from the hip. They were coming fast and a full platoon was able to get halfway in that mine field before they realized what that single strand of barbed wire meant. It only took a few seconds before every one of the forty men who'd vaulted the fence was scattered in little pieces.

I'd designed that field myself and the engineers had filled it with Bouncing Betty's. Basically, they're mortar shells. They weren't as sophisticated as the stuff we got now, but they did the trick. It was a Rube Goldberg contraption. You stretched out black trip wires from them and when a foot hit that string, it pulled a cord that set off a shotgun cartridge that sent the mine flipping up head-high—and then it popped off with a big frigging bam. That night there was a mass of yellow flashes, with spinning fragments nipping jugular veins and whacking off chunks of skull, sometimes whole heads. A lot of people in Easy Company were firing as fast as they could load and to hell with fire discipline; they added more to the confusion than to casualties.

The second platoon of Chinese hesitated at the edge of the wire just long enough to be caught standing straight up by a long burst from Johnny's 50-calibre machine gun. At that range a 50-calibre bullet hits like a pneumatic hammer; it just rips off hands, arms, and balls. Thirteen more Chinks were dead and 30-calibre bullets were wounding others.

The poor bastards from the second Chinese platoon hesitated only a split second before turning tail and running head-on into the charging third platoon. Then the panic really spread, because just then Kasten finally got the word to the battery of 105-mm howitzers. A few completely confused—or totally dedicated, I'm not sure which—gooks made it back to the wire and leaped over the fence, adding fresh hunks of flesh to the piles of lifeless meat. But most of the two platoons just wanted to shit and git. They swung around to the north and, in a bigger replay of the first collision, ran smack into the oncoming second company.

Red flares went up, then green, then yellow flares. Whistles were shrieking and bugles were tooting all over the frigging place. If we hadn't been using live ammunition it would have been as funny as a Keystone Kops movie. It was pure slapstick, laced with blood and gore. Shouting, cursing Chinese officers turned one squad from the third platoon around, but just then what was left of the second platoon came running north like a herd of horses in front of a forest fire. Another long burst of fire from the 50-calibre gun sang through the trees, and four 105-mm shells blanketed the ridge with sweet black smoke and whirring fragments. Wounded lying on the ground were begging for help, but instead they were being trampled to death. Then the 105's really started putting down their normal barrage.

It was midnight before the Chinese battalion commander could get his troops back into something that looked like order. He had to pull them back more than a mile north of Hill 915. The lead company was a raggedy-assed rabble. The survivors of the mine field, the machine guns, and the artillery barrage had stampeded way up north. I'll bet some of those gooks made it to Manchuria by morning. His officers managed to round up about thirty stragglers, most of them unarmed. They could work as stretcher bearers—there was a hell of a need for them—but not for any more fighting that night. The other two companies were in decent physical shape; their panic had cooled down to where they were just shit-scared. With an hour's rest, both could be used again, but any military man would know they'd fight poorly that night, if they'd fight at all.

A twenty-four-hour rest would give them time to remember they were soldiers—it's an easy thing to forget when the bullets are flying by your frigging ear—but time was something these people didn't have none of no how. The Chinese plan called for them to own Hill 915 by 0100, and the regimental commander was having a shit hemorrhage at the delay. There were some real red-assed messages in those unit diaries. If you think that Chink in command of the regiment was pissed at the battalion, you should have read what the division commander was saying to his regimental commander. As I read later, he was mightily leaked off at his gooks, I shit you not, boysan. The division was supposed to occupy the Sochon valley before dawn, and two other divisions were ready to move through Yanggu and be on their way to the Soyang valley. If this part of the attack screwed up, the entire corps of six divisions of slopeheads would either have to stop their advance or move on with their left flank naked—and no laundryman in his right mind would want a regiment of hairy-assed marines on his bare flank. They'd learned that much up north at the Chosin Reservoir.

The Chinese regimental commander said there was nothing to do but tangle titties with another frontal attack that night. He promised the poor bastards more mortar fire, but still only a fifteen-minute barrage because ammunition was short—our aircraft had been pounding the shit out of their supply lines. The Chink colonel also ordered a second battalion to start climbing up the valley floor to the west ridge that ran south from Hill 915 to catch us in a vise. The sneaky bastard also sent a company from his remaining battalion to make a diversion around the southern edge of Caspar's triangle to try to suck off our artillery and mortar fire. He set the new attack for 0315. In the meantime, Division had promised some of those big-assed Russian 122-mm howitzers to fire counterbattery against our 105's.

What the Chinese battalion commander didn't know was that his division commander was shifting a second regiment from its march down the Sochon valley and sending its forward elements to look for a weak spot south of us. Because of their higher ground and our kids' refusal to pay the slightest frigging attention to basic principles of camouflage—you can't ask them to do everything, you know—the Chinks had been able to draw a pretty good map outline of Caspar. I saw it and it wasn't bad. Their only mistake was to underestimate our strength by a full battalion. The division commander wanted to make sure that there were no marines between Caspar and the main American lines, so that if the next frontal attack crapped out he'd be free to wield a regiment in the gap and attack Caspar from the rear. By moving that regiment tonight, the Chinese division commander was putting it in position to attack us the next night—he wouldn't have the guts to hit us in daylight—or, if Caspar fell tonight, head on into the main American lines.

Back on Hill 915, Johnny Kasten had lost only eight killed and nine wounded—all but one from the mortar barrage. The last wounded man had been hit in the scalp by a stray splinter from a Bouncing Betty that had flipped off at an angle back toward the top of Hill 915 rather than leaping straight up. You can never tell, especially if it rains. You set those things in just right, and the rain packs the dirt in different, and then you've got yourself a frigging accident.

Well, the first attack had gone as well as we could have hoped. The delay in getting artillery support had actually helped us, because the Chinks had kept up the momentum that had carried them so far into the mine field. The only trouble I could see was that most of our mines had probably been set off. Still, I bet there weren't many laundrymen who'd climb that fence to find out for themselves.

Johnny Kasten used the lull to make a quick check of his lines. I knew him well enough to know he went out to get away from his telephone as much as to pick up firsthand information. Walsh had held him on the phone during most of the firefight and would be back again in a few more minutes. Other than more ammo, a new artillery forward observer was all that Walsh could send up, and he couldn't get either moving until dawn. I never had a chance to talk to Kasten about it, but I think what he wanted more than anything else was a few moments of quiet, to be able to thank God that he was still alive, and to shake in privacy, before having to tell his men that they could beat the gooks again that night.

Walsh, too, had left his command post. "Big Foot would like to have me tied to that telephone," he complained to the Smart Money. "The Gunny and I are going over to the Fire Direction Center. You stay here and talk to him. Treat him like the mushroom he is—keep him in the dark and feed him horse shit. I've spent half the night trying to keep him informed. All he really wants to know is if we've given the enemy 'cold steel.' Tell the son of a bitch what's going on here—if you know—and remind him that Kasten has got to have a new FO at dawn. Bug him about ammo too. Kasten really doesn't need it, but he'll feel better if he has it."

"I'll give the wagon master your love, Mein Colonel."

As soon as we were in the Fire Direction Center—another soggy, sandbagged tent—Walsh grabbed the telephone operator. "Get me Captain Kasten in Easy Company, son." Then he went over to Major Fritz Morstein, the Weapons Company commander. You know in combat the battalion Weapons Company splits up into a dozen small segments to help the rifle companies, and so the Weapons CO, with most of his men farmed out, gets the job of coordinating all the supporting arms that the battalion can call for.

"What have you done about artillery concentrations for Kasten?" As he talked, Walsh opened a can of C rations—"Ground Meat and." The "and what" was never mentioned out of fear of offending us marines from Italian families. We think of spaghetti as good chow, not a frigging disease, and one whiff told you which those C rations were. As the colonel began to eat the food cold, everybody in the FDC backed away a few feet. Hot, the smell of "Ground Meat and" won't make you barf; cold, it sickened even the starving Korean dogs who yapped begging around us when we were in reserve. Big Foot had lots of little tricks the troops loved to talk about, but the "Ground Meat and" was one thing about Walsh that awed them, maybe amazed them would be more like it. I never saw another marine who could eat that shit cold. Damn few could eat it hot.

"Well, Colonel," Morstein began.

"Sorry, sir," the operator interrupted, "Captain Kasten is out checking his lines."

"I'll bet he is. That asthmatic old devil is running away from me." Walsh dipped his plastic spoon into the C ration can. "Just like I am from Big Foot. At least I know everything's all right. If he needed anything, he'd bellow down without the telephone. What were you saying, Fritz?"

"There isn't anything much we need to do, Colonel. Kasten has his exec in direct communication with the artillery battery."

"Thurman? That reserve idiot Duncan Thurman?" Walsh always carefully distinguished between idiots who were professional soldiers and idiots who were reserves. "He'll shell the battalion CP."

Walsh put down the half-empty can of "Ground Meat and." A radio operator quickly threw it outside the tent.

"All he has to say is 'Normal barrage,'" Morstein protested.

"He could never remember that. Have him contact you, and you relay the information to the guns. It'll take longer but it'll save a few lives—probably yours and mine."

The major nodded to an assistant, who picked up a field telephone and began grinding away at the crank on the side.

"Let me see the fire support plan again, please." Walsh walked over to the FDC map board. It was a mass of numbered boxes and circles, each one showing a point at which a mortar or artillery piece had registered—zeroed in—so all we had to do was tell the battery something like "concentration nineteen," and they could put a frigging shell right on target—give or take a hundred yards.

"If I were the Chinese, and one should never put oneself in the enemy's position except that it usually works," Walsh was saying, "I'd swing around to the south and come up one of those ravines—unless I were in a hurry. Then I'd hit Hill 915 again. I wouldn't like that mine field on the east ridge, so I'd try the west ridge. What have you got plotted there?"

"Four-deuces, Colonel." That meant 4.2-inch mortars. "If nobody else needs them we can get all eight mortars. The angles are pretty steep there—better targets for mortars than artillery. As you notice we have a couple of artillery concentrations we can call on the high points. I'd rather keep the guns aimed in on the east ridge until we know what's happening."

"No. Switch everything to the west ridge. You can put them back on the east if you have to. You've got thc forward slope covered with 81-mm mortars. What about Kasten's 60-mm mortars?"

"They're on the same slope."

"Okay. Now suppose there's a penetration in that small ravine behind us. What can you do besides notify our next of kin?"

"That's Regiment's problem, sir."

"The hell it is. That ravine leads straight up into my tent; I don't want to meet any strangers in the night. Put it down to normal heterosexuality." Now that's what he said. I heard him. That's the kind of shit he was always saying.

"81's and 60's are about all we could put down there. That's much too close in for the 105's or 4.2's."

"Grand. Have one of your people plot a few concentrations down there. And have the ammo men from the 81 platoon ready to protect their guns from the rear. Make sure they've got plenty of hand grenades."

"Yes, sir."

The phone jangled angrily. As the operator gave Walsh the receiver, he made a face to warn the colonel.

"Walsh? Walsh?" It was Big Foot. "Where the hell have you been? I've been looking for you for twenty minutes. My staff can't get a casualty report out of your people. I don't know what the devil's going on."

"Colonel, I'm busy. I'll let you know when I know. All I can tell you now is that we've beaten off the Chinese and Easy's casualties seem to be light."

"I don't care if you're as busy as a one-legged man in an ass-kicking contest. What are the gooks doing?"

"Probably pissing in their pants; maybe they're playing with themselves. How the hell should I know? Their CO doesn't check in with me."

"Colonel Walsh," Big Foot began.

"All right, all right. I'll play the game. The Chinese are probably regrouping. We've got artillery firing harassing stuff out on the east and west ridges. Don't fret; they'll be back tonight. I'd watch that small ravine in the First Batt area, the one leading. . . ."

"You watch Hill 915. I'll watch the ravines, Professor," Big Foot roared. Then he added in a more kindly voice, "What do you need?"

"Kasten has got to have a new artillery FO by morning and we could use some small arms ammo and grenades. If they hit Hill 915 again I'd like priority on the 4.2's and 105-mm howitzers. If they come again, they're likely to hit from two sides—a diversion from the east and the main attack along the west ridge. We'll be short of ammo after an extended firefight."

"Well, there's nothing like cold steel to frighten an Oriental. I'll see what I can do. Let me know as soon as. . . ."

It was exactly 0315 and a couple of tons of mortar shells

suddenly began rocking the whole frigging ridge. We didn't get a warning because the rain muffled the tap of the rounds leaving their tubes. There'd only been a hissing whoosh in the final split second before the first shell exploded. The crest of Hill 915 was a mass of black smoke and spinning chunks of metal. A few badly aimed rounds would occasionally explode near us in the battalion CP, but Johnny Kasten and Easy Company were taking the brunt of the barrage.

"Walsh! Walsh!" the telephone sputtered and went dead. A few minutes later the radio started: "Silk Hat, Silk Hat, this is Topper. Over. Silk Hat, Silk Hat, this is Topper. Over."

The radio operator picked up the handset, but Walsh shook his head and said, "Get me Easy Company."

The call "Silk Hat Easy, Silk Hat Easy, this is Silk Hat Six," went out every few seconds for four minutes before there was a reply. Finally an excited voice broke through the static: "Normal barrage!!! Normal barrage!!! For Christ's sake, normal barrage!!!"

"Oh shit," Walsh snorted, "it's that asshole Thurman clutching again. Alert the guns, Fritz, but wait a while." (In a situation like this, the artillery people, when they're not actually firing a mission, keep their guns loaded and set on their normal barrage readings. It only takes a split second for them to give an "on the way.") "This stuff hasn't been going seven minutes yet. The Chinks got six minutes for the last attack. They'll at least double it for this one, after what we did to them. At twelve minutes cut loose with the four-deuces; and at fourteen minutes with the 105's."

The shells kept coming, rocking and rerocking the hill like a big ship in a storm. More and more were falling over the crest and down near us in the CP as the Chinese started to walk their fire away from their avenues of approach. Suddenly somebody cranked off a rifle shot, then another. They sounded almost questioning, as if the rifle was asking if some son of a bitch was really out there in the darkness. Then we could hear the electric quick burp of a Russian-made tommy gun, followed by American M-1's, automatic rifles, and heavy machine guns, plus the whistling boom of a 90-mm tank gun loaded with canister.

Now you know, that's really something. Canister's just

old-fashioned grapeshot. It's like a shotgun shell three and a half inches in diameter. You can make them yourself if you run short of the GI stuff. You take the armor-piercing head off a round and fill up the casing with nails, nuts, bolts, pieces of beer cans, or other kinds of shit; anything metal will do. It'll really clear a swathe about twenty yards wide. Tankers don't like to use them because they tear up the rifling in those beautiful guns, but tankers can't see very well in broad daylight from inside those iron alligators and at night they're blind as bald-headed bats. They get nervous and to hell with the rifling. It's a comforting sound if you're a snuffy in a damp hole and need some help. Generally though, I didn't like to dig in near tankers. They're too nervous, too frigging ready to cut loose if you get up to take a leak.

"That means the big ravine," Walsh said. "At least it gets Big Foot off our back. He'll be busy looking for some poor laundryman to stab with that bayonet he's been carrying in his footlocker since World War I."

I could imagine Johnny Kasten up on Hill 915 flattened out in a foxhole. Every blast would lift him up and bounce him down hard. His eyes would be as tightly closed as his fists and asshole, just like on the 'Canal. "Oh Christ," he used to pray out loud when the Jap battleships would belt us, "Oh Jesus, not this way, not mangled or blown to pieces. A quick bullet when they come at us, but not hacked to pieces." He'd get sick about then with a violent vomit that'd send his bile and lumps of C ration fruit spewing into the mud. Old Bugle Butt McIntyre, his company first sergeant, would have pulled his sleeping bag over his head and be whimpering in terror.

Then Johnny would recite the Forty-fourth Psalm. He was raised in hardshell Baptist country in Georgia. All those yamheads can quote the Old Testament like it was yesterday's sports page or something. I remember this one because I heard it on 'Canal every frigging night for two weeks. Besides, I looked it up after you talked to me on the telephone.

> Awake, why sleepeth thou O Lord? Arise, cast us not off forever. Wherefore hidest thou thy face, and forgettest our affliction and our oppression? For our soul is bowed down to the dust; our belly cleaveth unto

the earth. Arise, for our help, and redeem us for thy mercies' sake.

I heard this Chinese bugle sing out, and you could bet your douche bag that'd snap Kasten out of his hockey. When he heard it, he'd imagine he could also hear the feet churning through the mud toward his men. I was right. Every bit of good sense in him said to keep down, to cleave his belly to that soft frigging earth, but he forced himself to stick his head up and shout to Thurman and the 4.2 forward observer: "Normal barrage!!! Normal barrage!!! Now!!! They're coming!" With one more effort Kasten pulled himself out of his foxhole and crawled to the crest of the hill. "Here they come!" he bellowed. "Everybody up! Kill the bastards!!!"

The 4.2 observer got hold of his shaking long enough to send Kasten's request on his radio, while Thurman shouted and babbled into his set. Walsh and Kasten's timing was just about perfect. The Chink battalion commander on the east ridge committed what was left of his two companies together, and the commander on the west committed two of his. Both officers brought their troops in right under their own barrage. They were smart, tough cookies. They knew they'd kill some of their own men, but they knew they'd kill less than we would if the Chinese tried to move the last hundred yards with marines shooting at them. But the 105's and 4.2's started dropping in before the Chinks on either ridge could fully deploy. Man, it was bloody, enough dead meat to stock a supermarket butcher shop for a week.

Now there were also gaps in Kasten's line. The Chinese barrage had hurt him. It killed fifteen marines and wounded three dozen more. Seven more had been buried alive, and three machine guns and two bazookas had been destroyed.

At the same time the Chinese barrage lifted, their machine guns opened up. This second attack was a more carefully planned military maneuver than the first, wild, frigging banzai. The machine guns from Easy Company answered, and the marines and the Chinese locked assholes again. Just as Walsh had expected, the two companies on the east ridge weren't much trouble. None of the gooks would cross that single-strand barbed-wire fence, even though they had been told by their officers—you can bet your sweet ass they were standing well back—that all the mines had been set off by the first attack and the barrages and counterbarrages. Easy had no trouble pinning them down with machine-gun fire, and at 0350 they were still seventy-five yards from the marines' position, happy to stay put.

On the west ridge the story was different. The first Chinese company had been too close in to suffer much from the 4.2's and they came thundering up toward Hill 915. A burst of machine-gun fire and a volley of grenades slowed them, but the lead squad charged straight up the left side of 915 and through our lines, cleaning out four foxholes as they punched through. The seven men then turned to hit the marines from the rear, but as they whirled, Kasten, Bugle Butt McIntyre, and two navy corpsmen leaped up from their foxholes and cut loose at five yards with automatic carbines. Before he died, one of the gooks managed to turn his burp gun and fire a short burst into McIntyre's chest. None of the other six shitheads ever saw who shot them in the back.

While Kasten was playing soldier, his platoon leader in the area was shifting his men around to plug the gap in his lines, and the second gook rush was stopped twenty yards short of the top. But another eight kids died.

Meanwhile, the 4.2 barrage was taking an awful toll of the reinforcements the Chinks were trying to send up the mountain to keep up the attack's momentum.

Walsh had the battalion's 81-mm mortars pounding the west ridge, and along with Kasten's 60-mm mortars, they were tearing up human flesh like exploding meat grinders. By 0415 it was pretty clear to the Chinese regimental commander that his attack wasn't going to make a frigging nickel and that he'd had one battalion wiped out and the balls clawed off the other. Later I learned that his recommendation to Division, when he called up to get permission to break off the action, was that Caspar be bypassed and mopped up later. He got the okay to withdraw, but no comment on his advice.

Getting an okay to break contact and breaking contact are two different things. And boysan, I shit you not, there just ain't no frigging maneuver harder to execute than retreating in the face of an aggressive enemy. Walsh and

Kasten knew the Chinks had busted it, and they were all set to twist a repulse into a rout. Walsh had begun thinking about a local counterattack as soon as we had first eyeballed that ground, and he'd worked out a neat little plan with Keller and the company commanders. All he had to do was fire off a warning order at 0420, and at 0450 Dog Company struck down the east ridge and Fox down the west, both trailing a rolling barrage of 105's and four-deuces.

At dawn, with the rain clouds blowing away to the south, Big Foot was bubbling like a little kid at his own birthday party when he reported to Division. He had insisted on talking to the division commander personally. "General, we rolled them up like a rug—an oriental rug. We stopped 'em dead, then two companies of marines with fixed bayonets made a night attack with cold steel, the first time in this war." Big Foot hadn't bothered to say that there had been some predawn light. "Those ridges are thick with Chinese blood, General, thick. Walsh estimates 700 enemy dead and three times that many wounded." Johnson was yelling now, not so much in joy but so he could be heard over the roar of the helicopter engines as the whirlybirds shuttled back and forth carrying out the worst wounded. Since they could carry only two kids a trip, it would be dark before the three 'copters were done. The dead would have to wait until another day.

The general congratulated Johnson, but he didn't sound too happy. Even Big Foot—and Walsh was right that Big Foot wasn't the most sensitive guy around—could tell something was wrong. "The Sixth ROK's, the Sixth ROK's, Colonel," was all the general said. "Your communications people will get a scrambled warning order in a few minutes."

It was dawn, and for a marine in Korea dawn meant more than a new day; it meant life it-frigging-self. "As a sentinel waits for the dawn," King David wrote—or so Johnny Kasten told me—but even those old Jews couldn't have looked for dawn with greater longing than we did in that shitty Korean War. Night was the dirty black that hid the slimy Chinks and North Koreans and limited our firepower. In daylight we could mangle the gooks; we could blast them at long range with air and artillery or, if we could see the bastards, pick them off with a rifle that at 600 yards could lift a foreskin as neat as a rabbi's knife. The Russian burp gun can spit out a shower of 920 bullets a minute. But at seventy-five yards it's inaccurate, at one hundred yards as useful as tits on a bull. It was a damned fine weapon for close-in night fighting, say fifty yards and less, but it was a toy in a long-range, daylight shooting match.

Big Foot was usually full of piss and vinegar early in the morning, even after staying up all night. But this morning he was down in a pit. The general had put a pin in his big balloon. The decoded warning order said that the battle had gone well in the First Marine Division's sectors, but the Sixth ROK Division had bugged out west of Chunchon, leaving our left flank bare-assed. What was even scarier was that Intelligence had picked up another big Chinese force moving south toward Inje, east of us. The only thing between this new Route Army and the one road linking the entire First Marine Division with the south was a ROK division. Christ, no one ever expected South Koreans to fight unless they were South Korean marines. The guts of the warning order was clear: "Be prepared to abort Rat Trap and retrograde south of Soyang river on one hour's notice." "Retrograde"—we just don't like the word "retreat" in the Marine Corps. It's dirty.

Poor old Big Foot. A dream of glory, another dream of glory really, was being smashed. My ass could ache for him. He was fifty-three years old. He had an outside chance to make brigadier general before retiring, but it would take luck or something great, and he wanted something great a hell of a lot more than he wanted a general's star. I knew how he felt. Like me, he'd had no time for a wife or family. The corps was his wife; occasionally he may have humped a stray bimbo, but he never loved anyone else. He needed a victory to remember in his old age, something to look back on during those cold, lonely years of retirement, waiting for death, something to have made life worthwhile, some mark on the frigging world that would tell new marines that James McLaughlin Johnson had been there. I used to feel that way too; I got over it. I don't think Big Foot—or Walsh—ever did.

Big Foot'd given thirty-five years of his life to Uncle Sugar. He enlisted in 1916 when Woodrow Wilson sent

Black Jack Pershing into Mexico to chase Pancho Villa and his bandits. In World War I, at Chateau Thierry, Johnson had been wounded twice. They'd given him the Distinguished Service Cross (the Fifth Marine Regiment was attached to the Second Army Division) and a field commission. Through those long hot years of Caribbean dysentery and the Depression, when I was just a shitbird in high school or starting out at Parris Island as a raw-ass recruit, he had kept the faith in the corps.

World War II had frustrated the hell out of him. As a major on Guadalcanal he'd been wounded by a Japanese naval bombardment before his battalion got any real combat. Then he stayed for six months in a hospital in New Zealand and two years back stateside. I had seen him once or twice. He was spending half his time fighting to get back the use of his legs and the other half ducking a medical retirement. He won both of those fights, but until June 1945 the best he could get was a desk in the Navy Annex Building over in Arlington. Finally he begged an assignment to a replacement draft and joined the First Marine Division three days before we nuked Hiroshima.

Big Foot had come to Korea in the Inchon Landing, and he'd been up north at the Chosin Reservoir; he'd been a division staff officer then. He didn't get the regiment until Christmas, and Operation Ripper wasn't all that exciting for a regimental CO. Caspar was his big chance, and his last one to prove just how good a marine he was. He was due for rotation back to the States in another month. Now the Sixth ROK's were bugging out and dragging his dream in a trail of shit down the Korean hills.

Old Big Foot knew that the real danger to the whole operation right now was from the Chinese around Inje, to the east of us. The ROK's on our right flank would run as fast as the Sixth ROK's had on the left, and then both flanks of the Tenth Corps would be open. In a matter of a few Christ-precious hours after the breakthrough, at least the First Marine Division would be surrounded again, like it'd been at the Frozen Chosin. It must have really pissed Johnson to remember that a few days earlier Walsh had outlined almost the exact strategy the Chinese would use. Not that Big Foot said a single frigging word to the battalions about what was going on around Inje. He didn't believe in worrying the troops about things they couldn't do anything about. He always kept a tight lip and a tight asshole.

Major Stambert wasn't so tender, and he sent on the gist of the warning order to the three battalions. Walsh and Keller, who'd been busy reshuffling our lines to shorten the ground that Easy Company had to defend, drew up three evacuation plans, one for each of the most likely situations. When they were done, Walsh asked Keller, "What's Kasten's situation."

"He started off with 285 men, including his attached units. He took 93 dead or evacuated wounded. Fox Company took only 8 casualties in its counterattack and 3 more from the mortars. Dog took 9. They've each taken over 12 foxholes from Easy and I've given Kasten Dog's heavy machine-gun section. I've also organized the ammo carriers from the 81's and the clerks and cooks from H and S companies into a flying platoon to cover the back of the ravine or to counterattack. Our mine field on the east ridge is probably all gone, but they didn't touch the one on the west ridge. Little buggers learned fast. Guicciardini's surprise is pretty much intact, it seems."

My surprise was a mess of ankle-high barbed wire strung around between the mine field and Easy Company. Nobody could run through that in the dark unless he was a tank; crawling through it would mean leaving your balls hanging on the wire—maybe your wickerbill, too. I'd put some on the north slope and on the east ridge, but not on the west ridge the Chinese had used in their second attack. I hadn't had time.

"Okay," Walsh said. "We're in for another long night. I'm going to nap. I'm disconnecting the telephone in my tent so if you need me come and wake me—but try to get some sleep yourself."

I envied the colonel the way he could fall off to sleep as soon as he hit the sack. He could order a ten-minute break in a march and get eight minutes of shut-eye and be on his feet again before I could loosen my boots. I've seen a lot of old soldiers with that trick. They must be born with it. I've never been able to do it, and I've tried; believe me, I've had a shitpot full of trying.

We could sleep that morning, but the gooks couldn't. They'd been marching for seven days before reaching the Yanggu area, and had had only one full night in place before attacking Caspar. But with us still owning Caspar and their timetable almost twenty-four hours behind schedule, sleep was a luxury. You know what I mean? They had a hell of a lot to do—ammo to be distributed, replacements to be slipped in, dead to be buried, wounded to be moved, and lots of plans to be made and coordinated. And it was harder'n a whore's heart for them to move around in daylight with our OY observation planes buzzing around, ready to call in artillery or air on anything that looked peculiar, much less hostile.

The Chinese regimental commander had begged Division to bypass Caspar. He argued—pretty smart, it seemed to me—that when the column on the east struck down through Inje, Caspar would be isolated. When the rest of the First Marine Division began to retreat to protect its flank, the marines on Caspar would have to get their asses out or be starved off. An ambush between them and their main forces would wipe out them or any rescue attempt at small cost and no risk. And it would avoid more delay to the advance south.

The Chink division commander listened, but I don't know if the son of a bitch heard. Military men, I don't care what their frigging nationality, are usually proud people, and defeat tastes like shit in their mouths. Anyway, his corps commander was goosing him to clear the valley so it could keep the big offensive rolling. Corps was making noises about "an enemy bastion"—that's what the gooks called Caspar—astride a main supply route being sort of intolerable or some such big word, especially when American air was already clobbering the living shit out of their motor traffic. He had something there you know. So the gooks would try one more night to get Hill 915.

The Chinks' unit diaries had a copy of their plan. It called for two regiments to hit us on Hill 915 at the same time. Last night's probing around the rear of Caspar hadn't sucked off any big amount of artillery fire, but it had given the gooks some valuable information. They knew now the big ravine was nearly impregnable—they learned that lesson by losing a full platoon that had tried to assault the five tanks. That must have been legalized murder. But they didn't think the smaller draw was as heavily defended—it wasn't—and it led straight into the rear of Hill 915. So the Chinese division commander had decided that he would send two battalions from his other regiment against this smaller ravine. He'd send his third battalion south of Caspar, and hold it in reserve to take advantage of a breakthrough.

The first objective of the gooks attacking the small ravine would be to grab the high ground between the two ravines and to bring our artillery and mortars in the bigger ravine under small arms fire. Their third battalion would then pass through and sweep down from the high ground into the big ravine, capture the artillery, and take the tanks from behind. A second objective would be to put more pressure on the rear of Hill 915; this was secondary because if our artillery got zapped, any marines on Hill 915 would be up shit creek pretty quick. Since the Chinks already had their regiment in place south of Caspar, the attack would begin at 2230.

FIVE

At 2200, as the doggies' song "Bugout Boogie" went, the Chinese mortars started to thud. This was no barrage, not yet, just a few rounds a minute slamming into the face of Hill 915. But I didn't like the way that about half of the bigger shells were sprinkling the small ravine, rather than falling near the crest of the hill. Walsh got up on the telephone to Regiment.

"Stambert, they're going to hit that ravine, and I don't think the Third Batt can stop them with only the little bit of fire support they're going to get."

"Now, Colonel, you know Big Foot thinks they can."

"I know what Big Foot thinks. Who's your reserve company from the First Batt?"

"Charlie. I got them in a blocking position before dusk, if that makes you feel any easier."

"It does, Major." He talked too much, but Stambert had good tactical sense, even though Walsh called him "Lever" when he got mad and made fun of Stambert's potbelly. (Sometimes the colonel's being cute could be cruel. Pussgut's not a nice name. "Lack of imagination is not necessarily fatal to technical competence," is what

Walsh said about Stambert when he was calm.) "Major, please tell Charlie that in case of a breakthrough I've alerted Fox Company to bend back around the head of the ravine and try to make contact with them. I've organized my headquarters people into a reserve platoon and we should be able to seal off any penetration—as long as it's not a big one. I hope you've told our Chinese friends that under the new Uniform Code of Military Justice, penetration, no matter how slight, constitutes intercourse."

"Yes, sir." I don't think Stambert laughed. The picture of being raped by a Chinaman didn't strike me as being very funny either. It was too likely to happen. "By the way," Stambert reported, "Division sent another warning order similar to the one I gave you this morning. We'll get sixty minutes to execute, very likely tomorrow morning. I could hear artillery around Inje right after dark; with only ROK's there, the chances are the Chinese will break through before midnight."

"Sure'n shit they will if they try."

"Yes, sir."

Right at 2230, the mortar barrage started in earnest. It came just as the clouds opened up with a heavy, cold-pissing rain that stung the face of the troops. Nobody liked that wet chill, but the rain was welcome to the kids in Easy Company because they knew it would make the ridge lines slippery and slow the Chinks. As a little bonus, it would also keep down the smell from the dead who were piled up along the ridge.

Johnny Kasten would be shivering in his sleeping bag. He'd be telling himself that it was the cold that made him shake, but he wouldn't believe it. He'd be wondering why the barrage seemed so much lighter tonight than last. Then the truth would hit him as sharply as the cold rain. Most of the shells were whistling overhead at the artillery and mortars in the big ravine. For some reason, the Chinese usually didn't try much counterbattery fire. This was stupid since the best way to break up a large attack is by artillery, and as long as our artillery was left alone they could blunt, even if they couldn't *stop* it by themselves, any attack. Tonight, the gooks were playing the game with a few more smarts.

Bugles started blaring again, then flares spread their Fourth of July colors across the wet sky. You could hear shouts from people trying to be heard over the crash of the mortars. "Normal barrage!!! Normal barrage!!!" "Get your '60s on the north ridge." "Grenade!" "Fire, fire! Here they come!" "Corpsman! Corpsman!" "Jesus, help me! I'm blind!" "Kai! Kai! Die, you mother-fucking gook bastard, die!"

In the small ravine to our rear, the scenario was almost the same, but the first phase of the fight didn't last very long. The two frigging battalions of Chinese hit into a single marine company—it was Item Company of the Third Battalion—holding the ravine floor. For a few minutes, the Chinks took gory casualties. Each gook battalion attacked in a column of companies, each company in a column of platoons. The lead platoons of both battalions got their tits caught in the wringer and were wiped out to the man, the second pair of platoons ripped to shreds and halted. But the third brace of platoons got into our positions, and the next pair of companies pushed through easily and headed up the ravine toward the rear of Hill 915. Only six marines from Item Company made it up the ridge to the reserve company's area, and two of those poor bastards were killed before they could convince Charlie Company they weren't gooks.

We didn't need Stambert's radio message. From the command post we could tell by the quick halt to the firing what had happened. Walsh immediately ordered Fox Company to bend back its lines, leaving a gap to the west. In seven minutes our Fox Company, George from the Third Batt, and Charlie from the First were pouring small arms fire into the ravine like a herd of cows pissing on a flat rock.

It was at 0030 that Big Foot pulled a brilliant maneuver—so Christ-awful stupid it was brilliant, Walsh claimed. That wasn't kind but it may have been right. Item Company had had responsibility for the small ravine, and its commander had put one platoon facing west and south around the nose of the ridge that formed the west rim of the ravine. This platoon tied in with our Fox Company, while the two other platoons ran across the ravine floor and up the eastern side of the ridge. The Chinks had rolled down the middle of the small ravine and gobbled up the two platoons of gyrenes on the floor without touching the third platoon that was tied in with Fox.

As soon as he saw the breakthrough up the ravine, Walsh ordered the Fox Company commander to assume command of the third platoon of Item Company, but before Fox could execute this order, the sergeant in the operations tent at Regiment realized that the platoon was cut off on three sides and asked Big Foot what he wanted done. Big Foot roared out, "Let them cut their way out, goddamn it! What the hell do you think they've got bayonets for?" Whether he meant that as an actual battle order no one will ever know except Big Foot and he's dead now. But, well, it's pretty frigging unusual—I never heard of it before or since—for a regimental commander to bypass his operations officer as well as his battalion commander and personally maneuver a rifle platoon. But without hearing anything else, the sergeant—and in the colonel's name—told the platoon leader to counterattack with fixed bayonets.

At this point the Chinese in the ravine were in a screwed up mess. They'd just broken through our lines but they'd had the shit kicked out of them. Jarheads die hard. Mopping up was still going on as isolated kids, most of them wounded, kept on fighting to the death. Besides, the ravine was under fire from three companies up on the shoulders, and in the darkness the gooks were having a tough time reorganizing. In a spot like that, with stacks of dead piled up and wounded crawling around bellowing for help, bullets clipping around, ammunition low, officers and NCO's looking for their troops, and the troops looking for a place to hide—it's like getting caught in the middle of a big, gooey turd rolling across the stage of a shooting gallery. You know, a frigging Chinese fire drill.

It was just at the height of all that screwed up ball of shit that the third platoon of Item Company came roaring into the Chinese flank. Screaming more from fear than rage, the marines pounded down the nose of the hill on a dead run, bayonets fixed and rifles and machine guns held at the hip, blazing wildly. They shot and stabbed their way through the Chinese company on the left, taking a terrible toll of the poor gooks as they charged. The Chink company on the right suffered less, but only because their casualties had been so heavy that fewer of its men got in the way of the maniacs.

But one platoon of seventy-eight men, even with more courage than you can expect from humans—and a little luck from good, maybe accidental timing—can't win a firefight against a couple of thousand. Still, the surprise attack gave us a couple of extra minutes before the gooks could regroup and continue their advance. Those minutes were critical. The third Chinese battalion entered the ravine shortly after the marine counterattack had swept across it. Fresh troops added to the confusion, and were infected by it.

By 0130 we'd contained the Chink penetration of the ravine, and pinned down the enemy with small arms and mortar fire, though as Walsh had said would happen, our battalion command post had been turned into front-line foxholes. The first few Chinks weren't more than a hundred yards downhill from us. Meanwhile the fight on Hill 915 raged on. The number of Easy Company's dead got bigger—the wounded just lay there and fought like everybody else; there was no other choice except to die, and a lot of them did. Walsh had Dog Company assume more and more responsibility for the east ridge, which was quiet anyway. Easy was still being slammed from two directions. Now the battle split up into a series of individual and squad-level fights. Neither side had any centralized control. At one place a Chinese squad would rush a foxhole, kill a pair of kids, and then itself be cut down by another group of marines. A few yards away, panting marines and Chinks were in holes or behind rocks four paces in the dark from each other, both sides desperately low on ammunition and each waiting for the other to make a move that would justify firing a precious cartridge or flipping a hand grenade.

This kind of battle goes to the side that can commit fresh troops. The frigging slopeheads had plenty; with half of our artillery and mortars in the big ravine silenced by counterbattery fire, they were now moving their troops around pretty easily. The Chink commanding the regiment attacking Hill 915 had committed two of his three battalions, just as the regiment south of us had committed two against the ravine. Probably by sheer force of numbers the sons of bitches could have succeeded in a drawn-out fight, but since time was critical the commander of the regiment facing Hill 915 decided that now was the moment to use his reserve. At 0200 he ordered the reserve battalion, which was deployed along the east ridge, to strike immediately at Hill 915 with all three companies. Last night's debacle along that ridge wasn't a good omen, but the regimental commander said the American lines would now be thinly manned.

Actually Dog Company now occupied positions guarding the east ridge, and the Chinese reserve battalion piled into a fresh company at almost full strength. A few mines left from the previous night gave the marines a couple of seconds' warning—and a morale boost—but the three Chink companies from the reserve battalion, covered by machine guns and 82-mm mortars, kept coming on right through a withering stream of small arms fire and volley after volley of hand grenades. My little surprise slowed them. A shitpot full died screaming, caught in the wire as machine guns shredded their yellow hides.

Most of the first company was still hanging on that wire two days later, but it was much the same frigging story as down in the ravine. The second and third companies came swarming through, and the fight was hand-to-hand. M–1 rifle butts crushed into Chinese skulls, and big red hands throttled brown necks while Russian-made burp guns tore the intestines out of nineteen-year-old kids. Then it was rocks, knives, and fists. The size of the Americans gave them a great advantage. A big marine could throw a Chinaman like he could a large dog, but for every gook whose back was broken three more leaped in to take his place. The shrieks and screams of anger and agony were now as loud as the noise of the guns. The second Chink company was pulverized, but the next wave came pounding through.

Walsh dived over behind the sandbags protecting the Fire Direction Center and sat next to me. He was breathing hard. The tent had been hastily struck. The rain was gentle now, but it was still cold. It didn't play any favorites. The frigging stuff wilted maps, marines—both dead and alive—radios, cots, and, we hoped, Chinks. "I couldn't see a thing in the ravine," Walsh said. "I think we've got them stopped there. What's new with Hill 915?"

"I don't know, Colonel," Major Morstein shivered. "We've had no radio contact with Kasten for twenty minutes"—it was now 0400—"and they've just broken through Dog Company."

"Get me Rockey quick."

"Rockey's dead, Colonel. There's only one officer left in Dog."

"Oh, Christ. How was Kasten when you last talked to him?"

"Bad. He didn't know what he had left. He was fighting for his own life. The Chinese were all around his command post. I'm afraid Hill 915 is gone."

"Gone? There's still shooting up there."

"Yes, sir, but they've been hit by at least a full regiment, probably more. There'll be shooting for a while, but it'll be mostly marines who're getting shot and Chinese who are doing the shooting."

"Have you told Regiment?"

"Yes, sir. Big Foot says to be prepared to retake Hill 915 at dawn."

"With what, newsreel cameras? Easy is gone. Dog is cut up, and Fox is pinned down here. Maybe the four of us will have to do it ourselves." Walsh looked over at Keller and me.

"Havva no, Colonel," the Smart Money piped up. "This ichibon boysan wouldn't be caught dead in a situation like that. We've got a couple of hours to think about it—unless the Chinese are so gross as to come swarming down here on top of us uninvited. That's not likely because while you were out snooping I got Fox to turn around a bit and tie in with what's left of Dog just above us."

"Good. But that means we're now cut off from direct linkage with both Regiment and Easy Company."

"Si. Should I try to change anything?"

"No. You had no other choice, except suicide."

"Don't think the Smart Money hasn't thought about that one."

The telephone jangled. "You'd think the gooks could do something useful with their mortars and cut that fucking line," Walsh said as he grabbed the phone before the radio operator put down his handset. "Silk Hat."

"Professor, this is Johnson."

"Roger, Johnson."

"I won't bother with code. If the gooks have tapped our lines, we've had the course. Division has said we execute our order at 0700 hours. Do you have any more word on Hill 915?"

"Nothing, Colonel. We have no radio contact with Easy. It looks like Dog has been partially overrun on the east slope of 915. There's still a lot of small arms fire going on, but we've got no reason to believe that it's anything but a mopping-up operation. Two companies can't stop a regiment."

"Jesus Christ, Colonel, don't bitch to me. Your troops have fought like wild men. If they've killed half the gooks they claim, they've crucified most of a regiment tonight. . . ." Big Foot's voice trailed off. "This last part is hard for me to say."

"This is no time to pretend to be decent."

"All right, Walsh. I want your men to cover the regimental withdrawal by a counterattack against Hill 915 at 0645. Don't worry about the ravine. I think the gooks are trying to sneak out while it's still dark. The First Battalion and the tanks will clean them out at dawn, if there're any left.

"Now, for your counterattack," Big Foot went on, "I can't give you any artillery or 4.2's to speak of. Frankly, we've got only a couple of the 4.2's operating and we're almost out of ammunition. I think I'll blow the rest of them up before we leave. Those doggie self-propelled 105's brought along a wad of canister, and we'll take those that can run with us and use them with the tanks to help us break out in the morning. I suspect we'll be blowing them up before we get more than a few hundred yards outside. Division Recon Company and a company of tanks is holding. . . ."

"Are holding, Colonel."

"Goddamn it, Colonel."

"It's probably my last chance to teach you to speak your native language."

"Don't make me waste time arguing with you, Professor. Recon Company and a company of tanks *are* holding the pass to the Hongchon valley open for us. They can hold it until nightfall, but then they'll have to get the hell out. The Chinese have broken through south of Inje and are rolling down the Soyang valley parallel to the Hongchon. They'll be well south of Recon a couple of hours after dusk tomorrow—or today or whatever the hell the time is."

"And what?"

"And if you don't make it to that pass before then, you don't make it at all," Big Foot blurted out, half in tears. "I'm throwing you to the wolves, you son of a bitch, you and all your men, and I'm doing it to save the regiment."

"You're a real jewel, Colonel. Do you expect me to stand up and salute you and say we'll be happy to stick our peckers in the pencil sharpener while the Chinks grind away? Don't worry, Brigadier, we'll save Inja for the empire."

"Goddamn it, Walsh, I hope you live through this crap just so some day you can bleed like I'm bleeding now. All right, here's an order. Retake that hill and cover us. I can't give you enough supporting fire to protect you, but we've been promised four Corsairs at 0600. They're all yours."

"Thanks."

"Shove it—and good luck."

"The same to you, Colonel, the same to you. It's our turn in the barrel. I hope Syngman Rhee and western civilization appreciate what we're doing—but they won't, and I'm not sure I blame them. We who face the Yellow Peril alone salute you. All right, what about my wounded?"

"Able Company is sending up a detachment to carry them down. They'll go out with the rest of us."

"Good. Tell Able to hurry. We've got an awful lot of men stacked up here." With that Walsh slammed down the phone.

"You all right, Dec?" Keller asked.

"Yes. Mike, I want a platoon from Fox and every man you can gather from Headquarters and Weapons companies. The regiment's pulling out at dawn. We're covering with a counterattack on Hill 915. I'll lead it myself. Since we don't have an executive officer, you'll have to take over the battalion."

Walsh turned to the Weapons Company commander. "Fritz, Keller knows more of what's going on than anyone else. If anything happens to me, he's to take over. You're the senior officer and you can have the battalion—if you want it and if it exists—tomorrow."

"Yes, sir."

"Major, get your air team up here with me and find out if your 81's have any ammunition left. We're going to counterattack and retake Hill 915 at 0645. Keller, when we jump off, I want you to take what's left of the battalion and get the hell out of here. No rescuing heroics. I advise heading east. The main Chinese attack is around Chunchon. That column at Inje is a threat, but if that were their major effort, they would have smashed Recon Company off that pass in twenty minutes. Circle around them and ride that tall ridge south. If it looks like the Chinks have made it big, head for the coast and let the anchorheads sail you out. If it looks like we've stopped them, cut west and rejoin the war."

SIX

I DON'T REMEMBER the rain's stopping; there was too much other shit happening: like silence, dead frigging silence both from the ravine and from Hill 915. I read years later, when I was at Headquarters Marine Corps, an explanation of the silence that night in the ravine. Big Foot was right. After we'd sealed off the penetration, the Chinese had hauled ass fast before first light. With the advantage of altitude and M–1's, we'd have picked off every gook in that gully by noon. Of course, we didn't have until noon, but they didn't know that, thank God. All we could see after the sun came up was one hell of a lot of bodies, dead stiffening bodies and some that still wiggled and moved a little. In a few days that mammy-jamming hill mass would stink with rotten flesh and maggots.

At any rate, it was light by a few minutes before 0530. The sky turned from black to silver grey and then a bright blue. The Corsairs would have great visibility from their bombing runs. They came on station right on time, but sixteen of them, not four. Walsh looked up at the slowly orbiting aircraft, and at first he was excited—sixteen planes in a mass napalm attack on Hill 915 might give us enough shock power for the counterattack to come off. Then we saw four of the aircraft peel off from the formation and start circling north and west of 915. "Big Foot's all heart," Walsh said to Keller. "He gives me a pep talk and offers me his last material possessions, four Corsairs, a final talisman of his love. Then he keeps twelve more for himself."

"I never worry my troops with troubles they can't do anything about," Keller replied, aping Big Foot's deep, rolling voice, "and you can't do anything about his keeping twelve of those planes for himself."

"You're right. May the syphilitic chancres he inherited from his mother never heal. All right, how's my task force coming?"

"It's all ready. I've got two platoons from Fox with a light machine-gun section, and we've reorganized what we can find of Dog into one forty-five-man platoon plus a light machine-gun section. George Paraskovakas will lead it."

"My intelligence officer a platoon leader again? A few months ago he couldn't wait to get away from the troops."

"He didn't volunteer. I was afraid to ask him. He might have said no. All the officers from Dog are dead or missing, probably dead. George was with Dog before he rotated back here, so he's a logical candidate. Besides, he was the hardest charger in the battalion. I thought we could put Dog on the right—the east side—going up to Hill 915 and split Fox's two platoons. Princeton's gift to the nation, Charles P. Randall, III, can have one—mostly his own troops. And the Ginny Gunny here insists that all this smell of cordite has his hoary gonads working again; he'll take the other platoon. They can move up the left—the west." Keller looked over at me. "What's the rest of our freshly revised Table of Organization, Gunny?"

I looked at my notebook. It was a pretty shitty mess for a battalion. "Dog Company: 60 men, no officers; Fox Company: 117 enlisted, 1 officer; Weapons Company: 38 enlisted, 3 officers; H and S Company: 120 marine enlisted, 6 marine officers, 8 navy enlisted, 3 navy officers —2 doctors, 1 chaplain; Attached: 4 USMC enlisted, 1 USMC officer from the Forward Air Control Team. All that plus 6 walking wounded from Easy Company who refused evacuation a few minutes ago. That's a total of 355 USMC enlisted, 12 USMC officers, 8 USN enlisted, and 3 USN officers."

Walsh didn't blink, but his stomach must have been

turning. Two nights ago we'd had, with attached units, a little over 1400 enlisted and 46 officers. He looked at me sort of sick, like a man who'd just been kicked in the balls by a very large elephant. "How many of my staff officers are left?"

"Well, sir, there's Rogers, the Air officer, Captain Keller, Major Morstein, and Mr. Turner." Mr. Turner was our supply officer, a commissioned warrant officer, about six cubits wide and four cubits high, but all muscle, a sort of WASP Two-Ton Tony Galento. The troops called him "The Human Sewer Lid" or just "The Lid."

"I thought," Keller cut in, "we'd have Turner take over H and S and form a ragtag tactical unit. He could do it."

"Yes." I knew Walsh hadn't even heard. "Where're the rest, Gunny?"

"Dead, Colonel. Either mortars or those cats in the ravine this morning. They got pretty close."

The colonel looked up at the peak of 915. "Only 300 meters. A good track man should be able to do that in less than two minutes. I suspect it'll take us just a bit longer. We'll jump off when the regiment looks like it's ready to pull out. We'll go as you suggest, Mike."

"Yes, sir."

"Now send me my glorious lieutenants and the forward air controller. I'll explain to them how they die."

In a few minutes First Lieutenant George Paraskovakas, Second Lieutenant Charles P. Randall, III, of Fox Company (he didn't like poker even though his father was one of *the* richest men in the world), and Captain Harry Rogers, the unlucky throttle jockey assigned by the First Marine Air Wing to liaison with us, came crawling through the mud and flopped down next to us behind the parapet of sandbags around the Fire Direction Center. The lieutenants were both in their early twenties and had been in Korea since the Inchon Landing in September. Rogers was a fighter pilot, bald at twenty-eight. He'd gone through basic training with marine ground officers, so he could talk our lingo and understand the problems of both grunts and fly-boys.

I guess I was the oldest son of a bitch in the battalion. I wasn't the reckless type, at least not any more. It wasn't like on the 'Canal, when I was still a kid and didn't believe I would ever die; but I could keep the troops going.

They liked me. I needled them and shouted at them, but I knew my business and they knew I knew it. We got along. The colonel decided to put my "platoon" in reserve. I think he was doing it in case things got sticky—and only an idiot'd have thought they weren't going to get *very* sticky and *very* shitty. He thought I could give the troops a little zip to get them up that hill. I was hoping he was right, but mostly I was thankful I wasn't going to have to be the first bastard to try to retake 915.

Walsh unfolded a limp and soggy map, more like a wilted head of lettuce. "Dearly beloved, we are gathered here today to cover the regiment's evacuation of Caspar. We do it by performing a minor miracle out in front of God and a few hundred thousand gooks. We retake 915. The uniform will be skivvies, a light coat of oil, and a good Act of Contrition. We're here"—he pointed with a dirty fingernail to the CP—"300 meters due south of the crest. We jump off in about twenty minutes. I don't see how we can do anything fancy, just go straight up the ridge, kill all the gooks we can find, and retake 915. I'll try to get our bird boy here to act cute. Randall, you'll be on the left. When you've cleared the top of 915, get your men quickly in a position to defend against an attack from the west and north ridges. Paraskovakas, you're on the right. You have responsibility for taking the eastern half and then defending the east ridge. Gunny, I want you to take over all our machine guns and lay down covering fire for us. And get those two bazookas to throw a couple of rounds in front of us. And when I call for you, come running. We'll need help in a hurry.

"I'm not any good at pep talks, and I needn't tell you how difficult it's going to be to get that hill back, and when we get it how tough it's going to be to hold it. We'll have to keep the Chinese engaged until Regiment is clear of Caspar and what's left of the battalion has gotten out, too. It's the kind of job that a decent CO would only ask volunteers to do—in this case I just volunteered all of you.

"Paraskovakas, you and Randall are going to have to have tight control of your troops, especially the first 200 yards or so where the ridge is narrow. I want you to fan out fast and attack on as wide a front as possible." Walsh turned to the forward air controller. "Now, Captain, what have you zoomies got for us?"

"As you requested, Colonel, the four Corsairs all have napalm, four tanks each. They've also got some 20-mm stuff for strafing."

"Good. I want them to come in from the southwest, straight up the west ridge. Bring them in as low as possible, and to hell with the shrubbery."

"We'll clip the trees, Colonel."

"Good. Tell the pilots I'm going to two-block Fox"—Fox is the flag an aircraft carrier flies at the top of the mast (two-block) when she's about to land aircraft—"and I want you to mix up the runs. On the first run I want all four to come in together and each drop one napalm tank. After that, single runs. Vary them. Strafe once, napalm once, make a dummy run, maybe two dummy runs in a row. Get in a position where you can see us and make the final two runs strafing and dummy. That last batch of POW's said they figured twenty minutes of grace between an air strike and an infantry attack. Let's take advantage of that. Time the runs so that we're on top while the planes are still flying over the target making their last dummy run. I want every gook on that hill with his head down and ass up so we can insert a bayonet in his rectum. Can do?"

"Yes, sir, can do."

"I'll be with you on the left, Randall. Keller, get me an SCR–300 radio and an operator."

"I think we have two of each left, Colonel, but as far as I know we only have one extra 536 radio."

"Throw it away. No point in carrying that extra weight. The damned things won't work half the time anyway."

"Colonel," the telephone operator said, "Topper has just broken wire communication. I think Topper Six will be up on the radio in a minute."

"Thanks. Now any questions, gentlemen?"

There was a long moment of silence, then a heavy burst from an American 30-calibre machine gun and two distinct grenade explosions followed by a series of single blasts from an M–1 mixed with the smoother burp of a Russian tommy gun.

"It's from 915, Colonel," Keller shouted. "There's still marines up there. Listen to that machine gun."

There was a long burst of fire, ending with a playful "shave and a haircut, two bits," that only a practiced finger can give. The burst was followed by a chorus of burps and two more grenade blasts. Captain Rogers put down his radio headset and looked at Walsh. Walsh waved his hand, but it was a signal that didn't mean a thing. The obvious thing was that some of Kasten's people were still holding out. We could all imagine the guts of a small group of jarheads, fighting all frigging night against a couple of million gooks, now surrounded and just about out of ammunition but still cocky enough to hammer out a ditty. "Can you raise Kasten?" Walsh asked the radio operator.

"I've tried every five minutes since 0430, Colonel. Once about an hour ago, I thought I heard a voice that sounded like Mr. Kasten's but I couldn't read him."

"Listen," Keller cut in.

The machine gun banged again. This time there were three single shots, three short bursts, and then three single shots. "Three dots, three dashes, three dots—SOS, Colonel, SOS," Lieutenant Randall yelled as he started to climb over the sandbags, but I grabbed him around the knees. "Where the hell are you going, Lieutenant?" Walsh asked.

"Up that hill, Colonel. There's marines up there. They're asking for help. Jesus Christ, you aren't going to let them be burned alive?"

"Sit down, son, sit down." I patted Randall on the butt with my left hand but I kept my right arm around his knees.

"I don't know what I'm going to do, Randall," Walsh said, "but you're going to sit here until I make up my mind. Maybe Big Brother can get us off the hook. Get me Regiment, operator."

"Don't need to, sir; they're calling us."

"Silk Hat, Silk Hat, this is Topper."

Walsh took the handset. "Topper, this is Silk Hat Six. Give me Topper Six or Topper Three. Over."

"Silk Hat Six, this is Topper Six. We stand ready to vacate premises. When do you execute lease? Over."

"Topper Six, this is Silk Hat Six. Complications. Some friendly family still paying rent on premises. Over."

The radio went silent. We could hear more scattered shots from the top of 915. "Topper, Topper, this is Silk Hat. Do you read me? Over. Topper, Topper, this is Silk Hat. Do you read me? Over."

"Silk Hat, this is Topper. I read you. Execute your orders any way you see fit, but seize your objective. Begin within fifteen minutes. Acknowledge. Over."

"Topper, this is Silk Hat. Wilco. Out." Walsh put down the radio. "The oracle is silent. Captain, get your planes ready."

Randall almost tore himself out of my grip as Captain Rogers's radio man started cranking the handle to juice up the radio. "Let me go up there, Colonel," Randall begged. "Kasten got Fox out of a trap last winter. We were cut off and Easy came in like a herd of John Waynes. I owe my life to Kasten and so do a lot of my friends."

"Negative, Lieutenant, you'd never make it alone and if you did you wouldn't be a bit of help. Your troops won't make it either without air support. If you want to talk about a debt, you owe one to your men not to throw their lives away."

Walsh looked around at the rest of us, questioningly. Nobody said anything, not a peep. We just breathed hard. I don't know about the others but I was God-awful grateful it wasn't up to me. I had my own ideas, but I didn't have the responsibility. Walsh had the wheel and I never knew any officer in the whole Crotch with more smarts than him.

After a couple of minutes of silence, Walsh looked back up at the hill. "Well," he said, "it doesn't make any difference what any of you would have said anyway. It's my decision. Bring your planes in, Captain."

"Now, Colonel?" Rogers looked up from his radio set. He'd been relaying Walsh's instructions to the Corsairs.

"Now, goddamn it, start them now. Bring them in. Two-block Fox."

Rogers picked up the handset again, and Randall looked straight at Walsh. "You cold-blooded, murdering bastard, I hope you burn in hell for all fucking eternity." He didn't yell it, he just said it softly as the tears trickled down his face. He was crying, and like most men who cry for dead, or about to be dead, friends, he didn't feel any shame.

Walsh reached out quick, like a big cat, and slapped Randall across the face. His hand was open, but he was strong and fast. The pop knocked Randall back into the mud. He came up with a big red print on his left cheek. "You're hysterical, Lieutenant," Walsh said. His voice was quiet too, but it had a mean edge to it. "Get hold of yourself. You'll probably get your wish, and it's likely I'll start serving my sentence soon enough to please you. Get to your platoon, Lieutenant. Keller, you've got the wheel now."

"Dec, about Johnny, I . . ." Keller began.

"Never mind. The Smart Money can second-guess me at leisure if he can get the rest of the battalion out of here."

I turned my back so I wouldn't see those orange flashes and black smoke puffs from the napalm. The colonel stood straight up and looked right at the top of 915. He could be tougher on himself than on anybody—and that was pretty tough, I shit you not.

If it had been me, I'd have had the planes strafe and make dummy runs until we found out how mean it was actually going to be. We might have been able to make it without the napalm. The strafing and diving might have kept the gooks' heads down. And those old Corsairs could have stayed on station for a couple of hours if we needed the napalm later.

But for Christ's sake, don't get me wrong. I loved Johnny Kasten, maybe not as much as Walsh did, but I loved him. Still, I know that if those gooks hadn't kept their heads down we'd have had the course. We might not have been able to put enough distance between us and them to bring the Corsairs back to use napalm. Remember what I told you about that "disengaging" crap. It's a tough frigging thing to do when the other side's using live ammunition. And I don't care what those fly-boys say about how good they are. About the best they can deliver is to hit the right mountain. All that stuff about putting a bomb in a barrel is bullshit, unless the barrel's got a mouth like a volcano, and even then it would have to have hair around it.

It's a matter of how you play your cards, I guess. Our objective was to retake Hill 915, and Walsh put that first, way on top of everything else. I'm just glad it wasn't my hand to play.

After he'd given the platoon leaders enough time to get back to their troops and brief their squad leaders, Walsh stood up and motioned them to start their men up the hill. I gave him the thumbs up signal. It was corny, but I couldn't think of anything else to do. Then he said something that only he and I understood since we'd both been altar boys: *"Introibo ad altare Dei."* And I answered. *"Ad Deum qui laetificat juventutem meam."* Before Pope John and all this English crap, that's the prayer we used to say at the beginning of Mass, when the priest finished his prayers at the foot of the altar. It was the altar boy's signal to stand up. "I shall go unto the altar of God," the priest would say, and the altar boy would answer, "To God who giveth joy to my youth." Neither of us felt very young right then, or joyful, and I guess neither of us expected to live through the next few hours. But it wasn't a bad prayer to go out with; it reminded us of better times.

The troops started slogging up the hill, and the Corsairs came screeching in over our heads for their second runs, now strafing with 20-mm cannon, now making false passes, now another feint, then another tank of blazing napalm, now another napalm, now another dummy pass, now another strafing run; and so it went. With every tank of napalm—one fell so close that its scorching heat singed my eyebrows and the hair on the back of my right hand—each of us was praying that some frigging miracle would protect the marines who were dug in on top of the hill.

Walsh's trick with the Corsairs worked so well that the two platoons made it within ten yards of the crest before the Chinks knew they were under attack. While the planes were still roaring over in their last dummy run, Walsh let out a shriek of "banzai!" and both platoons swarmed into the Chinese. As the big marines hacked and shot the gooks to pieces, Walsh turned and used a police whistle I'd given him to signal me to commit my unit.

Unlike the night's fighting, this was short, but it was bloody enough. At point-blank range an M–1 doesn't put a little hole in a man; the bullet flattens out when it hits bone or gristle and blows out a steak that would feed a professional football player for a full day. Big chunks of meat went flying through the air, as the surprised Chinks stood up to try to fend off our shock power. Once again the physical size of the marines paid off. We just bowled the little gooks over, and crushed skulls with rifle butts and broke arms, ribs, necks, and backs like big butchers hacking up chickens.

As Walsh turned around after signaling me, two Chinese leaped up five yards ahead. He fired quickly with his 45 and winged one, but the other got off a short burst from his burp gun just as another marine cut the bastard's head off above the eyebrows with four quick shots from an M–1. Walsh slipped a few yards down the hill before he could get his footing back. He said later the only way he knew he'd been hit was that his mind went fuzzy. He sat down and felt himself. There was blood along his left cheek and the side of his head, and his left shoulder was numb. Neither wound was serious or even painful—yet.

There isn't much else to say. Walsh had to act like one of the troops. Once the planes were done and he'd committed my platoon, the only frigging thing left for him was to fight for his life like every other son of a bitch. And he did. The troops had never seen a light colonel in hand-to-hand combat, but even with only one working arm, Walsh did his share of killing gooks. It was a real boost to morale for the kids to see him snake quick to dodge a burst from a machine gun and then flip a grenade into the nest, or thump a Chinaman on the gourd with the barrel of his 45 when the damn thing jammed.

By the time I got to the top of the hill, there wasn't much to do but poke around in the holes, kill the few Chinks that were left, and then organize a defense. Our casualties had been light—nine killed and twenty-eight wounded. That asshole Randall made it, but his right arm was mangled. He was still tight-lipped, not on a high like people usually are who have lived through a firefight, or in shock like the badly wounded. He had a lot of hate left in him, and he knew that if he lived it would be without that flipper.

I took charge of setting up the defense, and Walsh—he was carrying a burp gun in his good hand now—walked around the area where Johnny Kasten's command post had been. I came up behind him a couple of minutes later. It was a god-frigging-awful sight. Not the couple of dozen dead gooks strewn among the bunkers—you don't mind that—but Kasten was in a bunker with two kids huddled over a machine gun. They were sitting bolt upright with their eyes open. Except for their skin being sort of parched, they seemed all right. Johnny had a 45 in his left hand and an automatic carbine in his right. It was easy to see what had happened—a napalm tank had exploded about twenty yards away and burnt up all the oxygen inside the bunker.

Kasten and his men had had their lungs burned out, instantly suffocated by the burning oil.

Walsh was just standing there, not saying anything, not doing anything, just staring like he was in a trance or something.

"Colonel, Colonel!" I spoke as sharply as I could. I had guessed that Walsh had found Johnny, but it was only then that I saw him. "Oh my God, oh my God, oh my God." I was praying, not swearing. "Come away, Colonel. I'll have some of the men bury them." I took Walsh firmly by the right shoulder and pushed him along. "Don't look back."

Walsh was silent. Then he muttered, "Do you think I have to? I'll see Kasten's face until the day I die."

"That may not be so long, Colonel. If you don't get hold of yourself, you'll take a lot of these kids with you. We've known each other since 1944. I don't recall ever Dutch uncle-ing you before, not even when you were a second lieutenant, but I'm going to do it now. If Johnny's radio had been working, he'd have called those planes on himself, and I shit you not. Johnny was a marine before he was anything else. God rest his soul." That much was gospel. As a marine, Johnny *would* have called those planes in on himself. Whether he would have called them in on somebody else, at least without trying something else first, is another question. I guess the colonel knew that, too.

I wiped the sweat and tears off my face. "I almost forgot what I came after you for, Colonel. We've got company coming."

"All right, Giuseppe." He looked up at me clear-eyed. He always could turn that switch, and I'd just seen it snap back. "Have we got enough ammo for a long fight?"

"Nope. In a few hours we might find some more around these bunkers and foxholes, but we won't need much right now, just one bullet for your friend the Smart Money. He's coming up the hill leading what's left of your battalion; the shithead's risking my hard-earned poker winnings."

Walsh waited until Keller was close. "You're a stupid, mutinous son of a bitch. Captain, you haven't even got the military sense it takes to be an Egyptian general. I told you to get the battalion out."

"Well, Colonel, regimental orders were that we should cover their withdrawal. You did that and they got off without too much trouble. I could hear firing and see the planes going in a couple of miles back, so I knew that job was done. Once you made me battalion commander, I was legally free to change the orders of the previous battalion commander. I elected to come up to 915 and take a look at the scenery. I have a legal right to overrule my predecessor."

"You're a chiseling, shithouse shyster."

"I learned from a master, Colonel. Besides, I don't think the troops trusted me to get them out. You know I get lost trying to find my tent if I have to go out at night to shake the dew off my lily."

"I'll court-martial you later. Gunny, show this fugitive from the funny farm where he can put his men. Get him out of my sight or I'll shoot him on the spot."

"Before you do, Dec," Keller whispered as he walked by, "see a corpsman. Your face is a mess, and that ain't strawberry jam on your shoulder."

Everything seemed queer to me. We had quiet. I looked around and saw that a thick layer of clouds had settled in at about the 800-meter level. We were a couple of hundred feet above a lot of the carnage, and the thick milky clouds were shielding us from noise. The only thing we could see clearly were the peaks of the tallest hills around the valley. Christ, it gave you an eerie feeling right after all that frigging shrieking and slamming of war. You could even see the holes in the clouds that were made by the 155 shells that went fluttering north. By noon, it was all over. The clouds had blown away, and we had a crisp day, with the ground sprinkled with smelly, twitching bodies.

We ate our C rations cold, put out dead friends into some foxholes we weren't using ourselves and filled them in. A few of the kids played "roll the gook"—they tucked the heads of dead Chinks between their ankles and tried to see who could roll a body farthest down the hill. In the tradition of the marines we buried only our own. It was grim work and at the end we had to scratch out a few common shallow graves. We didn't have much time, and after fighting for forty-eight hours straight we had less energy. I went around collecting dog tags from the bodies. I found 137 and did some quick figuring. I'd made up the casualty reports the night before and knew how many men had been left in the battalion outside of Easy and Dog companies. It was a frigging miracle—only a little miracle and not a useful one—but I could account for every marine in the Second Battalion. Most of the poor bastards were dead or wounded. I couldn't do much with those dog tags except maybe hit some gook in the chops when the Chinks tried to retake Hill 915.

I had other things to bother me. Walsh was the first and the biggest. I don't mind saying it now, but I was scared shitless he had battle rattle; that switch in his head could flip back in a second. He was obviously in pain, and I knew damned well his shoulder and face were causing only part of it. A corpsman had cleaned out both wounds. Neither one was serious. The one on his face was only a deep gouge that would probably leave a scar that broads would get all sexed up about—if he lived. The shoulder wound was worse because it was deep—right through on both sides, in fact—and we didn't have any antibiotics left. Still, the corpsman thought he'd be all right; the bullet had missed the bone and any major muscle. But Kasten's death had Walsh close to shock. I was afraid that any fresh strain would turn him into a babbling idiot—and in a war you get fresh strains every time you take a leak.

Major Morstein, the Weapons Company commander, was the next senior officer, with Keller after him. There were only five other officers left and two of them were navy people. You can't trust the best of those anchorheaded bastards to do more than piss downwind. Our two didn't even know that much. One was the chaplain, a red-faced, hard-drinking Lutheran. He was great for morale, but running a battalion in combat wasn't his line of work. The other navy man was a battalion surgeon. Like a GI jackass going down with his ship, he stayed with us himself, and sent his assistant out with the wounded that Regiment picked up. He'd be too busy with our fresh wounded to help anywhere else. Captain Rogers, the fly-fly boy, was the next senior to Keller. He'd do all right and the other officers, too. But they might be too afraid of Walsh even if he lost his nerve. All except that rich, Princeton mammy-jammer Randall, that is; but the surgeon was working on his right arm. I suspect he'd have chopped it off right there if he'd had the stuff to keep Randall out of shock. Rogers would have been more help if his radio still worked, but a burst from a machine gun had turned his communications gear into a jangled bundle of shit.

The Smart Money'd been joking about his crappy sense of direction, but the joke wasn't far off the mark. His misreading maps was a standard battalion joke. That's usually a fatal flaw in an operations officer, but Walsh had a sixth sense about such things; he always knew where we were in spite of the Smart Money. I thought about it a little and decided I'd have to squeeze Major Morstein to take over the battalion if Walsh cracked up. I can remember hoping that if the colonel went, he'd go apeshit rather than just lose his nerve. I could get him out if he started screaming or something but if he just clutched, I might not be able to do a frigging thing.

By mid-afternoon two-thirds of the kids were sleeping like the exhausted bastards they were. The noise of the regiment's firefight had faded away. Way off to the south, there was a new group of Corsairs, marking the regiment's line of retreat like a frigging flight of benevolent buzzards. Still there was no counterattack from the Chinese. Walsh dozed off a few times, but he always woke up with a start. I guessed either somebody was kicking him in the shoulder or Johnny Kasten was staring at him from Easy Company's command post. I stayed close by. At about 1430, Walsh sat up quickly. "Mike, Mike, wake up. I've got an idea."

"Good. Let's sleep on it, Colonel. You know what Mr. Justice Frankfurter said: 'Good ideas, like good wine, need time to mature.' "

"It wasn't ideas that Frankfurter was talking about. Let me have your map case."

Keller sleepily handed the packet over and Walsh spread out the wrinkled, torn maps. He asked me to get Major Morstein and I obliged, though if my eyes were as red as his, we couldn't have done anything for the colonel's morale. "How long can we hold out against a stiff counterattack, Gunny?" Walsh asked me.

"Depends on how stiff is stiff. If they throw in only one or two companies, we've got a fifty-fifty chance of making it through the night."

"Then what?"

"Then nothing. No ammo, no medicine, and no shit."

"More than two companies, say a full battalion?"

"Three to one chance we'd be done for ten minutes after the third company was committed. There wouldn't be any survivors." I was looking as close at Walsh's face as I could without provoking him, trying to guess whether he was going to start talking surrender. As soon as he did, I was ready to tell Major Morstein and Keller about finding Walsh frozen by Kasten's body and to tell Morstein he had to take command. I thought about telling the major anyway.

"That's what I calculate. We'd use all our ammo on the first two companies. I don't think we ought to wait to be caught. Regiment's well out of the trap—at least as far out as anything we can do will get them. How many men do we have left, Gunny?"

I pulled a notebook from my jacket. "327 USMC enlisted, 12 USMC officers, 8 USN enlisted, 2 USN officers. Total: 335 enlisted, 14 officers."

"How many of them wounded?"

"More than half of the men are wounded, sir, but if you mean those who can't help themselves, only about fifteen."

"Any prisoners?"

I just looked up but didn't say anything. I was tired right down to my cajunes, and the colonel should have known better than to ask silly questions. Prisoners in our kind of combat are a luxury that egghead professors talk about in college classrooms.

"All right. We'll head east and then south and take our chances on getting out. It's better than waiting here to die."

Everyone must have heard my breathing go back to normal, but nobody said anything. "Yes sir, Colonel. When?"

"As soon as it's dark. The Chinese must be feeling pretty cocky. They haven't even fired any mortar rounds since we've been on the top."

"They might not even know we're here," I said. "I don't think we let any of them get away, and might have come up too fast for them to get a radio message off."

"That's a possibility, but we can't get much more grace. Under the circumstances, it's not likely they'll try to attack much before 2200. It'll be dark tonight by 2000 or shortly before. We'll be ready by 1800 to move out as soon as it's black enough to cover us."

"What about the moon, Colonel?" Major Morstein asked.

"What about it? We're not going out there to neck. I haven't seen the moon in over a week. It's been too cloudy. What kind of moon would it be?"

Nobody said anything.

"Lousy lovers you'd all make. All right. If we move out shortly before 2000, moon or no moon, the worst we can do is to run head-on into an attack up the east ridge. That would surprise them as much as it would us. If we can get onto that ridge and make the turn south without being caught . . . well, we'll be on our way. Gunny, have the surgeon make some litters for the wounded. We'll take turns carrying them. Let H and S companies handle that first. They took the least punishment."

"Aye, aye, sir." I couldn't wipe the shit-eating grin off my face.

SEVEN

WITHIN A FEW DAYS of the Second Batt's retrograde from Caspar the east central part of Korea quieted. We'd pretty much stopped the Chinks all along the front—if you don't count the ROK's, and none of us who were fighting the war did. Those yardbirds deserted from the North and South so many times they must have confused *themselves* about which side they were on. Well, I don't blame them too much. I never saw a mammy-jamming thing in Korea I'd fight for, if I had a choice; and maybe the world would be better off if we'd all just turn tail and haul ass when somebody starts tooting on a bugle. But I was a professional soldier. It was a good life, and when you draw the pay you do the job. My job was to go wherever the commandant of the Marine Corps sent me and to fight. He sent me to Korea, God bless him, and I went and I fought.

Well, anyway, the whole Eighth Army had to pull back all along the peninsula to even out those big gaps the Koreans left when they bugged out. We'd been pounded—you don't bang assholes with 280,000 men shooting live ammunition without somebody getting hurt—but the Chinks hadn't really punched through anywhere against a respectable outfit. And we'd made them bleed. At Caspar, we'd done better than most, but that's what you expect from marines. The British and the dogfaces probably did their share, I guess, and air and artillery gave old Mousey Dung a little slack in his population problems. Once the Chinks counted their dead and saw that all they had to show for their blood was thirty miles or so of godforsaken hills, they decided to rest, regroup, and resupply some fresh flesh.

In some ways that helped us in the Second Batt. Every mile the gooks pushed south was another mile we'd have to walk—and risk running into a firefight. On the other hand, since they weren't concentrating on banging through at a couple of points, there were a lot more of those slopeheaded hummers spread out for us to stumble over.

Meanwhile, the rest of the First Marines had gone into reserve after Caspar. The Fifth and Seventh marines and the attached Korean marine regiment were on-line, waiting for Phase II of the Chinks' effort to push us off the peninsula. Every unit in the whole division had taken casualties—not as bad as at the Chosin Reservoir, but bad enough if the dead are your friends. With us supposedly wiped out on Caspar, the First Marines would get the bulk of the replacements due to dock in Pusan in early May. With a new batch of troops to stitch into the outfit and a new battle ahead, Operation Rat Trap would fade into a kind of myth. Caspar would be another name in a mishmash of nightmares. For me at least, the last operation always became unreal, like a dream or something, as soon as the next warning order came down. And that big balloon was going up again, quick.

Like I say, during the last few days of April I didn't know a damned thing about all of this, and I didn't give a rat's ass. All I wanted was to find a friendly unit, get a decent meal, and sleep for two or three days. I wasn't even thinking about bimbos, and in those days I used to think about nookie a lot. The night we left Caspar, we snuck down the east ridge in the dark and did some long, slow hill walking. That mountain range between Yanggu and Inje is a mean mother, and we couldn't use the only real pass in the area. Worse than that, we'd have to cross the Soyang River to go either south or east. North and west opened only to POW camps or a graveyard or maybe both.

Now it wasn't just the river. The Soyang isn't too deep that time of year, and we could find lots of places to wade across. The hitch was that the road through Inje generally went right along the river bank, and that was the only road the Chinks could use in this area. You could bet it'd be crowded with hostiles and that our air and artillery would be clobbering it. And most of the way south of us, the valley was wide—for Korean valleys, I mean—and flat, lots of open sand flats. We'd have had a bitch of a time getting 350 people across any of those fords without attracting a few million gooks, plus a lot of American fire.

But that's where Walsh was smart. He didn't take the quick, direct way to the river. We could've followed the east side of Caspar's V, where Dog had defended, and had a fairly easy downhill walk to a couple of fords—and probably strolled into a pair of Chinese regiments. Instead, we went almost straight east, around Easy's old mine field, for about 2000 yards. Now that might not sound so far when you think about it like a daylight walk in the States. Try it on a dark night on a mountain top when you're shit-scared, haven't slept for forty-eight hours, and you're toting a pack of wounded on litters, plus all the ammo and C rations you can carry, and you can't make any noise, and all around you are shell holes to fall into and dead bodies to fall over and even a few poor bastards just getting around to dying.

That little move took us a full hour. We rested for fifteen minutes, then turned down the ridge line and headed southeast on a fairly gentle ridge that humped up and down like a fifty-dollar whore toward the Soyang. We made better time there, and it was just as well. We stopped for our second break at 2215. We were almost 3000 yards down the ridge, at about the 600-meter contour level, when the shit hit the fan back on Hill 915. A good twenty minutes of pounding, then an attack from the east, right across our wake. I didn't know how many gooks then. Walsh moved us out just as fast as our frigging little feet would take us. He knew the noise from the shooting would cover our clatter, and he didn't want the rear end of our column to tangle with any gook stragglers.

When I read the Chinese unit diaries I saw that the division that had been attacking us had used its only intact battalion. They were in reserve by then, with a new division commander, and were a screwed up mess. We'd beat the living shit out of them. They had over 1500 dead and missing and about 7000 wounded. That's pretty stiff for a unit that started out with only 11,000 men. You could tell that from their dead still lying around. Those bastards were almost as good as marines about taking care of their dead and wounded. The North Koreans were pretty sloppy —or maybe they were South Koreans. Like I say, I never could tell one gook from another. I don't think they could either.

Anyway, we walked that ridge for another hour and then turned straight east on a big spur. Walsh must have sensed that turn; you couldn't see it. I kidded him about it, and he said something about genetics—I didn't know then what that meant. He said his ancestors must have been hunters or sailors, and those who didn't have a good sense of direction got lost and died before having too many kids. How'd he put it? Oh yeah: "Their gene pool was lost." I'll forgive a guy a lot if he can find his way around in the dark good enough to keep me alive.

Walsh pulled us off to the east because the main road was about two miles ahead. He'd chosen a great spot to cross it, the only place in twenty miles it cut away from the river, so we could get across the road, have a nice hill to fade into, and then cross the river later at a narrow spot in the valley. Trying to cross the two together would have meant getting caught by the Chinks or killed by our own air and artillery. Three times that night our planes plastered the road where we could hear them, and God knows how many other times, and every few minutes a shell would come screaming in. I guessed from the sound and the range that it must have been a tank. You know, we'd roll up tanks on a little knoll with their noses up high and their guns at maximum elevation and crank off some long-range H and I stuff—that's harassing and interdiction. I don't know about the interdiction, but just hearing those high-pitched whistles harassed the hell out of my ass.

It was 0300, too late to try to cross both the road and the river, and the hill in between wasn't big enough to hide in by daylight, so we found—actually I found it—a tight little ravine on the northeast slope of a hill numbered 593. We ate a can of C rations—I made sure that everybody buried their cans—and then we tried to get some cover and concealment for the day. We couldn't see the town of Inje, even though it was just a mile due east. And this wasn't a likely spot for a Chink patrol, but we sure as shit didn't want to be plastered by an American air strike in daylight—or at night for that matter.

We stayed tucked away all the next day. It was pretty

quiet. We would hear lots of artillery to the south, and occasionally some heavy traffic going out of Inje. We had four air strikes on the town that day. The colonel figured that with Inje being such a prominent town, the air force would clobber it every few hours and so the gooks wouldn't keep many troops close by. I don't know whether he was right or wrong, but we got through the day without any of the bastards spotting us.

Right after dusk we started out and got to the road about 2200. We had to cross in small groups, in between trucks—the traffic picked up after dark. I was happy to see most of the northbound stuff was loaded with troops. I guessed they were wounded. I didn't get close enough to see. We crossed near the top of a little pass. It was steeper going and hard on our wounded, but that way we could tell when the trucks were coming. They had to downshift and rev up their engines to make the climb. It took us another two hours to all get across. But we made it—scared shitless, like 350 kids in the pumpkin patch with Farmer Brown and his shotgun at the ready.

The river was tougher. Just as the first group started to wade, one of our Fireflies came over—that's a specially rigged C–47 but you probably knew it as the DC–3—and popped a string of flares to light up the area for an air strike. Well, there was a platoon of marines ass-deep in ice water out in front of God and everybody. They were good troops and they froze—I mean both ways—until the bombs started. Then in the confusion they splashed over to the other side. The planes were going after the two road junctions just north of Inje—I doubt if they hit either one —so we used the noise to cover the racket we made. The attack lasted fifteen minutes, not enough time to get all of us across, but it was a good start.

The river was deeper than we hoped. We couldn't use either of the two fords marked on the map because it was too likely a Route Army or two would be there. We had to wade in chest-high water, water coming from melting snow. That's tough for hungry, tired men; it was too tough for some of the wounded. Eight of the fifteen were dead within twenty-four hours. The doctor said shock, exposure, and a few other technical words. We buried them at night in shallow graves; the chaplain said a few words; and I had more dog tags to carry.

We climbed the rest of the night—long and slow and ball-busting hard. We still had some of the badly wounded, and a lot of the others were having more trouble. Legs were stiffening and arms were getting weak. We had a lot of infections and almost no medicine except what the doctor called vocal anesthesia. Walsh kept us going. I helped and so did Paraskovaskas. We were up and down the column, tripping and falling in the dark, carrying a rifle for a kid for a few hundred yards or taking a turn with a stretcher, or just kicking ass if somebody was dogging it.

We kept on until a few minutes before first light. The colonel thought that we were on the Chinks' extreme left flank, and they were more likely to have patrols out here than in the wake of one of their main attacks. We got two or three more miles south and east of the river and found another ravine—thank God they're a dime a dozen in that part of the world—to hide in. It was near a big double-peaked hill numbered 734.

We started to follow the same routine the next night and that's when we had our big trouble. First off it was raining. We even had the first thunderstorm of the season. Now any noise'd help and the rain and the thunder gave us lots. But the rain made the ridges slippery as whale shit, and our stretcher bearers were slipping all over the place. I think that's what killed another of the wounded. The kids slipped, and the poor bastard slid about twenty feet down a hill, hitting trees and rocks all the way. The doctor said he bled to death. We scratched out a grave for him.

We went sliding on for about an hour and a half until we reached the edge of a small valley. Half of it had a stream running west toward the Soyang, the other half a little brook that wiggled east into the next big compartment, the valley of the Naerinchon. On the other side of that was the sea. We'd come to a gentle hump of a watershed. Because of the wounded Walsh decided to use the hump rather than have a steep walk down in the slick greasy mud, another stream crossing, and a hard climb up. Fortunately for our asses, he sent out a patrol to scout first.

Sure enough, they came back and said there was some noise, and even a couple of small fires on the sheltered side. The colonel and I decided to play Injun and went snooping and pooping ourselves. His left shoulder was stiff now, but like me he carried a burp gun and three grenades—you know, I never could walk around with more than three of those damned things. I never liked them, I guess, because one of them rolled between my legs on the Tenaru-ri. I know what a head shrink would say and he might be right. Anyway, I never could bring myself to put one of those things in my pocket. Well, we came in real quiet. For once I was thankful for cuckoo birds. We were in a forest and the place was full of them and what we called radio birds, noisy sons of bitches that went dit-dit-dat-dit all night long. Rain, thunder—nothing seemed to bother them. They kept it up while we sneaked in.

We stayed about forty minutes. As far as we could tell there were only six gooks. I couldn't figure what the hell they were up to, and it didn't look like they knew either. In that forty minutes all they did was crawl under a couple of shelter halves, munch rice, and giggle. They might have been deserters or a flank guard or even a patrol. They acted to me like a bunch of fags having a couple of quickies. We looked the best we could on both sides but couldn't see a frigging thing, even when the lightning was flashing. Well, we couldn't wait much longer.

There were too many of them for any hand-to-hand stuff, and I don't think either of us could have whipped anybody much tougher than a kitten anyway. So we took out our grenades and put them in front of us. As soon as the six gooks were close together under the two shelter halves, we got ready for the next flash of lightning. We'd been timing about seven seconds from flash to crash. Our grenades had five-second fuses. For once, I was thankful they didn't make a pop when the fuse started burning, although that can be dangerous as hell—so we counted to three and each flipped one into one on the shelter halves. We had the second pair in the air just an instant before the first went off. The thunder rolled in beautifully. A hundred yards away you couldn't have known anything had happened. We moved in quick, but they were pretty messy.

Just as we started back I was looking to the east when I thought I saw some lights flicker. Then four big flashes and lots of boom—122-mm howitzers, probably self-propelled. It must have taken a hell of a lot of doing to get them there. They were down by a village called Lahyon off a creek leading into the Naerinchon. They'd decided to use the storm as cover, too. We'd flushed their flank guard.

I went back and got the battalion. With scouts out fifty yards in front we got across the hump and into the big hills on the other side. I was just itching to get down there and clean out those four, frigging Chinese guns. The colonel was, too. I could see him fighting inside himself, worried about getting the battalion out, and wanting to get in close and maybe flip a few grenades in the ready ammo pits that would be by the guns. Finally, the battalion won out, and we slogged ahead, climbing some pretty rugged countryside. We had a choice of almost straight south or southeast, and Walsh picked southeast. Those guns, he said, probably meant there were some Chinks straight south, although it seemed to me the guns were firing more southwest than straight south. But the colonel had two hands and two feet on the wheel, and so I wasn't about to argue.

It went that way for three more days and nights—hiding all day, walking all night. Each day we ate—were supposed to eat—only one can of heavy C rations and one can of light, plus maybe a chocolate bar. Explorers have had it a lot worse. We came close to a couple of streams so we had all the water we needed—not all we wanted, but enough to get by.

I could tell you a pisspot full about that march. I'll admit it, discipline was a problem. Not anything like desertion or mutiny, but it was tough work keeping those kids quiet all day, keeping them from going down to a stream to get some water. Not the first day. They were too tired and shit-scared. It was after the first few days, when they got more used to this kind of fear, you know, and hunger started to drive them. Some of them by now had eaten all their C rations and were complaining and begging from their friends. Nobody had enough to eat and you burned up a lot of sweat climbing mountains all night.

Some of them wanted to quit—not necessarily to surrender, just to lie down and die. But the colonel wouldn't let them do it, not easy anyway. He'd talk to a kid who was ready to quit, reason with him, order him, remind him of home, threaten to shoot him on the spot—I thought he would and so did they—but all the time, his basic message was "Trust me, son. I'll get you back alive and in one piece. Trust me." We did. Everybody knew that if anybody could get us out, the colonel could. It was just that some were so weak and shit-tired they didn't give a donkey's dong anymore.

I think I told you that the colonel had more juice than a bull elephant in heat. Sometimes he was dog-tired like the rest of us from no sleep and not enough to eat. But, except for those few minutes in front of Johnny Kasten's body, I never saw his morale at half-mast. He could always "get up" as fast as a tom cat's dick. Fifteen years later with all that drug shit, you'd had thought he was on speed or something; but that stuff pumping inside him came from his own two balls, no frigging foreign crap *a-tall.*

We needed that "upping" on our little walk back to friendlies, and I shit you not. Like I say, Walsh got tired, so tired the circles under his eyes had their own circles. But that steam engine he had tucked up his behind kept his morale two-blocked all the time. He'd be as ass-dragging as the rest of us when we'd stop before dawn and settle in for the day. But give him two hours of shut-eye, and he'd come roaring out of his sleeping bag all full of panther piss, ready to go. I could fake it somctimes, maybe most of the time, but he didn't have to.

The troops weren't bad, like I say, only risking all our asses and their own. The last few of the original stretcher wounded died the fourth day, but by then we had twelve more stretcher cases. All the guys were getting weaker, though that wasn't all bad. They were sort of—what do you call it?—lethargic the sixth day, too weak to get into any trouble, but pretty near the edge of despair. That day we didn't pick up any hostile sign, or that night either. Then just before dawn when we were up pretty high, sweet Christ, we saw some headlights over in the west, about seven or eight miles away, I'd guess.

EIGHT

BIG FOOT wasn't the kind of soft CO who let his troops lie around on their asses getting fat and feeling sorry for themselves. He let them sleep and lick their wounds for forty-eight hours, and then on the third day he started the regiment on a tough training schedule—not Mickey Mouse, but useful stuff. He sent them on conditioning hikes, had them practice assaulting mountains—man, that's tough on the legs—and he even got a bulldozer to whack out the side of a hill for a rifle range.

That day, 1 May, Big Foot was out with Lieutenant Colonel Lucker's Third Battalion, watching them cross the Hongchon River, attack a steep hill in the middle of the valley, and then set up a hasty defense. He wasn't happy about the way the troops went through their maneuver, but he wasn't pissed either. The tactical planning was good; it was the execution that was sloppy. Big Foot expected it would be. The troops had been playing for keepsies too long to play hard for funsies. Their officers were still sharp, and the kids were getting some of their strength back. Those were the important things.

He was looking down at the troops, when he barked at his radioman, "Get me Colonel Lucker, son." A few moments later, the radioman handed him the phone: "Lucker, Johnson. Let's critique." (He said it *cry*-tique.)

"Johnson, Johnson, this is Lucker. Roger, Skipper. Please join me for lunch. Over."

"Lucker, Lucker, this is Johnson. Thanks. Out."

As Big Foot and his staff began to pick up their gear, the radio phone crackled. The message was weak. Even the operator sitting in the jeep could hardly hear it, and he kept on reading a Superman comic book.

"Topper, Topper, this is Silk Hat. Over."

"Silk Hat, Silk Hat, this is Topper. You're not modulating. Over," the operator called back without looking up from his comic book.

"What the hell are you talking about, son?" Big Foot was irritable.

"Silk Hat isn't modulating, Colonel."

"Silk Hat? Are you drunk, son?"

"No, sir." Then it dawned on the operator what he had said. "I thought he said Silk Hat, Colonel, but it was awful fuzzy. I must've read it wrong."

"Put down that goddamned comic book, Private, and pay attention to your work or I'll stuff my boot up your shit chute," Big Foot growled. Given the size of Big Foot's boot, it was a pretty frigging impressive threat.

"Topper, Topper, this is Silk Hat. How do you read me now? Over."

The voice was still weak, but it was clearer. Big Foot grabbed the handset away from the operator. "Silk Hat, Silk Hat, this is Topper. Silk Hat, this is Topper. Who the Christ are you? Over."

"Topper, Topper, this is Silk Hat from Caspar. Over."

"Silk Hat, Silk Hat, this is Topper. Give me Silk Hat Six. Over."

"Topper, Topper, this is Silk Hat Six. Send your message. Over."

"Silk Hat Six, this is Topper Six. Who are you?"

"Topper Six, this is Walsh, Declan Patrick, Lieutenant Colonel, Uncle Sugar Mike Charley Roger, 0206271. I report my return, sir. Over."

"Walsh, this is Big Foot"—that's what he said, honest to Christ, Big Foot. "What's your condition and where are you? Over."

In the next valley, five miles north and east of where Johnson was, Walsh looked at us. We were hungry, ragged, cruddy to the point where shit would've looked clean. Our eyes were red-rimmed and sunk deep back into our skulls. Like most troops who'd been in combat awhile, we looked bigger than we were because of the way the dirt and crud hung on us. Tattered hunks of clothing stuck to our bodies, and every one of us reeked of stale sweat, clotted blood, and lots of dried turds from diarrhea without toilet paper. Almost all of us had at least minor wounds with infections, and we were near total exhaustion.

Walsh winked at me and said, "Topper, Topper, this is Silk Hat. Condition excellent. We have buried our dead and are carrying our wounded. How else did you expect marines to come out of a fight? Over."

The radio was quiet. For once in his life, Big Foot Johnson was speechless. "Walsh, where the hell are you?" he finally asked, forgetting all about proper radio procedure.

"Topper Six, Topper Six, this is Silk Hat. I can't rightly say. I would judge we're about nine miles northeast of Hongchon. Is that within friendly lines? Over."

"Affirmative on your last. You're well within friendly lines. What can you see? Over."

"Topper, Topper, this is Silk Hat. There's a river to my left front as I face due west. It runs southwest. I think from the other landmarks that it's the stream that comes into the Hongchon near Simnae, if those names mean anything. Over."

"Silk Hat Six, this is Topper Six. Welcome home. March down the river, we'll be waiting. There's a battalion of Ivanhoe in reserve there, so be peaceable. Over."

"Silk Hat Six. Roger. Out."

Big Foot was like a little kid again, just like he'd been after we'd creamed the first big attack on Caspar. "Get me Wizard Three—no get me Wizard Six—Christ, son, just get word to Division. Tell them the Second Battalion, First Marines, has cut its way through a Route Army and is meeting us at the Ivanhoe reserve area at the river junction near Simnae." He turned to his operations officer. "Stambert, take my jeep and get back to my command post. Make damn sure Division has my message. Round up every truck you can. I want the First Battalion there to meet them. I'll get Lucker over there too. Better call for ambulances, too. And for God's sake bring back a shitpot full of photographers."

Stambert hurried off toward the road.

"Wait a minute, Stambert," Big Foot called. "Bring the regimental colors back with you. I'll meet you at Simnae."

As Stambert roared away, the colonel grabbed his intelligence officer. "Jenkins, get me my jeep."

"Colonel, you just sent Major Stambert off in your jeep."

"Well, get me another."

"Colonel, that's the only jeep we have. Where can I get another one in the middle of Korea?"

"Goddamn it, Captain, I don't care if you have to squat and shit one. I want a jeep here in five minutes." Big Foot turned to his radio operator.

"Tell Colonel Lucker what's happened and to start marching his men up the road. The trucks will pick them up on the way. Let's get started!"

Johnson didn't have to get his bowels in an uproar. We were only four miles from the river junction, and in good condition we could've made it in less than an hour; but we were pooped. Picking up one foot and putting it in front of the other took fantastic concentration and brought grinding pain. Stumbling like drunken Bowery bums, it would take us two to three hours.

Back at Division the CP was really hopping. The general

was a quiet old cuss; he had about the tightest asshole of any gyrene I ever knew. He hardly ever smiled, even when he was a major, which was when I first met him. His chief of staff, a cocky little rooster just 5′5″ tall, had the reputation of being the toughest martinet in the whole corps. He didn't have a tongue; he had a whip. But I heard they were about as schoolboy-happy as Big Foot had been. The G–1, a bird colonel, practically carried Lt. Harvey Richards, the Division PIO—that's Public Information Officer—into the general's van. Richards was sober, thank God, which didn't happen often. His old man was a southern senator and got him and some of his buddies pulled off the Fifth replacement draft back in February and assigned to desk jobs in the rear with the gear back in Japan. That worked pretty well for a couple of months, diddling little gook girls, and boozing it up pretty regular until one of his buddies got shit-faced at a party and started bragging to a visiting general. The next day he and Richards were on the mainland. He got a rifle platoon—and turned yellow the first time a shot was fired. But Richards was smoother; he talked himself into the PIO slot. But it didn't help. The story was around. He had a few friends, guys who wanted political favors from his old man, but most of the officers cut the mammy-jammer cold. He drank a lot.

His NCO ran the show pretty much—"Light Horse" Harry Leigh, an old buddy of mine from the 'Canal. He wrote a lot for *Leatherneck,* a real savvy guy. He's the one who helped me write my stuff. Well, anyway, I got the story from him, so it's straight poop.

Richards came stumbling into the van with Leigh right behind him. The general was just sitting in his chair with a shit-eating grin all over his face. The chief of staff reached up and pushed Richards down onto a locker box. "Boy, this one is big! We've really got it. The Second Batt, First, just reported in by radio—cut their way out through a Chinese Route Army. Walsh says, 'We've buried our dead and are carrying our wounded.' How do you like that? See that one in the *Washington Post* tomorrow for that freaking haberdasher to read with his coffee! It'll grab him where he lives, right by the stacking swivel."

"Richards, the general wants this one played big. That piano-playing politician is going to have to hang so many Congo medals around marines' necks he's going to get lumbago from stretching. You round up every reporter in the Eighth Army and call Seoul and Tokyo. Who's in the CP?"

Richards looked blank. Leigh spoke up. "There's that guy Twisdale from the *St. Louis Post-Dispatch* and an AP man."

"Good, they'll do for openers. Get them on one of the 'copters; make sure you round up every photographer within twenty miles. Sergeant Leigh, start writing a handout. I want something on Walsh, who he is, and all that sort of shit. Call the Regimental Rear Area One at Masan. Walsh's file jacket should be there.

"Colonel"—the chief of staff looked at the G–1—"the general wants the division band up there. I don't care if you have to hum it yourself. The Old Man wants the Marine Corps hymn echoing down that valley when the Second Batt gets within camera range."

"Yes, sir, I'll leave now and give the orders."

"Now," the chief of staff turned back to Richards and Leigh, " 'The Lost Battalion.' That sounds good enough to snatch headlines in every newspaper in the country."

"It's been done before, Colonel, in just about every war," Richards said sullenly. A good afternoon's drinking was obviously frigged up.

"Not with the marines it hasn't, and it hasn't been done by anybody in this cruddy little war. Christ, this can be big. Don't bother the *Stars and Stripes* boys. Those pogs would rather write about some doggie division getting its ass whacked for the hundredth time than about marines whipping Chinks. Let those clowns tag-ass along later. Now get the hell out of here and get the job done. I want everybody at Simnae in seventy minutes."

It was mid-afternoon as we came stumbling along the creek. Actually it was a pretty little stream, not wide and only about a foot or two deep, but it went along quick and clear over a pebbled bottom, the kind of creek you dream about wallowing in when the temperature's ninety-five. We were tripping and falling, but it was still too cold for wallowing.

Up ahead I could see all sorts of troops. We'd been circled by helicopters twice. I looked back at the kids. Christ, they were a shitty mess. They weren't marching, they were lurching like drunks. They stunk—I mean it. None of us had had a shave or even a real wash since before we'd got on Caspar. We smelled like somebody who'd had his socks on for a week and then peed in them while he crapped in his pants—and that's pretty much what we'd been doing. At least their eyes looked good. They were still red and bleary, but they'd lost that glazed punch-drunk look.

I speeded up my stagger and got alongside the colonel. He was helping a corporal along and humming quietly—you know I think once he got over (I don't mean really over, just under control) the Kasten business, I think that crazy son of a bitch enjoyed himself. Anyway, I told him we looked like a bunch of beaten bastards, not marines. "Gunny," he says, "you're right. Let's do something about that." He tried to lift his left arm, but it wouldn't come up. That shoulder must have hurt pretty bad. I raised mine, and the column came to a stumbling halt.

"All right, you people!" the colonel bellows out, "we're going in like marines. We fought the Chinese and we beat the shit out of them. March up to these dogfaces and jarheads with your heads high. Now fall into two ranks and carry your weapons at sling arms." There was a lot of shuffling and cursing, but the order was carried out. "All right. Forwardddd march! Sergeant Major, count cadence." I yelled out as best I could, "Hut, two, rip, four! Hut, two, rip, four!"

Three hundred yards later, when we got a full view of our reception committee, Walsh shouted out: "Count cadence, count!"

"One . . . two . . . three . . . four . . . one . . . two . . . three . . . four . . . ," the battalion shouted back in unison as their left feet hit the ground. Then "one, two, three, four, one, two, three, four" each time either foot came down.

When we got about a hundred yards from Big Foot, the band started playing the Marine Corps hymn. Above the music, Walsh called out again, "Count cadence, count!" The same sets of shouts rang out. Cameras flashed and ground away, afraid to miss a split second of what was happening. The reporters stared at us, not believing a frigging thing they saw, just like the marines and the turdbirds from Ivanhoe, the Second Army Division. We were the filthiest, stinkingest pack of mammy-jamming jarheads they'd ever seen. Except for the cameramen, no one outside of the Second Battalion twitched a muscle. "That theatrical son of a bitch," Big Foot said out loud. "That theatrical son of a bitch must have stayed up every night planning that little bit of melodrama."

As we came up abeam of Big Foot, Walsh called out, "Battalion, halt!" then, "Left face!" He passed the corporal off to Keller and marched stiffly over between the battalion and Johnson. "Sergeant Major, front and center." I limped out behind the colonel and gave him my collection of dog tags. "Sir," Walsh's voice was thick but loud as he saluted, "the Second Battalion, First Marines." Then he switched the dog tags to his right hand and tossed them at the feet of Big Foot's personnel officer. "All men present or accounted for."

Big tears burned down Big Foot's cheeks; I knew those were as much tears of pride as of envy. This was the most dramatic moment of his life—it was a little too dramatic for my taste but I'm just a simple old sergeant—and Big Foot would've gladly given both balls if he could have played the leading role. But he had just missed it again. At least he had a part on stage. A little later I heard him mumble something about playing the old king's ghost many times, but never Hamlet. Still, he could admire a professional job, and Walsh's performance at Caspar and getting us out showed a shitpot full of military skill; and his public relations were excellent to outrageous. "Dismiss the battalion, Colonel," Big Foot said, returning the salute. "Welcome home."

Walsh saluted and spun around unsteadily on his left heel. "Battalionnnnn, parade rest!" He took a few unsteady steps toward us. "All right, you people." He spoke harshly, then quickly changed his tone and smiled. "Well done. I'm proud of you. If I were given to flattery I'd say you've been magnificent. But well done should do the trick. You can always remember how you clobbered a Route Army." Then, "Sergeant Major, dismiss the battalion!"

I never had a chance to carry out that order. As soon as the word "dismiss" was out, every man in the Second Battalion who could move broke ranks and hobbled for Walsh. He was lifted roughly up on tired shoulders, and we all cheered as loud as we could. (Lieutenant Randall was on a stretcher then, but I don't think he would have moved even if he'd been able.)

"I think, General," Johnson whispered to the division commander, "we could wait a few minutes to get Walsh's report."

"I expect so, Colonel. I want to stay around and hear what he has to say. My public information officer will be along to take notes. It'll save time in writing up the citation for the Congressional Medal of Honor. Under the circumstances I think we can persuade Washington to up that posthumous Navy Cross you recommended for him."

"Yes, sir," Big Foot agreed. He had twice tried to give his own life to earn that little patch of blue and white ribbon, and for the third time in his life he was going to help another bastard get it. While we were talking some reporter brought a couple of us a canteen cup full of bourbon. It's funny, none of us more than half touched it. We got lots of questions—mostly silly. How can you explain something like that to people who've never heard kids—American or Chink—screaming in terror when they see their guts spilling out on the ground like a mess of grey snakes, or had never felt the cold hand of death grabbing their shoulder, or waited for the snap of a grenade fuse or the whoosh of a mortar to turn them into basket cases?

Well, that's where I knew Colonel Walsh best. Like I say, he was a funny—well, not—yeah, he was funny in some ways, but I mean strange. I think that march from Caspar to Hongchon was the best time of his life—just like that minute he saw Johnny Kasten was the worst. But I'm just an old soldier, not a shrink. I was with him a lot afterwards, but I never got next to him again. You know what I mean? Really close. He was a marked man after that, a water walker, and not just to the Marine Corps, but to the rest of the world, too. The magic had touched him, with his Congressional Medal of Honor, and the book he wrote, and working in the White House, and all that other shit. Well, you know all about those things.

A lot of guys have asked me was I surprised at what happened to the colonel. In a way, but not really. I mean, you know, you see a guy and know he'll make it big or he'll go crash in a pile of crap, nothing in between. I had that feeling about him when he was a second lieutenant. I didn't know he'd do the kind of things he did, you know, but when they happened I wasn't surprised.

Leadership? You said you were interested in leadership, and all I've given you is a long sea story. But it was all about leadership—the way he planned and thought, and cared, or seemed to care, anyway, and taught and drove. He was good people, a little rough sometimes, maybe a little too sudden, but good people. Christ, he had smarts. If he was on the other side in a war, I'd hang up my jock or blow my brains out. And he was as stubborn a mammy-jammer as ever put on a tin hat. Without him, we'd have never held onto 915 for so long, or taken it back, or gotten through the Chinese alive. We needed him. But you know something? I think he needed us to need him just as much.

PART II

THE GREAT PULPIT

once he got it into his head
to lay his hands on a Silenus

Three days he chased him
till at last he caught him
hit him with his fist
between the eyes and asked:
—what is best for man?

The Silenus neighed
and said:
—to be nothing
—to die

—ZBIGNIEW HERBERT
"King Midas Does Not Hunt"

ONE

COME IN, young man, come in and sit down. There, in that chair, and put that awful recording machine on the coffee table, where it can spin away our lives without disturbing our conversation. I'm sorry but I can't get up from this couch very easily. My therapist insists that my progress is not unpromising. I have, after all, fully recovered my speech. Nevertheless, I still have only small use of my left arm or leg. That is a bother, but it isn't important in the eternal scheme of things. Apparently very little is, once one leaves the Court. Well, I shouldn't have allowed myself to be paragraphed out of my place, but I did. So there's an end to it. Now we must focus on your problems, on the claims of history.

You wanted to talk about Walsh—a fascinating creature, absolutely fascinating, my dear fellow. He had a great deal of atmosphere about him, but his was not truly a first-rate presence—close to it, but he missed, just missed. Great native intelligence, to be sure, and a dead keen wit. A man of fantastic drive, absolutely fantastic—and not devoid of vision, either. But for reasons I shall try to develop, there was a dimension missing, a lack of true understanding of the limited mission of our Court. In the very near future, historians, mesmerized by their own addiction—an understandable addiction, mind you—to the values he fought for, will overestimate his performance on our Court. But, mark my words, mark them well, soon their successors will drop his name from the rolls of the big chief justices. I offer that prediction on the basis of a lifetime of study of the oracles of the law.

Withal, he was a fascinating creature, and since we should follow the classics' mandate to praise famous men, one must concede that he has an honored place in our pageant—not as honored as he wanted or as he liked to think he enjoyed, to be sure, but still he lived a not unuseful life.

I had met them a few times in 1951 at various White House affairs. My company was much courted then, much courted. Harry S Truman, the Fates' punishment on us all for thinking that dear Franklin was immortal, was president. (Even after all these years, all these long years, linking the words *Truman* and *President* still sours my tongue.) Walsh was serving as the president's special military aide, having recently returned from the war. Kathryn, his voluptuously sculptured wife—she was a few years younger than he, you know—often came to White House parties. She was a tall woman, with soft, long blond hair that contrasted with the darker gold of her skin in the summer. She was one of those Scandinavians whose complexion the sun burnishes rather than burns. In the winter it was the color of rich cream, during the warmer months that of antique jewelry. Her eyes were green rather than the expected blue, adding surprise to beauty.

No one could deny her beauty. No, I misstate that—her magnetic attractiveness. She would have been an ideal priestess for an orgiastic pagan cult. I saw even Harry casting sidelong glances at her, and Bess looking at them both with a touch of fire. I know, I know, my dear chap, you didn't come here to listen to an old man prattle about sex goddesses, but she is not irrelevant to my narrative. Bear with me another moment.

Mrs. Walsh's Christian name was, as I indicated, Kathryn, but she preferred to be addressed as Kate, a privilege she bestowed quite liberally. I know, I know, it was not a promising omen, but what can one do? She had been one of Walsh's students at Chicago. Understandably, she did not return after their wedding to complete law school there. Equally understandably, Walsh sought employment elsewhere. In those more civilized times, we understood the nature of the chasm that separates student and professor.

It was a pity, however, that she did not complete her academic work at some other institution. She had a mind, and the legal profession might have provided a happier outlet for her energy than the one she eventually took. She also had a tongue that could swiftly slash those who offended her. It was not a trait dulled with age. In all, however, she was an intelligent woman for whom it was easy to feel sympathy. Marriage to a man as ambitious as Walsh, one could have said even in 1951, would bring a full share of sorrow.

She also, I gather from comments of others—for I have

no skills in such matters, none at all—possessed a shrewd sense of political maneuvering, inherited, no doubt, from her father, a hardy Scandinavian who had built a reputation for political acumen in the ethnic politics of Minnesota. I have it on the very firmest of authority that even Harry consulted her wisdom on occasion, doubtless partaking of her vista as well as her vision. Along with political interest and her sharp tongue went a not inconsiderable talent for mimicry. I once observed her perform an acerbic —and perfectly to the point, perfectly—imitation of that piously pretentious fool who was India's ambassador to the United Nations.

She and Walsh were happily married then. Given the brief passage of time between their wedding and the war, Washington was hardly more than a continuation of their honeymoon. It must have been exhilarating to have been thrust into the vortex of power, with no responsibility other than to enjoy the drama. I could not help but notice that when he was not in uniform the two would hold hands walking down the street or on the back lawn of the White House. It was all very touching, very touching. To be young and in love is such a preciously fleeting moment.

In my narrative I shall refer to Walsh's lady as Kathryn, as I did when I knew her. I must add that, to my knowledge, I was the only one who ever addressed her in that fashion. For clarity, I should also confess that I was not overly fond of her. We were on pleasant enough terms, do not misunderstand me, please, but we were never close. I think you will understand why more comprehensively when my tale is done.

In those days, there was no escaping Walsh's status as a great war hero. That's why, I imagine, he could sport that horrid reddish blond handlebar mustache. I can assure you, absolutely assure you, that hair on his face upset several senior officers of my acquaintance. But what does a mere general say to a lieutenant colonel who has won the Congressional Medal of Honor and whom the President of the United States has made his special aide?

Walsh had just written—I believe it was published while he was in the White House—that popular, vulgar but popular, book that bore the title *Silk Hat Six,* or some such gaudy appellation. Really, what the public will buy! We talk about television destroying national taste and culture, but the mob *has* neither taste nor culture to destroy. Television merely panders to a void, just as do publishers who put out self-glorifying adventure stories about hirsute brutes killing and maiming one another. As one who has spent a lifetime in his nation's service, I am surely not immodest in counting myself a patriot, but I decry exploiting the base cravings of the mob for violence, even in the name of national morale.

Well, I confess to having had a certain preformed opinion about Walsh, but when I met him I was not unfavorably impressed, not unfavorably at all. I had not then realized that he had been an associate professor of law at the University of Chicago. Still, it was not lacking in congruence. Like the institution itself, he was bright, quick, and intellectually just a bit raw for more cultivated eastern tastes. He always wanted to leap and tear the throat out of a problem. He took no aesthetic pleasure in measuring a problem and living with it for a time before deciding whether it was even desirable to try to slay it. In short, he was more quick than wise. He never appreciated the comfort that a worthy enemy could provide. That and a certain lack of judicial humility were his most obvious flaws as a jurist.

When I speak of rawness, I mean in an intellectual rather than a social sense. He had grown up abroad in diplomatic circles and was certainly socially polished, very polished. His father had been in the foreign service, supposedly a brilliant man, but there was some cloud in his career. I never indulge in gossip, but I understand there was a severe drinking problem. There so often is with the Irish, you know. His wife, I've heard, kept his career alive by judiciously dispensing her favors to higher ranking officers. To be sure, I myself put no stock in such vicious stories.

I became rather fond of Walsh. God—if He exists—knows I tried to help him. I believe it would not be immodest to claim that I enjoyed some small success in those endeavors. Except for that jugular reflex, he showed signs of being educable; and, as one who spent a lifetime in pedagogy, I was delighted at the opportunity he presented. When he was in the White House, knowing that he had the ear of the president, I used our brief encounters to give him the benefit of my reflections on several national problems. We would all be better off had the president deigned to carry out those ideas.

After Mr. Truman returned to his natural level in Missouri, and the general came to Washington, I lost touch with Walsh for some years. You know how one does in this town. A new crowd enters the White House and old faces quickly fade. Besides, Walsh really had not been around that long. It was in late 1951 or early 1952 when Mr. Truman finally realized that if we were ever going to extricate ourselves from Korea short of another world conflagration, we needed all the diplomatic means available. And whatever else it may be, the Vatican is an excellent diplomatic listening post. As a hard-shell Baptist himself, Truman knew that designating a representative to the Pope was going to raise hackles. And so, shrewd political creature that he was, he dispatched Walsh. Now no one, simply no one is going to attack the red-blooded Americanism of a marine with a Congressional Medal of Honor and chest full of Purple Hearts from two wars.

Walsh completed Truman's term in Rome, and the general retained him for some months, perhaps six or seven. Your standard biographical sources can supply that sort of information. I saw him briefly a few times in the late 1950s or early 1960s. He had affected a beard by then—so many academics do. They look horribly itchy to me, but I suppose they do save time normally spent shaving in the morning. While teaching law at the University of Michigan, Walsh also served as a member of the Commission on Civil Rights for a few years—that's only part-time work—and was on one or two special presidential commissions. He was establishing quite a reputation for himself as a scholar. I kept seeing his name on books and articles. He wrote too much like a social scientist to suit my tastes, but I am a purist when it comes to law, a purist. On the other hand, I concede that his writings showed considerable erudition and, on the whole, were not unsound.

Sometime later he became dean of the law school at Michigan—a terrible job, simply terrible. All those academic jokes about deans demonstrate how little faculty respect them. It's sad, very sad, to see fine minds contenting themselves with shuffling papers. I remember what old Harlan Stone said about being a dean—before coming to our Court he was dean of Columbia's law school, you undoubtedly recall. He said a dean does all the things that the janitor feels are beneath his dignity. Well, apparently being a dean planted some seeds of political ambition in Walsh's mind, and I heard from the grapevine that he was thinking of running for the Senate.

That was all in the last part of Clarence Bowers's first term as president. The old chief justice was fading. He had suffered two coronaries in the past year, and could not last much longer. We all knew that, all of us. Our docket would fell a healthy young Celebes Ox, much less a feeble old man. Most people have no idea, my dear chap, no idea at all, how hard we work on the Court. Old Man Holmes used to greet new justices with "Welcome to our chain gang," and the work was immeasurably less burdensome then than now. Well, the question was whether the chief justice would soon die or soon retire. I was not unconcerned—to be sure, we were all curious—about his successor. The austere functions of our Court require us to isolate ourselves from the political maneuverings that inevitably accompany such changes of high office, but at least we could watch with amusement the playing of the political game. And, when in late July, the chief justice announced his intention to step down, the Washington rumor mills immediately began grinding at top speed.

As you are no doubt well aware, my name was mentioned by intellectuals and by the better classes of politicians and journalists. Alas, those categories excluded the honorable personages to whom Clarence Bowers would look for guidance. I never took my own chances seriously, not at all, although it was gratifying to see that some still remembered with favor my long years of dedicated and, I believe, not altogether unmeritorious service.

I recall a cocktail party in Georgetown just about that time. It was an abominably muggy Saturday afternoon, and Senator Philip Amherst and I had gone for a stroll in the garden. Amherst was a long-headed Massachusetts man. He had just sought out my considered judgment on a candidate for the federal district bench in Boston. Having spent a lifetime studying closely the judicial systems of the English-speaking world, I had urged him to put aside petty partisan advantages and to present to the president a personage of character and learning—and I had two specific names for him from the Boston bar, both sound men in the prime of life. I knew they were sound because I had taught them both at Yale Law School. My dear fellow, it's a sad commentary on our system, a sad commentary indeed, but we appellate judges receive so much publicity that people tend to forget that judicial business starts in trial courts; and if the trial judge has a sufficiency of wisdom and integrity, most judicial business ends there as well.

Well, as Amherst and I were walking back to rejoin the mob inside, I inquired if he had any inkling of who our new chief justice would be. (Mind you, I was not fishing for support for myself.) I remember being astounded simply astounded, at Amherst's reply.

"Walker," he said—I have always preferred to keep even respected elected politicians away from first name familiarity. Only my closest intimates call me Bradley, and I am proud to say that no one has ever dared call me "Brad" or append some other silly soubriquet. "Walker, if I were a betting man," Amherst went on, "I'd keep a weather eye on our learned and distinguished senior senator from Michigan."

I recall lifting an eyebrow to show that I could appreciate his little joke, even on a muggy day. "My dear Amherst," I said, "Clarence Bowers is a vulgarian but he is not a barbarian or a clown. I am an old friend of the senator; and, as distinguished and learned as Harwood Trimble may appear to be in *your* chamber, he would be far beyond his depth in *ours*. When our Court sits, peasant cunning is no substitute for scholarship and judicial wisdom. Even if that creature Bowers were so lacking in intelligence as to consider Trimble, Trimble himself is too shrewd not to realize he'd drown within a term on our Court, within a single term. After all, his title of Wizard of Ooze indicates he is not without a certain native intelligence."

Amherst merely smiled. "I can't say that I agree with your assessment of our respective institutions, Walker, or even of the president." (I always respect loyalty, especially when, as in Amherst's case, it is tempered by prudence and combined with good manners.) "But, the Wizard of Ooze doesn't covet the place for himself, only for his own purposes."

I stopped before we reached the steps. This piece was

simply too delicious to be shared with the long ear of some potential gossip inside. "Please, my dear Amherst, are you implying something nefarious?"

"No more nefarious than survival; self-preservation is beyond any law, moral or statutory. The Wizard is in his late sixties, and he's coming up for reelection in two years. The Democrats are already falling in line behind a strong candidate, the dean of the law school at the University of Michigan."

"I know the man slightly," I said. "He would not become another trophy for the Wizard's wall, not easily at any rate."

"No, indeed. He's a toughie, smart, still rather young but old enough to be mature and to have made lots of friends, a big hero in not one war but two. He's also rather well off financially, and he has friends both in the United Auto Workers and in Grosse Pointe. Believe me, Walker, I know of what I speak when I say that there are few nightmares worse to an aging senator than a bright young war hero with a chestful of medals for killing Japanese and Communists."

"And you, my dear Amherst, one of the soundest of Massachusetts men, think the Honorable Harwood Trimble will persuade the President of these United States to nominate this Walsh creature to be chief justice, merely to save Trimble's seat in the Senate?"

"Precisely." Amherst spoke without any emotion beyond his usual wisp of cynicism. "And there is precedent for it. I recall that Woodrow Wilson tried to remove Charles Evans Hughes as an opponent for the presidency in 1916 by offering him the chief justiceship, and the story has persisted that Lincoln eliminated Salmon P. Chase from rivalry for the 1864 nomination by naming him chief justice."

"In Lincoln's case, there probably is something to the story, but surely you don't believe that Wilson tried that with Hughes?"

"I believe that we political animals know how to survive, and the Wizard knows that he would not survive a campaign against our war hero-dean."

"Well," I mused, "when he was chief justice, Taft did persuade Harding to offer a seat on the Court to John W. Davis to keep Davis out of the 1924 presidential race, but Davis would have none of it. Yes, yes, it makes sense from

Trimble's point of view, but does it make sense from the president's point of view?"

"The Wizard will persuade our president," Amherst explained, a bit more in detail than he needed; after all, I had accumulated a lifetime of experience studying *homo politicus Americanus* in his natural habitat. "He will explain that the nomination is in the national interest. The president will have the opportunity to name a distinguished scholar, brave soldier, learned diplomat, and gifted administrator to the nation's highest judicial post. Further, the president will have the opportunity, which he always readily seizes, to rise above petty partisan politics and engage in statesmanship by choosing a man from the opposition party."

"As those other great nonpartisans, William Howard Taft and Franklin D. Roosevelt did," I noted.

"Precisely."

"But what if there are other candidates equally as qualified? And I would venture to say there must be dozens of them, and they will all be crawling out of the woodwork."

"In that case," Amherst replied, "the Wizard will remind our president—who as you know must be reelected this very November to maintain his lease on the White House—that as leader of the great, but minority, Republican party he will be presented with an opportunity to name a Catholic and thus to win over Catholic votes and insure a steady hand on the tiller of state, or wherever it is that Clarence likes to keep his stately hands."

I did not succumb to the temptation to ribaldry. I wanted to remain with the subject. "But, my dear fellow, there are likely to be other Catholic candidates, aren't there? After all, those people breed like flies."

"The Wizard would still have one trump card. Clarence Bowers served for fourteen years in the Senate under Harwood Trimble's tutelage. In our jargon, he owes—and Clarence Bowers is an honorable man who pays his debts. In the end it could be that simple. In our circles a man who does not pay his debts is lost."

Back inside with the mob I caught a glimpse of the senior senator from Michigan and invited him for a bite of supper at my apartment here in the Hay-Adams. We were both bachelors and at an age when we were apt to be celibates as well.

He popped in about nine. "My dear Trimble," I took the senator's umbrella from him. It had begun to rain, one of those awful Washington thunderstorms. There isn't much one can do about them, but one doesn't have to pretend to enjoy them, does one? "Good of you to come on such a beastly night."

"Ah, Mr. Justice, a man reaches the stage where he cherishes good company and conversation above all else. It's just as well that the taste comes late or the human race might die out." The "Mr. Justice" was one of Trimble's typical affectations. The man was so outrageously flowery and insincere that it was impossible not to warm to him immediately. After he relaxed among friends, he would gradually peel off that unctuousness, like a snake losing its skin. Is that a good analogy? Yes, I'll stick with it.

I always tried to let my man have Saturdays off, so I ushered the senator into the library myself. I had a bit of rarebit warming on the table, some toast, and a nicely chilled bottle of white wine, probably a Moselle. (I don't pay much attention to such things.) He sat in the very chair you're in, the very chair, my dear chap, and I lounged here on the sofa. The furniture was more comfortable then, when I could move out of it on my own.

"It's been a long time, my dear Trimble."

"Too long, Mr. Justice, too long, but we dedicated servants of the public must constantly labor to earn our daily bread and protect our people's rights. Indeed, I fear we overdo it. We owe it to the taxpayers to get a bit more recreation so that we'll be sharper."

As we sipped the wine and began to eat, we chatted about mutual old friends in the Senate, not the most interesting of creatures, but we were both waiting for the polite moment to introduce our issue of mutual concern. After all, there is something unseemly in leaping at a thing. We both preferred to edge around the mountain. It was Trimble who first brought us to business.

"Tell me, Walker, do you think the president will be moved by the Holy Spirit to do the wise thing and name you chief justice?"

I could not forego smiling at the man's effrontery; it was disarming, absolutely disarming. "My very dear friend," I responded, "I strongly suspect that the president will be moved by that very corporeal elf from Michigan."

"Ah, old friend, you always were too sharp for me. Perhaps it's all that time you fellows have sitting around listening to learned lawyers babble while we drones of democracy gather the honey for our sovereign masters, the people. No doubt you've been listening to some rumors. Washington is a grand place for rumors. A senator talks to the president on the most trivial affair, and half the town has the two in a conspiracy."

"Then you haven't been offering the president advice on the chief justiceship?" I teased.

"Now, I didn't say that. If the President of the United States asks a senator to give him advice, it's the senator's moral duty—probably even legal duty, but I leave that to you folks who know a lot more about such things than we country lawyers—it's a senator's duty to offer help where he can. That's what makes our great democracy work." Trimble could not help smiling at the sincerity of his own hypocrisy.

"If the distinguished senator from Michigan will permit, I think I can bring this discussion to a useful point. I have it on impeccable authority, impeccable, mind you, that you have been laboring in the White House's vineyards for Declan Walsh, a gentleman with certain senatorial ambitions."

Trimble smiled and paused a few seconds. When he spoke, he abandoned much of his Chautauqua rhetoric. "Forgive me, old friend, I know how desperately you would like to have the center chair." (Actually, my dear fellow, you should make it clear in your book, as I shall make it clear in mine, that I did not want it *desperately* at all; I merely thought it would be a fitting capstone to a lifelong, and, I believe, not undistinguished, career in public service.) "And I know how richly you deserve the honor," Trimble continued, "but with this administration you do not have a chance, not a chance. Of course, it isn't lack of talent, you know that." (I most assuredly did know that.) "It isn't even that you're from the wrong party. That can help in an election year, and above all else this is an election year for some folks.

"The real reason," Trimble went on, "is that you're from the wrong crowd. Clarence Bowers identifies you with the

New Deal and the Fair Deal." (New Deal to be sure, but linking me to the Fair Deal was an insult.) "Further, you're a WASP and wouldn't help us with the Catholics at all—they're to be our number one target this year. If the president can break the Democrats' hold on the Catholic vote, we can have another four years in the White House and perhaps even control of Congress. Worse still for us, you're Harvard—undergraduate and law school—and Yale as a professor. That won't appeal to the Midwest at all, and that's where we will make our second biggest effort. Just being the best isn't good enough."

I smiled easily. His message was one that I had long ago understood and accepted, fully accepted. One receives only imperfect justice in this world; only fools, children, left-wing Democrats, social scientists, and a few demented judges expect anything better. "And, of course, as a realist, you are fighting for a cause that has a chance," I said.

"Exactly put. And I admit that I have some selfish interest. We aging senators have an ugly and recurring dream: a young, energetic, handsome war hero with money, talent, and political ambition. For me, Dean Walsh *is* that nightmare."

"I can well understand that, well understand it. Now, what can I do to help you? Let me put you at ease, my dear friend," I immediately added. "One with scrupulosities as sensitive as mine about the delicate nature of the Court's position in the American political system would not do anything, or seem to do anything, that touched even the periphery of judicial propriety. But, there are some things that I might legitimately do. I do not want to see Clarence Bowers drag the judicial ermine through the mud by offering the center chair to one of his cronies."

"That's generous of you, Walker, very generous."

"No, realistic. You are correct in your evaluation of my chances, absolutely correct—and I suppose you're right about Walsh, too. I knew him slightly some years ago, and formed a not unfavorable impression of his mind. I also spent the last hour perusing two of his articles in the *Harvard Law Review*. He's bright and erudite—a bit too social sciency for my tastes, but a lifetime in the study of law has left me an ascetic in such matters. Still, Walsh understands our Court and the issues we have been facing. He might just make a big judge; and, as I perceive the competition, they're all small men. If I err in that judgment, it is on the side of generosity. Several whose names have been mentioned in the press are venal, quite venal. Indeed, if the truth were known, they would make Richard Nixon appear a man of probity. But we should not worry about the press, at least not yet. Who are the real front-runners?"

Trimble paused and looked at the ceiling for a moment. "In my judgment, Walker, there are only two real competitors. Your colleague, Marvin Jacobson, has artfully beslobbered the president, but there's no political mileage in a Republican president's appointing a Jew to be chief justice. I am afraid"—here Trimble's voice lapsed into his senatorial style—"that Marvin's Republicanism is a rare exception. Few of our Hebrew friends have ever been able to appreciate the virtues of the Grand Old Party. As far as we are concerned, all Israel is a lost tribe."

"In this particular instance," I nodded, "the country and the Court are the better for it, much the better. But if my brother Jacobson is out, who is in?"

"Probably only our esteemed Attorney General Roger Neilson, and our learned Chief Judge of the District of Columbia Circuit Geoffrey Earl. It is difficult to tell at this point which of them is attempting to apply more pressure on the president. Both have impressive papers as party workhorses, and both have had distinguished careers in the law."

"Neither, however, is overly endowed with grey matter."

"That," Trimble mused, "may be true, and in the case of our learned chief judge may disqualify him. He made the mistake of sending the president a half dozen of his opinions."

"I can't imagine any president having time to read them," I interjected. "And even if he had time, certainly Clarence Bowers wouldn't understand them unless they were written on television cue cards."

"That may be true enough." Trimble smiled his most professionally ingenuous smile. "Therefore, I took the liberty to suggest the names of a few scholarly Republicans, whose party loyalty and legal learning are beyond reproach and who might act as impartial referees. It seems that their remarks to the president fell somewhat short of flattering the learned chief judge. But he's not out of the running, Walker. What he lacks in intelligence he makes up for in persistence. And, before going to the bench, he was a stalwart worker for the party. There are many people here in town who owe him. Besides, we must never overestimate the value that our president places on intellectual power. However, Earl is a WASP and that will hurt him in terms of our national campaign strategy. He is from the Midwest but I've questioned whether his connections there, after six years on the District of Columbia bench, are still strong enough to bring us votes."

"Well, all of those arguments should eliminate Neilson. Earl is a man of brilliance in comparison. Neilson is also a WASP and Philadelphia doesn't qualify as the Midwest except perhaps to New Yorkers and Princetonians."

"All true enough, and in Neilson's case the president is also seriously worried about the problem of grey matter. On the other hand, that lack has caused the president some difficulties with the Department of Justice. Neilson is honest enough, but he's allowed some pretty stupid things to happen that could embarrass the administration. Unhappily, Clarence can't fire him. Neilson swung Pennsylvania for us in the last election almost singlehanded, or at least so he's convinced the president. A promotion to the Court might be the graceful way out for everyone."

"Dear me, it is a complicated game you chaps play. But with all that said, what are Walsh's chances?" I asked.

"I am not, Walker, one of those stupid Washington egoists who thinks he owns the President of the United States. But I think it fair to say that I can neutralize the political pressures that Neilson and Earl are applying. I have a lot of IOU's out in this town, too, and many of those have Clarence Bower's marker on them. What it boils down to is this: If we can make an honest case that, on the merits, this man Walsh is a better candidate than the others—and can help us more in November—our chances are very good, very good indeed."

"Let me then repeat my query: How can I help?"

"Do you know anyone in the upper echelons of the American Bar Association?" Trimble asked.

"Not especially well. As you know, I am apt to be anathema among the troglodytes who populate the nether reaches of that reactionary pressure group. It happens, however, that Justice Albert is more tolerant than I of fools and has remained on very friendly terms with some of those creatures. In fact, his former law partner is a member of the ABA's Committee on Federal Judiciary, and one of his classmates from Stanford is chairman."

"They are the ones who pass judgment on our judges?"

I nodded.

"Perfect, Walker—if you think that Mr. Justice Albert would. . . ."

"Gerald Albert and I sometimes vote differently on the Court, but we share a concern for the things that really matter—a puritanical concern to keep our Court out of politics and a concern that our Court always live up to its highest traditions. I think he finds not unreasonable my fear that both those values would be threatened by the appointment of either Earl or Neilson—or, heaven spare us, some of those other worthies whose names the press is bruiting about. Yes, I think you can consider the matter done."

"Wonderful. That will be our weakest link. I've heard that pompous idiot, Porter Smythe, testify before. As you know, Walker, I've never been noted for left-wing tendencies, but he looks on anything north of William McKinley as, 'ahem, ahem, unsound.' And he won't cotton to anybody who hasn't been a conservative lawyer owned body and soul by some corporation. I may as well tell you that if his committee turns thumbs down on Walsh, the president will look elsewhere."

"Well, my brother Albert is not unknown for his diplomacy."

"Wonderful. Let us hope so. Now Walsh will have to give us a hand with some letters from the Catholic hierarchy. We'll need a nice mix of cardinals and archbishops. Clarence Bowers is impressed by pomp and circumstance. He also felt right at home with 'regular guys' like Spellman. You know the type—bourbon-drinking, card-playing 'just folks' who can raise lots of money because they're natural-born used car salesmen. Please don't get me wrong, Mr. Justice," Trimble said, for a few moments reclothing himself in his Chautauqua robes. "We are here to serve the 'just folks' of our country; but, Christ, they give me a pain in the ass when they wear red hats—or brass hats, for that matter." (I apologize for the language, but most senators have a streak of vulgarity in them. I suppose it is functional if one wishes to win the mob's votes.)

I got up and fixed a pair of ginger ales. We'd both been around Washington too long to imbibe alcohol late in the evening. "That leaves our good Judge Ruskin, the deputy attorney general, and his staff," I mused. "I assume that the president has followed the usual procedure of delegating to the deputy attorney general responsibility for choosing most judicial nominees."

"Yes, but in this case the deputy and his staff won't be as important as they usually are because the president knows damned well that the attorney general would sell a soul—anybody's, including his own or the deputy's—to get the center chair on the Court. Clarence Bowers is shrewd enough to discount anything the deputy tells him."

"But what if—I'm only thinking out loud now, my dear Trimble, merely thinking out loud—what if the deputy, while giving a strong endorsement, to be sure, to his chief, would also have some kind words to say about our dean? Do you think that might help?"

"Indeed, I do; indeed, I do."

"Well—still thinking out loud, mind you—it happens that the deputy was a student of mine at Yale and I gave him a small boost some years back when he nourished a petty ambition to become a state judge. We've been rather close since, despite marked differences in political outlook."

"Do you think . . . ?"

"I think," I continued, "that I can chat with Judge Ruskin. He's a man with an open mind, and he has integrity. And, off the record, his opinion of that poor Neilson creature is somewhat lower than either yours or mine."

"Splendid, Walker. But you must be careful."

"To be sure, my dear Trimble, to be sure. As one who has spent a lifetime preaching the necessity of judicial aloofness from the processes of politics, I am acutely cognizant of the danger of slipping into those morasses. After finishing reading three or four of Walsh's articles and glancing through a book or two, I thought I might write a personal and confidential memorandum—unsigned, to be sure—to Judge Ruskin. I'll see that he receives it myself—by hand. I can arrange that. He and his charming lady have invited me to tea on several occasions."

"Splendid, Walker, simply splendid."

"Then," I added, "after you let me know that the judge has passed these evaluations to the president—I shall stress to him that the president should only know that it comes from a senior and respected member of the judiciary—I think it would be appropriate if Bartholomew Riddock, the man who covers our Court for the *Washington Post,* were to receive a Xeroxed copy. I can arrange to have it sent in one of the Justice Department's envelopes, so the leak will seem to have come from within that department. It might look good in print, give our man the image of the most qualified candidate even in the real, as opposed to the official, judgment of Neilson's own staff."

"That would indeed be a nice touch, Walker. I am just glad *you* are not a Michigan man with senatorial ambitions."

That was very high praise, very high praise indeed, coming from the Wizard of Ooze himself. We talked for another hour or so, ironing out incidentals of timing and so forth. It was all grand sport, really. I would have dearly loved to see the face of my colleague Marvin Jacobson when he read Riddock's column.

After Trimble left, I sat down and wrote a brief note to Walsh. Here, I asked my secretary to make a copy for you. It's right there on the desk. Take it.

August 2

My dear Walsh,

You may have read in recent days that I myself have been a candidate for a certain high office or have been lending my support to others. I know that even our brief acquaintance in 1951–52 and your knowledge of my judicial career would leave no doubt in your mind about my jealous concern for the austere functions of our tribunal in a democratic system of government.

Let me add that if a lifetime of experience in navigating the Serbonian Bogs of Washington bureaucracy and the weird world of senatorial solons can be of assistance to you in your own plans, you have only to lift a telephone. The Court is my life, the law my religion. If I can maintain its steady course by aiding recruitment to the bench of men of proven courage, integrity, wisdom, and learning, I count my life useful.

Yours faithfully,
C. Bradley Walker, III

TWO

A WEEK OR SO LATER I was sitting here in my study perusing a batch of "bloody certs"—petitions for writs of certiorari. You, of course, know that most cases come to us that way. The side that loses in the highest state court—providing a question of interpretation of a federal law or treaty or the Constitution is involved—or the losing party in a U.S. Court of Appeals can petition us to review the case. The petition is technically for a writ of certiorari ordering the lower court to send the case to us for examination. We have absolute discretion, absolute, in deciding whether to grant or deny these petitions. When I came to the Court we were receiving about 1500 of them a year; when I retired the number was approaching 4000, a thousand or more of them scribbled by prisoners in penitentiaries. We treat them all seriously, although it would take the Deity himself to explain why.

Our Court does not sit in panels or committees. Every justice receives the papers on every case and has a vote and a voice in its decision. For certs, as we call them, we have a rule of four—a rule that Chief Justice Taft promised legislators in 1925 we would follow if Congress would give us absolute discretion over most of our docket. That rule means that if four of the nine justices vote to grant a petition, then the full Court must hear the case. Agreeing to hear the case does not mean, to be sure, that we shall decide in favor of the petitioner, only that we are willing to listen to his arguments. If we decide not to grant the request, we simply say "denied," and offer no explanation.

Practice in handling these petitions varies among my brethren. My custom was to ask two of my three law clerks—bright young men (I never hired a female) fresh out of Yale Law School—to read all the petitions, and, without consulting with each other or anyone else, to write for me a paragraph summarizing the problems involved and offering a recommendation to grant or deny the request. I would examine those memoranda, take home the petitions that seemed most interesting, and make up my mind on the basis of my own reading. Even with help, it was a back-breaking task, back-breaking. Fortunately, most of the petitions are frivolous, sometimes written by lawyers trying to earn an extra fee or catering to a client's emotional desire to take his case to the Supreme Court; often, as I have indicated, they are sent by a jailhouse lawyer who has read an article in a prison library and fancies he has found the key to his cell. We never granted more than 200 requests a year, and perhaps in half or even two-thirds of the rejections the Court was unanimous.

Well, as I was sitting there that August afternoon, the telephone rang. I immediately recognized the honeyed words. "Mr. Justice, this is Trimble. Could you spare me a moment of your precious time?"

"I am always at your service, Trimble."

"The Justice is always a gracious as well as a learned jurist. America needs more public servants of your intelligence and integrity."

I said nothing. What can one possibly say to such an audacious creature?

He went on. "I must be in New York day after tomorrow to offer some humble words of advice to a UN committee, and the thought has come to me that, with the Court not yet in session, I might take advantage of your offer to instruct me in some of the finer points of the New York theater. I'll be staying at the Plaza."

(My dear chap, I must tell you that Trimble always assumed that his telephone was tapped. Of course, I had never made any offer to take him to the theater, as he well knew. But it would sound plausible to any eavesdropper. After all, as one who had spent a lifetime as a student of culture, I had built up a not inconsiderable reputation, not at all inconsiderable, as a critic of the performing arts.)

"My very dear sir," I replied, "it will be a pleasure. I'll ring up some friends and see what's available. This is a grand surprise. I'll try to stay at the Plaza, too."

I flew to New York the next morning and spent the afternoon with some old friends who were producing an off-Broadway drama that was not scheduled to open until fall. At eight that evening I responded to a message from the senator and went up to his suite. Trimble was there, of course, and with him were Walsh and another man, whom I recognized as Sidney M. Keller, a rather vulgar creature, I must say—bright and agile enough, to be sure, and there was no doubt that he knew as much law as any attorney, but he wasn't deep; he didn't have a big mind. And, he *was* vulgar. As you are no doubt aware, I have followed a lifetime practice of never engaging in gossip, but the man was a womanizer, almost compulsively so. He was also something of a buffoon, behaving rather not unlike a mischievous child.

I also noted that Walsh still had his beard. I suppose hair had remained in vogue in academia. But I believe I've already told you that. In any event, his was quite neat, although full. There was a touch of copper in it, but it was mostly dark brown, grizzled with more patches of grey than a vain creature like Walsh would have liked.

"Come in, Mr. Justice, and do have a drink," the senator said effusively. Then to Walsh and Keller: "Justice Walker has consented to give us the benefit of his wisdom in this matter." Walsh started to say something, but Trimble cut him off with a wave of his hand. "Now, Dean, let us be clear that neither the justice nor I want any thanks. We are merely public servants trying to further the welfare of our country as best we can. If we can actually do some good, we have our reward."

Walsh looked a bit quizzical. That Keller creature smirked.

"Now, let me suggest," Trimble continued, "that we spend the evening together laying our plans. I propose that we have dinner served in this suite. I don't think it would be prudent for the four of us to be seen together. We wouldn't want to give the press the impression of a cabal."

The senator handed us menus and we went through the ritual of ordering. Trimble offered drinks, but only Keller accepted.

"Let me summarize the situation," Trimble said, his voice now several decibels lower and less hollow. "I have seen the president on two occasions recently, and he has warmed to the idea of the dean as chief justice. He remembers you well from your military record. I took the liberty of leaving him a copy of *Silk Hat Six,* and last week he told me—and I believe I quote him correctly—'By golly, it's good to see that America still produces real fighting men.' "

(I believe that the senator did not inaccurately quote our glorious Clarence Bowers. That was precisely the sort of simpering statement that creature would make about a vulgar book. Of course, Walsh had aimed the book at an audience with subnormal IQ's, and in Bowers he had hit the mark, hit the mark exactly.)

"Now the next step," Trimble continued, "is to secure some letters from the Catholic hierarchy, certainly from several archbishops and at least one cardinal."

"I have some reservations there," Walsh said.

"Dean," Trimble rejoined, "I share your opposition to involving the cloth in matters of politics. But surely you would not deprive any American citizen of his constitutional right to petition his government merely because he had chosen to serve God rather than amass personal wealth? In conscience, we must allow priests—and ministers and rabbis, as well as agnostics and atheists—to exercise their constitutional rights. Besides," he added, "if we don't approach your friends in the hierarchy, someone else will approach any enemies you have there. I should emphasize to all of you just how important this religious issue is. The president wants—needs—the Catholic vote. If he doesn't have some overt indications that the nomination of Declan Walsh will be looked on with favor by the powers within the Catholic church, he will turn elsewhere for a nominee. Let me suggest a compromise, Dean, one that will ease your conscience and still accomplish our objective. Let us restrict our solicitation of clerical views to members of the American hierarchy. We shall contact no Canadians, Mexicans, or even Italians."

"Now," Trimble continued, "do you know any cardinals whom you might approach, Dean?"

"One."

"Any archbishops?"

"A couple."

"Mr. Keller?"

"Don't look at me, Senator. I'm just an agnostic Jew from Chicago who travels around in the great man's shadow. I hardly know a rabbi. My last contact with the clergy came in Korea, when I got potted one night and pissed on the chaplain's tent by mistake. And he was a Lutheran."

"Very well," Trimble said. (To his credit, he did not even smile at Keller's vulgarity.) "That ball's in your court, Dean. All you have to do is ask those people if they would respond to an inquiry from the White House. You needn't ask them to volunteer opinions. I'll see that they are contacted. I merely need their names. I assure you the president will get their messages."

Walsh nodded rather glumly. I had not expected such squeamishness in one infected with the political bug. But I may do Walsh an injustice. Perhaps the thought of the chief justiceship had purged him of political ambition.

"The next step," Trimble instructed us, "is to open a limited campaign in the press. We want to attract enough attention so that it is clear you are a serious candidate, but we don't want so much attention that we look like a front-runner and draw the fire of all the others. Mr. Justice Walker has generously prepared a memorandum for the deputy attorney general who is nominally in charge of judicial recruitment. That memorandum is a cold intellectual analysis of some of your writings, Dean, but the grade is A."

"Not A plus?" Walsh smiled at me.

"At Yale," I said, "I enjoyed the not totally undeserved reputation of being an exacting critic."

"Well," Trimble broke in, "I learned this morning that someone has leaked a copy of that memorandum, fortunately unsigned, to Bartholomew Riddock of the *Washington Post*. I am not privy to all the details, but the memorandum came in an envelope from the Department of Justice. There is no point in our speculating about the source of the leak. Riddock will, I understand, use the document and it can only help us—help us immensely. But we shall need more. Dean, do you know anyone on the *New York Times?*"

"I know Kenneth Willard passingly. He's a passionate liberal activist who seldom bothers to get his facts straight. I suspect Justice Walker knows him better and may have a higher regard for his work than I do."

Let me emphasize, my dear fellow, that I hastened to make it clear, very clear, that I held fewer journalists in lower esteem. Really, the creature was worse than an enemy. He would espouse good causes but for all the wrong reasons. He was an embarrassment. I suggested that we go to someone else, but Trimble thought that Walsh was just the sort of man that Willard would warm to and that a good liberal senator from Minnesota, an old friend of Mrs. Walsh's late father, could be persuaded to butter Willard up a bit and get a favorable story.

"How good is the *Chicago Tribune* for our purposes?" Keller asked.

"Gold, Mr. Keller, pure gold," Trimble responded. "The president prefers Republican newspapers, especially," the senator took on a truly puckish expression, "especially those that do not care for ideas. And there the *Tribune* is without peer. What do you have in mind?"

Keller looked at Walsh rather than Trimble. "Dec, you remember Bob Twisdale? He covered the Second Batt a couple of times in Korea and you gave him several hours after we got off Caspar. He's been wandering around like a nomad the past few years, talking about writing the great American novel, but to pay the grocery bills he's been writing a syndicated column that appears in the *Trib* and a few other papers."

"Splendid, simply splendid," Trimble intoned. "Now, just what do we want him to write?"

Keller pulled a yellow pad from his briefcase. "How about something like this for openers? It would come, say, after a cool assessment of the leading contenders:

> Probably the most gifted and qualified of those whose names are being discussed around Washington is Declan Walsh, the Congressional Medal of Honor winner from the Korean War whose best-selling book, *Silk Hat Six,* won him a Pulitzer Prize in 1952. An eminent legal scholar now serving as dean of the University of Michigan Law School, Walsh was also personal representative to the Vatican for two presidents. Despite his intellectual qualifications and broad experience as a lawyer, scholar, soldier, and diplomat, most informed sources here discount Walsh's chances. Politically he's from the wrong party; and although he is well known professionally, he has no connections with any of the politicians who will be hounding the president to nominate their friends."

"What do you think of that, Senator?"

"I'd have given you a C minus," Walsh snorted.

"Basically good, basically good, Counsellor," Trimble crooned, "but it needs a little barb at the end that will twit the president. Let me see, how would something like this sound as a closing sentence: 'Indeed, cynics claim that the people in the Department of Justice are leaking Walsh's name only to reassure the public that the Administration does consider men whose only claim is merit.' "

"Great, Senator," Keller agreed. "If you're ever out of work, the firm of Milbank, Hughes, Hudson, and Webster can use you."

"The only question, Counsellor," Trimble put in, "is whether your man Twisdale will print it. It is a bit heavy, but good—and what counts, of course, is that it is honest."

"I've never cottoned to Twisdale," Keller said. "He takes the world and himself much too seriously. But he'll print it, or something very close. He owes us. Besides, he's not too bright—he thinks our dean here is an honest to God hero."

"Clearly a journalist of perception," Trimble imparted sanctimoniously. Then more crisply: "Timing. When? We want to crescendo. Perhaps I could ask our Mr. Riddock to hold off for a day or two. Let me see. Today is Tuesday. Do you think, Counsellor, that you might, aah, prime your man Twisdale to produce on Sunday? The president loves the funnies. He won't miss Sunday's *Trib*. It'll be waiting for him when he gets in from his afternoon round of golf."

Keller nodded.

"I have it on good authority," Trimble smiled, "that next Monday morning a bipartisan group of senators—six of them—will send a letter to the White House supporting our good dean. Here, gentlemen, we have the essence of American democracy: six honest public servants rising above party for the good of the country. It's the sort of thing that makes America great."

(My dear chap, I can't tell you how difficult it was not to predict that these six senators would be old friends of Trimble or deeply in his debt, or both. They would not be unaware, decidedly not, of what Walsh's appointment would mean to Trimble.)

The senator looked at me. "Mr. Justice, has your distinguished colleague, Gerald Anthony Albert, agreed to talk to his friends on the American Bar Association's committee?"

"I can report that Justice Albert is now deeply impressed with Dean Walsh's qualifications and is prepared to talk to the chairman of that committee. We thought it best to await your signal."

"Very wise, Mr. Justice, very wise. You have that signal now. Perhaps late this week, perhaps early next week, the committee will receive some names to evaluate. As you know, practice for submitting names of Supreme Court nominees to the ABA varies. President Bowers would like to give the ABA the names of the three or four leading candidates so that he won't be considering anyone whom the ABA thinks incompetent. I really don't know how much weight he will place on their views of the relative merits of the candidates, other than that I am dead certain he will not nominate anyone who does not have the ABA's approval."

We were interrupted at that point by a waiter bringing our dinner. I have a firm rule, one in which Trimble concurred, never to discuss business over meals. Walsh was of a different persuasion, but wiser heads prevailed. While we ate, we chatted pleasantly. Afterwards we returned to work. There were more details to discuss, but we had already made the basic decisions. The baby was born.

Later Walsh told me of his meetings with the clergy. I can't recall now who the two archbishops were—I should, you know, but there is no entry in my diary, none at all. Those were busy days, busy days indeed. I am not a religious man, to be sure, but I respect the pageantry of the Roman Church. Indeed, as one who has spent a lifetime studying psychology, I think the Church erred, grievously erred, when after the Second Vatican Council it stopped using Latin and discarded some of its more elaborate rituals. Those sorts of things appeal to the mob. Heaven knows you can't reach them with reason and logic.

Well, the cardinal whom Walsh knew was Charles Pritchett, a man I had known fifteen or twenty years earlier at Yale. He had been a visiting lecturer in the law school. Unlike most of the American Catholic hierarchy, he was an intellectual and a scholar of some repute, a noted authority on canon law, already marked twenty years ago as one of those bright young men whom the Church singles out for great things. He'd been educated at the North American College in Rome, the one that now stands on the Gianicolo Hill overlooking the Vatican on one side and the old city on the other. Later he had taken a doctorate in canon law at the Jesuit university there, the Gregorian, and then taught at the Lateran, the Pope's own university, for several years. It was during that period that he wrote a remarkable treatise on medieval law. It was because of that book that we had invited him to Yale.

He was a creature of overwhelming charm and, mind you, of tautly disciplined energy, tautly disciplined. A lifetime of studying the careers of successful men has convinced me that what my friends in the social sciences call "the critical variable" in success is not intelligence, at least not above a certain minimal point, but rather disciplined energy. Pritchett had that quality, and he also had good judgment, as well as a certain serenity. I knew even then that some day he would receive the red hat—incidentally, when he did, he became the youngest American cardinal.

Forgive me, I seem to have forgotten the point of all this. Ah yes, Walsh's visit to Pritchett. To be sure, to be sure. Well, the two knew each other. They had met several times in Rome when Walsh was Truman's personal representative. And later their paths frequently crossed, since Pritchett was archbishop of Detroit.

Because we were old friends and former colleagues, I did not hesitate—some years later, to be sure—to interrogate Pritchett about the meeting. He recalled it vividly, very vividly. Walsh had been obviously uncomfortable. "Eminence," he had begun, "I don't like to put you in an embarrassing position."

Pritchett smiled quickly. He knew precisely why Walsh had come to him. One does not, Pritchett himself once confided in me, become a cardinal—or even a bishop—by prayer and fasting, at least not *alone* by prayer and fasting. "I don't embarrass easily, and I'm rather good at saying no."

"Unfortunately I do and I'm embarrassed now. Here's the nub of the matter. Apparently I am being considered as Chief Justice of the United States. It's unlikely, of course, that lightning will strike me, but some friends in Washington believe that an endorsement from you would help.

The White House will contact you. My rationalization for asking is that my friends and competitors will soon be after you as well. I can protect you from my friends but not from the competition."

"I understand from reading the opinions of that tribunal," Pritchett mused, "that there is a wall of separation between church and state, a wall that cannot be breached unless your politicians or we clerics find it convenient to do so. If you'll pardon the alliteration, we're as pragmatic in our practice as we're dogmatic in our dicta. If I found political involvement distasteful I'd have to enter a monastery—God forbid. I never could stand the early hours and all that quiet meditation. The only problems I see are ones of prudence. I must avoid partisan stands that might be construed as helping one party or the other, unless a question of faith or morals is directly involved—and the leaders of both our parties are so clever at mincing their words and taking fence-straddling positions that it has exceeded my theological perception ever to discover a clear-cut question of faith or morals between them."

"We're all against sin, Your Eminence. Like Mammy Yokum, both parties stand for the proposition that 'good is better than evil because it's nicer.'"

The cardinal smiled blandly. "I once heard that quotation used to describe some Catholic theologians' justifications for natural law."

Walsh smiled back, remembering the occasion before the Newman Club in Ann Arbor in which he had used the same analogy.

Pritchett broke the silence. "I may well be imprudent, but I think I shall get involved. And I shall not wait to be contacted. I would also like to elicit the support of one or two of my colleagues. It would truly please me to think that I had helped you along."

"Thank you, Your Eminence. I'm sure anything that you do will help."

"I'm not certain you'll thank me in a few years, and I deserve no thanks from you now. I said it would please me to think I have helped you along. I meant that literally. It would please me. You are in many ways an extraordinary man. Some of our separated brethren would say that you've been touched by fate; I prefer to think that you have been touched by God. You have been given great gifts, and you've used them well."

"I've done no more than a thousand others in my generation," Walsh said even more uncomfortably. The creature always had a certain personal modesty that accompanied his intellectual arrogance.

"That is probably true, but don't you think it a bit odd that almost every thing you have done has been so visible?"

"Luck, I suppose."

"I do not deny luck; I just do not understand what it means. What you have done is remarkable. What is even more remarkable is that in this age of anonymity you have been given full credit for your accomplishments. I see more than talent and more than luck in that combination of apparently accidental circumstances. Of course," Pritchett's eyes twinkled, "in my profession one is supposed to discern more than the workings of mere chance."

Walsh could think of nothing to say other than to mutter that he sincerely hoped the cardinal was wrong; then it was his turn to smile. "But I'm not sure I do, Your Eminence. I have enough ego to nourish the secret hope that you're right."

"If I am, your life will be miserable, and it will be wasted—forgive me if I play the priest along with the politician—unless you retain and strengthen both your humility and your faith in God."

"I'm not a particularly humble man, Your Eminence, or even a very religious one. I have a great deal of hope, but very little faith."

"Neither am I religious in the sense that you mean it. The professional piety of some of my colleagues of the cloth either annoys or amuses me. But when I first met you in Rome I decided that we had much in common besides an interest in the law and in leading men—something deeper. I cannot put a name to it. In my case, it touches my fundamental religious . . . not beliefs, but feelings."

"I fear I have never looked closely at mine, Eminence."

"You should take the time. It's an interesting and enlightening experience, a bit like glimpsing the next world without having to make the trip. Well," the cardinal looked at his watch, "I hate to appear abrupt but if you will excuse me I must tell a delegation of holy nuns that I do not have the money to assist them in opening a halfway house for former drug users. Their work is worthwhile and I bless it, but I cannot finance it. Alas, ladies, even nuns, are apt these days to look on clerical poverty as a sin rather than a virtue. I suspect the chancery will soon be picketed by gentle ladies and to make money available to them I shall have to sell my Ford, just as I sold my Lincoln three years ago. Pray for me. I am far too tall to fit comfortably into a Volkswagen."

THREE

OUR PLANS quickly began to bear fruit. Even one who stands as aloof from politics as I could enjoy the play. Bartholomew Riddock's article appeared three days after our meeting in New York, and the column by that Twisdale fellow was published in Sunday's *Chicago Tribune.* Riddock closely followed the script that I had prepared for the deputy attorney general and, of course, made no mention of the author of the memorandum other than to identify him as a senior judicial official with a reputation for sound judgment. Those intimately familiar with our work would suspect, but they could never be certain, not really certain. Twisdale changed hardly a comma of the text that Keller and Trimble had drafted. (Really, my dear chap, I laugh at the hypocrisy of those journalistic creatures. They cry to the heavens about their integrity at the same time that they allow themselves to be used as prostitutes by anyone with a printed handout.) Well, in any event, our gospel was in the wind. Walsh was now established as the most deserving but least likely candidate.

All the sailing was not silken, to be sure. The attorney general, poor cretin creature, was intensifying his campaign. A more bothersome note came from all those horrid women's organizations. They were trying to pressure the president to name a female. I was annoyed, but one could not resist admiring their effrontery. A woman on our Court! Indeed! Can you imagine a woman keeping the secrets that we must? Or being able to refrain from gossiping about colleagues behind their backs? Impossible! It simply cannot be. Ever. Still, Clarence Bowers was a politician, and that's not a breed noted for courage. I was genuinely fretful that he might cave in before such pressures. More amusing and far less dangerous were the pathetic efforts of our colleague on the Court, Marvin Jacobson, to push himself forward as a candidate. I shan't embarrass us both with the details. It was not a nicely nuanced campaign, but then Jacobson was not a man of taste or breeding.

About ten days after our meeting in New York, I telephoned Trimble for a progress report, but he declined to say anything. In fact, he would not even allow me to ask a question. Then I recalled his paranoia about tapped telephones. An hour or so later he rang back from a booth in a restaurant to apologize and to say that the FBI were conducting a complete investigation of Walsh—surely a not unpromising omen—and that several representatives from the wire services had been trying to interview Walsh—another not unfavorable augury.

No sooner had I replaced the telephone in its cradle when my brother justice, Gerald Albert, one of the most able men ever to grace our bench, rang. He reported that he had been in contact several times with the Smythe creature who vets judges for the American Bar Association's Committee on Federal Judiciary, and that Smythe had just telephoned to make an immediate appointment to confer with Albert at his home in Chevy Chase. There was barely enough time for me to commandeer a taxi. (I take some pride in the fact that I have never diverted myself from serious activities to learn to drive an automobile.)

Elizabeth, Albert's lady—an absolutely charming creature—ushered me into the study. You don't hear Albert's name mentioned among the big judges of our Court, but he was that. The old chief had called him "my chancellor," and that title explains a great deal. Albert had an impediment, a writing block. Composing an opinion was a cruel ordeal for him. No chief justice could assign him more than two or three a year, leaving the rest of us with an average of about fourteen each in addition to our dissents and concurrences. But, mind you, Albert had a gloriously capacious mind. As a critic of the writings of others, he was magnificent. His logic was sharp as a surgeon's scalpel and his knowledge vast. It would not have surprised me to have heard him recite the entire U.S. Code from memory.

He had the sort of memory that allowed him not only to recall the names of cases—I confess they constantly slipped my mind—but also the volume number of the U.S. Reports. That was no small feat since during our joint tenure the Court's opinions went past their 450th volume.

Albert brought us more than a photographic memory and total recall. He was a wise man, a grey beard who gathered his wisdom from literature as well as from personal experience. He loved to read and his tastes were truly catholic—Proust one evening, Hemingway the next, then one of Disraeli's political novels, then a play by Arthur Miller or a treatise on the development of common law under the Plantagenets. His mind was an intellectual Eden, illumined by Elizabethan poets as well as by the lore of the law, and tightly disciplined, very tightly disciplined, closely controlled, but also not without gentleness.

He was by no means an impressive-looking man. Indeed, he was rather heavy, even a bit obese, with long, thin white hair and bright blue eyes. His skin was pale, an unhealthy color brought about by his inability to tolerate sun even in small dosages. That paleness was accentuated by the large yellow liver spots on his hands and cheeks. He was an inveterate pipe smoker and kept several pouches of tobacco—of which he always reeked—on his person. Yet he was always misplacing them. That's a dreadful habit—smoking, I mean. It was Albert's sole vice. His voice was cultivated—he was, after all, a cultivated man—but a trifle hoarse, due, no doubt, to all that hot, foul smoke he drew into his throat and lungs.

Albert had been a Rhodes scholar—he did his undergraduate work at Harvard, to be sure—and returned to graduate first in his class from Harvard Law School. His family was rather well connected both financially and politically, and Albert began his career in the foreign service. After a few years of that, he settled down for a decade or more with one of the larger Wall Street law factories and became a partner. He might have become just another prosperous attorney if he had not contracted the political virus when Eisenhower first ran in 1952. Albert took a position as a speech writer for the general. He didn't write many speeches himself, but he was wonderful at revising what others drafted. Later he became an assistant attorney general, then solicitor general—and a marvelously competent one, precise, elegant, and honest. Finally he joined our Court and became a long-headed judge. At sixty-eight his mental faculties were at their apogee, but his obesity—you will notice, that even though I am five feet seven inches tall I have never weighed more than 135 pounds in my life—and smoking caused me concern for his physical well-being.

Well, that day in Albert's home, the three of us—I include Elizabeth—chatted pleasantly for a few moments. Relations among us were always easy; no, cordial and genuinely so. Not five minutes later the doorbell rang and Elizabeth brought in J. Porter Smythe, the pompous chairman of the ABA's committee. Albert invited us to have some refreshment. The thought of some of Albert's Madeira was pleasant, but Smythe, boor that he was, and still not able to grasp that he himself was too old—and too stupid—to become a federal judge, insisted that he was in somewhat of a push. At that point I turned on this little pocket machine. It's not as fancy as yours, but it does the trick. I thought that posterity should not be without a verbatim record of J. Porter Smythe's banality. Listen to the tape; I'll identify the voices.

ALBERT: I asked Justice Walker to sit in, Porter, because he knows Walsh rather well.

WALKER: Only in a professional way, my dear Smythe. I've met the fellow a few times but I hardly can claim intimacy. I am rather closely acquainted with his scholarly work, however.

SMYTHE: Ahem, uh, how do you, uh, how do you rate him as an attorney, Mr. Justice?

WALKER: As one who has spent his entire adult life in the service of the law, I can speak not without authority. Walsh is clearly—clearly—a very intelligent and learned lawyer. I do not see room for any doubt that he has mastered our science. As for leadership, his career from Iwo Jima through Korea, the White House, the Vatican, and now the deanship of a major law school speaks for itself.

SMYTHE: Uh, yes, learned, uh, yes, there's no doubt there; but, ahem, but is he sound?

WALKER: Sound?

SMYTHE: Yes, uh, politically sound, that is.

WALKER: My dear Smythe, one who is as insistent as I that the Court and its members must retain an antiseptic aloofness from the virulent botulism of partisan politics simply cannot respond to such an inquiry beyond noting the obvious facts that Dean Walsh is neither a Fascist nor a Communist.

SMYTHE: Ahem, I, uh, I beg your pardon, your honor. I, uh, what I meant to say, ahem, what I was getting at, is whether he would be one of these radical judges who think their job is to reform the world. He made some critical statements about the war in Africa and he does have a beard, after all.

WALKER: My dear fellow, many of our big judges have had beards. I need only mention Charles Evans Hughes and George Sutherland to recall to your memory an association on our Court between beards and judicial conservatism. Now, as to the war in Africa, Walsh publicly said he is opposed, but not for some bleeding heart, emotional reason. He said that he has no sympathy for the rebels but believes that the cost in lives that accompanies use of American troops is not worth the strategic value of the area to us.

SMYTHE: Mr. Justice, do you, do you find such views sound? I am using the term in its, uh, broadest sense.

WALKER: Smythe, were I a legislator or an executive official, I would want to think long and hard about such an opinion. I am not sure what I would do if, heaven forbid, I were president. But as a judge, I need only say that Walsh's views are both reasoned and reasonable. Those who disagree have the opportunity to debate him in an open forum. In a nation supposedly dedicated to democratic ideals and the free exchange of ideas, we can hardly ask for more.

SMYTHE: Well, uh, Mr. Justice, what about his soundness as an, uh, attorney? I mean he has very little trial experience and more seriously he, he lacks any judicial experience at all.

ALBERT: Porter, you're asking the wrong people on that last one. As you remember, before coming to the Supreme Court, neither Justice Walker nor I had sat on any bench, except on a ball field.

(In my own case, I must point out, that bit of levity was decidedly inaccurate. I have always abhorred athletic contests. But I let the remark pass.)

SMYTHE: Well, uh, that is, . . .

WALKER: My dear Smythe, as a literate lawyer you have undoubtedly read my book on the history of the Supreme Court. I demonstrate there on the basis of irrebuttable evidence—absolutely irrebuttable—that greatness in the law has nothing, absolutely nothing, to do with prior judicial experience. Some big judges have been promoted, so to speak, to our Court—Field, Holmes, and Van Devanter, for instance. Others had no prior judicial experience—Marshall, Taney, Brandeis, Hughes, and Black, for example. For every big justice on one side, there's a big justice on the other. The only conclusion that squares with the evidence is that prior judicial experience is irrelevant to greatness on our Court.

SMYTHE: Yes, well, I hadn't, I hadn't meant to stress judicial experience except as, uh, a counterweight to absence of experience as a trial lawyer.

WALKER: My dear Smythe, what we do on our Court is unique, at least in the United States. A lifetime of study of the Supreme Court has left me unconvinced that lawyers are better qualified to staff such a tribunal than would be philosophers, historians, or litterateurs. Surely having toiled in a trial court would be of trivial significance in our multifaceted tasks.

ALBERT: Porter, I think you may report to your committee that the two of us feel many kinds of experience are useful on our Court and that in addition to being a learned attorney, Dean Walsh has had more of those experiences than most of us had. In our judgment, they more than compensate for lack of work at the trial level, either as lawyer or judge.

Here, let me turn that thing off. Smythe was such a terrible boor, a dreadful creature. He really hadn't read my book nor, I suspect, even heard of it. Truly, an intellectual pygmy. There is more of that exchange. Albert and I gave it to him straight from the shoulder, as you would expect; but he simply could not comprehend what we were talking about. I tell you in all candor that I shudder at the thought of boorish little minds like his daring to advise presidents on the qualifications of federal judges.

What I did take comfort in was the fact that Smythe had asked nothing about other people. I interpreted that as a sign that Trimble was making progress with his friend in the White House. It was difficult to discern from coverage in the press. I subscribed to the *Washington Post* and the *Star*—in addition to the *New York Times,* to be sure—and all three were filled with guesses and gossip. The attorney general's name still appeared most often, and even our colleague Jacobson was mentioned—and far more favorably than he deserved. Walsh's name came up now and then as a dark horse rather than as a leading candidate—which was just right, just right. As Trimble had said, everybody shoots at the front-runner; as a dark horse Walsh was relatively safe from partisan attacks.

It was about eleven-thirty an evening or two later when the telephone rang. I was sitting up in bed reading that fascinating but flawed book by John Rawls, *A Theory of Justice.* I immediately recognized Trimble's voice. "Mr. Justice, I thought that you would like to know that our friend has an appointment at ten o'clock tomorrow morning with the big boss. From where I sit, it looks like virtue will triumph. I think that the two of us can take a good deal of pride in what we have accomplished for this wonderful country of ours."

I would have dearly loved to be present at the meeting between Walsh and Clarence Bowers. Bowers had been in the navy during the Korean War and liked to affect nautical argot even though he had never been outside the Pentagon. And, according to one reliable report, he would get seasick on a cruise down the Potomac. I can hear him admiring the cut of Walsh's jib. Apparently all was like glass, at least so Trimble, who was there, related.

One could now only wait. I had other things on my mind, to be sure. The Corcoran Gallery had borrowed a gaggle of impressionist paintings from the Jeu de Paume in Paris; there were some rehearsals for the off-Broadway production my friends were doing and I wanted to attend those; I had promised to give a lecture at the University of Virginia Law School; that business of the district judgeship in Boston was still unresolved; one of my former students who was an assistant U.S. attorney in Denver wanted me to talk to someone about his being seconded to Washington; and, as always, the "bloody certs" were piling up. Then on a Sunday in early September, a story on page one of the *Washington Post* reported that a source in the White House said that the president would drop a small political bombshell the next day by sending the name of Dean Walsh to the Senate. Neither the *Star* nor the *Times* carried a similar report, but the *Times* said the president was nearing a decision, and the *Star* noted that the attorney general had flown to Los Angeles to attend a conference of law enforcement officials.

Promptly at noon on the first Monday in September, a special messenger from the White House delivered to the Senate Walsh's nomination to be chief justice. Senator Lawrence Fletcher, Trimble's Democratic colleague from Michigan, spoke quietly and, if I may say so, with some elegance, welcoming the nomination as richly deserved and evidencing a highly desirable display of nonpartisanship. Trimble spoke equally briefly, albeit with greater lubricity. Without objection the nomination was then referred to the Committee on the Judiciary. The chairman of that committee, Archibald Swinton Timrod Rutledge, a curious creature—for centuries he had graciously misrepresented the whites of South Carolina and with a lotal lack of grace had expectorated, if you will forgive the vividness of my imagery, on the rights of South Carolina's black citizens —announced that hearings would begin in exactly one week. There was hope, although a slight one, that when our Court met a month later on the first Monday in October we would have a new chief.

FOUR

MY DEAR YOUNG MAN, I have a capital idea. You can read the *Hearings* for yourself, but I talked to Walsh and Trimble about them so many times that I can paint in a few shades of color that you can't possibly insinuate from the record. Bring the *Hearings* over to me. They're over there in the green paper covers on the middle shelf behind the desk. Now, you stand here next to the couch and read over my shoulder. I'll skip through and point to the places where I can add something.

First of all the hearings were held in the Old Senate Office Building—don't ask me why. I've long forgotten if I ever knew. My hearings had been held in the very same room; perhaps that's why I have a fondness for the place. Its ceilings are elevated, making it a dignified chamber, reminiscent of those bygone days when public officials considered architectural beauty rather than cost per cubic foot. In the front of the room on a raised dais was a semicircle of desks. Each desk had a microphone and the senator's nameplate. In the middle of the semicircle was a slightly lower set of desks for the committee's counsel, staff, and stenographers. (In some committees the counsel was the chief interrogator, but not here, when Senator Rutledge was in the chair.) Directly facing them were a table and a pair of chairs for the witness and his attorney, if he cared to bring one.

It was still early in September and the air conditioning was straining to keep from falling too far behind the midmorning heat. The room was not especially crowded; although a dozen reporters and photographers were sitting around talking among themselves, relatively few interested citizens were in attendance. The mob is so stupid. Senate hearings often provide informative, intellectual debates and occasionally vulgar circuses, but the hordes of tourists who people Washington's torrid months prefer the usually boring and typically meaningless debate on the floor of either house.

Sharply at 11 A.M. the hearings were called to order by the chairman of the Committee on the Judiciary, the

Honorable Archibald Swinton Timrod Rutledge, senior senator from South Carolina. The senator was not related to the great man's families, but his aristocratic mother had always admired their names. His plebeian father, on the other hand, could not abide them and negotiated a compromise with his lady that their son—I make the charitable assumption that he was the product of their joint endeavors, although the senator's behavior suggested other origins—would be called Archibald for his paternal grandfather in exchange for appending Swinton and Legare. This compromise, the senator liked to say, made an auspicious beginning for a politician. In a quaint Charleston accent—as one who has spent a lifetime studying the language of Americans I can tell you that it has a ring and a rhythm not unlike a slow Bostonese. It's a tidewater intonation, rather than the drawling "up-country," you-all patois.

Well, as I was saying, Rutledge explained that these hearings were to be conducted by a special subcommittee of the Committee on the Judiciary. As the chair was speaking, the other two members of the subcommittee ambled in. First was Carol Vanderbilt, Democrat from New Mexico, a thirty-eight-year-old freshman who had already established a reputation as a crusading liberal and had made himself nationally known because of his opposition to American intervention in Africa. (Just between ourselves, he was also building a reputation as a Casanova. Gossip, to which I never give heed, had him in half the beds in Washington. To his credit, that gossip always identified his partners as females, something that was never said about bedmates of the senior senator from South Carolina.)

The other senator was Frank Alexander, a Republican from New York. He was a handsome creature, silver-haired, in his fifties, with a ready though heavy wit, a nimble political foot, and a chameleonlike devotion to principle. Trimble, who was hardly a novice in the fine arts of mending fences and evading issues, told me—in a voice hushed with awe—that he was a great admirer of Alexander. When he was not attending every wedding, christening, and bar mizvah in New York state, Alexander was a deadly man in a fight. "The trouble is," Trimble complained, "you never know whether he is going to stab friend or foe in the back. The only thing you can be sure of is that someone who isn't looking will lose a lot of blood. He's as steady as a weather vane—liberal today, conservative tomorrow, reactionary next week. If he had his ear any closer to the ground he'd have grass growing out of his head. We'll have to watch him closely."

The chairman next announced that the subcommittee had permission to sit while the Senate was in session and also that the subcommittee was going to allow the Honorable Harwood Trimble, senior senator from Michigan, to participate in the hearings.

We would need Trimble's presence, for Rutledge, as an unreconstructed white supremist, would be an implacable foe. Alexander would be equally dangerous and far more irascible. If he smelled political blood he would discard, for the moment, any thoughts of loyalty to party and eagerly injure the president's prestige by slashing his nominee. If, on the other hand, Walsh seemed sure to win, Alexander would be our fawning servant. Vanderbilt represented another kind of problem. He was a doctrinaire liberal who would delight in most of Walsh's views on internal public policies, but his current African fixation and his pacifism threatened uncharted shoals. I distinctly recollect joining Trimble and Keller in warning Walsh to steer away from matters of foreign affairs.

Thus the subcommittee would have one hostile and one fairly friendly interrogator as well as one mugwump. Trimble, to be sure, would do all he could in his professionally suave manner.

The chairman announced that the attorney general was ill that morning but hoped to be available in the afternoon. Thus the subcommittee would hear first the senators from Michigan. There was a ten-minute delay while Trimble's Democratic colleague, the Honorable Lawrence Fletcher, finished his talk with a constituent in the hallway outside the hearing room. When he finally deigned to appear, the creature spoke unenthusiastically of his enthusiastic endorsement of Walsh. It was in sharp contrast to his earlier oration on the floor. The situation, you can readily perceive, was not untouched by irony. The senator had come, slowly, to understand that, as a Catholic from the Midwest, Walsh was an expensive gambit in the Republicans' strategy to retain the White House. On the other hand, the good senator could not retract his earlier remarks, nor could he oppose confirmation of a man who everyone, simply everyone, knew had been supporting the senator's own campaign for reelection and whom the senator had been prematurely touting as the Democrats' best hope to unseat Trimble in two years.

For his part, Trimble was unstinting in praise. Although by nature more adept at condemning sin, he could also laud virtue with not inconsiderable eloquence. Only the truth suffered. In his mouth, Walsh's military record shamed those of Ajax, Hector, and Ulysses. As a diplomat, Walsh became a conscienced Henry Kissinger. As a professor, Walsh was no less than a pillar in the temple of the law. In all, anyone who took Trimble's words at face value would have wondered whether the president should not have nominated the learned dean for membership in the divine Trinity.

With just a spot of dry wit, Senator Rutledge thanked his colleagues for their succinct remarks and then directed the clerk to call the first witness, a good maiden lady from Boston, secretary of the American League to Expel the United Nations. She explained that her group pleaded with the Senate to reject the nomination of a man who would undermine American sovereignty by supporting the United Nations. Indeed, she asserted, in one of his books, "horrid, immoral books," he had revealed himself as no less than a one-worlder.

The subcommittee listened politely to the Boston lady, thanked her effusively when she was done, and offered to accept for the record any written statements she cared to make. The next witness was from Detroit, representing the Greater Huron Civic Association for Constitutional Government. He, too, spoke against Walsh, charging that in working with the American Civil Liberties Union, Walsh had used legal technicalities to free criminals and make the streets unsafe for the wives and children of decent folk. The second and related cause for attack was that Walsh's support of the efforts of National Association for the Advancement of Colored People to integrate housing in Detroit threatened fundamental property rights of the majority.

The third witness was Harold Wilson, a graduate student in sociology from Columbia University, claiming to speak for the Students for Democratic Action. He asserted that Walsh's military career, the aggressive tone of his books on international politics, and his popular work, *Silk Hat Six,* glorified war. "No man," Wilson stated with that solemnity and certainty only the young can affect, "who revels in blood and profits from the suffering that war brings is fit to serve a people's democracy."

Again there were no questions. Even senators have enough sense not to take such beasts seriously.

The next witness was that shocking creature, Ms.—how does one pronounce *m* and *s* together? Miz, I venture—Ms. Cynthia Faber. She was rather well-dressed, although her blond hair must have come straight from the shelves of her cosmetologist. Her voice showed that she had spent hours trying—but without total success, I might add—to remove all traces of New York City from her accent. But it was what she said that was outrageous, my dear fellow, not how she said it. She made no attempt to criticize Walsh. Indeed, she conceded that he was probably quite qualified. Rather the gravamen of her semihysterical peroration was that the Senate should refuse to confirm any male until there was at least one woman on our Court. The mind boggles, simply boggles at such nonsense. But, as one of my colleagues once said, the price of freedom of speech is that we must put up with, even pay for, a good deal of nonsense.

The worthy solons on the dais appeared embarrassed by Ms. Faber's foolishness. Senator Alexander found himself beset with a minor coughing fit. Senator Vanderbilt picked a spot high on the rear wall of the room and fixed a glassy stare upon it. Rutledge toyed with pencils and papers in front of him. Trimble, on the other hand, looked directly at the creature and smiled benignly, if deafly, throughout her address.

When she rested, Senator Rutledge said: "We thank you, ma'am, for taking the trouble to come down and visit with us. Your suggestion is most interesting, most interesting indeed. The subcommittee and the full committee will want to consider it very seriously."

Ms. Faber's temper flashed. "We shall not be satisfied with 'serious consideration,' Senator, or even 'very serious consideration.' The time has passed for that—and for condescension. We shall be satisfied only with action, a firm policy of 'no woman, no appointment.' And, I need not warn you that we form a majority of the voters in this country and that my organizations will see that women remember who defended their rights and who merely talked about defending them."

"Yes, ma'am," Rutledge agreed feebly as Ms. Faber marched out of the room. Two reporters scrambled out behind her. Rutledge waited until the door had closed, then recessed the subcommittee until one-thirty.

The first witness after lunch was the attorney general, a man not without capacity to evoke pathos. His goal, frustrated only by his own dim intelligence, was to have been the nominee rather than the witness. He looked pale and drawn, and his voice was weak. He apologized for his health, explaining that he had suffered an attack from some kind of virus—acute disappointment, no doubt—and asked if under the circumstances, Deputy Attorney General Charles Ruskin might testify for the Department of Justice.

At his courtly Charleston best, Rutledge wished the attorney general well. Trimble got up from the dais and walked to the door with the attorney general, graciously supporting the gentleman—who was at least fifteen years his junior—on his arm. Meanwhile, Ruskin strode to the witness table and took a single sheet of paper from his briefcase. Because early in his career he had served as a state judge for two years, he was always accorded the courtesy of the title "Judge"—anything, my dear fellow, to distinguish him from those crawly political creatures. He was a laconic, brusk New Hampshire man, tough-minded, long-headed, and, if I dare say it and I do, well trained in the law. I took some not unjustified pride in that training.

"Judge Ruskin," Rutledge greeted him, "it's always a pleasure to welcome you."

"I thank the chair," Ruskin nodded, then plunged directly into his work. "Mr. Chairman, the chief justice's retirement took no one by surprise. We in the executive branch have canvassed the field thoroughly for a suitable replacement. We considered a number of highly qualified men—and despite what Ms. Faber implied—women. On balance we thought that Declan Walsh was the best candidate. We made that judgment without regard to race, sex, religion, or region. My mandate was to find the *person* who was best qualified. In my judgment, Declan Walsh is that *person.*" Then Ruskin gave a terse but accurate summary of Walsh's career as the justification for the nomination He ended crisply: "May I answer any questions?"

"The chair would like to bring out a few points for the record, Judge," Rutledge stated. "Did the FBI investigate Dean Walsh?"

"Yes, sir, just as they do all prospective nominees for the federal bench."

"What was the nature of their report?"

"The FBI is a cautious organization. They try not to evaluate a person's fitness or to draw conclusions. They simply gather evidence. The evidence shows that Dean Walsh is a man of the highest moral character and of the strongest loyalty to the United States."

"Did the American Bar Association also check on Dean Walsh?"

"Yes, sir. Before the president reaches a final decision on any judicial nominee, we submit the name of that person—and occasionally several others—to the American Bar Association's Committee on Federal Judiciary. That Committee checks on the candidate's professional standing and reports back to me. The ABA reported that Dean Walsh was qualified."

"As I understand it, Judge," Rutledge continued, "the bar association reports that the candidate is exceptionally well-qualified, or well-qualified, or not qualified. What was the report in this instance?"

"Qualified."

"Not well-qualified, or exceptionally well-qualified; just qualified," Rutledge mused. "Why not exceptionally well-qualified, if you and the president are so enthusiastic?"

"You will have to take that up with the American Bar Association's representative, Mr. Smythe. Nothing that he told me made us less enthusiastic."

"Did you try to pressure Mr. Smythe to raise his committee's endorsement to well-qualified or exceptionally well-qualified?"

"I did not, sir," Ruskin snapped. His voice took on a hard edge. "I resent any inference that I would act improperly."

"Now, Judge," Rutledge said soothingly, "you know the chair has to ask many unpleasant questions. We mean nothing personal. People will be asking themselves these questions, and it's better that we get the evidence out on the table."

Better that the chair plant seeds of doubt was what that rascal really meant.

"Senator, the evidence is all on the table. If you have questions about the ABA's report, I respectfully suggest you ask Mr. Smythe."

That, of course, was precisely the answer Rutledge wanted: an open invitation to twist poor Smythe like a piece of twine.

"Thank you, Judge, I'll make a point of it," Rutledge replied. "Are there any other questions from the subcommittee?" The chairman looked around at his fellow senators.

"Just one," that boorish Senator Alexander said. "Judge, did the FBI give Mr. Walsh a clean bill of health?"

"They never do that, Senator. They only report what their field investigation showed."

"So they didn't clear him?"

"The FBI doesn't *clear* anyone. They only report on the evidence they found."

"No derogatory information against our learned dean, none at all?" Alexander raised his eyebrows.

"I did not say that. No man is loved by all his neighbors."

"What you're telling us, Judge, is that you discount what his neighbors said." Sensing one of Alexander's famed assaults, the journalists began taking careful notes. Before Ruskin could respond, Alexander continued. "I'd like to see the raw evidence. Could we have that FBI report?"

"No, sir, it's confidential. I went over it with the chairman two days ago; no one else outside my office may see it."

"That sounds suspicious to me, Judge. The Senate of the United States has a higher duty than the staff of the attorney general. We have to pass on this man's fitness, yet you deny us evidence we need. Mr. Chairman, can we subpoena the FBI file?"

Rutledge responded shortly. "The chair will take it under advisement, Senator, but frankly I don't see any point to it. I'm not nearly as impressed with Dean Walsh's qualifications as is the deputy attorney general; but I did go over the FBI file with him, and I concur fully in his evaluation of the evidence. Any further questions?" The senator paused for only a split second. "Call the next witness, please."

That worthy was none other than Porter Smythe, chairman of the ABA's Committee on Federal Judiciary. Smythe explained the nature and function of his petty cabal and said that after an intensive investigation, the committee had concluded that Walsh was qualified.

"Just qualified? Y'all didn't think he was exceptionally well-qualified or even well-qualified?" Rutledge slowed his cadence.

"No, uh, sir. We did not."

"May I ask why not?" Rutledge's voice dripped honey.

"It's . . ." Smythe replied in his usual halting style. "It's always hard to give, uh, an exact reason for a group decision, Senator; but more or less I think we all felt that Dean Walsh's experience in law was too academic to deserve a higher rating. He's a man of fine, uh, character, but he has no judicial experience, none at all; and he has practiced law only part-time while teaching at the University of Chicago and the University of Michigan. In addition, we . . . we didn't think that his books and articles on constitutional law showed that kind of fundamental, uh, soundness in American legal history that makes a man—a person—well- or exceptionally well-qualified for the Supreme Court—not that we thought his writings were not scholarly. We, ahem, we just thought that they weren't truly as sound as they should be for the highest ratings."

"Mr. Smythe," Rutledge asked, "did the deputy attorney general discuss your recommendation with you?"

"Yes, on, uh, several occasions."

"What was the nature of these discussions?"

"Very pleasant, Senator; we . . . we have excellent relations with Judge Ruskin."

"How did the judge react when you gave him your report?"

"Well, he thanked us and we discussed the report and the record at, uh, some length, sir."

"Did he try to persuade you to change your recommendation?"

"Well, that might, that might be putting it a bit strongly, but the judge said he didn't see, uh, why we couldn't say well-, or even exceptionally well-qualified. We, the two of us, discussed that on at least two occasions, maybe three."

"How would you describe these discussions?"

"Well, Senator, as I said, they were all pleasant. They, they were also quite lively. The judge is a fine lawyer; he really fights for his client."

"He fights tooth and nail with every weapon at his disposition, I'll bet," Rutledge interjected.

"Yes, sir," Smythe fell into the trap—willingly, gladly, I suspect—"tooth and, uh, nail."

"He fought you, but you're not the kind of man who gives in when you know you're right, are you?"

"No, sir. I . . . I am not. Besides, it wasn't only my recommendation, though I think, uh, it was the right one. It was the committee's. I did promise Judge Ruskin to talk to the committee again. I did, but they wouldn't budge; they, uh, just didn't think Dean Walsh was sound enough to rate more than a report of qualified."

Senator Trimble smiled his most ingratiating smile: "Mr. Chairman, may I ask Mr. Smythe something here?"

"Of course, Senator."

"I gather, Mr. Smythe, that Dean Walsh's lack of judicial experience weighed heavily with your committee."

"I . . . I think that's fair, uh, to say."

"Mr. Smythe, who was the greatest chief justice that the United States ever had? I'd be interested in your opinion."

"John Marshall, sir, and I . . . I think all lawyers and historians would agree."

"John Marshall, John Marshall," Trimble mused. "Yes, that would be my opinion, too, Mr. Smythe. Tell me, did John Marshall ever sit on a court before being appointed chief justice?"

"Well, no, sir, I, uh, don't believe he did."

"Did he practice much law or was he a professional politician?"

"Well, Senator, I'm afraid you've got me there. I don't know that much history."

"Let me refresh your memory, Mr. Smythe. I'm sure you do know a great deal of history or you would not have judged that Dean Walsh's view of our history was not very sound. But I can understand," Trimble smiled as brightly as an oil slick struck by a sunbeam, "your mind is burdened with so many important facts that you can't be expected to remember all the details." If possible, Trimble's smile became even more radiant. "When he was appointed chief justice, John Marshall was secretary of state, and for some weeks he continued to act as secretary of state while he was chief justice. In addition, he had been a congressman from Virginia and one of the special emissaries to France in the XYZ affair. Marshall's career was eminently political. He had some law practice, but no real judicial experience, mostly a military, political, and diplomatic career—remarkably like Dean Walsh's, except Marshall's education was not so broad. How about Marshall's successor, Roger Brooke Taney? Do you recall if he had any judicial experience? Or his successor, Salmon Portland Chase, or his successor, Morrison Waite, or his successor, Melville W. Fuller?"

Smythe shook his head at each name. "I don't . . . I don't believe so; some of those men are just names to me. My field . . . my field is tax law, not constitutional law."

Like a genial bulldog Trimble continued to smile as he pressed his attack. "Did Chief Justices White or Hughes or Stone ever sit on any court other than the U.S. Supreme Court before becoming chief justice?"

"I don't think so. I'm . . . I'm really not sure, Senator."

"Did Taft?"

"Yes, sir. That one I . . . I remember. Mr. Taft did. He was a federal judge."

"Do you remember for how long?"

"No, uh, sir."

"I do, Mr. Smythe. It was only for a couple of years, nothing compared to his service in the Philippines, the cabinet, and the White House. And although Fred Vinson served on the Court of Appeals here in the District for a few years, his pre-Court career was largely that of a congressman. And Earl Warren was a governor. Now, wouldn't you say, Mr. Smythe, that the American tradition has been not to appoint men with judicial experience to the chief justiceship?"

"I, uh, suppose so, Senator."

(My dear chap, think how easy, how very easy, it would have been for Smythe to have avoided that exposé of his stupidity. All he had to do was to read my book, or for that matter to have remembered our conversation at Justice

Albert's house. But, as I have explained, Smythe was a dunce, an absolute dunce.)

"And wouldn't you say, Mr. Smythe, that we have the finest legal system in the world?"

"There's doubt there," Rutledge cut in, "we may have the finest legal system in the world, but many of us have grave misgivings about where this Supreme Court is taking us. Do you have any other questions, Senator?"

"Yes, I do, if the chair will indulge an old man. I enjoy the chance to chat with an attorney of Mr. Smythe's competence. I always learn something useful from our conversations. Now, Mr. Smythe, as I recall, you said your relations with the deputy attorney general had always been pleasant."

"Yes, sir. Judge Ruskin is a fine, uh, gentleman and a fine lawyer, too."

"Has he ever been anything but a fine gentleman in your dealings?"

"No, sir."

"A gentleman would never try to pressure another gentleman on a matter of principle, would he, Mr. Smythe?"

"No, sir."

"And you really don't want to leave the impression with this subcommittee that Judge Ruskin tried to pressure you, do you?"

"No, sir. No, sir. Our relations have always been very, uh, pleasant, very amiable. I . . . I couldn't speak more warmly of the judge. He's a fine gentleman. We don't always agree, but we, ahem, we discuss our disagreements like civilized men."

The reporters were quietly chuckling among themselves, whether at Trimble's oleogenous adroitness or Smythe's obtuseness I could not say.

"And that was all that was done here?" Trimble pressed on.

"Yes, sir."

"That's all I have, Mr. Chairman, and I thank the chair for its indulgence. It's always a pleasure to see Mr. Smythe, even on business."

"Are there any other questions?" Rutledge asked. "If not, we thank you very much, Mr. Smythe." Smythe stepped down, aheming all the way to the door. After a polite pause, Rutledge continued: "We've invited Dean

Walsh to appear before us, and he has agreed to do so. Dean, if you would like to come and sit at the witness table, the subcommittee would appreciate hearing from you. We'll allow the photographers three minutes for their work."

At that official invitation to have at the star witness, several of the newsmen picked up their cameras and popped flash bulbs at Walsh and the subcommittee. When everyone was properly blinded, the subcommittee's counsel asked Walsh to state his name and address for the record. Walsh did so and then added, "I've taken the advice once given to an English judge who was contemplating a libel suit against a newspaper: I have retained competent counsel. This is Mr. Sidney Michael Keller, who practices in New York and occasionally here in town."

"Very wise, Dean," Rutledge responded. "We're all familiar with the old saw, the lawyer who argues his own case has a fool for a client. The chair has met Mr. Keller and he is competent counsel indeed. Dean, would you begin by giving us what you think are the pertinent facts in your biography."

"I am a professor of law with a joint appointment in political science at the University of Michigan and, at the moment—pending student and faculty revolts—I am also dean of the law school there. I was born in Rome and grew up there and later in Dublin. My father was in the diplomatic service. I went to University College, Dublin, for a year, then graduated from Georgetown here in Washington and attended law school at the University of Chicago for two years. I was commissioned in the Marine Corps in 1943 and spent some time with the Fifth Marine Division as a rifle platoon leader. I landed at Iwo Jima, was wounded, and shipped home.

"After the war, I went back to law school, finished my degree quickly, and then obtained a Ph.D. in political science. I stayed on at Chicago teaching jointly in the law school and the department of political science. My professional interests have been in constitutional law and international law. I stayed in the Marine Corps Reserve and became commanding officer of the Ninth Infantry Battalion in Chicago.

"In July 1950, we were recalled to active duty. I went to Quantico for retraining and then to Korea in January 1951.

I joined the First Marines as commanding officer of the Second Battalion. I was wounded twice in April 1951 and again shipped home. My wars have been violent but quick. I was assigned to the White House staff from late July 1951 until January 1952, when the president made me his personal representative to the Vatican."

"Excuse me, Dean," Rutledge interrupted. "Why did the president pick you for that position?"

"There were some obvious reasons for his choice. I speak Italian fluently. Because of my father's long service in Rome, I knew passingly a few of the more influential people in the Vatican and knew fairly well several other people, who though somewhat farther down the official hierarchy were nevertheless important people in Vatican affairs. Most of all, though, I suppose it was because the president liked me and trusted me."

"Isn't friendship a dangerous basis for making government assignments?" Senator Alexander asked.

"It can be, Senator," Walsh agreed. "But a president has to rely heavily on friends. He can only work with those whom he understands and trusts. I can add that the next president, a member of the other party, kept me in the Vatican for about six months. When I left the government, I returned to academic life at the University of Michigan, and except for occasional service on governmental commissions, have stayed there."

"You have published a number of books and articles, have you not?" Rutledge asked.

"Yes, sir. My fifth book is in press now—it deals with constitutional law—and should be published later this fall. Four of these books are professional and they relate to governmental processes, either domestic or international, and the other is *Silk Hat Six,* an account of that part of the Korean War in which I participated."

"Financially *Silk Hat Six* did rather well, did it not?" Senator Alexander asked.

"Quite well. I don't have the exact figures, but it sold about a half million copies in hardback and probably twice that in paper."

Alexander quietly slipped in his knife: "How much did you profit from those sales?"

Walsh pretended not to notice the blade. "Again, I can't

be precise, but the total royalties came to a bit more than a half million dollars."

"Do you think it right, Dean, that you should make a fortune out of the sufferings of others?" Senator Vanderbilt posed his first question.

"Senator," Walsh paused as he watched his hands curl up into tight fists. He strained to keep both of them on the table. And, according to that infallible source, the *New York Times,* when he spoke his voice was flat and very quiet. "I did not make money out of the sufferings of others. The men who suffered, at least those I wrote about, were dead or wounded long before I put a word on paper. My writing did not affect or exploit their suffering. I described that suffering and tried to explain the spirit behind it. That book was meant to be a memorial to many of my friends."

"But you did accept royalties for your friends' memorial, did you not?" Alexander leaped in.

"I did."

"If the chair will again indulge an old man," Trimble put in, "I should set the record straight here. Dean Walsh is a modest man and he hesitates to tell you that he put half of all the money *Silk Hat Six* earned into a special trust fund for any needy survivor of his battalion and for the families of all men killed when he commanded that battalion. I think that was a generous thing to do, a very generous thing."

Senator Vanderbilt—remember, dear fellow, he was our knee-jerk liberal pacifist—switched course. "Dean Walsh, one witness testified this morning that *Silk Hat Six* glorified war and that your other books encourage war. What would you say to that?"

"No, sir. One of my books is on the judicial process and another on constitutional law. Neither has anything to do with war. The other two professional books argue in part that we must think the unthinkable. War, as horrible as it has been and would be now that we have biological and thermonuclear weapons, is still a real possibility. I think we make it more, not less, probable by pretending it can never happen. To use an analogy, we don't avoid coronaries by making believe nothing could go wrong with our hearts. As for *Silk Hat Six,* it in no way glorifies war. No decent, intelligent person could glorify a bloody process that violently snuffs out precious lives. I do speak highly of the courage of many brave men—just as I would of comrades on Iwo Jima. If anything is glorified it is their selflessness, their sense of duty."

Vanderbilt leaned forward intently. "Dean, would you spell out your views on war? Do you see any war as justifiable?"

"As you know," Walsh began, "the historic answer of most Christian theologians has been that it depends on the purpose of the war. If that purpose is economic profit or something similar, the answer is clearly no. If the purpose is to preserve our own independence or lives, or the lives and independence of others, then you have a different situation."

"Does that answer satisfy you?" Vanderbilt asked.

Walsh hesitated for a full minute before responding. During that interval there was absolute silence; both Keller and Trimble assured me that it was absolute.

Finally Walsh smiled. "You've touched a raw nerve, Senator. No, that kind of answer doesn't satisfy me, not intellectually. It only provides a crutch to soothe my conscience. You've posed a dilemma that I can't resolve. On the one hand, my reading of Christianity is that it requires pacifism. I honestly don't see how we can love our neighbors while killing them on a mass, organized basis. On the other hand, in this world the alternative—maybe not for an individual but for a nation—to being willing to fight is usually to be enslaved. I just can't bring myself to accept slavery in this world in return for the hope of reward in the next world. That probably shows a lack of faith. It may also signify a lack of courage, fear of not being in control of my own life. I don't make this sort of confession easily, Senator, but it's the only honest answer that I can give you. I speak from a troubled conscience."

Vanderbilt was impressed, deeply impressed. He told me so himself some months later. "I understand, Dean, and I respect the honesty of your reply. Just as a follow-up, do you think we're justified in getting involved in this war in southern Africa we seem to be backing into?"

"No, sir, and for prudential as well as moral reasons. The rebels may be murdering a lot of people, but using American forces will only make it worse. Intervention by a predominantly white country will win every battle but lose the war. It'll cost thousands of American lives and perhaps hundreds of thousands of African lives. And for that cost I see few returns. We really don't have a viable alternative to communism to offer those people. God knows a military dictatorship isn't constitutional democracy."

Rutledge's face reddened. However he might disobey the Constitution in domestic affairs, where international relations were involved, the Senator was a chauvinist. But Trimble broke in smoothly.

"Mr. Chairman, Africa is an interesting and important subject on which we all have strong feelings. We have heard Dean Walsh's views. I suggest that we move on to another topic."

Both Vanderbilt and Rutledge tried to respond, but Senator Alexander was quicker. "Dean Walsh, forgive me for a personal line of questions, but you are a Catholic, are you not?"

"Yes, Senator, I am. At least I think I am. The Church has been changing so quickly over the last few years that one can't be absolutely sure from day to day."

That brought a few laughs, not because it was funny, but because the talk of morality had made those creatures very tense.

"Do you see any problem—I know this question has come up before, but I want to give you a chance to dispose of it for the record, because as I see American history, Catholics and Jews have played an important role along with Protestants in making this country great."

"Sorry, Senator, I didn't get the question."

"I hadn't come to it yet, Dean. I was speaking by way of preface. Now, do you see any problems, moral or legal, in your being a Catholic and at the same time Chief Justice of the United States?"

"No, Senator, I do not."

"Suppose—and forgive me but I don't want to leave any loose ends—suppose Congress passed a law about something, say abortion, that went directly contrary to the teachings of the Catholic church. Would your being a Catholic mean you would feel obliged to vote against the constitutionality of such legislation?"

"Senator, if I were a member of the Supreme Court and the constitutionality of such a law were challenged, my task would be to interpret the Constitution of the United

States and determine if the legislation squared with that Constitution. To say that the Constitution permits something is not to say—or even imply—that that something is morally good. Many immoral laws can be constitutional. Let me add, however, that if I were called upon to enforce a law that I thought so grossly immoral, even though constitutional, that no rational man could doubt its immorality, I would resign before enforcing it."

"Can you give me an example of that?"

"Suppose in a wave of hysteria, Congress proposed and the states ratified a constitutional amendment authorizing the police to execute without trial anyone whom they caught possessing marijuana. I can't imagine anything like that happening in this country, but I would be dishonest not to say that there are limits to my loyalty to my country."

"So," Senator Alexander tried to sum up, "what you are saying is that, as a practical matter, you wouldn't be influenced by your religious views?"

"No, Senator, I did not go that far."

"How far did you go, Dean? I'm afraid you're confusing me."

(My dear chap, confusing Alexander was not among the world's more difficult tasks, but I must confess that Walsh was trying to state his position so precisely that he sacrificed clarity.)

"I'm sorry, Senator. Let me be as clear as I can. Every one of us is influenced in his decisions by a number of factors. Some of them we may be aware of, others are buried in our subconscious minds. Certainly our religious beliefs are among those factors. I have no doubt that, where the Constitution is vague, where history does not provide an answer, my choice among alternatives will be influenced by the same sorts of subconscious factors that influence every other human being.

"What I am trying to say," Walsh continued, "is that we have succeeded pretty well in separating church and state, but we cannot separate morality from politics or from law. And we cannot send to the bench—or to the Senate—mature, intelligent adults who have not formed certain moral frameworks. We can ask—we can demand—that a judge be absolutely neutral between the individuals who come before him, but we cannot ask that he not have formed any opinions about the moral worth of certain principles and policies. We can demand that a judge examine those moral judgments and do his best to make as sure as is humanly possible that it is the law that speaks and not his private biases. We can ask him to realize that he is fallible and to be willing to re-evaluate his opinions, but we cannot ask him to be without opinions."

"Where does that leave us, Dean?"

"It leaves me with a denial that my being a Catholic requires me to interpret the Constitution in any particular way. I shall 'call 'em as I see 'em.' But it also leaves me with the admission that, like the rest of mankind, how 'I see 'em' will be influenced by a host of personal factors, many of which I shall not be aware of, but among which will certainly be my moral views."

"I'm doubly sorry I began this line of questioning," Alexander said. "I had hoped for a simple, direct answer."

"I tried to be direct, Senator, but your question was not simple."

It was Rutledge's turn. "Tell me please, Dean Walsh, do you believe in judicial legislation?" The ears of the reporters perked up. It was Rutledge's typical opening question when he had decided to skewer someone who believed that the Thirteenth Amendment had truly freed the black man from slavery.

"Well, sir, that reminds me of the Gallup pollster who asked a Vermont farmer if he believed in baptism by immersion. The farmer said he did and the pollster asked why. 'Because I've seen it done,' the farmer replied. I'd have to say the same about judicial legislation."

The audience laughed—again more from nervousness than amusement, I suspect. Rutledge, however, did not betray even the ghost of a smile.

"Yes, Dean, I'm sure you have, just as I have, far too often. Let me rephrase my question and ask if you believe a judge should legislate."

"Of course not, Senator, but no more than the chair can I prescribe a general rule that distinguishes judging from legislating in all circumstances. Our Constitution is so wonderfully vague in many places that a judge has to be creative in interpreting it."

"I find those to be damning words, Dean, damning words," Rutledge solemnly intoned.

"They are truthful words, Senator. If the chair would offer a definition of 'due process of law' or of 'unreasonable searches and seizures' both general enough and precise enough to settle all cases, he would prove himself to be Solon and Solomon rolled up in one neat ball."

At that the reporters guffawed loudly and even the subcommittee's staff members had difficulty suppressing their laughter. You see, my dear fellow, the senior senator from South Carolina was both short and obese. The Malicious Butterball was what one hostile journalist had dubbed him, and a well-known Washington cartoonist often caricatured him as a basketball with hair. It was a splendid shot that nicked the senator's vanity, his most vulnerable—and probably his only vital—area. But there you have an excellent example of my criticism of Walsh. To be sure, the remark was a gem, slicing an evil man down to size. On the other hand, there's little to be gained in publicly humiliating the chairman of the Committee on the Judiciary. Quickness even when mixed with brilliance is not the same stuff as wisdom.

Rutledge rapped his gavel loudly. Red-faced, he barked angrily if not coherently, "The chair does not need to offer any definitions or to prove anything to you, Dean Walsh. It is you who must satisfy us of your competence and integrity. The chair will only indulge a small amount of levity."

Obviously Rutledge wanted to wade into the attack, but the creature was too flustered to formulate more piercing questions. At that point Alexander cut in: "Dean, how much do you think a Supreme Court justice should stick with the law and how much should he be concerned with politics in his decisions?"

It was at this point, I later learned, that that Keller creature did some good. He leaned over and quickly whispered in Walsh's ear: "Careful, Dec. I see a coin of tribute being offered." Walsh did not take his eyes off the senator.

"If you mean," Walsh responded, "partisan party politics, not one iota. Helping or hurting a particular political party or faction should be totally irrelevant. But if you mean concern for public policy, then a responsible judge has to be very concerned with politics. What we call the law is often what other judges have said about questions of public policy, ranging from whether it would be bad for public morals for courts to enforce gambling contracts to whether it would be realistic for courts to require instant desegregation. A court that decides who can vote, how far government can regulate citizens' speaking out on public issues, or who can go to what public schools, is vitally affecting public policy. And a judge has to look at the future—at what public policy will result from his decisions—as well as at the past. If you'll pardon my profane use of Scripture, I think the only general answer is 'render unto politics that which is politics' and to the law that which is the law's.' "

"A clever answer, Dean."

"Neither your question nor my answer is original," Walsh remarked drily.

As Alexander fumbled for a response, Rutledge broke back in. His voice was still trembling. "Dean Walsh, since you work for the NAACP, could you ever give a truly neutral decision in a Negro case?" (In Rutledge's mouth, the word was *Nigra.*)

Walsh sighed audibly, then spoke with exaggerated patience. "First of all, Senator, I never worked for the NAACP in the sense of being paid by them. On several occasions when I was especially impressed with the justice of their cause and they were having difficulty finding a local lawyer, I volunteered. On several other occasions, I helped in writing briefs. In neither sort of situation did I ever accept a fee. Second, if a case in which I had participated in any way ever came before me on the bench, I would recuse myself. That's standard practice. Third, and getting back both to your earlier question and that of Senator Alexander, no intelligent person can be without strong views on matters like race relations, criminal justice, or freedom of speech. All we can reasonably ask of judges is that they be aware of their views on issues of public policy, be willing to re-examine those views in light of any new evidence, and be sensitive to resist the temptation to read those views into the Constitution."

"Nothing you've said," Rutledge replied, "has convinced me that you could be neutral on any important constitutional question."

"That's too bad, sir. I think I can, but I have to confess that my judgment on that issue is not unbiased."

Walsh smiled as he made the last remark, and once more there was a small ripple of laughter. Rutledge tapped his gavel again. "The chair will have order or the chair will clear the room." Then turning to Walsh, he asked heavily: "You spoke of justice, Dean. Now just what do you think of the justice of busing little children over half a county just so we can mix up the races in the schools? Do you see any justice in that?"

"Senator, I cannot speak on any issue that is likely to come before the Court."

"Dean, if we accepted that excuse you could remain silent on anything. These days almost any issue is liable to come before *that* Court." Rutledge gave the journalists a self-satisfied smile.

"Perhaps, but in one form or another the issue of school segregation has been before the Court for decades; the basic question was settled as a matter of law in 1954, but I would bet there are several cases on the Court's docket right now involving the proper remedy for *de facto* segregation. I can't answer you without risking prejudging such cases."

"I'm still not satisfied, not satisfied at all," Rutledge shook his head.

"Senator, all I can say is that if you want a segregationist, I'm not your man. I think the Court was right in 1954 in ruling segregation unconstitutional and Congress was right in 1964 in adopting the Civil Rights Act. I can't say more."

"That's still not good enough, Dean. I'm not asking you how you would vote in any particular case. I'm just picking up on your earlier statement about having views on issues. What are your views on busing little children?"

"Senator, I have to give you the same answer. I just can't, as a matter of propriety, express an opinion on an issue that's so likely to be before the Court."

Rutledge shook his head. "That won't do, sir, that won't do at all. We have a right to know your judicial philosophy."

"Sir, I've explained my judicial philosophy in several books. Those are available. But here I can only repeat my reason for respectfully declining to answer your question—or any other that so directly relates to the Court's business."

"Very well," Rutledge snapped. "Since you are not going

to be cooperative and since there are no more witnesses to be heard, the chair declares these hearings adjourned." He slammed his gavel down again and, turning his back to Walsh, began talking to one of the subcommittee's staff. The newsmen hurried out to file their stories of a stormy session.

FIVE

AH, YES, where did we leave off? Yes, the nomination and confirmation, to be sure. The subcommittee came down two to one against Walsh. He had thoroughly alienated both Rutledge and Alexander, but Walsh said he counted both among the lost sheep anyway. Perhaps that was accurate, but he need not have demonstrated his superior intellect in such a blatant way. There is a world of a difference, a world, between a senator who merely votes no and one who tries to influence his colleagues to vote no with him. In any event, due in no small part to Trimble's skills and also to Vanderbilt, the full committee was a different story. Our logorrheic senator from South Carolina simply could not muster the votes to defeat Walsh there. The senator could, however, drag those dainty feet that underpinned his obscenely rotund body; and that is precisely what the churlish creature did.

It was not until Congress came back into session to clean up business after the November election—an unusual display of public spirit for those sybarites across the piazza—that Walsh's supporters could pressure Rutledge into convening a meeting of the full committee and allowing a vote on the merits. Walsh won by the not too comfortable margin of 9–5. On the floor of the Senate, the script was much the same. An affirmative vote of 53–27 may not seem close, but it raises a few hairs when one knows that many of the 27 were bitter and a goodly share of the 53 unenthusiastic. The Democrats had lost the presidential election and some of them placed the blame on Walsh for accepting the nomination as chief justice. They felt that the president had indeed benefited from Walsh's Catholicism and Midwestern residence.

I express no opinion on those points, none at all. My antennae were never calibrated to communicate with the mob; I have only the certainty that the moving force is not informed reason. Republican solons, to be sure, should have been grateful to Walsh, but only a naif would expect gratitude from politicians, especially Republicans.

The very day after the Senate's vote—it was the Wednesday before Thanksgiving—Walsh appeared in our Court and took the oath of office. As senior associate justice I administered it. We were not in session that week—I'll explicate our schedule later—but we held the ritual in the courtroom anyway. Walsh's Kathryn was present. Years had passed since I had seen her, but she seemed little changed, a compliment no doubt to the skill of her cosmetologists. I would have recognized her anywhere. Her most obvious charms were still making their presence known even though her dress itself was rather modest—for her.

There were others in attendance, though I confess she attracted far more of the newsmen's attention than did the eight associate justices and their ladies combined. There must be something about journalism that attracts lechers.

I also observed that Keller creature, and several other undistinguished but athletic males and their ladies. I assumed they were marines, and was grateful they did not attempt to sack the building or assault the women. Even Walsh himself had once remarked—only half-jocularly, it seemed to me—that one should never trust a marine around a white woman. That, at least, implied that Justice Kelley's wife was relatively safe, although her skin was three or more shades lighter than her husband's, and central casting would hardly have classified him as a Nubian.

The congressman from Ann Arbor and the two senators from Michigan also graced our chamber. All three gentlemen smiled professionally, and continuously, absolutely continuously, for the photographers. (We relaxed our rules and let them take flash photographs for a few minutes; we also allowed the brief session to be captured on video tape for educational television.) The attorney general was there—an interesting gesture, I thought, and wondered what scheming lay behind it—as were the solicitor general and his staff of attorneys. These fellows, you may realize, argue almost all the government's cases before us, and they seldom miss an opportunity to impress us with their bubbling intelligence and deeply rooted integrity.

We were also blessed with no less than the personage of the vice-president. He had been sent on direct orders from Clarence Bowers himself. The vice-president had complied willingly enough. Poor creature probably thought we would serve alcoholic beverages. He was sorely disappointed. On this side of the piazza we work rather than romp, and few of us drink during the day—and, with one unhappy exception, seldom during the night, for that matter.

At least I was able to make the vice-president's visit worthwhile by asking him to convey to the White House my endorsement of the candidate for the vacant district judgeship in Massachusetts whom Senator Amherst and I had selected. I also dropped several sage suggestions about our policy toward the latest military junta to seize power in Greece. As usual, our State Department appeared utterly baffled by developments there, though for the very life of me I could never understand why. As an educated man, you undoubtedly know that Plato explained convincingly, quite convincingly, why democracy cannot work in Greece. He was, to be sure, making a general argument —which I have never seen rebutted—but his remarks have always had special applicability for Greece.

The ceremony itself was brief. I led my seven colleagues, clad in black robes, into the courtroom to take our places behind our chairs. As senior associate justice, I said: "This special sitting of the Court is held to receive the commission of the newly appointed Chief Justice of the United States, Declan Patrick Walsh. At this time, it is a great pleasure to recognize the Vice-President of the United States. Mr. Vice-President."

The vice-president, the only less worthy officeholder than Clarence Bowers himself, bowed, obviously ill at ease in his not too well-fitting morning clothes. He approached the bench and said stiffly: "I appear here this morning as a member of the bar of this Court"—alas, it takes only twenty-five dollars and prior admission to a state bar—"to officially inform"—the poor creature split the infinitive—"this Court that the nomination of the Honorable Declan Patrick Walsh to be Chief Justice of the United States has been consented to by the United States Senate. The president has signed the commission and the attorney general has attested to it. Mr. Walsh is present in the courtroom, ready to take his oath. I request that the attorney general be recognized to present the commission to the Court."

I nodded, giving the creature far more dignity than he merited. "Thank you, Mr. Vice-President. The Court now recognizes the Attorney General of the United States." That august gentleman, looking a bit hangdog, I cannot forego telling you, approached the bench.

"Mr. Chief Justice, may it please the Court. I bear with me the commission issued to the Honorable Declan Patrick Walsh as Chief Justice of the United States. It has been duly signed by the president and attested to me as attorney general. I move that the clerk read this commission and that it be made part of the permanent record of the Court."

Once again I nodded. "Your motion is granted, Mr. Attorney General. If you will hand the Commission to the attendant so it may be delivered to the clerk, I shall request that the clerk read the commission."

Upon receiving the commission from the attendant, the clerk proceeded to read it in his somewhat loud but not unpleasingly stentorian voice:

Clarence R. Bowers
President of the United States of America
To All Who Shall See These Presents, Greeting:

Know Ye; That reposing special trust and confidence in the Wisdom, Uprightness and Learning of Declan Patrick Walsh, of Michigan, I have nominated and, by and with the advice and consent of the Senate, do appoint him Chief Justice of the United States, and do authorize and empower him to execute and fulfill the duties of that Office according to the Constitution and Laws of the said United States, and to have and to hold the said office, with all the powers, privileges and emoluments to the same of right appertaining, unto Him, the said Declan Patrick Walsh, during his good behavior.

In testimony whereof, I have caused these Letters to be made patent and the seal of the Department of Justice to be hereunto affixed.

Done at the City of Washington this twenty-third day of November. . . .

[SEAL]

By the President: Clarence R. Bowers

Roger M. Neilson

Attorney General

With that recitation done, I said simply, "Mr. Walsh."

He came before the bench. He was still considered, I suppose, a handsome man. (Have you ever noticed, my dear fellow, how our society bestows accolades on the tall? As if height were related to beauty and either were associated with virtue.) Walsh's beard was still full; he had not deigned to mark his entry into a new life by shaving. That scar that ran from behind his left eye back across his temple had faded but was still visible. (For reasons that I could not even begin to fathom, keloid tissue on a male face stirs romantic pulsings in female bosoms. Several Washington women had displayed rather obvious animal interest in him when he was in the White House. I recall hoping, as he came toward the bench, that we would be spared such performances. Walsh had, to the best of my knowledge—though I would be the last to know about gossip—virtuously ignored that sort of interest, but, to be sure, he had been practically a honeymooner at that time.)

Well, where were we? Yes, the oath and the ceremony. What we were doing was not exactly the custom, but rather something of an innovation that I designed. I pride myself that I am nothing if not creative. In any event, I walked around the bench and met Walsh at the lectern as the marshal proferred Walsh's family Bible on which the chief justice designate placed his left hand. He then repeated after me:

I, Declan Patrick Walsh, do solemnly swear that I will administer justice without respect to persons, and do equal right to the poor and to the rich, and that I will faithfully and impartially discharge and perform all the duties incumbent upon me as Chief Justice of the United States according to the best of my abilities and understanding, agreeably to the Constitution and laws of the United States. So help me God.

Later he would sign that same oath, but with its pronouncement Declan Walsh was metamorphized not merely into a judge, one of the mouths of the law, but into the most prestigious of judges on this planet. He was not, to be sure, the best man for such an elevated throne, but he was the best man possible. Polite applause among the associate justices and the small audience marked the passage from human to oracle.

I could not help but note—indeed, I made a point of noting—the page to which Walsh had opened the Bible and the verses he had circled in green ink. I confess that I was surprised. The marked passages were from the eleventh chapter of Isaiah:

> But a shoot shall sprout from the stump of Jesse,
> and from his roots a bud shall blossom.
> The spirit of the Lord shall rest upon him:
> a spirit of wisdom and of understanding,
> a spirit of counsel and of strength,
> a spirit of knowledge and fear of the Lord,
> and his delight shall be the fear of the Lord.
> Not by appearance shall he judge,
> nor by hearsay shall he decide,
> but he shall judge the poor with justice
> and decide aright for the land's afflicted.
> He shall strike the ruthless with the rod of his mouth,
> and with the breath of his lips he shall slay the wicked.
> Justice shall be the band around his waist,
> and faithfulness a belt upon his hips.

The choice was fascinating, simply fascinating—Isaiah the prophet, not the New Testament. It gave me an insight into Walsh that few, perhaps none—yes, I think none—of the brethren shared. But I shall discuss that later.

Well, before continuing my narrative, I must offer you some instruction on the mechanics of our tribunal. First of all, our term begins on the initial Monday in October and runs until we have exhausted our docket or ourselves. Without exception, without any exception at all, we fall long before the docket. Indeed, if there is an eternal being its name must be The Docket of the United States Supreme Court. The time of our collapse is usually in late June or early July. Within those nine months we sit—are in session, one might say—for two weeks, and recess for two or even three weeks if a holiday such as Christmas or Easter intervenes.

When we are in session, we hear oral arguments on Mondays, Tuesdays, and Wednesdays for those cases that we have decided to review—the wheat left after we have shaken out the chaff from the bloody certs. Traditionally, the Court began a sitting at noon, but recently we had shifted to a new schedule, beginning at ten, recessing at noon for an hour's lunch, then sitting again from one until three.

Normally we give each side in a case thirty minutes to argue. That may not seem long, but remember this is at least the third opportunity counsel have had to enlighten our minds. Each side has petitioned us to review or not to review; then if we granted certiorari each side presented elaborate written arguments—briefs, we call them, though the title misfits; whatever else they are, these arguments are seldom brief. Each side can also present reply briefs if it feels that something said by the other party merits fuller response. After that deluge of paper, thirty minutes of talk is hardly niggardly.

Strictly *entre nous,* my dear chap, strictly *entre nous,* thirty minutes is more than adequate for most lawyers to make complete fools of themselves. After a lifetime of study and reflection about our Court, I can say without fear of contradiction that the average intellectual level of oral argument before us would embarrass a first-year law student at Harvard or Yale.

Really, most of those creatures who come to us are either ignorant or intellectual frauds—and sometimes both, sometimes both. There is, to be sure, an occasional bright spot. The solicitor general's lads are usually not without intelligence, and the attorneys for some of the interest groups like the NAACP or national labor organizations that regularly have cases before us can be dead keen. But, by and large the other lawyers whom we see—and worse, far worse, hear—are abysmal.

We don't need speeches; we are not a jury of ignorant laymen. Nor do we need an attorney to explain to us what we meant two years ago when we decided a particular case. *We* decided that case, thus *we* know—far better than he—exactly what *we* meant.

Illuminating the judicial mind is a delicate art, and the American legal profession seems heavily staffed with journeyman dolts and apprentice dolts. Occasionally, as with the leadership of the American Bar Association, we are afflicted with master dolts. To spare ourselves the agony of oratory, we generally pepper counsel with questions. Typically they quickly fold, making it plain as a pikestaff, a quite large pikestaff, that they really don't even understand their own case.

Well, don't let me become distracted and run on about the dismal state of the lawyer's art. Rather, let us return to our subject. I said we hear—forgive my use of the present tense; I never psychologically left the court—argument on Mondays, Tuesdays, and Wednesdays. On Wednesday afternoons after argument, we confer together. We try to keep Thursdays free for reading and reflection. Then again on Fridays at nine-thirty in the morning we meet once more in conference, with a pause for a bite of lunch, until five or even six in the afternoon. During those conferences, we discuss among ourselves—I concede that "argue" may be the more accurate word—the cases that we have just heard.

During the two weeks that we are not formally in session—that is, not hearing oral argument—we spend most of our time researching, writing drafts of opinions, sometimes for the Court, sometimes concurring separately, sometimes dissenting. We also read and comment on the drafts of opinions that colleagues have written. (Every justice, I must assure you, every one of us, is supposed to read—and carefully, too, very carefully—any opinion that another justice circulates.) And it is a practice unheard of, absolutely unthinkable, for a justice to issue an opinion, even if he speaks only for himself, that has not been circulated to the full Court.

During those two weeks between sittings, we try to hold as few formal meetings as possible, but it is usually necessary to meet at least during the second week so that we can settle the matter of what decisions we can announce at our sittings during the following week. Then, too, the number of petitions for certiorari may so mushroom—if you will forgive the martial analogy—that we must confer to reduce the backlog to manageable proportions.

Those petitions complicate our work immensely, for they know no schedule, none at all. They pour in day by day, even night by night, at the rate of almost 4000 a year, plus another 600 or so cases that come to us by other routes. It was a burden. One had to stay in harness seven days a week. But, let me assure you that it was a sweet burden. Its rewards were as great as its difficulties were heavy. One could take true satisfaction in that work. One could look at a finished opinion and know that it would shape the future course of the law and perhaps even western civilization.

Even though we were not in session that week, I had, knowing all the brethren would be available because of the ceremony, scheduled a conference for 3 P.M., hoping to dispose of most of the more than 200 petitions for certiorari that were with us. I had alerted Walsh to our plans and assured him that I would handle the matter and preside. I suggested that he might wish to join us for a few moments to get the feel of the conference, so to speak, but that no one expected him to stay, much less preside. After all, he had not yet read any of the relevant papers. The important thing was for him to be at the luncheon that I had scheduled and socialize with the justices and their ladies. (Six of the brethren were married; I was a bachelor and Jacobson a widower. No doubt his wife had died of chronic embarrassment.) Like it or not, we are a very small and intimate, perhaps too intimate, group; cordial relations with all the brethren are a must for the chief.

The luncheon itself was a success, in no small part due —and here I pay a debt to history rather than modesty—to my careful planning. There being only seven wives and nine justices, I invited the old chief's administrative assistant, Elena Falconi. We were all on easy terms with her (and she plays a not unimportant role in my story—but more about that later). In any event, her presence added both charm and beauty. The unbalanced number of males and females allowed me to place Justice Kelley's tawny-skinned lady on Walsh's right and Justice Albert on his left.

I wanted Walsh to become acquainted with Albert as rapidly as possible, and I thought that a woman who called herself black—attractive, no doubt, if one appreciates non-Caucasians—would provide less of a distraction. If nothing else, such women are not accustomed to being center stage, so to speak. Albert and Walsh hit it off right from the start, just as I thought they would. Indeed, their friendship became quite close, though not, to be sure, as close as mine with Albert.

I sat at the other end of the table facing Walsh and placed his Kathryn—by then "Kate" to everyone—on my right. Directly across from her I stationed Elizabeth, Justice Albert's dear lady, hoping that she could help acculturate Kathryn to our mores. On her right I placed Justice Kelley. He was a good sort, lively without being obtrusive, neither what is popularly called an Uncle Tom nor one of those civil righters who do not feel comfortable unless accusing all Caucasians within earshot of indulging in incest. Whatever pains discrimination had inflicted on him he bore with no outward sign of bitterness. (I confess to the Machiavellian thought that having a member of a racial minority as her companion would slow ignition of Kathryn's temper. I also confess, and not without some glee, to having entertained the thought of placing Jacobson next to her. The pyrotechnics would have been marvelous. But my concern for the Court outweighed my pleasure in such a wondrous display.)

Well, in all fairness, all fairness, I must say that Kathryn acquitted herself admirably. She could, you know, when it pleased her. Elizabeth, whose kindness was a bottomless well, was actually quite taken with her. They, too, struck up a friendship so that the Alberts and the Walshes became a frequent foursome, though, again, I assure you, that they were not as close as Albert and I. For his part, brother Kelley was also fascinated, though for reasons quite distant from those of Elizabeth. No doubt Kathryn flirted a bit with him—she did with me on several occasions. I, of course, pretended not to notice, but I marked it down in my memory.

Well, I was talking about my offer to Walsh to preside for him at the conference. After a brief visit with us there, he could leave, I pointed out, and cope with the myriad details that inevitably attend moving across the country. Can you believe it? He refused, absolutely refused. Oh, he was polite enough about it. Despite his education at the University of Chicago and life with those hirsute brutes in the Marine Corps, he could be knightly in his ways. In a word, my dear fellow, a single word, he excused himself early from the luncheon to prepare for the conference.

As you know, each justice has a small personal staff, usually a secretary (we have a typing pool to draw upon when work becomes very heavy) and three laws clerks. These latter are generally young men and now—much to my dismay, I hasten to assure you—women who have recently graduated from law school. Because of the double burden of presiding over the Court and being responsible for the Administrative Office of U.S. Courts, the chief has a second secretary, a fourth and perhaps even a fifth law clerk, and an administrative assistant who has a staff of his or her own.

Most of us retain our clerks for only a single term, but some justices keep one of their fellows for a second year to train and direct the newcomers. I never followed that practice, but the old chief did and Walsh continued it.

We use these youngsters—all extraordinarily bright, usually the top men in their classes at the very best law schools—we use them in diverse ways. Some of my brethren routinely allow them to write first drafts of their opinions; others let them do only research; some permit them to edit and revise opinions. The custom of allowing a clerk to write first drafts is unusual, at least on a regular basis. To be sure, toward the end of a term, I might permit an especially gifted clerk to try his hand at drafting an opinion for a rather simple case—all of us probably do that—but only one or two of my brethren made it standard practice to delegate to their clerks the initial task of writing. Intelligence, even of a very high magnitude, desperately needs experience.

Yes, I know what's crossing your mind, my dear chap. Perhaps Justice Gerald Albert *would* have enhanced his public reputation had he used his clerks in this fashion and then applied his marvelous powers as an editor. Perhaps. But Albert was a man of fastidious conscience. He could not bring himself to put his name on what was not totally his. Indeed, we talked about it and at length, at great length, several times. I respected his decision. We all did, with the possible exception of Jacobson. A fastidious conscience was surely not included among such moral luggage as that creature carried through life.

Well, I was speaking more generally of the clerks. I freely concede—indeed, gladly concede—that I drew much inspiration and vigor from these fresh young minds. They sparkled with energy and enthusiasm and even optimism. They were so wonderfully oblivious to their own mortality! But then the young always are. In any event, however else we on the Court differed in particular customs, we all employed our clerks to help us sort through the petitions for certiorari. I have already told you how I used mine. Some of the brethren pooled their clerks for such purposes, but as I may have told you I find it difficult to evaluate the judgment—and the accuracy—of a person, especially a young person whom I do not know well.

Well, I apologize for this wordy prolegomenon to Walsh's inaugural performance, but it was a necessary exercise, one in which I shall indulge from time to time because I want you to understand comprehensively what transpires within our tribunal. We faced 208 petitions for certiorari that week. As has been the recent custom, I had circulated a "discuss list," if you'll forgive the literary barbarism of using a noun as an adjective. As I explained, most of the petitions are frivolous. We simply cannot discuss each in conference. Merely multiply 4000 times two minutes per justice, if you could keep those verbose creatures to such a disciplined schedule, times nine justices and you'll see that we would spend thirty forty-hour weeks just deciding what we would decide, not counting, to be sure, the time it takes to read the dreadful things. Our solution has been for the chief to circulate a short list—the discuss list—of petitions that he thinks we should take up together. If no one objects, our agenda are so limited. Let me assure you, however, that one or more of the brethren often do object, especially Jacobson. As I recall that particular day, my own discuss list had contained less than a score of petitions. By the time each of the brethren had added his pets, we had thirty-two.

Walsh excused himself, as I was saying, and retired to his office to read summaries from the pool of law clerks, and whatever papers he chose to delve into. I had offered him my personal notes, but he had declined. Such a silly goose. He almost had a fetish about appearing to be independent. I assure you, I only had his interest at heart. What he did that day was to display one of his basic characteristics—a deeply felt need to be in command and, even more deeply felt, a need to know all that could be known about our business. He was, in sum, my dear chap, not only a compulsive worker—a trait, a lifetime of study of human nature convinces me, that tries to cover severe personal insecurities far more than it evidences devotion to duty—but also a person with a paranoia about dependence. The two formed a fascinating syndrome, absolutely fascinating.

We disposed of that afternoon's business with dispatch. As you know, we convene in conference in the room at the rear of the building behind the courtroom itself. It's a rather large austere chamber. One wall along the longer axis of the room has two windows onto Second Street, N.E.; the other long wall, except where broken in the middle by a door, is consumed by bookshelves. There is a fireplace, with a portrait above it of John Marshall in his red robes, on one of the shorter walls. At one end of the room is a table around which the nine of us sit, the chief justice at the head, and the associates ranged in order of seniority, the most senior opposite the chief, the next at the chief's right, the next at the senior's right, and so on.

When Walsh first joined us, there was a large desk and chair in the opposite end of the room. The old chief had used the chamber as his office when we were not in conference, a disposition that many of us—I among them—viewed as an unintentional but insensitive usurpation. It is true that the chief has the least spacious accommodations in the Court, and that he had a larger staff to house. (Each associate justice has a three-room suite of offices around the outside rim of the building: a large office with a fireplace as well as a private shower and bath for himself and an equally generous office for his secretary. The clerks shared a similar room, adequate for two persons, but somewhat cramped for more. We each had a second suite on the floor above. I used mine for my clerks and turned their chamber into a sitting room.)

We all understood the chief's problems with space, but traditionally the conference room had been neutral ground on which we could wage intellectual battle. The old chief's converting it into his private office meant that, as my brother Jacobson, for once not inaptly, put it, we played on the chief's turf.

Well, after our handshaking ritual—as you know, each justice shakes hands with every other justice before and after each session of the Court and each conference. Tempers can flare, and that ceremony reassures us of our solidarity as brothers, though I confess, quite candidly confess, that it was often difficult for me to imagine familial relations with some of those creatures. But, I use the term *brother* as symbolic of my own humility.

After that ritual, Walsh offered us his maiden speech: "Lightning strikes pretty much as it will, and it has now struck me. I assure you that I have no illusions that I deserve this chair." Then he looked up with a rather wry smile, "But then I have no illusions that anyone else does, either. So, here I stand—or rather sit—for better or worse until death, retirement, or impeachment do us part. First of all, I don't think that we should meet in the chief's office, even if the chief is as benevolent, gracious, and objective in judgment as the incumbent. As soon as I can complete arrangements with the marshal, my office will be moved to another suite." (In fact, my dear chap, within the week Walsh moved into a set of not very commodious offices in the front of the building.)

"A second point," Walsh continued. "I understand that some of the justices would like to move the Court's sessions back to noon, with an hour for lunch at 2 P.M. That arrangement gives us at least the mornings free for work. I would like that. Are there objections?"

Jacobson spoke up immediately, even though he was second in seniority among the associates. "I prefer to get the day over as quick as possible, Chief, so I can sip a little syrup in my branch water. But, I'm a hoss-swapper. I didn't cotton to meeting in the chief justice's office; and if you're serving that up, I guess I can postpone my syrup sipping a couple of hours."

Some of the brethren actually chuckled at that vulgarity. To be sure, I made no move even to acknowledge the usurpation of my prerogative to speak first among the associates. Instead I merely replied affirmatively to Walsh's proposal, as, indeed, we all did. One does not, after all, respond negatively in the face of such a generous gesture.

"And," Walsh said, "as a further compromise, let's begin our Friday conferences at nine-thirty, as you have been, and our Wednesday sittings at ten. That should accommodate both sides." Need I say that that was another gracious gesture to the three members who still preferred to meet in the morning?

"Now let us attack the discuss list. The first case is #984, *Giancana v. Ohio,*" Walsh continued as he picked a file from the library cart near his chair. "The facts are that the grievance committee of the Ohio Bar Association suspended George Giancana from practicing law for two years because of alleged inattention to the needs of his clients. Giancana appealed to the association's Board of Governors, as provided by the association's rules, and they sustained the committee's decision. He sought review in Ohio courts, claiming that his property—his right to practice law—had been denied without due process of law. He argued that only a court of law, after a regular judicial proceeding, could take away his right to practice law because, in reality, removal of that right is a painful penalty, more analogous to a heavy fine in a criminal case than to an administrative proceeding.

"The trial court," Walsh went on, "held that Ohio statutes gave full authority to the state bar association to determine who was qualified to practice law. The trial court held such provision not to violate the Fourteenth Amendment's prohibition against a state's taking away a person's life, liberty, or property without due process of law. The state supreme court affirmed. Giancana filed with us a timely petition for certiorari. I notice that my predecessor put this one on the dead list, but Justices Jacobson and Campbell disagreed. I would grant. The issue of control over individuals' lives by nongovernmental organizations touches important questions under the Fourteenth Amendment. Mr. Justice Walker?"

And so he went around the table, giving each of us several minutes to summarize, thanking each, and moving on. To be sure, his performance was not flawless. He missed the more subtle sinuosities of several cases, and at least twice allowed brother Jacobson to vent his spleen-filled views at too great length. But, on the whole it was a good show. We disposed of the thirty-two petitions—granting only three—in just a trifle over three hours. That is efficiency.

I must add, however, that the brethren were on their best behavior, often saying merely "I agree with Mr. Justice Walker," rather than orating. Still, the tenor of Walsh's performance and the practiced ease with which he presided—mind you, I have not yet used any form of the word leadership—augured for the sort of efficiency that one associates with Chief Justice Charles Evans Hughes. Hughes, who, incidentally, also had a beard, had marched the conference briskly along in step with the drum that thumped in his head twice each second.

Gerald Albert and I did all we could to assist Walsh, and, as I told you, the brethren behaved well that first day. The honeymoon continued for several weeks. Even our quarrelsome sibling, Marvin Jacobson, restrained—perhaps stored up would be more accurate—his usual outpourings of vitriol. My dear chap, can you imagine a born-again Jew from Texas? Now, please do not misunderstand me, some of the most cultivated people I know—especially in the performing arts—are Jewish. And, if being "born again" gives an emotionally insecure person comfort, I am not at all opposed, not at all. But picture, if your mind can entertain such a horrid image, picture the combination: the superabundance of chutzpah of an aggressive Jew, the narrow self-righteousness of the born again, joined to the capacious mouth, the coarse manners, and the arrogant ego of a Texan! I do not think it presumptuous to say that such a man would be an insufferable boor, and Jacobson was no exception to that rule. He possessed, I assure you, all those nonqualities to the nth degree. He was physically more like a bear than a man, sprouting thick black hair from every follicle of his skin, big, about 6′3″ and 240 pounds, with gross features. I am certain that he had two voice boxes, each located near his ankles. (If I were less fastidious I would locate them elsewhere on his person.) He never spoke; he rumbled with that loud, discordant southwestern twang that so offends civilized ears.

We avoided each other socially—I suspect that he perceived my austere notions about life and law as squeamish—and we were far apart in jurisprudence. I confess that on the few occasions I heard him echo my thinking, I paused to re-examine my own basic premises. Jews are supposed to favor social justice in economic affairs and to be hypersensitive to claims of civil liberties, especially by other minorities. That Jacobson creature, however, was a rationalizer of dog-eat-dog capitalism, a former tame tabby of a house-lawyer for one of those immense oil corporations. He was the personification of all the evil in which that business revels.

To be sure, he was intelligent enough. Indeed, one might even assert, not without evidence, that he had a brilliant, albeit savage mind. No, no, that cretin's problem was not a lack of grey matter, not at all. Rather he lacked any sense of social morality. He had the values of a troglodyte, the instincts of a barracuda, the ethics of an oil man, and the disposition of a shrew. I once entertained for some pleasant weeks, very pleasant weeks, the impish thought of posting a sign on his door: Beware of the Troll. Naturally, I did not succumb, but I confess that rolling the temptation around in my mind created a fair amount of sensuous pleasure.

Jacobson loved, I emphasize *loved,* to play nasty tricks on the innocent. He could affect a certain reptilian charm and would deploy it during oral argument to lead a lawyer, especially a young lawyer, down a primrose path of reasoning. Then, at the very moment that youngster would reach the summit of his presentation, Jacobson would confront him with a basic flaw in the premises of his arguments. That the poor chap had endorsed those premises in response to Jacobson's coaxing made the lawyer's ignominy all the more delectable to this horrid creature.

It surpassed my understanding how most of the brethren tolerated him with such apparent ease. They *must,* simply *must* have despised him as much as I did. After all, they were, by and large, civilized human beings. It also surpassed my understanding how he could have ever made it to our Court. Certainly merit had little to do with it, but then that had seldom been the critical desideratum. (I do not imply that most of the justices have not been able men, but, with only a few exceptions, far abler lawyers were never considered for elevation.)

I suppose the crucial elements in Jacobson's case were that he had collected large sums of money for Republican candidates. Texas oil men, natural gas producers, executives of multinational corporations, even—despite his own ethnic heritage—Arab oil sheiks were his cronies. Their price was that Jacobson become attorney general. In that post he controlled, of course, prosecutions under the antitrust acts, and one can be certain, absolutely certain, that none of his friends had reason to fear the federal whip during his incumbency. The lump in the pudding, however, was brother Jacobson himself. Too powerful to fire, too savage to retain, he was promoted to our Court, even as Clarence Bowers had considered doing with his attorney general. I need not tell you, my dear chap, what a shabby, absolutely shabby thing it was for us—and for the country.

I have already spoken to you at length about Gerald Albert, a peach of a man, a veritable peach. He was as chivalrous as he was learned. Moreover, Albert was a model of probity as well as of discretion. Alas, if only he had not suffered from pen paralysis the beauty of his mind and sweetness of his character would have been manifest to those outside as well as inside the Court. But, few of us are perfect.

The other five were not an uninteresting group. Ian Campbell, our dour Scotch outdoorsman, you know, of course. He was Colorado's gift to our bench, not really a bad sort, although he was a cipher in our deliberations on constitutional issues. Physically, he was constructed much like Jacobson, except, to be sure, he was much more attractive, sandy blond—really white by the time he joined us after three years in the cabinet as secretary of interior—while Jacobson was dark as a Moor. Campbell was bright enough, despite his addiction to athletics. Almost every day that the Court was not in session or we were not in conference, he played basketball at noon with some of the young clerks. Did you know that we have a small basketball court on the top floor of our building? A dreadful waste of the taxpayers' money, simply dreadful. But what can one do? It is there. But there or not, I cannot forego saying that it is unseemly for a jurist in his late fifties to be running around in his BVD's with similarly unclad youngsters less than half his age, all trying to throw a ball through a hoop.

Well, to be sure, Campbell was bright enough, in fact, very bright indeed—and quick, too quick. Like Jacobson, he shared Walsh's fault of having a reflex, more appropriate to the jungle, that made him leap at the throat of a problem. He was . . . how shall I put it with precision as well as accuracy? Yes, he was gruff and somewhat common in his language. But that commonness masked a great deal of erudition, and the gruffness concealed the fact that socially he was rather shy. I suspect—only suspect, mind you—that he only fully relaxed around others when he was chasing that basketball. He and his wife never, absolutely never, entertained except for very old friends who antedated his incarnation in Washington. At our conferences he seldom spoke more than a few sentences, unless a constitutional issue was involved in the case. Then, he would deliver a set speech, insisting on *literal*, word-for-word, I mean, interpretation of the Constitution. His fundamentalist Baptist approach to religion completely suffused his constitutional jurisprudence.

Literalism—especially since it did not extend to nonconstitutional issues—was not, however, his major flaw as a jurist. But perhaps I am too puritanical in my image of the Supreme Court's proper role in the American system of government. What I am intimating—no, let me say it straight out; after all, our duty to history includes directness. Despite his social shyness, Campbell was, and remained, a political animal. He was often too involved with members of the other branches, the political branches of government. Twice when we had Democrats in the White House, he had the president's ear, so to speak. And, so I was apprised by people who should know, he talked to the White House about foreign policy, about domestic policy, and, as far as I know, even about judicial matters. I shall say no more. You know my feelings, my very strong feelings, on such matters. We on the Court *must*, absolutely *must*, stay out of the policy-making processes.

On nonconstitutional issues Campbell and I tended to vote together, but I am certain that you will note that, almost without exception, I never joined in a concurring or dissenting opinion that he wrote. At root was my fastidiousness about the proper model for judicial reasoning. Now no one, simply no one, in his right mind pretends that a judicial opinion is a *description* of how a court came to decide a case; nor is a judicial opinion even an *explanation* of why a court so decided. No one ever fully understands *that* psychological process, least of all a judge. An opinion, rather, is a justification for a decision, an argument, if you will, supporting one particular choice as the best among available alternatives.

I found Campbell's style in this regard too abrupt, too elliptical, aesthetically unpleasing to my craftsman's eye. He did not manifest—because, I suspect, he did not feel—the appropriate respect that we should accord to our former self by explaining carefully how a current decision fits into the mosaic of past rulings. The duty of a judge includes not merely laying down abstract pronouncements for the unfolding future, but identifying the path the law has taken so that the present and the future become more intelligible. We must never forget that law, like the people it serves, is rooted in history.

To be sure, there was also Senator Henry Leigh Breckinridge, that self-righteous scion of Virginia's ancient aristocracy—a monument to the moral deterioration of a race of giants. Physically, he was rather average for a man in his late sixties—tall and thin without being gaunt, not yet but almost bald with wisps of white carefully teased to cover as much scalp as the laws of optics would permit. A quite natty dresser, he was not without claim to a certain distinction, a claim authored more by his tailor than his own accomplishments.

But, my dear fellow, he was anything but average. Mind you, I deliberately chose not to characterize him as either normal or abnormal. Part fanatic, part demagogue, he could be a fearsome opponent in debate, though one more suited in oratorical style to the tastes of the mob, or to their panderers in legislative chambers, than to the rigorous intellectual demands of our august tribunal. The nub of it, the very nub of it, is that, although a Democratic tenant in the White House saw fit to elevate the senator to our Court, the creature never really crossed the piazza to enter our temple in spirit as well as in body. It was far more a physical transfer of his office than it was a psychological translation from legislator to judge. Upon entering our domain, he took on one objective that drove him with fiercely unprincipled determination: to write into law all that he had failed to accomplish in the Senate. Failed, let me underscore, heavily underscore, not merely because he was but one out of a hundred, but also because, as senator from Virginia, he had felt constrained to speak and vote on the wrong side of every issue of social justice that arose during his eighteen years.

Once ensconced on our Court, he believed he had freedom to atone for his sins of omission and to indulge the social conscience that he had so long and effectively stultified. He found his conscience, but at the price of losing his integrity. But perhaps I flatter the creature; there is no evidence, no hard evidence, that he *ever* had integrity. Intelligence, yes, more than a modicum, although he was the product of a consistently second-class and splendidly expensive education at William and Mary for undergraduate work, the London School of Economics for a year's graduate study, and then the University of Virginia for his law degree. In sum, he possessed a keen if not finely honed cerebrum.

He used his position and employed the intellectual resources at his disposal to play the great social reformer. He simply—and totally—disbelieved in law. To him law was not man's groping toward general principles upon which to build a better society, but a means to achieve, and instantly, the particular social reform that was that day troubling his new-found conscience.

He was not, I hasten to stress, totally devoid of learning. Even a second-class education imparts some knowledge. Like his brain, his tongue and poisonous pen were not linked to any viable concept of law—or morality, for that matter. To him a judicial decision differed in form rather than in substance from a statute. In each, the senator was convinced, one saw a goal and attempted to achieve it. Logic and learning were the dumb, pliable slaves of the will, not sentient instruments that a jurist deployed in a tireless search for truth, justice, and wisdom.

One would hardly have needed to consult a seer to predict that the senator and I would not become intellectual bedmates—if you will forgive the earthiness of my metaphor. My conscience seldom allowed me to join his opinions, even when they were thoroughly researched and cogently argued—which they not at all infrequently were. The difficulty lay in my foreknowledge that the elegance of his prose and the apparent solidity of his reasoning united to form a mere façade to rationalize the specific public policy that he wished, at that moment, to fasten upon the nation.

I tried—you simply will never know how urgently I tried—to spare the Court his presence. To be candid, I essayed to persuade the last Democratic tenant of the White House to designate the senator as his ambassador to the Court of St. James. Not only did I approach the president directly, I also spoke to several fund raisers for the party and to two or three solons whose discretion I trusted. Actually, I suspected that Breckinridge's early years as a student at

LSE would have made London compellingly attractive to him. It would have formed a splendid capstone to his career and surely it would have raised the level of both institutions. Alas, the president turned a deaf ear to my entreaties. The good of the Court was not at the center of his concerns.

Well, enough for now about the brethren. We were nine, as every schoolboy knows. Rather than proceed with the call of the roll, let me talk about a few incidents during Walsh's chief justiceship and mention something in that context of the character—or lack thereof—of our colleagues. To be sure, I shall not run down many cases. After all, we pluck about 175 disputes a year from the petitions for certiorari; to discuss even a fair sample of them would have me in my grave long before we have Walsh completing his first term—and he served almost four as you know.

Wait, my dear fellow, before ending our talk today. Permit me to mention something that happened very early on and gave me some pause at the time. To be absolutely candid, it still does. First a bit of background. Among the Court's supporting staff is a small police force. Congress, perhaps unconstitutionally but surely not imprudently, has delegated to us complete authority to formulate and enforce rules to preserve order within the square block that encompasses our building and its grounds. The old head of our police had retired on June 30 before Walsh's appointment, and he had been temporarily succeeded by his deputy, who we all expected would formally accede to the office upon the advent of a new chief justice. Such was not to be. Walsh brought his own person.

I should inform you that, while technically the whole Court makes such appointments, the associate justices have allowed, indeed expected, the chief to handle these matters. It would be diplomatic of the chief to consult the brethren, and Walsh did so. We consented, I concede that. We did consent, although Justice Albert and I were not without reservations. We felt that there was an odor of patronage about the appointment. The person whom Walsh named was a tall, overly slender, oily, foul-mouthed creature, a former marine sergeant named Guicciardini. To be sure, I recognized the supreme irony in the name of a great historian being carried by such a brutish person.

Worse yet, far worse, Walsh and this Guicciardini were

manifestly fond of each other. They even saw each other socially, if you can conceive of such a thing. I fear that Walsh never appreciated the long-established rule that cultured people simply do not socialize with the servants. But then, what could one expect from a man who married one of his own students? The largest lump in the pudding was that this Guicciardini creature never referred to the chief justice by his proper title but always as "the colonel." Moreover, I feel it is my duty to inform you that he and Walsh's lady called each other "Kate" and "Gunny," if you can imagine such an appellation for a grown man.

Well, Guicciardini was efficient enough in his handling of security. I do not deny that, not at all. But one simply does not bring one's friends into public positions, especially friends who find it arduous to utter a single sentence free of metaphors relating to sexual acts or the more private bodily functions. Neither does it seem to me proper that a mere policeman should have free access to the chambers and to the home—the home, mind you—of the Chief Justice of the United States. Equality before the law by no means imports social leveling. Let me emphasize that I tell you these things not to carp, but to shed what light I can on the kind of person you are studying.

SIX

THE MONDAY FOLLOWING Walsh's installation, we assembled in the robing room, an oak-paneled chamber behind the courtroom itself. There, with the aid of our batmen, we donned our black robes, and, after performing our handshaking ritual, we were ready for whatever the day and barely competent attorneys would offer us. The "we" in this instance, as so frequently was the case, excluded our brother Jacobson. As was his wont, he was tardy. He arrived, huffing and puffing like an antique steam engine, a mere second before noon, grabbed, literally grabbed, his robe from its closet, and threw it around his shoulders in a heap of wrinkles. All the while his batman looked on in obvious embarrassment before his confreres. It was a stance he was often, very often, forced to assume.

As the two hands on the clock touched twelve, we could

hear the marshal slam down his gavel three times; and, as the dark red velour draperies behind the bench parted, we began our stately entrance into the courtroom to the accompaniment of the crier's chant:

> The Honorable, the Chief Justice and Associate Justices of the Supreme Court of the United States!
>
> Oyez, oyez, oyez! All persons having business before the Honorable, the Supreme Court of the United States are admonished to draw near and give their attention, for the Court is now sitting. God save the United States and this Honorable Court.

(I am old enough to remember the salad days of the New Deal when we, who gathered at Roosevelt's feet, would chant: "God save the United States *from* this Honorable Court." But those were other days—glorious days, gone to earth with dear Franklin himself.)

We swiftly seated ourselves in our highbacked, black leather chairs arranged behind the massive mahogany bench, facing the small but lovely courtroom. To me that tall, gracious room with its twenty-four columns of Siena marble, its dark red drapes enclosing it on all four sides, its bench and bar separated from the general public by what to all the world was an altar rail, had the serenity of a compact episcopal cathedral—high church, to be sure, very high church—which conveyed precisely the image of mystery and holiness that old William Howard Taft, the building's persistent godfather, intended. Precisely. Others have been less spiritual in their impressions. One pair of reporters likened the room to "a classical icebox, decorated by an insane upholsterer." But one cannot hope to please reporters, my dear chap, at least while maintaining good taste. And, despite my theological agnosticism, I, for one, felt very much at home in that chamber. It was and is what it should be—a temple of the law.

Walsh, now firmly in the center chair on my left, made his first public pronouncement as chief justice: "Number 1206, *Hilton v. California.*"

A beaming and bespectacled young man, a thick and disorderly sheaf of papers in his hand, stepped up to the podium in front of us. He was dressed in a dark blue business suit, with a silverish tie. Alas, the day had long and sorrowfully passed when no attorney would dare to appear in our Court unless he were attired in the frocked coat and striped trousers of morning clothes. Indeed, during my last few active terms on the bench, I can recall only the solicitor general himself ever wearing the proper costume. Well, so be it. It is ever the fate of old men to recall happier times.

Our young man nervously arranged his papers on the podium, making certain not to cover the portion of the panel occupied by a pair of small lights. When he would have only five of his thirty minutes remaining, that light would flash white; when his time had expired, it would flash red. Argument halted instantly. Thirty minutes in our Court does not mean thirty minutes *and* one second. Before we were blessed with such modern gadgetry, the chief justice would announce when counsel's time was over. Charles Evans Hughes, so the story goes, once cut off a prominent attorney in the middle of the word "if."

"Mr. Chief Justice," the young man began, "may it please the Court: This is an action brought by my three clients, applicants to the University of California Law School at Berkeley (or Boalt Hall, as it is popularly called) who were not admitted despite the fact that they scored higher on the two criteria that this state agency established for admission than did many persons who were admitted. Those persons who scored lower but were nevertheless accepted were members of so-called minority groups. All three of my clients are white, non-Hispanic males. When they initially filed this suit two years ago, they ranged in age from twenty-two to twenty-three. Each was and is a resident of California. All three graduated the same year from San José State University and applied for admission to Boalt Hall well within the time limits established.

"As required," the young man continued after adjusting his spectacles, "all three had taken the national Law School Aptitude Test, the LSAT. Each received a numerical score that ranged from 648 to 667, placing them within the upper seven to ten percent of all persons who had taken the test within the previous ten years. Forty-eight successful applicants, forty-five of them either blacks or from Spanish-speaking families, had scores on the LSAT that were significantly lower."

"What about grades in college?" my black brother Franklin R. Kelley asked. (The *R,* to be sure, was for

Roosevelt.) Although he had come to the bench as an effort by our last Democratic president to hold onto the black vote, he was not a bad appointment at all, not at all; he was not a big judge, but he was not lacking in competence.

"Yes, sir, I was just coming to that, Your Honor. That is the second criterion which Boalt Hall claims is critical. At San José, my three clients maintained grade point averages—they figure these things by giving an A a 4, a B a 3, and so forth—ranging from 3.51 to 3.59, which translates into an average of A minus. Of the forty-five successful minority-group applicants who had lower scores on the LSAT than my clients, thirty-seven also had lower grade averages, and lower to the extent of putting them in the B range—two as low as B minus, most B, and a few B plus."

"Tell us about the people who were accepted, those other than the forty-five from minority groups. What were their scores and grades?" brother Kelley persisted.

"Well, sir, Boalt Hall accepted 405 'regular' applicants that year. According to the university's records, the average grade point was 3.78 and the average score on the LSAT was 702."

"Did the 405," I asked, "include any members of minority groups?"

"According to the testimony of the dean of admissions at the trial, those accepted included twenty-one people of oriental background, six blacks, three Chicanos, and four foreign students."

"Did any successful white applicant score lower than your clients on either the LSAT or on grades?" Jacobson asked.

"Yes, sir. Again according to the university's records, thirty-two of the successful applicants had a lower grade point average and three had lower scores on the LSAT."

"That's not responsive to my question," Jacobson snarled. "I wanted to know whether any successful applicant scored lower on both."

"I'm sorry, Your Honor, I thought you said either."

"Don't waste our time, Counsellor. Just answer my question."

The young man blushed and stammered just a bit, but only a bit. "No, sir. None of them scored lower on both criteria."

"So what's the problem?" Jacobson snapped. "They wouldn't have let your boys in anyway."

"No, sir. That's not the point. They—"

"What is the point, then?" Jacobson cut in again.

"The point, Your Honor, is that they—Boalt Hall—did admit candidates who scored lower on both criteria than my clients. Boalt Hall and—because Boalt Hall is established by, financed by, and operated by the state—thus California discriminated against my clients on the basis of their race. That's a plain violation of the Fourteenth Amendment: '. . . nor shall any state . . . deny to any person within its jurisdiction the equal protection of the laws.' "

"I've lost the track," Justice Nathaniel Putnam said gently. (It was, my dear chap, undoubtedly a true statement. Putnam was a splendid New Hampshire gentleman, as splendidly white-maned as an aging lion, splendidly well mannered, splendidly attentive to the work of the Court, and, unlike some of the brethren I could name—but, of course, I shan't—splendidly open-minded. Unhappily, entering that open mind was not unlike being trapped within an intellectual vacuum. One found oneself gasping for oxygen. He was seventy-five and several of the less sensitive younger brethren ascribed brother Putnam's vapidity to onrushing senility. The creature's memory *was* fading a bit, but I can assure you, absolutely assure you, that, in the fifteen years we had sat together on the bench, that flinty stanchion of Republican individualism had never once been able to grasp an intellectual abstraction, much less adhere to a consistent jurisprudence.) "I've lost the track through all of these numbers," Putnam repeated. "What's the essence of your argument?"

"Yes, sir," the youngster smiled gratefully. "We argue that, while California can set intellectual standards for admission to law school as high as it deems proper, it cannot apply substantially different standards to applicants solely because of their race or their ethnic heritage. That is a clear denial of equal protection. If my clients had been black or Chicano they would have been admitted to Boalt Hall. On both criteria, they scored well above most of the successful black and Chicano candidates."

"Please read the relevant clause of the Fourteenth

Amendment for us again," our taciturn brother Campbell requested.

"Yes, sir: '. . . or shall any state . . . deny to any person within its jurisdiction the equal protection of the laws.' "

"Thank you, Counsellor. Now," Campbell's bright blue eyes focused like a pair of laser beams on the young man, "tell us exactly what protection, equal or otherwise, California denied your clients. It seems to me that your only complaint is that California did not bestow a special benefit on your clients. What protection did California deny them? Did the state refuse to guard them against criminals or anything like that?"

"No, sir, Your Honor, of course not. The term 'equal protection,' at least so this Court has held since the first time it interpreted that clause, has a much broader meaning than merely the defense of certain rights. As this Court said as long ago as 1880 in *Strauder v. West Virginia,* the amendment must be liberally construed. There, the Court said the clause meant that 'the law of the states shall be the same for the black as for the white; that all persons, whether colored or white, shall stand equal before the law. . . .' And over the years this Court has extended 'protection' to include all governmental activities, positive programs as well as prohibitions."

"Yes, you put it well," Campbell mused. "This Court has extended the Constitution. But is that our legitimate task? Is not the Constitution itself the true standard, not the extensions that well-meaning but mistaken officials have hooked onto the Constitution? And that Constitution says nothing about equal benefits."

"In a sense, yes, sir; of course, Your Honor." Perspiration was beading the lad's forehead. Clearly he had not done his homework. Any close student of the Court would have known that brother Campbell thought of the Constitution much as a fundamentalist Christian viewed his Bible: as a collection of self-evident truths that needed neither priest nor judge as interpreter, merely an honest man to read and apply what was written. Our young attorney should have been ready to cope with if not satisfy our fundamentalist. Alas, the creature could only shed water, not light. "We concede, Your Honor, on that narrow, literal interpretation of the Constitution, our case fails, but so would—"

"Narrow? Literal?" Campbell asked. (If I had not known him better I would have actually believed he was surprised. He was disappointed, to be sure, but surprised? Hardly, my dear chap, hardly. He had fought and lost this battle far too often to be surprised.) "I must remind you that we, when we became judges, and you, when you became a member of the bar of this Court, took oaths to defend that document, not to add to it. If we amend it, we stand forsworn." With that, brother Campbell spun around and presented the back of his chair to the grieving lad.

Obviously the time had come to restore some intellectual order to the argument and rescue the young creature from his less than adequate preparation. "Let us assume," I interposed, "merely assume for the sake of argument, that every justice but one who has sat on this Court has not habitually violated his oath; let us further assume, again merely for the sake of argument, that this Court is not quite yet ready to renounce its entire past and erase from the margins of the constitutional document the gloss of a century of history. Now, on those two assumptions, shaky as they may seem to some jurists, what is the nub of your argument?"

"Yes, sir." I thought the poor lad would swoon from relief. "It's a simple and straightforward argument: the Fourteenth Amendment forbids *all* racial discrimination in *all* governmental policies. It forbids discrimination against whites just as firmly as it forbids discrimination against blacks; it forbids a state to give greater benefits to one person or group solely because of race just as firmly as it forbids a state to impose greater punishment on one person or group because of race. And here California has discriminated against whites, who by the law school's announced standards are more qualified for admission, in favor of blacks and Chicanos who are—"

"Some blacks and some Chicanos," I injected.

"Yes, sir, in favor of some blacks and Chicanos who are less qualified, again according to the standards that the law school claims to apply."

"What you are saying, Counsellor," brother Kelley interpolated, "is that the Fourteenth Amendment absolutely forbids all forms of racial discrimination. Is that right?"

"Yes, sir." The little twit began to stumble again.

"But," Kelley continued, "has that been the doctrine of this Court? Have we been so rigid, so absolute?"

"Well, sir—"

The creature looked at me, but I had done my knight errantry for the day. The question was fair. If, indeed, the matter had been as simple as the not overly competent young man had claimed, we would not have granted certiorari; nor, in fact, would his clients have needed to go to law.

This time Walsh broke in, a mere millisecond before brother Jacobson committed mayhem. "Isn't what you are saying that we have held racial classifications to be 'inherently suspect' and that we must exercise 'strict scrutiny' in such cases to require a state to show a compelling public interest to justify such a classification?"

"Yes, sir. That's what I meant, Mr. Chief Justice. But this Court has struck down racial classifications so many times that there don't seem to be any exceptions—"

"We know what we have held," Kelley interrupted. "And we have always stopped short of laying down an absolute rule. Under what conditions might such a classification be constitutional?"

"I can't think of any, Your Honor."

"You can't think of a compelling public need that might make a racial classification constitutional?" Kelley sighed audibly. "Would you say that there was a compelling need in this country for certain groups—identifiable by such characteristics as the color of their skin or the accents of their English—certain groups that have historically been discriminated against, flagrantly, even violently, discriminated against, a need for such groups," my brother's emotions were garbling his usually impeccable syntax, "to have their own members in professions like law and medicine?"

"Yes, sir, I agree that that may be an important public interest, but as important as it is the Fourteenth Amendment forbids a state to give preference in admission to publicly funded schools to members of one race over better qualified members of another race."

The light on the lectern flashed white, but there was no stopping our black lion from Columbia. "Better qualified? Better qualified in what sense?"

"In the sense of the two criteria that the law school says

are the most relevant to its decision to admit a student: score on the LSAT and grade point average in college."

"These are the only two factors," Kelley asked sarcastically, "that make a man—a person—qualified to practice law? Not a passion for justice, not a concern for the suffering of one's fellow man? Not a deep-seated honesty and integrity?"

"No, sir, that is not our argument at all. What we are talking about are not *our* standards—the standards my clients would use—but the standards set up by the University of California. We don't defend those standards. We simply say that if those are California's standards, then she must apply them in an evenhanded way to whites and blacks and Chicanos and anybody else. If my clients had been black or their last names had been Gomez or Diego, they would have been accepted. But because they are white and their names show English and Italian origins, they are turned away by the state. We—"

"Doesn't California give some preference to California residents?" Justice Albert inquired. "To the extent that it does—or could—doesn't that indicate that certain other standards besides grades and LSAT scores are really relevant?"

"Well, sir, to the extent that—"

The red light flashed, and our battered young man quickly sat down, suffering no doubt from adrenal insufficiency.

The attorney general of California rose, preened himself for a moment, then approached the lectern. "Mr. Chief Justice, may it please the Court—"

"General," Jacobson was at him like a bullet, "what's a Chicano?"

"Sir?"

"What's a Chicano? I heard your opponent talk about blacks and Chicanos. I read in both your briefs about blacks and Chicanos. Now I think I know what a black man is, and if I didn't"—Jacobson affected a smile that made his face homelier than usual, if such a feat were possible—"one of my brothers would remind me. But what's a Chicano?" (Several of the brethren chuckled. I did not. I found the remark in bad taste.)

"Well, sir, it's a name that some people have more or less put on themselves, people who come from Spanish-speaking backgrounds, usually on the West Coast from families of Mexican origin, though I understand that isn't so true back here in the East."

"How do you identify a Chicano? I mean, he doesn't belong to a separate race, and I suppose we can assume they're normally distributed according to sex. How do you know if an applicant is a Chicano?"

"The best way is from the last name. If it's a Spanish name, the man or woman is apt to be Chicano. It's not an infallible test, but it's a good rule of thumb."

"In this case—these cases," Jacobson twanged on, "these people listed as Chicanos, you identified them merely by their last names—Gomez or Alvarez or something like that. Or did the law school make some check to insure that they had real, live Mexican-Americans?"

"As I recall from the trial record, Your Honor, the law school classified people only according to last names. With the staff available, the school couldn't—"

"So," Jacobson almost lunged out of his chair, "if these three petitioners had changed their names to something like Alvarez all three would have been accepted?"

"Well, I couldn't say, Your Honor. But—"

"You couldn't say? General, I don't think you're being candid with us."

The attorney general's face flushed deep crimson, more in anger than in embarrassment. "Mr. Justice," he spoke very slowly, "I am being as candid with this Court as it is humanly possible to do. In all honesty, I cannot tell you what a group of law professors whom I do not know and have never met would do if faced with a hypothetical situation."

"No rational man," Walsh put in gently, "would predict what a group of law professors would do, except disagree with one another—and this Court." We laughed, and tensions momentarily relaxed. Then Walsh continued, "Let's look at the basic policy involved here. Does the law school have a quota system?"

"Not in any formal way, Mr. Chief Justice, but we do have a double policy that some people claim—wrongly, in my judgment—amounts to a quota system. On the one hand, we keep tabs on the people whom state agencies hire and promote and whom universities and similar institutions admit and reject. If we find that the percentage of minorities is below the general distribution within the population, we make inquiries. If we find any hint of discrimination, we come down hard, very hard. The other and much more important side of that coin is that we encourage state institutions to hire or admit or whatever they do, minorities. In particular, in the state universities we have established programs to encourage admission of disadvantaged persons."

"All that sounds very interesting," that Jacobson creature interjected, "but, in fact, your program is just for minorities, is it not?"

"No, sir; technically, officially, the program is open to any disadvantaged person."

"Has a white, even a poor farm white or a poor white from a city center, has any poor white ever been in that program at Boalt Hall?"

"No, sir, I'm afraid not."

"Well, you're right to be afraid," Jacobson said heavily, "because I don't think that you can convince this Court there isn't somewhere in the great state of California at least one white student who's bright but disadvantaged. And you don't have to go beyond the census data to know that a lot of blacks aren't disadvantaged in this country, not by any economic standards."

There was a moment of silence. Given Jacobson's belligerent tone, there was little the attorney general could say that would not turn the colloquy into a nasty display of temper. Walsh broke the silence: "What's the essence of your constitutional defense against petitioners' claims, General?"

"We have several, Your Honor. First we argue that the purpose of the Fourteenth Amendment is to protect whole groups—classes, if you prefer—of people as well as individuals within those groups. The protection is against discrimination. We think that it's sound constitutional doctrine that, where a group has been grievously injured by past discrimination and its members are still suffering from the effects of that wrong, a state can—indeed should—bestow a greater share of benefits on that group in order to right the scales. Were we writing on a clean slate, we'd agree that a state has to be color-blind. But to give everyone the same benefits when some, through no fault of their own, start off a couple of miles behind everyone else, is to continue the inequality that the Fourteenth Amendment tries to eliminate. Now, please, sir, note that I said benefits, not rights, not basic protections of police and fire departments and so on. The University of California would possibly, even probably, not have admitted these three petitioners even if it had not admitted the blacks and Chicanos. So we argue that we didn't deprive petitioners of any right. There is no constitutional right to attend a law school."

"But there is," brother Putnam brightened, "a constitutional right, is there not, to be considered on the same basis as everyone else? The state has to give all an equal opportunity."

"That's precisely the point I'm arguing, Your Honor," the attorney general said, betraying just a wisp of impatience. "We argue that in the abstract the answer to your question is yes. But, where one group has suffered from discrimination in the past, where because of that discrimination many of its current members are still disadvantaged, then the state can recognize that situation by giving current members some benefits that it doesn't give to all. Boalt Hall could bestow a benefit on some blacks and Chicanos that it didn't bestow on whites—"

"Even whites who have been as much or more disadvantaged than blacks or Chicanos?" Jacobson cut in.

"Your Honor, as this Court said in *Dandridge v. Williams,* a classification doesn't have to be perfect to be constitutional. We concede that we haven't helped everyone who's suffered from past discrimination, but we're doing the best we can. We've been what this Court calls 'under-inclusive.' But this Court has said that isn't necessarily a constitutional sin."

"At least not a mortal sin," Walsh noted.

The attorney general smiled. "Yes, sir. We aren't trying to discriminate against anyone. We're trying to undo past discrimination. Because we're fallible human beings we aren't doing a perfect job—and it's likely we'll never do a perfect job. But we're trying to accomplish the purpose of the Fourteenth Amendment—to make people equal before the law, truly equal, not just equal on paper but equal in fact."

The attorney general paused, probably expecting another onslaught from brother Jacobson. He was not to be disappointed.

"Some of your applicants apply for scholarships. Do you screen those people for financial need?"

"In a general way, yes, sir. Nothing very detailed or especially close. I'm sure it would be easy to cheat."

"Well, if you can screen out the rich from the poor, why can't you screen out the Chicanos in a more effective way than simply by last name?"

"Your Honor, each year Boalt Hall receives from 3000 to 4000 applications for 300 or so places. The law school accepts about 450, on the assumption that about a third of those chosen will elect to attend other law schools, delay entry to Boalt Hall, change their minds about law altogether, or die or have some sort of serious illness. But it is only those among the 450 who ask for scholarships—about half or less—whom the university subjects to any real financial screening. The committee just couldn't handle many more cases."

"How would they screen 4000 petitions for certiorari each year?" I could not resist asking.

The attorney general waited for the laughter to subside. "They couldn't, Your Honor. Only miracle workers could do that," he smiled. Again there was an appropriate titter of laughter. Then the attorney general continued. "On a related subject, we also argue that one of the two intellectual criteria, scores on the Law School Aptitude Test, do not measure the abilities of minority group members as accurately as they do the abilities of the white majority. In short, the test is culturally biased."

"Is that why people of oriental ancestry do very well, possibly even better than whites?" Jacobson's sarcasm was heavy.

"Well, sir, because of tight family structure and discipline some groups are able to overcome the disadvantage—"

"Without special state benefits, but by discipline and hard work—yes, if there is bias in the test, they overcome it themselves," Jacobson injected. "Why isn't that a sufficient prescription for everybody? Is government our Big Brother?"

"Sir, perhaps because of slavery, and for other reasons that we don't understand, black family structure just isn't as tight as that of Oriental, that—"

"And Spanish family structure? I grew up along the Rio

Grande, General, and the Mexicans I knew had a tight family structure, very tight." (I would wager, my good chap, that our brother never knew a Mexican except as a servant, or someone he could push off the sidewalk.)

My brother Albert tried to remove us from Jacobson's cul-de-sac. "During the last few years what percentage of blacks and Chicanos admitted have obtained their law degrees, and has your special program made any difference?"

"Well, sir, according to the information that the university gave me, I can report that over the last four years some seventy-five percent of the people who were admitted under the special program for the disadvantaged successfully completed their first year of law school. Those are the only figures that I have."

"Do you know what proportions of blacks and Chicanos, as compared to whites, received law degrees?"

"No, sir, I just don't have that information. I can try to get it for you."

"Please do that."

"Let me go back, if I may," the attorney general continued, "to my answer to the chief justice's questions about our constitutional defenses. We have a second argument. We concede that our program has so far given advantages based on race and ethnic background. Now race, we are well aware, is a suspect basis of classification. We justify that classification by a compelling need, a compelling interest of society as a whole. A good law school, after it has insured that its students are intelligent and sufficiently well trained to study law and practice law, should try to provide an environment which reflects the larger world in which these attorneys will live. It isn't enough for a lawyer—it may be all right for a philosopher but not for a lawyer—to study about discrimination in a book. He or she should know people who've felt the sting of discrimination, who can speak from experience; while a lawyer has to be learned, even more he has to be a practical solver of real problems of real people who live in a very real, sometimes too real, world.

"He gets some of that experience in a law school that has whites and blacks and Chicanos and Orientals and Indians and rich and poor, and so on. We feel that the state has a positive obligation not merely to the members of minority groups but also to members of the majority to provide such an environment in law school.

"We also think," the attorney general added, his voice becoming a bit too oratorical for my tastes, "that there's another compelling need, a need to provide legal services for members of minority groups, people—"

"Is your argument," Jacobson interrupted, "that blacks and Chicanos can't get legal aid from white lawyers or from the best lawyers regardless of race?"

"No, sir. Our argument is that minority groups who've suffered from discrimination in the past and may still be suffering from the dregs of past wrongs, those people are more likely to go to people like them, people they instinctively trust rather than distrust, for legal help."

"Do you argue," Walsh asked, "that black and Chicano attorneys are apt to be more sympathetic to the claims of black and Chicano litigants than are ethnic strangers?"

"We don't claim they will, Mr. Chief Justice, not in a sense that we can prove. We hope they will, but we know some won't. Most human beings are pretty selfish, and blacks and Chicanos are not more or less human than the white, Anglo majority. But, I'd note in passing that the National Association for the Advancement of Colored People didn't become the powerful force for racial justice that it did until blacks were firmly in command. White liberals helped found it and fund it and even run it for many years. But it didn't become *the* force for black civil rights until it had become a black organization for, by, and of blacks. One case doesn't prove a thesis, but it gives our hopes some reasonable basis."

"In sum, you want us to validate California's violating the constitutional right of one group—here whites—to be treated equally because you find a 'compelling societal interest' in the chance, the hope, that those who benefit are members of groups who have suffered discrimination in the past? Is that the gist of your argument?" The questioner was my brother Stanley Svenson, who was giving us the initial indicium that he had not grasped a word of what had been transpiring. (You have undoubtedly heard, my dear chap, the rumors that he drank heavily. My duty to history compels me to overcome my deeply seated aversion to gossip and to confirm these stories. Usually—usually—he confined his drinking to evenings. Stories of his faux pas at dinner parties were legion; every civilized hostess in town dreaded, simply dreaded, having that creature on her guest list. Not that he ever drank—at least to my knowledge—while the Court was sitting, but I suspect that his metabolic system was never clear of alcohol except for the first few days after his return from one of his periodic trips to a rest home in Connecticut where the rich and famous could—what is the euphemism?—dry out in private. I can tell you that sitting next to him at conference when the windows were closed could be a trial—yes, a trial; I like that. He exhaled far more alcohol than carbon dioxide, and inhaling spirits at one remove has never been among my pleasures.)

"No, sir, that—"

The white light flashed.

"—is not our argument, not at all. The only right that a person has to enter a state law school is that he be given a fair chance. On that fair chance, these petitioners did not make it. We gave, for *all* the reasons I've just mentioned, some other people a second chance, an additional chance. There's a point here I'd like to stress while I still have a moment. There's another compelling interest here: that of providing positive images for young blacks and Chicanos, showing them that they have a real chance of success in America, letting them see people with whom they can identify serving as doctors, and lawyers, and executives. We must reach the bright young members of minorities and convince them that our society means what it says about equality, that there are ways of life open to them outside but not necessarily divorced from the ghetto and the barrio. We have to show those people that pushing drugs, pimping, running numbers, and mugging senior citizens don't represent their only hope for a share of American affluence. No white person can provide that sort of image for a black or Indian teenager; no Anglo can provide that kind of image for a Chicano youth. We need these people, Your Honors, these young minority lawyers. We—all of society—need them if we are truly to become one people and not a collection of angry, frustrated racial and ethnic groups ready to use violence against what they conceive to be 'the system.' We need them."

The attorney general's timing was perfect. Not five seconds after his last sentence the light flashed red.

"Thank you, General," Walsh nodded, then glanced at the papers in front of him. "Number 768, *The United States v. du Pont de Nemours and Co.*"

A few seconds later, another gentleman, not so young as our first lawyer and not so suave as our second, strode to the podium. "Mr. Chief Justice, may it please the Court. . . ."

And that, my dear fellow, is illustrative of one of the most significant facts about our Court. A case may be freighted with dramatic import for the country at large; its issues may be exquisitely complex. Howsoever all that may be—and let me assure you, that it often does be—that case is preceded by another case and followed by yet another. No matter how dread the import of a case, it is but one item on an assembly line that inexorably rolls through our courtroom and our minds. Rarely do we have the pleasure of pausing to savour at leisure the intellectual delights of any particular controversy. Always, simply always, there are other disputes competing for that scarcest of all resources, time itself.

Each of us reacts to that condition in his own way. I believe I have made my position not unclear: I learned to live with that fact of life and thus to live with problems so long that they seemed old friends rather than enemies. Like brother Jacobson, Walsh reacted by leaping at the problems as they came by. To a point, but only to a point, that method begets efficiency; it seldom sires wisdom.

SEVEN

OUR DOCKET typically reflects the unsolved political problems of the day. I mean political here in the highest sense of the word, problems of public policy, not partisan advantage for this or that party or individual. For the nonce, let me concentrate on the California law school dispute, even though it was only one of twelve cases argued that week—and, of course, its importance did nothing to diminish the exfoliation of petitions for certiorari.

It came up for discussion that Friday. Because such broadly reaching issues were involved and because our time was so limited, Walsh asked that we suspend our usual rule against shoptalk at lunch and have coffee and sandwiches brought in the conference room at twelve-thirty so that we could devote a full ninety minutes to an informed discussion, postponing a vote on the merits until the following week. I did not relish the thought of debating while eating. Besides, my dear chap, my digestion suffered merely from proximity to Jacobson's mouth and Svenson's breath. But what could one say?

The morning's work had gone well. We had disposed of twenty-five petitions for certiorari, given final approval to three opinions to come down during the next week we sat, and discussed and voted on the antitrust case that had been argued directly after the dispute about California's affirmative action in law school. Shortly after noon we adjourned for twenty minutes to tend to any business pending in our chambers, and then returned for our lunch.

Sandwiches and coffee were at our places as we strolled back into the conference room. Dessert and an extra pot of coffee were on a rolling tray off to one side. No one, but no one, comes into our conference room when we are at work, neither secretaries, nor clerks, nor even messengers. If there is an urgent message, someone knocks at the door and the junior associate justice—then Franklin Roosevelt Kelley—answers it and receives the communication. There is only one seeming exception. If we pause for coffee or other refreshment, we allow a waiter to wheel his tray into the sanctuary; he rarely trespasses more than a few feet into our holy of holies before one of the brethren quickly eases him of his burden and speeds his exit. In sum, while war may rage within the conference, it is internal war. We are cut off from, if not at peace with, the outside world.

Before I could even lift my sandwich to sample its rather mushy contents, our compulsive new chief justice had snapped us down to business, reminding us that, since this was, in effect, a preconference meeting, we should think out loud, play devil's advocate, and, when we met again to rethink the issues and vote, not feel at all committed by any arguments that we ourselves might now make. Having dispensed with that prologue, Walsh addressed the merits.

"I come up to this case like a skittish horse before a brass band. The issues are volatile and visible. I would like to see the United States a country in which a person's race was as irrelevant as the color of his eyes. But I know that won't be true in my lifetime. Race cuts too deeply. It's an ugly scar on our bodies that we have to live with. In this case, I see two different injustices—first, a large social injustice that has severely disadvantaged some people, usually members of particular minorities, and, second, a more specific injustice in that California has not used the same criteria to choose among candidates for admission to law school. Whichever way we decide, we are going to have to live with one of those injustices. We didn't cause either of them, but any decision we make will fail to right one of those wrongs.

"For me," he went on, "the decisive factor is the fundamental purpose of the Fourteenth Amendment—to help the newly freed slave retain his status as a free man and eventually to become an equal man. I think that the changing nature of American society has deepened that purpose, in part because waves of immigrants meant other groups also needed equal protection and in part because the white majority has made 'eventually' read more like an eternity for blacks and Latins. For generations, the dominant majority ignored the promise of the Fourteenth Amendment. Until recently, we made no more than a halfhearted pass at equal education; even now it is not yet a reality in many areas. And where physical facilities are equal for black and white or for Anglo and Latino, and where all are mixed together in the same schools with the same teachers, those children whose parents were systematically denied an equal education are not likely, as a group, to receive equal benefits."

Walsh paused for a moment to inhale a large gulp of black coffee and then continued. "I do not see how there can ever be equality for more than a trickle of truly extraordinarily talented—or extraordinarily lucky—individuals, if we do not reach out and relax the rules just a bit. Admitting students by academic merit without regard to race, religion, sex, wealth, political influence, or political affiliation is the fairest way. But for most young people academic merit is heavily influenced by their parents' education, social class, and appreciation of learning; it's also heavily influenced by the support of peers and their belief as well as one's own that an education is both possible and useful. To say to people who have been denied advantages in these respects that they will have chances equal to those who enjoyed these advantages is like telling a runner that he has an equal chance but only if he begins the race where he is now, a hundred yards behind the starting line."

"Well, now, Chief, I just don't see it that way," our boorish brother Jacobson cut in. For him "I" was a three-syllable word, full of *a*'s and *h*'s, twanged in an ugly tone that was closely congruent with the thing for which the pronoun stood. To be sure, it was my prerogative to speak immediately after the chief justice, but once again I held my tongue. Walsh was familiar with the custom, just as was Jacobson. I deliberately determined to let Walsh see Jacobson *au naturel,* so to speak, to let the pattern form and be recognized.

"As I see it, nobody in his right mind ever thought this world was a fair place," Jacobson continued. "Nobody gets an equal chance at the big banana. We set up rules and we play the game by those rules. When I've got a pair of jacks, I can't claim the pot just because the hombre with three aces had a rich poppa while my daddy ran off when I was six and my momma had to take in washing just so's we could eat. Rulewise, California said this game would be won by the highest college averages and the highest scores on the Law School Aptitude Test. And that's the way the chips have got to fall. Nobody gets any Brownie points because he's white or black or Mexican or Jewish or, God forbid, goy."

Jacobson paused, hoping no doubt to allow this homey wisdom of the frontier to penetrate our skulls. Before he could renew his war with the English language and our sensibilities, I assumed my rightful role. I looked straight at Walsh as if Jacobson were not between us.

"Chief, like Greek tragedy, this case presents a clash of rights rather than of wrongs. A lifetime of association with struggles against racial injustices impels the Blue Danube side of me to join with you. But, as a judge, I am neither liberal nor conservative, neither black nor white. Actually, I come to the same conclusion as you do, but I believe, earnestly believe, we need a different algorithm from that which you have articulated.

"It is not our function," I explained, "except within very constrained limits, to decide whether affirmative action is necessary, useful, or desirable. We have before us a competing set of interests; I would ponder long and hard before I could feel certain about where to strike the most wise or most just balance. But that is not our task. We must keep in mind that we are not the primary resolvers of this clash. 'Courts,' as Harlan Stone reminded our predecessors, 'are not the only agency of government that must be assumed to have capacity to govern.' "

As you can well imagine, my dear chap, I held Walsh's rapt attention. "A lifetime of study of the history of this Court convinces me that our proper approach in such cases is not to attempt to weigh the multifaceted values in conflict, but to look at how the political branches have weighed them and then to ask if that weighing is reasonable. If it is reasonable, then our task is at an end. And here I find it to be so."

Several of the brethren were rapidly scribbling notes on what I was saying. I continued my instruction. "The Fourteenth Amendment's broad prohibition against a denial of equal protection is pregnant with the ambiguity syntactically inherent in the use of the double negative. The amendment's command is for a state not to deny equal protection. For a state to do nothing where inequality of state benefits exists involves, one might cogently argue, a denial of equal protection of the laws. For a state to act as California has in this case, to take affirmative action to wipe out inequality in the distribution of benefits from state action, also involves—and necessarily so—a certain amount of inequality. There are no doubt other alternatives in this post-Edenesque world which we inhabit, but I would guess—and that is not a curbstone opinion—each is equally flawed."

In conclusion, I summed up the issues. "Is California's judgment reasonably designed to effectuate equal protection of the laws? That is the only question before us. The question we face is not whether this is the best policy or the fairest policy that could be devised in a perfect world. But is it a reasonable policy? Given the fact that any other policy that I can imagine is also imperfect, I am slow to condemn. Our lodestar must be that we have no concern with the wisdom or unwisdom of policy, only its permissibility as a reasonable regulation. I go no further and this Court should go no further, because with that answer we reach the very boundary of our jurisdiction."

(I confess, that I spoke a bit lengthily here, but I was trying to contribute to the chief's education about the limited function of our Court as much as to forge an outcome in the specific case before us. Walsh, I believed, was educable, and it was my duty to assist him.)

"I think Justice Walker has summed up my views quite adequately," dear Albert said; then he went on to restate the problem and its optimal solution with his usual silken precision. "So resolving this case would put us in the great tradition of Holmes and Brandeis. What we would do as legislators is beside the point. We should, as this Court has done since the days of John Marshall, presume the statute constitutional and place the burden of proof for unconstitutionality on the challengers. In my judgment, those challengers have shown only that California's policy is not perfect; they have not demonstrated that the policy is unreasonable. If we are unanimous or nearly so, I suggest a brief *per curiam* opinion that says no more than that."

(A *per curiam* opinion, as you may not be unaware, is an unsigned opinion, typically quite short, used in cases where the law is settled and needs only succinct restatement to resolve the dispute at hand.)

"But we are not unanimous, not by a long shot, not yet anyway," Jacobson snorted.

"I am afraid that brother Jacobson is correct," Putnam, our beloved New England ninny, said. "A state must give every man the same break and judge his performance by the same standards. That's what equal protection means to me. Here California used different sets of standards for different people because of their color or national origin. That won't wash. I sympathize with California's honest efforts to solve a very difficult problem; but she chose a path forbidden by the Fourteenth Amendment."

Next spoke the senator from Virginia. He prefaced his remarks with a long recitation of cases. Really, my dear chap, it was a façade of erudition that should have fooled no one; indeed, that logorrhea should have put us all to sleep, and would have had it not been for the coffee. "The gist of our jurisprudence," he finally concluded, "is that reasonableness is not always the standard for determining if a classification fits the equal protection clause. There are, we have held time and again, certain 'suspect' bases of classification, and the worst offender is race. Where race —or alienage or, although we differ on this point, I believe, sex—is the basis for a state's distinguishing among people, it is not enough that the state show the classification is reasonable. We have consistently held that, there, the proper test is that of 'strict scrutiny.' We do not—I repeat, do not—presume that statute constitutional under such circumstances. Rather we throw the burden onto the state to justify the classification by showing a compelling public need that cannot be met in any other way.

"For the reasons given by the chief justice," the creature prattled on as if he were addressing his former colleagues in the Senate, "I think California has met that burden here. And because the issue is so fundamentally significant to the whole problem of equality in America, I urge that we say foursquare that California has met the very stiff test of 'strict scrutiny' and that her plan for affirmative action is in accord with the highest constitutional standards unanimously announced by this Court in the School Segregation Cases."

Our brother Svenson, who, after his sandwich and coffee, exuded only the faintest tincture of the previous evening's libations, grunted a few remarks. Obviously, his law clerks had failed to pump enough information into his ear. In short, he agreed with the chief and the senator, though he was unable to articulate his reasoning. It was a poor show, but not atypical, not at all atypical.

Brother Campbell, our Celtic literalist, treated us to one of his sermons about the plain words of the Constitution. We had only heard it a million times before. I took advantage of the opportunity to sketch the outline of a concurring opinion. My conscious mind returned to the conference room as Campbell was droning: "The Fourteenth Amendment says explicitly that a state shall not deny any person the equal protection of the laws. California has denied petitioners no protection to which they are entitled, and I cannot understand how they could claim to have been denied any right to liberty or property. No one is at liberty to attend a state-supported law school, nor does one have a property right in that school."

It was an absurd argument, utterly absurd. Its only virtue was that it was now completed.

Our junior colleague, Franklin Roosevelt Kelley, spoke

last. His tone was gently mocking. "I prefer to think of myself as one of those extraordinarily talented people of whom the chief justice spoke, rather than as one of the extraordinarily lucky. In fact, I've been wondering whether I shouldn't recuse myself in this case because someone might claim I have a vested interest in the status quo that only lets a few blacks into the system. Seems like most of the last twenty-five years I've moved up the political ladder as the house nigger" (I have never accommodated myself to that word, not even in the mouth of a black) "giving legitimacy to what you honkies have been doing at the moment."

We all chuckled, except that Jacobson creature. He put his head back and roared with laughter. It was overdone. Irony deserves a quiet smile, perhaps even a soft chuckle, not paroxysms of loud laughter.

Kelley's tone shifted. "I can't become serious in this matter without becoming impassioned. Three generations of preacher-man genes can make me give the hottest fire and brimstone sermon this side of low country Georgia. So let me just say that I associate myself with the chief justice's views and the views of Justice Breckinridge." Really, it would have so shortened our conferences over the years if the other brethren would have merely referred to Breckinridge as "the Senator." "We've got to face up to the substantive issue here and declare that what California has done is right—morally right and constitutionally right. I don't want us to use any cute tricks of presuming constitutionality. I think brother Breckinridge is right. I think that we've got to place the accolade of constitutionality firmly on affirmative action."

You will notice, notice well, that I did not interrupt, even at the mention of "cute tricks." Cute tricks, my eye! Presuming constitutionality of legislation is a practice as old as this Court. I shan't bore you by calling the roll of the big judges who adhered to that doctrine. Those were grey beards, indeed! Cute tricks, just imagine! But I forbore to interrupt. I have found that blacks tend to be very touchy; I suppose it's because they are so very unsure of themselves—often not without reason. An unhappy byproduct of giving blacks an extra chance is that many of them have made it who really do not deserve it. Worst of all, they know it—and, more frequently, suspect it even when, as with brother Kelley, it is not true. In any event, I thought it wise to wait until Kelley was done to try to engage him in a dialogue. I probed gently, very gently, lest I bruise his tender ego.

"My Brother," I said, "a lifetime's work for the cause of equal justice impels me to praise your remarks—and the chief's—to the echo, to the very echo. But my judicial robe constrains the flow of those sweet juices of life. We are not free, as are our confreres across the piazza, to speak our own minds on substantive issues. Our limited powers and our thus limited capacities caution us to be humble. We should keep in mind Brandeis's sage dictum: 'The most important thing we do is not doing.' We, if we are to act within the four corners of our jurisdiction, have a very limited function. Here the issues of policy are subtle, complex, and, as the chief reminds us, politically explosive. Whatever solution is proposed to the sorrowfully vexatious problems of race, it must have widespread popular support to succeed. We are not a representative institution. We are out of touch with the public pulse—as, indeed, we should be. Our task is the restricted one of deciding cases agreeably to the Constitution. We have no mandate to serve as roving knights righting every wrong in the realm. Our task of constitutional interpretation is completed when we have satisfied ourselves that another branch of government has not unreasonably deployed its powers."

"We are not monks or eunuchs!" Alas, it was the senator who responded, not Kelley. "We have a duty in deciding constitutional issues to *decide* them. As much as I admire the erudition of Justice Walker"—as well he should have, as well he should have—"I cannot accept his reading of the history of the Court or of our practice under equal protection. As I demonstrated in some detail"—"flatulently argued," would have been more apt than "demonstrated," much more apt—"this Court has demanded more than reasonableness when the basis of classification has been race. To fail to say that California has met those stricter standards would be to cast doubt on a long line of decisions and do injustice to California as well. Furthermore, we have the duty to set down clear guidelines to other public officials and to the public at large, so they can all know what their rights and duties are. This Court knows no finer hour than when it cuts through formalities and technicalities to enunciate great constitutional principles."

"But," Putnam put in, "we can't be blind to a state's using race as a standard to bestow privileges. I agree with brother Campbell that a citizen has no property right to attend a state law school, but if a state sets up a law school, it cannot use racially tainted criteria to determine who shall be admitted. Besides, as attorneys ourselves and members of the bar, we have a duty to see to it that standards for admission to the legal profession are kept high. We need better lawyers, not worse ones."

"You know," the chief mused, "I used to sit in on a lot of decisions to choose students for law school. I think that at Ann Arbor we got about the same number and quality of applicants as they do at Berkeley. I can tell you that all our follow-up studies of how well students did in law school convinced me that the Law School Aptitude Test was good but far from infallible. It probably told us who could not do the work at all or who would be pretty poor at it. But even when we took college grades into account, we'd miss on those we admitted at both ends of the scale. The correlation was high enough to please statisticians, but it was too low for me not to choose every now and then according to my own gut feeling.

"Look," he went on, "in the early 1960s the scores on the LSAT that these minority candidates got would have admitted them to any law school in the country—Harvard, Yale, Berkeley, or Michigan. We aren't talking about California's lowering standards, we're seeing the results of a tremendous boom in the number of applicants to law school. What the facts show is that this case is not about how a state distinguishes qualified from unqualified candidates, but how it chooses among those who are highly qualified. At that stage, when you're dealing with only those who are highly qualified, I can't see why it's wrong to try to put some ethnic or racial leaven into a class, any more than it's wrong to try to get some out-of-state students or to get a proportion of people from private colleges as well as state universities. As the attorney general pointed out, every decent law school tries to pick a class that will represent a cultural mix that will expose students—and faculty—to a range of outlooks. That's an important aspect of education. Parochialism is bad for education at any level; it's absolutely debilitating in graduate school. I'm still assuming, of course, that the pool consists only of qualified and highly qualified people."

"At the undergraduate level," I interjected, "being an athlete or the child of an alumnus can be a critical factor for admission. And God knows neither is positively associated with intelligence. Indeed, we all have ample evidence at hand that the relationship between athletic prowess and intelligence is probably inverse."

Jacobson, a former football player for the University of Texas, scowled, but the others—even brother Campbell—smiled at my riposte.

"Well," Walsh wound up, "I just cannot say that the Constitution forbids California to try to right past wrongs, to provide models for young people to emulate, and to fulfill an important educational function by guaranteeing the entry of a small number of highly qualified blacks and Chicanos. Those all seem to me to be compelling public needs, and I don't know how else they can be met—not that I am positive that California's method will meet them. But it's a try, an honest try."

"A few minutes ago," Jacobson rudely interrupted, "brother Breckinridge mentioned great principles. Now, Constitution-wise, what's the great principle involved here? Affirmative discrimination? If we want to give extra benefits to people whose grandparents suffered, then show me the line. My maternal grandparents went back to the old country in 1935 and they were both burned at Auschwitz. And before that, my ancestors were for centuries herded into the stinking ghettos of central Europe. How're y'all planning to reward me?" (The *re* of "reward" consisted of two heavily accented syllables.) "Hell, I figure if those people were sheep enough to take that crap, they probably got what was coming to them. If those Jews or those blacks had stood up on their hind legs and fought instead of knuckling under, people would've respected them. Look at the Israeli. Nobody pushes them around. Nobody's got any respect for a man—and he doesn't even respect himself—who lets the world stomp on him."

"You've got your reward, Marvin," Kelley joked, "just being privileged to sit here with us Christian dudes." Jacobson guffawed loudly. Then, more drily, Kelley added: "You've got a strange jurisprudence. You condone violence and revolution, but you won't approve peaceful change within constitutional limits. What ever happened to the rule of law?"

"I don't think this change is within the Constitution; that's what happened to the rule of law. And sure as hell if any change like this comes, it won't be peaceful. White people may be willing to foot the bills for welfare and a lot of other special privileges for those who're too lazy to work or too dumb to cut the mustard test-wise, but they're not going to give up their professional schools and their universities, not by a damn sight."

Before our brother Kelley could reply, Walsh broke in: "Well, we've accomplished at least one thing: we've put a lot of ideas out on the table. And several of us," he nodded toward Jacobson, "have played the role of devil's advocate—perhaps too successfully." (Jacobson guffawed again.) "I suggest that we put this case first on the schedule for next Friday's conference and in the meantime we pray over it. I consider—I hope I consider—my own views tentative, and I hope you all do the same. Let's adjourn now for fifteen minutes, stretch our legs, and get back to other business."

As we rose, Jacobson put a hairy paw around Kelley's shoulder, and the two walked out of the room together. I could hear—one could hear both the original and the echo—the beginning of Jacobson's opening remark. "Little Brother, I've got me ten dollars that says this Sunday my big Dallas Cowboys are going to blow your teeny-weeny Redskins right out of the ball park and into the river so fast your boys'll all be drowned by the first half. I'll give you five points."

"Five points for blowing us out of the ball park? Man, you people in Texas must have real small ball parks." I lost the rest—it was hardly a loss—as they went into the anteroom. How Kelley, or any of the other brethren, could fraternize with that creature always exceeded my comprehension.

The next week's conference showed small changes in position. Putnam had weakened a bit, but that was normal. I am certain, absolutely certain, that he did not change his mind so much as he forgot what he—and we—had said the week before. When the Court voted, the lineup was 7–2 to sustain the constitutionality of California's plan. The seven, however, were badly divided in their reasoning. Albert and I wanted to speak with Doric simplicity and preserve our proper deferential stance toward the other branches of government. (I do not need to enlighten you, I am sure, that I entertained no illusion that the other branches of government deserved that deference. But that is the attitude that the Constitution prescribes for our Court and that is the attitude I take.)

On the other hand, Walsh, Breckinridge, Svenson, and Kelley wanted to address the merits as if they were legislators and pronounce the plan clearly constitutional. For his part, brother Campbell stuck like glue to his position that petitioners had not made out a case. What a mindless creature!

"Well, it's time I got my feet wet," Walsh said when the voting was done. "I'll take the job of writing the opinion in this case. I'll follow the usual custom and let you know about the other assignments in a day or two."

I should be less than candid, less than candid, were I not to confess that I had hoped to have that task myself. Oh, don't misunderstand me, there was no question of ego involved. Where the Court is concerned, I have no ego, none whatsoever. I could say all that I wanted in a concurring opinion that I was certain Albert would join. Rather, my concern was for stern observance of the austere functions of the Court, to keep it as insulated as mere humans can from the dangerous bucking of that unruly horse, public policy.

I tried, I tried but I could not. Immediately after our conference ended late that afternoon, I accompanied Walsh to his office. I gave him a full hour, a *full* hour. I pulled out all the stops, calling the roll of the big judges, as I had forborne doing in conference, who had forged the doctrine of self-restraint. He listened and I believe he learned something—surely I gave him some needed instruction in the history of our Court. But in the end, he stubbornly refused to concede the unwisdom of his stance. The most he would yield was to agree to think about my principled argument.

Not being especially sanguine about the possibility of converting Walsh—although I was determined to continue to try at every opportunity—I decided to bring along with me enough of the other justices so that he would have to capitulate. One must keep in mind that the magic number on our Court is five. If five justices are willing to sign an opinion, then that document becomes the opinion of the Court. If five justices are not willing to sign, the opinion is that of a group of judges, respected but neither definitive of the issues nor authoritative as a precedent to settle future litigation. Walsh had only four votes for his general approach, his own plus those of Breckinridge, Svenson, and Kelley. I had two, my own and Albert's. Campbell, as usual, was isolated, and Putnam was confused. Jacobson was unyielding in dissent. Because Walsh needed only to persuade one additional justice to join him and I had to convert three, my task was far more difficult—but the difficulty was proportionate to our skills, I can say not immodestly.

My first step was to draw up a brief memorandum concisely stating my views. By nine that evening I had pecked out a draft on my secretary's typewriter. The next morning I brought it, as messy as it was, to Albert's home in Chevy Chase, and he gave it the benefit of his capacious mind. By nine-fifteen Monday morning my secretary had it neatly typed and duplicated, and I took it by my own hand to brothers Campbell and Svenson. They were the two weakest links in the majority. I sat with each while he read it and gave him the benefit of a few additional minutes of explanation.

My work was not without some fruit. With Campbell—who was not simpleminded enough to believe his literalism could capture another vote—I reasoned that my approach, while quite different from his, was far closer to his than was Walsh's. With Svenson I used the same direct argument that I had at conference. I had some optimism there. Before his problems with drink, he had had a passable if not fine mind.

Next, I spent a full hour with brother Putnam, who, as you recall, had joined with Jacobson on the merits but had seemed to be weaseling toward the end. He was a weak reed, indeed, but, withal, something of a realist. He knew—or at least I reminded him—that his position had lost, and, as with Campbell, I put forth the thesis that my approach would do less damage to the values he wished to protect than would Walsh's. He seemed interested in what I said, but one could never be sure what Putnam *thought* one was saying.

I by no means counted Walsh as a totally lost lamb. Twice more during the next week I talked to him, leaving him a copy of my memorandum. I candidly told him that it was a working draft of a concurring opinion that I might later circulate to all the brethren. I also found it tactically useful to keep track of the progress of his own opinion. I wanted to circulate mine at exactly the same time as he did his so as to minimize the impact of his prose, which, I feared, would be not ungracefully composed.

To that end, I consulted with one of my clerks, Franklin Adams, a bright young lad fresh from Yale. I was not unaware that one of the law clerks whom Walsh had inherited from the old chief, a rather homely young woman from Harvard, had taken more than a professional interest in young Adams. The lad played his part splendidly, if somewhat reluctantly. Apparently the lady's imagination was monopolized by two interests, sex and law; after I made a point of inviting her for tea, I concurred in Adams's judgment that she was not *rather* homely but *very* homely, with a figure not unlike that of an overweight male adolescent.

Be that as it may—and I tried to assure young Adams that true beauty went deeply beyond the physical—she was far more helpful than she meant to be. (It was the sole benefit of our lowering the barriers to allow female clerks.) We had a running account of Walsh's progress and sent our draft to the printer within hours after he dispatched his. (You know, of course, that we have our own printing press in the basement. Not only are all the final opinions done there but so are the drafts that we circulate within the Court. It's expensive but worth every penny, every single penny. One is able to comprehend so much more fully when one sees an argument on a printed page than on a sheet of typescript.)

I devoutly wish I could weave a happy ending onto this narrative. Alas, quite the contrary was the case. The decision and its import for the function of our Court aside—and these were important, indeed potentially momentous especially when seen in conjunction with other decisions that Walsh tried to effect—the affair gave me an insight into the new chief's character, an insight that was not at all flattering. The creature had been stalking the halls of the Court, dropping in on other justices—not on me, I assure you, and not on brother Albert—pressuring them to join his opinion. To be sure, he would claim that he was only trying to reason with them, but I knew better. He even had the bad taste to call on Putnam. He badgered that poor feebleminded creature for almost an hour.

You won't believe this, but it is gospel. He even had the effrontery to try to persuade *me—me,* my dear chap. During one of my visits designed to educate him, he made a little speech to me about *our* duty to decide constitutional issues that were properly before us. He said something to the effect that courage was a judicial virtue no less important than modesty. He has that phrase in his opinion. You can look it up if you have time to waste. I can assure you, absolutely assure you, that I only pretended to listen. With the omniscience that hindsight always brings, I suspect that I was quiet more out of shock at his audacity in thinking that *he* could instruct *me* in constitutional jurisprudence, than out of respect for the merits of his argument.

I do not claim, not at all, that there is anything illegal or even unethical in our trying to persuade one another. Indeed, because we are a *court,* we play orchestral roles rather than solos. Mutual give and take is the essence of our work. If each of the nine of us went off in the direction he liked best, the law would quickly become a shambles. How could even a good attorney make sense out of nine different opinions? It sometimes happens that that is what we write, to be sure, but the resulting chaos only proves my point.

What I am trying to say is that we must *negotiate* with one another if any opinion is to command the assent of five or more justices. The real question we face is how shrewdly to negotiate with each other. Mark my use, I beg of you, of the word "negotiate." I abhor the word "bargain." Some vulgar political scientist once wrote a book entitled *Elements of Judicial Strategy* in which he asserted that we bargain with one another. Nothing could be further from the truth. We do not bargain, not at all. We negotiate. After all, if one has been outvoted 8–1, one might, in all prudence, express a willingness to make the decision unanimous if the opinion writer would substitute a few softer paragraphs for those the putative dissenter found especially objectionable.

Even more often, when you are with the majority, you find the opinion writer has taken a quite different tack from the one that moved you. You inform him and explain your preferences, seeking some middle ground of accommodation. The opinion writer's refusal to listen and at least attempt to adjust his draft could—I do not say it always does—lead to your circulating a separate concurring opinion, which, if persuasive, might bring the rest of the majority to your side and leave the original person assigned the task of writing the opinion of the Court speaking for himself alone.

The sanction of a separate opinion need not be expressed, though some, like that Jacobson creature, might be so unsubtle as to use it as an open threat. I also need not add that as the vote is closer, this sort of sanction becomes more effective. To take the extreme, when the vote is 5–4, defection of a single member of the majority to a concurring opinion means that no one speaks for the Court. And, if one truly believes that what one is writing is jurisprudentially sound, one wants to speak for the Court, not merely for a minority of the justices.

Here, I have an excellent illustration of what I have been talking about. It's a carbon of a note that I sent to the senator on a very different case:

> My dear Breckinridge:
>
> Re #251: I have read your opinion and, as usual, am salivating at the array of luscious plums you have set before us. Who, after reading this splendid essay, could ever again complain that antitrust law is dull?
>
> We are very close in our reasoning. So that you may have the full flavor of my views—reflecting, as they do, a lifetime's study of giant corporations and the law's never quite successful efforts to civilize them—I have attached a brief memorandum. In the face of your legal and literary masterpiece, I hesitate to ask you to peruse my stumbling sentences. I am, however, emboldened by the respect that we have for each other and the profound concern we share for the proper development of the law.

Well, my dear chap, I believe you now can comprehend not inadequately what I have been saying and in that general context can appreciate my criticism of Walsh in this instance. He carried on a veritable campaign within the Court, parading from door to door like a Fuller Brush man. I needn't tell you how his conduct offended my scrupulosities. There is no denying that his efforts paid off, but that is not the real measure of rightness nor even of greatness, is it? Be that as it may, Walsh garnered four other votes for his view. In the end, that silly goose Putnam came over to Walsh's side, leaving Jacobson to fume alone in dissent.

It was not a pleasing performance. For the Court—I do not deny he spoke for the Court, for he *had* won over his five votes—Walsh leaped at the throat of the constitutional problem, just as he had at conference. I think you can now better understand what I meant when I said that he was not one of our big judges. *Hubris,* sheer *hubris.* His view of the Court's function in our system was overly grandiose, and his opinion of his own intellect exceeded arrogance.

I was concerned, even during his first term on the Court when new justices are supposed to experience what scholars have christened "the freshman syndrome." That is, during their first year or so on the Court, most justices feel their way around the parameters of the institution, writing for the Court mostly on relatively trivial issues, joining, on the more important questions, several different sides of the doctrinal debate among the brethren, groping for some purchase on their new role. Not Walsh. If I may resort to a vulgar athletic analogy, he came out of his corner like a prizefighter who knows he must win in the first round or not at all.

There was no doubt, none whatsoever, about where he stood on the substance of any issue. The poor, the downtrodden, these people formed, so to speak—and the analogy is not misplaced—his special constituency. He voted not only to extend the requirement that states provide free counsel to indigents accused of *any* crime that carried the possibility of a jail term, but also to compel states to waive filing fees for poor people seeking divorces, and for the federal government to waive similar fees for those poor people trying to persuade a court to declare them bankrupt. He was the perpetual friend of those on welfare, voting to strike down state residency requirements for eligibility for medical care, unemployment compensation, or aid to dependent children.

"The poor, the sick, the downtrodden," he wrote in one opinion, "are entitled to rights under the Constitution no less than are the healthy and the wealthy." I realize that sentence hardly touches the profound, but it was widely quoted. It was, as I recall, the caption that *Time* used when it featured his picture on its cover. *Newsweek* preferred his remark, "The dignity of man rests at the core of the galaxy of American constitutional values. Its spirit suffuses every clause. Government's duty to protect and cherish that dignity is the moral and political motive force of the whole constitutional system."

I don't disparage those sentiments, not at all. Representing as they do the values of a lifetime's work in the service of justice, I had adopted them as my own long before Walsh knew the difference between an injunction and a mandamus. The true milk in the coconut is that such sentiments, noble as they may be, have no rightful place in the pronouncements of our Court. I shall not repeat my judicial philosophy, the philosophy of all our big judges. Let me only say that we are not preachers of morality or political wisdom. We are judges, not legislators, not executives, not even ministers of the gospel, unless it be the gospel of self-restraint.

For Walsh, on the other hand, the Court was not the country's highest legal tribunal but a super legal aid bureau. It was even more—or less, depending on your legal theology. To him it was a pulpit which he mounted to preach what he considered to be social justice, natural rights, and limitations on governmental control over the individual.

I suspect—suspect, mind you, for scattered dicta do not a jurisprudence make—I suspect that he was moving toward a doctrine of positive governmental responsibility. Now that doctrine has largely been triumphant in the White House and Congress since Franklin Roosevelt and the New Deal. As a follower of FDR I supported that doctrine. At the polls I always voted for it. But in the Constitution as seen by our Court—at its best, at least—there are many ideological mansions. We allowed, after some struggle by the troglodytes, that the Constitution could fit FDR's New Deal. But, we never ruled that the Constitution *required* positive governmental responsibility for social and economic problems.

That, it seemed to me, was the direction in which Walsh was moving—a constitutional duty laid on government not merely to refrain from violating the rights specifically enumerated in the Constitution as well as what he dubbed their "penumbras"—a veritable armada of lesser rights that he deduced from the specific rights taken individually and collectively. Even further, he was implying that agencies of government had a duty, a duty that was judicially enforceable, to take positive action to foster that welter of rights. It was a dangerous course, very dangerous, for the country as well as the Court, presuming as it does that its author has a near monopoly on political wisdom as well as a surfeit of integrity.

And always, he patrolled the halls of our Court seeking a majority, even unanimity, for his views. At conference, debating him was a bit like arguing with a Jesuit. He always gave the impression of listening closely, of having an open mind. He was never ill-tempered personally, or offensive like Jacobson; he was never adamant like Campbell, never a speechifying orator like the senator. Moreover, he soon became a storehouse of knowledge about our Court, not that history was ever more than another arrow in his quiver of arguments. As a worker, he was indefatigable. Indeed, some of the brethren called him a workaholic. He was at his desk at home or in the Court by seven, and when he left at six or later in the Court's limousine, there were typically papers bulging from his briefcase.

One must give him credit. He was always well prepared, extraordinarily well prepared. In fact, he was normally far better prepared than any of us. Albert's encyclopedic mind and power of total recall gave him certain natural advantages, but Walsh could hold his own even there. He tossed his learning out—and I use the verb "tossed out" after thoughtful deliberation, for that is precisely what he did—in an offhanded manner, often mockingly, as if it were a piece of trivia that one should not take overly seriously.

Beneath those layers of study there was also a sharp sense of logic, and even further down, a firmly held set of principles. Those principles, however, were the wrong ones for a judge. Still, one must give the devil his due; he was true to his notion of the Court as a last refuge of justice for those whom our society had mistreated. Admirable in its way, to be sure, but so sadly mistaken—and so very dangerous to read into the permanence of constitutional law the passing policies, or agonies, of the day.

That sense of logic, dauntless pursuit of information, and a knowledge of the Court's history (not theoretically sound, to be sure, but factually full) were disciplined by his energy and self-control, and—surprisingly for a former military person—guided by a concern and talent for clear literary exposition. He spent not hours but days on each opinion, putting a satiny gloss on the phrases, arranging the words so that their meaning was clear. I would not judge his opinions as generally eloquent. They certainly were not always elegant in the literary sense. Yet they were clear and precise. Indeed, in places they sparkled.

That concern for clarity and his acute sense of logic caused the one rough spot in his relations with the other justices. As a critic of the writings of the brethren, he was without peer. Even brother Albert was less acute, for he felt it beyond his jurisdiction to suggest literary changes, restricting himself to matters of substance. Walsh, on the other hand, savagely attacked every slip opinion, whether he was with the majority or the minority, as if he were once again waging war against the Communist hordes. Often, especially with the productions of brothers Jacobson and Kelley, he would write as much as they did, substituting words, restructuring sentences, rearranging paragraphs, adding or subtracting citations. He was the professor displaying to first-year law students that they were guilty of nothing less than rape of the English language.

That he typically managed to intersperse his comments with good humor did little to soothe chaffed egos. Indeed, as I shall explicate later, I do not think he intended his wit to soothe. Here, he made no effort to conceal the arrogance that was implicit in his view of the function of our Court. What he was demonstrating to the brethren, so they felt—and not without reason, not without reason—was his fundamental intellectual superiority.

To some extent, perhaps to a great extent, they should have been grateful. More than once, the passages in their opinions quoted with approbation by legal and even popular commentators were sentences that Walsh had fashioned out of the clay of their drafts. Generally, he was, as he should have been, respectful of my literary endeavors, though I must confess that on occasion he took unwarranted liberties with what I had written.

That particular relationship was congruent with our more general association. He and I remained on rather close terms. Naturally, he felt more affection for me than I for him. I judged him to be educable, though wrongheaded. In retrospect, I probably overestimated him in the former respect. But still, he was a fascinating creature—quick, clever, doggedly hardworking, ruthless, and not without wit.

He was, to be sure, a hero to the do-gooders, but I always sensed that he took their worship with a grain of cynicism. They were softheaded; he was hard. They ached for the poor out of sympathy not unmixed with guilt. He responded to the cases from principle. I don't think he had a modicum of sympathy for any oppressed individual in this world—for the oppressed *of* the world, yes, yes indeed, but not for any particular human who happened to be suffering.

In my judgment—and a lifetime of study of men of the law allows me to speak not without some authority here—Walsh responded to social injustice not as a warmhearted liberal but as a tough-minded, very self-centered, self-oriented man. He rationalized to himself that it was the Constitution that spoke through his mouth. In another age, he would have made a splendid oracle at Delphi. It is, to be sure, a typical symptom of the activist judge, typical. God—if He exists—knows I have seen enough of it in my time. But I do not want to move ahead of my story. I shall later return to the labyrinthian ways of Walsh's psyche. Let me provide more narrative before opening the inner doors to you.

EIGHT

WALSH'S FIRST FEW YEARS as chief justice slipped rapidly by. It is amazing, simply amazing, how one's life accelerates with age. As a lad, I can recall an hour being an eternity; as a middle-aged man, my years became minutes.

One moment we're young and ambitiously striving and the next moment we're cold, old men whose bones are warmed only by the memories of those marvelous milliseconds between infancy and senility. Well, enough self-pity. The alternative to growing old is to die young. In all, I think fate bestowed on me the more interesting option. Let us return to the narrative.

Rather quickly Walsh became an efficient administrator. No, I have misstated that. Walsh was born an efficient administrator. Such people are not made. A lifetime of experience in, as well as study of organizations large and small has convinced me that an ability to administer is genetic. Walsh had an orderly disposition. Mind you, I did not say neat. Indeed, his office was often a shambles; when they took tea with me, his clerks not infrequently complained that *they* did not understand what they were doing. The point they failed to grasp was that *he* understood, and they were working for *him,* as much as it pleases youngsters to believe that the world, especially its senior citizens, work for them. The papers and the people that were often strewn around his life were parts of a gigantic jigsaw puzzle that dovetailed only in his mind.

As a result of Walsh's efforts and despite the complaints of his own staff, there was a minimum amount of confusion about the Court's work in other offices, a condition that enabled the rest of us to concentrate on substantive issues. We realized that this situation obtained in part because of the efficiency of Elena Falconi, the old chief's lovely administrative assistant whom Walsh had inherited. (I believe I mentioned her to you earlier—a truly lovely and, I must say it, efficient woman.) Our lives were made easier not only by Elena's skill but also by Walsh's willingness—eagerness may be more accurate—to work harder than the rest of us. I deem it fair to say, quite fair, that we all appreciated his efforts, even brother Jacobson, although he to a lesser extent than the civilized brethren.

One of the things that would have most fascinated a psychiatrist about Walsh—next to what I diagnosed as tremendous anger kept within bounds by an astounding, simply astounding self-control, but I'll tell you more of those things later—one of the things that would have most fascinated a psychiatrist was his tolerance of chaos and ambiguity. Some people, brother Campbell with his literalism, for example, need simplicity and neatness; they squeeze the universe into a parsimonious but misshapen mold. On the other hand, some people—and Walsh surely ranked high among them—willingly, perhaps even joyfully, accept the inherent messiness of the real world. That there were no simple solutions and few "correct" answers was not a problem for him because it never occurred to him that such were possible, much less desirable. That absence did nothing, nothing whatsoever, to diminish the fervor with which he worked to achieve his goals.

More particularly, he reveled in what to many of us on the Court is the greatest difficulty we face: securing agreement among enough of the brethren to produce a judicial opinion that is both jurisprudentially principled and practical in application. Articulating a principled explanation of why we prefer one decision to another is seldom easy. To grasp fully all the ingredients in the omelet you must couple that task with the mind-boggling difficulties of persuading one's always strong-willed and often wrongheaded brethren to accept some sort of mutual accommodation of their conflicting views while maintaining thematic unity and a modicum of intellectual integrity in our collective reasoning. Simultaneously achieving those ends requires the combined skills of a professional tightrope walker with those of a superb juggler and a gifted chef.

While, for the reasons I have heretofore explained, I do not count Walsh among our big judges, I have seen no one, no one at all, who could more efficiently sort out, accommodate, and integrate conflicting views. "I seek consensus much as Captain Ahab sought the white whale," was what he once remarked—in a sardonic tone, let me hasten to add. For him accommodation was not a search for the lowest common denominator but an opportunity for creative planting of his own policy goals in a form acceptable to a majority of the Court. Invariably, his consensus was an extrapolation from, not merely a distillation of, what had been said in conference and afterwards in memoranda and conversations. And equally invariably that extrapolation, one would later discover often to his sorrow, had been clandestinely but effectively impregnated with Walsh's values.

Had one not known the truth, one might have guessed that before coming to the Court he had been the permanent and cunning secretary of a Quaker meeting rather than a military man. Perhaps it was his experience as a dean—a post of responsibility without power—that honed his talents; or again, perhaps like administrative orderliness, such skills are innate rather than acquired. There is yet another explanation, one that I prefer. During two wars Walsh had led by *commanding*. He was now setting before himself a new challenge: to lead by persuading. In fine, he may have been playing a game, as much with himself as with us. I often, quite often, felt that to be the case. In any event, to an extraordinary degree, truly extraordinary, Walsh possessed the necessary talents; if he was playing a game, he played it artfully and with pleasure.

By no means am I implying any lessening of my criticism of his substantive views, nor do I recant my critique of the intensity with which he sought to convert others to his causes. One can admire his professional skills while lamenting both his grandiose conception of the function of our Court and his overly ambitious image of his own role. What I wish to stress is that he was adroit, ruthlessly adroit if you will, in navigating through the labyrinthian intellectual channels of his colleagues' minds. And he was also a marvelously self-controlled negotiator. One could sense an inner churning, but he always forebore to return in kind Jacobson's studied ugliness; he listened patiently to the senator's orations; he was generously chivalrous in coping with Putnam's vapid meanderings.

To be sure, his ability to enjoy easy relations with us all, even Jacobson, was of central significance to his success. But amiability, even if coupled with zeal, provides no magic key. Brother Putnam's dismal record stands as a shining testament to the necessity of a first-class mind to effectiveness on our tribunal.

All of which causes me to reiterate that I cannot for the life of me yet, even yet, comprehend how Walsh could have shared Jacobson's and Kelley's interests in that violent game for gladiators, professional football, and at the same time have enjoyed, as I am certain he did, the more literary and philosophic conversations in which Albert and I gamboled. Walsh would even spend an occasional Sunday afternoon with Jacobson and Kelley at the stadium—I inferred from the innuendoes of his lady that it was one of his few diversions from the work of our Court—to watch the local team, the Indians or some such equally silly appellation. In all, however, he carried his own learning easily; it was no small amount of intellectual luggage. Indeed, he tended to conceal it beneath an insatiable, almost childlike, curiosity. That last was a winning trait, one that caused us to forgive, even if we could not overlook, the hot core of ruthless ambition that fired all his activities.

Well, I believe you comprehend not inadequately what I am saying. We often negotiate, and Walsh was quite adept—no, *very* adept—at it, though, as I have noted, sometimes a trifle too strong or flattering for my austere tastes. My colleagues, however, sometimes exacted a high price in doctrinal purity, since none of them totally shared his vision. Strictly *entre nous,* my dear chap, strictly *entre nous,* it was not a bad thing, for, as I have already explained, he did not understand the proper function of our tribunal. The rest of us put a brake on him. He often gathered four or five or even six more votes for the results that he wanted, but he had far greater difficulty in massing the Court behind early drafts of his opinions. Each of the others would insist on important jurisprudential changes. Indeed, I recall his once complaining—I do hope you will forgive the vulgarity, but one must be willing to sacrifice taste for accuracy in these matters—"The brethren delight in cutting at least one of the balls off my opinions." It was, to be sure, a vulgarism, but it was not inapt as a metaphor.

The compromises that he ably effected did not always enamor him to those Simple Simons who populate the ivory towers of academe. They pursue doctrinal chastity as if it were the Holy Grail. Those learned professors, who have never grubbed about herding a gaggle of judges behind a single opinion, would prefer a clear defeat and a dissent uncontaminated by compromise to a partial victory. I cannot help but wonder how long those creatures would maintain their doctrinal pudicity on a collegial tribunal that had to decide—decide, not endlessly debate—real cases. Walsh, however wrongheaded, was also tough-minded. He accepted what the brethren would yield, every millimeter, and smiled at the wrath of the vestal virgins of the law schools.

On the other hand, liberal journalists, political activists, social workers, and bleeding hearts throughout the nation were much less finicky. They cared only for his votes; they could not bear to read opinions. He became and remained their darling, their absolute darling. I believe the editors of *Time* and *Newsweek* ran a special contest to determine who could write more vapidly laudatory stories about him.

At this point I must, absolutely must lest I be unfaithful to Clio, inject a note of tragedy. Walsh's zeal for our work was not without negative repercussions in his marriage. I believe that earlier I related to you, albeit elliptically, that when he was posted to the White House in 1951–52, he and his bride were in the midst of a quasi-idyllic state of freshly and frequently requited love. Kathryn's tongue could show an edge even then, but their marriage seemed mostly honey and harmony—not unmixed with a great deal of eroticism, one would suspect.

When they returned for Walsh to take the center chair, there were some obvious changes. None of us is impervious to the eroding friction of passing years. Yet initially one could still sense a closeness there, some abrasions, to be sure, but still a closeness that could be perceived, admired, and even envied. And, in a city that dotes on the real and fictitious amatory adventures of the great and near great, not even a hint of Walsh as a philanderer reached my ears. His friend, that Keller creature, yes, to be sure. But that had become such a salacious commonplace that only the worst wags noticed, and then only when their supply of interesting gossip had been exhausted.

Still, there was evidence of marital problems. I recall a winter evening at the Alberts' house during Walsh's first year on the Court. It was late. We had enjoyed an adequate performance at the opera, dined well if lightly afterward, and were in that brief but mellow state between satisfaction and fatigue. Elizabeth had been reminiscing about another opera, enjoyed some thirty-five years earlier when she had first met Albert. He had then been a young diplomat seconded to the ambassador in Paris. She and her father, a wealthy industrialist who contributed heavily to the Democratic party, had been vacationing there when the old gentleman had been suddenly summoned to a conference in Germany. Rather than leave Elizabeth to amuse herself among the decadent French, he had telephoned the ambassador and had him nominate an aide to escort his daughter to the opera. That aide turned out to be Albert, of course.

It was, I suppose, a romantic tale, though of a genre

that generally does not engage my interest. But dear Elizabeth, always sensitive to the presence and needs of others, inquired of Kathryn how she had met Walsh. You are well aware of my aversion to learning the intimate details of the lives of others; but feeling it my duty to the Court to know, I overcame my reluctance and listened.

"It was in Chicago, at the university bookstore," Kathryn informed us. "I was a freshman law student ready to start my first quarter. I was standing in a long line to pay for a couple of those fat and expensive casebooks, when I began talking to a handsome young man"—I have heard other women speak of Walsh as handsome, but why, I could never fathom. To me he always seemed very ordinary in appearance. But what mere mortal can account for female tastes?—"who was waiting behind me. After we paid, he bought me a Coke. We were very simple in those days: a boy, a girl, a couple of law books, and a Coca-Cola and you had all the ingredients for a love story. After that he walked me over to my first class at the law school—it was on the north side of the Midway then, on the main campus.

"It was just the right season for a crush," she went on. "I was alone in a new city and at a frighteningly intellectual university. At Radcliffe and Harvard, people played at being intellectual," Kathryn noted in her usual tactful manner, totally unconcerned that Albert and I were alumni of Harvard. Incidentally, that, as I recall, was the first time I realized she had been exposed to such a splendid undergraduate education. "But at Chicago they really were intellectuals. It gave me a scare. Then suddenly I met a sweet young man who oozed sex appeal. I thought he would have held my hand, if either of us had had fewer books, and I was sure he was going to ask me out. I went from fright to bliss."

"I thought you were cute, too," Walsh interjected facetiously.

"I'll bet you did," she said as she ran her hand through his hair. (He was sitting on the floor by her chair in front of the fire, a pose that I found beneath the dignity of the Chief Justice of the United States, but in a small, intimate group it was something he often did, as did that Keller creature. Perhaps it reflected some strange military malady they contracted in the Orient.)

"Do you know what this evil genius did to me?" she

asked the rest of us. I assumed the query was rhetorical and made no reply. "He knew I thought he was another student. He even told me he was going to the same course as I was, the first meeting of Legal Process. Then he let me prattle on about all I'd heard from second-year students about the horrible ogre who taught the course. I tried to share my fear by telling him about the blood-thirsty marine war hero who looked on students as leftover Japanese to be flushed out of law school as quickly and painfully as possible."

"Even then I knew that overpopulation was a coming crisis," Walsh chuckled.

"Shut up," she said mockingly. "When he left me and walked up to the podium and began to explain what the course was all about, I panicked and ran out of the room."

"But you came back for the next session," Walsh noted.

"I had to, the damned course was required. But I huddled in the back with the three other girls in the freshman class. They thought you were cute, poor innocent babes. I knew you were a sadist and I told them they'd better be careful or Bluebeard up there was going to eat them alive. They learned," she was looking at us, "as soon as he called on them for his special torture session. 'Miss Torgerson,' he'd say, 'please brief *West Virginia v. Barnette* for us.' It was like having to face the Spanish Inquisition and the Star Chamber at once, with all the irons heating there on the fire in front of you. If it hadn't been for Mike Keller—he was a third-year student then—I'd have never made it through the course. He taught me a lot of the big woolly bear's tricks."

"Mike was always anxious to teach young girls tricks," Walsh observed.

"That's true," Kathryn agreed. "For a while it was like being helped by an octopus who lived on a steady diet of Spanish fly. But he calmed down after I told him that I was dating the good professor on the sly."

"It was a bald-faced lie," Walsh said.

"Of course, but it worked. It was like invoking the incest tabu. When I got an A minus in the course, and the next summer when the monster himself asked me to be his research assistant, poor Mike was sure I had been telling the truth. To be honest, I was surprised at both the grade and the invitation."

"You had impressive talents."

At that Kathryn gave a ribald laugh that we all, I confess myself included, joined in. She was never the least unaware of her physical allure.

"Seriously," she went on, "it wasn't until the next spring that I think St. Declan here finally began to realize that girls were different from boys and that I was a girl."

"I knew you were a girl and I had a fair idea what the difference was. It just hadn't occurred to me that girl students could also be women. Remember, I was turning thirty, and thus staring old age directly in the face."

"I was twenty-three. That's too old to be a girl, but you would never have learned that from that skinny sociology instructor you were dating."

"I admired her mind."

"You must have; there wasn't anything else there, unless you've got a thing for broomsticks. But mind doesn't have a chance against matter," Kathryn confided to the rest of us. "After a few months as his assistant, I decided that I'd been in love with him since we met in the bookstore and he'd been in love with me, too, only he didn't know it. I was going to help him find out. And that was not an easy job. We shared a lot of interests and got along well; from the way he looked at me, I could tell that he had a few impure thoughts. But he never so much as made the beginning of a pass at me. Those inhibited Irish think sex is the greatest possible sin." Ostensibly she was being playful, but one could not help but feel a tingling sexual vibrancy in the air.

"You were a young student. I thought I might have been taking advantage of our relationship."

"Relationship? We didn't have one until May, when you took off that weekend to a friend's house on Lake Michigan."

"I needed to be alone," Walsh explained, not altogether willingly, "to think over what was happening. I thought I was falling in love; it was a new emotion for me, especially in that context. I'd never even been tempted before to get involved with one of my own students. It's hard to feel romantic about someone you've just heard butcher the briefing of a simple case."

"Thanks a lot," Kathryn snorted.

"Well, you had me confused, alternately 'coming on'

and 'turning off.' I had to walk the beach and think things out all by myself," Walsh protested.

His lady laughed, not in the same ribald tone as before but still a sound musky with sexual aura. "Loneliness is what you didn't get, and I don't know how you could have found a minute to think. I found out where he was going," she explained to us, "borrowed Mike Keller's car, and drove up behind him. I believe he honestly thought I was carrying books for him in my overnight case." She tussled his hair again. "I thought I was going to have to rape him to make him understand my message."

"You make sport of my innocence," he said in mock ruefulness. "I couldn't help it if the Church and the corps had made me pure. That's why my strength was the strength of ten."

She laughed again. "That was about the right number. And when he got his strength back a few days later there was nothing his puritanical Irish conscience would let him do but make an honest woman out of me. I wonder," she mused, "how it would have turned out if all that had happened two weeks later, when some of the other cottages had been open. I can see the *Trib*'s headlines: CHICAGO PROFESSOR ARRESTED FOR CAVORTING NUDE ON THE BEACH WITH COED. Your tenure would have been zapped and there'd be no Court. Maybe," her voice suddenly became quite soft, "we'd just be two quiet people in a little midwestern town with a little college watching the world go by—living and loving together."

We laughed a bit at the newspaper fantasy. I suspect the others were turning over in their minds the salacious image of Kathryn's nude, Junoesque body throbbing in passionate entwinings. It would have been a heady thought indeed, one, of course, in which I would never indulge.

I glanced at Walsh. He had now left us. He was staring into the fire as if he were alone. Whether he was embarrassed at this rupture in his usual wall of privacy or was retracing certain critical junctures of his life I do not know. But it was plain that he was no longer with us. It was a trait, I must say, that I had seen before and would see again and again. He could abstract himself from a conversation for some few minutes and retreat into a private nether world. Usually when he returned it was with a plan or idea, but that night the trancelike state lasted for at least ten minutes, and he returned in silence, not exuberance. By then, the conversation had switched to less bawdy topics, and it was almost time for me to make my excuses for the evening. I would have never imagined our hyperzealous chief vulnerable to concupiscence or to any sin except overambition.

What I did not then realize—and I confess I should have but one cannot always be astute—was that Kathryn's concluding statement was far more revealing about her own current state than the rest of the story was about Walsh. She was, I have since realized, trying to call him back to her in a way that he could not ignore. Alas, she was fighting his ambition, and few women have ever won a battle against a man's vision of himself. For Walsh to perform the tasks of the chief justiceship according to his standards—that is, more effectively than they had ever before been performed—required many sacrifices. Kathryn was one of them. Do not misunderstand me, please. Walsh was not a cruel man—ruthless, certainly, and sometimes not overly considerate of the sensibilities of others, but not cruel. I do not think he consciously sacrificed her, though, in effect, that is precisely what he did. Consciously, it is my diagnosis, he accepted the risk that she and their marriage would not survive his neglect.

Closer, more detached examination at the time would have indicated just how perilous the risk was. As you know, they had no children. Apparently Kathryn had several times become pregnant—given his religion and her figure one would expect such a result, and frequently—but on all except one occasion she had early on suffered miscarriages or whatever is the proper medical terminology. The one child she carried to term lived only a few weeks. It had a congenital heart defect of some sort, and cardiac surgery was not in the 1950s as developed a science as it now is.

That was an unfortunate state of affairs, especially so when coupled with the fact that Kathryn had not completed her law degree. Thus she was alone without either children or a profession at an age when her wedded contemporaries were marrying off sons and daughters and expecting grandchildren. (Women really seem to enjoy infants though for the life of me I cannot equate joy with a squawking alimentary canal. Were I a legislator, I would not be untempted to classify infanticide as only a minor misdemeanor.) And, of course, Kathryn's female friends who were professionals were experiencing successes in their careers. She, for her part, had only Walsh, or what little was left of him after the certs and the brethren had eaten away at him for fourteen hours a day.

Furthermore, Kathryn's main outlet in Michigan, involvement in practical and very partisan politics, was now tabu. At Ann Arbor she apparently had been able to give her political genes free rein. She chaired the local branch of the Democratic party and was an assemblywoman or whatever it is they call state legislators in the hinterlands. In sum, she had a hand in a dozen liberal political causes—a fact that must have nourished her husband's late-blooming ambitions in that area.

As you have by now undoubtedly inferred, I was not especially fond of the lady; yet I was not unfeeling about her plight. A lifetime of experience has convinced me that the weaker sex never construes any sort of neglect as benign, and Walsh's prodigious energies were manifestly monopolized by the Court and the world. What, simply what, does a woman do under such circumstances? Honorary committee memberships was one possibility, a real possibility. Every charity in town wanted the wife of a justice on its letterhead and Mrs. Chief Justice was a gorgeous plum they all sought. To her credit, she wanted no part of that sort of thing.

The other alternatives are equally obvious: other men and/or drink. She chose, as far as I know—and to be sure, my disdain for gossip restricted the ambit of my knowledge—only drink. I am confident in my own mind that Kathryn genuinely and deeply, very deeply, loved Walsh. Some of the old hero worship never wore off. One could see it in her eyes. And she was bright enough and informed enough about the law to recognize that his was a major talent. But for most of us, loving a legend provides less than adequate fulfillment for lonely days and nights.

Her choice, I believe, came slowly, no doubt imperceptibly to her. My first intimation of the problem came when, a year or so after our conversation at the Alberts', I could not help overhearing a distressing exchange between the Walshes just before a dinner party at their apartment on the southwest side. You know, of course, that area of glass, high-rise buildings erected after urban renewal had cleared away the dilapidated housing and forced the local blacks to seek other slums.

I had arrived a bit early, which is to say that I was precisely on time, promptness being not the least of my virtues. I was sitting in the living room, enjoying the Potomac's panorama and trying by sheer mental effort to blot out the words coming from the dining room. Well, Walsh was suggesting, rather sharply, to his wife that she forego another drink for a time. She snapped back at him, literally snapped: "Mrs. Chief Justice doesn't embarrass Mr. Chief Justice by drinking too much. Mrs. Chief Justice doesn't embarrass the Supreme Court by messing in politics. Mrs. Chief Justice doesn't complain when she only sees Mr. Chief Justice a few hours a week. Mrs. Chief Justice goes to lots of committee meetings. Most of all Mrs. Chief Justice smiles all the time."

I suspect she took the drink. I would have guessed so by her slightly slurred speech and the very precise movements of her hands that one who has just a bit too much to drink affects. Thereafter I saw other evidence of a general problem there. Not that I ever witnessed her badly inebriated, but on more than one occasion it was plain that she should have imbibed several ounces less of alcohol.

I am not an expert on such matters, but I am positive she became at least a borderline alcoholic. Needless to say, the poor creature was caught in a proverbial vicious circle. It has been my experience that, an occasional seduction aside, absence of sobriety makes females quite unattractive to males, thus increasing the loneliness of women who overindulge.

What more is there to say? Friends tried to help. I, to be sure, was not close enough to the lady to be of tangible assistance though I tried to keep my finger on the situation's pulse through dear Elizabeth, Albert's charming wife. She was truly fond of Kathryn and was most attentive and solicitous, as was brother Kelley's black bride. Even that Keller creature, so I heard, became involved. Whatever his defects as a hedonistic vulgarian—and they were legion, simply legion—he was loyal to Walsh and his lady.

For months, Elizabeth tried to persuade Kathryn to see a psychiatrist. It was, in my judgment, a suggestion more well intentioned than well aimed. It has been my experience that those people fail most miserably in dealing with alcoholics. Surely if they had any skill, our brother Svenson, who placed a small fortune in their pockets, would have been as sober as the eight other judges who sat with him. The only hope that I have seen in a lifetime of observing human weaknesses is to get such people to Alcoholics Anonymous. Their mystic treatment defies rational analysis, but it is effective. We did not succeed with Kathryn. She remained a cross for Walsh to carry. And he carried it in silence. He never spoke to me about it, nor, to my knowledge, to anyone else among the justices.

NINE

EARLIER I MENTIONED to you that Walsh quickly became the darling of the liberal press and social reformers. I also noted that he had the approval, though not without carping criticism of most of those liberal pundits who second-guess us from the safe halls of academe. On the whole, these admiring expressions were not transient emotions. Indeed, this affection ran sufficiently deep to survive even the trauma of his dissent in the abortion cases. Why, my dear chap, why is it liberal to allow a woman to kill her fetus? I can tell you candidly, quite candidly, that I do not like children. Indeed, I abhor the little savages, especially in a world already overpopulated by adult savages. If a woman wants to dispose of her offspring prenatally, I would, as a matter of personal values, be happy to have her do it. But I would hardly be so intellectually dishonest to claim that I was following the tenets of liberalism, unless the word connotes selfishness.

Well, as I was about to say, the liberal elements ascribed Walsh's dissent to his Roman Catholicism. They were quite cognizant of that flaw in his character; as you must be well aware, anti-Catholicism remains the anti-Semitism of the intellectual—not that intellectuals any more than liberals generally will not forgive that religious failing if a judge usually votes their way. How religion accounted for my joining Walsh's dissent, they blithely and totally ignored.

You probably know the background of those cases. Unmarried but pregnant women—one would think that in this day and age people who intend to copulate would have the good sense to stop off at a pharmacy on the way to their trysting place—filed class actions in federal district courts challenging as a violation of a woman's right to privacy laws in Georgia and Texas that permitted abortions only to save the mother's life. (Georgia's statute was more complex, but my summary is not inaccurate.) Before proceeding, however, let me explain one technical point. A class action is a suit begun by one or more persons not only on their own behalf but also on behalf of all other persons similarly situated. Thus the suit does not become moot—dead—if the original plaintiff no longer has a case (in this instance has a baby or obtains an abortion elsewhere).

Well, the lower federal courts sustained those statutes in part and declared them unconstitutional in part. Both sides sought review by us and we—improvidently, to say the very least—granted their requests. The cases threatened to turn the Court into a veritable multiring circus. Several of those awful, screeching women's groups tried to file briefs as *amici curiae*—friends of the Court—as did various medical associations, the American Civil Liberties Union, the American Jewish Congress, the American Legion, the National Conference of Catholic Bishops, two right-to-life organizations, and about a dozen state attorneys general.

As a judge, I, of course, put all these emotional arguments to one side. I visualized the basic issue as pivoting on an exquisite legal conundrum: a clash between, on the one hand, a woman's supposed constitutional right to control her own body and thus to expel the fetus and, on the other hand, the fetus's supposed right to life. Complicating the conflict was the question of the dimension of the authority of the state to intervene to protect the one or the other, or perhaps to some degree both. If one *assumes* —mind you, I stress assumes—that the fetus is neither a human being nor a "person" protected by those clauses of the Fifth and Fourteenth Amendments that forbid the state and federal governments to take a person's life without due process of law, the answer flows easily and obviously.

But, and there is always a but, if one *assumes* that at some early stage in its development the fetus is either a human being or a person in the legal sense, then to kill it at or after that stage is to commit murder. For the state or federal government to cooperate under such circumstances could well constitute a denial of life without due process of law; for government to stand idly by while others take the fetus's life would surely raise grave questions of equal protection.

Alas, my dear chap, medical science offers us scant evidence on which to ground either assumption about a fetus's legal status. We know that life begins almost immediately upon conception, but what kind of life? Who knows when a zygote, embryo, or fetus—or whatever—becomes a human being? I do not delude myself that I know the answer; I envy those on both sides of the question who claim that they do. As is typical when knowledge is lacking, partisans fill the void with acrimony and rhetoric. Each time I listen to the proponents of abortion, I am tempted to enroll in a right-to-life organization. Each time I hear the right-to-life people speak, I conclude that abortion on demand must be a very sensible course.

I needn't tell you about the low level of oral argument we were forced to endure, and I certainly shan't bore you with the actual words. History as well as charity are better served if those arguments are lost to memory. There is a line, a sharp line, between advocacy and intellectual prostitution; unhappily, those who argue before us tend but dimly to perceive the distinction. At conference, discussion was somewhat more elevated, although largely irrelevant to the central issue before us as judges, which as you will see, had little to do with the merits or demerits of abortion.

"Because these cases come to us on stipulated facts," Walsh opened our debate, "we need only look at the basic question itself. Abortion raises moral arguments that engulf, even threaten to overwhelm, the underlying constitutional issues. I have never heard anyone discuss the problem without moral fervor. I doubt if we shall break that record today. I've had to think longer and harder about these cases than any others that I've faced in my four years here, except perhaps the capital punishment cases that are scheduled for argument in a few weeks. Part of my difficulty arises from the clear teaching of my Church that abortion is morally wrong. The issues before us, of course, are constitutional, not moral, but it sometimes takes superhuman effort to separate the two. I have tried and am continuing to try to mark that separation.

"In all candor," Walsh continued, "I must admit to another force that may be influencing me. I grew up in Mussolini's Italy and as a teenager several times visited Hitler's Germany. My German was fluent then, and I can still remember arguments about Jews not being human beings, arguments about the necessity of sacrificing 'life-unworthy life' for the good of society, the purity of the race, and so forth. Those memories aren't pleasant."

"Chief, is that a fair analogy?" brother Kelley asked.

"Of course it isn't fair to equate the motives or the morals of those who favor abortion with the mentality of the Nazis," Walsh replied. "And I do not mean to do so. I only mention this business to lay all my cards on the table.

"Now that confession is done," Walsh mocked himself, "we can attack the issues. Is the fetus a living being? That much is clear. Is it a separate being from the mother? That, too, is clear. It has its own unique genetic code. And it is alive and can react to stimuli, including pain, and in a properly hospitable environment can and has survived outside the mother's womb. But is it a human life? I wish I knew, but I don't. It is potentially human; that much is also obvious. But I don't know when it becomes human and I don't claim to know. Because I do not know, I feel I must—constitutionally must, not morally must, unless one looks on our oath of office as merely imposing moral obligations—come down on the side of life.

"As you know," Walsh added rather whimsically, "I go further than many of you on questions of civil liberties. I firmly believe that government—state and federal and local—has a duty to protect certain rights, not merely not to *injure* those rights but an obligation *positively* to protect them. And I believe that the whole spirit of the Constitution cries out for the protection of the dignity of human life as its highest value. Until someone proves beyond a reasonable doubt that the fetus is not a human being, however imperfectly formed, I do not believe that we can say, as a matter of constitutional law, that a state may not protect that life. If we were confronting a statute that forbade abortion even where the fetus presented a real threat to the life of the mother, we would have an entirely different problem. The statutes before us, however, allow abortion to save a mother's life."

"Chief," brother Albert asked, "are you arguing for a hands-off attitude for this Court?"

"In these cases, I am," Walsh replied. "I am largely presenting only one side of the moral argument, but I realize that there is something to be said on both sides—medically, morally, legally, practically, and politically. Under those circumstances, I am not prepared to overturn the states' judgment that the life of the fetus should be preferred over any discomfort the mother may suffer, short of a threat of very grave injury or death." Walsh then nodded to me.

"I believe," I said, "that in his closing words the chief has starkly posed the central issue and articulated the proper solution. Let me echo some of his accents. As so often happens, we face a clash of rights, not of wrongs. As always we must, absolutely must, bear in mind that we are not the primary resolvers of that clash. Were I a legislator, I would need to ponder long and hard to vote for the mother or for the fetus. For that very reason, I cannot, cannot as a matter of constitutional interpretation, say that the legislatures of Georgia and Texas here acted unreasonably. They have tried to strike a balance between the rights of the mother to privacy and the rights of the fetus, if any, to life. That they did not strike that balance at the exact point where I might have is immaterial. They did strike it at a point that I cannot, in constitutional conscience, say is unreasonable; and because I cannot say it is unreasonable, I cannot say it is unconstitutional.

"That is all that need be said about the constitutional issue," I continued. "But, if I may hold the floor a moment longer, a lifetime of study of the history of this Court compels me to add more about the specifics of this issue. Like affirmative action, capital punishment, reapportionment, and many other issues that come before us, abortion is politically explosive. I do not take pleasure in speaking in cataclysmic terms, but I beg of you to consider the inherent weakness of this Court in our governmental system. We lack purse as well as sword. Let us not become enmeshed in this political thicket, where we as an institution could be torn apart by thorns and brambles.

"As judges," I reminded them, "we draw our peculiar

strength from our aloofness from the partisan issues that divide our people. Our function is to unify, not to fracture, to set limits and define boundaries within which the political processes can operate, not to ordain specific solutions to vexatious, divisive, and perhaps insoluble problems of public policy. Here we should preserve our position above the fray by leaving specific solutions to this problem where they properly belong: to the elected representatives of the people. If those representatives stray beyond the bounds of reasonable constitutional interpretation, then, but only then, should we hurl our constitutional thunderbolts.

"The solutions offered by the legislatures of Georgia and Texas," I concluded, "may not be the wisest possible; certainly no intelligent person would expect wisdom from either state." (I could not forego the opportunity to barb the barbarians.) "But those solutions are not unreasonable. If the people of either state wish different solutions within the bounds of constitutional reason, they may elect new legislators. I simply cannot find any specific clause of the Constitution, nor can I logically deduce from any relevant grouping of its clauses, nor can I infer from its general terms any language that forbids states from striking the sort of balance that Georgia and Texas have here sought to achieve."

"I," Jacobson again began with his polysyllabic personal pronoun, "hate to disagree with such respected jurists, but it seems to me that this is a pretty simple case. As I read the law—the common law—a fetus was not a person until it was born and born alive. Until then, its only rights were really the rights of its parents. It couldn't sue for injuries it suffered; its *parents* could sue for its injuries—but as injuries to them as parents, not to the fetus as a juridical person."

"Yet don't forget," Walsh put in, "that the statutory laws of a few states immediately before, at the time of, and for a century after adoption of the Fourteenth Amendment have treated abortion of a 'quickened' fetus as manslaughter. That indicates that at a relatively early stage the law has treated a fetus as a person, and we now know that the fetus quickens—begins to move—within a few weeks of conception, perhaps within days."

"Maybe, but you folks are always telling me that what's important is not what went on a century or two ago, but how the Constitution fits our modern society." (Touché. As much as it grieves me, deeply grieves me, to acknowledge that a creature like Jacobson was ever correct, for once in his overly extended and boorish lifetime he had thrown one of Walsh's dangerous principles back at him.) "So, as much as I hate to vote against those good ole boys down in Austin, I can't,"—actually, my dear chap, he said "cain't," but I shall not essay to mimic that coarsely grating accent—"Constitution-wise, see how a state has any authority to forbid a woman to control her own body. If she's married and the husband objects to an abortion, that may be something different, but if she's single, she and her doctor, providing he's licensed, are all you need. Just as long as she doesn't hurt the legal rights of any other person, she's free; that's what individualism means."

"Can she poison wild horses that belong to no one, or torture her own pets because they annoy her?" Walsh asked quietly. (Actually, it was a less foolish question than one might think. For all his uncouthness toward humans, Jacobson doted on animals. Have you ever noticed how often misanthropes love animals? I cannot abide four-footed creatures. I simply cannot abide them. Well, in his Washington apartment—I do not proffer firsthand witness because I can assure you I was never there—Jacobson kept two dogs, three cats, and a pair of Gila monsters; furthermore, he maintained a rather large ranch in Texas with a herd of horses.)

Jacobson threw back his head and laughed loudly. "Well, now, Chief, that's a different story. We all know that animals are worth a hell of a lot more than most people."

Walsh grinned rather amiably and nodded to brother Albert.

"As you would have guessed, brother Walker has adequately stated my views. If we were sitting as legislators, I would probably vote against the chief, but since we sit as judges, I must vote with him." Albert was a brick, a veritable brick.

"I agree with Jacobson," poor Putnam said. "Our whole system of government is one of individual rights. 'Freedom is the general rule, and restraint the exception.' *Adkins v. Children's Hospital,* 1923. That decision and that sentence sum up for me the heart of our constitutional adjudication. If a woman has a right to privacy, and we have held that she has, surely that right must extend to this most personal of spheres: her sexual relations and her decision to have or not to have a child. I respect the moral views of those who see a fetus as a person, perhaps a human person, but for me priority must go to the rights of the person we *know* to be a human being."

Next, the senator from Virginia treated us to a long oration on the right to privacy. He searched it out in the penumbras of freedom of speech, association, and religion, as well as in protections against self-incrimination, against quartering of troops in civilian homes, and against unreasonable searches and seizures. Then he traced the beast to its lair in the vague contours of the Ninth Amendment: "The enumeration in the Constitution, of certain rights, shall not be construed to deny or disparage others retained by the people."

It was a dreary speech, but, like Jacobson's remark about keeping the Constitution in tune with modern needs, it repaid Walsh for his use of similar arguments on other—too many other—occasions. Perhaps our chief now appreciated the wisdom as well as the propriety of my more austere and modest approach to constitutional interpretation. Be that as it may, Senator Breckinridge offered us another of his panegyrics on limiting governmental tyranny and liberating modern women from ancient social fetters. (He did not mention, to be sure, that he and his ancestors had hammered those fetters on white females as securely as they had shackled black slaves.) It was a pity that we lacked a gallery in our conference room; he would have been applauded to the sky. There, however, where reason is sovereign over rhetoric, we greeted his peroration in stony silence.

Svenson merely nodded agreement with the senator. I suspected that his head was troubling him too much to permit him to speak. I was grateful.

"I get nowhere with this talk of privacy," our literal brother Campbell began. (One should never, simply never, look a gift-vote in the mouth, but if it's Campbell's mouth, one should not have to listen either.) "I value my privacy as much as any man, but I see no protection for any such general right in the Constitution. The Constitution protects some aspects of privacy, yes. Brother Breckinridge listed those in his usual succinct fashion." (How droll, how very droll; on occasion Campbell displayed a preciously dry wit.) "But the right is limited to just such circumstances as are specified in the document and its amendments. Abortion was punishable as a crime when the Bill of Rights was adopted; even more specific and stringent laws punishing abortion were in force when the Fourteenth Amendment became part of the Constitution, eight decades later. No one seriously suggested at either time that the amendments restricted state authority, or within its limited jurisdiction federal authority, to regulate or even forbid abortion. It's clear that neither the Bill of Rights nor the Fourteenth Amendment had then or has now anything whatever to do with abortion. If these women's groups want to legalize abortions, they belong in the lobbies of legislatures, not at the bar of this Court."

Our black brother Kelley spoke last. His voice was soft. "Like the chief, I fight to keep my emotions out of this. I see poor families, I see families already burdened by too many children—the parents too uneducated to know about birth control, too poor to have decent food much less human housing, too poor to get an education for themselves or for their unwanted children. What does a woman living in stinking poverty do when she's pregnant for the eighth time in eight years? Have another child that she can't feed or clothe or house or educate or even love? Does she have to die at thirty, worn out from carrying in her womb the conscience of middle-class whites?

"I agree," he spoke more in a whisper now, "that the right to life should be sacred, but in the ghetto where there's not enough work or food to go around—but more than enough roaches and rats and disease and crime—life isn't sacred at all. It's just dirty. If constitutional liberty, if privacy, individualism, and all the Ninth Amendment's unspoken rights mean anything at all, they mean that a poor woman does not have to further burden herself with a load she *cannot* bear and a society *will not* bear. Those rights mean her freedom not to bring into this world a child who will be abused as an infant, socialized into crime as an adolescent, and ultimately imprisoned or on welfare as an adult.

"Let's not fool ourselves by talking about life," Kelley went on, "either the fetus's life or the mother's life. Sustaining these kinds of statutes will kill them both. There is no way a state can enforce laws like these, not in a society that accepts abortion as legitimate, not in an urban, atomistic society like ours. The rich and the middle class can find doctors, with skill and sterile equipment, who will take care of them or their daughters for a handsome fee. The poor can't afford competent abortionists, not as long as the procedure is illegal; medical men, after all, have their ethics. They won't perform illegal operations except for a fat price. So poor women, black women, Hispanic women, have to go to quacks and butchers to get the job done—and they do go now and they will go in the future as long as we have laws like these. Thousands of those women will be injured or killed and those fetuses will be just as dead as they would have been were a competent physician in charge. And all of those women will be poor and most of them will be black. Today, with birth control and abortion morally accepted, laws like this make no sense, unless we want to punish the poor even more than we already do.

"I don't question anybody's motives here," Kelley concluded. "I think they're all good. But meaning good and doing good just ain't the same. In our society, our right here-and-now society, these sorts of laws take lives instead of saving them, and the lives they take are all poor and mostly black and Spanish-speaking."

It was quite an impassioned speech, the other side of the moral dilemma that Walsh had begun to sketch. As you can see, the vote was 5–4 to invalidate both state laws. As senior associate justice in the majority, Jacobson assigned Senator Breckinridge the task of writing the opinion of the Court.

To be sure, Walsh did not surrender merely because he had lost at conference. That was not his style. A change in one vote was all he needed, and the majority included two of our weakest links, Svenson and Putnam. Walsh focused his attention on Svenson, and I tried to persuade Putnam.

I had the more difficult assignment, far more difficult. Being inside Putnam's mind greatly increased my admiration for the astronauts. In a vacuum, everything is weightless and floats aimlessly. It is a disorienting, very disorienting experience. I appealed to reason, though I had little hope there. I also appealed to emotion, to his rigid Calvinist upbringing, to the possible criticism of our Court as a tribunal of death. I even conjured up the spectre of government's operating large clinics that performed abortions on an assembly line basis.

His response was a reflex: "Freedom is the general rule, restraint the exception." (Actually, my dear chap, that was a slight misquotation of *Adkins v. Children's Hospital,* but I thought it impolitic to correct him.) In the end, both Walsh and I failed. Emotion prevailed over reason, ambition over modesty.

The senator circulated an opinion that, like his statements at conference, read like a speech on the Senate floor —an apt phrase, that. For the floor was precisely the place for such an emotional screed disguised in legal language.

Walsh circulated a dissent. Albert and I joined it, happily joined it. Campbell wrote his own, of course. Walsh's opinion did not, to be sure, put matters exactly as I would have, but it was not at all bad. As I have told you, he paid attention to writing, and what he said he said clearly and not without grace. Here, let me read you a few passages in which he neatly skewered the majority—and more important, the senator, who in another set of cases had unsuccessfully advocated our treating river basins, trees, and bears as legal persons. The particular subpoint was whether a fetus was a person:

> The fact is that today we face for the first time the problem of whether or to what extent a fetus is a "person" whom the state must protect under the Fourteenth Amendment. If the law treated, as the majority seems to imply, only those born of woman as legal persons, our task would be easy. Courts and legislators, however, have not been so rigid. For instance, after some initial hesitation, this Court held—and continues to hold—that a corporation is a person covered by the terms of the Fourteenth Amendment and thus entitled to the state's protection. So, too, a ship is a legal person, similarly protected in its rights. Furthermore, to cope with problems in protecting our natural environment, one member of this Court has eloquently argued that courts should treat river basins, trees, and even bears as persons. His argument, which I find persuasive, is that, in the life they create and preserve, these objects and animals have at least as

much claim to the status of persons as do corporations and ships.

The usual process of growth in the common law is reasoning by analogy, responding to novel problems by selecting among existing rules and, if necessary, adapting them to the new circumstances. A judge examines situation X and decides that it is closer to situation A than to situation B, then applies to X the rule governing A or adapts that rule to fit X. It takes a greater capacity for logic chopping than I can muster to argue that a fetus is less like a fully developed, adult human being than is a corporation, even one as benevolent as Dow Chemical, or than is a ship, even a supertanker happily spilling its oil into our rivers and onto our beaches.

Thus, with all deference due to the reasoning of my brethren, I feel compelled by the laws of evidence, sensory perception, and plain common sense to conclude that one cannot, with any degree of rationality whatsoever, simultaneously hold that a ship, a corporation, or even a bear is a person, and a fetus formed by the union of two human cells and growing within the womb of a human mother is not a person.

Whatever one's opinion of a fetus's actual humanity, no one can doubt its potential. Not since the days of Jakob and Wilhelm Grimm, however, have bears and ships become people, and neither tellers of classical fairy tales nor modern scientists have yet succeeded in transforming corporations into human beings.

It follows that if the fetus is a real person then it has certain rights that the state can, perhaps must, protect; and if the state can protect some fetal rights, surely it must also follow that the state can protect the fetus's very existence.

To be sure, Walsh said too much. I would have preferred a few paragraphs restating the fundamental principle that the balance struck by the legislatures of Georgia and Texas was reasonable in terms of their constitutional authority. That answer would have closed our examination. Alas, life is neither simple nor easy. I went along with Walsh because I still entertained the faint hope that his writing such an opinion would educate him away from his activism. As one who has spent a lifetime as a teacher, I am convinced that such an exercise has immeasurable, absolutely immeasurable, heuristic worth. Furthermore, it publicly committed him to the proper approach to constitutional interpretation, one that, if he valued consistency, he would find difficult to repudiate.

Public reactions to the decision were precisely as I had foretold, precisely. Those horrid women's groups danced in the streets, while Catholic bishops spoke mournfully of our having legalized mass murder. Some lower-court judges enjoyed a Dionysian holiday, wreaking havoc with state statutes. Abortion on demand soon became the law as well as the practice in many jurisdictions. At the same time, other states soon enacted, or already had on their books, statutes that were more sophisticated than and somewhat different from those of Georgia and Texas; attacks on those regulations generated fresh waves of litigation. Meanwhile, right-to-life organizations were clamoring for a constitutional amendment to reject the principles which the senator's opinion for the Court had endorsed.

To be sure, my dear fellow, to be sure, one might reason not unintelligently that this clamor was a positive indicium of the health of a democratic polity. I would not disagree except for one point: our Court was at the vortex of that political tornado. Foes of abortion condemned us, likening us to the German judges who abandoned the rule of law before the Nazis' brutal power. Those who favored abortion on demand lauded us as the liberators of women, the saviors of society from the spectre of over-population, and the protectors of human rights generally—though how one reached the third conclusion escaped me as completely then as it does now. We were at the fulcrum of the debate on a divisive issue of public policy, identified, not with the overarching principles of the Constitution, but with one set of partisans in a bitter dispute. Such identification only saps our authority, which is ultimately grounded in the public's perception of our Court as above sectarian clashes.

As I related earlier, Walsh himself initially emerged unbruised from the controversy. The abortionists, who wished to keep him "liberal" on other issues, publicly said that they understood how his Catholicism had "forced" him to vote and speak as he had. (Had he been more successful in his efforts—and those efforts were strenuous indeed—to form a majority behind his views, the abortionists might have been less understanding. It is always easier to be generous when one has been victorious.)

Walsh's Church, of course, reacted favorably to his dissent. It was not overly prudent of them to do so, at least not publicly, but other than dear Cardinal Pritchett of Detroit, I have found few Roman prelates in America who are deft at politics; efficient at raising money, yes; adept at conniving with local political bosses, to be sure; but their peasant cunning (and most of them *are* peasants, my dear chap, but a single generation removed from the effluence pumped onto our shores from the bilges of the immigrant ships), their peasant cunning stood them in poor stead when they dealt with someone above the level of ward heeler.

Be all that as it may, the following June the University of Notre Dame, that great midwestern breeding ground for professional football players, conferred on Walsh an honorary degree—for whatever that was worth. (Have you ever heard the tale that at that institution they print diplomas on pigskin rather than sheepskin?) A few months later, Walsh flew to Rome where he was made a papal knight. Pope Paul personally bestowed on him the Order of St. Gregory the Great. Roman pomp is much too rich for my simple tastes. Had I been religiously inclined I would have chosen to be an Essene rather than a Pharisee, a monk rather than a cardinal. But I confess such ritual is grand for the mob, and, on occasion, can even be in excellent taste.

Well, I needn't tell you what a reaction exploded in Congress at the sight—and with satellites beaming pictures to American television, it was *the* sight—of the Chief Justice of the United States receiving papal knighthood. For a time, I thought—and I confess the thought did not altogether displease me—that an epidemic of apoplexy would cleanse the Augean stables of Congress of many of its white southerners, those good fundamentalists who firmly believe that one cannot display true Christian love without hating Catholics, Jews, and blacks. There must have been scores of resolutions in the House to impeach Walsh and certainly many more to require him—can you imagine, my dear chap, to *require* the Chief Justice of the United States?—to repudiate the honor. He ignored it all, which, I suspect, was all the more infuriating to those raging creatures who charged him with violating the federal statute against officials of the United States accepting awards from foreign governments. His liberal defenders in the law schools sprung to his defense, of course. They explained *ad nauseam* that he had accepted the award not from the Pope as head of a foreign country, Vatican City State, but from the Pope as chief priest of a religious sect. Surely, they argued, and not without reason, that if it was kosher to have Billy Graham publicly imparting his benediction on conservative Republicans, there could be nothing wrong with the Pope's blessing a liberal Democrat.

The whole matter gradually blew over, as you know. But it did not help enhance the image of our Court as aloof from the factors that divide rather than unite us. I thought the basic issue silly, but the whole incident unfortunate.

But wait, my dear chap, wait. I had thought not to divulge this tidbit out of a sense of propriety. But I cannot forego relating to you a delicious incident. Let us tell the full truth and shame the devil. I preface the story by repeating my general disapprobation of the sabrelike instrument that flicked out of the mouth of Walsh's official lady. But this once, just this very once, her vulgarity was put to good use. It was at a reception for the new Canadian ambassador, and, as I happened to be near the punch bowl, in the immediate vicinity of Kathryn, I offered her a cup of refreshment. At that moment, that very moment, who insinuated himself upon us but that pompous senator from South Carolina, the Honorable Archibald Swinton Timrod Rutledge, the gentleman, you recall, who had presided over Walsh's confirmation hearings. I suspect that he really approached us to reconnoiter from closer range the lady's somewhat exposed charms. Be that as it may, he opened the conversation with a direct sally. "I hope, madam, that your husband understands the anger of Congress and will soon return this thing to the Pope."

Kathryn looked at him coldly—and I assure you that her cold glare would have frozen a penguin. In distinct tones that carried twenty feet, she said: "Don't hand me that shit, you fat faggot." She then turned on her heel and sinuously slithered across the room, her twitching cheeks the object of the stares of every male present save one.

It was delectable, absolutely delectable! I believe Rutledge's jaw was still hanging open ten minutes later. Even one with tastes as puritanical as mine has to admit that there are times, few and far between to be sure, but there are times when vulgarity has a rightful role to play in life.

Well, let us return from ribaldry to more serious matters. My account of the abortion cases and of my efforts to educate Walsh does not have a felicitous conclusion. Alas, I again overestimated his educability. A few weeks later we heard and decided the capital punishment cases. Once more the proper constitutional course was clear. The Fifth and Fourteenth Amendments, however unwisely or unjustly, only forbid state and federal governments to take life without due process of law; those amendments do not absolutely forbid government to take life. I make no bones about my opposition to, indeed, my abhorrence of, the death penalty. A lifetime's work and thought convinces me of its barbarity. But, my judicial commission is not a license to read my reasoned values, however deeply felt, into the Constitution's clauses and impose them on the people of the United States. I do not, to be sure, argue that the world is better for my self-restraint; only that the Constitution requires such modesty from judges. You see, I can live with the fact that most of mankind is stupid, venal, and corrupt. I expect neither wisdom nor justice from my fellows, and I am seldom surprised.

Walsh, unhappily, chose anew the path of policy making. He freely conceded that at one time the death penalty had been constitutional, but, he claimed, we had to interpret the Constitution "according to the maturing standards of a civilized society." And those standards, having matured, now outlawed capital punishment. (How we, as judges, could discover those standards or distinguish among those that had matured, were still ripening on the vine, or were but seedlings, he did not enlighten us.) It was human dignity—his usual *cri de coeur*—that he claimed the Constitution protected and the death penalty violated. By killing a convicted felon, he argued, the state treated a human being as an animal, a thing beyond rehabilitation; the state denied the sacredness of his existence. I shared his emotions as well as his values, but above both I place my limited function as a judge.

At least one could say that Walsh's views on abortion and capital punishment were consistent, as, indeed, were brother Jacobson's. In both instances Walsh voted to protect what he saw as a right to life—strange conduct from a man who first came to public notoriety as a killer in Korea. Jacobson, on the other hand, approved killing both fetuses and criminals. Some of the brethren, however, saw no inconsistency in voting that a state could not forbid a woman to kill her unconvicted if not innocent fetus, but that that same state had to respect the right to life of a convicted murderer. The senator and brother Kelley were as eloquent in defending a convicted fiend's constitutional right to life as they had been in rejecting a fetus's right to life. It was all very confusing for one whose votes are based on general principles, untainted by any ambition to make public policy.

TEN

I SHOULD TELL YOU something about that fascinating, very fascinating aspect of Walsh's life, his relationship with his Church. To be sure, except for that one fray over his acceptance of papal knighthood, there were no crises in church-state relations while he was on the Court, unless one counts the issue of abortion. But there, even I, as devout an agnostic as ever ignored formal religion, found his views constitutionally and jurisprudentially impeccable, though I thought the opinion less simply direct than it could have been. To be sure, questions of state aid to parochial schools arose, but he was as faithful as I in hewing to our line of decisions on such matters.

I suspect—it is only an inference, mind you, but, as one of the fruits of a lifetime of studying human behavior, not to be lightly disregarded because of its inferential nature—I suspect that religion played an important but subtle part in his character. I do not mean that he was overtly, or even covertly, for that matter, pious. I refer to a different syndrome. Earlier I talked to you about his vision of the Court and the country. That vision was both moralistic—in the very best sense of the word, one I would delight in having applied to my own views—and optimistic. The moralistic aspect could have been that of any Christian or Jew or humanist, perhaps even—I am ignorant in the field—of a Moslem, Hindu, or whatever. Certainly I found nothing sectarian in wanting all people treated with fairness and justice and tender regard for their dignity as human beings. One does not have to be a religious fanatic or even a humanistic idealist—and I confess to neither fault—to accept that sort of moralism. As I pointed out to you, the biblical passage on which he placed his hand at his oath-taking ceremony was from Isaiah. Its language summed up not inadequately Walsh's obvious goals of public policy. Insofar as that moralism applied to legislative and executive action, I wholeheartedly endorsed it.

But let me not rehearse our differences over the Court's role; rather let me return to the religious dimension of Walsh's character. Papists have no monopoly on optimism, to be sure, but I have noted a marked degree of optimism in that religion. Somewhere deep down there has to be a self-generating core of optimism in a religion that believes that creatures like men and women can earn some sort of eternal bliss. I think, too, that the Church's opposition to abortion is grounded in the belief that, however unwilling she may be, a mother will come to love her child; similarly, the Romans' opposition to euthanasia is based—not overtly, I concede—on a dual faith, first that someone can love even the old and the hopelessly ill, and second a faith in divine mercy.

Please don't misunderstand me; I've said before that I'm not at all convinced, not at all, that the world would not be better off with abortion as well as euthanasia on demand. Insofar as I seem to be awarding moral approbation, it is to a certain psychological consistency, indeed, to a stubborn courage to hold on to values when reality offers little hope of success. And, to a degree, to an important degree, Walsh had that optimism and the stubbornness, one might say the indomitability, that can accompany it.

He seldom talked openly about religion, except for extracting an occasional entry from his repertoire of scandalously indecent jokes about the clergy. I add, however, an observation that a lifetime of experience among the great and the talented has taught me: intelligent men often ridicule what they admire most. Be that as it may, the nearest thing to a theological discussion in which I heard him engage came after a diplomatic reception somewhere in town. I forget where, probably one of those Latin American or African affairs. I always wonder how officials of countries where starvation is supposedly rampant can entertain so lavishly and so frequently.

In any event, several of the brethren were there, and among the other dignitaries was the Pope's ambassador. No, that's not the proper title. What is it he's called in the United States? Yes, the apostolic delegate. Diplomatic titles tend to ooze pomposity. The gentleman in question was Ugo Galeotti, the first churchman, I was told by people who should know—I confess I have no idea—to hold the post as a cardinal. Apparently the Pope had previously posted no one higher than an archbishop as a diplomatic representative, but he retained Galeotti in Washington, even after his promotion, as a signal to the world of the special significance of American Catholicism to the Church. (My more cynical Roman friends said the "special significance" lay in American contributions to sagging papal finances.) This particular prelate was an old friend of Walsh's family, dating back to Walsh's childhood in Rome. I gather a formidable social bond had formed between the two, and the relationship was avuncular. That is a relationship that I instinctively mistrust, instinctively.

As I recall, I was chatting with Walsh and Kathryn near the exit of the reception hall. She, incidentally, had acquitted herself well, being, as far as I could discern, quite sober. It was past six, and we were all quite ready to make our respective exits. At that moment Galeotti joined us and insisted that the four of us take supper with him and his chief aide, a Monsignor Carlo Sartori, at his apartment. I say four because Elena Falconi, Walsh's administrative assistant, was draped on my arm. Let me hasten to assure you, my good fellow, that it was only a friendly drape. As I may have confided to you, I was genuinely fond of the lady and, of course, she of me, but I was twenty-five years her senior. I looked on her as a niece. I would add only that Kathryn did not approve of that part of the invitation. Apparently she sensed something that I had not yet grasped. The cold fire shooting out of her green eyes made that as factual as a flagpole, a very large flagpole, an indication that alcohol had not befogged her perception of Elena as a potential danger.

Galeotti's apartment was quite an elaborate affair. Rather than living in a monastic cell, he resided in a penthouse in the Watergate complex. It was an appropriate lodging, very appropriate. The Vatican had once owned a controlling interest in the firm that had constructed the buildings there. Happily for the Church, their holdings were disposed of shortly before Mr. Nixon's assorted felonies occurred. The view across the Potomac was panoramic, the carpets thickly plush, and the furnishings quite tasteful—nothing modern and no strict adherence to the style of only one period, although there was that marked Italian tendency toward the baroque. There were several pieces of art displayed—all religious, to be sure, but not totally uninteresting. Indeed, one was an original by Fra Angelico, a small canvas of the Madonna. I can recall admiring its subtle beauty while Kathryn was curtly dismissing it as "bland and overdone at the same time. Look at that face—so insipid that it's almost sacrilegious." She and I agreed on very little, except, perhaps, that Elena Falconi was a very attractive woman and that Declan Walsh might be vulnerable.

Galeotti was a fascinating creature, simply fascinating, though not, I admit, among my favorite personages. He was short and portly—no, no, my dear chap, if the truth be told, and that tape of yours reminds me of my duty to history, if the truth be told, he was short and fat, a caricature of Pope John. It was a likeness, I suspect, on which he had capitalized in his advancement through various ecclesiastical ranks. Actually, I could take him or leave him—Galeotti, that is, not dear Pope John. He was fascinating, as I said, full of knowledge of international affairs, philosophy, and even art; we knew many of the same people in Paris, London, and Latin America.

Our stout cardinal boasted a consuming interest in gourmet cooking. (I hope you'll forgive my play on words. I simply could not resist it.) He also affected a connoisseur's knowledge of wine. I am willing to admit that his choice of wines was delicate, but I abstain from further judgment. I can claim no expertise in oenology. On the other hand, a decent respect for the truth compels me to say that he was a gourmand at best, not a gourmet. You're aware, to be sure, of the vast difference, the very vast difference.

That evening's "supper" was an excellent example—no, a simply horrid example—of what I mean to convey. There were three courses in addition to dessert. First came some sort of cold, mixed shellfish in an acidic dressing of lemon, vinegar, and a bit of olive oil—and green olive oil, at that. Can you imagine serving anyone *green* olive oil? I later discovered that the chewy things shaped like onion rings were slices of octopus. Other tidbits were pieces of conch. Had I known then, I would have been ghastly ill right at the table.

The second course was magnificent to look at—something called Venus's Jewel Box, cooked and served in individual baking dishes. Each was a bright yellow pasta shell stuffed with green noodles, mushrooms, fresh ham, cheese, cream, and onions. The pasta shell was tied at the top with a single green noodle. It was a thing of beauty, no question about that, none at all. But no person of taste could enjoy anything so rich and heavy, especially on top of shellfish marinated in acid and green oil.

As if those two courses were not enough to gorge a hungry elephant, we were served what the cardinal called the principal plate, a "mixed boil" he termed it. The butler placed in the center of the table a long, narrow bowl that the six of us could reach and from which we could extract the contents: chunks of sausage and various cuts of veal, beef, and chicken, all sliced paper thin and mixed with carrots, celery, potatoes, and onions. It was surprisingly palatable, I must concede that much, but despite its not unpleasant medley of aromas, I could barely touch it. As it was, I never went to bed that night. My stomach was convinced that someone had poured into it molten lead that solidified even as it scorched. In fine, the dinner sat like the combined nightmare of a cardiologist and a gastroenterologist. I shan't even mention the salad of spinach and bacon, served with a heated dressing, the side dish of fruit marinated in a mustard sauce—no, I did not misspeak, mustard—or the sickly sweet dessert of chocolate-flavored rum cake, accompanied by thick espresso and followed by cognac. To eat at the same pace as the cardinal was to participate in a collegial effort at gustatory suicide.

So much for that digression into indigestion. I simply had to make it clear to you, very clear, that, for all his other talents and not inconsiderable charm, Galeotti was much more the glutton than the gourmet.

Now, where were we? Ah, yes, the conversation at dinner was intriguing. Galeotti held forth on some recent developments in the Caribbean; he had been posted some years ago in Cuba and maintained many of his contacts in the region. Monsignor Sartori's last station had been Beirut, and he was a veritable gold mine of aperçus about that sadly afflicted country. Still sober but quite out of sorts, Kathryn tossed sarcastic peccadilloes randomly, striking a tender spot in her questioning of Sartori about the sexual preferences of a newly designated French cardinal who, years later, was to drift into schism from Rome. I gathered from the monsignor's blushes that heterosexual affairs were not among the new cardinal's sins. I know nothing of ecclesiastical scandals, and you know my oft stated position on gossip. I could not help but observe, however, that Galeotti's face visibly colored during the discussion of that topic and that he adroitly switched the conversation at the very first opportunity.

There was more than conversation to make the evening interesting. I especially enjoyed two subplots. Elena and Kathryn carried on a marvelously nuanced fencing duel, featuring ripostes of exquisite politeness. Jealousy always provides capital entertainment. What surprised me and set me thinking was its appearance in this context. I recalled that two weeks earlier, at my annual dinner for the Court, Walsh had spent a good deal of time with Elena. It was food for thought, but, since I was not one to pry into the personal affairs of others, I put it aside.

For the second subplot, we had a morality play. Young Monsignor Sartori—well, I should not say too young, probably in his early forties—was having the devil's own time. (I really didn't intend that pun, my dear fellow; it simply burst out of my subconscious.) The monsignor was having awesome difficulties keeping his eyes diverted from Kathryn's generously—I might even say lavishly—displayed bosom. I have willingly granted that for all her problems she possessed a rare physical beauty. She was some seven or eight years younger than Walsh, you recall. Indeed, even now, well into middle age, she could be breathtaking—which is a not inapt description of the monsignor's reaction. I myself was at a stage in life when such sights gently stirred memories but no longer generated imaginative anticipations. Thus I could enjoy the drama without being dazzled by the leading lady. Her dress that particular evening must have been designed and sewn onto her skin

—and by a genius, nothing less than a genius. Really, my dear chap, some of those designers of women's clothes missed their true callings as architectural engineers. It was astonishing, simply astonishing, how that creation so flagrantly flouted the laws of gravity.

Our monsignor's interest, I fear, was not as scientifically detached as my own. His guardian angel was putting up fierce but only partially successful resistance. The poor fellow was trying desperately to look anywhere in the room but at Walsh's lady. Unhappily for virtue, she was seated directly opposite him at the table, and often leaned over to help herself to a portion—one very small portion at a time—of the "mixed boil" or the fruit. The ethereal atmosphere of a seminary, the cloister of all male manses, and the plentifully draped figures of obese nuns had ill prepared him for such a vision at close range. I am certain, absolutely certain, that later that evening he spent some hours with his rosary. I confess to more than a mild curiosity as to precisely what it was he told his beads.

After the meal—engorgement would be a more fitting description—Kathryn mentioned that the Kennedy Center was having a late evening preview of an art show sponsored by some diplomatic charity or other. She made it apparent that she would like to attend. It was also apparent that the cardinal wanted some time with Walsh.

"Allora, cara," Galeotti said, "perhaps one of our other gentlemen might escort you, and you could spare me a moment of your husband's precious time."

I sat silent. I assure you that escorting Kathryn, clothed—or rather unclothed—in that particular dress, was a task I considered far above and beyond the call of duty. After what could well have become an embarrassing pause, diplomatic tact—or perhaps Satan himself—triumphed.

"I would be honored, *Eminenza,"* our young monsignor volunteered, "if I might act as escort."

Kathryn smiled a bit too greedily, it seemed to me. I have no doubt, no doubt whatsoever, that she was not unaware of having aroused clerical concupiscence and was thoroughly enjoying the monsignor's discomfort. Elena, however, divine creature that she was, intervened on the side of Sartori's guardian angel.

"If I may, I'd like to come along." While that did not

eliminate the monsignor's difficulties, at least it spread his temptations a bit thinner.

Their departure at a little after ten left me alone with Galeotti and Walsh. For a few minutes the cardinal, obviously not yet fully relaxed, sparred conversationally, mentioning a recent off-Broadway production he had enjoyed on his last visit to New York. Slowly, however, he changed from the gracious, ebullient priest-diplomat-host into a tired and rather saturnine old gentleman.

"La chiesa santa," he sighed as he slumped into an easy chair—"the Holy Church."

I must preface my recounting this episode with a warning concerning a trait that annoyed me—Galeotti's propensity to sprinkle his English with Italian, a language for which I bear no great fondness. Have you ever noticed in your many travels how often Italians, even cultured, educated Italians, carry over into English that repertoire of throw away words from their own language? At least every third sentence opens with *ecco,* which means literally "behold"; *allora,* "then"; or *senta,* "listen." Galeotti demonstrated that trait to an extreme degree. Elena found in it a quaint reminder of her family. It apparently did not disturb Walsh or Kathryn. They, after all, were fluent in Italian; Walsh, indeed, was bilingual. I confess, however, that the habit grated on my ear, as did the cardinal's penchant for transliterating Italian expressions: *without other* for *of course, all and two* for *both,* or *of truth* for *really.* Predictably he would choose English words with Latin roots. For him things never began, they commenced; rooms had portals, not doors; people enjoyed sanity, not health. Worse yet, he never could fathom the differences among *speak, say,* and *tell,* while English prepositions remained as great a mystery to him as the notion of the Trinity to me.

Well, *la chiesa santa* was a typical lapse into Italian.

"What's the matter, Ugo?" Walsh asked. Some gentle solicitousness was apparent in his tone.

"I speak you in confidence," Galeotti replied. "I am an old man, and to old men the future is always dark, perhaps because it is so short. But at times I despair for the Church. Since the Second Vatican Council in the middle of the 1960s, we have known only turmoil. *Ecco,* we have extended our hand in friendship and understanding toward the other religions of the world, but, within our own

Church, we verge on bitter civil war. The Vatican itself has become a nest of intrigue."

"There was always that aspect," Walsh put in softly, "and some of it is inevitable in any human organization."

"Of truth, of truth. You have reason," Galeotti conceded. "But I see a rancor now that I do not remember myself from earlier years. I confess you that it may be a failing of the old, visualizing the ideal in the past rather than in the future. But I remember myself, in earlier years, clashes of personality, inevitable as you tell, and also even less elevating clashes of ambition. We can all look back in sorrow on the division between Monsignor Tardini and Monsignor Montini when they were substitute secretaries of state for Papa Pio XII. That was bitter and, without other, resulted in Montini's being denied the red hat and exiled to Milano."

"At least until dear Pope John," I put in, more to make the point that I was not totally uninformed about matters ecclesiastical than to add substantively to the discourse. "And, to be sure, Pius's ill-treatment helped Montini become John's successor."

"Ecco," Galeotti nodded, "it was thus. But what I view now are not those sorts of affairs, not merely sad but human conflict. Now I see more: a Church paralyzed by chaos. Perhaps I am only dead tired—you have that expression in English, too, no?" We nodded. "I had three reunions today. First I convened with a representative from your American bishops protesting the Vatican's rejection of their plans to bring divorced and remarried Catholics back to the practice of their faith. I found the argumen of the Americans appealing, but the position of the Holy Office firm. Next, I convened with a group of laymen from Virginia protesting their bishop's and their pastor's refusal to honor a past agreement concerning participation by the laity in operating a parish. Last, I was visited y a delegation of Dominican nuns to discuss the possibility—*ecco,* the impossibility—of women being ordained as priests.

"There was much rancor in all three reunions, a rancor that is abundant in the Church today," the cardinal sighed again. "Bishops denouncing the Pontiff, priests denouncing their bishops, theologies of liberation and revolution, and supposedly charismatic babbling in tongues. *Allora,* it is no wonder so many of the laity play golf or siesta instead of attending church.

"Above all," Galeotti continued, "there is a trend toward official indecision, interrupted by foolish pronouncements such as *Humanae Vitae,* condemning birth control. Papa Paolo has, how do you say . . . streamlined? . . . the Curia. And with his own former secretary, Giovanni Benelli, functioning as his real if unofficial chief of staff, the Vatican operates more like a controlled machine than ever before in all its history. But it runs for the sake of running. No one knows where we are going, least of all Papa Paolo. He could be a great leader, but he is filled with self-doubts. He does not trust his own instincts."

"Would you go back to the old days before Vatican II?" Walsh asked.

"No, *caro,* no. Those were calm days, but they were not good days. Their order concealed a volcano that, like Vesuvio, silently threatened to bury us under a hot sea. In ventilating these forces before they destroyed us, Papa Giovanni and Vatican II made a marvelous cause. But now, I view only confusion. Papa Paolo seems the most confused of us all."

"I remember him very well as Monsignor Montini when I was Truman's special representative," Walsh said. "In fact, I dealt with him as much as with any other man in the Vatican. I liked him a great deal. He was shy, even a little awkward in personal relations, but he had a powerful mind. No, that may be wrong. He was extraordinarily intelligent, but he was not a man of power, intellectually or physically. I sensed understanding more than power, but I also sensed a burning ambition."

"Of truth, of truth," Galeotti sighed. *"Ecco,* the tragedy. Intelligence but not power. Stubbornness, yes, and certainly ambition. He is not only the most intelligent—and cultured and learned—of modern pontiffs, he also labors hardest and longest, from five in the morning until near midnight, with only a brief siesta and very small wine. But he is not a man to whom decisions—or people—came facilely. He has been torn apart as Pontiff. Perhaps it was the unjust treatment that he received from Papa Pio XII that scarred his soul. Perhaps," Galeotti shrugged in that inimitable Italian fashion, "he merely suffers the curse of the intellectual—the ability to see all sides of a problem and the inability to arrive at a clear selection. In politics he is a liberal, perhaps —I would tell yes—a Socialist, a Christian Socialist but nevertheless a Socialist. You have read his encyclical *Populorum Progressio,* in English *The Development of Peoples?"*

(The translation was for my benefit, but I can assure you, my dear chap, that while I make no claim to being a polyglot, a lifetime of study in the academy has given me more than a nodding acquaintance with Latin. But I said nothing lest I distract a fascinating stream of consciousness.)

"That document is a call for social action, for sharing by rich nations as well as by rich individuals, a sharing with the poor. It is a call to return to basic Christianity."

"But *Humanae Vitae?"* I asked, able to restrain myself no longer. "How can one reconcile his attitudes, his pronouncements, on birth control with a concern for the poor?"

Galeotti lifted his palms upward and repeated the classic Italian shrug. "How no? *Ecco,* that is Papa Paolo's cross. Politically he finds himself on the left, theologically on the right. His social conscience cries out within him, but his theological conscience triumphs. He cannot tolerate any manipulation of what he considers to be a doctrine of the faith."

Walsh started to say something, but Galeotti lifted his hand. "I know, *caro,* I know. Birth control is not a matter of faith. There is no dogma there. In fact, and I speak you in gravest confidence, the draft of *Humanae Vitae* that the Holy Office itself prepared was much less rigid than the version Papa Paolo issued. Someone—according to me, a certain theologian in the secretary of state's office—reworded it; but, whoever he was, he reworded it of accord with the wishes of Papa Paolo. The ultimate document is his, Paolo's, in tone and in substance."

Walsh merely shook his head. I could not help smiling at this capital piece of information, truly a golden nugget to be stored away and treasured. I offer it now as a legacy to history.

"Allora," the cardinal continued, "the basic problem is —and it displeases me much to say thus—that Papa Paolo is an Italian. We are a strange people in many respects, not least in our attitudes toward sex. At one level, we are earthy; machismo and the sex act are open parts of our

daily lives. At the same time that our culture is so candid and earthy, some of us—most of our saints and I have fear almost all of our clergy—recoil from these things and associate sex only with sin and spiritual death, with life but not with love. *Ecco,* unlike the Irish whose attitude toward sex is consistently of an unhealthy puritanical sort, it is as if we Italians were culturally Manichean. According to me, Papa Paolo—and of truth, at times most Italians—have a neurotic vista of sex. He believes that most people in the secular world hold it as a pleasure relentlessly to be pursued to the exclusion of all else, including God. Just so, it is a vile sin to be avoided, not only under the Sixth Commandment but also under the First. *Humanae Vitae* springs from a belief that artificial birth control is a manifestation of a false god."

"There's no doubt," Walsh agreed, "that *Humanae Vitae* has driven people from the Church. At very least, it has made 'the false god' seem rational."

"Without other, without other," Galeotti half moaned, "another facet of the tragedy of *il Papa.* His goodness creates evil results. But only part, one out of many, as the inscription on your money tells us. The rigidity of his views on birth control has assisted to drive many laity, and even priests, from the Church. But there is much more to the problem. We now have within our own ranks radically different models of the Church bitterly competing not only among theologians but also among pastoral bishops and even within the Roman Curia itself. I see nothing but chaos. *Allora,* perhaps my faith should be stronger. We have Christ's assurance that the gates of hell shall not prevail against us. Still, there is great temptation to surrender to despair as age saps our energies."

Walsh's face lit up as it sometimes did at conference when we confronted an especially challenging case. "I can understand that temptation, Ugo, and I'm sure that Justice Walker and I share your vulnerability."

(Let me assure you, positively assure you, that I have no recollection of ever as an adult despairing about anything. I have never believed in nor hoped for things beyond the immediate, tangible world that we inhabit. That leaves nothing to despair about. "Leave the cosmos alone" has been my philosophy as much as it was old man

Holmes's. To be sure, I said nothing. After all, I was only a spectator at a fascinating dramatic vignette.)

"The Church," Walsh was saying, "along with all of western society is in chaos. But why not look on this chaos as an opportunity rather than as a menace, a challenge rather than a threat? People aren't rejecting religion or God so much as they're looking for new answers that fit new problems. The old catechism's approach doesn't help. These people are yearning, not rejecting. It's only when we question accepted facts and values that we progress.

"I also disagree," Walsh went on, "that the years under Pius had a volcano seething under them. Quite the contrary. We were fat—at least in our dumb acceptance of ideas. I don't mean acceptance of doctrine, but of the conclusions that some very unimaginative but closely orthodox theologians claimed inevitably followed from basic doctrines. John's service was less in venting the discord that was welling up within the Church than in helping create the resentment, the restlessness, and the discord that we should have felt—and expressed—as Christians about the gap between our moral roots and our humdrum acceptance of evil as inevitable."

"Of truth," Galeotti commented drily, "that fury, Discord, accepted the invitation rapidly enough."

"Yes, but out of that chaos, out of this questioning, the Church now has the opportunity for new leadership, for someone with perception, judgment, imagination, and intelligence to lead us—maybe to lead us back—to a sense of community and Christianity as it should be practiced both to be true to its fundamental ideas and to operate in *our* world."

Galeotti merely looked at Walsh quizzically. Our good chief justice, suddenly metamorphosed into theological engineer, raced on, much taken, much taken indeed, with his own thoughts. I was surprised, though I should not have been at all, to learn that his intellectual arrogance did not stop with our Court or our Constitution. The creature really believed he had cosmic answers, cosmic!

"I don't think Catholicism is in such bad shape with its real constituents, the believing laity, or its potential constituents among the unbelieving. Sure, there's a lot of turmoil and confusion and staying away from Mass. But much of that is a reflection of a healthy concern for the Church.

You people in the hierarchy have made the horrible blunder of confusing ecclesiastical reform with ripping up ritual. Most laymen are too sensible to make that mistake. You've substituted an ugly audience-participation show for an artistic performance by trained actors, substituted atonal cacaphony for Gregorian chant." (You can see why I thought Walsh was educable: his artistic sense was sound, even if untrained.) "In part, the laity is telling the hierarchy that you good prelates sit on your taste buds.

"That's not the only reason people are staying away from church," Walsh rolled on, "but it's a large part of it. *Humanae Vitae* with its atrocious logic and faulty physiology is another. Poor Paul didn't even bother to learn about how reproduction occurs. For the life of me, I can't put that kind of stupidity together with the quick, sensitive intelligence of the Montini whom I knew."

"In general, I am of accord, but—," Galeotti began to say, but Walsh overrode him.

"But dissatisfaction with poor taste and rejection of a logically and morally indefensible argument about birth control augur well for the intelligent faith of our people. And you people in Rome should remember your roots and pay more attention to auguries and omens. Catholicism was the dominant force in the western world for centuries, and it can become so again, all the more so with an intelligent laity rather than a dumb herd of sheep, but only if you people who claim to lead us seize the opportunity not only to reclaim traditional followers but to reach out and bring in the rest of a seeking world. You don't conquer by whining in self-pity as poor Paul, for all his massive talents, tends to do. You act and you justify and you convince and you convert and change the world. Remember Machiavelli said that fortune was a woman who must be seized."

"Ecco," Galeotti smiled, "that may be the heart of the problem, *caro*. As celibates we have no skill at seizing women. Where will our leadership come from? Not from Papa Montini, as much as I respect his mind, his dedication, and his personal sanctity; not from that collection of holy men called the college of cardinals, nor from our spiritual bureaucrats in the Roman Curia."

"Perhaps from the next Pope. Papa Paolo can't live forever, although it might seem that long."

"How no? He cannot survive for much longer, but his

successor is apt to be a . . . how do you say? . . . dishwater compromise among the factions that are warring within the Church, a man who will mark time with prayer and fasting, resolving nothing."

"Well," Walsh joked, "you clerics don't let us poor laymen in on that game. We can't vote, much less run for office. Seriously, Ugo, you underestimate your Church. You can overcome, as our black people said some years back."

"Let us pray," the cardinal nodded.

I don't really believe, my dear chap, that our portly prelate was greatly solaced, but pity, even self-pity, having played, as the poet says, soon tires. What would have surprised many people—not me, of course, but many people who claimed to know him well—was Walsh's fervent interest in affairs ecclesiastical, his sense of a popular yearning for closer contact with religion. To be sure, I would never profess to have the vaguest idea about what the mob was yearning for—or the slightest concern. To me, however, that evening revealed an aspect of Walsh's personality that, I believe, truly believe, I alone of his secular acquaintances grasped. If nothing else his exhortation to Galeotti reflected much of his own ambitiously expansive philosophy about the role of the chief justice and our Court.

ELEVEN

As I HAVE not undeliberately intimated to you, Walsh and I were on cordial, very cordial terms. Our relations were more than pleasant, much more. If you will permit it, I might say parenthetically that Walsh was very close to few people. He got on well with all the justices, even with our Neanderthal from Texas and the senator from Virginia, but only Albert and I touched his inner life. Basically, Walsh was friendly, but he possessed a charm that could keep people from approaching his real self. He could exude warmth—and occasionally rather sharp sarcasm, to be sure —but much more often warmth. Yet it was as if the amounts of warmth had been carefully measured in calories. They came out in dosages meticulously metered in his cerebrum rather than in surges pumped from his heart. In fine, he typically said and did the right thing, but he did so because he had thought about it rather than because he was following his emotions—his instincts if you prefer.

That diagnosis is not irrelevant to what I now want to relate to you. It was sometime during the early spring of his fourth year that an ominously intriguing morsel dropped in my ear. Well, as I have heretofore informed you I have no patience for gossip or gossipy creatures. But one does have an obligation to tell the whole truth, doesn't one? Besides, you have probably heard something of this from others, and it would be negligent for me to withhold probative evidence from you.

Perhaps I am moving slightly ahead of my narrative. Let me retrace my steps at the risk of some repetition. With his fetish for neat administration, the old chief had engaged an administrative assistant for his office. Please do not confuse this functionary with the Administrative Office of U.S. Courts; that is an entirely different institution, a rather large bureaucracy nowadays. What I am speaking of is a single person with one secretary. The chief charged his administrative assistant with supervising the Court's personnel—other than the justices, to be sure—and expediting the flow of paper around the Court. Those tasks are much more important than they might seem to outsiders, and responsible performance of the work involves judgment as well as tact.

The first incumbent was a male political scientist. I confess, freely confess, that initially I had serious misgivings about such a person's operating within our Court. This man, however, performed competently, very competently indeed. He soon made himself indispensable, and like all indispensable men he was noticed and left us to become dean of a university program in judicial administration.

His successor, who arrived during the old chief's last year, was that handsome woman, Elena Falconi. Handsome, yes, that fits, but she was quite feminine; perhaps comely would be a more apt description. As I have several times intimated to you, Elena was very much a female, although hyperefficient and, even by male standards, able to exert leadership. Actually the law clerks lived in trembling awe of her, while the justices were all, as far as I know, very fond of her. I suppose the differences in ages had a great deal to do with it. At thirty-five she undoubtedly appeared to the young clerks as an "older woman," while to us—at forty-nine Kelley was the junior associate justice in age as well as in service—she was most assuredly still a young woman.

Elena was tall, with long, rich black hair that she usually kept tightly disciplined in a knot at the back of her head. Her pale grey eyes and somewhat lentiginous skin contradicted her name, though Falconi was, to be sure, her married name. Later, I discovered that her family had in fact immigrated from Italy, but from the north, Trent, where people are apt to be more Nordic than Latin in appearance. Her figure was adequately proportioned. I believe that description is appropriately delicate without being misleading. I do not mean to infer, not at all, that she was carved by the same erotic scalpel that had fashioned the chief justice's official lady. Physically and temperamentally they were very different, although I had good reason to believe that each had a will of steel.

When she joined us, Elena was already divorced. Thus I escaped the dubious honor of her spouse's acquaintance. I do not hold with gossip, I need not repeat, but the rumors around the Court had it that that worthy, a citizen of New Jersey and of no definite profession, had been connected to the Mafia. To be sure, I put no stock in such tales, none whatsoever, but it was interesting that her sponsor with the old chief had been the senator from that state whom several investigative reporters later named as a recipient of monetary favors from organized crime in Jersey City. It is also worth passing note that her husband was several times subpoenaed to testify before the state crime commission, but somehow evaded the writs and was killed in an automobile accident when it seemed he would soon testify. Her own family background—her father had been a rather well-to-do banker who came to this country as vice-president in charge of the international operations of one of the New York conglomerate houses and she herself was a graduate of Smith College—indicated she was free of any taint except bad judgment in men, a fault that is rampant among females.

Be that as it may, it was in the fourth year of Walsh's chief justiceship that, in response to my commenting to one of my clerks that I had been unable to contact Elena, he remarked that she was probably with the chief justice.

His rather heavily affected tone caught my ear, and my eye was arrested by the knowing smirk that tone elicited from my secretary. I noted their reactions, but said nothing. One does not, after all, discuss one's peers with the servants. That does not mean, to be sure, that I dismissed the incident from my mind. Far from it, for those knowing looks my staff exchanged recalled a few other facts that had lodged in my subconscious. Now I seldom—not more than twice a month—socialized with the Walshes as a couple. To be sure, they invited me to dinner several times a year, and I reciprocated. We would also meet rather more frequently at the Alberts', as we had on the evening on which Kathryn had discussed their romance, or at formal gatherings, as on the night we supped with Cardinal Galeotti. As a threesome, however, we were not close.

Yet even at that remove, I had noticed during several recent encounters that Kathryn and Walsh had been rather distant with one another. She, to be sure, could be coolly aloof to others or even sharply cutting in her remarks, but between the two of them there had almost always been an obvious electric field. I say "almost always" to exclude the occasional flareups about her drinking. The snapping sarcasm she so freely turned on others, she had not, in my presence, ever launched against him. Recently, however, she had reserved a few choice barbs for her spouse, referring to him as "our glorious chief hero, or is it hero-chief, darling?"

Kathryn's problem with alcohol was becoming more obvious. Mind you, I did not say more acute or more serious, only more obvious. She undoubtedly realized that Walsh's zealous devotion to his work was not something that would fade as he became more accustomed to our routine. His neglect of her, she must have realized, was likely to be a permanent condition. It was not a state of affairs that she was cheerfully accepting. No doubt absence of outlets for her interests and energies worsened her condition. Indeed, she was displaying many of the classic symptoms of depression.

There was also mounting, if indirect, evidence of a complicating dimension. Her behavior at Cardinal Galeotti's toward Elena and the clumsily coded message between members of my staff left me frightened—actually, I was terrified—that there was another woman and it might be

Elena. I hoped that Kathryn's behavior was due to no more than the sort of paranoia that usually accompanies emotional upset; I could not so easily explain away my staff's communication.

This was definitely something I had to look into. Please do not misunderstand me, my dear chap. I was not motivated by some prurient curiosity. There would not be an iota of verisimilitude in such an assumption. Rather, I felt a responsibility for the integrity of the Court. I was concerned lest some yellow journalist pick up the scent of scandal and drag the judicial ermine through the mud. In addition, I was genuinely fond of Elena and appreciative of her services to the Court. To be sure, that personal loyalty was secondary, quite secondary, to my loyalty to the Court as an institution to be kept above reproach; nevertheless, it was not without weight.

What does one do, what does one do? To discuss the problem with others is to give it notoriety and even credibility. I brooded in solitude for a few days, then took the matter up with Justice Albert—at his home, away from the prying eyes of colleagues and staff and also perhaps away from the long ears of persons unknown. You may not realize it, but on several occasions we have suspected, not without reason, that someone had implanted listening devices—what is the current argot? To be sure, bugs. We suspected someone had "bugged" our conference room. In fact, we once called in the Federal Bureau of Investigation to sweep the place, as they say. The agents claimed to have found nothing, but since, as brother Kelley noted, they were the ones most likely to have placed a device there in the first place, we had to discount their report.

Well, I can assure you that Albert was as perturbed as I over my intelligence. We had no hard evidence, to be sure, but the net of circumstance was tight. For all her effusive sexuality, Kathryn's sharp temper alone could easily propel a man from her bed to seek solace in the company of another woman. Her drinking would only have increased that probability. That was not at all an implausible scenario. And Elena Falconi was not only attractive herself, she was extraordinarily intelligent and, of course, she shared Walsh's intense interest in the Court. One could easily imagine their slowly slipping from shoptalk to more intimate matters, from intellectual co-workers to a closer, physical relationship. After all, they also shared the experience of a curdled marriage. I say these things to make it plain, perfectly plain, that I approached the problem without morally judging the principals.

Albert insisted that there was nothing we could do at the moment. I suggested that the proper course, the only course that would protect the reputation of the Court, if and when hard evidence were at hand, would be to approach Walsh and demand that he yield either Elena or the center chair. Albert was less firm on that point than I. He asserted that, given human nature, many males in all branches of life were not without problems involving females. He doubted that we were confronting the first case of adultery within our Court. Besides, he argued, there was a custom, seldom violated among Washington journalists, not to divulge anything about the sexual conduct of public officials unless that conduct became a matter of official record. It was only when it became a police matter that drinking and womanizing by public men, common knowledge among journalists, were reported in the press. I was less sanguine than Albert about keeping the Court a total stranger from scandal, but I agreed to talk again with him before taking any tangible steps to eradicate the problem.

I decided that the least I should do would be to continue to gather intelligence so as to obtain a closer purchase on the affair. The next day, the very next day, that the Court was not in session, I asked Elena if, on her way home to her apartment in Georgetown, she might stop by my place here at the Hay-Adams and bring some papers that I had left in my chambers. It was, I fear, a rather transparent ploy; I had a secretary and three clerks who could have performed that task, and the Court has a pride of messengers precisely for such purposes. But Elena and I were fast friends, and I covered the matter as best I could by suggesting that she take tea with me, as she not infrequently did in my chambers. It was one of my principal and most enjoyable forms of socializing. As you may not realize, entertaining poses knotty problems for bachelors. Well, when Court was not in session I would several times a week have a few friends in for a cup of tea—always, to be sure, with something else available for those whose preferences ran to more powerful stimuli. It was refreshing to have that small break of conversation with intimates—and not only with those from the Court, but also old friends in academia, the arts, or even in the other branches of government. In all, it was a most satisfactory way to begin to unravel from the day's cares.

After her arrival and our performance of the usual rituals of entry, we began by my questioning her about a problem in the typing pool. The senator, it seemed, was dispatching a heavy portion of his official work there, reserving his secretary's time for preparation of the manuscript of a book—perhaps propaganda for his brand of judicial activism would be more appropriate. The chief thought—and wisely, let me add—Elena's intervention would raise fewer hackles than would his own. Next we discussed the way in which several of the justices were sharing the fruits of their clerks' labors in the exfoliating jungle of petitions for certiorari. Although Roman by religion and Italian by origin, she had absorbed enough of the Protestant ethic to feel as I did—and almost as strongly—that each member of the Court should do his own work.

After about fifteen minutes of this sort of shoptalk, I said: "And you, my dear, I'm more than a trifle concerned about your health. You have looked worried these past few weeks, burdened beyond limits proper to a beautiful young woman."

She smiled. "It shows?"

"It shows," I replied as gently as I could. "It always shows to those who care deeply about the people involved. Strain takes an obvious toll. Now, what can I do to help?"

"There are 'people' involved," she said. "It's easy not to think about that at the beginning, but these things always involve a lot of people, not just two."

It was a most curious response, curious but still healthy. "I am not inexperienced in such matters, my dear," I said. "A lifetime of study of human nature has left me not without some wisdom."

She stared out the window toward the White House. "It's not an easy thing to explain, Judge. It hurts my pride; in fact it wrecks my self-respect. I'm not some silly teenybopper; I'm a mature woman with forty racing at me like an express train. I've been in love and in bed and married and divorced and in bed again a few times, a couple of times with men whose faces I can't even remember. But I'm pulled toward Declan like a fourteen-year-old groupie chasing after the Beatles."

"My dear," I started to say.

"Don't fret, Judge. It's not likely there'll be cause for scandal, at least not likely there'll be any more cause. He's not going to 'keep me' in some Georgetown love nest and we can't maintain a torrid affair in the chief's chambers. I'd be willing to accept either, or both, but our great leader is far too noble."

"There's always the possibility of a divorce," I said. (Mind you, I was not suggesting that route, far from it. I was merely sounding her out on all the more obvious options.)

She laughed, more at herself than at me, I presume. "I've thought of that one, but it's as likely as *your* being the next president. With all that Irish Catholicism floating around in his soul, could you see him divorcing Kate and marrying me? His religious conscience would destroy him, if his moral conscience didn't do it first—and they're both eating at him now. Kate's finally started seeing a psychiatrist about her drinking. She's accepted the fact that she has a problem. Even if he weren't a true believer in Holy Mother Church, Declan wouldn't leave her to sink or swim on her own. He knows the chances are she'd sink. If you ask me, she'll sink anyway, and I think he thinks so, too. But that doesn't matter. Sir Lancelot wouldn't deny her the chance."

"Are you truly as ready as you say," I asked, "to put aside your Church's doctrines? That sort of thing usually runs deep."

She laughed again. "We Italians have had the Church on our backs for too many centuries to let it get on our consciences as well."

"Well, where does it leave us then?"

"In a mess—not a very original answer."

"Perhaps not," I agreed, "but not inapt. Well, to clarify the present and the future, I've often found it helps to retrace the past. How did it all begin?"

"How did it all begin? With Adam and Eve, Judge, and that damned apple."

I smiled at her feeble efforts at bravado. "We need not return quite that far. Let us seek more proximate roots."

"Part of the story you know. We've been together for

almost four years. For most of the time, I found him merely attractive and amusing. He likes to speak Italian and I can still do that. He appreciates my work, and I think he prefers a reasonably good looking female assistant to a male without really being conscious of it. What man wouldn't? I admit I had an occasional sexual fantasy about him, but nothing more serious than the sort of picture of him that would flash through anyone's mind." (I assure you, my dear fellow, firmly assure you, that no sexual fantasy involving Walsh ever flashed through *my* mind, but I thought it better not to interrupt.) "We had a comfortable relationship. I was his girl Friday, a sort of female Mike Keller, who's always ready to do whatever Declan wants the second Declan wants it. Actually, he's become quite dependent on me in running the Court."

"Yes," I agreed. Actually it was true, but only up to a point, only up to a point. Again, however, I forebore to press for accuracy.

"I got a great deal of satisfaction from my job. Some of the Court's magic rubs off on all of us, you know, even on the janitors. My social life was pretty much elsewhere, except for formal affairs." She laughed in the brittle way that females affect when they're upset with the world. "That's a word I must learn to avoid. Well, then this year, there was a difference. There's a time, I guess, when we all feel like chucking it, and Kate's drinking plus the burden of the work here began getting to him. He's a very lonely man."

"Most only children are, but they become accustomed to it," I remarked.

"Yes, that's true and it's also part of the problem. He's lonely but so used to it he's not even aware of it, not consciously anyway. But deep down somewhere or other he knows it, and he cries out for help—silently. And he's also a very attractive man."

(I recall musing to myself that I did not understand why that was so. That it *was* so I had direct evidence. It was merely that I could not, not for the life of me, comprehend *why*. But then I have never pretended to understand the gentler sex and their peculiar perceptions and convoluted needs.)

Not knowing that I temporarily deserted her, Elena was still talking: "I guess I was the aggressor, but gradually he wasn't just a friend anymore. I developed, almost without realizing it, the same sort of silly crush I had back at Smith for a Yale fullback. And my sexual fantasies weren't fleeting anymore. And they were a lot more detailed. I wasn't sure at the time—I knew I was hoping too hard to be dependable—but I felt he was coming on to me, too."

"You're a very attractive woman," I said.

"Thanks, my ego needs a lot of that," she smiled. "We were together a great deal, perhaps no more than usual. Maybe it just seemed that way. We'd talk more about personal things. I realized, I thought I realized, what I was getting into, but love is a disease that destroys the rational processes first. One evening in January, I knew he was planning to stay late because I'd heard him order a sandwich. I ordered one, too, and about seven-thirty brought in a bottle of Spanish wine and invited myself to supper with him. (I was sure everybody else was long gone.) We chatted innocently enough, but I think he could read my eyes. Nothing happened though, not until he tried to open the wine. It slipped and we both grabbed for it. We caught the bottle, but we also caught each other. Then we were kissing and groping like two characters in a cheap novel. That black leather couch made a great bed, and I'd had the good sense to leave most of my underthings in my office—just as I had on three other nights when he worked late."

(Really, my dear chap, I had neither expected nor desired such lurid details. I divulge them to you now only to purge my memory of them. What I had wanted was a more abstract description of the pattern of events, hoping that discussing that pattern would illuminate a path of escape from its grasp. But, there was no stopping Elena. She was determined to tell all. There was nothing to do but listen.)

"It was a passionate explosion, but I can look on it dispassionately now. Once we touched he may have been the leader, but I was the seducer. Afterwards, we lay scrunched together on the couch, drank some wine, got out of the rest of our clothes and made love again. This time slowly and deliberately and tenderly. I suppose those people who write books on sex would say the second time was more physically pleasurable, but I've never experienced anything as emotionally satisfying as that first explosion. It was sudden and violent and cleansing."

"That night both began and ended the physical aspects." It was more a question that I asked than a statement.

"Hardly. He might have preferred it that way. I'm sure his good Catholic conscience did, and he probably could have carried it off. But women aren't that simple. No, it went on until three weeks ago, two months of passion neither of us thought we could still muster. Don't look shocked, Judge. We didn't repeat our sacrilege by making love at the Court again. We used the apartment Mike Keller keeps in town. Then, as though a curtain fell, we stopped. At Declan's insistence. Kate suspects, he realized. I don't think she suspects; I know she *knows* and not because of anybody's telling her or any sort of direct clues. A woman can tell about those things. I think that's what's made her decide to do something about her drinking. I've read it takes a powerful shock to make such people admit they've got a problem." Elena suddenly broke off. "God, she must have been a beautiful woman."

"She was, indeed," I said, "she was indeed. What will happen to you now? That's the important thing."

"Nothing, if you don't count anguish and heartache and crying myself to sleep at night. Declan wants me to stay at my job on the Court. As I told you he depends on me."

"Doesn't he realize," I asked incredulously, "what that's likely to do to you?"

"No, he really doesn't. In his own case, his remedy is just right, but for reasons that are all wrong for me. I love Declan for what he is, a thinking type, not a feeling type. In the right situation he can be passionate, but that's a different story. No, he thinks he's figured life out: you face up to problems and either stare them down or beat them down. You don't budge an inch. That's what he thinks he's doing. What he's really doing is indulging his Irish Catholic guilts. He wants me around as a reminder to atone for his mortal sin. I'm to be a form of penance for him, a bit of purgatory right here on earth. I thank God I liberated myself from the Roman religion a long time ago."

"And what will it be for you?"

"Pure hell. That's the difference. He's so damned rational that he *knows* in time we'll forget. He's a Jesuit. And in his intellectualizing way, he believes women are just men with breasts and vaginas instead of balls. His work is the center of the universe, not his personal life. He's beyond selfishness in the usual sense. He'd sacrifice himself just as quickly, maybe even more quickly, than he would anyone else. Well, he may be right in the long run, if I'm still alive." She was ready to weep. Really, I simply cannot abide it when women weep. I cannot abide it.

"My dear, what can I say?" I already regretted my efforts. I had intended to clear up a scandal not to become the recipient of the lady's life story or her adviser in the devious ways of Eros.

"You can say: 'Elena, stop being a fool. Resign and take a job in the White House or on Capitol Hill, where people find it possible to work a little, diddle a lot, and even occasionally love, and all in the same lifetime.' Or you can say: 'Young woman, go to church and beg God's forgiveness for screwing your neighbor's husband.' " (My dear fellow, that is the last, absolutely the last, thing I would advise her or anyone else.) "Good God, sometimes I feel so sorry for Kate I could shoot myself for adding to her pain, and then sometimes I hate her so much I could shoot her."

While not intrinsically without interest, the conversation had become both too personal and too earthy for my tastes. Still, I tried to shift the onus for assistance. "Have you talked to Mr. Keller about this problem?" I asked. "I thought for a time that you two were becoming—what's the current expression?—tight. Apparently he's aware of what's transpiring in his apartment."

"Yes, at one time we were close. If Mike could ever be serious, we might have made a go of it. But to him, the world is just one big lay after another. He calls himself the Original Humpmobile. And yes, he knows exactly what's been going on in his apartment. Curiously, given his philosophy of 'if she moves, lay her,' he's been very upset. I think he's torn in his loyalties. He's really very fond of Kate, too. But despite all that, he's been a jewel, holding my hand for the past few weeks. I must have cried in half his handkerchiefs. Every time he's in town, he comes over or we meet somewhere. I don't know how I'd survive without him. Now he's the kind of man I can understand, trying to bed down with every female between sixteen and sixty that crosses his path. It's Irish puritanism that I can't cope with. Those Irish mothers must have a special method of castration."

"What's Mr. Keller's advice, if I may ask?" A lifetime's association with Catholic lawyers left me with no need for a lecture on Irish neuroses.

"He says that he and I both have chronic cases of the same disease. He calls it 'hero worship à la Dec.' He's right. Declan exploits poor Mike constantly. At least the government pays me for my time."

"I've had the impression that Mr. Keller enjoys his fate," I said. I was becoming desperate for any opportunity to extricate myself from the trap into which I had cleverly, too cleverly by half, led myself.

"Yes, he does; and he says that I do, too. And that's part of the problem. I probably do." She gulped the cold remains of her tea, then dabbed at her eyes. "I hope you don't mind mascara on your napkin, Judge. You're great to listen, and don't worry. I won't cause a scandal—or Declan won't. There'll be no more trysting on the chief justice's couch. If I ever change my mind, I'll give you plenty of warning so you can summon the Court and demand that I be turned out as a wanton woman."

Before I could deny any such intention, she kissed me on the cheek and was on her way out the door. That *was* an experience, an experience I would never care to repeat. While I had been of no tangible help, the conversation had not been without profit. At least it provided a view of another facet of Walsh's character, confirming some of my insights and offering yet fresh ones. It also offered some, albeit faint, hope for Kathryn's personality.

TWELVE

To ME, the news came like the proverbial thief in the night, although I suppose to others, in the vicinity of the Washington Beltway, its arrival was more like a thunderclap. I can recall, vividly recall, that morning. It was early spring, less than a week after my conversation with Elena, just before we moved to daylight saving time. It is a season that I especially cherish. Dawn comes early, creeping softly through my window before six. It's a pleasure to waken to gentle sun and have a whole new day ahead, even a day filled with bloody certs.

It was not yet half past the hour, and I was shaving as the telephone rang. Now as you are aware my number is not listed in the directory. I knew my young clerks would still be asleep; indeed, they would have all slept until noon had not my secretary telephoned each of them when she awoke. I do like to have my staff in the office by eight-thirty, eight-thirty sharp. Among the brethren, Walsh and Albert were the only two apt to be stirring as early as I, and neither liked to use the telephone. Well, there was nothing to do but address the noisy monster.

It was Albert. A chill came over me; his voice was heavy with death. "Walker, have you heard the news?"

I had not and I did not want to hear his news or anybody else's news. In fact of my own free will I never listen to a radio and I do not own a television apparatus. I prefer newspapers with delay between event and report cushioning shock. But there was no help for it. I would have to know.

"Kathryn Walsh was killed in an auto accident early this morning."

I was stunned, simply stunned. I had—we all had—been expecting brother Putnam to leave us soon—none too soon, I might add—for what he doubtless imagined would be more Republican environs. I had also feared that dear Elizabeth, Albert's charming lady, might have slipped away. But Kathryn Walsh was among the last I had expected to go.

I hastily completed my toilet and within minutes of Albert's call was at the corner of Sixteenth and H hailing a taxi. Walsh's apartment was, as I told you, located in one of those glass towers along the waterfront in the near Southwest. It was that Guicciardini creature who responded to my ring. He actually appeared pleased to see me, and, for once, he did not punctuate his speech with foul epithets. Indeed, he spoke in a most formal even stilted fashion in a voice that scarcely rose above a whisper. "It was good of the justice to come, sir. The colonel could use help, even if he won't admit it."

"What can I do?" I asked.

"The justice can be with him, sir," he said.

"Would it help if I knew how it happened?" I inquired.

"Probably, sir. That's part of the colonel's problem right now." I noted how calm, although obviously fatigued, the creature was. "They were supposed to go to the cocktail party at the Italian embassy last night; then they were going to meet the captain and his latest broad"—I assumed that the captain was Keller—"for dinner afterwards. Anyway, at the last minute the colonel called from the Court that he'd be tied up. You know how he is. Nothing in this flaming world comes before his work. You can bet Kate was furious. Things between them haven't been too good lately. She stalked out. You know her temper." (I did, I did indeed, but the circumstances dictated that I withhold comment.) "She went to the embassy party; then she met the captain and his new bimbo at the Normandy Farms about nine. He says they saw her to her car a little after eleven. (That's about the time the colonel got home.) The Maryland state police called him before one—that's when he called me. We don't know anything more yet, other than that she must have been going like a bat out of hell. She had the Lincoln and you know how she loved to drive that old tank with her foot on the floor."

"Did she hit another car?" I asked.

"No, sir; she missed a turn. And there was no one else in the car with her—and I thank the justice for not asking that," Guicciardini smiled sadly, almost as if he, too, were capable of human emotions.

"Is he alone?"

"The captain is with him. He was here when I arrived about two this morning. There's damned little family on the colonel's side, and Captain Keller telephoned Kate's people. She has two sisters in Minneapolis, and her mother's in a nursing home out there. The sisters will fly in later today."

I went into the study. It was a large comfortable room, with one of those modernistic picture windows opening toward the marina and the Potomac down below. Most of the other walls were occupied by bookshelves and filing cabinets. A marvelous U-shaped desk fashioned out of walnut and black leather—real leather, not the slick vinyl material one sees so much of today—dominated one end of the room, while at the other, two easy chairs and a small sofa were arranged around a handsome stone fireplace. All the furniture was done in the same walnut and leather motif as the desk. Clearly, someone had gone to considerable effort—and frightful expense, frightful—to select just the right appointments for this salon.

Keller was lying on the couch, his long, hairy legs and stockinged feet draped over the arm. Walsh was seated, as if in a trance, in one of the easy chairs. Someone had started a small fire in the grate. For the first time I noticed that there was a decided chill in the air that morning. Keller looked dreadful. His eyes were bloodshot and he needed a shave. Walsh was ashen. One could not tell with that full beard when, if ever, he had last shaved; but his scar, which I had long ceased to notice, was now a brilliant scarlet lump of keloid tissue running from the corner of his left eye back behind his ear. He stood when I entered and clasped my hand in both of his, but from the expression in his eyes—I should say lack of expression, for there was none, none whatsoever—I believe that had he been asked ten minutes later if I had been there, he would not have been able to recall.

Keller waved in a not unfriendly fashion as I sat down in the other chair. There was nothing to be said, so we sat in silence until about a half an hour later when Elizabeth Albert arrived. She quickly brought in a pot of coffee and a tray with glasses of orange juice, some sweet rolls, toast, and a plate of butter. Guicciardini left his post as doorman and slid quietly into the room. Keller swung his legs over the couch and began pouring coffee for all of us. Elizabeth sat on the arm of Walsh's chair and squeezed his hand. If he responded, it missed my practiced eye. She took a glass of juice and offered it to him, but he shook his head. After a few minutes, she left and the four of us resumed our deathwatch in silence.

Later others arrived, first Albert, with more food as Elizabeth had requested, then brothers Kelley and, believe it or not, Jacobson. A marine general whom I did not recognize entered with his aide. To make room for them, Guicciardini and Keller seated themselves on the floor on either side of Walsh's chair, like a brace of temple dogs guarding their idol from evil. I noticed that Guicciardini's eyes were puffy and red. Italians love nothing better than a good cry, even the men.

Then, our obese Cardinal Galeotti arrived. He went to Walsh and embraced him. *"Caro,"* he said, half the tearful mourner, half the comforting priest. *"Caro,* we suffer, all and two. 'The Lord giveth and the Lord taketh away; blessed be the name of the Lord.' "

"No!" Walsh responded in a sharp voice that cracked the room's funereal silence. He leaped up and walked to the large picture window overlooking the river. Then softly and with a bitterness I'd never heard: "I don't believe in a god who wants people to crawl on their bellies to him like beaten dogs. Job did that and got nothing but a bigger ration of shit each time he surrendered his dignity." (My duty to history compels me, however apologetically, to report accurately rather than to edit.) "*My* God wrestled with Jacob, and when Jacob fought back He promised him that he would be the father of a great nation and his descendants would be as numerous as the stars in the sky and the sands of the seashore. I am Jacob, not Job!" Walsh suddenly shouted.

He shook his fist at the window. "Come down and wrestle with me, you yellow bastard! You can beat me but you can't make me lick your hand for murdering my wife. I'll burn in hell before I'll crawl. Fight me like a man, you frigging coward!"

The room was stunned. Galeotti crossed himself. The rest of us sat in shocked silence at what surely must have been the ultimate in blatant blasphemy. (I pretend no expertise in such matters, none whatsoever.)

"Can you forgive, *caro?*" Galeotti asked softly.

"Forgive?"

"Yes, forgive, *caro*. Is your God beyond needing forgiveness?"

"I don't know what you mean, Ugo."

"Ecco, I am not secure either. God confuses me. That is His mode. I speak what finds itself in my heart, not in my mind. Know your God first, then curse Him if you must, but then forgive Him. Do not condemn the stranger, least of all if he is your God."

Walsh waved his hand. He was a man I'd never before seen. "I cannot fight you, Ugo, and *He* hasn't got the guts to fight me," he said, then sat back down again. Within a few moments he reentered his semitrance, blankly staring at the fire.

Sometime in the mid-morning I left the study to have a few minutes alone with dear Elizabeth, who had graciously assumed the role of hostess. "Have you ever seen him like this before?" she inquired.

"No." I did not feel it kind to say that I had never seen anyone like that except for a victim of a recent stroke. But someone so afflicted was not likely to leap up and shake his fist at the Deity. "He's had a severe emotional shock. I think a physician should see him."

"Yes," she agreed. "It might not be a bad idea, but who?"

"Let me handle it, my dear," I said. "As you well know, we on the Court have the privilege of availing ourselves of the government's medical facilities in town. The chief justice and I give our favor to the same man at Bethesda. He's a naval captain. I'm sure he'll be happy to pop by just as soon as he can navigate"—it was a good choice, though unpremeditated—"the traffic."

My prediction was accurate. The captain literally snapped to attention through the telephone's receiver and promised to leave within the minute. In fact, he was there in just a few instants more than a half an hour, via a flashing, clanging ambulance. "The traffic," he explained, motioning toward the machine.

After his examination, the captain came into the kitchen, where Elizabeth, Albert, and I were closeted. Keller and Guicciardini insinuated themselves along with him, making the quarters close indeed. "Physically, he's all right, I think," the captain muttered. "There's always the possibility of a stroke in such situations—he's at the right age for that. But his reflexes are within normal limits, and I see no positive symptoms or anything but psychological shock. The anger you report is normal, but it doesn't fit with a stroke. The sudden death of a loved one often triggers just this sort of syndrome, but I want to keep an eye on him. I gave him a shot of Thorazine. That's powerful stuff, but he needed it. He should sleep anywhere from four to twelve hours. Call me when he wakes up—this afternoon, tonight, at 3 A.M., I don't care when. I don't want to prescribe anything or do anything until I've seen him after he's had some sleep; but I want to see him just as soon as he's awake. If it were anybody else and conditions were different, I'd put him in the hospital for a few days, but we all know that wouldn't work here."

Keller and Guicciardini walked the captain to his red

and white chariot, though I cannot for the life of me, the very life of me, imagine what an attorney and a physician found it possible to say to a mere policeman like Guicciardini.

Well, with Walsh sedated and dear Elizabeth very securely in control, there remained nothing for me to do there, and so I went to the Court to try to keep ahead of my own work. For it was plain as a pikestaff that Walsh would not be functioning for some days and that, as senior associate justice, I would once more have to absorb many of the chief's responsibilities. I also wanted to spend a few moments with Elena Falconi. She would need comforting—and she would have to be dissuaded from going to Walsh's apartment or from doing more than attending the formal services and making whatever other visits minimal standards of civility dictated. It was not an easy task, as you can well imagine, well imagine. In crises, women react with their emotions, not with their reason. Her initial and almost overpowering impulse was to race straight to Walsh's apartment. Happily, I was eventually successful in persuading her otherwise, although it consumed the remainder of the morning.

The funeral was one of those magnificently orchestrated Roman affairs, a High Mass, concelebrated—I believe I use the canonically correct term—by Cardinals Pritchett, Galeotti, and the young cardinal archbishop of Washington. Given the rank and mixed nationality of the concelebrants and Walsh's own station and wish—he said it was also Kathryn's wish—the elaborate service was sung in Latin. As was also her wish, the ceremonies were held in that charming Franciscan monastery in the District, an oasis of serenity in a city of chaos.

Had the occasion not centered around death, it would have been a grand spectacle. The all-male choir was the Franciscans' own. Their Gregorian chant was exquisite, simply exquisite, and I was pleasantly surprised to learn that the three cardinals could each more than carry his part of the chanting. I was reminded of Walsh's philippic to Cardinal Galeotti about the Church's new ritual. The chief had been right, dead right. Indeed, I simply do not understand how the fathers of the Roman Church can retain any claim to sanity after abandoning that majestic ritual for the shabby shows that they nowadays sponsor. One would at least think that the way their flocks stay away from church would have shaken them back to reality.

On the day of the funeral, Walsh, though hardly normal, was physically much more animated than he had been the day before. (I never learned the results of the captain's second visit.) Still, that glaze in front of his eyes shielded him from reality.

In contrast to the ornate filigree of the rituals at the main altar of the monastery, the burial at Arlington was simple and brief, something for which we could be grateful, for the day was damp and cold, with a rain that, mist-like, enveloped us rather than fell on us. Because of Walsh's rank, the cortege was met at the gate by a guard of honor, marines in their gaudy blue and red uniforms. Despite the raw weather, they wore no raincoats. They preceded us to the grave site and stood at rigid attention during the service —this time in English—then silently and swiftly marched away.

There was a jarring note at the grave site. When the prayers were completed, the casket was still above ground, held by straps that would lower it into the excavation. At that point, the funeral director began to usher us from under the canopy where we had been sheltered and toward the waiting limousines, but Walsh shook his head.

"Lower the casket," he ordered.

When that was done, he walked to the edge of the pit and picked up several clods of the soft, wet earth, crushed them in his fist, and gently scattered them into the hole. One could hear the muffled taps as the dirt came to rest on the metallic covering of the casket.

"It's an old Irish custom," he said quietly as he returned to the canopy. "When a man has laid the earth over his wife's body, he can never deceive himself. He knows she is truly dead and gone."

I was afraid the gossip columnists would play on that incident, but there was hardly more than a line or two in the news columns. Speaking of gossip, there were some ugly stories bruited about concerning the circumstances of Kathryn's death. I have it on unimpeachable authority, absolutely unimpeachable, that the medical examiners found enough alcohol in what was left of her veins to intoxicate a bull moose. To be sure, there was no mention of that in the newspapers. Occasionally those creatures of the mass media do evidence a flicker of decency.

There was no concealing her vehicle's speed, however. She was a bit of a car buff and drove one of those old Lincoln convertible sedans that they stopped making centuries ago. It ploughed through a metal guardrail, leaped a ditch, flattened two small trees, and careened off the concrete and steel footings of a tower for a power line before overturning with enough momentum remaining to continue forward another ten yards, its windscreen flattening out and digging into the terrain. I do not imagine the driver was a pretty sight.

Three days after the funeral—it was a Monday and we were scheduled to sit that noon—Elena came into my chambers and handed me a copy of a letter. I read it in astonishment, utter and dumbfounded astonishment. Here is a Xerox for your notes:

Dear Mr. President:
I herewith resign my commission as Chief Justice of the United States.
[signed] Declan Patrick Walsh

It was hardly a complicated epistle, but it was full of dread import for the Court and the country. And worse, we had no warning, none whatsoever. Oh, I expected Walsh would want to miss the next two weeks of the Court's sitting; then our two weeks of recess would have given him a full month to regain his composure. On the other hand, I would not have been very surprised—surprised, but not *very* surprised—had he appeared in Court that morning. Resignation? It never entered my mind, never for an instant.

"He wanted you to see this first," Elena said, emotions reined in. "You'll have to make the announcement at noon and run the Court. A messenger is carrying the original to the White House right now, and his clerks will be taking copies to the other justices in a few minutes. He will prepare the usual letter to the brethren in a week or two; in the meantime he would appreciate your saying a few words to them in the robing room. He said you'd use all the proper adverbs and adjectives to express his regret at leaving them."

"Organized and orderly at the very end," I smiled as we sat down together on my couch. I poured her some tea that had been steeping in its pot on my table. "What is he planning to do?" I inquired.

She looked at me rather strangely. "Can't you guess? What would be in perfect keeping with his character?"

"God only knows," I replied wearily. "He might join the French foreign legion or even a monastery. The range is—" Then I saw the tears on her face.

"A Trappist monastery in South Carolina," she said quietly.

"Impossible, my dear. That kind of thing takes time. Even I know that one doesn't join a religious order like one posts a check to become a member of a Book-of-the-Month Club."

"You do if you're Chief Justice of the United States, a papal knight, a former special envoy to the Vatican, and a friend to all sorts of cardinals. His plane leaves National Airport at twelve-fifteen."

"Can't we stop him? We—you and I and if need be whoever among the brethren are in the building—we can talk some sense into his head. Surely—"

Again I looked at Elena carefully. For all her efficiency, she was a gentle person, a woman both attractive and vulnerable, and every ounce of her vulnerability had now been actualized into pain.

She just shook her head. "If only—but no ifs. You know him better than that. He's not only stubborn, he's so filled with guilt that he can barely live with himself. Mike spent hours with him, and the two of us were with him until three this morning. This is better than suicide. He feels totally responsible. That's enough to unravel any man, but there's a lot no one else can understand. It has to do with things other than Kate. Without Mike and the Gunny"—she referred, of course, to that Guicciardini individual—"I think he would have killed himself after the funeral. It's an amazing quality alcoholics have. They screw up their own lives and the lives of those around them, and manage to make those who love them feel guilty."

She looked up and smiled very softly. "Well, now I'm the one who's following her head, and he's following his heart. All the things that made him strong and good have twisted inside him. Now he's weak and bent on self-destruction. He's lost to us and most of all to me. He'll never again be able to love, if he ever really was."

"I think you underestimate the man's resiliency," I said, affecting a cheerfulness I did not feel. "Give him a few weeks of silence and all that praying and manual labor the Trappists do and he'll be roaring to escape and return to something useful."

"You're sweet," she said and leaned over and kissed me on the cheek, then stood up. "But I really don't think you understand him." (She was wrong, absolutely wrong, but my ego is sufficiently secure not to require affirmation. I merely smiled in return.) "Thanks for the comfort," she continued. "I've leaned on you and you've helped."

When she left I picked up pad and pencil and began to sketch what I would say at noon. I wanted it to be as simple and direct as Walsh's own statement. I found it difficult to concentrate, however. I was distracted by the recurring thought that Walsh might be taking the rotund cardinal's advice. Perhaps he was trying to learn more about *his* Deity. Perhaps he was. I thanked the Fates that I have never been attacked by any theological virus, for I have observed many men who have been so stricken. One does not, simply does not, expect rational behavior from them. Normal behavior for them runs along precisely the sort of lines Walsh was following: to curse their God one moment and then to spend months or even years in fervid prayer to the accursed one.

We are indeed strange and fascinating creatures. And, of course, Elena had been right, dead right, about the Irish. I would give a pretty to be alive when scientists completely decipher the human genetic code. I am certain, absolutely certain, that the Irish—and the Jews, with the exception of Jacobson—will be found to have a vast oversupply of the protein molecules that collect, store, and possibly multiply guilt.

Fortunately, I could not for long indulge my speculations about our resigned brother. Confronting me were the demanding tasks of composing a message to the brethren, drafting a letter from them to Walsh expressing their regret at his departure, formulating the discuss list for the coming week's conferences, and insuring agreement about what decisions were ready to go down. Immediately, the burdens of the chief justiceship once again fell on my shoulders, at least until some younger man better politically connected than I entered our Court to claim the chair of honor.

THIRTEEN

MY DEAR CHAP, I promised you my interpretation of Walsh, and you shall have it. To be sure, I am not a licensed psychiatrist, but as one who has spent a lifetime studying human nature—as any intelligent jurist must, for the law is, at bottom, nothing more nor less than a systematic striving to regulate human behavior—I believe that I can speak on this matter with some authenticity, albeit without formal jurisdiction. Let us break the man down into his component parts, or aspects, if you prefer. One part of Walsh embodied in many respects a caricature of what Max Weber called "the Protestant ethic." To be sure, Walsh was a Roman, not a Calvinist, but he was filled with the same sorts of needs for reassurance.

Weber claimed that Calvin's doctrine of predestination generated immense tensions and neurotic insecurities. If before all time God has decided whether each man will be saved or damned, and if men are too sinful to merit anything, then neither faith nor good works, alone or in combination, can be a means toward salvation. Such a situation is pregnant with the seeds of despair. But, Weber claimed, Calvinists eased their tensions by viewing secular successes as hints from the Deity that the achiever was among the elect. Yet a hint is hardly firm assurance, and its comfort quickly evanesces. Thus, Weber reasoned, the Calvinist had a compulsive need for constant material success—for a stream of hints and their transient reprieves from the terror that God had condemned him to hell.

That is the bare bones of one part of Walsh. Constant achievement was as necessary to his spirit as to the most pious sixteenth-century Calvinist. But Walsh's personality was multidimensional, and so a useful explanation must be heterodox. Let us look at a second aspect of the man. My own belief is that his father's alcoholism and the likely reaction to it by family, colleagues, and even strangers had created a sense of shame and disgrace as well as *anger* against those who, perhaps unconsciously, perhaps deliberately, or perhaps only in Walsh's imagination, displayed disdain toward the drunkard and his family.

That disdain shook his sense of self-worth, but genetically he also had a powerful enough ego to be angered, profoundly angered, rather than crushed by that treatment. If the stories about his mother's judicious allotment of her favors are correct, they would reinforce to an extraordinary degree those self-doubts as well as feelings of disgrace and rejection and, again, anger. I contend that at one level, a primitive level to be sure, he saw the world as sneeringly hostile; he hated "them," bitterly hated "them" whoever "they" might be. In sum, through all of the rat's maze that formed Walsh's psychological life, I am absolutely certain of one thing: he needed, desperately needed, his frequent triumphs to reassure himself that "they" were not sneering, and that those who had once sneered had been proved wrong, wickedly wrong.

Actually Kathryn was one integer on this side of the equation. Her physical beauty made her magnetically attractive in an obvious sexual way to all healthy males. But she was his, completely his. Others could gaze and envy, but they could not partake of this luscious fruit. I am certain, dead certain, that Walsh enjoyed the lustful stares she received. It was a way, to speak colloquially, of rubbing "their" noses in it. She cooperated—I do not say at the conscious level but I do say she cooperated—by wearing in public those erotically clinging gowns.

If one understands this much, one can readily comprehend the aggressive aspects of Walsh's personality, the intellectual fascination with brute power evidenced in his academic writings, his willingness to discuss frankly the obscene possibility of thermonuclear war. His own competitiveness becomes more intelligible as well. To be sure, I need not tell a person of your perspicacity that this explanation also accounts for his fondness for those horrible gladiators, the marines, and his success in the cruel arena of savage physical combat.

His addiction to work was another element in this syndrome. He always—not sometimes, or occasionally, or even usually, but *always*—had to be the most knowledgeable, the most learned on any problem. Furthermore, he found it necessary to have thought out, tested, and perfected his reactions, lest "they" again have an opportunity to sneer at the drunkard's son. Moreover, he had a compulsive need to prove to himself that "they" were wrong and he was better than those snobs. And, to be sure, by exposing "their" ignorance he vented his anger.

But there was more milk in that coconut, much more. Life is never simple. There is a third aspect here, his self-control. Except for occasional orgies of war, Walsh generally succeeded in masking his self-doubt and hostility, at least to the extent of expressing them in such socially accepted ways as intellectual competitiveness. I am confident, fully confident, that while, at a conscious level, he remained ignorant of his gnawing self-doubts, he was very much aware of his aggressiveness and tried manfully to repress it. Indeed, he detested that streak within himself; and that hatred of an integral part of himself increased his self-doubts and, at the same time, provided further fuel for a necessity to excel. To cope with that bundle of competing emotions, he developed a marvelous self-control. I do not like to dramatize life—actually, there is no need to do so, no need to at all—but I have never encountered anyone with that degree of self-control over his emotions.

On an intellectual level, he found his own aggressiveness utterly revolting. And on a different, less primitive but still emotional level, he was deeply committed to the values of Christianity. Now, as I have reminded you, I am agnostic; a lifetime of investigation and thought has convinced me that that is the only viable intellectual stance. But, I must tell you in all candor—indeed, I speak, so to say, in italics—that Walsh was an absolutely committed Christian. I know very well that there was nothing in his early or middle life that obviously pointed that way, and a moralizer would surely condemn as serious sin his affair with Elena Falconi. Certainly he himself did. But I felt that commitment burning within him. Put it down to my not untrained intuition. His notion of constitutional law was a Christian gospel of social justice. His concept of himself as chief justice was as a St. Paul—or perhaps St. Francis—bringing that gospel to a heathen world.

The commitment not only contradicted his aggressive impulses, but birthed its own litter of tensions. It was not merely that at a conscious level Walsh abhorred violence and conflict; more important, much more important, he genuinely wanted to love his fellow man. Now, we both know what a foolishly impossible task that is, and how setting absolutely unattainable goals for oneself can only lead to frustration, anger, guilt, and more aggression. Be that as it may, I can tell you with full assurance that without the traumae of his childhood he might have become another Francis of Assisi. Almost alone of those who knew him, I found his later career completely in character—at least it was congruent with a strong cable that ran through his personality.

As I have indicated, without his simply stupendous self-control, the centrifugal force of those fiercely orbiting tensions would have disintegrated his personality into a hundred discordant pieces. He would probably have become a murdering maniac or regressed into a catatonic trance. But even that marvelous self-control could never fully succeed in curbing his competitiveness. Indeed, that was undoubtedly an essential safety valve for his anger and aggressiveness.

In his personal life he was typically kind and gentle, though one sensed that a cauldron was darkly bubbling here. As I have already indicated, one of his ways of venting hostility—and of reassuring himself that no one could dare sneer again—was by constantly showing that he was quicker and brighter and more learned than "they" were. His humor—which many of his friends dubbed earthy but which to me never seemed more than vulgar—had a double aspect. In one sense it was an effort to say "not only am I brighter and quicker at this than you, but I can beat you at whatever you do while thinking about something else." In another sense, his humor was often a way of degrading the strivings of others. He was saying that what others were trying to do with their lives was actually worth very little. As a concession to Christianity, or perhaps his own self-doubts, he might include himself in the humor and thus demonstrate humility if not charity.

Let me now guide you through an apparent, but only an apparent, set of contradictions. I have hypothesized not at all unreflectively about Walsh's anger, his self-control, and his internalization of the norms of Christianity. Indeed, at one point I noted that, under different conditions, he might have opted for the life-style of a Francis of Assisi rather than of a marine killer. The apparent contradiction, my dear young man, hinges on the fact that, while he wanted to love his fellow man, he found it difficult to become closely emotionally attached to human beings and individuals.

I believe those statements do not really contradict one another. I also believe that his inability to love deeply—people as individuals, not abstract mankind but the specific thee and me—was partially the result of his father's frequent binges, which to a child would have been equivalent to rejections and desertions. In part his incapacity to commit himself fully to other people as individuals was a price exacted for the self-control he exercised over his anger and aggressiveness. By exerting almost superhuman efforts to extirpate one set of emotions, he succeeded in crippling all of his emotions. Elena, in her wonderfully imprecise feminine fashion, intuitively comprehended what I am saying. I believe that Keller creature also understood, as did Kathryn but she herself was too emotionally committed to him to live with that understanding.

This angry aggressiveness, sublimated as it was into competitiveness, his addiction to work, his sharp-edged, if vulgar, humor, and his wife's sexuality were clear indicia of one side of his personality. His immense self-control tempered his aggressiveness; his commitment to Christianity rationalized what society demanded. It also moved him toward peaceful persuasion. That accounts for his irenical manner at conference and within the Court, his efforts to seek peace and harmony—after, to be sure, demonstrating his own cerebral superiority. In presiding over the Court, in deciding cases, and in assigning work to colleagues, he was always scrupulously fair. I have already described these gentler aspects of his character. I re-emphasize them here. His frequent endeavors to smooth over differences, to heal cuts, and mend divisions, I am satisfied, were signs that he was convinced in his mind that he was practicing Christianity by example if not by precept.

With his wife's tragic death for which he, not without justification, felt responsible, the steel strands of his personality all began to snap. His decision to enter a monastery was therapeutic biologically as much as spiritually. Of that I am convinced, totally convinced. One might even look on that decision as a subconscious, albeit very Chris-

ONE

You asked me to commence with my name. I am called Ugo Galeotti, Monsignor Galeotti, as I prefer, or as my official title reads, Ugo Cardinal Galeotti. Once in my diplomatic career I was Titular Archbishop of Numida. *Ecco,* Numida is not a real see, as you probably know, and I was never a real bishop in the sense of being the shepherd of a flock, but I became, and shall relate you how, the shepherd's dog. That is enough if the flock are the people of God and the shepherd is no hireling.

Allora, most of my life I was a professional diplomat. And at some stage in his service, a papal diplomat needs, if not to speak with the authority of a bishop, at least to be treated with the dignities of that office. And, because of the Arabs' conquests centuries ago, the Church counts many ancient sees that exist in name only. Still, I would not seem overly modest. I became a prince of the Church, a member of the Sacred College of Cardinals, and during a time when there were not so many of us. In my retirement, I am returned to wait for death here at Torri del Benaco, not a hundred meters from the house in which I was born eighty-one years ago. According to me, that death has been a long time coming, but, as *il Papa* once told, it is a free gift of God, and we have no claim to its mercy.

When I grew up here my father owned a long stretch of vineyards that commenced near Bardolino, a few kilometers to the south, and ran, with some interruptions, to what are now the suburbs of Verona. Here in our house on the Lake of Garda our table wines were Soave for white and Bardolino for red. (I inherited my father's preference for Bardolino over the rougher Valpolicella or even the heavier and more elegant Amarone.)

In that house we spoke as much German as Italian, and my father insisted us that we learn French—that was before the Great War when English was not taught and spoken everywhere.

Do not ask me when I decided to become a priest; I did not decide; I simply always knew I must be a priest. In any case, it was inevitable that a bright young priest from a good family that could afford to send him to Rome to study for a doctorate in canon law and who was already bilingual and had knowledge of a third language as well as an appreciation of fine wine would drift into the papal diplomatic service.

God has been good to me. As you can see from my size, I have possessed more than my fair share of material things. *Allora,* I have also enjoyed my share of more spiritual things, even though I have never commanded my own flock. In the morning, when I celebrate my Mass, I can look at my lake—it is lovelier now in the winter when the tourists are gone and the snow has crept down from the Dolomites into our hills—and I am grateful for all God has given me.

Ecco, I do not mean life has always been easy or interesting. For a young man the papal diplomatic service is mostly difficult drudgery: reading and summarizing cables marked urgent but usually containing only trivia; listening to complaints from priests against their bishops and from laymen against their priests; trying to learn what madness modern governments are plotting against one another; compiling dossiers on priests who might be elevated to bishops; drafting letters to present the Church's interests to dictators and democrats, knowing that in neither case were you likely to exercise any influence. There was sometimes physical danger as well. I found myself in Havana from 1956 to 1961 as what you would call a first undersecretary. Those were exciting days. First we had to deal with the decay of the Batista regime, then Castro. Many of our younger priests viewed Fidel as a savior. Soon, however, they found themselves in prison or in exile or in the tomb.

Later, after Castro had expelled or imprisoned almost all priests, I returned. My task was to consecrate as bishops two young priests in hiding in Havana. Castro's police captured one of those men when he was driving to our rendezvous. (He died in prison a few months later, without the solace of the final sacrament.) When I had consecrated the other priest a bishop—*allora,* it was the briefest ceremony since the time of the Apostles—I departed the island by the same secret route I had entered.

Ecco, you do not want to hear an old man prattle about his life. According to Cardinal Pritchett and the *avvocato*—you say lawyer?—Keller (you please all and two of them, by the way), I may trust you and be perfectly candid with you, even though you transport that little tape register. In reality, I am at liberty to talk as I want about this thing in which you are interested.

Before I say you anything about the Vatican, I must warn you to look at us who are in the Curia—*mi scusi,* those who were in the Curia—for what we were, men, whole men. We were not a group of saintly ascetics who came from a life of solitary prayer in monastic cells to pray in the shadow of San Pietro. Nor were we—how does one say?—neurotics or cynics. We were priests, bishops, and cardinals, but in honor of truth, we were also men, with all the strengths and weaknesses of our fellow humans. We were not, as one says, a cross section of humanity or even of priests. We were an elite, even an elite among priests, very intelligent, highly trained. But because we were more intelligent and better trained does not mean we did not feel temptation or on occasion give in to it.

According to me, as I sit here on my lake, pride was our most frequent sin, a failing I have found common among very intelligent men who possess power over their brothers. But I must confess you that some of us also drank too much, some were envious of others, some were less strict with the truth than we should have been, and *anche,* some of us, a few of us, had problems with women, and fewer with other men. Many of us were—of new, how does one say?—neurotic, immature, childish, selfish, narrow-minded; at some time all of us displayed these faults. Yet I think most of us were healthy, normal adults. And most of us tried—we may have sometimes failed but we tried—with all our souls to serve God by serving His Church.

In sum, in many ways we were not too different from your very senior civil servants, or the management of Fiat, IBM, or people like that. We followed much more austere sexual lives and our language was less vulgar; but, while we prayed more, I am not secure that we were more holy. We tried harder to be holy, perhaps, but that is not always enough.

Allora, I am not criticizing my colleagues or apologizing for them. I merely say you that if you want to understand us, you must not think either that we were a group of otherworldly saints, cynical sinners, or neurotics. We were men who tried to serve God, and being men, often served ourselves.

Enough so. Let us commence with the conclave itself. *Senta,* I pray you not to think of me as one of those Vaticanisti who violates his oath of secrecy and sells gossip to the newspapers. We who participate in a conclave do take an oath of secrecy, although it was not always so in the past. We can tell no one of the things that transpire when, with the help of the Holy Spirit, we choose *il Papa.* We can say nothing about what went on inside those sacred walls unless we enjoy the permission of the Pontiff. The punishment is excommunication, automatic excommunication. But, *ecco,* I possess that permission.

Declan—*il Papa*—I now think of him all these ways; I cannot separate the Pontiff from the man, understand? That is natural, perhaps. *Dunque, il Papa* wanted those around him not only to speak what we knew of his papacy but also of it to write. Now it is too late for me of it to write, but perhaps I can help you write his story well. I can only talk. We Italians can always talk. I pray you, at one time my English was quite fluent; now it lacks practice. But it will return me as I use it. If I am unclear, I pray you interrupt me. It would not please me to seem to speak with hair on the tongue.

Allora, I do not know at what time to commence even when I speak of the conclave. Perhaps it is best to explain you the idea, even though I do not know when it first came. I am certain that I did not possess it before Declan and I had our long talk at my apartment of the Watergate, when he was still Chief Justice of the United States. It was not arrived at that time. Sometime after, I am not secure when, it came to me like a child's soap bubble, teasing me, floating in the warm sunshine of a Roman midday. It danced there in my mind and then was gone; then it returned of new only to go. But I knew it would come of new.

I can myself remember of the time when I first commenced to consider it seriously, as something more than a fantasy. It was at a moment of great sadness. As a member of the Sacred College of Cardinals I was returning to Roma from my post as apostolic delegate to Washington. My task was to bury one Pontiff—a thing I have now done too many times—and to elect his successor. It was dawn below, but it was only two hours more than midnight by the time in which I had been living. We had flown all night across the Atlantic into the morning sun. Such crossings always leave me confused and unclear in my thinking, and I usually try to sleep through them with a capsule. But I myself remember well that the idea then became fixed in my mind. I do not mean that I instantly accepted it, but it was then firmly in my mind and would not vanish.

I remember that the grand 747 was descending rapidly, making my ears—how does one say?—pop. We passed high over the coast south of Roma, and, as we reached the outskirts of the city, the aircraft went into a slow, banking turn. With the wing well behind my seat, I could look below into a magnificent vista. Directly beneath me was the Colosseo, then the Imperial Forum and the glistening white marble of that atrocious matrimonial cake, the Vittorio Emanuele monument. As the plane continued its sweeping turn, I could see the Borghese Gardens, then the brown and yellow of the muddy Tiber, and finally the vast expanse of the Piazza di San Pietro and the dome that Michelangelo designed for the basilica.

According to me, for all Michelangelo's talent, San Pietro's—I pray you, I mean St. Peter's but I think of it in Italian—lacks the beauty of those gothic marvels like Chartres, Notre Dame, Milano, or Toledo, or the spidery elegance of the cathedral of Barcelona. San Pietro is not perhaps even a pretty church; its discolored and yellowing marble façade might even be called ugly. *Ecco,* its beauty rests in its authority, its immensity, accentuated—you say that?—by the crablike arms of Bernini's colonnade, threatening to collect the entire world into the Fisherman's net. The basilica possesses the kind of beauty that accompanies pomp and splendor rather than grace. The stolid, squat building shouts like a fat Trastevere *signora* that here is the center of the world.

It was during that sweeping turn that the idea of Declan Walsh as the bishop of Roma firmly fixed itself in my mind. I looked from the window and tried to dismiss the thought by reading of new the headlines of yesterday's *New York Times,* succinct and to the point as headlines are: POPE KILLED IN PLANE CRASH. The new Pontiff had been progressing on his way to attend a special session of the World Council of Churches at Geneva, to listen to a discussion on justice and peace. As the aircraft had prepared in ugly weather for a landing at Geneva, a Swiss fighter plane had broken through the clouds and crashed head-on into *il Papa*'s transport. The only survivor had been the fighter pilot, whose condition was reported as critical; he was alive only because his automatic ejection seat had thrown him from the mass of machinery that had tumbled into Lac Leman.

I confess you that I had not felt altogether secure during my flight from New York. According to me, our God has the perverse kind of humor that would smile at the irony of the first cardinal's dying in a plane crash on his way to attend the funeral of the first Pontiff to die so. I pray you, do not think me callous or believe that I think God cruel. It is only that He will call each of us home some day, and as the years go by that fate seems less terrible.

Ecco, I was speaking you about the funeral. I was wondering what kind of funeral the Church would make *il Papa.* The *Times* reported that the jet had exploded at impact with the fighter and that the wreckage had fallen into the lake. I doubted that there would be identifiable bodies. That lack would present my colleagues in the Vatican with bad problems of protocol. We of the Church prefer to follow precedents than to make them. My brothers in the Curia have boasted that in the Vatican nothing is done for the first time. But here there would be no choice.

Without question, a few rites would be performed. Already Giovanni Cardinal LaTorre, the *camerlengo* (you would say chamberlain) of *il Papa*'s household, would have removed the Fisherman's ring of the last Pontiff from the papal desk and disintegrated it with a special hammer. Already the clergy in Vatican City would have removed the purple and red decorations from their cassocks. Most would dress themselves completely in black, with cardinals and other prelates permitted to wear their colored robes reserved for official ceremonies. The staff of the papal palazzo would be wearing black morning coats and black ties. The great bells of San Pietro and of San Giovanni in Laterano, *il Papa*'s own church, would be slowly tolling their deep voices, reminding Romans of their sorrow. Mercifully, the rules of Paolo VI and the air accident had spared *il Papa* the medieval ceremony of having his head tapped three times with a small silver mallet while the *camerlengo* called his name to make secure he was truly departed. I myself was in grief, but I was obliged to smile at the picture of the bull-like LaTorre tapping the delicate Pontiff on the forehead with a mallet. If His Holiness was not already dead, LaTorre's heavy hand would have rapidly dispatched his soul.

Soon more than a hundred cardinals would be arriving in Roma from all over the world, to bury a Pontiff if not to elect one. Papa Paolo's constitution for the election of the Roman Pontiff had removed from cardinals who had more than eighty years the right to participate in papal elections. That would mean that only 82 of the 120 living members of the sacred college could vote.

But even with fewer cardinals eligible to participate, the process of selection would be more difficult than usual. Old national jealousies would flare up of new. Undoubtedly some Italian cardinals would want to bring the tiara home, so to speak; some cardinals from other countries would love it for one of their own. According to me, no prominent Italian could easily obtain the necessary vote of two-thirds plus one. There would also be problems far deeper than nationalism. More bitter were divisions among so-called liberals, traditionalists, and moderates that good Papa Giovanni—you say Pope John?—and the Second Vatican Council had brought into the open.

I must say you something about these terms *liberal, conservative,* or *traditional,* and *moderate. Traditionalists* or *institutionalists,* according to me, has some meaning, signifying those who do not desire the Church to change, at least not change much, its mode. The other terms make less sense. Differences within the Church are not so much over change of itself, for the liberals charge conservatives with changing the character of the Church just as much as the traditionalists level that charge against so-called liberals. Nor is the dispute exactly over freedom versus authority. For our liberal bishops can be as authoritarian as our conservatives. Witness their canonical rage at clergy and laity who prefer the stately Latin liturgy over that melange of bad translations and poor taste that characterizes the liturgy since Vatican II.

Ecco, the real point is division over ideas about the Church's nature—you say, models of the Church? Those whom the press calls conservatives tend to view the Church in the mode that is associated with the era after the Reformation, the Council of Trent in the sixteenth century. That is, primarily as a hierarchically organized society, a visible institution created by God to save souls. The clergy possess the functions of teaching, sanctifying, and governing. I stress you the last, governing. The laity also possess their roles: believing, professing, and obeying—what you Americans sometimes jokingly tell means pray, pay, and obey.

Allora, the object of the Church is to save souls, and that task according to this model can best be performed within a society that announces clearly defined rules in order that all men may know what to believe and how to act not merely in order to avoid sin, but also to receive God's grace and, when they fall, to receive God's mercy.

Most of us, traditionalists, liberals, or moderates, view the Church as a communion of believers—what theologians and especially Papa Pio XII called "the Mystical Body of Christ." *Ecco,* according to me the true divisions meet here. The traditionalists stress us the necessity of the communion's hierarchical nature, its orderly character, and its clear, firm rules of moral conduct. The liberals talk us more of the "people of God" interacting, if not as perfect equals at least as independent adults whose lives and societies are too complex to permit clear, simple rules to be useful.

Liberals and traditionalists, all and two, view the Church as the mediator between God and man within this Mystical Body, but the liberals look at the hierarchy's principal roles of teaching, sanctifying, and governing in a different, perhaps broader mode. In their model of the Church, they tell, clergy are servants as well as governors. The liberals—the which is why I prefer to call them *servants*—make their departure from Mark, 10:43–45: "Any one among you who aspires to greatness must serve the rest; whoever wants to rank first must serve the needs of all. The Son of Man has not come to be served but to serve—to give His life in ransom for the many."

The servants also picture the secular world as possessing a dignity and a legitimacy that the traditionalist's institutional model ignores—not denies, merely ignores. For those who accept the model of servant, the end of man—and so of the Church—remains salvation, but they see other institutions as playing important and proper roles in that process.

Rather than describing the Church's primary functions as pronouncing rules of conduct and condemning deviations, the followers of the servant model view the Church's overriding task as fostering the brotherhood of man, healing, reconciling, and helping create a climate of trust in which the kingdom of God, and of His love, can become reality. The Church remains the teacher, but—how do you say?—the leader—do you know that we have no equivalent for *leader* in Italian? Even had we been spared Mussolini's making the word an international joke, *duce* is closer to your "commander" than to "leader." That may be a problem with our theology as well as our political philosophy. We can say director or commander, but not quite leader. *Ecco,* I wander. Those who accept the servant model, view the Church teaching as a warm leader of an intimate seminar rather than as the austere lecturer to a huge audience. Perhaps more important, the servants desire that the Church, and especially the clergy, teach by example as much as by words.

Allora, forgive me. I was once a *professore,* and on occasion I still make a lecture. But there is necessity to explain you these things. The traditionalists' love of directing by clear rules causes them to stress us faith and dogma and avoidance of sin. The servants'—I use that word instead of liberals—desire to lead by encouragement causes them to emphasize us good deeds. It is an old division within Christianity. We who are moderates—and that word has no meaning unless you comprehend the forces between which we stand—see all and two sides.

I do not mean you either that most traditionalists or most servants—and certainly none who are moderates—claim the others speak falsely. (*Ecco,* I concede you that there are charges and countercharges of heresy, but only from the extremes on either side.) There are wide varieties of views among each school, but their fundamental differences are on things of emphasis, or words such as *primary* or *principal.* No traditionalist denies the necessity of the Church's fostering the brotherhood of man any more than servants deny the Church's obligation to teach and sanctify. But traditionalists sometimes believe—I confess you not always without reason—that the servants are willing to sacrifice some articles of our holy faith to create harmony. For their part, many servants—they, too, not always without reason—see traditionalists as posting the formal institutions and the prerogatives of the hierarchy of the Church above the task of saving souls.

We moderates possess the unhappy task of trying to maintain peace in our own homes. Sometimes we wonder, as Papa Paolo VI must often have, if the Sermon on the Mount did not really tell: "Blessed are the peacemakers for they shall be reviled by everyone."

Allora, these divisions within the Church are complex, and the lines, if not sharply drawn, can still make for bitterness, even rancor. These differences also cross national lines. With the exception of Ireland, whose three cardinals are so traditional as to suspect that even a deviation from the punctuation of the decrees of the Council of Trent is evidence of heresy, every national hierarchy names cardinals in all three groups. And at risk of sounding the boor, I say you of new that there are differences as wide within servants as among traditionalists. Indeed, I confess you that a few servants—that Dutchman Gordenker, for instance, but I describe you him later—would reduce the Church's teaching role to proclaiming the message of the Gospel and leaving all moral conduct to the individual conscience so informed. That, according to me, is hardly more than Protestantism.

Ecco, I say you no more about this thing now. But I pray you to maintain it in mind as I talk. For without understanding this thing, one can neither understand what happened at the conclave nor Papa Francesco's reign.

Allora, I myself remember making while yet on the aircraft a list of the names of the more probable candidates, the *papabili.* Each would be objectionable to a sizable portion of the sacred college. Thus, unless there would be some unlikely compromise or direct and prompt intervention by the Holy Spirit, the choice would probably come to an old man, one intended as Papa Giovanni had been to serve as an interim Pontiff, maintaining, as you say, the warmth of the chair of San Pietro for a successor selected at a more propitious time. Or we might decide on a relatively unknown candidate who was, if not pleasing to all, not displeasing to many. According to me, the second alternative appeared more likely, but preceded by a very long conclave during which all sides would appeal to heaven, to reason, and ultimately to self-preservation before a decision was accorded.

As yet, in the few hours since *il Papa*'s death, I had had no direct communication with other cardinals, but earlier general conversations in the Vatican and in America gave me fear that both servants and traditionalists were—how do you say it?—"compromised out." They had several times in recent years entombed their differences to choose a Pontiff who was not the first—or second—selection of either. Now, I sensed, both sides would be stubborn. *Allora,* I would soon learn more.

I pray you to understand something about our rules of the conclave. Since the thirteenth century we have been expressly forbidden to—how do you say in American politics?—canvass and campaign for votes. But, *la mancanza* —how is it called?—*ecco,* the lack of a miraculous inspiration makes some discussion necessary for the college to arrive at the required extraordinary majority. While warning against the sin of bargaining over candidates, Papa Paolo's constitution says us specifically: "We have no intention, however, of forbidding the exchange of views concerning the election during the period in which the see is vacant." Such "exchanges of views" commence early in the Vatican. In fact, as soon as one Pontiff is selected, we curialists commence to think about his successor, although we are prohibited to discuss the subject. Without other, the thinking becomes much more pointed after a Pontiff has died. I knew that at that very moment LaTorre would be selecting a candidate and speaking encouragement to his friends within the Curia, just as I myself might also talk to those princes whom I knew.

In Milano, the handsome, charming aristocrat, Paolo Cardinal Fieschi, would be busy telephoning friends in Roma and Paris and Cologne and Vienna. In the end, LaTorre and Fieschi would likely side together. But as a descendant of one of the oldest and noblest families of Genova, one that had already provided the Church several Pontiffs, Fieschi—I hope I do not sin against charity—regarded LaTorre with personal disdain because he had been born in the Sicilian hinterlands of a peasant family. LaTorre was aware of Fieschi's feelings, but, according to me, even before the conclave LaTorre migh' well decide that Fieschi should be *il Papa.* For all his stubbornness, nothing, certainly not personal pride, took precedence in LaTorre's mind over the good of the Church. (I should explain you also that we Italians are more accustomed to arrogance than you Americans; we look on it as a common venial sin rather than a major flaw in character. As my fellow countrymen would ask, what good are power and status if you cannot use them and even abuse them?)

More subtle than the activities of either of these two princes would be the labors of the youngest member of the sacred college, Mario Cardinal Chelli. He was regarded as a traditionalist colleague of LaTorre, and he, too, would seek a traditionalist Pontiff. But, according to me, Chelli, unlike LaTorre, coveted the supreme post for himself, if not today, then tomorrow. *Ecco,* that makes another story.

I told that Chelli and LaTorre were of accord in their regard for an image of the Church. Of truth, but few men could be so different in all other modes. LaTorre, whom we—even his enemies—affectionately called the Holy Mule, was a huge man physically. He weighed almost 120 kilos —about 250 pounds by your standards—and was almost two meters tall—about 6′6″. Chelli was rather short—I make these computations in my head—about 5′9″ you would say, and fully dressed weighed no more than 135 of your pounds.

LaTorre's bulk was topped by a mane of silver hair that remained as thick as it had been forty years earlier, when we had been young priests together, students in the Pontificia Academia Ecclesiastica, and its color had been black-black.

Chelli's hair was sparse; thin wisps of it retreated helter-skelter—is that the proper phrase?—from an already naturally high forehead. His family had been rather well-to-do bourgeoisie from Naples, but as evidence of that city's varied foreign rulers, the cardinal's coloring was fair; his eyes were blue, and what remained of his hair was brownish. His thin face, as he often remarked us, looked much like that of Machiavelli, a likeness, he would join, that had made it difficult for him to receive a good grade in his seminary examinations in ethics. At that point he would laughingly flick his blue eyes into a fanatical gaze.

The mind of LaTorre was like a crusader's broadsword: honest, direct, and heavy. Chelli's intellect was more like an Arab's scimitar: sharp, swift, and curved. We were all and two canon lawyers and I respected Chelli's learning and the quality of his mind. And also, the young cardinal possessed a quick but gentle sense of humor. In a personal mode, I found him what we Italians call *simpatico*—that is, congenial not sympathetic. He was sensitive to the feelings of others, at least—I hope I do not sin against charity—of others of equal or higher rank. He was often able to use his charm to soothe if not persuade those whom his logic and learning left unconvinced.

Chelli, I have said you, was identified with the traditionalists in the Curia, but he was not so dogmatic either personally or theologically as LaTorre. Let me give one example. LaTorre's approach to ecumenism was to quote from the fourteenth-century bull *Unam Sanctam:* "Indeed we declare, announce, and define that it is altogether necessary to salvation for every human creature to be subject to the Roman Pontiff." Chelli, on the other hand, was apt to listen intently to the words of our separated brethren and to stress them our points of agreement, leaving it clear, although untold, where we disagreed. It was an approach that at least left open the possibility of future discussion. (I do not imply you that LaTorre was rude in his dealings with people of other faiths. His rough honesty and good humor usually softened the impact of his stentorian voice and imperious words, and many Protestants preferred to talk with LaTorre rather than with some of our fuzzy-minded liberal cardinals.) In any event, these men cannot be compared with the rather supercilious attitude toward ecumenism that our dear French brother Claude Cardinal Bisset demonstrated. His solution for relations with anyone who did not fully accept Catholicism (as Bisset understood it) was the formula of the Council of Trent: *Anathema sit*. Let him be cursed.

According to me, each of these men would be a formidable opponent in the conclave, and, with the exception of Bisset, each was as dedicated to the Church as was I. Furthermore, on the other side there would be men equally active, although usually not so powerful. While the traditionalists had been able to concentrate their power in Roma, those who were pressing for the servant model of the Church were scattered across northern Europe, Africa, Asia, Canada, Latin America, and, in a few instances, the United States. Because of this dispersion they found it more difficult than the curialists to consult and form what you Americans call a winning coalition even when in actual numbers they might have made a majority.

A few minutes' meditation on these problems convinced me that saving Holy Mother Church from the loving embraces of her quarrelsome children would be a most difficult task. I also understood about jet lag and how it makes intellectual activity and especially judgment to suffer. I concluded that it would be wisest to postpone for at least several hours, if not some days, any discussion with my holy brothers.

Passing through the customs control made no problems; it never does at Fiumicino even without a diplomatic passport, but recapturing one's luggage always consumes much time. At least my car was waiting for me and drove me rapidly to my apartment in the Palazzo di San Calisto. The palazzo—the term palace is an accurate translation in this case, although it often is misleading—is a huge edifice that Pio XI constructed in the middle of the Trastevere to house curial offices. The more important congregations have always refused to find themselves so far from San Pietro and the papal palazzo; as a result the San Calisto is inhabited only by the unimportant officials. The top floor, the *attico,* is used as a series of apartments for cardinals, and I had managed to retain mine even while away on diplomatic missions. The noisy, garbage-littered streets of the Trastevere were not pleasing to me, but it did please me to be somewhat removed from my curial brothers; I also appreciated the fact that the area is crowded with the best restaurants in Roma.

I hoped that in a few days the sun of the early Roman summer would warm my brain so that it would tell whether I should try for the papal tiara myself—for, according to others as well as myself, I was *papabile*—or whether instead I should try that other teasing plan that remained with me. As always when I have a problem, I prayed God for an answer. He was somewhat slow in responding, but that is His style. *Ecco,* I suppose if we were eternal, time would seem less important and patience would come more easily.

TWO

THE FUNERAL RITES for the dead Pontiff were executed with that full measure of pomp and circumstance which, according to me, only we Italians can provide. What things the methodical Swiss could identify as *il Papa*'s body were placed in a sealed coffin and dispatched via special train from Geneva to Roma. The Swiss government provided a military escort, and the Bundespräsident and the president of the Constitutional Court accompanied the body. The official sorrow of the Swiss was sturdy and stolid, like that of a banker who hears of a misfortune to a client who does not wish to increase or extend a loan. That businesslike sorrow paled beside the emotional outpouring of our Italians. *Ecco,* as the funeral train wound its passage down the Alps, crowds knelt in prayer along the concrete aprons of the rural stations; along the tracks in the countryside small clumps of people stood at their vineyards, sobbing loudly as women kissed their rosaries and men made the sign of the cross. The faces of these peasants reflected the anguish and grief that are such vital parts of the joys of our Italian life.

Allora, in Domodossola, the official Italian escort came aboard—the president of the Republic, the president of the Constitutional Court, the prime minister, and a representative from each party with seats in Parliament, including the *Comunisti,* accompanied by a platoon of infantry, gorgeously uniformed in blue and scarlet. From the Curia, LaTorre came himself, together with the senior cardinal from each order, two patriarchs of the Eastern Rite, fifteen *monsignori,* and a platoon of Swiss Guards in their Renaissance costumes and even carrying their pikes.

(I should explain you before I continue that we have three orders of cardinals. The least numerous, most prestigious, but not necessarily the most influential of the princes of the Church are called cardinal bishops. They are all members of the Curia and are titular—not real—bishops of the six suburban dioceses of Roma. They elect from their own number the dean of the sacred college. Next in rank are the cardinal priests. These men may be curial officials or they may be archbishops of real dioceses like Paris or Dublin or New York or Milano. In either case, they are assigned churches in the vicinity of Roma for which they are nominally—I stress you nominally—responsible. Finally come the cardinal deacons, in whose ranks I find myself. We are all curial officials or diplomats. We, too, possess titular churches. By virtue of their office, patriarchs in the Eastern Rite have been, since the time of Papa Paolo, members of the Sacred College of Cardinals and rank with the cardinal bishops, although the patriarchs are not assigned titular sees or churches in Roma.)

The police had fear that a large turnout at Milano might precipitate trouble between political factions, but Italian *Comunisti* are more Italian than *Comunisti,* and the *Fascisti* always protest their love for the Holy Church, even as they rape her. *Ecco,* when the train arrived into the station for a brief ceremony and a special blessing from the cardinal archbishop of Milano, almost a half million people, monarchists, Christian Democrats, Republicans ,every shade of *Socialisti, Comunisti,* and even neo-*Fascisti* from the Italian Social Movement stood as solemnly reverent as had the peasants in the countryside.

By the time the train had arrived in Roma's gleaming *Termini,* it was late afternoon. I had enjoyed my siesta and had joined a group of fifty-two cardinals, all of those already assembled in the city. *Allora,* the Pontiff's former throne bearers gently lifted the casket out of the railway wagon and, transporting it on their shoulders, commenced the long, slow walk to the Basilica of San Giovanni in Laterano—you call it St. John Lateran. That is the traditional church of the bishop of Roma, standing on the site given by Constantine himself. Ahead of them, as the bells of all the churches in the holy city tolled, we cardinals marched. Behind us strode the Swiss and Italian governmental officials, then the platoon of Swiss Guards. Behind the body came the Italian military escort.

We went through the main portals of the station and turned left to proceed down the dingy Via Cavour. (Every time I return to Roma, I recall how dirty a city it really is, but one soon ceases to notice trash and garbage and views only baroque grandeur.) In late afternoon the Cavour is usually a bustling thoroughfare lined with hotels, *pensioni,* shops, cheap *trattorie,* and bars. Rattling trams, snarling buses, and honking taxis maintain the noise high, even for Roma. But this afternoon, all traffic was blocked and the shops and eating places were tightly shuttered. The sidewalks were crowded with people, but, for Roma, there were few sounds—a crying child, a sobbing old woman, tinkling rosary beads, shuffling feet in the procession, and only an occasional exchange of angry shouts as someone blocked someone else's vista.

At the Basilica of Santa Maria Maggiore, the cortege turned down the even dingier Via Merulana, with its old brown stuccoed homes now housing bars on the ground floor and on the upper levels assorted dentists, surgeons, attorneys, and accountants. In another block, however, past the Alfonsiana, where Redemptorist theologians taught young priests doctrines that LaTorre was privately convinced were heretical, the Merulana assumed a more prosperous face. The shops, even though closed, were more elegant, the thoroughfare wider, and most important to us old men, there was shade from big trees lining all and two sides of the street.

We paused here for the pallbearers to catch their breath, for in two steps the street would go uphill. Then we commenced of new, walking past the obelisk that Constantine had brought to us from Alexandria. We went around the Palazzo Laterano, built supposedly where Constantine had lived before he donated the area to the Pontiff. The cortege then slowly marched into the basilica itself, through the 2000-year-old bronze portals pilfered from the ancient Roman senate, and halted before the main altar.

To the posterior of the basilica, in niches high up in the wall, were the bodies of Leo XIII, the first Pontiff who had evidenced any understanding of the modern world (according to me the last until Giovanni), and Innocenzo III, whom many scholars more than 750 years after his death still regard as the greatest of the Pontiffs. (According to me, Gregory VII would be a better choice, but in such matters all tastes are tastes. I report you them without judging them.)

Once the casket was in place on the catafalque before the papal altar, we paused for a short prayer and then retreated to a cool, cloistered, thirteenth-century courtyard that sits on the church's left flank. The Vatican staff had wine, coffee, soft drinks, mineral water, and a pair of physicians on hand, ready to give aid and comfort. It was in that courtyard that I experienced my first conversations about the next successor of San Pietro. Several of us exchanged laughs about LaTorre's heavy-handedness in routing the funeral train into the station in Milano so that Cardinal Fieschi, whom it was now obvious would be LaTorre's first choice at the conclave, might receive some extra notoriety.

LaTorre had planned every step of the obsequies—not that the authority was his, even as cardinal *camerlengo,* cardinal dean, or all and two. Our law provides that between the death of one Pontiff and the entry of the cardinals into conclave there should be daily "general congregations" of the sacred college. All cardinals are eligible to participate in these meetings, and here are decided, formally at least, all the important things regarding the governance of the Church and more particularly the special arrangements regarding the burial of the old Pontiff and the election of the new—all, without other, within the framework of the law of the Church, which itself can be changed only by the new Pontiff.

Allora, I said you that the general congregation possessed formal authority. In facts, LaTorre expressed us detailed ideas on almost all things that occurred, especially the funeral and the conclave; most of us knew little and had less care about these things. Besides, LaTorre was a respected, if not always properly appreciated and revered, man. It is, I understand, typical of large groups in such situations to defer to an energetic leader who will give the time to think through the problems that do not interest the others.

Let me tell another word about the post of LaTorre. Not only was he the prefect of the Holy Office, historically the most prestigious of curial offices, but he was also acting secretary of state, the office which in the modern papacy is potentially the most powerful except that of *il Papa* himself. In addition, as I have told, he was *camerlengo,* often described as the dictator pro tem of the Church, and dean of the sacred college, a post that carries more prestige than power.

Rarely in the modern Church has one man simultaneously held so many posts. The deanship was a sign of the affection in which he was held by the other cardinal bishops, who, as I spoke you, were all curial officials themselves. The old Pontiff—I call him that although he did not reign long enough to lack the accolade of "the new Pontiff" during his own lifetime—had been drawn to LaTorre not only because of the Sicilian's obvious talents but also because the Holy Father knew that he was not thereby appointing a crown prince. LaTorre was too marked a traditionalist, his ideas too well publicized and controversial, and his personal style too abrasive for him ever to be seriously considered *papabile.*

Va bene, as you understand, the constitution of Paolo VI provides that the cardinals celebrate funeral services for *il Papa*'s soul for nine consecutive days. The body did not arrive in Roma until the evening of the third day after the accident, but, because he had realized that such a delay was probable, LaTorre had provided that services would commence the day following the tragedy. Under the circumstances, LaTorre specified that Masses concelebrated in San Pietro by three or more cardinals would suffice until the body arrived.

We, the general congregation, had agreed that once the coffin arrived in Roma, it would lie in state, closed, in the basilica of the Laterano for five days. On the morning of the sixth day (the ninth since death), the cortege would of new assemble. It would include dignitaries from every nation in the world as well as more than a hundred cardinals and perhaps four or five times as many bishops, archbishops, and abbots. Those who were able would march the streets of old Roma from the Laterano across the Tiber and down the Via della Conciliazione through the marble arms of Bernini's colonnade and into the main door of San Pietro.

Under the circumstances LaTorre had persuaded us to dispense with most of the usual ceremonies except the funeral Mass in San Pietro. After that rite, *il Papa*'s body—*ecco,* we all prayed earnestly that we were indeed burying the mortal remains of the Supreme Pontiff and not those of a pilot or steward or one of the several *monsignori* who had been on the aircraft—would be sealed in the traditional triple coffin and placed in a temporary niche in the crypt below the chapel of Pio XII until an appropriate tomb could be constructed in San Pietro or in San Giovanni.

Like every other event in Italy, the funeral commenced

twenty minutes retarded and was subjected to a half dozen mishaps, but they were all minor, praise God, for it made ugly weather for mid-May. The warmth meant that the streets were packed; the Piazza di San Pietro alone held 200,000 people. I had lived in Roma long and often enough to sense a *cambio*—how do you say?—a shift in popular mood. One sign was the number of unpleasant scuffles along the funeral's path, as the Romans pushed and shoved each almost as rudely as they did foreigners. *Senta,* while the predominant atmosphere in the city was yet that of mourning, the melancholy that had engulfed earlier crowds was now less deep. Sorrow was mixed with expectation and concern about who would be the new Papa. Already newspaper pundits around the world were touting favorite cardinals among the *papabili,* and the special treatment accorded His Eminence Cardinal Fieschi received much attention.

As LaTorre wished, we approved the opening of the conclave for Sunday, 19 May, fifteen days after the crash, the exact minimum specified by our rules. According to me, that is too long an interval. One can reach Roma within a day from almost any part of the world. And many cardinals who preside over real dioceses have anxiety to return rapidly to their people. In this case that anxiety was increased, because other princes shared my fear of truculence within the Sacred College of Cardinals and thus of a lengthy conclave.

Within the walls of Vatican City, cardinals would be talking to each other but without making commitments. Indeed, by the law of the Church, any previous commitment, even one freely made under oath, is not binding within a conclave. Each of us, when he casts his ballot, is obligated to swear that he is voting for the man whom he thinks to be best qualified to be Supreme Pontiff; and at the four conclaves I have attended, I have never found a prelate who made this oath lightly.

There is some of what you Americans would call electioneering among the candidates and their supporters, but, *senta,* it is difficult to explain you what electioneering means in this context because you are accustomed to the bargaining that transpires in secular governmental processes. We do probe the feelings of others and try to sort in our own minds the strengths and weaknesses of those whose names are likely to be seriously considered—and, being human, we like to try to gauge the number of votes any candidate will collect on the first few ballots. But we do not exchange overt promises of support for future rewards—and we try not to imply covert promises except regarding general policies.

I must also say you that it would need a college of saints—and no one who knows my brethren in red hats would characterize them so—for such considerations to be totally lacking. We do what we can to exclude them from our minds; we focus on what we believe will be good for the Church, and we pray a great deal that our judgments possess integrity.

I tried to avoid most of the inevitable discussions with my brothers, not because I did not believe them to be useful but because I needed time to gather my own thoughts before I could expose them to others. *Allora,* after the funeral, I returned to my apartment in the Palazzo di San Calisto and dictated a series of long reports to LaTorre, as acting secretary of state, about certain problems in the United States.

Then, to prepare myself physically and spiritually for the ordeal ahead, I made a retreat at a monastery in the Abruzzi. I had secured LaTorre's consent to the absence. He was of accord that it was a wise move and spoke me that he envied the opportunity. I am certain that he did. We of the clergy urge retreats on laymen for the simple reason that we find them so useful ourselves. To sit in a monastery for even three or four days, free from the day-to-day tasks of normal life so that one can pray and meditate, refreshes the soul and the body, all and two.

Allora, when I returned the Friday morning before the conclave—one can be in the quiet heart of the cool Abruzzi in two hours from the noise and heat of Roma—I found an invitation to lunch with LaTorre. I realized that this would be more than a social gathering, but I felt better prepared to resume of new the burdens of a prince of the Church.

I arrived a little delayed at LaTorre's small apartment on the top floor of the Palazzo del Sant' Uffizio, the historic Holy Office, the site that tourists remember only as the place where Galileo was tried. Three other guests were already present: Chelli, of whom I have already told; the French theologian Claude Cardinal Bisset, who was now prefect of the Sacred Congregation for the Clergy; and Sean Cardinal Greene, the—how do you say?—exuberant Irish ultraconservative who was prefect of the Sacred Congregation of Divine Rites and Sacraments.

These two men were as different in their own ways as were LaTorre and Chelli. Greene was less—how do you say?—sharp, intellectually, than Bisset. *Senta,* I do not mean that the Irishman was not a person of impressive intellect. He was, but he lacked Bisset's slashing mind and tongue. I myself like to remember Greene mulling over a statement, his lips pursed, tapping his long fingers together and saying in that wonderful, lilting way in which the Irish sing English, "just so," if he was of accord. If he was not of accord, one might be subjected to an excited oration that piled layers of scriptural quotations on top of references to papal encyclicals and then loosely tied the bundle together with cords of Thomistic logic. Perhaps his arguments were more ordered than they seemed to me, for I was always distracted by the rush of words that poured out in English as fast as a Roman's Italian, and by the way His Eminence would continually run his hands through his hair and make that ample, though thinning, mass of red-speckled grey stand on end.

According to me, Greene was charming. He was a man of culture, a prelate who knew his Dante as well as his Joyce, and all and two as he did his Aquinas and Augustine. In art he preferred, as did I, the painters of the Italian Renaissance to those of the modern world. He could also be amusingly witty and was always thoughtful. At bottom, he was a gentle man, lacking that streak of meanness one so often finds in Celts. He possessed, however, that tendency toward dark moods that, according to me, characterizes the Irish. *Ecco,* as you have without doubt heard, he also demonstrated the national failing. The Irish name it "the drink"; Cardinal Greene referred to it as "the sickness." It struck him in a peculiar, although predictable mode. At times he would be stricken by a fit of depression —"my melancholia" he called it—and would retire to his apartment for several days of constant drinking. Because he did not venture outside of his bedroom or do anything more than maintain himself in a state of total insensibility, there was never scandal.

Allora, after a few days of "sickness," he would return

to his labor, as outwardly jaunty as ever, but inwardly torn with that self-contempt and accusing guilt that prepared the road for the next onslaught. Between attacks—and they would seldom arrive nearer than several weeks—he was as efficient a prefect as one would find in the Curia.

Ecco, Bisset was—how do you say in America?—a horse of a different color. He was a theologian by profession and a Frenchman by birth, a most unhappy combination, according to me. He did not look French. He was tall, thin, fair, and even rather handsome. Perhaps he had Celtic blood. He had once said me that all and two of his grandmothers had been Bretons, although he himself had been born in Paris. He had fifty-nine years and was arrived in the Curia several years after Vatican II, but it was during that council that he had made his basic contacts in the Holy See. He had established himself through his writings and more important through his labor as a *perito,* an expert, in traditionalist theology. He had been called to Roma not to the Holy Office but to the Secretariat of State, during the time when a powerful and conservative undersecretary feared—not without reason, I confess you—that the Holy Office was turning liberal.

Allora, Bisset performed brilliantly as the undersecretary's theologian, tightly checking any liberal tendencies within the Holy Office, until, with LaTorre's promotion to the prefectureship, such meticulous oversight became redundant. In recognition of Bisset's theological writings, Papa Paolo made him first an archbishop and later a cardinal. Neither was among Paolo's more popular acts.

According to me, one can speak easily of Bisset's vast intellectual capacity. It is more difficult to describe him as a person. In most people, the eyes give the clue. With Bisset it was the hands and the fingers. They were long and slender, but actually they were bony and ugly, even though always perfectly—and recently—manicured. They reminded me of talons like those that El Greco had painted on Don Fernando Niño, the Grand Inquisitor of Spain.

To understand Bisset one must, as I told, understand not only that he is a conservative theologian but also French, and like Greene he suffers from a national malady: a self-image of Napoleonic grandeur mixed with sad memories of Waterloo and all that has happened to France since—her rout at Sedan in 1870, the mutiny of her armies during

World War I, the rabbitlike courage of her troops before the German advance in 1940, her misguided and bloody efforts to retain her grasp first on Vietnam and then Algeria. This line of defeats, all lacking intelligence as well as valor, would have turned most people toward an Italian acceptance of national military mediocrity. *Ecco,* according to me, one of the charms of Italian culture is that we do not pretend ourselves or others that our talents lie in massing the brute force of modern armies. We have come to terms with the fact that we shall never be a "great power," and neither we nor the world appears any the worse for that lack.

But to many Frenchmen, the dream of Napoleonic grandeur is stronger than either the reality of their ability or the record of their failures. Nor, according to me, is that self-esteem made more rational either by the fact that their language, once the tongue of civilization, has become a mere curiosity, borrowing heavily from English, or that their culture, once the envy of the world, now finds its major expression in the nude spectaculars of Parisian night clubs, the filthy postcards on sale outside their cathedrals, or the heroin factories that poison children around the world.

In sum, reality eats at the Frenchman's dream of the past, turning his pride into insolence and his wit into waspishness. According to me, the only mode that many Frenchmen can recover their self-esteem is by trying to destroy that of others.

Perhaps I sin against charity by speaking in such general terms. The syndrome that I describe you may not fit all Frenchmen. On the other hand, I would sin against justice if I did not affirm that it goes far to explain the complex and not very pleasant personality that encapsulated the gifted intelligence of Bisset.

Allora, I was saying you about the luncheon at the apartment of LaTorre. Margherita, LaTorre's sister and housekeeper, came from the kitchen to greet me, briefly but rapidly, and tactfully returned to her task of supervising the cook and the butler. I could see from the brevity of her stay that LaTorre was playing to my principal weakness, the pleasures of the palate. That weakness shows in my 100 kilos—220 pounds in your system. Without other, that is not especially heavy but I am only 173 centimeters tall

—about 5′9″ by your reckoning. (I am not indulging in false humility when I say that one of the reasons I was considered *papabile* was that I am constructed rather like good Papa Giovanni was, even though I lack all and two his peasant piety and his peasant cunning.)

The conversation commenced easily enough. The *aperitivi* were dominated by questions about internal American politics and changing American attitudes toward Western Europe. Then we entered the small dining room with its petite but ornate crystal chandelier and its cupboards along the walls filled with antique silver—gifts from the rich faithful to the princely son of poor Sicilian peasants.

During the first plate (a chilled, moulded *risotto* generously stuffed with tiny *gamberetti*—you say shrimp?—garnished with mayonnaise, and served over a bed of lean, thinly sliced prosciutto) we talked of continuing defections from the clergy. *Allora,* as the butler commenced removing the dishes, we commenced discussing the health of some of our brother cardinals, those in the Curia as well as those whose sees were inhabited by live people rather than by ghosts. The chilled, white Frascati, which the butler served from a magnificent crystal carafe, matched the cool, delicate style in which we probed each other's minds.

Ecco, I must pause of new to explain you that that wine, because normally to me the Frascati—indeed none of the Castelli Romani—is not pleasing. But LaTorre's Frascati was fit only for the most delicate palate. The secret, LaTorre claimed, was that Frascati does not travel well. According to me, that is very doubtful, but let us accept it as a hypothesis. An old friend of his owned a vineyard in the hills just south of Roma and dispatched the wine to LaTorre in a special mode. First, the casks were filled so that no air remained inside; then they were packed in straw and transported at night, when traffic was easy, by slow-moving lorry. It needed four men to lift each cask onto the small elevator in the Holy Office and carefully carry it into the cool inside pantry of the apartment. Because of my affection for this wine and to honor my host, I permitted the butler to refill my glass three times; out of prudence I accepted two servings of the *risotto* to prevent the alcohol from going to my head.

Allora, the second plate was more hearty—roasted chunks of chicken and pork, also served on a bed of thinly sliced prosciutto, and garnished with quarters of lemons and what you call green beans. The butler brought several bottles of 1967 Barolo, a red that some critics say is the greatest of Italy. According to me, however, either Gattinara or Carema deserves that honor. All and two are made from the same Nebbiolo grape as Barolo, with the Carema grown rather high up in the Val d'Aosta and the Gattinara coming from the low ground in the Po Valley. I find their taste lighter and more pleasant. Unfortunately, authentic bottles are difficult to locate. The vineyards are small, the demand large, and Italian wine merchants unscrupulous in the mode in which they paste labels onto bottles. I have found that Ghemme, Sizzano, or Masserano make passable substitutes for Gattinara, although one always prefers the best when he can obtain it. In any case, Barolo is a little heavy with lunch and certainly much too heavy with chicken. The year, however, was excellent. (I should explain you that while we do not have as wide a variation from year to year in our wines as do the French, one can taste a real difference when one is drinking the best of our wines. And the products of the Nebbiolo grape improve with age.)

All things considered, it appeared to me that it would be lacking in appreciation of my host not to enjoy several glasses. Now we spoke of the ability of specific men, although, of course, no one mentioned for what task; we talked only of ability in the abstract.

I noticed that LaTorre, Greene, and Bisset were eating as heartily as I, but, as always, Chelli merely picked at his food. According to me, the way he was fondling the bread sticks showed that he wanted very badly to smoke one of his long, thin Cuban cigars, but the dining room was small and Margherita had worked too hard on the lunch to have the table surfeited in cigar smoke.

At the third plate, *zuppa Inglese,* a layered cake soaked in rum, Margherita joined us for a glass of champagne—Piper Heidsieck. It is not the optimum certainly, but well chilled and served in hollow-stemmed glasses it was appropriately bourgeois for five prelates who lived lives of poverty. While Margherita was with us, we chatted of the unreasonable warmth of mid-May and the horrors it augured for July and August. Only half joking, Margherita urged us to finish rapidly the affair of choosing a new

Pontiff so that we might enjoy the coolness of Castel Gandolfo and the Alban Hills. Not joking at all, I offered the suggestion that her brother might have performed the Church a cardinal service by persuading the college to conduct the conclave there, where we could at least listen to orations without enduring the Roman heat.

Margherita departed to supervise the fourth course, a melon with part of the center removed and replaced with sliced fruit that had been marinated for some weeks in brandy. The butler uncorked a third bottle of champagne, and, *ecco,* the talk commenced to drift of new to the capacities and failings of our cardinal colleagues. Chelli pushed aside the marinated fruit—something of a sacrilege, according to me—and ate about half the melon before finishing his first glass of champagne, now unappetizingly flat.

When we had done eating, the five of us went into LaTorre's drawing room for coffee and brandy. It was a small chamber, and the heavy red wallpaper and the ornate gold brocade on the furniture made it seem even smaller, but it did have a window that offered a partial view of San Pietro and its piazza. LaTorre had opened that window to circulate the smoke that he and Chelli would be puffing up. On the table were a pair of glass-lined silver decanters; one was filled with Courvoisier for LaTorre's guests, the other with that raw Grappa that he loved. All and two decanters went untouched. We each thought it best to sample the hot, syrupy *espresso.* I declined Chelli's offer of a cigar. My doctor forbid them, and they really are not pleasing to me. I like to be able to smell wine and food, not smoke, but I confess that their aroma was preferable to that of LaTorre's Murati cigarettes, which remind me of smouldering damp straw and always seems to seek out nonsmokers.

Allora, I was about to gulp my second *espresso* when Greene asked bluntly. "And who, my dear Ugo, would you see as our next Pontiff?"

I smiled and used the moments it took Chelli to relight his cigar to try to think of a gentle parry. I looked at the only decoration on the wall facing me. It was an oil portrait of a handsome, vigorous, and much younger LaTorre. Somehow it did not inspire subtle thoughts.

"One of the disadvantages," I told lamely, "of being an

apostolic delegate 6000 kilometers from Roma is that one is not able to form a firm judgment about such a question. How do you think the Holy Spirit will move the conclave?"

"I fear as much as I think, don't you know?" Greene riposted. "I see our liberal servants, whom our overly patient prefect of the Holy Office here should have declared heretics years ago—"

"Sacred Congregation of the Doctrine of the Faith, not Holy Office," LaTorre intervened good naturedly.

"Ah well, whatever you call it, these heretics in shepherds' clothing will fight for that Dutchman Gordenker or even worse that Austrian atheist Wildenmann, who calls himself a theologian." Greene was commencing to play his long fingers through his hair; according to me, it was time to intervene to prevent a torrent of biblical quotations from drowning us all.

"But of certainty neither of them has a chance. Who does?"

"I think we should—" Chelli commenced, but Greene cut him off.

"Only one or two really. Paolo Fieschi. He is a man of courage and determination and scrupulous orthodoxy. He comes from Genoa; and in Milan, don't you know, he has the most important see in Italy, excepting Rome, to be sure. He has administered that see very well, certainly as well or better than Montini did before he became Paul VI."

"An able man by any standard," I agreed. "Who else?"

"Why yourself," Chelli said me smiling.

I smiled back and just as blandly. Imagine you that scene: two wily Italian canon lawyers smiling at each other. "I do not think so. So soon after Papa Giovanni the throne bearers could not stand another fat Pontiff. Besides, I have neither the charisma nor identification with any of the factions within the sacred college, and I am too old to cultivate such connections. It has been many years since I have dispatched Christmas or Easter cards."

"Just so," Greene told, "just so. That is why you are *papabile*, don't you know? The heretics within our ranks do not fear you, and we in the Curia trust your orthodoxy."

The others were looking intently at me. I knew that I was being given the opportunity to make my candidacy by asserting my belief in the fundamentalistic Catholicism which they espoused. If I did so in a convincing style, I would probably become their choice if Fieschi could not be elected on the first five or six ballots—and that was an extremely likely event. It was highly improbable that anyone closely identified with the servant or the traditionalist factions could command the two-thirds plus one required for election. And I truly had many friends among the servants as well as among the traditionalists.

But—and I say you in all candor—although the idea had its temptations, I did not seek the post or even want it. I pray you to understand that there was little noble in my motive. During his own lifetime, Papa Paolo, whom I had known well and had been fond of, had been called by friends and enemies the Pope of Agony. According to me, it was a just title. Trying to preside over a divided Church and fighting to exist in a world he did not understand, he had courageously but unsuccessfully attempted to walk a tightrope. His failures, gallant as they may have been, had not only made his own life here miserable, but they had also left him with thousands, perhaps millions, of lost souls for whom to answer to God. The Almighty might have been sympathetic, at least amused, by a man of my girth trying to walk a tightrope, but it would not be facile to explain Him why I had not moved the Church. *Allora,* I confess I lacked clear ideas on that problem.

I decided to forego the opportunity to make my candidacy—not to reject it totally since I could not be secure how the conclave would develop, and some sacrifice might become necessary. (In which case, I remember myself hoping, the Lord might change His statement to read: "Greater love hath no man than that he lay down his soul for others.")

"I am not a fearful man," I said them, "but partially for that reason, I doubt that I would be, or even should be, elected. Let us talk of others."

"Not yet, my old one." LaTorre persisted. "You are too humble. Tell us how you view our northern colleagues and that 'new catechism' they published back in the 1960s."

"I view the Dutch and even the Belgians with confusion and, I hope, with compassion. I confess you I do not understand them. Their ways of expressing God's truth are different from those in which I was taught. But, neither do I think that we can continue to do God's work by repeating the anathemas of the Council of Trent. Perhaps we have obligations to rephrase in modern language our ancient faith. I only wish we could do so in language I could understand."

Greene's blue eyes flashed. "The word of God should suffice to do the work of God, don't you think?"

"Of truth, it does, as it always has," I agreed, "and always will. But we must not confuse the truth of the Holy Spirit with the groping efforts of man to express that truth."

"That is hardly a precise response," Bisset snorted.

"You have reason. I find it unsatisfactory myself. I see my Church in turmoil and I do not know how to bring peace. That is one reason why I prefer to think of others sitting in the chair of San Pietro. The archbishop of Bologna has had much publicity in recent days."

"I fear His Eminence is hardly more sound than some of our northern colleagues," LaTorre moaned. "He says less about theological matters because he is less interested, not because he is more sound. I do not know, however. His position may be strong since many think of him as a man in the center. He is, after all, an Italian, and that usually is an advantage."

"It may not be any longer," Bisset put in, without effort to conceal the pleasure that the words brought to his mouth. According to me, the French have not felt the same about the papacy since 1420 when Papa Martino V returned the Curia from Avignon to Rome.

I looked at Chelli. "Do you think the Holy Spirit will shed His light on our most reverend brother from Genova and Milano?"

Chelli fenced with me. "I suspect that the Holy Spirit has already shed His light on the archbishop of Milano. The real question is whether He will shed His light on the conclave."

"What do you think are the chances of such illumination?"

"I truly do not know. Small, I would guess. I fear we may be about to experience the longest conclave in modern history. We of the Curia cannot tolerate a man like Gordenker or Wildenmann. Their friends in the sacred college, misguided or heretical," Chelli smiled at Greene and La-

Torre, "will not tolerate one of us. I intend to bring several boxes of cigars into the conclave."

"Perhaps a bit of poison might be more useful for God's work," Bisset observed in his usual sardonic humor.

"I wish," I said to LaTorre, "that Your Eminence might establish a special rule for his conclave that would allow Margherita to supervise the cooking. I do not know how long I can survive the kitchen of our good nuns."

We dispersed shortly thereafter. I enjoyed a brief walk in the bright sunlight across the Piazza di San Pietro. In the middle of siesta time on a prematurely hot afternoon, the piazza was almost deserted, although the smell of horse manure hung heavily in the air about the carriages. I could see no sign of life in the papal palazzo, but then one rarely can from the street level. On the other hand, I did see three of my brother cardinals walking in the opposite direction. Without doubt, they had been participating in a ritual similar to the one I had just attended. I waved to them and then turned to watch three young—you say hippies? (I think two were boys, but one is never certain about such things these days.) They were huddled in the narrow shade from the obelisk in the center of the piazza, singing softly to themselves as one of them gently sounded a guitar. For a few moments I envied their lack of responsibility. Then I walked back to my car and chauffeur, parked inside the courtyard of the Holy Office, and we drove back to the Palazzo di San Calisto.

THREE

AT TEN-THIRTY, Sunday, 19 May, 105 cardinals, attired not in their broad red hats and red silk robes but in somber —and very warm and scratchy—purple wool, gathered in the Hall of the Congregations inside the papal palazzo. Preceded by a contingent of Swiss Guards and led by Monsignor Valerio Anguillara, the old Pontiff's *maestro di casa,* we departed the palazzo through the bronze portals and trooped through Bernini's colonnade. Then, as a light rain fell, we marched through the narrow, arcing passage that the Swiss Guards and Italian police had cleared across the piazza into the majestic basilica. There, LaTorre, as dictator pro tem of the Church, had the honor of celebrating at the posterior altar the traditional Mass of the Holy Spirit. (Some of us had suggested a concelebrated Mass, perhaps with the Patriarch Aspaturian of the Eastern Rite, an Asian cardinal, and one from Africa—all to symbolize the catholic reality of the Church. I thought I had convinced LaTorre, but someone—according to me, Bisset—persuaded him to say the Mass alone.)

The sermon was delivered by Monsignor Antonio Gaetani, the *rettore magnifico* of the Lateran University, a noted authority on patristic theology, and brother of one of the most significant papal advisers on financial affairs. Appropriately, the Latin homily was entitled "De Elegendo Pontificis"—"On Electing a Pontiff." Gaetani's initial words capsuled his message and were sufficiently nonpartisan neither to exacerbate differences within the sacred college nor to inspire us new ideas: "The Church of Rome needs a man of holiness and of strength to guide her. To fulfill his duties he must be statesman as well as saint, for he must take up the cross of Christ and carry it in peace, honor, and love to all men of this earth."

According to me, the learned *rettore magnifico* might have, with more spiritual profit to us and with better reflection on his judgment, restricted himself to repeating the Epistle for the Mass for Electing a Pontiff, San Paolo's letter to the Hebrews:

> So let us confidently approach the throne of grace to receive mercy and favor and to find help in the time of need.
>
> Every high priest is taken from among men and made their representative before God, to offer gifts and sacrifices for sins. He is able to deal patiently with erring sinners, for he himself is beset by weakness and so must make sin offerings for himself as well as for the people. One does not take this honor on his own initiative, but only when called by God as Aaron was. Even Christ did not glorify himself with the office of high priest; he received it from the One. . . .

After the procession had made its way back across the crowded piazza to the palazzo, those of us who were entering the conclave were allowed three hours (in Italy that means four or five hours) to place our affairs in order and eat lunch before being locked up for a period of indefiniteness. *Allora,* without special permission founded on motives of health, we could bring no one into the conclave. Not that we would be alone. The *camerlengo* would provide us confessors, physicians and other medical personnel, janitors, and even plumbers, lest our deliberations be disturbed by malfunctioning toilets. (Right now, I knew, LaTorre's staff would be visiting nunneries and monasteries, trying to locate for us enough *"gli zi Peppi"*—how do you say in English?—the Uncle Joes. *Ecco, vasi da notte?* "Night vases?" *Dunque,* "chamber pots." The distance to toilets, even those that functioned, might be too far for old men to traverse at night. It was merely another problem of what you call logistics.) The *camerlengo* would also command a staff of clerical assistants including the papal master of ceremonies; the architect of the conclave, with several assistants, would also remain inside with us. In all, there were eighty-eight conclavists locked up with us.

Because of the scandalous reunion at Viterbo in the thirteenth century, when the cardinals dawdled for thirty-three months of banqueting and carousing before selecting a new Pontiff, custom provides that until we agree on a successor to San Pietro, our food, God save us, is prepared by the good sisters of the Daughters of Charity of San Vincenzo di Paolo. These holy women operate the kitchens for the poor of Roma and have notoriety for their gentleness as much as for their ability to make even plain spaghetti inedible. One of the few concessions to civilization was a stand-up bar in the Borgia Apartments. It would mainly dispense *espresso* and *cappuccino,* except after meals, when it would be stormed by cardinals seeking *digestivi.*

Until a new Pontiff was elected, we would eat (if we could), sleep, and live together in a restricted area in the papal palazzo, Vatican museums, and attached buildings. Guards were now stationed all around the area of the conclave to seal out worldly contacts. The museums and library had been cleared of scholars, tourists, and staff to ensure quiet and privacy for our sleeping accommodations —mostly cots in small cells—hastily constructed in the space within the great halls around the San Damaso courtyard. Two of the larger chambers in the Borgia Apartments would serve as common dining rooms, at least for those of us who boasted good appetites and insensitive palates.

At the first general congregation of the college of cardinals after the death of a Pontiff, the constitution of the Church regarding a vacancy in the apostolic see and the election of *il Papa* is read us, and we, I quote you, "bind ourselves and swear" to follow the constitution for the election of a Pontiff and, "above all . . . to observe with the greatest fidelity and with all persons, including conclavists, the secrecy concerning everything that in any way relates to the election of a Roman Pontiff and concerning what takes place in the conclave or place of election, directly or indirectly concerning the scrutinies"—*ecco,* a *scrutiny* is what you name a ballot—"not to break this secrecy in any way, either during the conclave or after the election of a new Pontiff, unless we are given a special faculty or explicit authorization from the same future Pontiff."

The conclavists—the assistants, lay and clerical, all of whom fall under the jurisdiction of the *camerlengo*—take a similar oath of secrecy. The punishment for violation of this oath, by anyone within the conclave, is automatic excommunication that can be removed solely by *il Papa* himself.

Allora, there is another provision to the oath that cardinals and conclavists make, a promise not to transmit to any member of the sacred college a secular government's "veto" of any particular person as Pontiff, even if that veto has been communicated to one of us as a mere wish. The purpose of that provision is obviously to protect the independence of the conclave, and it may still be needed. As late as 1903 the cardinal archbishop of Cracow delivered to a conclave the Austrian Emperor's veto of the papal secretary of state, Cardinal Rampolla del Tindaro.

Because my personal affairs found themselves in reasonably good order, I had asked my secretary, Monsignor Alessandro, to have my driver await us after Mass inside the Porta Sant' Anna. Once the crowd from the piazza had dissipated, we drove rapidly to the Trastevere, to the Piazza di San Cosimato, for our final decent meal at my favorite *ristorante,* Il Galeone. Elio, my usual waiter, had our first plate prepared: *spaghetti al Corsetti* (only a *mezzo*—you say half?—portion for the monsignore). It is spaghetti cooked *al dente* with a white sauce of olive oil, garlic, and parsley, and then mixed with heaping mounds of small shrimp, whole fresh baby squid, and mussels and young clams still in their shells. We had Soave with the spaghetti and a good but undistinguished Pinot Grigio with the principal plate of grilled crayfish and cold *spinacci* with lemon. Monsignor Alessandro accepted only coffee for after, but, thinking of the future misery that was even now ripening in the kitchens of the holy nuns, I decided on small portions of *zuppa Inglese* and *Saint Honoré*. As we paid the account, Elio, knowing the sins that would soon be committed in the conclave's kitchen, brought me a large bag stuffed with fried squid and shrimp. At least I would enjoy a decent supper and perhaps even a nibble for the first collation in the morning.

By five-thirty in the afternoon, a half hour after the conclave was officially scheduled to commence, each of the eighty-two cardinals with voting rights had entered the restricted area. Promptly at six (*ebbene,* six-fifteen, but that is close enough for us Italians), we all assembled in the great hall outside the Sistine Chapel. Then, headed by various clerics assisting the conclave and accompanied by a flock of bishops and archbishops, we followed the master of ceremonies as he carried the papal cross into the chapel.

First came the cardinal bishops, then the cardinal priests, and last the cardinal deacons. At the altar, LaTorre, as cardinal dean, recited the prayer *"Deus Qui Corda Fidelium."* Then Monsignor Cencio Dell'Aqua, the master of ceremonies, gave the command *"Extra Omnes"* for all but cardinals to depart the chapel, and we assumed our places on our small canopied thrones, arranged in two levels. Those canopies may have reminded us of our princely duties, but they also restricted our views of Michelangelo's marvelous frescoes on the ceiling and even of the Last Judgment on the anterior wall. The restriction of vision was aggravated by the fact that the thrones were tightly packed in the chapel. With eighty-two of us present, this conclave was among the largest in the history of the modern Church.

A babble of hushed whispers ran among the cardinals until LaTorre rang a small bell for silence. He then read us once more the constitution for the election of a Pontiff. When the reading was finished, each of us made anew the solemn oath to follow the provisions of the constitution, to observe strict secrecy, and not to transmit a veto from any secular government.

As commanded by the constitution, LaTorre, in his capacity as cardinal dean, gave us a discourse on our sacred duties. Knowing that we had each read the constitution many times in private and had at least twice heard its provisions in plenary reunions, he was brief. After a short prayer, the first formal session of the sacred college was completed, and we retired to our cells so that the labor of closing the conclave could proceed swiftly.

Monsignor Carlo Silla, governor of the conclave, rang a bell three times as signal for all persons not specifically authorized to participate in the conclave to depart the area immediately. After turning on all the lights in the building, he, LaTorre, the senior cardinal from each rank, the secretary of the conclave, and the architect of the conclave made a thorough search of the entire area to insure that no unauthorized person was present. With them were two technicians who carried electronic equipment to detect—how do you call them?—bugs? Papa Paolo had a near obsession about secrecy, and his constitution not only forbade bringing into a conclave tape registers—like yours—cameras or similar devices, but also specifically required that the area be—how do you call it?—*ecco . . . swept* for listening devices.

With that search completed, Monsignor Silla summoned the marshal of the conclave, Prince Gallori Giacomo Chigi. Dressed in strikingly colorful Renaissance costumes, the prince and his entourage came to the door of the conclave area and accepted the keys from the *monsignore.* The area was now officially sealed.

All the conclavists, lay and clerical, were then obligated to file singly into the chapel, where each was identified. Moreover, the cardinal dean and the three senior cardinals were each obliged to visit periodically the area of the conclave and even the cells of the cardinals to insure that no unauthorized persons were present.

I said you that the area was officially sealed. That is something of an exaggeration. Generally we are all removed from contact with the outside world. We cannot, for example, see newspapers or periodicals. In an emergency, however, someone from the outside may approach the area of the conclave and, in the presence of an attending group of bishops or archbishops who are fluent in the language used, talk to a cardinal or other conclavist. Those within the conclave may also transmit and receive letters, but they must all be carefully screened by a committee of censors to insure that no news of our deliberations exits and that there enters no news of the outside world that would affect our votes.

There is one exception to this last rule. Any duly sealed communication between the Cardinal Grand Penitentiary and the Tribunal of the Sacred Penitentiary may enter and depart without examination. I should explain that this tribunal decides important cases in which individuals wish special guidance in problems of conscience, dispensations from Church law, or forgiveness for trespasses. Freedom of communication in this regard symbolizes the priority of God's mercy over all duties of the Church, including electing a Pontiff.

Following tradition, we held no voting or other affairs on the first day. Instead we rested, prayed, and consulted. Yet labor was being made, despite the obliqueness of many conversations and the lack of what you Americans call "a pork barrel." Those cardinals who wanted to remake the Church into the image of the servant model were especially active, gathering in small groups of ten and twelve. For many of them, it was the first time they had personally encountered each other. Those of my brethren who were more concerned to preserve the primacy of the institutional model were, apparently at least, more united. Most of them knew each other well.

The next morning, the Patriarch Aspaturian celebrated Mass in the Eastern Rite for the entire conclave. There were several concelebrations, but these we ourselves arranged. Then, after breakfast, all but the cardinals were excluded from the Sistine; after we had sung *"Veni, Creator Spiritus"*—"Come, Holy Spirit"—and said a brief prayer for His guidance, the affair of selecting a Pontiff moved into its next phase.

Like its predecessors, the constitution of Paolo VI permits three modes of selection. The first is "by inspiration"; that is, if a cardinal feels himself divinely inspired he should stand up and propose the name of a candidate, offering us a very few words of explanation. Our rules suggest a form: "Most Eminent Fathers, in view of the singular virtue and probity of the Most Reverend———, I would judge him worthy to be elected Roman Pontiff and I now choose him as *il Papa.*" If others feel similarly inspired, they call out *"Eligo"* ("I elect"). If the sentiment is unanimous, the candidate is thereupon elected without recourse to further ceremony.

The second mode of selection is "by delegation." According to this procedure, the sacred college may—unanimous consent is also required—delegate to a small committee, of at least nine cardinals but not more than fifteen and in any case of an uneven number, authority to elect a candidate. If the college adopts this mode it must also provide specific instructions to the delegation about whether it must report the name of its candidate to the full college before electing him or may proceed directly to election, and whether the vote must be unanimous or may be by simple majority or by some extraordinary majority. It must also be made clear whether candidates are restricted to members of the sacred college or to a broader field. In addition, the college must set a definite time period in which the commission's decision will be valid. Lastly, the resolution of the college should close with the statement: "And we promise to regard as Supreme Pontiff the person whom the delegates shall have decided to elect according to the aforementioned form."

The third and most common mode of election is "by scrutiny," which in effect means by secret ballot—very secret ballot, as I shall later describe. The extraordinary majority of two-thirds plus one is required for election.

The conclave sat in silence for a full ten minutes. Each of us waited quietly to see if anyone would move election by inspiration, but apparently the Holy Spirit was keeping His own counsel that particular Monday morning. Like most of those present, I used the silence to seek consolation if not inspiration in Michelangelo's genius. In all the world, that is my favorite room. The majesty of that art—the finger of God reaching out to radiate life to Adam—has many times touched me as no other work ever has. Adam was uncircumcised—perfectly proper since he antedated Abraham—but he had a navel. I hoped that this represented a demonstration of Michelangelo's knowledge of anatomy rather than of doubt about the authenticity of the account in Genesis. And God—a vigorous, white-bearded man, old but ageless in his filmy pink nightshirt—was that a satire on religion? *Allora,* whatever Michelangelo meant, according to me, that portrait of God, created to man's image and likeness, was a comforting one.

It suddenly occurred me that Declan and Kate had disliked the chapel, especially Kate, God rest her troubled soul. They found it "busy." I could hear Kate's voice: "Get those paintings off the side walls and leave only Michelangelo's frescoes on the ceiling and the Last Judgment in the front, and you'd make the chapel far more attractive. Now it's too cluttered—Michelangelo, Rosselli, Perugino, Signorelli, Botticelli, and Ghirlandaio, all one massive jumble, plus that ornate tile floor." Then she would add in her typically tactful manner, "You Italians are so rococo." Perhaps that is why Italy pleases me, why I, a northerner, love Roma and the Church: I am rococo and I have need to live in a rococo jumble.

"My Lord Cardinals and Most Reverend Brothers," LaTorre brought me to reality, "since no one moves election of the next Pontiff by inspiration and since we hear no suggestion that we proceed by delegation, we propose that the sacred college begin the process of election by scrutiny."

The master of ceremonies then distributed to each cardinal a packet of a dozen small, rectangular ballots. Stamped on each was the formula in Latin: "I elect as Supreme Pontiff———."

The sequential step was the choice by lot of three cardinals to serve as scrutinizers—you would name them tellers—to examine and count the votes. Next, also by lot, we selected three *infirmarii,* cardinals who would go to the cells of those members of the sacred college who were in conclave but too ill to enter the Sistine, collect their ballots, and transmit them to the chapel to be counted. Lastly, once more by lot, we selected three cardinals as revisers to recount the ballots after the scrutinizers had finished their labor—and I quote you our rules—"in order to make certain that they [the scrutinizers] have performed their task exactly and faithfully."

We were ready for the actual process of nominating, debating, voting, and, we hoped, electing. Immediately after the three *monsignori* who assisted us left the chapel, Henri

Cardinal Fournier, primate of Belgium, arose. His intervention was concise. The Church, he told, faced a choice: to follow Papa Giovanni and the Second Vatican Council or to stultify by returning to a sterile past. Historic formulas, rituals, and even institutions could no longer serve to communicate either with our own people or those outside of our community.

"We must grow or we wither," Fournier related. "We have Christ's word that we, His Church, will endure forever, but we have no assurance that, if we fail to understand problems of the real world and fail to communicate with the people of that world, we shall save souls. We may indeed be a perpetual institution, but we can also become a whited sepulchre, clutching in hands of stone the dead bones of a glorious past. Today we have a great opportunity, one equaled perhaps only in the time of the Apostles, to bring a hungry, searching world to Christ. Now is the time to advance, not to be content with holding on to the status quo."

Near the close, Cardinal Fournier noted that he spoke for many members of the college, "more than one-third of the conclave." Since a vote of two-thirds plus one was necessary for election, he, in effect, pronounced a canonically permissible veto. "We have no concern about the nationality or race of the next Pontiff, but we pledge that we shall not agree to anyone who is timid, blind, a captive of the past, or a captive of a bureaucracy, however holy the intentions of that bureaucracy may be."

When the murmurs from curialist cardinals quieted, Fournier went on. "We say bluntly, out of love for Christ and His Church, that we shall insist that the next Pope be a man who is ready to take on the mantle of John as well as the burdens of Peter. We are ready to sit in this conclave for days, for weeks, for months, or even for years to ensure that end."

There were a few whispers of *"vergogna"*—"shame"—and a few soft handclaps from under the canopies. Fournier bowed to LaTorre.

Senta, we all knew what such signs meant. My fears were at least partially confirmed. The servants were determined and united, if only in opposition. As I had heard the previous evening, they were divided in their support between two candidates: the Dutchman, Henrik Cardinal

Gordenker, and Angelo Cardinal Corragio, archbishop of Bologna. Everyone realized that the liberal Austrian theologian, Wilhelm Cardinal Wildenmann, did not have, as you Americans say, a prayer; and in a conclave that is a serious lack. Of the two principal candidates of the servants, Corragio had what you call the edge. Gordenker was closer, perhaps, to the hearts of the northern Europeans and many of the prelates from the Third World, but his frank statements on birth control and clerical celibacy would make it difficult for him to attract support from those of us in the center and would totally alienate him from the traditionalists.

Corragio was less outspoken. In fact, his appeal to the servants was based largely on his judicious silences. He had quietly ignored LaTorre's urgings that he instruct confessors in his archdiocese to deny absolution to those penitents who refused to abjure birth control or who utilized the Italian courts to obtain a civil divorce. Similarly, he had not reprimanded a group of young priests who had been saying Masses in private homes, and in the pulpit had been preaching that the Church and her hierarchy seemed to have more care for edifices than for souls. The archbishop's sole public statement on the affair was: "There may be something to what they say. Let us set about making rather than asserting the statement false."

Because he was a Venetian and because Papa Giovanni himself had consecrated Corragio archbishop, he gained a certain halo that would win him votes from the center. His record as a war hero assisted, too. As a young priest stationed in Vincenza he had fought with partisans. His record of opposition to communism in Bologna was also favorable. His courage and tenacity were universally acknowledged, although there was some confusion about his theological posture.

On the other hand, Corragio had a great disadvantage. A record of failure—heroic failure, yet failure. *Ecco,* the Germans had all but obliterated his partisan band and in retaliation for guerrilla activity had executed more than seventy-five civilians. He himself had been badly wounded and had escaped capture only through the willingness of his bishop to perjure himself. The later campaign against the Communists had been less disastrous, but it could hardly be named a success since the Communists had for decades governed Bologna. A history of defeat could tarnish the chances of even the most capable man.

The servants, I had also heard, were in accord that each cardinal would support his own candidate through the first five or six ballots, unless it became likely that a traditionalist was coming close to being elected. Then they agreed that to win they would need to unite behind a single candidate. Most of them knew, as men of the world, that although they could block an election, they were not likely to elect a Pontiff from their own ranks. It was very probable that they would be obligated to compromise eventually—which was why some servants were supporting me—but to talk openly of compromise *now* would weaken their position vis-à-vis the traditionalists from the Curia and might even splinter their group.

After Fournier sat down, Sean Cardinal Greene of Ireland spoke. He had been laboring late the previous evening consulting with LaTorre and Chelli. Like Fournier's talk, this intervention would represent the views of a group of cardinals. According to me, there were thirty-one of them: fourteen Italians (almost all from the Curia itself), two Spaniards, two Portuguese, a pair of Frenchmen, a pair of Latin Americans, three North Americans, all three of the Irish, one Englishman, and two men from Eastern Europe. Another five to ten members of the conclave identified themselves with this hard core of traditionalists, but without the degree of commitment shared by the inner group.

Allora, as had Fournier, Greene arrived directly at the point, a mistake no Italian would ever make. He agreed that the primate of Belgium had put the matter well. The Church was facing a crisis brought on by those who would desert sacred traditions, rewrite holy doctrines, and deny the very authority on which Christ had built His Church. Greene claimed not to believe that any member of the conclave would knowingly join in any such nefarious activities. But in sympathizing publicly with popular clamor for sexual license, fads about ritual, or demands that nonbelievers be allowed to partake of the Holy Eucharist, clergy elevate the vagaries of individual whims above the explicit commands of God.

"We must remember," Greene stressed, "humans are weak and temptation is rife. They need our firm guidance and correction. Utopian phrases like 'freedom of conscience' mask rather than justify this surrender of what is God's. We commit the sacrilege of attacking Christ's Church no less in not correcting such errors than if we ourselves directly challenged the validity of the sacraments or the primacy of Peter's successor."

Greene then reminded us that his group, too, possessed a veto, and they would support only "a man of iron will and firm commitment to our holy and historic teachings. His task will be to lead our people back to the hard, narrow road toward salvation, not to pipe the way to hell with promises of worldly freedom and material happiness.

"Let us also assure our most reverend colleagues," Greene continued, "that those who share our views are also prepared to deliberate at length and to implore, for however long it takes, the divine grace of the Holy Spirit to enlighten the minds of His faithful here in this conclave. We came to choose a Pontiff who would preserve and rebuild our Church, not one who would destroy it under the guise of reform, not one who would personify the spirit of modernism so effectively condemned as a vicious heresy by our saintly Pontiff, Pius X."

Greene had no need to explain us, as he had implied at lunch on Friday, that he would support Paolo Cardinal Fieschi, the patrician archbishop of Milano. According to me, Fieschi was a candidate to be received seriously. He looked as a Supreme Pontiff should, tall, erect, with the clear-eyed image of energy and dedication that one associates with youth. Of truth, he was not as flashingly quick as the young Neapolitan, Cardinal Chelli; he was a man of deeply intelligent judgment rather than of brilliance. In sum, he had that quality which the ancient Romans considered essential for greatness—*gravitas*. He not only was serious, but he imagined himself serious and fully expected the world to do so. Moreover, in his aristocratic if condescending charm, he was not so adamant in his conservatism as LaTorre. Perhaps his noble upbringing and wide travels had made him less provincial than our son of Sicilian peasants.

His record as a bishop and cardinal evidenced great administrative skill, but—and this is what made him attractive to the traditional institutionalists who were all apt to give him their votes, at least after the first few ballots when it was proper to bestow a few honoraria on venerable cardinals—he possessed neither interest in nor patience for theological dispute. He would follow in the traditional mode precisely because it was the mode of tradition, the sound, secure, proven mode that permitted one to utilize one's energy most efficiently for the more important tasks of directing, and thereby saving, souls through the Church's historic apparatus. If elected, he would probably reorganize and—how do you say?—streamline the Curia so that its business would flow in and out much more speedily and at less cost. But it was not likely he would understand, much less be sympathetic to, demands for fundamental reforms. Suggestions for doctrinal change he would greet in the incisive but firm style of a headmaster confronted with a request from the boys that examinations be abolished.

Because, as I have said to you, I had no intention of accepting the tiara unless it became the only way of saving Holy Mother Church from her sons, I judged that Corragio and Fieschi were now the serious candidates. Gordenker's name would attract votes, perhaps for many ballots, but he would never come near to victory. I thought that the others, except for myself, would receive only token support. I estimated that my support would be small initially but would probably increase as the deadlock between Fieschi and Corragio became more apparent.

Ecco, when the orations were done, we proceeded to the first scrutiny. Each cardinal took a sheet of paper from the table in front of his throne and wrote the name of his candidate, trying as best he could to disguise his handwriting. Then LaTorre first marched up to the altar, holding the folded ballot between the two fingers of his right hand so that it could be plainly viewed. At the altar he knelt and prayed silently for a few moments, then loudly recited an oath placed before him: "I call to witness the Lord Christ, who will be my judge, that my vote is given to the one who before God I consider should be elected." He then placed his ballot on a gold paten and slipped the paper into a large chalice on the altar.

When, in order of rank, we all had completed this same rite, one of the scrutinizers covered the chalice with the paten and shook it vigorously to mix up the slips of paper. A second scrutinizer then received the chalice and one by one transferred the ballots to another chalice and counted the total number cast to make secure that every cardinal had in fact inserted a ballot. Only then did the actual tabulation commence. The first scrutinizer opened the ballot, read it to himself, passed it to the second scrutinizer who also read it to himself, and then gave it to the third scrutinizer, who read the name aloud. Each cardinal noted the vote on a sheet in front of him that contained all names of the members of the Sacred College of Cardinals. When the counting was done, the three scrutinizers offered us the totals for each candidate. *Allora,* as I had expected, the conclave was badly divided. Fieschi had received twenty-six votes, Gordenker ten, the archbishop of Bologna twenty, I myself thirteen, and the rest were scattered among four others.

As a final insurance against error or fraud, the three revisers then recounted the ballots. As expected, their tally accorded with that of the scrutinizers. With a needle and thread the ballots were then strung in a garland and prepared for burning.

Since no one had received the fifty-six votes required for election, a second scrutiny was immediately completed. Our rules allow one such immediate repetition after each balloting. The results were quite similar. Each of the four leading candidates was augmented by one or two votes at the expense of the other four. Again the counted and recounted ballots were strung in a garland, and, in our view, LaTorre put both sets into the makeshift stove, mixed them with a chemical pellet to make black smoke, and set a match to them.

At eleven-forty-five in the morning, wisps of smoke could be seen from the Piazza di San Pietro. Since few observers had expected a rapid decision, only about 15,000 people were milling around. The first puffs were white, but a moment later the chemical began to function and the smoke turned unmistakably black. Knowing we would now recess for a midday collation and siesta, the crowd decided to emulate their reverend preceptors. The decision was a wise one. At five-fifty that afternoon another cloud of dark smoke wafted slowly over the Sistine Chapel, and the college, still divided much as in the morning, formally adjourned for the day. Informal discussions continued through most of the evening. The arguments were largely moral and theological.

Twice more on Tuesday and Wednesday, the wisps of

black smoke puffed lazily over the chapel, for a total of twelve unsuccessful ballotings. Papa Paolo's constitution commanded that, if three days passed without an election, we should pause for a maximum of one day's "prayer, free discussions among the voters, and a brief spiritual exhortation given by the senior cardinal in the order of deacons." He asked only that we all earnestly pray that God might give us the grace to recognize His will and to discern what was truly optimum for His Church.

On Friday we resumed, a bit refreshed; as before, however, the results were inconclusive. We did not know, of course, but we suspected that Saturday the piazza would be crowded with people (the newspapers that I later read told about 150,000) who were confident that we would arrive at a decision before Sunday. The first cloud of smoke would only strengthen convictions that a decision was at hand. Sitting in the cool, quiet of the chapel, I could picture the scene outside. The late morning sun would be hot, and children would be splashing in the two fountains. Even an occasional adult would soak a handkerchief to sponge his face. The vendors in the small motorized carts would be selling their *gelati*—how do you say?—ice cream, soft drinks, and wet slices of coconut so rapidly that much of their time would be consumed driving for fresh supplies. The streets would be so crowded that obtaining a table at one of the small bars along the Via della Conciliazione would entail standing for more than an hour in what we Italians jokingly call a line.

Inside the chapel, we were still badly fragmented. We had heard few interventions since Tuesday. There had been a tacit agreement to talk only privately. Most of the words spoken in formal sessions had been in prayer. There were now only three candidates being seriously considered, the Dutchman Gordenker having stated that he wanted the election of the cardinal archbishop of Bologna. After the first ballot on Saturday afternoon, Fieschi had thirty votes, Corragio thirty-eight, and I had fourteen. Solely Corragio was close even to a simple majority, and no one was remotely near the fifty-six votes needed for election.

Sunday morning, at the seventh session since our day of prayer, discussion, and recollection, the vote was identical. Our rules provided for another pause and formal consideration of how we should proceed. But before LaTorre explained us the options, he recognized Cardinal Greene. I sensed that our tacit truce was about to come to a finish.

"My Lord Cardinals," the Irishman's usual lilting voice was sharp and a bit unsteady. After all, he was seventy-six years old, and a week of incarceration with more than eighty cantankerous prelates, while being fed from the kitchen of the holy nuns, would tire the most athletic youth. "My Lord Cardinals, we are at an impasse. Christ's Church is paralyzed. In the name of God Almighty and His beloved Son, I ask"—"we" was a victim of fatigue—"what is it that our so-called liberals want? Do they want to destroy our Church? To tear us apart? To make us the laughing stock of Communists and Protestants alike?"

"We want," Henrik Cardinal Gordenker responded, "to go forward, not backwards, to serve Christ by serving His people."

"You want," Greene snapped as he ran his hand rapidly through his thin hair, "to make life easy for your people; you want to tell them they can have sexual license. You claim to serve them by catering to their weaknesses. You cannot bear to tell them they cannot have pleasure if it is sinful pleasure. You reject this world as a place of testing, of pain, and of suffering. You would destroy morality and turn their lives into wild, fornicating orgies. You would take us back to the Roman world that Christ condemned."

"That is a damnable lie," Gordenker angrily riposted.

LaTorre's head snapped up in amazement.

"It is the truth, God's truth!" Greene shouted. "You are not merely a heretic, you personally condone a vile libertinism that would destroy holy purity."

"For you sex is morality, all of morality—sex, sex, sex," Gordenker retorted loudly. "While you condemn the sins of others you revel in idolatry, falling down and worshipping the Church as an institution, ignoring its mission of preaching love and justice to all mankind. You serve yourselves, not your fellow man and certainly not Christ."

LaTorre had been vigorously sounding his bell for order, but neither cardinal had heard. Finally, the Holy Mule slammed his heavy fist on the desk in front of his throne. "Silence! Silence! We shall hear no more of such talk in this holy place. Brothers, we are all tired, but we must curb our tempers and our tongues. This kind of conduct borders on sacrilege. If such language reoccurs, we shall use our power as dictator pro tem to excommunicate the offenders. Now, we demand that our two most reverend brothers ask the other's—and God's—forgiveness for the harsh words with which they have offended each other and the Holy Spirit."

(*Ecco,* I say you in confidence that I was grateful that Greene's intervention had been spontaneous, lest we have been suffocated in pillows of theological citations.)

Greene and Gordenker rose and faced each other, looking like two schoolboys who were sorry to have been caught fighting but not sorry to have fought. They mumbled a few words of regret, then rapidly sat down.

"Under the circumstances," LaTorre announced, "we declare a recess until tomorrow morning. At that time, because we have experienced seven unsuccessful sessions since our first pause, we must decide how to proceed. I remind you of our choices. First, we may continue as we have been, though without the rancor that so ill fits princes of Christ's Church. Second, as at any time, someone may be moved by the inspiration of the Holy Spirit. Third, we may proceed to delegate to a committee authority to elect. These last two can be adopted only by unanimous consent. A fourth set of options that opens after a week of balloting also needs unanimous approval: allowing election by only an absolute majority plus one or, alternately, narrowing the eligible candidates to the two with the highest number of votes. I now adjourn us until five this afternoon, when the senior cardinal priest shall, as our rules require, give us a spiritual exhortation."

(Because I do not wish to sin against charity, I say you nothing about that exhortation, made by the Korean Cardinal Su. It was a *capriccioso*—you have that word? It means goatlike and signifies a great, leaping mixture—*ecco,* hodgepodge. It was a hodgepodge of primitive Christianity, Confucianism, and the epistemology of Teilhard de Chardin. Its sole effect was to ensure that no sane cardinal would ever cast a vote for Su.)

When we returned to the chapel on Monday morning, my old friend from Trieste, the venerable Virgilio Trentin, stood up to speak. His father had been a follower of Don Luigi Sturzo and, naturally, an ardent foe of fascism. After Papa Pio XI had decided that fascism might not be a bad thing for Italy and had ordered Don Sturzo to disband his party, Trentin's father had remained an outspoken foe of the regime. For his writings he was three times beaten up by blackshirted gangs, but the man had courage as well as eloquence. Finally Mussolini drove him into exile by having local thugs set fire to Trentin's home when he was away. His wife and children had barely escaped with their lives, and the *signora* had been painfully burned.

Virgilio was then a young reporter for a Venetian newspaper and he, too, had been beaten several times by Fascist gangs. He moved with his family to Belgium and returned to school to study history at Louvain. When the Germans overran the Low Countries in 1940, he and his parents fled, of new, this time to Switzerland, where they found permanent shelter. From there, Virgilio slipped across the border into Italy to fight with partisan bands against the Nazis. He was, in fact, one of our few authentic partisan heroes. After the war, at a rather advanced age, he entered the priesthood, and eventually was recognized as a leading biblical scholar. It was because of that immense reputation of erudition that Papa Paolo had given him a red hat in 1975, one appointment that had brought universal acclaim.

"My dear Brothers," he commenced, as usual speaking and thinking in the first person singular, "we have sat here for seven days—as long as it took the Almighty to create the world—first discussing amiably, now quarreling bitterly. Tempers have become short as weariness has conquered reason. Since my eightieth birthday is approaching, I know I shall never vote for another Pope. Indeed, if we continue to move with the speed of the last week, I may not live to vote for this one."

Trentin's gentle smile helped break the tensions left in the wake of the outburst between Gordenker and Greene. The old man went on: "I am the oldest present, but three of you are also in your eightieth year. Another seventeen are over seventy-five, and only nine of us have less than sixty years. I fear that the spirit of fatigue, rather than of God, will soon rule here. I am still the man I was thirty years ago, but only for an hour or two a day—and then only if I can rest on weekends.

"We must not go on like this, exchanging angry words rather than increasing the love of God. I propose that we adopt the delegation and allow a committee to bring us the next Pope."

As I listened to the debate, I reviewed my decision—*ebbene,* my half-decision. I had been thinking of my plan, I have confessed you, since arriving in Roma. I had brooded over it in the Abruzzi, praying for guidance. Although by now it had grasped firm hold of my mind, I still had fear of it. I may have had fear because it would not be good for the Church, because I would be laughed at, and you know that we Italians live in less dread of the last judgment than of making a *brutta figura* here on earth. I decided to let God decide whether the idea was good or bad for His Church. I would wait to see the outcome of Trentin's proposal.

It was not until seven-thirty that evening that the vote came. The proposal was adopted unanimously, as required. By that time, I should say you, the idea was Trentin's but the specific proposal on which we voted was Chelli's. The commission was to consist of nine cardinals, with Trentin as president. The other eight represented a good—how do you say?—cross section of the conclave. Bisset could speak for the traditionalists, José Martìn, archbishop of Buenos Aires, was a noted servant, although not a woolly-headed one. There were three other Europeans; a German, a Spaniard, and a Pole. All three possessed solid reputations for solid orthodoxy and equally solid reputations for open-mindedness; in short they were moderates. There were also three men from the Third World. One was a black African, another a Chinese, and the third was an occidental Jesuit who had lived in India so long as to be more Indian than the natives. (I hasten to assure you that although English by birth, he was not a homosexual.) To these three from the Third World, the disputes between traditionalists and servants were intelligible, but not interesting; each had his own model of the Church in mind. The delegation was, according to me, an excellent group—with the exception of Bisset—holy men of experience and charitable judgment.

Chelli's resolution also provided that the delegation would proceed to election without further consultation with or notification to us; that a vote of six of the nine would be needed to elect; that choice should be restricted to members of the sacred college; and that the delegation had five days in which to make its decision. As was canonically proper, the resolution closed with our vow to accept the committee's decision as determining the election.

Allora, the delegation proceeded to a separate area in the chamber of the maps in the museums that had been set apart for precisely such an occasion. There they would be sequestered until they reached a decision or their time expired. For the next four days we waited, at first patiently, but soon more and more impatiently, for the committee to tell their decision—or if they had been able to arrive at a selection at all. The food, according to me, became, if it were possible, even more ugly. There was at least one small blessing: the scale revealed that I had returned to God more than four kilos—almost ten pounds.

By Thursday evening there were many running voices—you say rumors? One had it that the committee had chosen a traditionalist from the Curia, another that the next successor to San Pietro was a black man. Another told that I was the choice, while yet another denied that there was any selection at all. I suspect that I prayed more fervently than the rest of my brothers, although I was never quite secure in my own mind what to pray for.

On Friday morning, we gathered again in the Sistine to hear the delegation's report. As president, Trentin spoke. "Most Reverend Brothers, we report with heavy heart that, despite long labors and ardent prayers, we have not been able to select a Pontiff. Because no six of us can agree, we have concluded that there is no further point in this committee's continuing, and we respectfully recommend that, if delegation is still the will of the conclave, another committee be chosen."

Paddraigh Cardinal O'Failoin, archibishop of Armagh and primate of all Ireland, stood up. "We have listened with sadness to the report of the most reverend president. We urge our brothers not to appoint another committee, but to resume ourselves the burden of choice. There are not among us nine—or even six—who exceed in piety, judgment, and tact the members of the present committee. If they cannot agree, it is because it is the will of the Holy Spirit that we return to our work."

Gordenker then made the shortest intervention of the conclave: "We agree wholeheartedly."

There were, however, other opinions. A large group, including many of the oldest cardinals, wanted to select another committee. Five days of rest within our prison had sharpened tongues if not wits, and the debate rapidly became acrimonious. LaTorre wisely postponed a vote until Saturday morning. Then, by a division of forty-two to thirty-eight, with four abstentions (including mine), the motion failed. It had been apparent it would, since unanimous consent is obligatory. We dismissed the delegation with appropriate appreciation and returned to the task of choosing a Pontiff ourselves.

LaTorre reminded us of our other options, but no one sought recognition. He then suggested that we forego further discussion and take another ballot immediately. *Senta,* that tally was interesting but inconclusive: Fieschi had thirty votes; Corragio had thirty-two; I had sixteen, and Trentin had four. The customary second vote showed essentially the same division, but with three of Trentin's votes going to me and one to Fieschi. Of new we had reached an impasse, this one more serious than that six days earlier because then each of us could have in his mind the escape of delegation. No one, apparently, seriously thought that we should resort to election by means of a majority plus one of the conclave; and neither servants nor traditionalists dared ask for a narrowing of candidates to Corragio and Fieschi.

FOUR

Allora, my idea took firmer root in my mind as one sterile scrutiny followed another. After the unsuccessful delegation, two sets of three fruitless days of voting dragged painfully by. We, of course, paused after each trio to concentrate on seeking divine guidance rather than imparting our own. I recall spending the second day of rest in almost constant prayer that my idea was in the interest of the Church. As usual, I gleaned nothing of God's pleasure in the matter. As I may have told, He has always kept His own counsel where I have been concerned. Yet, if He did not indicate I was right, neither did He imply that I was wrong.

By then, our ritual was firmly established. Most of us rose at six, said a Mass alone in our cubicles, though a few concelebrated, ate a piece of the holy nuns' charbroiled toast and drank the liquid that smelled like tea, looked like coffee, and tasted like neither, then appeared in the Sistine Chapel at eight to commence discussion. There were few formal interventions, although those that now occurred tended to be long-winded. According to me, it is a rule of life that as there is less and less to tell, it takes longer and longer to tell it. After lunch and a siesta to recover from the assault on our palates, we returned to the Sistine to cast new words and new ballots.

I sensed that another crisis was at hand. *Ecco,* we had now been imprisoned for almost three weeks. Delegation had failed and inspiration was lacking. Old men were now heavy with fatigue. Stomachs were sour from poor food and inconvenient toilets—sometimes we were obliged to walk the length of the museums to the tourists' entrance to find a commode. In sum, a clash of theological styles had largely deteriorated into personal bickering among old men. I resolved to propose my idea that Saturday morning.

Before I could seek recognition, Thomas Cardinal Arusha of Nigeria stood at his throne. When the others had seated themselves, he spoke in a voice that was nervous and sad. Chelli graciously translated his speech into Latin. "My Most Reverend Brothers, I must report a most tragic happening. During the evening, I was approached by a member of our conclave and asked to intervene with my colleagues from Africa and Asia to secure the election of a particular cardinal. There is nothing specifically sinful in this although it violates the spirit of our rules. What is most regrettable about this incident is that I was offered the prefectorship of the Sacred Congregation for the Propagation of the Faith if the cardinal in question were elected." Thomas Cardinal Arusha pursed his lips. "That is a crass violation of our sacred trust. However innocently meant, Cardinal Chamberlain, that offer is tantamount to simony, a sin against God and a violation of our constitution. I report this act to you and to the whole conclave. The lord cardinal who approached me was Henri Del Val."

The conclave was absolutely still, not even a robe rustled. LaTorre looked gravely around the chapel. I wondered how much of this affair the Holy Mule had known in advance. Del Val was a French Canadian, a member of the Curia, the prefect of the Congregation for Catholic Education. He was an independent—you say tough-minded?—man, whose thinking was much closer to that of LaTorre—perhaps Chelli would be a better reference point—than to cardinals like Fournier or Gordenker. I wanted very much to know the name of the candidate for whom the bargaining had been attempted. I had strong suspicion that Del Val had not intervened for Fieschi, but for another candidate to whom the traditionalists could accommodate themselves. I hoped it had not been for me.

Finally LaTorre spoke, and when he did it was in sonorous Latin. "We are fully cognizant of our authority as cardinal dean and as *camerlengo* and dictator pro tem until a new Pope is chosen. We bear heavy responsibility for discipline in the Church. We are prepared to exercise that authority. My Lord Cardinal Del Val, you have heard our Most Reverend Brother Arusha's charge. Do you wish to speak?"

Del Val looked around the chapel. "My Lord Cardinal, I only crave the forgiveness of My Lord Cardinal Arusha and of the conclave. My zeal to end this marathon, to see our Church governed by a new Pope, triumphed over my reason. I have sinned. I offer fatigue and devotion as explanations, not as excuses."

LaTorre nodded gravely. "We are all fatigued, My Lord Cardinal. Christ's work is tiring business. Your violation of the sacred constitution that we have all recently sworn to follow is a serious one. Under our authority as cardinal *camerlengo* during a time when the Apostolic See is vacant, we declare you excommunicate. You have our leave to appeal our decision to the new Pontiff. Like the rest of us, you must stay in this sealed conclave, but articles thirty-five and eighty-two of our constitution leave your status unclear. We adopt, subject to appeal to the members of the sacred college here assembled, the interpretation that as an excommunicate you may take no further part in our deliberations but you may vote. Please also keep in mind you are cut off from the grace of the sacraments until our decision is altered."

The sentence was harsh but traditional. In 1922 two cardinals—one later considered for sainthood—who offered similar bargains were also excommunicated. Without doubt, the new Pontiff would immediately lift the ban, but for the moment the traditionalists were embarrassed. More important, according to me, was the strong probability that this bargaining indicated that some traditionalists were now willing to abandon Fieschi to rupture the deadlock.

Ecco, the time had arrived for me to make my proposal. If the impasse were about to be broken, the advantage would go to the one who first suggested a solution. I took one last look at Michelangelo's finger of God imparting life to mankind and prayed once more that my idea was truly a part of that divine transmission.

"My Lord Cardinals, Most Reverend Brothers." Rather than Latin, I used English and then French, knowing that each cardinal was reasonably fluent in one of these tongues. "There are many holy and able men among us, but we are hopelessly deadlocked. One group, supporters of our most holy and able brother from Bologna, wants us to go in one direction; a second group, supporting our equally holy and able brother from Genova and Milano, wants us to follow another route. Many of us are insecure about all and two paths, although we are impressed by the sanctity and talents of our two brothers. Because those princes of the Church who support each man represent more than one-third of this conclave, it is not possible for us to elect either cardinal, unless we unanimously agree—as apparently we do not—to a majority plus one. To continue balloting on this basis is to continue an impasse that can only be resolved by a miracle or by the deaths of a sufficient number of us to permit an election." There were a few smiles; *ecco,* some of them were grim. "We have tried delegation, but that mode has proved fruitless.

"In your charity," I continued, "some of you have mentioned Monsignor Galeotti in your votes. We are deeply honored, but we do not think that circumstances yet occur in which we would accept election, even in the unlikely event that it were offered. We, therefore, feel entitled to tell plainly what is in our mind and in our heart, to speak candidly not only out of filial love for our Holy Mother Church but also out of fraternal affection for you, our brothers in Christ.

"It is clear to us that not only can this conclave not select either of the leading candidates, but also, as the failure of the delegation shows, when the choice was limited to the sacred college, we cannot choose one of our own members. We are too divided, too ridden by honest, intellectual strife that is now degenerating into personal recrimination. We therefore propose a course that at first may seem radical, yet we are convinced that it is a prudent mode."

I paused to make certain my words were being comprehended. "*Allora,* we suggest that we go outside of this conclave. We suggest that we go not to a bishop or even a priest but to a simple monk who joined the clergy in his mature years after a distinguished secular career. He has not yet received any holy orders but he has taken temporary vows of poverty, chastity, and obedience preparatory to taking permanent vows."

LaTorre sounded his bell to quiet the murmurs of those who understood English so that my translation into French could be heard.

"Before we dismiss this suggestion as the senile wanderings of a tired old man, let us remember that in earlier times the Holy Spirit also passed over eminent cardinals and bishops to choose a monk to guide the Church out of crisis. We name only San Gregorio VII of the eleventh century as the most notable example. And, lest fatigue dull our memories of ecclesiastical history, we recall that the holy orders of the episcopate or even the priesthood are not a requirement of election. Innocenzo III, the greatest of Pontiffs, was not a priest, though he had taken some minor holy orders. Indeed, by our rules laymen as well as monks are eligible for the chair of San Pietro. Let us also remember, as we were reminded at the Mass on that distant Sunday that marked our opening, the Church needs a Pontiff who has the qualities of a statesman as well as those of a saint. It also," I added as wryly as I could, "needs a man on whom we can agree. The Church needs a Pontiff who can make real the good implicit in many of the unfulfilled promises of the Second Vatican Council, one who can aid us make the Church more relevant to—and thus more useful to—the sufferings of the people of our own time, just as the truly great Pontiffs of the past made the Church more relevant to the people of their times. In effecting such a transformation, *il Papa* must have the capability to maintain our traditional heritage intact. He must preserve the integrity of our sacred doctrine.

"These are difficult tasks," I continued. "In fact, many here speak as if they were incompatible tasks. We think not, at least not to the right man. But the new Pontiff's duties will transcend these difficulties. He must also restore in the minds of the laity the legitimacy of the labors of the Church.

"*Allora,* we, as princes of the Church, face two simple, ugly, yet overpowering facts. First, modern man is suspicious or even hostile to us in the hierarchy; even younger priests are suspicious of us. If we examine our own consciences, we may find that, while the causes of these suspicions and hostilities are exaggerated, they are not without foundation. Let us remember what our English brother, John Henry Cardinal Newman, said: 'Nothing great or living can be done except where men are self-governed.' We who have labored all our lives for the Church may doubt that men in any age, and certainly not modern men, can rightly govern themselves in affairs spiritual. Yet there is no blinking the fact that modern man not merely resents rule imposed on him, he rejects it. It is our personal opinion that the crisis of the Church in the modern world is essentially a crisis of legitimacy, the legitimacy of *our* rule, the rule of a clerical hierarchy. That crisis demands that we seek a dramatic yet prudent solution, one that will preserve the integrity of our holy tradition and still permit us to serve the people of God, the people who live in this world at this very time. Any solution to our crisis demands that we bring the laity and the lower ranks of the clergy more meaningfully into the government of the Church and at the same time instill new vigor into that government.

"*Ecco,* the second ugly fact is that men must be ruled. We cannot mistake self-government for anarchy, although by denying men self-government we may be inviting anarchy. We must have a Pontiff who can rule and do so in the name of our Church and with the support of all of our Church. We need a Pontiff who will keep us in the tradition of the Holy, Roman, and Apostolic Church. What would it profit us to elect a man who would lead the world but who would not lead that world to Christ?

"We think it a foolish vanity for any of us to believe that only we who are cardinals can love the Church and rule her. None of us can claim that he has earned a right to rule the Christ's Church because he is holy and because he has devoted his life to that Church. The See of San

Pietro is a gift—more aptly a burden—from God. We have no authority to use it as a reward; it can only be given for the benefit of the Church herself. San Paolo says us that 'no man takes the honor to himself; he takes it who is called to God, as Aaron was. So also Christ did not glorify Himself, with the high priesthood, but He Who spoke to Him.'

"My brothers, men outside this conclave, even men outside holy orders, are called to God. San Paolo says us that the Holy Spirit allots 'His gifts to everyone according as He will.' As *He* will, my brothers, not as *we* will. As *He* will. And Vatican II reminded us of that distribution. *Lumen Gentium,* the Constitution of the Church, tells: 'He distributes special grace among the faithful of every rank.' If we accept the fact that the Holy Spirit's call is broader than our elite brotherhood of cardinals, we can read the impasse we have now reached as a divine blessing, an opportunity to go forward. We may possess the opportunity for which our recent Pontiffs so earnestly prayed and mentioned so often—a fresh wave of inspiration from the Holy Spirit."

Again I paused. I confess you I wanted to dramatize the moment, but I also wanted to ensure that my message was being received. I believe it was. Every face I could view was taut with expectation.

"The monk whom we would elect is an American, although we ourself are Italian. He is called Declan Patrick Walsh, the former special emissary to Papa Pio XII and Chief Justice of the United States. He is now a humble monk in a Trappist monastery."

Again LaTorre had to sound his little bell for silence. I could read surprise in the murmurings, but I could not discern the degree of approval and disagreement.

"We doubt," I continued as soon as quiet returned, "that this is such a radical proposal. We have recently had a non-Italian Pontiff, and Walsh is part Roman. He was born here and was baptized in Santa Susanna, not four kilometers from this chapel. He grew up in this city, and he also spent part of his youth in Dublin." Not without pangs of guilt, I confess you, I was hoping to appeal to the three Irishmen.

"After winning his country's highest award for military valor in a war against Communist aggression in Korea," I went on, "he returned here in 1951 as special representative of his president. Many of us knew him intimately during the eighteen months he was here. We ourself were acquainted with him as a child when we were a friend of his parents, but we think we really knew him for the first time in 1951. All of us who labored with him in the Vatican were impressed with his wisdom and his candor—and with his courage and his ability to lead men of different views.

"As Chief Justice of the United States, he led his country toward justice for the poor as well as the rich, the black as well as the white. He came to that Court after its historic decisions outlawing racial segregation in public schools, but his life on the bench was in great part devoted to the fight for racial justice." It pleased me that the Asians and Africans be clear on that point. "Furthermore, it was also he and he almost alone on that Court who spoke out on the merits against abortion. It was a brilliant and courageous opinion that earned him enmity from many, but respect, however grudging, from the more intelligent foes of the sanctity of human life.

"As you all know, we possess firsthand knowledge of American affairs since we have recently been apostolic delegate in Washington, and two things impressed us. First, his mode of achieving consensus on his tribunal, perhaps the most eminent in the secular world. He was tyrant over no one. He showed respect for the views of others, yet he led, gently, firmly, but still effectively. He did not destroy the institution, nor did he radicalize it. Rather, he preserved it by forcing it to confront the problems that faced his country.

"Second, and here we evidence a bias shared within this chapel, was his willingness to surrender the most prestigious of worldly goods to seek God in the solitude and sacrifice of a Trappist monastery.

"Let us be absolutely candid, Most Reverend Brothers. *Ecco,* let us declare, as is the custom in the British House of Commons, our interest in the affair. He is dear to us. Yet we think that our judgment is not influenced by this fact. Indeed, we pray that our judgment is formed despite this fact, for it has given us great concern. We all know that try as we may to avoid it, we may each be influenced by personal considerations, although we say ourselves that we are acting only for the good of our Holy Church. Let me simply tell"—I recall slipping from "we" to the personal "I"—"as the Lord Christ will be my judge, this is the man whom I think we should elect."

Immediately there came what you Americans call a great hubbub. At least sixty voices spoke at once. It was LaTorre, however, whose deep basso commanded our attention. He addressed us rapidly in Latin, and for the first time during the conclave he acted as a partisan rather than as an impartial presiding officer. "Incredible! We know nothing of this Walsh. We ask the lord cardinal how it is possible to vouch for the doctrinal understanding much less orthodoxy of such a man, layman or monk? New World Catholicism, even among the clergy, seems to us to have little regard for the sacred dogmas of our Church."

The Holy Spirit, operating in His usual indirect way, had apparently moved LaTorre to intervene against my proposal in an assisting mode. I could see Chelli wincing at the outburst, and I also noted that even two of the traditionalist cardinals from Latin America appeared as offended as did the three or four cardinals from the United States whose faces I could observe. I rose slowly to respond, first gathering some notes from the small table in front of my throne. It pleased me to allow the full impact of the contemptuous remarks about New World Catholicism to sink in.

"The monk Declan Walsh is not a theologian, but then many of our most effective Pontiffs have not been theologians either. We have even heard it told, although we are secure that it is without truth, that some members of this sacred college are not theologians, at least not good theologians." Even the traditionalists could not suppress smiles at my reference to LaTorre's well-known penchant for labeling, only half in jest, as heretics colleagues with whom he disagreed. "In our conversations with Walsh, we have never heard him speak in a heretical fashion. We doubt that even at its prime the Holy Office could have found fault with him. Nor, let us add, do we consider his being from the New World a failing. He seems to us to have the best of both worlds."

"There is no question," our slender Cardinal Chelli put in suavely, "that in his radical suggestion My Lord Cardinal Galeotti has presented an able man to us, one in whom the Old World can take as much pride as the New.

But his training and his work have been in secular government, and without doubt there he has made a contribution to God and to mankind. Now as a simple monk he undoubtedly lives a holy life of prayer. But these contributions do not mean that he should sit in Peter's chair. Peter's successor must be a man of personal holiness. And that, we believe, can only be achieved through *many years*—not a few well-intentioned years, but many years—of training, self-discipline, sacrifice, and hard testing. Only a long career in the clergy provides reasonable assurance of such qualities. A few years in a monastery are laudable, but they do not turn a layman into a member of the clergy. In Naples we have a saying, 'A cowl does not make a monk.' We doubt that any layman, no matter how talented and well-meaning, can put on those habits of personal holiness as easily as he can slip on a monk's material habit."

Charles Cardinal Pritchett, archbishop of Detroit, who once many years earlier had intervened on Declan's behalf, spoke us in a swift, beautifully accented Latin that was unique among Americans. "With My Lord Cardinal Chelli's permission, I shall try to speak to that point. I think Walsh has those qualities of personal holiness, although through much of his life he did not pursue a clerical calling. I knew him here in Rome and later he became a member of my archdiocese. I have felt in him, in a quiet way, those very qualities of which My Lord Cardinal Chelli properly inquires. I once spoke to Walsh about it, and I fear I embarrassed him. The very fact that he was embarrassed is some evidence of humility, and we should keep in mind it is one of the great virtues in a Christian, however"—and now Pritchett looked directly at LaTorre—"absent it may be among some of us who wear red hats."

Another American, Philip Cardinal O'Brien of New Orleans, intervened in an annoyed voice, speaking in English which Chelli translated into Latin for the conclave, "Holy is as holy does. When faced with racial injustice or murder in the form of abortion, Walsh did not pussyfoot." (I well recall those words because Chelli asked me how to translate them into Latin. I suggested a pleasing phrase: *Sine fuco a fallaciis dicere.*) "He spoke out clearly and unequivocally, just as he acted courageously to save the lives of his people in a war. I call that personal holiness—a willingness to lay down his life for his fellow man. I believe there is some scriptural authority for that judgment, and"—O'Brien looked directly at Chelli—"it is a pity that one of your recent Italian Popes trained in your Old World traditions of self-discipline and after a long career of sacrifice and testing in the clergy and the Curia saw fit to watch in silence and in shame the mass murder of six million Jews."

Wisely, Chelli declined to defend the refusal of Pio XII during World War II to condemn the Nazis' death camps. Instead, the young cardinal shifted the site of his attack. "Was this man not married?"

"He was," I replied. "His wife died more than two years ago."

"How many children does he have?" Chelli's voice oozed innocence.

I tried to conceal my anger at what I knew well was the underlying point. "His wife, tragically, was unable physically to bear healthy children. One child died within a few weeks of birth. Other pregnancies, several others, resulted in miscarriages. We were with her on one such occasion and we know the grief it caused. Perhaps God had a purpose in allowing such sorrow."

Chelli again shifted his attack, this time using the other hook of his question. "Would not a widower as Pope, a man who had not always practiced celibacy, be a source of scandal among us?"

"Less than some of your Italian Popes who kept mistresses did," O'Brien intervened in English. "We are not proposing to bring back the Borgias." (His use of "we" was pleasing to me.)

"My Lord Cardinal O'Brien is aware, of course," Chelli said urbanely, "that the Borgias were Spanish."

"Catalans," the primate of Spain interrupted, "not Spanish." (The primate had been born in Madrid.)

"Thank you," Chelli continued. "In any event, it has been centuries since the finger of scandal has been pointed at the papacy, and we would like to keep that record."

"There is no reason to believe the record will be in greater danger from this monk than from a cardinal," I spoke. "If nothing else, the defections from the priesthood of the last decades and the death under mysterious circumstances of one of our own recent brothers of the sacred college should have instructed us that we are no more immune to the temptations of the flesh than others.

"There is," I told, "a certain advantage here. The monk Declan Walsh has no near relatives. His parents are both dead, and he was an only child. We all know that there is always the danger of scandal from relatives of Pontiffs and cardinals." (I thought it necessary to tell no more. Every family in the world has what you Americans call its black sheep, and in Italy such people make free use of the names of their cardinal uncles. Even Papa Pio XII had been afflicted with such problems.)

"We are concerned," the Patriarch Aspaturian put in, "more by the nationality here than by the fact that the candidate is not a cardinal. Would not an American Pope rekindle the ashes of the Cold War? We had hoped that the struggle between East and West had receded and that the next Pontiff might continue to play a role in completely ending that conflict. Could this Walsh mediate among the Chinese, Americans, and Russians?"

"My Lord Cardinal raises a serious point." It was Jozef Cardinal Grodzins, archbishop of Warsaw, who spoke us. Because his grandfather had been Jewish, the Nazis had dispatched Grodzins, even though a priest, to Auschwitz along with his family; his parents and two younger sisters had been burned in the ovens of gas but Jozef had survived. The Communists had been more lenient: after he had been consecrated a bishop and had spoken against the government, he had been imprisoned for five years and had lived for many years thereafter under virtual house arrest. In later years he had been permitted some freedom—which he had immediately used to criticize the tenuous and informal understanding that marked a suspicious truce between communism and Catholicism in Poland. He had been a thorn in the side of Church and state, all and two. Now he was suffering from lung cancer, and the more "liberal" regime felt strong enough to tolerate a man near death. But to Grodzins death was an old enemy to be beaten as long as possible, and for three years he had been clinging tenaciously to life and to office.

"A serious point," Grodzins said us, "but let us be candid, though sorrowful. Which of our recent Popes has been able to mediate the conflict between East and West? During the Cuban missile crisis of 1962 John was active, but surely his role was small. Sadly we must concede that

Paul's voice was seldom heard, and his successors did not survive long enough to make a real impact.

"We admit that an American in the chair of Peter would bring some problems, but his long career as a layman might solve some as well. In Poland we still see our young people drifting away from the Church, not because of the appeals of communism but because we are not reaching them. My Lord Cardinals, we bore them. Our brother Cardinal Galeotti has said that we have no legitimacy with them. We would go further and say that we have lost our capacity to attract their attention long enough for them to care about us. It is well known that our personal days are short, but we are willing to try something new, something dramatic. It is a prudent political principle to co-opt the best of those on the outside. Besides, we remember one of the old sayings of a seminary teacher, that one look at the Roman Curia should convince even an atheist of the divine nature of the Church. Who but a benevolent and omnipotent God could keep an institution going for 1900 years under such incompetent management? We have survived almost twenty centuries of misrule by professional clerics. If we truly have a Church against which the gates of hell cannot prevail, we would survive another quarter of a century under the rule of a monk."

"We shall survive forever, My Most Reverend Brother," Chelli put in, "but it is written 'thou shalt not tempt the Lord thy God.'"

"It is also written that the master was not pleased with his servant who kept his talent wrapped in a napkin," Grodzins countered. "We must take a chance. We think that the gain is worth the risk."

The debate continued for several hours. As the talk went on, it became more and more clear that my suggestion had struck a spark. It pleased some of the northern Europeans and Africans to have an excuse to abandon the archbishop of Bologna and his gallant defeats, but it was also apparent that some of his supporters were prepared to remain with him to the finish. The Americans, servants as well as those identified with the traditionalists, and even the three Irish, were intrigued. Pritchett and O'Brien, the two most intelligent among the Americans—I do not mean to sin against charity but you Americans have produced few members of your hierarchy in whom you can take intellectual pride—had immediately identified themselves with Walsh's candidacy.

The Italian supporters of Fieschi and the few Spaniards who were with them were all adamant, but some of the Latin Americans were wavering. LaTorre's contemptuous outburst had not cemented them into an alliance against a man from the New World. In fact, it was José Cardinal Martìn, archbishop of Buenos Aires, who mentioned that Clement IV had been a widower. (I could read the unsaid words on Chelli's lips: "Since he was a Frenchman, one could have expected worse.")

At a certain point, Su, the Korean cardinal, told that he had known Declan Walsh the soldier and diplomat. It was a laudatory intervention. Given Su's wandering mysticism I was uncertain if it was helpful—until, that is, near the finish when he spoke of the attractiveness of a Pontiff who had shed his own blood for Asians and would be sensitive to the budding Church of the Third World.

Ecco, a few hours later, Martìn made an important oration. Returning to Grodzins's point, he said us: "We are fast becoming shepherds without flocks. I do not think that Europeans or North Americans understand the Church in Latin America, but to some extent there has always been —and even now more so—a divided Church in which many clergy, especially bishops and archbishops, go one way and the mass of the people another. It is difficult to say how much of what our people practice—their glorification of particular saints, for example—is based on primitive ideas about magic, and how much is Christianity. But what is clear is that our message, the message of Christ, is not being heard by our people. And I fear that that message cannot be heard until we take steps that are at least dramatic if not radical."

"The Church is no stranger to anticlericalism," LaTorre responded. "Here in Italy it is always rampant."

"What My Lord Cardinals Galeotti, Grodzins, and I are speaking of goes far beyond anticlericalism," Martìn explained. "In Latin America we do have opponents who directly attack us and even on occasion persecute us. But, among the people we are often, too often, ignored. We are tolerated like ancient fountains in a city that has a modern, piped water supply, tolerated neither because we are useful or even beautiful but because we represent a piece of quaint folklore. Our people suffer far less from anticlericalism than from *a*clericalism.

"The most anguishing aspect is that the people—and we know this—feel a deep need for our message," Martìn continued. "They turn to communism—whether out of frustration or despair I do not know—with its political religion and its preachments about social justice—preachments that we should have been shouting. Or our people are turning to penitential Protestant sects for spiritual nourishment.

"I would prefer to see a South American rather than a North American in Peter's chair, but I am willing to take a chance that a man outside the ranks of the sacred college can bring the message of Christ to our people. For we within the college cannot now do so. I realize that there are high risks in bringing in an outsider. But," Martìn smiled in an effort to take some of the sting from his words, "I have faith that our most reverend colleagues in the Curia could prevent any theological disasters, for surely they have been able to stultify genuine reform during the many years since the Second Vatican Council."

Pierre Cardinal Tascherau, archbishop of Montreal, made similar points, stressing that three decades ago the Quebecois had been among the most pious and observant of Catholics. Now what Cardinal Martìn had said of Latin America was each year becoming a more accurate description of French Canada.

Ecco, the objections that the traditionalists continued to repeat were those that LaTorre and Chelli had outlined. According to me, they were serious objections, and I had been restrained by their weight. Declan Walsh had demonstrated himself to be a man of judgment, courage, diplomacy, and, as a layman, of steadfastness in his faith; still, even though he had become a monk, he was without systematic theological training and his inner piety had not been tested by years of loneliness as a cleric. LaTorre, Bisset, and Greene were bitterly scornful in their attacks on these lacks. I detected in Chelli, however, a curious attraction to my proposal. He was opposed, but unlike his colleagues he was intrigued by the prospect of a different solution to an old problem.

It was thus fitting that it was Chelli who p-sed the crucial question. I confess you now that, in fact, I had—

how do you say?—sandbagged him. I could have included the information in my own presentation, but I had deliberately omitted it in the hope that someone, preferably someone hostile to the fundamental idea, would raise the issue so that the answer could be all the more effective. Knowing Chelli's orderly mind, I had suspected that he would notice the gap in my presentation and would place the question. It was he who asked: "Let us grant for the sake of discussion, but only for the sake of discussion, that the Church would now benefit from the rule of a monk-layman. Why this particular man? Are there not hundreds, even thousands of others equally or perhaps even better qualified?"

"The question," I commenced, "is fair, although it is difficult to answer since none of us knows all monks any more than any of us knows all members of the laity. Even many of us in this chapel are strangers to each other." I paused. "But let us try a more positive response to such an important question. Why Walsh? We offer two sets of reasons. The first is not inconsequential but it is not as fundamental as the second.

"Let us discuss those reasons in order. First, he is well known in the secular world for his great abilities, and he is knowledgeable about our world. His former position of judicial leadership and his unstained reputation give him an advantage of stature and respect that few laymen or clergymen even within this chapel could equal. In addition, we know that he has fought, ably fought and publicly fought, when he had nothing personal to gain, on an issue of central importance to our moral code, abortion. Moreover, he has demonstrated his love of the Church by taking vows, not holy orders but vows.

"This set of reasons, as we told, is not inconsequential; but, we repeat, according to us the second set is more weighty, although more difficult to demonstrate in an objective way. Walsh has been touched by the finger of God. He was a hero, not merely a participant, but a wounded hero in two wars, one against fascism, one against communism. He was born here among us, grew up among us, and returned to us as a mature man, the representative of his government. Since that time he has been selected for the most prestigious judicial office in the secular world. He relinquished that office in the midst of a distinguished career. He relinquished it not for material advancement but to enter a monastery in the service of God, not even as a priest but as a simple brother. We do not look on these events as fortuitous accidents, random events for which reasons are lacking. We see the finger of God illuminating for us the shape of a man to lead us. We do not claim inspiration. But, if in your charity, you put aside the possibility of our senility, we can offer no other satisfactory explanation of why we have been brooding over this man's name since our last Pontiff died, why we in this conclave have not been able to select a Pontiff from among the very capable and holy men in our midst, and why the delegation failed. We believe that God is giving His Church an opportunity to save souls.

"Most Dear and Reverend Brothers, as we consider this proposal, let us keep in mind what says the Prophet Joel:

> In the days to come—it is the Lord who speaks—I shall pour out my spirit on all mankind. Your sons and daughters will prophesy, your young men shall see visions, your old men shall dream dreams; even on my slaves, men and women, in those days I shall pour out my spirit. . . .

San Pietro quoted those words in his very first sermon after Pentecost. They are good words for us to hold in mind. The spirit of God in all mankind. We old men may dream dreams, but unless we can somehow reach our people, young men will continue to see visions only of materialism, not of Christ's gospel. We offer the Church a man who beyond any of us here can reach our people."

As usual, we had commenced that morning at eight, and as I finished it was almost noon. We had enjoyed no respite from debate, and the time for the nuns to risk our health was rapidly approaching—as was the time of the final direct flight from Roma to America.

I gazed across the chapel at Corragio. I thought I saw something in his eyes. I seized the chance and told: "My Lord Cardinals, we would value the opinion of the archbishop of Bologna on our proposal."

Corragio stood up slowly, wearily. He looked around the crowded but silent chapel and said simply, *"Eligam*

Walsh." ("I shall elect Walsh.") I say now, if there was inspiration at the conclave, it was at that moment.

Everyone in the chapel knew what those two words meant: for the archbishop, the third great defeat in a courageous life; for the Church, the first Pontiff in centuries from outside the Sacred College of Cardinals; for Declan Walsh, power and suffering.

"We see many practical difficulties here," LaTorre intervened. "He is not a priest much less a bishop. We do not know if he would accept election at all. We would look like a pack of fools—and we are all agreed we need no more of that—announcing that we had chosen a Pontiff who did not choose us."

"We are secure," I riposted, "that under the skillful direction of the *camerlengo* we shall follow the proper ecclesiastical protocol. Articles 88–90 of our constitution set out guidelines for us when the new Pontiff is chosen from outside the conclave. It is not an unprecedented event. The cardinal dean *immediately* consecrates him a bishop, if he is not one already. Let us keep in mind that in the early Church many bishops were elected before they were even baptized, not merely before they were ordained priests. Our own San Ambrogio, the man who converted San Agostino to Christianity, was only a catechumen when elected bishop of Milano.

"As for acceptance," I told, "if the sacred college elect Walsh, we have a very simple plan. After proceeding with the scrutiny"—I wanted that part settled and sealed before proceeding to any other step—"and if Walsh is elected, I shall fly to America—with the conclave's permission—and speak to him tonight. It now lacks noon. There is a flight at two-thirty. We shall immediately communicate his answer to you by telephone and return either with him, or alone. If he accepts, then we have no further problem, although he shall have many. If he declines, then we shall be obliged to lift our cross of new."

"What about burning the ballots?" LaTorre asked, reduced now to questions about petty details.

"We understand," I responded, "that although the constitution of Papa Paolo VI prescribes that the ballots shall be immediately burned, only tradition, not that sacred constitution, requires that we make black smoke when a Pontiff has not been chosen or white when he has been elected. Surely, we could dispense ourselves from that tradition. If Declan Walsh is chosen, we can add some of the black pellets to the ballots, as we have been doing. If he accepts, we can then burn some plain paper when he is here, and add the chemical pellet to make white smoke. It is a simple thing." (Not for nothing had I spent all those years studying canon law.)

"We propose," Chelli intervened, "that the conclave appoint a new delegation to choose a Pope, from within or outside the sacred college. We are fatigued, as the general level of debate indicates. Our minds are weary and our judgment shaky."

"We have tried delegation," I responded, "and it failed. We have considered a second delegation and have rejected the idea. We see no more merit to that plan than the conclave did last week. And there is an immediate practical objection. To be valid, delegation must be approved without dissent, and we—I myself—shall vote against such a proposal, if it comes before us. More important, My Lord Cardinal Chelli certainly has faith, despite the fatigue that we all share, that we are yet capable of selecting wisely. If the Holy Spirit restricted His wisdom to the young and fresh of mind, our Church would have perished 2000 years ago. We ask that another scrutiny be held, with the name of the monk Declan Patrick Walsh considered."

"We do not feel it within our power to prevent another scrutiny," LaTorre shrugged, "but we feel it our duty to vote against this proposal and to urge all those who love the Church to join with us in opposition."

Now, as my brothers filed to the altar to place their neatly folded ballots in the huge chalice, the air was charged with excitement as it had not been since our opening vote. It seemed to me that we crept through the voting procedures. Then, when the scrutinizers began their shuffling, tabulating, and announcing, I tried to keep count. But my head was spinning from my glands' final pulsing of adrenaline through a wearied body, spinning too much for me to maintain accurate figures. I put down my pencil, closed my eyes and ears, and prayed over and over: "Thy will be done."

When the counted ballots were strung on a garland, I was probably the only person in the chapel who did not know the result. As if in a dream, a faint, confused dream,

I heard the scrutinizer call out: "The Most Reverend Cardinal Fieschi has twenty-two votes; the Most Reverend Cardinal Corragio has one vote; His Holiness the Patriarch Aspaturian has one vote"—Fieschi, according to me, was too honorable to violate the tradition against voting for oneself, but he could not vote for Corragio and would not vote for a monk whom he considered a layman—"the monk Declan Walsh has fifty-eight votes. There is a majority of two-thirds plus one for the election of the monk Declan Walsh. The monk Declan Walsh is elected."

LaTorre sighed hopelessly as the three cardinals chosen to review the election concurred in the result. "If this be the will of the conclave, we have no recourse. We shall mix the chemical when we burn the ballots. We fear we are engaging in a comic opera, but let us suggest that our brother travel incognito. And may God, in His infinite mercy, forgive us all for this sin against the Holy Spirit."

"With your permission, My Lord Cardinals," I told, "we shall leave the conclave immediately, and, as our brother has so prudently suggested, we shall travel incognito. Let us now ask your prayers, not only for a successful journey but also that God give the grace to our new Holy Father to accept the cross that we offer to him."

LaTorre said nothing. The Holy Mule looked more like the stunned ox.

As the exhausted cardinals commenced to file from the chapel, I whispered to Pritchett of Detroit: "If I know our brothers Greene and Bisset well, there will be an effort to reverse this decision when I am gone. LaTorre and Chelli may join in that attempt. All of us will depend on you to see that this does not happen."

"It will not happen. If it is proposed, I shall use an old American political trick and talk until you return. So please hurry. An old man can talk for a long time, but the standing is painful."

FIVE

Back in my cell, I swiftly clothed myself in a dark business suit borrowed from one of the architect's assistants. It would have pleased me to appear as a distinguished layman, perhaps a lawyer or a physician, but from the architect's barely suppressed amusement it seemed that I was not making a good figure. Ten minutes later I was in a car and, through the Porta Sant' Anna, on my way to the airport at Fiumicino.

At the ultimate moment, Prince Chigi had made a reservation on TWA's afternoon nonstop flight to New York and then, after a delay of two hours, on to South Carolina. Fortunately, first-class seats are usually available. I have often felt wasteful at spending that much money. But because I would be, in all, ten and a half hours in the air, it was no more than Holy Mother Church owed me after the ordeal of the past few weeks.

As soon as the 747 had lumbered off the ground, the stewardess brought the first of what would be an endless stream of complimentary beverages. I refused and instead asked for a light lunch. In view of what we had been served during the previous three weeks, I contented myself with a first plate of Coquilles St. Jacques with a half bottle of Pouilly Fuissé (American airlines are ignorant of Italian wines), then a rather large steak Chateaubriand *al sangue* —you say rare?—an *insalata mista,* and a full bottle of St. Julien. When I had finished the meal, I took a capsule and asked not to be disturbed until the plane landed at New York.

After we had bounced to a stop, I rapidly traversed the public health control. At customs I merely displayed my diplomatic passport and was waved through. I carried only a small valise. Because our trip had been retarded an hour by winds near Nova Scotia, the wait for the flight to South Carolina was brief. I dozed as soon as I was seated and awoke in Charleston as the plane rolled down the runway past a line of gigantic cargo aircraft.

I stepped out into the soggy twilight. After the cool air conditioning aboard the plane, the atmosphere on the ground slapped my face like a warm, wet towel. It was even more—how do you say *umido?—ecco,* muggy, more muggy than I remembered Washington. Fortunately, the abbot of the monastery had dispatched a huge monk to assist me, Fra Stefano—no, you say, Steven. We departed the dingy airport building and walked in the dense atmosphere, with Fra Steven carrying my small valise as if it were a toy. I had difficulty breathing the blanket of air. No one who has endured summer in Roma or Washington is a stranger to a cruel climate, but this air was terrible. Only in Cuba have I ever felt anything so oppressive.

Fra Steven did not seem to notice, and not knowing what else I could do I meekly followed him to the abbey's machine. Once inside that small ship—you Americans prefer ocean liners to automobiles—he pressed a series of keys and blessedly chilled air commenced to restore hope that it would be possible to continue breathing.

The holy brother guided the ship through traffic signals; unlike an Italian, he stopped for each that was red and patiently waited until it had become green. Soon we found ourselves on a large *autostrada.* We traveled north for some kilometers past signs pointing to a nuclear submarine port, then slid off onto a smaller and less crowded road. Like a true Trappist, Fra Steven chatted constantly about life in Mepkin Abbey—a strange name—with its 45,000 chickens, its timber, and plans for reforestation to replace the tall pines the monks were cutting. I could imagine Declan laboring with trees, but the image of him among chickens was more than my mind or my sense of humor could support.

I must say you that the Trappists—originally they were a part of the Benedictines, but divided some few centuries ago in 1028, though they still follow the order of San Benedetto—the Trappists are a very strict and also very simple group. They are doers of difficult manual labor, not teachers or missionaries or preachers or pastors. Nor do they especially encourage scholarship or even, despite their long periods of silence, contemplation. True, they spend some time each day in prayer and meditation, and some Trappists have been famous mystics. But mostly they labor hard, frequently from two or three in the morning, and usually in silence. They pray hard, and they chant beautifully. It is not, according to me, a post for a man with ambition or a man who can better serve God with his mind than with his sweat.

We sped along in the night perhaps twenty or thirty kilometers to a village named—long before the Trappists were arrived, Fra Steven assured me—Moncks Corner. We turned right into a smaller road for several kilometers, then right again onto yet another road. By now a full moon had risen, showing us the ultimate turn onto a lane lined with bearded trees—oaks and cypresses, dangling silver tresses of Spanish moss. The road's surface became earth, and we arrived at a large swinging portal. To the left, through a decline in the land, I could see moonlight shimmering on the water of a large river.

"We walk from here," Fra Steven told as he lifted my valise by two thick fingers. I stepped out into dense air. It was cooler now but no less thick than at the airport, despite a small breeze. We found ourselves on a short hill—how do you call it?—a bluff overlooking a wide, dark river. The noise was incredible—not of man, but of nature. A million crickets were chirping, and hundreds of deep-voiced frogs—I wondered what fat legs they must have—were gulping; an occasional bird called out, while unseen insects buzzed about my ears.

Fra Steven strode to a tall pole by the side of the portal and tugged vigorously at a thick cord. About three meters high on the pole, a large bell sounded an ear-shattering peal. A few moments later, preceded by two monks carrying torches, the Very Reverend Father Abbot, attired in the white and black robes of the order, came to greet us. The Very Reverend Father Abbot, whose face I could not clearly discern in the darkness, insisted on kissing my ring, something I was not accustomed to in Americans. (In the Vatican, lower-ranking clergy spend much of their time bent over, performing this rite.) Then he conducted me to his office.

As we walked, he told that before your war of independence the area had been a rice plantation, the home of a famous patriot whose name I have now forgotten. The old palazzo, its ruins located several hundred meters farther up along the hill, had become too ancient to repair, and the monks had removed it. Here, closer to the river, they had constructed a cluster of low, modern edifices to house their community. There were individual cells for forty men, but only twenty-eight were in use. Thus, the Very Reverend Father Abbot assured me, there was ample room for me at this inn.

As we entered his office I received a clear vista of his face. It was rugged and lined, at the same time very familiar, but I was too tired to inquire. He must have observed my fatigue, because he kindly asked if it would please me to bathe and eat a little. I replied that my business with Fra Declan was urgent. The Very Reverend Father Abbot looked at me with gentle but piercing eyes that told he knew precisely why I was there. I am not sure that I read reproach in that glance or in my own conscience.

He led me two steps into the tall chapel that the monks themselves had constructed. Another hooded monk quietly appeared and placed on one of the arms of the monks' stalls in the chapel an opened bottle of chilled Verdicchio, two glasses also chilled, and a plate of biscuits.

"I shall fetch Brother Declan for you," the Very Reverend Father Abbot told, then added softly: "A little more than two years ago, he came to us a tormented soul. Now he is a whole man again. But have mercy on him, Eminence. We cannot go on breaking him and repairing him forever."

I nodded without comment or commitment. Our God often reserves His mercy for the next world and sometimes tortures us in this life beyond all human cruelty. It gave me no pleasure to be an instrument of that torture. I am secure that the abbot understood and gave me absolution. I could hear his woolen robe swishing quietly through the thick, damp grass as he went to find Declan. Before I had finished my first glass of the cool Verdicchio, Declan, wearing a monk's coarse, black robe, entered the chapel. For a few seconds, my fatigue allowed my mind to imagine a younger Declan, with Kate on his arm, attending a diplomatic reception. They had made a striking couple. She had been tall with a full figure, a trifle slender according to Italian tastes but ample according to those of Americans. Her long hair was the color of the fine wine of Soave. Declan had stood even a head taller and, with his heavy, red-tinged beard, made an imposing presence that enhanced her beauty.

I watched him now in the chapel. In some ways there

were only the shading changes of aging: his hair had more silver on the sides, his beard was more grizzled and not neatly barbered. The patches that were not white were sombre brown, with only an occasional red wire protruding. In other respects, the changes were more obvious. One could read much new in his eyes, a depth of feeling—no, that is not the exact word—perhaps a measure of suffering that carried with it a hint of some sort of understanding not possessed by the rest of us.

Suddenly he perceived me. "Ugo! What are you doing here? I thought that you would be huddled up in conclave with the other princes of the Church, gestating a Pope," he said as he released me from a bearlike *abbraccio.* At least some of his old humor remained.

"You have right," I told. "That is where I have been." I had carefully considered how to approach Declan. After hours of thought during the nights of the conclave, I had decided to come directly to the point. It was not the Italian mode, but Declan was an American and he might be impatient with more aesthetically pleasing approaches. What you called the "shock treatment" might be most functional. "We have elected a new Pontiff. The conclave has chosen Declan Walsh as bishop of Rome."

Declan stepped back as if I had struck him. He remained in stung silence for a moment; then he laughed but without any trace of humor. "You joke, *il mio vecchio,* but you joke badly."

"I am not making a joke, *caro.* I state the simple truth. The Sacred College of Cardinals has elected you to be the successor of San Pietro, the Vicar of Christ."

Declan looked at me, full in the eyes. The tanned skin above his beard grew ashen, making his scar stand out like a freshly bleeding wound. He did not fully believe, yet neither did he fully doubt.

"Pray tell me, how did this latest miracle come to pass?" His voice was harsh. "Did three wise men on camels suddenly appear in St. Peter's Square?"

"Under pain of instant and automatic excommunication no one in the conclave can reveal any of the proceedings without the permission of the newly elected Pontiff. *Ecco,* that means you will have to accept before discovering." There was levity in my words, but none in my heart.

"You are not joking." It was a firm statement not a question, but some of the harshness had gone from his voice.

"I am not making a joke. . . ." I commenced, but he was not hearing me. He got up and walked around the small chapel before opening the portal to the moon and the river. For several minutes we both listened to the discordant symphony of frogs, birds, and insects.

He brought us back to reality. "I can see what has become my world, so this is not a dream; it's only a living nightmare. There are times," he sighed, "when I miss Kate more than others. She would have said something to clear my head."

I nodded. It was true. She was the most direct woman I had ever known, and her mind was even sharper than her tongue. (I pray you, do not think I offend against charity. She was a person I loved dearly, as dearly as Declan himself. Fundamentally, she was one of the kindest people I have known, but when she spoke her mind she did not choose words to blur her meaning.)

Declan walked back to the stall in which I was seated. He stood towering over me, but he spoke gently. "Ugo, I know it's been said before, but I am not worthy. There're sins in my life that you know nothing about. Kate's death was the result of several of them."

I looked toward the side of the chapel at the purple curtain covering the entry to the confessional. "Is there one among us who has not sinned grievously? If there is, he is not a member of the college of cardinals, of that I am absolutely secure. You have fallen; so did the first Vicar, and far worse than you could have. Perfection is what we strive for, not what we achieve in this world." Then I returned his gaze. "I believe, truly believe as Christ the Lord is my judge, that you are he who should lead the Church." I clasped his hand and kissed it.

He pulled away as if burned. I could feel torment radiating through the room. "Do you realize," he asked, "what you are asking me to do?"

"Yes. To accept the most awesome responsibility that any human being can possess, and with it no life for yourself but only for others; and no escape except death."

"And no one with whom to share that responsibility."

"No one except God. He will be enough. Have faith in His mercy. If you accept the power to bind and loose in heaven as on earth, surely He will give the grace to choose wisely."

He looked at me quizzically, as if about to pursue my statement. I was relieved he did not. I would have had difficulty justifying many papal judgments, recent and ancient. But he was off again, making his own argument rather than responding to mine.

"Ugo, how can you ask that?" His voice was pleading, a tone I had never heard from Declan Walsh the marine, the diplomat, or the judge. Perhaps he had imbibed some measure of humility from the humble, sweating brothers here.

"God asks you, *caro,* not the Monsignor Galeotti."

"Perhaps, perhaps. But I have spent the last two years here in penance. I sacrificed Kate for my ambition and I rushed her death by my self-indulgence. I may have sacrificed others in Korea or in the opinions I wrote and assigned for the Court, maybe even in my academic work. I've seen myself as I am. I detest what I now recognize as a driving ambition, a ruthless readiness to use others. I cannot reconcile those habits with Christianity. I've prayed for forgiveness, and I have removed myself from temptation."

He stood up and again walked around the chapel. "I don't think you can understand. A part of me has a craving for power over others like a drunk craves alcohol. You don't realize what an intoxicating, almost sexually gratifying, feeling comes from putting your grubby finger on a map and causing a thousand men to attack behind a curtain of artillery and bombs, or from motioning to a man to move and watching him obey even though you both know that the reward for his obedience will in all probability be a painful death. Imagine the selfish gratification one feels whispering in the ear of a president or presiding over a Court that shapes the law and policy of a great nation. And those are *nothing* compared to the potential influence of the papacy."

He stopped his pacing. "Ugo," he cried out, "don't you realize what I'm saying? Perverted or not, I enjoyed Korea. I reveled in the games of intrigue in the White House and among diplomats—and, God knows, among academics. On the Court, marshaling a majority by converting one or two judges who originally voted against me was for me the ultimate fulfillment or so I thought."

He held up his hand before I could speak. "I know what you're going to say: I did those things to win a war as cheaply as possible, or to get wise and just public policy adopted. That may be true. I thought it was then and now I pray it was, but the fact remains: I loved the game itself. I wanted to win, not once or twice or usually, but always. Here I am safe from ambition and power. Put me back into the real world and the old fires will burn again. In ten years, maybe monastic life could discipline my drive, or age drain its strength. But two years have taught me only to recognize my weakness, not to cure it. I can still hear that lion roaring inside my head."

"If I may presume for perhaps the ultimate time to offer spiritual advice," I intervened, "I say several things. You no doubt exaggerate your sinfulness. Years in the confessional have taught me that, when we sincerely reflect on our lives, most of us exaggerate that darker aspect of our character. We must be careful, *caro,* for such an emotion can easily leap the bounds of repentance into the dangerous fields of narcissistic egotism.

"Also," I continued, "ambition and what you call the game played for its own sake have been dangers for all Pontiffs, indeed for any man of authority. But it need not be an evil thing. I recall once reading a statement about your President Lincoln made by an attorney-colleague. He said that the president's ambition was a little engine that knew no rest. If your ambition is for God's Holy Church and not for yourself, then what you name a personal flaw may, in fact, be a blessing. According to me, ambition is not the important question."

"What is?" He seemed to be preparing to dispute my response, whatever it was.

"Caro," I spoke hesitantly, for it was not an easy thing to ask a man to look deeply into his own soul. "Do you recall the morning of Kate's death? You challenged God to fight you openly, as He wrestled with Jacob. Then, within a week, you pledged me to shake what influence I possessed to obtain your admittance to a monastery."

"Do you think I could forget?"

"No, I remind you only because, according to me, the

critical question is whether you have now forgiven God and accepted Him."

"Ugo, it is a difficult. . . ."

"I do not want to know the response," I told quickly. "I have no right to know."

"You have. You deserve an answer. I cannot give an eloquent or perhaps even a clear one, but I'll try. You've more than suspected that I have never been a person of great faith. In fact, I've never been without serious doubts about the existence of God, the divinity of Christ, and almost every other so-called dogma. But I accept—totally and without trace of reservation—the social and ethical teachings of Christianity. I can see no other set of rules that humans can follow and attain a peaceful life with some real degree of justice among them. My faith there has never wavered."

"You have always intellectualized too much. I have told that before."

"Yes. Others have said it, too. Maybe I *feel* about Christianity's social ethics, while I *think* about abstract questions of theology. I've seen a different kind of theology here. Have you met the abbot?"

It—how do you say?—all came together suddenly in my mind. Now I remembered why his face seemed so familiar. He was the mystic poet, Robert Pryce. Declan told that the abbot had introduced him to his own forms of meditation. He spoke with respect and hope but not with exuberance. That much was comforting. He visualized it as possibly outlining a road that the intellect alone could not perceive. I was more skeptical. Whatever the merits of such modes for some people, they would never work for him. Even being passive was a strange experience for Declan. Of course, I was thinking of him before he had spent two years in a monastery, but even now he was speaking about mysticism in intellectual terms. Declan was fundamentally a man of action and of cold reason. I admired the brilliance of his mind and the sweet clarity of his writings. But, however firmly grounded they were in philosophy and founded on a vision of a better world here on earth, he was not a philosopher and certainly he was not a mystic. Except for that period immediately after Kate's death, he always exuded, as he did now, the restless energy of a man who tries to shape reality rather than to transcend it.

After ten more minutes of discussion, he returned to my question. "We have a truce, God and I; it's shaky but it's a truce. You told me not to condemn the stranger and that God might need forgiveness. I could spin a whole theology out of those statements, and I have, although not systematically. I won't bore you with it. The short answer is that I have come to believe that you and I were both right that morning. God does not want us to crawl to Him, and He may need our understanding and forgiveness. I find it easier to forgive Him than myself."

"Bene," I agreed. "It is often so. Our self-esteem can be such that we expect more from our own humanity than from God's divinity. But you think you have now found God?"

Declan smiled at me. "I am not sure what I believe, but at least you believe that He has found me. Ugo, you present me with a terrifying choice. If I say no, I reject what you believe is a divine call. If I say yes, I risk destroying myself in this world and the next—if there really is a next."

(I said you that Declan was different. He was in many aspects. But in one thing he was his old self: not once did he speak of the danger of his not leading the Church in the proper direction. His fears, at least those that he expressed to me, were solely for what the tasks would do to himself and through himself to others.)

"Yes," I concurred. "That choice should strike terror in your heart. I am asking you—God is asking you—not to risk your life for another. You have already done that, many times. He is asking something far more difficult—that you risk your soul for others."

Declan had been calming. I expected that in a few more moments he would resignedly accept his fate. But just as I thought I had won, he walked back and again stared out the open portal. When he spoke, his voice was angry again: "Why me, Ugo? Why me?"

"For the love of God, *caro.*"

"For the love of God? For the love of God, why me?"

"Why you? Why any of us? Why are we born? I have read that the chances are less than one in two billion for any particular germ cell a man deposits in a woman to fertilize an egg and then survive the full gestation period. God marks the sparrow's fall and each moment of our lives. Why did I devote my life to the Church, without the love of a woman to comfort me or hope in my children to console me for my failures? Why? For the love of God. But He has never sent me a vision or a sign. He has never even spoken me directly, nor, I have fear, has He always listened to my prayers. If He has, he has been very selective in answering them. But He has spoken within me.

"Why *you* as *il Papa?*" I went on. "*Senti,* have you not asked yourself a thousand times why you as a war hero? Another officer might have commanded that unit. Think of all the so-called accidents that placed you at that place in April 1951. The Chinese could have attacked a few kilometers to one side or the other of your hill. The bullet that raked your temple could have struck two millimeters to the right, and you would have died instantly. Later, you might have stumbled off course a few hundred meters and have all been captured.

"Why you as chief justice?" My fatigue had left me and I spoke in Italian. "You told once that it was a coincidence that there happened at the same time a president who owed a great deal to a shrewd senator, and this shrewd senator was frightened for his reelection. Why all of these things? Coincidences or the hand of God? *Eccomi,* I am an old friend who sees his Church in crisis and knows your ability, just as your regimental commander knew your ability and placed you at the critical point—and, according to me, you underestimate Senator Trimble. I have talked to Cardinal Pritchett about your appointment as chief justice. Trimble was frightened, but he also recognized your ability.

"*Caro,* you possess great talent, perhaps genius. It was given you by God. He touches you again and again with His finger. That is 'why you' in Korea, that is 'why you' as chief justice, and that is 'why you' as *il Papa.* God has given you talent and He has given you *His* opportunity. He exacts a price, *His* price. You must—we all must—pay it. There is no escape from Him or His justice."

"I have paid for what people call my talent and my success," Declan said me.

"I know some of your sorrows, enough of them to understand that Kate's loss has not been made easier by your own sense of guilt—according to me, an exaggerated sense of guilt. But without those sorrows you would not understand the grief of others. Without experiencing a sense of tragic failure you could not tolerate the failures of others and love them as you forgive them. Without these last years of loneliness after Kate's death, you would not be able to understand the depths to which loneliness and the fear of loneliness can drive all human beings, including priests.

"Why you?" I asked him again. " 'Who knows the mind of the Lord? Who has been His counsellor?' God's love is a heavy burden. It is a cross. You must pick it up."

"You can be eloquent," Declan was speaking now without anger, "but then you're Italian. You people learn oratory instead of baseball." He paused for a full minute. "How long do I have to make up my mind?"

"A very little. But once you said me that you had been trained to make a decision in the split second between the sound of the bolt of a machine gun cocking and the first shot firing."

"I talk too much. How much is very little?"

"I hope you decide tonight, and we fly to Roma tomorrow morning. A TWA 747 leaves New York at 9:40 A.M. I have two first-class reservations and an extra diplomatic passport for you. There is a plane leaving here at 6:50 A.M."

"You have everything planned. Can I seek any advice?"

"My oath of total secrecy does not bind you, but I would prefer that you did not talk to anyone."

"Not even the abbot?"

"I would prefer not, but the decision is yours."

"Very well," he responded, "no one."

In the heavy darkness, a brilliant flash of lightning leaped ahead of a black thunderhead to a small forest a few kilometers across the river.

"The finger of God," I told, not secure whether I was being melodramatic or sacrilegiously facetious.

Then, from inside the portal of the chapel, safe from the stinging wetness of the big raindrops, we watched the majestic display. "I've always loved southern thunderstorms," Declan mused. "I remember when I was about three or four I woke up crying because of the noise of a storm in Rome. My mother took me out on our terrace and showed me how beautiful a storm could be at night."

I said nothing, I was recalling his mother—and, less happily, his father, a brilliant diplomat who had become alcoholic. I was a young man in the office of the papal secretary of state. I remembered the nights we searched the dirty back alleys of Trastevere and the Borgo looking for him. When we found him, he was usually—how do you say?—*ecco,* passed out. We would have to drag him to the automobile. The three of us were close in those days, too close. She was, I confess you now, the one woman for whom I ever considered leaving the priesthood. But she was another man's wife, and God did not permit me to wander far into temptation because she communicated in many subtle modes that she would never leave her husband. Fortunately, the *Fascisti* did not approve of some of the things that I told and did, and Papa Pio XI sent me to Turkey to spare me the possibility of physical harm.

My thoughts were interrupted by Declan's voice. "The lightning has pretty well moved off. It comes mostly from the leading edge of the storm, you know." (I did not know.) "I think I'll go for a walk."

An hour later as I sat in the chapel reading my breviary and listening to the soft rain bouncing on the roof—I confess you that I was dozing a bit, too—the portal burst open and Declan strode in. He threw back the wet black cowl, obviously having reached a decision. "I believe the formula is '*accepto*' but after your speech I would prefer: 'My soul doth magnify the Lord.' " He told it quietly more in sorrow than in jest.

"May God help you," I whispered and knelt and kissed his hand.

"Via, via," he responded in Italian. "There will be none of that between us."

I was suddenly aware of shuffling feet outside the chapel. The door opened and more than twenty monks, clad not in robes but in the heavy work clothes of loggers and farmers, filed into the chapel. Declan took what must have been his accustomed place, and I picked up my bottle of Verdicchio (no longer chilled) and moved to the rear of the chapel, where the abbot stood. A young monk with a bright red beard and the rough hands of a manual laborer began the opening chant of matins. It was, after all, 3 A.M., time for the Trappists' day to commence.

I enjoyed the chanting for a few minutes, then looked at the abbot. He nodded and pointed toward his office, telling simply, "Telephone." Outside, the insects, frogs, and birds were now silent. The early morning stillness was broken only by the soft chanting of the monks thanking God for sending the earth yet another day. One could reach out and hold the serenity of the place. Even as I was making my call to Vatican City, I continued to pray that I had truly followed His will and not my own.

By the time my message was communicated, there was small point in sleeping. Instead, I invited the abbot to concelebrate Mass with me, for the success of the new Pontiff. (I had said nothing to him about the purpose of my visit nor, to the best of my knowledge, had Declan; but he was too intelligent a man not to guess why a member of a deadlocked conclave was secretly visiting a monk.)

Well before dawn we were again on the *autostrada* in Fra Steven's huge automobile. Declan was wearing slacks, an old sports jacket, and a tie that I recollected Kate giving him. The trousers and jacket sagged a little. The life of a Trappist makes miracles for the waist.

The plane from Charleston departed exactly on time, as did the 747 from Kennedy. Once we were safely headed toward Newfoundland, I ordered one of your large American breakfasts and was soon asleep without the aid of a capsule. Declan had only coffee. As I drifted in and out of sleep, I saw him alternately reading the *New York Times* and staring out the window. I was curious about the thoughts that must be racing through his head, but I was too exhausted to talk and he did not seem anxious to be recalled from the edges of his private world.

I awoke when we landed at Paris, and between there and Roma I enjoyed a light supper. Declan toyed with his food, eating fully only the roll. We had been traveling against the sun and it was eleven-thirty in the evening when we landed at Roma. According to me, my internal time clock was confused beyond repair. When the plane halted, Declan went to the rest room, carrying his small handbag; it was all the luggage he brought and, it turned out, aside from some books that later arrived in the Vatican, it contained all his worldly possessions. He returned a few minutes later, wearing the coarse, cowled habit of a Trappist. I gave him the extra diplomatic passport, and we rapidly exited through the various controls into the terminal, where a small cluster of Vatican police, dressed in civilian clothes, of course, moved us even more rapidly into an illegally parked Fiat sedan. Two of the police rode in our car; three leaped into the automobile ahead. The man next to our driver was armed with what yellow films—you say gangster movies?—call a tommy gun.

The terminal flashed by as we headed for Autostrada 201 and Roma. Although the driver was a policeman, he was also an Italian; thus, he believed that the only place for an accelerator was flat on the floor. Once on the *autostrada* we raced along at 160 kilometers per hour—that is about 100 miles per hour. At that time of night there was little traffic, even when we turned off the *autostrada* onto the Via della Magliana that leads through middle-class neighborhoods in the near suburbs of the Portuense Quarter. The driver slowed to a mere 90 kilometers to negotiate the Piazzale della Radio and the passage under the railway tracks to the wider Viale Trastevere. We picked up speed again, leaving red and yellow signal lights blinking helplessly in our wake. *Allora,* as we sprinted toward the Ponte Garibaldi, Declan muttered something that I could not hear, then spoke to the driver.

"We'd like to cut into the Trastevere and so up to the Piazza Garibaldi on the Gianicolo." I suspected what he was thinking, but I believed it best not to intervene.

"It is not possible, *Padre*. We have strict orders, and besides I do not think I could find my way through Trastevere at night."

"It starts already," Declan sighed, "but I'm not quite ready. Ugo, I'm not a prisoner yet. Tell this man to stop and I'll drive. Otherwise, we get out and take a taxi."

He was speaking in Italian, and the man with the tommy gun picked up the radio and talked to the car ahead as we screeched to a halt in the Piazza Sidney Sonnino. Declan leaped out and exchanged places with the driver. We scatted off again, leaving a trail of burning rubber and exhaust fumes as we made an illegal left turn behind a group of parked buses into a twisting alley that snaked parallel to the curves of the river. At a high rate of speed but with considerable skill—learned, according to me, from Kate—Declan negotiated the rat's maze of streets called Trastevere, barely missing several slightly tipsy pedestrians trying to leave a *taverna.* Suddenly we burst onto the lovely little Piazza Trilussa, and spun first to the left, then at a ninety-degree angle to the right as we went flying behind the fountain to the old Porta Settimiana where the street widened and became the Via Garibaldi. Suddenly Declan pulled to the side of the road and turned to me.

"Do you remember Kate's Vespa?" he asked.

"Yes," I said. I vividly remembered that the people from the American State Department as well as my colleagues in the Vatican were very concerned that a special envoy and his wife were driving around Roma on Vespas. They were afraid of his having traffic incident. They could see the picture on the front page of the communist newspaper, *L'Unita*. But Declan—perhaps it was Kate—insisted that it was the only intelligent mode of navigating Roma'- traffic. Declan also made some atrocious play with words about always having wanted a Vespal Virgin in Roma. He did not, of course, use the Vespa for official business.

He smiled and looked over his shoulder at me. "Do you remember what happened along this wall?"

"I remember." As he sat silently behind the wheel I recollected Kate on her Vespa. Truly she was a Viking goddess with her blond hair flowing in the wind from under the helmet that Declan insisted she wear. Here, at the old police academy a speeding car had barely missed her. The driver shouted something at her, and she shook her fist and screamed back, *"Stufa di gas!"* It means only "gas stove" in Italian, but she liked the vulgar way it sounded in English. The unfortunate man could not comprehend his ears. He leaned out the window to look back at Kate and—how do you say?—sideswiped the wall of the academy. She thought it was divine justice, but Declan was afraid the poor devil was injured and came over to the car. The man was a little stunned but unhurt. All he could say was, *"Signore, stufa di gas?"*

Just as suddenly as we had stopped, Declan sped us off. Within a few seconds, we were climbing out of the Trastevere along the hairpin curves of the Via Garibaldi. One third of the way up the hill we passed the overlook of the church of San Pietro in Montorio, then another brief climb and we were at the seventeenth-century fountain of Paolo V. The tires squealed loudly on the cobblestones around the fountain, and we spun through the portals into the park that crowns the Gianicolo. The Piazza Garibaldi was deserted at this hour—except for a few lovers—and Declan parked the car at the overlook.

Senta, I have lived in Roma from time to time for almost a half a century, but I yet feel its grandeur when I view its panorama, as we did that evening. The whole city was stretched at our feet. Despite the lateness of the hour, thousands of lights were still flickering in the hills and valleys beneath us. Through small wisps of fog I could see the hideous white marble of the Vittorio Emanuele Monument, outlined by searchlights; farther off to the right, the disintegrated buildings on the Palatine Hill, bloodred even in the reflected light, were visible; and behind them and even farther to the right one could catch a small view of the Colosseo itself. Much closer and directly ahead of us, I could discern the circular shape of the Pantheon. Trastevere was immediately below us; its garbage-littered alleys mercifully hidden among dark shadows.

With the police nervously following, Declan and I walked across the piazza to the posterior side of the hill. *Ecco,* far on our right was the dark, hulking mass of San Pietro. It seemed like a different church from this vista. Michelangelo's dome was as majestic as ever, but from here one could not view Bernini's colonnade nor any part of the palazzo, only the dome and the basilica itself. Its white sides—or so they seemed in that light—contrasted with the dirty yellow that I knew formed its façade. We stared silently at the huge bulk. Then Declan turned and was absorbed by a small country villa half concealed by a set of shadows about thirty meters below us, across the ancient Roman wall that girded the Gianicolo.

I maintained several paces from him. I knew he was remembering an earlier dream. In 1952–53 he and Kate often picnicked here. They talked of buying that little villa and refurbishing it with a veranda with a vista of San Pietro. Declan, so they dreamed, would retire and write novels and they would live together happily ever after. After a few minutes alone, Declan shrugged his shoulders and said quietly, "That's another dream that will never come true, at least not in this incarnation."

I nodded. What does one say to truth?

I signaled the police, and the cars gratefully roared beside us. With Declan again sitting beside me in the posterior seat, we wound our way along the crest of the hill, past the curiously out of place lighthouse, the children's hospital, and the North American College, then swerved and descended the slope. We hardly slowed for the blinking red light at the foot of the hill, made another of our illegal left turns, and raced through the *galleria*—you would say tunnel. On the other side, just past the Sant' Uffizio—the ancient palazzo of the Inquisition, where LaTorre now reigned—we made a right turn into a small portal in the Vatican wall, completely avoiding the piazza and either of the principal gates, which would certainly be watched by a few newsmen and curious Romans. Fortunately, the police had been talking on the radio before we entered the *galleria;* as we turned, the portal in the Vatican wall—normally closed behind the small open-air market—swung open. We received only the barest odor of stale fish.

Inside Vatican City, we drove around the railroad station, the governor's palazzo, the passage under the museums, in front of the library, and then twisted into the Cortile di San Damaso. Willing hands rapidly aided us out of the cars, accepted our two small pieces of luggage, and ushered us into the elevator and to the now vacant and spacious apartment of Alfredo Cardinal Monteferro, the aging archpriest of the Basilica of San Pietro.

Allora, we stayed there for the remainder of the night. At seven the next morning we were served rolls and coffee in the cardinal's dining room. Then at seven-thirty two archbishops escorted us through the labyrinthine ways of the papal palazzo to the anteroom of the Sistine Chapel. There, in the huge Sala Regia, with its murals of Renaissance paintings, Declan waited, while I accepted Prince Chigi's escort into the conclave.

Allora, once inside the conclave I went directly to the Borgia Apartments to meet LaTorre. He was sullen—which was unusual because we were always close friends even though often intellectual antagonists—but he agreed to summon the college into session at 8:00 A.M.

"My Lord Cardinals," LaTorre commenced when we had gathered in the Sistine. "As we learned yesterday, Declan Patrick Walsh, a former secular judge and now a monk of sorts, has indicated that he might accept election."

"Excuse me, My Lord Cardinal," Pritchett intervened in his beautiful Latin. "I think your syntax is incorrect. You used the subjunctive mood. The indicative is needed. We *have* elected Declan Walsh as bishop of Rome and he *has* accepted. There is no need—or place—for the subjunctive. *Habemus Papam.*" (I translate the historic formula: "We have a Pope.")

"My Lord Cardinal Pritchett is aware," LaTorre responded, "that there is feeling within the conclave that our action Saturday was precipitant, that we were moved by fatigue and despair rather than by the Holy Spirit. We are certain that my lord cardinal himself has heard sentiment for he has spoken, quite eloquently we might add, against it. Therefore we propose—"

"Very Reverend Brothers," I intervened in as loud a voice as I could muster, "*Habemus Papam.* Whoever so much as questions the authority of a new Pontiff between election and coronation is automatically excommunicated. A deed has been done in the name of the Lord Christ our judge. So swore fifty-eight of us on Saturday. We are bound to respect those oaths and the authority of the new Pontiff just as strictly as we are obliged to respect our vows to Holy Mother Church.

"Because it was our personal privilege to bring his name before the conclave, we ask the special privilege of escorting him into this chapel."

There was a babble of voices speaking out in Latin, Italian, French, Spanish, German, Polish, and various African and Asian dialects. Chelli sensed the mood of the conclave more rapidly than had LaTorre. According to me, we could have had a modern schism. Thirty-six additional hours of imprisonment had strengthened the wills of as many cardinals as that added time had weakened.

"My Lord Cardinal, Most Reverend Dean," Chelli said as he gained recognition. "We are all appreciative of your efforts to ensure that the will of the conclave and the directions of the Holy Spirit are carried out. It appears to us that at least the will of the conclave has been done. We are certain that the cardinal dean would allow Cardinal Galeotti the special privilege that he requests. We are also certain that the cardinal dean would insist on joining Cardinal Galeotti in escorting the new Pontiff to receive our fealty. As the youngest cardinal deacon, we claim our own privilege of calling into the chapel the secretary of the conclave and the other clerics who should witness the ceremonies of acceptance and adoration."

LaTorre looked around helplessly, like a bull in the ring

who has just been run through and awaits the *coup de grace.* "If that be the will of the conclave, we can do no other." He pointed to a sheaf of blank ballots. "Please be ready to burn those." Then to the conclave he added: "Please place all your notes in envelopes and pass them to the cardinal scrutinizers. As you recall, our constitution requires that all papers from the conclave be burned. Our own record of the scrutinies will be sealed and placed in the archives, to be opened only with the Pontiff's permission."

Allora, within a few moments, the portal to the Sala Regia swung open, and LaTorre and I invited Declan to walk between us into the Sistine Chapel. Once inside the great chapel before the thrones of the cardinals, LaTorre asked in Latin: *"Acceptasne electionem de te canonice factam in Summum Pontificem?"* ("Do you accept your election as Supreme Pontiff, carried out according to the canons?")

"Accepto," ("I accept") Declan replied. LaTorre looked baffled that the new Pontiff understood even a bit of Latin, then recovered himself enough to ask by what name would Declan be called.

"We shall be called Francesco," he said in Italian. No previous Pontiff had chosen that name; thus Declan Walsh became Papa Francesco I. I confess that the choice surprised me. He had not consulted me; in fact, he had barely spoken since he accepted election at the monastery. It was, of course, his father's name, but I knew, and sadly, that Declan and his father had never been close—indeed, quite the opposite. Why he would chose Francesco would gradually become evident, however. I shall explain it to you at the proper moment. Now you must feel my own puzzlement as part of my larger concern over what I had, with the help of God, engineered.

As our rules provide, we rapidly—and briefly—performed the barest essentials of consecrating Francesco a bishop. As cardinal dean, LaTorre officiated. As soon as that ceremony was finished, LaTorre knelt and kissed *il Papa*'s hand. At that moment, the canopies of our eighty-two thrones came rustling down, almost in unison. We each followed LaTorre in the hand-kissing rite, the first of three adorations. Francesco recognized several cardinals from his days as special emissary and spoke them warmly.

(Like a good priest or politician, he possessed great charm that he could unloose at the proper moment, and, as many cardinals later found, retract as well.) When this ceremony was completed, we sang the *Te Deum,* the most solemn hymn of joy in our liturgies.

LaTorre then gave a signal and a match was lit to the notes that we had surrendered and to the white chemical in the stove. Within a few moments, Roma and the world knew that we had at last chosen a new Pontiff. The Piazza di San Pietro immediately commenced to fill with thousands of people—newsmen, tourists, clerics, but most of all Romans.

Allora, Francesco was ushered into the sanctuary of the chapel to meet a tailor from the Gammerelli family. He had patiently waited these weeks to fit the new Pontiff with one of the four cassocks that he kept on hand. Meanwhile, the cardinals proceeded to the papal apartments, where Francesco would join them and break the seals that had been placed on the doors after the death of his predecessor. Then, we moved through the palazzo toward the loggia in the façade of San Pietro, from which the results of the election would be announced to the piazza below. As we hurried through the passages, we could hear the noise from the hundred thousand or more people who had already assembled.

On the loggia, the maroon, gold, and white papal colors were already draped over the railing. Alfredo Cardinal Monteferro, the senior cardinal deacon, grasped the microphone and spoke the historic formula to a suddenly hushed crowd: "I announce you a great joy. We have a Pope. He is My Most Eminent and Reverend Lord Declan Patrick Walsh, a holy monk from the United States of America. He has chosen to reign under the name of Francesco."

Ecco, there was only scattered applause. We Italians have never been noted as a taciturn people, but many people seemed disappointed that once again a foreigner had been elected as Pontiff of the universal Church. LaTorre did not even try to suppress his smile. "Holy Father, your people are anxious to see you."

Francesco's eyes flashed, but he made no reply. He stepped forward, grasped the microphone, and spoke in clear, Roman-accented Italian: "My people, especially my people of Rome, on this day and all days to follow, we ask your prayers. A cleric used to the cares of the Church needs much help as Pope. How much more help, then, does a mere layman need who has only been a monk for two years before being abruptly thrust into the midst of so many holy priests?"

It was a very clever ploy. Despite their love of pageantry and the fierce mode in which they covet the papacy for one of their own, Italians pride themselves on their anticlericalism. And a Pontiff whose accent bore traces of their own city replaced national with local pride. The crowd responded to Francesco's tactic by bursting into wild cheers. Then spreading his arms for silence, he made the sign of the cross, speaking still in Italian rather than the traditional Latin: "May the Almighty God bless you, the Father, the Son, and the Holy Spirit."

The silence for the prayer was shattered by a thunderous "Amen," then by more cheers and chants of *"Evviva il Papa! 'Viva il Papa! 'Viva il Papa!"* Francesco stepped back and, in the best American political style, opened his arms in a V. By now the crowd had grown to nearly a quarter of a million as the news spread around the city by radio, television, and rumor. Now reconciled, the Romans went wild with delight. *"Il Papa! Il Papa!"* was a constant cry for almost an hour each time Francesco returned onto the loggia.

After that time, Francesco, his face lined with physical and spiritual exhaustion, turned to LaTorre. "I would appreciate your asking the cardinals from Latin America to remain in Rome for a few days. I would like to see them tomorrow morning at eleven, and I would like to see Cardinal Martìn this afternoon. I would also appreciate it if you and Cardinal Yañez would join us for a moment in our private library."

SIX

WE—Francesco, LaTorre, Cardinal Yañez y Domingo, the primate of Spain, and I—assembled in the studio of the old Pontiff. It was a huge room, about thirteen by twenty meters, and cold despite the two ornate oriental rugs that covered the center of the pavement and even reached under *il Papa*'s desk. The desk itself was small and neat, standing a meter or so out from the blond paneled wall. The top of the desk was bare except for a large Bible. Behind it was a typing stand with an electric typewriter. Above the desk was a Renaissance painting of the Holy Family—exactly the style that had always irritated Kate—and on either side was a portal leading to the private papal quarters. The windows overlooking the piazza were flanked by heavy, gold damask drapes; thin white Venetian blinds could deflect the morning sun. On the wall opposite was a large crucifix above a Mediterranean-style credenza. A dozen straight-backed chairs covered in ivory-colored leather were arranged in—how do you call it?—a horseshoe facing a long table in front of *il Papa*'s desk.

Francesco motioned to the chairs. "Please be comfortable. I am deeply troubled and need your advice." He gave Cardinals Yañez and LaTorre his copy of the front section of the *New York Times* of yesterday—Sunday. "I am concerned about this story. Can you give me any more details?"

Yañez glanced at the front page. His English was not as comfortable as mine, but it was enough for him to read with understanding. Apparently about a hundred young priests from Catalonia had congregated in front of the magnificent medieval cathedral in Barcelona to protest continuation of the Church's concordat with the Fascist regime. They had planned to march a few blocks to the nearby Via Layetana to publicize their protest and then return to the cathedral, where groups of them would concelebrate Mass in the various chapels around the church. The archbishop had refused them permission to use the church, but he had also told that he would take no action against them.

According to the *Times,* the Spanish police had felt differently. As the priests had gathered in the Avenida de la Catedral, they were confronted by several phalanxes of police moving at them from several sides. According to the police, the priests had commenced shouting obscenities and throwing stones. To protect themselves, the police told, they dispersed the gathering. According to the priests, the police, without provocation, suddenly charged into them, flaying away with clubs. The priests claimed that they had retreated into the cathedral, but that the police had relentlessly pursued them into the church. Whatever the origin of the violence, fourteen priests had been hospitalized, three had been killed (all with fractured skulls, the *Times* reported), and several dozen others injured. According to me, the priests were probably not innocent of some name calling, but the police were Fascist thugs. I knew them under Mussolini.

Yañez handed the newspaper to LaTorre. "I have been locked up in conclave, Holiness. This is the first information that I have received of such a tragedy. As you know, newspapers are absolutely forbidden within the conclave. I shall secure the complete story from the archbishop himself in the morning."

"Within the hour, if you can, Eminence. Time is now short. I should particularly like to know why the archbishop has not excommunicated every policeman who participated in the attack and every Spanish governmental official who was in any way involved. I would appreciate it if you would put that question directly to His Excellency, but please emphasize to him that I want him to take no action now. Indeed, until I am satisfied that there were compelling reasons for his failure to act he should consider himself suspended from the exercise of all powers of his office as archbishop. And I mean all, excepting none, not even his power to say Mass. My Lord Cardinal LaTorre will send a dispatch in writing to that effect. Can you hazard a guess as to why the archbishop failed to act?"

Yañez blanched. *Il Papa*'s action, though possibly temporary, was severe in the extreme. After a moment's hesitation, the cardinal replied, "Nothing more than that, Your Holiness. The archbishop is not the most energetic of our shepherds in Spain. He is getting on in years. Actually, he has passed the retirement age, but he has stayed on because the Vatican and the government could not agree on a successor. I am also afraid that much that has transpired within the Church since the Second Vatican Council has not pleased His Excellency. In addition, like many of us, he is worried about political changes in our country. After Generalissimo Franco's death, the regime tried a bit of liberalism but has recently begun to show signs of regressing in the face of demands for speedy reform. The prince is not a strong man, and many old Fascists still hold office. Dissidents—they include Communists, Socialists, anarchists, radicals, liberals, young students, and old monarchists—have recently been threatening anarchy or revolution or both. There has been violence—terror, executions, kidnappings, and murder. I am afraid that the archbishop remembers—perhaps too vividly—our time of troubles in the 1930s, and he lumps all opponents of the regime together as Communists or anarchists. In his defense, let me say that at times it is difficult to distinguish—"

"I had supposed as much about His Excellency from the newspaper account," Francesco intervened. "I suspect that in a few days we shall be accepting his resignation. In any event, please be good enough to get all the details for me that you can by early evening. Cardinal LaTorre, who is our nuncio in Madrid?"

"Monsignor Orsini, a very gifted and astute man."

"Please telephone him and have him in Rome this afternoon. I want to talk to him as soon as he arrives. In the meantime gather what information you can. You must have many sources of intelligence. Use every one you can. I might use one of mine. The Spanish ambassador should be summoned to an audience here at six-thirty. I would like all of you to be present as well as Monsignor Orsini. I need as much information as possible before that meeting.

"I hope that the ambassador will be prepared to speak for his government. Perhaps, Cardinal LaTorre, one of your people could brief him about the gravity with which I view this incident.

"Now, Most Reverend Fathers, Cardinal Galeotti and I have had little sleep since Friday night, and it is 2:00 P.M. I suspect that you could also use some rest. I shall try to make clear to you in the next few weeks, after I know the situation better, the staff changes that I shall make. For the moment, I want everyone to stay on."

LaTorre's pain at *il Papa*'s abrupt dismissal was unmistakable, but he told only, "Yes, Holiness."

As the group departed, Valerio Anguillara, *maestro di casa* for *il Papa,* was waiting at the door to see what arrangements were lacking to us. We inspected the private apartments and saw that Francesco's simple luggage had been unpacked, towels were in the bathroom, and at the end of the living room a table had been set for one person. (I also saw that the furniture in the private apartment was as ill suited to Francesco's personality as that in the studio.)

Francesco asked that the table be set instead for two, and Anguillara sent a steward for us to order.

Francesco wanted only minestrone, cannelloni, and an *insalata* for himself, leaving me to select what pleased me along with a wine from the papal pantry. I walked there and chose a pair of bottles of Lacrima d'Arno, a rather common dry, white wine from Tuscany. It was not what I would have bought at a wine store, but it was the very optimum in the pantry. I had more fatigue than hunger, so I contented myself with ordering prosciutto and melon for the first plate, ravioli for the second, and for the principal dish some broiled lamb and cold spinach with lemons and a few mushrooms. To spare my health I asked only for a bit of cheese (the only kind available was a bit of Gruyère) and a peach for after.

Allora, when I returned from the pantry to *il Papa*'s studio, he was talking to Monsignor Luigi Bonetti, the old Pontiff's secretary.

"Monsignore," Francesco was saying, "I have heard that you served my predecessor well, and I realize it is the custom for a new Pope to retain the old Pope's secretary. But our ways—his and mine—are apt to be so different and our ideas also that you might prefer to serve the Church in another office. I intend to invite my former administrative assistant in Washington, Mrs. Falconi, to come here. She will handle many matters that once fell under your jurisdiction. You will have new responsibilities, broader in some respects, narrower in others. As yet, I do not know how to be more specific. I can say only that your work would be very different.

"If you think our differences in style, temperament, and ideas—and your different authority—would make continuing in office in any way difficult, do not hesitate to say so. I shall feel obliged to reward you with any post within reason as a tribute to your past services and future promise."

Despite the fact that chain smoking had ruined his palate, Bonetti was always pleasing to me. Being secretary to *il Papa* is an onerous function. Essentially he makes certain that the Pontiff can enjoy some time to think and pray. And the only way to provide that time is by firmly telling no to people—usually cardinals, archbishops, bishops, and *monsignori*—who want to see *il Papa*. Because speaking no so often creates enemies, a new Pontiff customarily protects a good secretary by retaining him in some important capacity. Bonetti had managed the task of speaking no with firmness and good grace. His labors had been made easier by the strong bond of friendship between himself and the old Pontiff.

"I do not know, Holiness," Bonetti said. "I could serve your predecessor well because I knew his mind as I knew my own. I do not know Your Holiness at all, but I would be honored to try to continue my service."

"Very well. I am pleased. Let's try to work together for at least a month or two. Keep my promise in mind, because I assure you that I am not an easy man to work with."

Allora, the food commenced to arrive in a few minutes and the two of us ate in tired silence. Francesco pushed aside his pasta before it was half-eaten. According to me, it was a wise decision. I know of no Pontiff in recent centuries who was a gourmet, and the late *Papa* never noticed what he ate. For Francesco there was some hope. He had an excellent palate for wines and, if one put aside strange Americanisms like using pasta as the principal plate, he had basically good taste in food. I made a mental note to discover him a truly fine chef and encourage that development.

"I don't know what you are going to do," Francesco said, "but I'm going to take a nap and then a fifteen-minute shower. Anguillara can find you a room somewhere in the palace, Ugo, unless you'd rather go home. What time does Cardinal Martìn arrive?"

"At six," I riposted. "He has a half hour, and you see then the Spanish ambassador."

Promptly at six I joined *il Papa* in his studio to meet José Cardinal Martìn, archbishop of Buenos Aires. He was tall, slender, with a natural tonsure around a wonderfully shiny pate. He spoke that ugly Latin American Spanish, which in aesthetic terms is to fine Castilian as Romanaccio is to the Italian of Siena. But Martìn did not look Spanish or that mixture of Spanish and Indian that characterizes so many Latin Americans. I later found that his ancestors had been among the "Wild Geese," the Irish officers who had fled their country after the failure of Wolfe Tone's rebellion at the end of the eighteenth century.

Martin, of course, was an Irish name, but the family had bowed to the inevitable and had called themselves Mart*ee*n.

Senta, while he possessed the reputation of being among the most liberal of Latin American prelates, the cardinal's liberalism was, according to me, based on Papa Leone XIII's *Rerum Novarum.* Namely, he was a liberal—in reality, as I earlier said, a servant—in terms of seeking social justice, rather than being merely woolly-headed about theological matters. Indeed, by the standards of the Dutch, he may have been a traditionalist. LaTorre had referred to him as a man who was fundamentally sound but too generous in tolerating error and too willing to dissipate his energy in attacking insoluble problems. What I had seen in the conclave was pleasing to me—directness and a keen analytical mind.

When the cardinal entered, he tried to kneel and kiss *il Papa*'s ring, but Francesco caught him and shook both hands.

"Thank you for agreeing to stay on in Rome, Your Eminence. We have much to talk about and little time," Francesco told in halting Spanish. "My Spanish is terrible. Would you prefer English or Italian?"

"English, Holiness. We Latins learn the imperial tongue early." Martìn smiled easily, as he had during the conclave.

Francesco's eyes twinkled in appreciation of the—how do you say?—cheeky humor.

"Good. The language suits the topic. We plan something imperialistic. Eminence, I fear the Church in Latin America is in shambles. I hear you agree. Tell me why."

"Does Your Holiness want my two-hour sermon or my ten-minute homily?"

"I'd like you to dictate your two-hour sermon and leave it with me. Since I have another group arriving in less than thirty minutes, your ten-minute homily is what I need now."

"Holiness, in Latin America we have in many ways been a kept Church. First, the Spanish used us. We thought that we were using them, but it turned out that our going to Latin America was less a way to bring salvation to the Indians, as we had thought, than a means of helping the Spanish rule and exploit the poor devils. We were at fault for being blind to political reality, for being less energetic than we should have in our missionary efforts, and for being less than courageous in preaching social justice.

"In any case, we—the hierarchy, at least—benefited from this arrangement. We received funds from the government to build churches, hospitals, schools, and orphanages for the poor, as well as mansions for bishops, to pay the clergy, and to buy property which could yield more income, prestige, political influence, and the means to continue charitable work. We also received a monopoly to preach the gospel. When, with the help of my great-great-grandfather, the people threw the Spanish out, the new governments saw that they could use us just as the Spanish had, and we again thought, mistakenly, that we could use them.

"From at least the last part of the nineteenth century, when the liberals began to attack the conservative regimes, until now, when liberals, Communists, anarchists, Socialists, and God knows who else attack the oligarchies that rule most of Latin America, they also frequently attack us. And many of us in the hierarchy have deserved to be attacked because we have often defended the status quo and have even sometimes become an integral part of the ruling elite. In recent years, many, very many, of us have tried to lead the Church in new directions; but memory still tarnishes the way the people perceive us.

"It is bad for the Church to become identified with any regime. It is worse when that regime, as have most in Latin America, neither practices nor preaches social justice—at least once it has come to power. Because many of those who want genuine reform, who want justice and peace, still look on us as partners in an outmoded and unjust establishment, they do not listen to us. Our history proves to them that we cannot be trusted; we still seem to be the natural allies of the rich and the powerful, of all those who benefit from social injustice."

"Obviously someone listens to us," Francesco intervened, "or else there would be no need either to subsidize or to hate us."

"Yes, Holiness, I exaggerate. Some people do listen to us, many do, in fact, but fewer and fewer each day in those areas in which we stand pat, as you North Americans say. We retain the allegiance of many devout Catholics, but in reality, if not in the numbers that pastors send to Rome, their ranks thin out. Where, however, we have been active in pressing for social change, we have managed to keep the faith alive in many of our people and to win back some of those who have fallen away."

"Do you mean the militarism of the new guerrilla priests?"

"I include them, but only for the short run. Those priests who take the open political road, who join revolutionary groups and rationalize, even urge, the use of violence to effect social change are bringing in some lost sheep. There is no denying that. But for the long run, they are repeating old mistakes. If they win, they shall have bound themselves to a particular political regime. Perhaps at first it will be a more just regime, but we know that all men are weak and that temptations of power are often stronger than those of the flesh. Thus it is highly likely the new regime will soon begin committing its own kinds of sin, and the new rulers will know how to use the Church—once more a kept Church—of these naive young priests. The ideologies will be different, but the results for the people will be the same."

"What then? Catholic Action as Pius XI proposed in the 1920s and 1930s?" Francesco asked.

"No, that is not the answer, although it is a better answer than doing nothing, which, as Your Holiness will discover, is the answer of many of our older bishops in Latin America. In Catholic Action we urged laymen to spread enthusiasm for Christ's teaching. But several things went wrong in Latin America. First, Catholic Action was under the control of bishops. That fact alone made it suspect in the eyes of many others who wanted social justice, especially those whom we wanted most to reach, the urban workers and the rural poor. As I have said, some of that suspicion was well founded.

"A second problem is that we often had great difficulty even within the ranks of the faithful in recruiting able and enthusiastic participants. In some situations we did rather well—Chile, for example, or Rio de Janeiro. And to some extent, Catholic Action helped encourage the creation and continuance of Christian Democratic parties. On the whole, however, the record of success has not been long."

"I come back to my question," Francesco spoke. "What then?"

"I can only respond in general terms, Holiness. First, we

need a renewal within the Church, a reorientation and rededication to our basic principles of human love and justice. We need to free ourselves from our close connections with existing political regimes and economic and social orders whether liberal—which is hardly ever the case for long—or military dictatorships. Those will be expensive and heart-wrenching processes, for our people do not contribute to the financial support of the Church. Most of them cannot and probably would not even if they could. The fiscal problems will be real, for we depend on governmental money to run our schools, hospitals, and orphanages. as well as to run our palaces and limousines. That is why the web that binds us to the regimes can be so strong. Even when we want only to do good and recognize the regime as evil, we can be caught in a trap. Our people are poor and need so much. We can give them some of what they need, but often only by first accepting help from the government; and, of course, the government exacts its price."

"You spoke of a renewal."

"Yes, Holiness, for that we would need leadership, strong leadership from Rome and from home. We have had very little of that from here, except admonitions to make sure our people were not using contraceptives. And, alas, I must say that we have produced little leadership of our own for the obvious reason that the hierarchy has included too few people who would fundamentally change the status quo."

"Is there more?" Franceseo inquired.

"Much more, Holiness. We need to preach social justice divorced from specific political systems or ideologies. In short, we need to return to religious matters while encouraging—creating if need be—within our people an enthusiasm to apply those principles in their daily lives. We need to supply moral guidance but not specific political direction. I know that nothing in this world promises immediate success, but when we have tried to exert some such influence, as in Chile before the generals' coup in 1973, for example, we have managed some progress.

"I am afraid that I am slipping into my two-hour sermon, Holiness."

"What you say interests me greatly. I want Rome to supply its share of leadership and to help you recruit your share. Let me tell you briefly that I want to make the Church in Latin America the main object of my first years of work. That is why I have asked your colleagues to stay on in the Vatican and to meet with me tomorrow. I want to start something like a Peace Corps. It will largely have to be the work of the laity, but we—the Church—must supply the moral impetus to begin such an operation. And I shall need you to help me with that and to counsel me on how to reform the structure of the Church itself. I think that bishops will be critical in my plans, and not only in Latin America. Are there enough able priests who share your views for us to recruit new bishops at the appropriate time?"

"Enough, Holiness," Martìn responded. "Not a surfeit, but a sufficiency."

"Would you be willing to serve as prefect of the Sacred Congregation for Bishops here in the Vatican? It is through that office that we shall do most of the hard work of choosing bishops for the whole world."

"I exist only to serve Christ's Church, Holiness. Buenos Aires is dear to my heart. It is an archdiocese where much remains to be done, and I would leave it reluctantly—less so, however, if Your Holiness would listen to my suggestions for a successor."

"Your advice on such matters is the principal reason that I want you in the Holy See, Eminence. Now, the appointment may not come for some weeks, even months. As my colleagues in the United States would say, first I have some political fence-mending to attend to. In the interim, let us keep this between ourselves."

"Of course, Holiness."

"I shall give you very brief warning when the time comes, so we must have your successor ready. Cardinal Galeotti should be our mutual contact. I suggest that you communicate with him at his residence in the Palazzo di San Calisto. One final matter: I have read of a bishop in Chile and the archbishop of Recife in Brazil—their names escape me—who have been giving Church lands to the peasants and turning over property in the cities for housing the poor. Do you know these men?"

"I know them well, Holiness. They are both young and able men who feel as I do. As you know, the military juntas in both countries have been angry at them. In fact, the archbishop of Recife has several times been subjected to virtual house arrest."

"So I have heard. What would you think if the first official act of my papacy were the bestowal of a red hat on each?"

Allora, Martìn beamed. He had been earnest but reserved, insecure how seriously *il Papa* took his words. Now he spoke with enthusiasm.

"Making them cardinals would be a dramatic move and would send a message that would be unmistakable—not to say welcome. In fact, at least some of my colleagues would be appalled and certainly the military juntas in Santiago and Brasilia would be enraged."

"That sounds fair enough. We shall not give the hats in the usual consistory; I shall make a special announcement of some sort, within the week if that is possible, perhaps even while the cardinals from Latin America are still in Rome."

(According to me, as I sought to say then, this was an unwise move. It is seldom prudent to alert one's enemies. But *il Papa* had not asked my advice on this matter, and, as I shall often explain you, I never offered him advice that he did not first request. When Papa Francesco made up his mind, he acted swiftly if not wisely, and he expected others to act just as swiftly.)

As soon as Martìn departed, the Spanish ambassador, the papal nuncio to Spain, Cardinals Yañez and LaTorre, and Archbishop Cencio Candutti, the *segretario* of the Council of Public Affairs, were ushered into the study. (I should explain you Candutti's position. The secretary of state commands two principal divisions: the Secretariat of State mostly coordinates the work of the Curia and other offices within the Holy See; the Council of Public Affairs generally handles what are essentially the foreign affairs of the Vatican. In sum, Candutti was *il Papa*'s chief diplomat, performing functions very close to what you Americans expect of your secretary of state, although, let me stress you, he is never expected to escort beautiful young ladies in the fashion of your Professor Kissinger.) *Ebbene,* where was I? Ah yes, Francesco was seated at the papal desk. He rose to allow the nuncio, Candutti, and the ambassador to kiss his ring, but motioned the rest of us to seats around the table.

"Your Excellency," Francesco commenced, "we should like to have what information you can give us about this affair."

"Your Holiness knows," the ambassador responded suavely, "that Spain is at the moment experiencing growing pains. After Generalissimo Franco's death, we chose a slow, steady path toward constitutional democracy. But we are a strange, moody people in love with tragedy and with little experience in the ways of representative democracy and its parliamentary manipulations and maneuverings. Some well-meaning but misguided liberals have tried to push us too hard and too fast; they have played into hands of certain radical elements that want to undermine the stability of the country and return us to the kind of Communist regime that God, the Church, and the *generalissimo* spared us in the 1930s. We in the government have felt it necessary to pause—briefly—in our progress toward constitutional democracy. Since His Holiness has not been active in European affairs, he may not know that the Catalans have been notoriously restive, and not only recently. Barcelona is the center of this disquiet. These people —some are merely nationalists, while others are Communists and anarchists—include many young clergymen. Now I do not claim that these young priests and nuns are evil; I am sure that most of them mean well. But they are being used by certain malevolent forces.

"My government," the ambassador continued, "regrets the action taken against these priests. We want order, not oppression. But here the police felt obliged to respond to provocation. They were first insulted then attacked, and they fought back. My personal opinion is that the police probably overreacted. They usually do. After all, the police tend to attract men who are inclined to violence. I have read much about American narcotics agents terrorizing and even murdering innocent citizens.

"In private, Holiness, my government conveys to the Vatican its sincere apologies and its firm assurance that we shall take steps to prevent the reoccurrence of such a tragedy. If we could quietly transfer to one of the accounts of the Vatican a small sum of money that would show our true regret in this matter, we should be happy to do so."

"Thank you, Excellency," Francesco said. "We accept the offer of an indemnity, although not of a small indemnity.

Now we seek additional ways for your government to demonstrate its regret. Does our nuncio, Monsignor Orsini, wish to add anything at this point?"

"I can only testify, Holiness, that the Catalan and Basque clergy are exceedingly liberal and nationalistic—some of them quite radical politically and even theologically. Spain is now threatened with turmoil and the government feels that it must show a firm hand. I agree that the police overdid things here—I would not say 'probably,' but 'definitely'—but I am satisfied that the government will exercise greater caution in the future."

"Cardinal Yañez?"

"I agree in general terms with Monsignor Orsini, although I would speak in even stronger terms about condemning the unnecessary violence of the police. I am deeply troubled by the police entering the cathedral. From what I have learned, it was in the cathedral itself that the police crushed the skulls of two young priests. Still, as tragic as this incident is, we must keep in mind that the government regrets the action and will see to it that it does not happen again. If we were to push harder and the government were to fall, we might find ourselves dealing with men who would persecute the Church."

"Thank you, Your Eminence. Cardinal LaTorre?"

"I would defer to the judgment of Monsignor Candutti. This is his field and I have been locked up in conclave."

"Very well. *Monsignore?*" (I should explain you that Candutti, like many of us in the Vatican, preferred the title *"Monsignore"* to the archbishop's *"Eccelenza."*)

"I think I can associate myself with what has been said here," Candutti replied. "The Church has been outraged and murder committed on holy ground. Yet we have to understand the situation in which the Spanish government finds itself and accept their regrets—and indemnity—for what has happened. The Church can survive many kinds of government; I am not sure we can survive anarchy."

Francesco looked at me. "Cardinal Galeotti?"

"I find myself even more disturbed by this tragedy than my colleagues appear to be. According to me, we should have some public statement of regret from the government."

"I am afraid," the ambassador replied, "that we could not do that at this time. A private expression and a private assurance and an indemnity—all of these things, yes. But a public expression of regret might have dangerous repercussions." The ambassador stood up and bowed to the Pontiff. "If His Holiness will excuse me, I must leave. I shall convey the essence of this conversation to my government."

"His Excellency is free to leave at any time," Francesco told, "but we would suggest that he and his government will be interested in what transpires in this room during the next fifteen minutes. Cardinal LaTorre, would you be so kind as to ask the projectionist to come in and show us the film he has? If someone would close the drapes, that grey wall will make a suitable screen. For your information, Excellency, an American priest happened to be watching the entire affair from the balcony of his room in the Hotel Colon, and used his movie camera to record the scene. He had the good sense to fly here to Rome with the film. It may be instructive to watch."

A projectionist swiftly brought in a machine and set it in motion. (Francesco's cryptic explanation of the appearance of the film left us all confused. I did not know what to expect, nor even, I could see from his face, did Monsignor Candutti.) *Ecco,* when the projectionist commenced his work, we viewed a horror movie of a group of young priests milling in front of the cathedral on the Plaza de Cristo Rey. Then the camera moved to the left and the right as steel-helmeted police with raised batons trotted down the Avenida de la Catedral toward the priests. Some of the priests dropped to their knees and prayed; others ran up the steps toward the portals of the cathedral. All were being clubbed in the head or body. A few, but only a few, offered physical resistance. The camera flicked toward a group of officials standing near a souvenir shop on the *Avenida.* One of the officials signaled a third squad of police to pursue the fleeing priests into the cathedral.

"Stop right there," Francesco commanded in Italian. "Give us the blowups of the slides." The movie projector halted and the slide threw a huge picture on the wall of the face of the official directing the police. "Does Your Excellency recognize the face of the man who is giving the police the order to violate the sanctuary of the cathedral?"

"He is the minister of security of our government," the ambassador told quietly.

"And do you recognize—new slide please—the short, fat man on his left, the one who is smiling so approvingly?"

"Of course, Holiness. He is our minister of justice."

"Lights, please. It does not seem to us," Francesco said, as LaTorre opened the drapes, "that this was merely an unfortunate incident caused by a few overzealous local police. And it is apparent that the explanation of priests' provoking the police is a tissue of lies."

The ambassador whitened. I could see how tightly he was clenching the arms of his chair.

"We take this," Francesco went on, "as a direct challenge to the Church, a challenge made clear by cold-blooded murder, personally directed by two members of your government. We are not appeased by your mendacious explanation or your offer to apologize in private and pay an indemnity.

"Your Eminence," Francesco nodded to LaTorre, "we would appreciate it if your office would prepare for us a decree excommunicating every policeman and governmental official who participated in or cooperated with the planning or execution of these murders. We want the minister of justice and the minister of security specifically named. Moreover, we want that decree to appear as an appendix to a brief encyclical expressing grave concern over conditions in Spain and expressly disassociating the Church from a government that appears to be following the path of Hitler. We shall also state that unless within seven days all persons responsible for the attack on the priests—and again we want the two ministers mentioned by name—have not been properly punished, we shall dissolve the oath of allegiance taken by any Catholic to this government. In addition, we shall declare excommunicate any Catholic who continues to work for the current regime as a civilian, a policeman, or a member of the military. Furthermore, we shall say that if within six weeks this government or any member of it is still in Spain—except in jail—we shall lay an interdict on the country. No Masses may be said, no babies baptized, no marriages performed, no confessions heard, no communion distributed, and the interdict will remain in force until this government has been destroyed."

"This is medieval, Holiness." The Spanish ambassador was smiling genially, but I noticed that he had not relaxed his grip on the chair. "No Pope has dared lay such a decree for centuries. I humbly submit that it is a power that has atrophied through disuse."

"*We* dare to use this historic power of the papacy to defend the rights of God's Holy Church. We shall see if it has atrophied."

"Holiness," LaTorre intervened, "the Church must take governments as she finds them."

"Your Eminence may be correct, but we need not leave governments as we find them."

Cardinal Yañez interjected: "Your Holiness, I am counted a liberal in political terms, but is Your Holiness aware just how much the Church owes this government and its predecessor?"

"Other than dirty hands, no. The Church's consorting with Fascists and Nazis has done only harm to her people."

The Spanish ambassador was still smiling, although now very tight-lipped. "Perhaps, Holiness, my government could see its way clear to make a public expression of regret. It will be difficult, but I may be able to persuade my colleagues in Madrid that His Holiness feels very strongly on the matter. I might add at this point that we were thinking of an indemnity of a half million pesetas."

"We were not thinking of money at all, Excellency, but of further revisions in the concordat between the Vatican and Spain. We would accept those changes as a sufficient demonstration of good faith if accompanied by several other conditions. First would be payment of four million pesetas. Second would be dismissal from office of the ministers of justice and security, and third would be a speedy trial on charges of murder for those two worthies as well as all policemen responsible for killing the priests. If those actions were immediately accomplished—or, in the case of the trials, immediately begun—let us say by tomorrow at noon, it might only be necessary to issue a decree excommunicating all those in the attack, without listing any specific names and permitting return to the Church after a suitable public apology by each individual concerned."

"Your Holiness drives a hard bargain."

"We do not bargain. You misunderstand our position as well as your own. As our predecessor Innocent III said, we have been 'set over the nations and over the kingdoms, to pluck up and to break down, to destroy and to overthrow, to build and to plant.' "

(I was amazed to hear Francesco quote Innocenzo III; I had had no idea that he knew anything about the history of the Church, certainly not the thirteenth century.)

"That is not the language of diplomacy, Holiness," the ambassador spoke stiffly.

"You have learned little from our conversation, Excellency. We are not a diplomat. We are Christ's Vicar. We have come to judge not to negotiate. You have our leave to go."

The ambassador rose, bowed curtly, and marched out of the room.

"Holiness," Candutti said solemnly, "I fear we shall have cause to regret this evening. The Spanish government will give in. They have to. A severe reprimand from *il Papa* would cause the government to fall and Spain to topple into anarchy. But these men will remember what we have done, and some day the Church may have need of them."

"If that day comes, *Monsignore,* they will treat our needs with no less respect than had we suffered this outrage in silence. Governmental gratitude is a luxury that only the very great or the very just can afford, and no one would place a Fascist regime in either category."

Francesco nodded to Candutti, Orsini, and Yañez. "If you reverend gentlemen will forgive us, we are still very tired and we have yet a few matters to discuss with these others."

After the two had left, LaTorre spoke quietly. "Your Holiness, it has been the practice of past Pontiffs to ask the secretary of state for a detailed investigation and a recommendation before making a decision so vitally affecting the foreign relations of the Holy See. That is why Archbishop Candutti and I exist."

"Please forgive me," Francesco replied gently, "if I have embarrassed you or seemed to have undermined your authority in any way."

LaTorre nodded solemnly. His authority and that of Monsignor Candutti had, without doubt, been severely undercut; more embarrassing to the two of them, that undercutting had produced results that their more official and organized efforts had not.

"Holiness," LaTorre said, "the terms of almost all of the

heads of curial offices automatically terminate with the death of a Pope. I think that Your Holiness should name my successor at this time so that he may carry out whatever plans seem best to you."

"Please, Eminence, have mercy on a poor soul. I need you and Archbishop Candutti. I ask you and shall ask everyone else in the Curia to stay on at least until I have a thorough understanding of the organization of the Holy See. To put it quite simply, I need you. I shall try to see each of the prefects personally, but I would ask you to prepare the papers formally extending their terms of office for one month from today."

"Very well, Holiness. These things will be done."

As LaTorre rose to depart, Francesco added: "By the way, when my wife was alive she had always wanted to live in the summer villa of Pius IV. It would please me to use that *casina* as my residence. I suspect that it will need a lot of work before I can move in, and I would appreciate it if you would see that the appropriate people are alerted. I shall engage my own architect, but I want the work finished quickly. Now, I would ask Cardinal Galeotti to remain a few more moments."

The moment the portal closed behind LaTorre I asked Francesco how he had obtained the film. He smiled at me —no, that is not exact; he *grinned* at me, quite pleased with himself, and explained that he had read in the *New York Times* that many of the priests were Jesuits. He suspected that they would not expose themselves to martyrdom without taking some precautions, so he telephoned— it was an extraordinary if not unique thing—a Jesuit official whom he knew here in Roma and asked for assistance. The film had arrived in the palazzo within the hour.

I wanted to remark something about the wisdom of using his own staff, but before I could speak *il Papa* was interrogating me. "Am I wrong, Ugo, in sensing that LaTorre would not have been brokenhearted had the Holy Spirit's lightning struck someone else?"

I shrugged. "I do not think you mistake his feelings; and, according to me, his offer to depart immediately was not to you a totally unwelcome gift. But, even knowing that his views on many theological, social, and political questions are far from yours—although less far on most social and political matters than you might now think—if you can win LaTorre you will possess a stouthearted friend. *Allora, il Papa* commands but his bishops do not always obey, at least as he wants them to. LaTorre is the rock of the traditionalists not only in the Curia but throughout the world. I know the Holy Mule can be pigheaded, if with permission I mix animals in my analogy, but he loves the Church with his whole soul. He once confessed me, when we were much younger, that he could not directly love God because God is an abstraction. He could only try to serve Him by serving His Church."

"I realize that I will not have a completely free hand," Francesco riposted, "but I cannot see LaTorre as my secretary of state, at least if I keep that office as the central coordinator of the Curia. Well, let's think about that later. Right now I have a request for you. I believe when you were in the United States you once gave a long interview to a reporter named Robert Twisdale."

I acknowledged that I remembered him well and respected the article that he wrote about the apostolic delegation. It evidenced good judgment along with a clear command of the facts. Francesco then related to me that he had also known Dottor—You understand our Italian fondness for titles? A man becomes *dottore* upon graduating from a university—Twisdale for many years, first in Korea, then later when Declan was chief justice. *Il dottore* was, *il Papa* believed, living in Paris writing a novel but also working occasionally for the *International Herald Tribune,* still writing a column—how do you say?—syndicated in the United States. He had married a wealthy widow and accepted journalistic assignments only when they were especially pleasing to him. In essence, Francesco wanted me to find this writer as a *portavoce*—you say call him a press secretary. I, of course, agreed, though I saw no reason to remove the incumbent.

Then as I was taking my leave, Francesco asked: "What do you think of the Pope's holding a press conference every few weeks? We could call it a special audience for journalists."

In fact, I was appalled. I covered my emotion by saying, "I pray you, Holiness, do not think that just because you are *il Papa* you can paint this palazzo white and plant a green lawn around it. We Italians will become very angry."

He laughed. It was good to see him discard the harsh mode that he had adopted in speaking to the Spanish ambassador.

I confess that when I left the palazzo that night—I returned to the San Calisto, where I could sleep once again in my own bed and eat my own food—I had much to think about. Pontiffs have differed in the speed with which they have exercised the power of the papacy. Papa Paolo VI had acted more swiftly than most when, within hours of his election, he was sketching plans to replace certain curial officials and to continue the sessions of the Second Vatican Council. But Francesco had been far swifter. I had expected a pause, some weeks, certainly at least some days, of study and reflection before taking any action of importance, but he had not hesitated for a moment. Without doubt, he was fatigued from the transatlantic trip, but he showed an iron will. I already sensed, as I had not when I had only observed him at a distance, what—it now seemed like ages ago—Fra Declan had meant when he spoke of his attraction to power.

Two things were obvious: he was enjoying playing what he called the game of power, and he was very good at it. I was not certain what these meant for the Church. I could only pray that we might channel that driving energy into constructive courses. To me, it was certain that the papacy was on the edge of a momentous change; what left me uncertain was what shape that change would take and whether it would be good or evil for the Church.

SEVEN

Allora, at eight-thirty the very next morning, the fifteen cardinals from Latin America who had attended the conclave assembled in *il Papa*'s studio. Francesco asked me to be present also. For almost four hours he pushed them about conditions in their dioceses. Although we heard different stories, there was a general admission that the Church was not strong. It was on the question of a solution that divisions were both sharp and bitter. The traditionalists demanded stricter rules, more formal rituals, and more priests, imported if necessary. The servants agreed about the need for more priests, but they argued along the lines Cardinal Martìn had sketched and gave highest priority to the Church's cleansing itself of its image as an ally of the oppressors rather than the oppressed.

Francesco listened and questioned, then listened and questioned more. He was the director of a seminar, leading strong-willed, intelligent, and stubborn students toward understanding what they knew, while he himself was extracting useful information from them. It was an exhilarating but exhausting performance. When we adjourned at twelve-fifteen, Francesco invited Martìn and me to share a bad lunch with him and continue the discussion.

Later, I gratefully accepted Monsignor Bonetti's suggestion that he have a room permanently set aside for me so I could siesta at the palazzo, for the lunch ended at one-forty-five and at three-thirty I was to return to *il Papa*'s studio to join a reunion of the cardinals who headed the ten congregations, or departments, into which the Curia is divided. As president of the Prefecture of Economic Affairs, Mario Chelli, our thin, young Neapolitan, was present. Francesco had also invited five other cardinals who were chiefs of secretariats and commissions, but no staff members were in the room.

Il Papa commenced by repeating his wish that all cardinals remain in their administrative posts for at least a month, until he was more familiar with the functions of the various offices. To speed his learning, he promised to spend during the next few weeks some hours with each prefect in his own congregation.

Then, Francesco came to the real point: "The principal reason for our calling you together is to solicit your views on our plans to reinvigorate the Church."

Out of the angle of my eye, I could see LaTorre look quizzically at Bisset, who rolled his eyes toward the ceiling. Greene visibly winced, but the other cardinals seemed curious, expectant.

In some detail, Francesco explained that he wanted, first, a spiritual renewal of the clergy, begun by retreats of several weeks during which time they would rethink their roles as witnesses to the gospel of Christ and rededicate themselves to live simple, holy lives serving God by serving their fellow man. Then he wanted similar programs conducted for the laity, though, of course, the retreats would have to be shorter. (I think you know this thing, a retreat. I believe I explained it when I spoke of my own before the conclave—a retirement to a monastery or similar haven from the cares of the world for some time of unbroken prayer and meditation. It is refreshing for both body and spirit.)

Francesco stressed that the clergy were to spread the gospel as much by example as by preaching, by involving themselves as humble workers in solving the problems of social justice in their own communities—using, for example, Church property to house the homeless, drunken derelicts, or drug addicts.

Third, Papa Francesco told he wanted to mount a massive campaign for social justice throughout the entire world. It was not to be merely a campaign of urging others to act justly but a campaign of doing. "We must spread the gospel of Christ by carrying out his teaching to feed the hungry and clothe the naked."

Recognizing the expressions on several faces, he raised his hand. "I know the works of charity that the Holy See now carries out are enormous and seldom recognized. God alone knows how many hundreds of thousands of black Africans are alive because Pope Paul and the Vatican cared about the Ibo of Biafra and later about everyone in the path of the drought. Few others cared, but you did. I want to continue that sort of activity, but I want also a focused effort to set an example by attacking poverty and hunger with the same zeal and drama that people in the Middle Ages employed to recover the Holy Land from the Muslims. I know the term is overused and abused, but 'crusade' is still the only word that adequately describes what I have in mind. Initially, we should concentrate our efforts on Latin America. I want to win back what is ours, then move to capture other areas, such as Africa."

"Ecco," LaTorre said as he exhaled loudly, plainly relieved.

Francesco then endorsed Papa Paolo's view that the Church's future development lay in the Third World. Catholicism, he told, had already influenced European and North American civilization, and that civilization had also influenced the Church to such an extent that Christianity itself had become a Western rather than an Asiatic religion. To shape the Third World or to regain power over the materialism and hedonism rampant in the West, the Church had to be true to its name and become less provincial and more catholic. The first step in this direction had to be an emphasis on Christ's message of universal brotherhood.

"Too often we have spoken boldly and acted timidly. Now we must speak humbly and act bravely. If we, the clergy, beginning here in Rome, can involve ourselves more deeply and more publicly in helping the less fortunate, we can also involve the laity more deeply. That is why I want a spiritual renewal of the clergy and want it followed by a similar renewal among the laity and then by a crusade to feed the hungry—an adaptation of the old American idea of a Peace Corps, young and old people who will not only help distribute food but help teach the poor how to use and develop resources, help them farm more scientifically, help them build schools and hospitals. Only after such a crusade is well along—it can never be finished—can our gospel of love and justice have credibility. Then, but only then, should we make massive and direct missionary efforts. We must first show that we believe what we preach and practice those beliefs."

Il Papa stopped and looked around. "Your reactions?"

"I think it is a wonderful idea," LaTorre bubbled. "It will take people's minds off sex and revolutionizing ritual. It will get them doing something constructive instead of sitting around criticizing those of us to whom God has given the care of souls."

"Just so," Cardinal Greene added. "Please God, we can return to the business of saving souls. We in the Congregation of the Sacraments welcome such an opportunity. The confusion of the world makes a ripe market for the gospel —not the gospel of licentiousness but the hard gospel of prayer, sacrifice, and salvation."

"I am sure that we all welcome the opportunity to spread Christ's gospel," Chelli agreed, "but has His Holiness thought of any budgetary figure for this plan?"

"Yes. Whatever it takes."

"It may take a great deal, Holiness. Charity is always an expensive business. We are not rich. How can we finance a massive campaign?"

"That is Christ's problem. He has commanded us to go to all nations, teaching what He has taught. We shall do as

He commanded. We expect Him to hold up His end of the bargain."

"Please, Holiness, I do not like to seem to persist," Chelli added, "but those were the very words of Papa Benedict during the First World War. His magnificent charity left the papacy near bankruptcy, and made it more attractive for your predecessors to accept a financial settlement not only with Mussolini but with other dictatorships as well."

"You do well to remind us," Francesco nodded, "of our predecessors' lack of faith in God's goodness. I assure you, our sins will be different."

"Holiness," LaTorre inquired, "would not emphasis on the purely temporal aspects of social justice open the doors of his crusade to others not of our faith?"

"I would hope so, yes."

"But then, Holiness, would we not be risking inroads by Protestants or, God forbid, Jews, or even Muslims?"

"Risks, yes, but I believe that the true faith can survive competition. Indeed, it would not be a bad thing for different religions to compete with each other to see who can do more to help his fellow man. But," Francesco conceded, "Your Eminence raises an important point. We do not want to neglect the spiritual for the temporal. We believe that our efforts to feed the hungry and help them help themselves will set an example of how God's love can and does work, an example that should encourage those who have not heard our message—or have ceased to hear it—to listen to us. Its effects will be indirect, but not less effective for that."

Chelli spoke again: "Your Holiness, I foresee an immensely serious problem here, as with all our concern—our rightful concern—for social justice. To speak and to act on social problems inevitably enmeshes the Church in secular politics. Surely Your Holiness is not proposing that we become some new political force in the world."

"You do raise a serious question," Francesco said, "and I do not pretend that I have an easy answer. When we—the papacy, local bishops, priests sharing parish property with the outcast, or the layman sharing his goods with the poor—speak or act on issues of social justice, we are, in one sense, in the midst of politics, for that's what politics is all about. We, as Christians, must work in this world. We must be in it but not of it. We shall be deeply involved in politics in the sense of shaping the larger values of society and having a voice and a part that much of society considers legitimate in determining the distributions of material benefits and burdens. But we need not be part of partisan politics. I do not mean to foster 'priests' parties.' I do not care what party our laymen endorse as long as they preach and practice the dignity of man, the sacredness of human life, and the necessity of justice among mankind."

"Your Holiness," Chelli observed, "is making fine distinctions."

"I acknowledge that. Caesar and God make overlapping demands on us. In following God's bidding we shall often offend Caesar in the future as we have, though perhaps not often enough, in the past."

I confess I was worried by the risk of persecutions and martyrs. I decided to intervene: "But what if a bishop views a government about to carry out a policy that violates the moral law? Let us suppose, for example, that a dictatorship were about to confiscate peasants' lands. Could the bishop speak out without entering partisan politics?"

"The bishop, or the layman for that matter, must speak out clearly and firmly, though the bishop has the greater obligation since he has no family. He must be willing to accept martyrdom—not to court it, but to accept it. Insofar as explaining and applying the moral law means affecting partisan politics, we have to accept that fact. But one can condemn a policy as immoral without condemning its supporters or endorsing its opponents, though inevitably some of that will result."

It was a just answer—just, naive, and very American.

"May we return to an even more fundamental issue, Your Holiness?" Bisset asked. "Can we learn more precisely what is in your mind about a crusade? I mean beyond an ecclesiastical peace corps?"

"Not as precisely as you or I would like," Francesco smiled. "In all honesty what you have heard are general ideas. Their generality is the reason we are meeting here today. I want to see if we, collectively, that is, can put some substance onto these rough outlines."

Bisset did not reply, but the prefect of the Sacred Congregation for Catholic Education asked: "More particularly, Holiness, how do you envision our carrying out this crusade?"

"Does His Eminence have any suggestions?"

"Not immediately, Holiness, but I shall try to present you with some very quickly."

"We would appreciate memoranda and personal visits from each of you. It will be difficult to sharpen this set of ideas into a coherent plan and far more difficult to carry out that plan. First, however, let me ask if anyone has any fundamental objection to such a policy? Cardinal Chelli has pointed to a serious problem. Our flippant response was a matter of personal style, not a reaction to the merits of his question. Our response is also in part a demonstration of our faith in Cardinal Chelli's capacity to finance cur vision. Others have raised different but equally pertinent questions. What I need to know now is whether anyone sees such a program as unwise or unnecessary."

Francesco looked around the room slowly. No one spoke.

"In that case, let us proceed. Obviously there are many problems. You have already raised some; let us try to raise others. I shall leave you and walk for about a half an hour on the roof. When I return, we can renew this discussion after you have had an opportunity to think out loud and talk among yourselves."

There was silence for a full five minutes after *il Papa* departed. Chelli had walked to the window to exhale the smoke from his Cuban cigar. Bisset idly rolled his pencil back and forth across the table top. Suddenly Chelli turned around. "My dear Ugo, tell us what you think."

"I think there are problems. The sort of role that *il Papa* wants the Church to play—and wants to use the spiritual renewal to encourage—contains a plethora of difficulties. Being politically nonpartisan in a stable democracy like the United States is vastly different from being nonpartisan in a chaotic situation where a whole range of forces, most of them evil, are warring against each other. But, I see his general point. I also see the necessity for the Church's becoming more involved, more dramatically as well as practically involved, in the search f... social justice. You all heard my intervention in the conclave when I spoke of our crisis of legitimacy, and Card:nal Grodzins told that we bored our people. I believe Francesco will give us greater legitimacy with our people, and certainly what he plans will not bore them. As for the problems, I think we should candidly raise them with ourselves and with *il Papa.*"

"I think," Bisset spoke with more than a touch of a sneer, "that our canon lawyer from Naples was asking a more subtle question: How serious is all this talk about a spiritual renewal?"

"What do you mean?"

"I mean is this just something for the laity's amusement—a sort of spiritual 'bread and circuses'—or do we take these pipe dreams seriously?"

I looked away from Bisset and tried to talk calmly to the group. *"Ecco,* we have heard *il Papa* speak what was in his mind. According to me, we must meet his honesty with equal honesty of our own."

"Fair enough," Greene told. "Fair enough. Let us think through the plan. Assuming that our brother Chelli can create the money, the main problems will be to define more clearly the objectives, then to decide who is to lead and staff the various phases. Third, and most difficult, don't you know, will be coordinating the activities of the local bishops. Collegiality often means anarchy."

Allora, after that the discussion went as well as could be expected among men who were not accustomed to—how do you say it?—laying their cards on the table. In the Vatican, we tend to be jealous of our prerogatives and to be wary, as good Italians usually are, of revealing our inner selves. When Francesco returned we continued in session for another hour. The results were not miraculous; indeed Francesco was disappointed at what he called the flabbiness of discussion. But, according to me, he sowed some seeds of trust, and he had excited the imagination of several of us. I shuddered at the thought of the volumes of memoranda that would soon be flowing because of this reunion.

EIGHT

By eight the next morning, Francesco was at his desk, scribbling outlines of his plans. Earlier that morning *il Papa* had gruffly rebuffed Monsignor Bonetti when he had asked if His Holiness intended to say Mass. Francesco had been consecrated a bishop, but, according to me, he always felt that these things were formalities. One can say that Francesco was a monk but never a priest—not, at least, in the psychological sense that the rest of us are. He confided to me that sometimes he prayed in faith, sometimes only in hope. According to me, those prayers were effective. But the Mass, the sacraments, these never became the intimate part of his psychology that they are to a priest. I do not say that this was bad for him, only that it made him different from us. *Ecco,* I *do* say it was bad for him, because he did not develop those fonts of grace that most of us in the clergy have found of such assistance. He possessed his own fonts, of course, but there were other sources of grace Christ had made available that Francesco did not try to use.

We cannot be all things and Francesco never made the mistake of trying. That morning he had complained of a muddled night's sleep. He described dreaming that he was in Roma as a child, wandering through the Trastevere searching for his father; then he had been in Dublin, at first looking for his father through the ruins of the buildings near the Coombe; then he was in Korea searching for a friend called Johnny Kasten. Sleeping capsules, hard work, and jet lag had left his mind—at least his subconscious mind—fuzzy, and after a quick breakfast he had gone to the roof for a passage in the fresh air and a view of the city through the early morning haze. He had long ago become accustomed to commence his labors early, but he always tried to do only routine tasks during the first few hours. This morning we had yet another series of conferences scheduled.

He was chafing because the Dutch Cardinal Gordenker, the outspoken leader of the servants, was already ten minutes late. Francesco looked at his watch for the third time and told me to commence my briefing on the character of the Curia. I was to pretend that he knew nothing. I opened by explaining that one of the two most important facts about the Curia is that it is not *a* Curia at all, but ten or more separate curias. Everyone of the *dicasteri*—you would call them departments or more formally sacred congregations—tends to go its own way. The secretaries, the men responsible for the day-to-day administration of each congregation, are usually career officials who have lived much of their lives here in the Holy See or abroad in diplomatic posts. They are bureaucrats, shaped by similar forces, but also with competing ambitions. They are usually *monsignori* when selected to be secretaries; they have normally served at least a dozen years in the Vatican, often longer. If they function well, they will soon become archbishops, but of titular sees, not real ones. If they do very well, they may some day gain the red hat. There is even hope for higher office. Three of Francesco's recent predecessors—Montini, Roncalli, and Pacelli—were all Vatican bureaucrats with very little pastoral experience, and only Roncalli, Papa Giovanni, that is, escaped the bureaucratic mentality, possibly because he lived so long in exile in the diplomatic service.

The secretaries, I went on, are to some extent rivals of each other, not merely to become cardinals, but to achieve their ideas. The jurisdiction of each congregation always overlaps that of two or more others. And despite their similar career experiences curialists often possess somewhat different ideas about how best to apply fundamental moral or theological principles to specific problems. Moreover, seeing the world from their peculiar institutional perspective, they tend to believe that their own congregation will handle any particular problem with greater skill and wisdom than will other congregations. In a sense, personal ambition, institutional loyalty, and devotion to God and Church reinforce separatism within the Holy See.

The prefect of each congregation is a cardinal, but each is apt to possess the same virtues and defects of the congregation's secretary, although a larger proportion of the cardinals have not been Vatican careerists. Those who have been pastors typically find more difficulty managing their subordinates, who know our Byzantine ways in a mode that a man who arrives in Roma late in life never will. *Ecco,* these cardinals also differ among themselves on many problems of theology, administration, diplomacy, and specific application of general rules.

Each congregation has a group of cardinals who are members—something you might call a board of directors. They meet only once or twice a year and usually exercise little control since by the time they gather most of the specific problems have already been dealt with. Besides, according to me, these cardinals are not likely to speak to each other with total candor or to labor together in close cooperation. The previous day's reunion showed how reluctant most cardinals are to commit themselves in the presence of their brethren. There is something of our morbid Italian fear of making a *brutta figura* (which I explained you earlier), something of distrust of the ability of others, and perhaps also some subconscious rivalry for the papacy, if not for oneself for one's candidate. "I would not want to overstress the last," I told.

"Why not?" Francesco asked. "Pitting ambition against ambition is not a bad way of checking power. It's the gospel according to James Madison and its holy writ is the American Constitution."

Not knowing anything about Signor Madison or your Constitution, I continued my analysis. "Those cardinals who are in Roma can see as much of each other as they want—or, in probability, even more—and that provides opportunity for real, if informal consultation."

There came a discreet knock; the portal opened and Monsignor Bonetti ushered Henrick Cardinal Gordenker into the studio. "Forgive my tardiness, Holiness," Gordenker knelt to kiss *il Papa*'s hand, but Francesco motioned him to a chair.

"Your guards insisted that I wait in the *camera.*"

"I fear your getting into the palace is about as difficult as my getting out of it. We were discussing the Curia."

"The Curia? Do not discuss it, Holiness; abolish it. It's a sea of bureaucratic jailers who will imprison you in paper chains just as they have the rest of the Church. Wipe it out and start the Church off fresh in the modern world."

"We would only have to create another bureaucracy," I said.

"I am afraid that for the present at least Cardinal Galeotti is right," Francesco nodded. "Let us first understand what it is we face. His Eminence was just explaining the two most important characteristics of the Curia. The first was lack of coordination. How did my venerable predecessors, of sainted memory, now that they are no longer with us, cope with that difficulty?"

"Ecco," I replied, "most of them did not cope with it so much as they learned to live with it. Historically, it has been an immense problem for the Church. Most Pontiffs have thought of themselves as absolute emperor. on the model of Constantine. In reality, they have more often been like feudal lords with tenuous control over supposed vassals. During the late middle ages and early modern period each cardinal would swear, before a conclave, that if elected *il Papa* he would respect the prerogatives of his brother prelates—one of the reasons that Church law now automatically absolves all members of the conclave of any oath regarding succession to the papacy."

Francesco muttered something; Gordenker looked bored.

"During the first half of this century," I explained, "curial independence was not as great a problem as it was historically or has become since. There were personal bickerings, but from the time Pio X purged the modernists from the Church before the First World War until Papa Giovanni opened the Pandora's box of Vatican II, curial officials tended to think alike on doctrinal lines; those who did not embrace the monolithic notions of our pious Pontiffs were soon not in the Vatican."

Gordenker nodded vigorously. "Even Montini was exiled, if it is not too much to imagine poor, agonized Paul VI being thought of as on the radical fringe."

"That was a more personal thing," I told. "Monsignor Montini feuded with Monsignor Tardini and Pio XII tired of hearing people refer to Montini as his heir. But, you are right, to some extent, the problems of division within the Curia existed then. Curialists were as jealous of their prerogatives, as secure of their capacities, and as devoted to the Church as they are now. But monolithic theology minimized problems, except when dealing with certain secular governments.

"For all that you may criticize Papa Paolo," I looked at Gordenker, "he tried to govern the Curia, and probably did so better than most. He made the secretary of state chief of staff, in fact as well as in title. All proposals for official action by the Holy See went to *il Papa* through that office, and that same office assigned tasks to curial departments. The Secretariat of State then collated and coordinated recommendations for action, so what *il Papa* received was more than unconnected pieces of a puzzle."

"That was how it was supposed to work," Gordenker intervened, "but Paul mucked it up by appointing a liberal Frenchman, Jean Villot, as secretary of state, and as undersecretary responsible for coordinating within the Curia, Giovanni Benelli, a traditionalist who was also Paul's old friend and former assistant. Villot's undersecretary was often more his under*cutter*. Paul and Benelli often left the poor Frenchman out in the cold—and he was very bitter about it."

"Be that as it may," Francesco told, "the idea of the Pope's having his own man—and his own pipeline—has a certain appeal." He looked at me. "But why not financial control?"

"Without doubt," I replied. "Papa Paolo tried that, too. In 1967 he created a Prefecture of the Economic Affairs of the Holy See—our brother Mario Chelli has been president for three years—to receive, approve, and control the budgets of all offices of the Holy See."

"And that hasn't worked well either," Gordenker said.

"Why not?" Francesco asked.

"It has worked well but not perfectly," I answered. "I suggest that we permit Chelli to explain the situation himself."

"All right," Francesco agreed. "So much for lack of coordination. What's the second critical characteristic?"

"*Allora,* absolute dedication and usually that equally absolute lack of humility that very dedicated people possess. Most curialists *know* what the Church must be and do. They are honest men, but this certitude inevitably colors what they see transpiring in the world, how they evaluate those events, what information they transmit, and what recommendations they make."

"Selective perception we called it in one of our former lives," Francesco told. "We all see life from a particular set of perspectives. The trick will be for us to use that dedication to the Church and make sure that we never have to depend on any single group of people as our sole source of information or recommendations. We'll have to create other sources so that I can exercise my own judgment after seeing the problem from several points of view."

"If Your Holiness can manage that," Gordenker remarked drily.

"Yes, if I can—if we can, you two and a few others. We have only a few alternatives open: destroy the Curia—or curias—and build a new organization; reform the Curia and try to work through it; bypass the Curia. Each course presents problems. A new or reformed Curia is likely to quickly develop its own interests and adopt its own obstinate patterns of behavior. It's also doubtful that we could consistently bypass the Curia without in turn developing a second Curia, which would then create its own problems. I can't keep all the proper forms in my head. I've already found out that I can't even name a pair of new cardinals without producing a ream of paper. I just cut through all that and sent cables to the two telling them they were cardinals and inviting them to come to Rome as soon as possible to receive their red hats. I scandalized some of our holy brethren. That doesn't bother me, but I can't make similar cuts every day and survive with enough energy to get other things done."

"Perhaps," Gordenker conceded. "Is there no other alternative?"

"Yes, there is: to swallow our hopes and work through the Curia as it stands."

"That would mean no real modernization of the Church," Gordenker protested.

Francesco nodded his assent. "So I opt for a mixed strategy. I have only a limited supply of energy and only a limited number of days. I'm to be assured at the coronation ceremony, as I recall, that I shall not see the days of Peter." Francesco looked at me. "How long was Peter Pope?"

"About twenty-five years, according to tradition; no one knows exactly."

"Hardly enough time to build and supervise a new organization."

"Christ had only three years, Holiness," Gordenker demurred.

"But He had the advantage of divinity," Francesco noted. "Lacking that quality, I shall depend on people like you and Cardinal Martin to help me reform and coordinate the Curia. The secretary of state will still be responsible for coordination, but I want other sources of information about what is going on—and not going on. Later this morning, we're talking to Chelli about the Prefecture of Economic Affairs. If I can control my lord cardinals' money, I'll have gone a long way in controlling their policies. Not as far, of course, as in secular governments, but still a long way.

"I also want the Curia to be even more international than it now is," Francesco continued, "and I mean international regarding not only the cardinals who are the titular heads, but also the secretaries and undersecretaries and minor officials who handle the day-to-day work. If the Curia is like every other organization that I've known, shifting cardinals around is going to be less important than changing the *monsignori* who make the everyday decisions. I want people whose minds are open. I don't want fanatical liberals any more than dogmatic traditionalists. I may be infallible, but I am also uninformed about many of the world's social and spiritual problems.

"I also plan," Francesco added, "on occasion to bypass the Curia by assigning problems to special task forces. If we can create, then quickly eliminate, organizations, we may avoid some of the stultifying effects of bureaucracy —and, I know," Francesco waved his hand at me, "pay a great cost in waste and inefficiency. But if the goal is to make wise decisions, then waste and inefficiency are only apparent. It may sound like textbook Franklin D. Roosevelt administration, but the object is to do well, not to do neatly."

"*Senti,* wouldn't a number of judicious appointments be sufficient?" I asked. "I fear the notion of a task force will grate on curial sensibilities."

"Very well. Let's change the name—that's the oldest legal way to cope with a problem. If a situation becomes intolerable and you can't change its essence, you change the problem's name. It's surprising how often that works. But I want to try the basic idea of task forces—let us call them special papal commissions."

"About appointments—" I tried to tell, but Francesco cut me off.

"Appointments alone won't do it. William Howard Taft complained that every time he made an appointment he created twelve enemies and one ingrate. The temptation to build one's own empire is pretty much universal and irresistible. Some of that tendency we can control by close supervision, some by putting people in charge whose empire building helps us for the moment, then transferring them before that tendency hurts us. And again, if I can pit some of these people against each other, I can gain several sources of information—from their quarrels if not from their reports. Competition might also force them to produce better ideas."

"If it works, Holiness," Gordenker shrugged. "I still think we'd be better off"—I was secure that Francesco had noted that the Dutchman had said "we" and meant it to identify himself with the plans of *il Papa*—"starting afresh. But I shall do all that I can to make our plan work."

"Ugo, would you and Cardinal Gordenker prepare a list of names of people whom you would recommend for every senior post in the Vatican? I want no one outside of this room to know what you are doing. Incidentally, don't hesitate to include men who are not yet cardinals. Like the Holy Spirit, we do not feel obliged to restrict our choices to the sacred college."

We nodded.

"I have one other idea I want you both to be thinking about: how to build up the World Synod of Bishops so that it could serve more effectively as a forum for debate, a kind of representative, advisory chamber where I can hear all sorts of views expressed. I know it does some of those things now, but so far not very effectively. I want the synod to compete with the Curia for power. Over the long run, the synod might well become a real ecclesiastical parliament. It might even challenge the authority of the Pope. But that would be a problem for my successors; it would not be fair," he smiled, "for us to deprive them of the fun of solving some problems. Brood over this and give me some ideas over the next week.

"Before we end our meeting, let me say," Francesco stood up and walked to the window overlooking the piazza, "I have more radical plans for the Church. I shall tell you some of them over the next days and weeks, but right now I want to get started on restaffing the Curia."

Gordenker smiled broadly. I must have looked concerned, for Francesco patted me on the shoulder and smiled comfortingly. "I believe the Holy Spirit will approve of my plans, Ugo, and so will you."

As Gordenker left the papal studio, Francesco turned to me. "We have ten minutes before the next conference; let's try and settle something. Ugo, would you accept the post of secretary of state?"

"Holiness, I cannot refuse *il Papa* anything, but I have not said you or anyone else that my health is not good. I fear that in a post that taxing I would be able to serve you for only a few months."

"Have you been to a doctor?"

"Many. The story is the same. You remember your Ovid: 'Old men are only walking hospitals.' My ailment is nothing dramatic, merely serious—leukemia. When I was in Washington, I received considerable treatment—in deep secrecy; only a few trusted members of my staff knew. For several months now, I have been enjoying a state of remission. How long it will continue, no one can predict, although the doctors have been moderately encouraging. Apparently my illness is vulnerable to a combination of chemical and radiotherapy. With proper rest and freedom from anxiety, the prognosis is good. Still, one does not hope for—or perhaps fear—too many more years when one passes seventy-five."

Francesco's face darkened and his voice trembled a bit. I knew his concern was genuine and I cannot speak how much it touched me. "Really? I had never asked, but I had assumed that you were in your mid-sixties."

"*Ecco,* that shows what a life of prayer and fasting will do," I said as I patted my ample stomach. "I am ready to serve you, Holiness, but I do not think I could serve you well as secretary of state."

"Of course, I respect your wishes. I had no idea. You will be able to serve as a close adviser and friend?"

"It would be my honor," I told.

"Very well," Francesco spoke a little impatiently. "Then who as secretary of state? Gordenker's too committed to one approach to be an effective coordinator. He would be enforcing his policies, not mine, even without meaning to. I'll probably have to put LaTorre somewhere. I don't want to alienate the traditionalists—at least not on an issue of personality—and I suppose being elected cardinal dean is an indication of some sort of trust. But I can't have La-

Torre as secretary of state any more than I can have one of those reactionary Irish like Greene or that snide Frenchman, Bisset."

"No," I agreed, "LaTorre would not do there. In any event, he is only acting secretary of state. You have reason about Gordenker and Greene and his colleague. Any of them would divide—no, fracture—the Church. *Senti,* have you thought of an African or an Asian as a demonstration of the Church's true catholicity?"

"I've thought about it, but I could never fire him. If he were bright, he'd realize that; if he weren't bright, the job would be too much for him. If I can't have you, I want someone who has what you call the servant image of the Church but not so publicly identified with that faction as Gordenker or Fournier. Martìn would be excellent, but I need him more somewhere else for the time being. I want someone whom I can either trust implicitly or fire easily. He has to be *my* man."

"Cardinals tend to think of themselves as Christ's men."

"Probably true—and to draw a fine line between loyalty to Him and to His Vicar. All right, I stand corrected. Any suggestions?"

"Yes, Holiness, one of your principal rivals at the conclave, Paolo Cardinal Fieschi, archbishop of Milano."

"He's too much a traditionalist," Francesco objected.

"Solely, according to me, in that he understands little of the world of the Church outside of canon law and administration. More generally, he's a man of considerable intelligence and stature. He's also a superb administrator. He knows how to give and to execute commands. He is the closest thing to a marine in the sacred college. If you want coordination in the Curia, he will give you coordination—and in the smooth mode that only we Italians can offer."

"He might do," Francesco conceded. "I'll think about it. I'm not sure I value coordination that highly. I've only met the man twice, but I know he's arrogant. Do you remember Kate's comment?"

I well remembered. After watching Fieschi's cool, self-assured handling of a diplomatic reunion, she had described him as "going through life able to sit down whenever the thought strikes him, confident somebody will slip a chair between his behind and the floor."

"He is," I concurred, "arrogant by American standards.

It was normal for him to be so with you. You were not then his superior or equal in rank. He is, after all, an Italian nobleman. You reacted as an egalitarian American. Remember that he will be dealing mostly with Europeans. They would think a lack of arrogance strange."

"Ugo, are you taking care of yourself?" Francesco broke off quickly.

"Of course, Holiness. I have little else to do but take care of myself and pray." (I came to regret those words.)

NINE

I CONTINUE MY NARRATIVE from almost the next moment so that you may have some sense—you say "feel"?—for how seriously Francesco worked. Besides, most laymen have a morbid fascination about the Vatican's finances; I shall indulge that curiosity.

Not five minutes after Gordenker left, Monsignor Bonetti ushered in Cardinals Chelli, LaTorre, Greene, Bisset, an American archbishop (titular only) named Giorgio—you say George?—Sullivan, and a layman, Cavalier Carlo Gaetani, brother of the rector of the Lateran University. The four cardinals were members of the Prefecture for Economic Affairs; as one of his few curial acts, Papa Paolo's successor had increased their number from three to four to include, *ex officio,* the president of the Administration of the Patrimony of the Holy See. Archbishop Sullivan was secretary of the Institute of Religious Works and Cavalier Gaetani was a former director of the Bank of the Holy Spirit (in which we hold an interest), one of the chief advisers among the *uomini di fiducia,* the "men of trust," who handle many of the investments of the Holy See.

After each of the cardinals had kissed *il Papa*'s ring, Chelli presented the archbishop and the layman. Francesco automatically extended his hand—according to me, to be shaken, but Sullivan and Gaetani knelt and kissed his ring. *Il Papa* quickly motioned the group to the white chairs around the table.

"Please be seated. The purpose of this visit is for you gentlemen to brief me on the Church's finances. We take it, Cardinal Chelli, that although we hold the keys to the kingdom of heaven, you hold the keys to the Vatican's treasury."

"Actually, Holiness, my task is more restricted. As president of the Prefecture of Economic Affairs, my duties are to formulate a budget and then to supervise the audit of the funds actually spent. As Your Holiness can imagine, our work involves mostly coordination. Toward the close of each calendar year, we receive a proposed budget from each office of the Holy See, consolidate those budgets into a single document, and submit it to the Pope for approval, together with a summary of thirty or forty pages and our own recommendations. Final decisions rest with the Pontiff himself."

Chelli then explained the origins of the Institute of Religious Works. It came into being in 1942 to safeguard the funds of European religious organizations who feared confiscation by the Nazis. As is obvious from the very name of the Bank of the Holy Spirit, the Vatican holds interests as well as deposits in other financial institutions, but the institute had gradually come to function as the Vatican's own bank. It was not huge compared to American conglomerates—its deposits probably never far exceeded $2 billion—but it was our own thing.

As Chelli detailed the institute's operations, only three points annoyed Francesco: the promise that the religious orders had extracted from the Vatican under Pio XII that the institute would never be ordered to reveal its accounts to anyone, not even to *il Papa;* the institute's exemption from supervision by Chelli's Prefecture of Economic Affairs; and the rather easy mode in which some secular financiers were allowed to use the institute and so to keep their operations secret from their own governments. Francesco said, as much to himself as to us, that, as a matter of diplomacy, he might have to live with the first, but he would not live with the second or the third. *Eccellenza* Sullivan commenced to say something in rebuttal, but rapidly thought better of it.

Chelli then outlined—without always supplying specific numbers of dollars or lire—the largest expenditures of the Vatican. Sometimes charity and relief constituted the largest items, but generally first place was won by missionary efforts, which always included a far greater outlay for charitable works—hospitals, schools, orphanages, and so forth—than for expenses such as salaries, churches, transportation, and the like. It was not unusual for either set of categories to require $100 million a year. The next largest category was subsidies to churches and religious organizations that were not self-supporting. Finally came the administration of the Holy See itself—the cost of operating the Vatican and its diplomatic offices around the world. Despite draconian efforts at austerity, that overhead had debited the Church many, many millions of dollars during each of the past few years.

"Obviously, Your Holiness," Chelli concluded, "I have not gone into fine detail. We have also made many arbitrary classifications. For example, part of our outlay for the Vatican radio station—actually the Jesuits pay most of the expenses—could reasonably be charged to missionary expenses, just as might our subsidies to religious institutions."

"Where does the money come from?" Francesco asked.

"Chiefly the Administration of the Patrimony of the Holy See provides our money, Holiness," LaTorre replied. "As acting secretary of state, I am president of that office, but I think that Cavalier Gaetani can better answer your question. He knows far more about the actual working than I do."

Ecco, Gaetani spoke in those confident tones that only bankers, brokers, physicians, and readers of tea leaves can affect. He explained that there were six basic sources of income for the Vatican. (I do not have to explain, I know, that the Holy See does not control the money of local bishops or of religious orders such as the Dominicans or Franciscans. These people are financially independent—at least in being beyond our control. If, however, they encounter more accounts than they can pay, then we try to assume part or even all of the obligation. Thus their money is not our money, but our money may become their money.)

The first source of the Vatican's income, Gaetani said, was the return from the investments of the historical capital of the Holy See, mostly from the money that Mussolini had given the Church under the Lateran Treaty of 1929 as an indemnity for Italian expropriation of lands belonging to the old papal states. Mussolini promised to pay us almost $90 million, but most of that was in government bonds. When the bonds matured they were seldom worth their supposed 1929 value and some were little more than beautifully decorated paper. Moreover, some of the money we actually obtained had to be used to construct new edifices and repair or enlarge old ones to compensate for the property the Italian government had seized.

The second major source of our income is the annual offerings of the faithful all over the world in the special collection (or sometimes merely a special gift by a bishop) that we call *l'obolo di Pietro* and you call Peter's Pence. Third, are funds from other special collections, typically set aside for particular purposes such as the missions. Fourth, are from the rents and sales of apartments and other real estate, mostly in Roma, that the Vatican owns. Fifth, is money from Vatican City-state, principally profits from selling stamps and coins to collectors, food and gasoline to residents of Vatican City, books and newspapers to anyone who wants to read, and fees paid by visitors to the museums. Last was a *misto,* what you call a hodgepodge, including such diverse items as bequests from wealthy Catholics and gifts brought by bishops to their annual or biennial visits to Roma.

"How are your investments organized, *Cavaliere?"* Francesco asked.

"At one time a large share of our money was in land, mostly here in Italy. We have disposed of many of those holdings, except for apartments and housing here in Roma. Otherwise, our portfolio is basically rather conservative. Something under one-fourth of our assets are in steady, income-producing paper not likely to fluctuate much, bonds of some of the more stable governments, for instance. Somewhat more speculative—and profitable—are our holdings of gold. Many of our larger ingots, incidentally, are stored in your Fort Knox. I said profitable because we bought most of our gold when it was selling at $35 an ounce. This morning's quotation in Zurich was $407. About half of our assets are in what you call blue-chip stocks, such as Italgas, AT&T, Olivetti, or IBM. We have invested another fifteen or twenty percent in more speculative common stocks. Some do reasonably well; some do little; but rarely do our firms collapse. On the whole, our gains exceed our losses by a considerable extent. I would estimate a real annual growth rate of about seven to ten percent—inflation makes the amount seem higher.

"Last, we have a small share of our capital out in what frankly is a highly speculative venture, dealing in international currencies. We have been in this business for many decades. The rates of exchange shift from day to day, sometimes from hour to hour. We buy and sell regularly. In 1973 when the dollar was weak we used our lire to buy millions at between 560 and 600 lire to the dollar. Within a few months we were able to sell all the dollars we wanted—unofficially at a minimum of 700 lire. We had, and have, sufficiently small faith in the Italian economy to take a lower profit by using our dollars to buy other currencies, such as Swiss francs, which by 1978 almost doubled in relation to the dollar. On other occasions, of course, we have lost, but on the whole we do very well."

"How are our stocks divided by country?" Francesco asked.

"About ten percent in Italy, Holiness, perhaps a little less. We have been cutting back there slowly so as to disturb the economy as little as possible. But political unrest, inflation, and new tax laws make Italy a poor investment. We have another thirty-five percent or more in the United States; the rest is mostly in Western Europe although some is in Japan. We own almost nothing in Latin America. In Africa we put a few million dollars into local organizations. Pope Paul initiated the idea. He started the Populorum Progressio Fund, named after his encyclical on development. But the scheme is designed to help black Africa rather than to make money for us. Certainly it has made nothing so far and has cost us in the sense of depriving us of the return that we could have earned on the investment. We hope, of course, that the money is helping the Africans."

"Let us pray," Francesco muttered, and then asked, "What are our connections now with the Società Generale Immobiliare?"

"None, Holiness. At one time we did some of our work through SGI but mostly in real estate and construction. After some unpleasant publicity in the 1960s, we disassociated ourselves completely. We had sold all of our shares before the Watergate scandals. As Your Holiness knows, SGI built and owned Watergate, though I believe they disposed of it prior to the scandals."

"What is the total value of the money we have invested or available for investment?"

"Holiness, that is a most difficult question to answer, for two reasons. The amount fluctuates hourly in stock markets in a dozen countries. I can say, however, that most of the newspaper stories that one reads about our wealth are greatly exaggerated. We are hardly comfortable, certainly not rich."

"You said there were two reasons," Francesco intervened.

Gaetani looked embarrassed. "Perhaps Cardinal Chelli could explain."

"Yes," Chelli said, "although probably not altogether satisfactorily, Your Holiness."

"Try me."

"Holiness, the second problem is that while we have a full set of records on the holdings of the Administration of the Patrimony of the Holy See, many of the other offices —Propaganda Fide or the government of Vatican City State, for example—have separately invested some of their own funds, and they do not always tell us exactly how much or where. We are trying and we are learning more and more each year, but as of today no one could produce an accurate balance sheet of all the holdings of all the offices of the Holy See."

"Incredible," Francesco muttered. "We'll come back to this in a minute. Right now, within the limits of your knowledge, give me a rough estimate of the net worth of our investments."

"My estimate is very rough, Holiness," Gaetani said, "but my best guess is that if we had to liquidate everything in a few weeks we could realize about a billion dollars; if we had two years to liquidate we could do much better, certainly by a margin of fifty percent, perhaps even double the figure."

Francesco frowned. "You're right. That is hardly wealth in the modern world, and it's not much comfort. Several American universities have endowments that approach or even equal our holdings—and far fewer demands on those resources."

"True, Holiness," Gaetani replied, "but we are still recovering from the losses we suffered during the Sindona scandals. We have recouped some, but we have still lost several hundred million dollars. Now Cardinal Chelli fights to keep our expenses down, and with Peter's Pence, special collections, and bequests, we do not have to depend entirely on income from our investments. That freedom allows us to invest in some ventures with long-range possibilities of growth rather than solely in those—like currencies—in which the return is likely to be exclusively immediate."

"How much do we get from Peter's Pence?" Francesco asked.

"I do not know, Holiness," Gaetani said.

"Nor I, Holiness," Chelli noted. "That money does not appear in our budgets. It goes directly to the Pope for whatever use he wishes to make of it. We see some of it, since we usually cannot make ends meet on what we have ourselves."

"I think I can give you an approximate figure, Holiness," LaTorre volunteered. "Last year the amount was just under $50 million."

Francesco frowned again. "Our people are taking the 'pence' too literally. Please remind me to do something about that."

"We find the money comes mostly from the United States and the English-speaking world, Holiness," LaTorre told. "We Italians *are* apt to take the 'pence' very literally. It is a rare Italian who will put more than a 100-lire coin in the Sunday collection."

"He knows, of course," Francesco added, "that his government is subsidizing the Church with his taxes. I wonder how much we gain in cash by such arrangements? Certainly we lose a great deal in moral power. But that's another problem for another day. If I recall correctly, one of the reasons for creating the Prefecture of Economic Affairs was to establish centralized budgeting for the Holy See."

"That's correct, Holiness," Chelli responded.

"To a considerable extent you have succeeded in that. I understand that your consolidated budget shows where all the money goes—with the exception, of course, of His Excellency's bank." Francesco smiled at Bishop Sullivan. "Another objective was to allow the Holy See to organize its resources and make decisions about operations and investments on a rational basis. From what you have said, we aren't there yet."

"That would be a kind way of putting it, Holiness."

"So, on the same day that one office in the Vatican is buying a hundred shares of IBM, another office may be selling a hundred shares of the same stock. Both transactions will cost us money because each office will pay a fee to a broker. Worse, our decisions and planning as Supreme Pontiff may be hampered because we may not know that either ever had those assets or the proceeds from their sale."

"Exactly, Holiness."

"If you agree, why does the situation still exist? Can't you force the congregations to produce the information?"

"We are making progress, Holiness," Chelli replied, "but my brother cardinals have been independent for too many centuries to surrender quietly or quickly."

"Why not a central investment pool controlling all the funds of the Holy See? It could make much more intelligent decisions and could exercise a great deal more financial leverage than a dozen or so smaller groups."

"Exactly, Holiness, I have been urging just such an institution for several years. Alas, as I indicated, not all of my brethren are willing to exchange independence for efficiency."

"Not even if directly ordered by the Pope himself?" Francesco demanded.

"Holiness," Chelli replied, "the Vatican is like an old lady. You can lead her gently and slowly by the hand, but you cannot push her without expecting her to fall down or to become very stubborn."

"It seems," Francesco mused, "that everyone advises me to go slowly with every problem."

"Here in the Vatican," LaTorre ventured, "we tend to think in terms of centuries."

"Yes, I have noticed, Eminence—mostly the sixteenth. Well, I'll brood on your suggestion for a few minutes. Let's move now to a related point, one that I hesitate to raise because I fear I know the answer. But I want to hear it from you. A third objective of the Prefecture of Economic Affairs was to permit the Pope to use this budget to control the bureaucracy, to force each curial office to submit in advance a detailed explanation of how much money it needed for the next year and why it needed that money. With that explanation in front of us, we could approve, disapprove, or modify items so that our own priorities would be carried out. To what extent have you been successful in that regard?"

Chelli shrugged. "So far, Holiness, as with investments, I can report progress but not success. My brother cardinals have not cheerfully accepted Mr. Robert McNamara's magic formula of Planned Programmed Budgeting. We ask that the next year's budget be submitted in November—what we call the *preventivo*. Most of the offices comply on time, or what passes for promptness in southern Italy, although not all give us much detail. The fiscal year is the same as the calendar year, so we do not have a great deal of time to make adjustments. In March, we receive the *consuntivo*, the annual accounting for the previous year's funds. Last March, for instance, we received the accounts from 1 January through 31 December of the preceding year. Unhappily, the amount planned in the *preventivo* is often smaller than the amount the *consuntivo* shows was actually spent. And since the money has already actually been spent, we can do little but complain."

"Is there any pattern of cooperation or lack of cooperation among the offices?" Francesco inquired.

"I would not say any is noncooperative, Holiness, only that some are more cooperative than others. The newer secretariats and commissions are the most anxious to cooperate. Some of the older congregations are less anxious, but they are moving. It is the same story as with investments. We ask to see the books; we are not told no; we are simply told nothing. We ask again, after a respectable interval. Then we are invited to talk—after another long interval, of course. At that point we negotiate a bit and we see a little. The next year we see more. We move."

(Chelli's face gave no clue about what was transpiring in his mind, but Francesco may have noticed, as I did, that LaTorre appeared distinctly uncomfortable. As president of the Administration of the Patrimony of the Holy See and as a member of the Prefecture of Economic Affairs, he had forceful reasons to cooperate with efforts at centralized investing and budgeting. But as prefect of the Congregation for the Doctrine of the Faith, he preferred to keep his own secrets. *Ecco,* I knew, as did the other cardinals present, that LaTorre was a notorious foot-dragger in this regard.)

"Let us hope the Curia is moving," Francesco said. "I intend to lead this old lady or even pick her up and carry her if I must. And I look on your office, Cardinal Chelli, as second only to that of the Secretariat of State in co-ordinating the policies of the Holy See and in providing information on which we can act. I would like you to draft, within the week, if possible, a set of procedures to tighten our budgetary processes and to create a central committee to supervise investments. I want within thirty days a complete listing submitted by every office—congregation, commission, secretariat, or whatever—in the Holy See of every piece of stock, every real estate holding, every bank account, and every other financial asset. Every one. No exceptions, no delays.

"Beginning this year," Francesco continued, "I also want departments to submit their proposed budgets by 1 October. I want you to have enough time and I want to have enough time to analyze those requests thoroughly. Perhaps we could also have a set of hearings in which prefects and secretaries could appear and explain their requests, and indicate why priority for scarce funds should be given to their work. I also want your draft to include an unequivocal statement that no money in excess of the amount approved beforehand can be spent. If an office runs out of money, it will have to come back to you—and then you to me—and justify additional funds being allotted or it goes without.

"We are going to lead, My Lord Cardinals. God has given us a Church and we shall govern her." Then Francesco smiled. "We hope to do so with more gentleness and decency and permanence than Oliver Cromwell, from whom I've just borrowed."

TEN

AS FRANCESCO HAD REQUESTED, I had, with the help of the Vatican press office, been easily able to locate the American journalist, Dottor Roberto Twisdale. He had been—you say covering?—covering the conclave for the *International Herald Tribune* and was also planning to write about the coronation. As in Washington, I found him to be a thoughtful, intelligent, if not altogether warm, person. I briefly explained my mission, which seemed to please him, and took him to Francesco. An hour later, *il Papa* had a *portavoce,* a spokesman. The two also told me of plans for a press conference within a few days.

According to me, that was not a prudent thing. Lacking armies or other means of physical force, *il Papa*'s authority rests totally on moral grounds—psychological grounds, if you prefer the secular term. That basis helps account for the pomp of papal ceremonies and the relative seclusion of most Pontiffs. The more opaque the veil of mystery about *il Papa,* the more cloaked he is in what Charles de Gaulle called the mystique of leadership. There must be much about a true leader that his people, even his aides, do not understand. If he is seen, fully and frequently, as a mere mortal, even as an intelligent and holy mortal, his psychological hold on the popular mind is apt to weaken. That is one reason, but only one, why we in the Church treat the person of the Pontiff with such awe. Another reason, of course, is the reverence we truly feel for the one who must walk the path of the Big Fisherman and also that of Christ. As an American, Papa Francesco distrusted awe and when he was not consciously thinking about it, as with the ceremonies of coronation, discouraged it in regard to himself. I tried to explain all these things, and he agreed. But he often did not—how do you say?—internalize my words. His habits of life were informal, something he only slowly learned to change.

Allora, at eleven o'clock on Saturday of the week after his election, the new Pontiff, Monsignor Bonetti, Dottor Roberto—*mi scusi,* you say Robert—Twisdale, and I walked into the Sistine Chapel for what you call a press conference. The others entered the Sistine because of their official duties. I came not because I approved, but because I wanted to view history made, even if wrongly made. The reporters, about eighty of them, had arrived through the museum entrance, still closed to the public while workers removed the remains of the conclave. Francesco was dressed in a white cassock, but without the *zuchetto,* the small white skullcap, as you call it, that *il Papa* has usually worn.

A pair of Swiss Guards snapped smartly to attention as we entered the chapel. At a stroke, the babble of talk and laughter died. Francesco stood on the steps in front of the altar, and, placing a sheaf of papers on a small podium, commenced talking in that rapid, clipped mode he used when lecturing. It was a style that emphasized his Roman accent when he spoke Italian.

"I understand that open press conferences with the Pope have not been frequent. We intend to have them follow Yaweh's ancient command 'Be fruitful and multiply.' We shall need ground rules. I'll lay down some now; after we gain experience, we may modify them. If we have a model, it is that of presidential press conferences in the United States.

"First, no question is out of order. We don't guarantee to respond directly or even at all, but responses are my problems. Questions are yours. Second, except where specifically indicated otherwise, there will be no direct quotations and no direct attribution. 'A highly placed Vatican source' will have to be sufficient."

Only the Americans displayed disappointment. The Europeans had not expected such generosity.

"We'll try to schedule conferences regularly, biweekly if possible. We encourage you to submit written questions in advance. We'd appreciate knowing what's on your minds and the time to find the answers. But the conference will not be limited to such questions. We'll try to answer you either in English or Italian. Please identify yourselves and your newspaper when you speak. After a time, we hope to know most of you by name. The conferences will be taped" —Francesco nodded toward Monsignor Bonetti who was setting up a small tape register—"for posterity. They will be placed in the apostolic library for future use. We would not want any of you to think that your, or my, pearls will be lost to history.

"We should go on from forty to seventy-five minutes. Today we'll limit ourselves to forty minutes. The representative from *L'Osservatore Romano* will have the privilege of asking the first question and will call us to a close at the appointed time.

"Now, we'll usually start off with some announcements. Today we have four. First, we have notified the bishops of Recife and San Carlos de Ancud of our intention to elevate them to the rank of cardinal at a special consistory to be held as soon after the coronation as is possible. You may note that their appointments constitute the first official act of my papacy. Second, we have appointed a press secretary

—a *portavoce*—Mr. Robert Twisdale, an American who has been associated with the *St. Louis Post Dispatch*, the *Chicago Tribune*, and the *International Herald Tribune*. He has lived in Europe and Asia most of his adult life. He will take over the old press office in the Palazzo delle Congregazioni in the Via della Conciliazione just outside the colonnade. He will establish a system of accreditation—God alone knows how—to get you people in and out of this fortress for our conferences.

"The third announcement is that, regretfully, we have accepted the resignation of Signor Carlo Bobbio, who has served so ably as editor of *L'Osservatore Romano*. We respect his wishes to reduce his responsibilities and to enjoy some of the repose that he so richly deserves."

(*Senta*, all of which was to say that Bobbio was a most conservative man from the Veneto whose right-of-center political views Francesco well remembered from 1952–53. Francesco had asked for the resignation, firmly but with generous provisions for a pension. *Il Papa* had a right to select his own man, but neither he nor anyone else ever questioned Signor Bobbio's professional competence or personal integrity.)

"We have been able to prevail upon Signor Alfredo Grottanelli of Milan to take over that post. Signor Grottanelli is well-known to many of you. He was born in Siena and has been a working reporter in Italy and South America for eighteen years, the last six spent as a senior editor of *Corriere della Sera*. We are fortunate to have a man of his standing to replace so eminent a journalist as Signor Bobbio.

"The fourth announcement is a kind of warning order. At our coronation on Sunday we shall make a major policy statement. Mr. Twisdale will have mimeographed copies for you sometime late Saturday afternoon or early Sunday morning. We shall only be able to provide semiofficial translations for you at that time—in Italian, French, German, Dutch, Polish, Spanish, Arabic, Swahili, and Chinese. The other languages will come later. The authoritative text will be English because that's the language in which we are writing the address. In case of doubt, refer to that version. There will be a ban on releasing the text or stories based directly on it before 5 P.M. Sunday. You can, however, alert your editors, and you can also write stories saying that leaks around the Vatican indicate an important announcement.

"We are still working on the final phrasing of the talk. And since, we have quickly learned, here in the Vatican even a misplaced comma can be construed as carrying some hidden meaning, we prefer to say nothing more at this time other than that we hope to set the Church firmly onto an old but still exciting path."

Francesco waited a few moments for these ambiguous remarks to be absorbed. "Now the questions. *Monsignore?*" Francesco looked at the stolid Swiss-Italian priest from *L'Osservatore Romano.*

The *monsignore* blushed and stammered. "Would, aah, would, that is, is your Holiness planning, like your predecessors of sainted memory, to nourish the souls of the faithful of the Church by offering new indulgences?"

Francesco regarded the *monsignore* incredulously. "No," he snapped. "His Holiness has plans neither for indulgences to provide spiritual sustenance nor for burning Protestants at the stake for temporal amusement." There was no laughter. In the Vatican one does not joke about such matters. "Next question."

"*Frankfurter Zeitung.* Has Your Holiness yet been ordained a priest and consecrated a bishop?"

"We have, in a set of private ceremonies right here in the Sistine immediately after we accepted election. The cardinal dean officiated."

"*Le Monde.* Could you tell us about the coronation ceremonies?"

"Not much, only that they will be as simple as is appropriate for such an occasion. Cardinal LaTorre is handling all the details. He is in complete command."

"Reuters. Has Your Holiness been able to keep abreast of the situation in Spain? I refer to the recent beating and killing of priests in Barcelona and the military tribunal's sentence of death against two cabinet ministers and three policemen."

"We know something about it, yes. This is for the record. You don't have to take notes right now. Monsignor Bonetti and Mr. Twisdale will take what we say from the tape and pass out mimeographed copies within the hour if you want the official version. You may say that His Holiness was appalled at the brutality displayed by the police and their commanders at Barcelona, and that he joins the Spanish people in mourning their martyred priests. He has been comforted, however, by firm assurances from the government that it treasures the civil rights of all citizens and that this was an isolated instance of a group of fanatics disobeying explicit policy directions. His Holiness has also been gratified by the swiftness with which the Spanish government has moved to punish the guilty, even within the ranks of its own cabinet. But he is opposed to capital punishment. He has therefore dispatched a cable to the Prado pleading in Christ's name for clemency for those accused who risk sentences of death. He fervently hopes that the government of Spain will temper justice with mercy.

"So much for direct quotation and attribution. Let us add, back now under our ground rules, that our decree excommunicating those involved in the attack requires only that the guilty confess their sins and make a public act of contrition if they wish to be readmitted to the Church and the sacraments. We should also note that we're pleased by the government's offer, as a gesture of its good faith, to give up their remaining rights under the old concordat. We have accepted that offer. We hope other countries will follow this selfless example."

(*Ecco,* it was then that I first realized that I had underestimated Declan Patrick Walsh. He was capable of a degree of dissembling that would have stirred the envy of any Italian and most certainly of every Vatican careerist.)

"*Time* magazine. Does Your Holiness always dress like this?"

"No. We wear pajamas at night, shorts when we play tennis." The reporters laughed more loudly than the retort deserved, but the man from *Time* was undeterred. "Your Holiness mentioned tennis. Do you plan to keep playing now that you're Pope?"

"Whenever we can. There's a vestige of an old court in the garden near the *casina* of Pius IV. We're having it repaired." (It was a vain thing. In the end he never played; there was no time.)

"What kind of tennis balls do you prefer?" the man from *Time* persisted.

"Round fuzzy ones. Next question, please." Francesco

gestured impatiently toward a hand at the back of the chapel.

"*The Irish Times.* Has Your Holiness any comment about the latest killings in Ulster?"

"No. Cardinal Greene here in Rome and Cardinal O'Failoin, the archbishop of Armagh, will keep us informed. We had hoped that the civilized world had outgrown religious and racial hatred. We don't believe we should say anything public at this time lest we increase that hate. Let us only note for the record that if Ulster ever has a Catholic government we shall not take up residence in Belfast."

Again there came an appreciative sprinkling of laughter.

"*Il Tempo.* Has your Holiness any plans for Italy?"

"Plans, no; hopes, yes."

"Did Your Holiness tell Signor Rinaldi anything in your meeting yesterday about possible entry of the Communists into the government's coalition?"

"We *told* the president of the Council of State"—the official title of our prime minister—"nothing about the Communists or anything else beyond our good wishes toward the Italian people. The two of us exchanged ideas about problems of mutual interest. That's diplomatese for saying that we just talked, trying to get to know each other more than anything else. The Pope, as bishop of Rome, is the primate of Italy, and that gives us special concern for the Italian people. But let us say two things. First, the Vatican is not a peculiar part of Italy, at least it cannot afford to be. For too long, the Vatican has seemed to be such. That must stop. One symbol of the new relationship is our terminating the arrangement by which Italian police operated within the Piazza di San Pietro to help keep order. We shall police Vatican City with our own officials.

"On the other hand, the charge has often been made that the Vatican interferes with Italian politics. We don't know enough recent Italian history to judge the accuracy of such stories, but we can assure you that, within the limits of the moral law, we do not intend to interfere with the internal workings of any government. We should, however, in all candor, ask you to note carefully the qualification 'within the limits of the moral law.' In another role, we said that church and state should be kept widely separate but that morality was an integral part of politics. We stick by that statement."

"*De Amsterdam Telegraaf*. Does Your Holiness plan any statement about birth control or clerical celibacy?"

"That's a hard question to answer without being naive or cunning. We can truthfully say that no, we don't plan to re-examine these questions at this time. But some people in the Church will be pushing us to say one thing, and other people another. You, here in this room, will devil us to say anything at all that you can use for copy. We have neither plans nor desires to fall into these traps, but we may not be able to avoid them. When one compares the scriptural promises with the realities of the Vatican, it would seem that the Pope's wishes often have greater force in heaven than here on earth."

The priest from *L'Osservatore Romano* looked at his watch and leaped up to recite his White House lines: "Thank you, Your Holiness." Francesco gave a smiling nod and, followed by Dottor Twisdale, Monsignor Bonetti, and me, walked out of the rear exit of the chapel.

"Well, how do you think it went?" Francesco asked Dottor Twisdale.

The *dottore* paused to remove his pipe from his jacket pocket. There was yet a blur of muffled voices in the background as the reporters were departing via the room of Paolo III. "Not bad, not bad at all, Your Holiness. In fact, much better than I had hoped. You were sharp, they weren't. They didn't know what to expect. But they'll get better."

"So will I. I haven't been grilled for a long time. It was actually fun. I'd forgotten that. On our Court, if there was any grilling, I'd be the grill*er,* not the grill*ee.*"

"Holiness," Twisdale asked, "some tv people want to know if they can televise a later conference."

"We'll have to wait and see. Right now I'd be inclined to say that, if we allow it, we'd have to restrict the questions to those submitted in advance. A chance remark could cause huge problems, and I'm not sure how long I can resist the temptation to be flip. What about radio and television coverage for Sunday?"

"I'm checking on that now. It shouldn't be too difficult. Voice coverage is absolutely no problem except for the echo around the piazza, and the lads have been televising papal doings for years. We can have cameras at a half dozen spots, and use zoom lenses where we can't get in close. Saturday night we'll tape your talk in English so we can dub it in while you speak Italian. Telstar will give us a worldwide audience. It's your boys who're causing most of the problems."

"We'll nudge them, for all the good it will do. John said that he felt like a prisoner here. I already feel the same way." (*Ecco,* I could have told him that that would only become worse.)

ELEVEN

IN MOST THINGS regarding the coronation, Francesco allowed LaTorre a free hand, knowing he would want to restore much of the pomp and grandeur that recent Pontiffs had thought overly ostentatious. By openly acknowledging LaTorre's role, Francesco hoped to gain some ground with traditionalists while allowing the Holy Mule to absorb the servants' resentment. The most important restoration of ritual was that of the actual placing of the triple crown on *il Papa*'s head, symbolizing his power over the nations, the Church, and even in heaven itself. In this respect, making a specific allusion to papal power, Francesco's will was at one with that of the traditionalists. His handling of the Spanish affair should have alerted all to his imperial—soon traditionalists would say "imperious"—concept of the papacy. Most servants would mute their earlier objections to papal pomp when it was used to their advantage. He wanted everyone in the Church to keep firmly in mind that *he* was the ruler of their Church.

LaTorre wisely prescribed an evening ceremony to avoid heat prostration. Our beginning at 6 P.M. pleased Francesco, for it would allow television coverage in Western Europe during the prime viewing hours of early Sunday evening and at noon the same day in North America. LaTorre had also suggested that Papa Francesco be carried in the historic way on the *sedia gestatoria.* Here Francesco was also in accord, but, according to me, more as a gesture to traditionalists, for he was always an impatient man who would have preferred his own brisk pace to the slow, cumbersome gait of the throne bearers.

LaTorre recommended that the ceremonies be held in the piazza, where a much larger crowd could be accommodated than in the basilica itself, and the problems of television simplified. Francesco added something of his own here. The procession would begin within the papal palazzo and enter the piazza not from the basilica but from the bronze portals, allowing many more people in the piazza a close view of *il Papa.* Rain would, of course, spoil all these preparations, and LaTorre had a contingency plan to perform all the ceremonies inside the basilica. I had no nerves about the weather, however. I knew that LaTorre had all the nuns in Roma praying for a clear evening.

Problems of security were much more troublesome. Not only would guards have to police almost a quarter of a million people pushing and shoving in the piazza, keeping clear the corridor from the bronze portals to the makeshift altar atop the steps at the entrance to the basilica, they would also have to protect the dignity and the lives of several dozen heads of state. Surely many demonstrators would hackle—no, you say *hec*kle—heckle some of these officials, and there was always the chance that an assassin would try to strike at one of them.

These difficulties of security were complicated by Francesco's wish to—how do you say it?—de-Italianize the Vatican. (I will tell more about that wish later; according to me, it was like our saying, an effort to straighten dogs' legs.) LaTorre met Francesco's wish by having arm bands of maroon and gold—the Vatican's colors—available for several thousand uniformed police whom the Italian government put at our disposal.

In all, including our own few personnel, we had 3500 officers in the piazza that evening, and the Italian government had stationed another 5000 regular police, *carabinieri,* and special troops around Roma. We were content that there would be no incidents, though I heard that the *scippatori* (thieves mounted on Vespas, motorcycles, or even motor bicycles) treated the police and troops elsewhere in Roma with total contempt, snatching purses within a few meters of the slow-witted and slow-footed officers, who would then argue with the victims rather than undertake the more dangerous task of pursuing the criminals.

By 5:00 that afternoon, the warm stones of the piazza already held perhaps 200,000 spectators and another 50,000 would soon be elbowing their way to the front. Within a few minutes the folding chairs on the left side of the temporary altar would be occupied by representatives from seventy-three countries, including royalty and near royalty: the prince and princess of Monaco with six of their fourteen children; the former king of Greece; the exiled grandson of the late emperor of Ethiopia; the latest Feisal to rule Arabia and three Muslim sheiks (all grateful, without doubt, for previous papal chilliness toward Israel and hopeful of a continuation of that policy); the president of Libya (encased in a human wall of bodyguards); the presidents of Guatemala, Ireland, Italy, Switzerland, France, the Federal Republic of Germany, Uruguay, and even the Soviet Union (but no official from Spain except their emissary to the Holy See); plus assorted prime ministers, cabinet members, ambassadors, and cinema stars. The United States was represented by your ambassador to Italy as well as Senator Harwood Trimble, Justices Albert, Walker, and, in a display of ecumenism, Justice Jacobson.

Francesco's old friend Sidney Michael Keller had also arrived from the United States. He escorted Signora Elena Falconi, Francesco's former administrative assistant, whom *il Papa* had somehow found time (when I do not know) to persuade to function in that same capacity in the Vatican. I confess I had grave misgivings about her appointment, and not because Signora Falconi was a woman. After all, a German nun, Sister Pasqualina Lenhart, had commanded Pio XII's office, though her authoritarian style and definite ideas about how the Church should operate did not make that precedent especially felicitous. In truth, my fear was that Signora Falconi was such an attractive woman that she might be a source of scandal. I do not mean of temptation to Francesco or any of us, but a source of calumny about the papacy. The Italian press caters to my countrymen's weakness for sexual gossip. When an Italian journalist finds no evidence of such sin between a man and an attractive woman, he is likely to ascribe the absence to homosexuality on one or both their parts. There is not much one can do in a positive mode, but one must be careful.

Allora, I was speaking of the coronation. As the crowds

were gathering in the piazza, we, the ecclesiastical notables, were assembling. At five-thirty *il Papa* entered the Sistine and mounted the *sedia gestatoria,* the portable throne that would be transported by eight strong men. Then, led by LaTorre, the rest of us joined *il Papa* in a brief prayer. Afterwards we proceeded down the magnificent Scala Regia through the bronze portals into the piazza. As soon as we came into view of the crowd, a sprinkling of clapping commenced, rapidly followed by cheers and shouts of *"Il Papa! Il Papa!"*

Ecco, the procession itself made a brilliant spectacle of color, a sharp contrast to the simplicity of recent ceremonies. First, the Swiss Guards came, resplendent in yellow, maroon, and purple Renaissance uniforms; then the Master of the Sacred Hospice, and the procurators of the various religious orders, each in the formal habit of his society, ranging from the coarse, brown wool of the Franciscans to the softly flowing white of the Dominicans. After them came the assistant to the papal wardrobe, displaying a plain iron tiara on a black velvet cushion. Next marched a line of red- and purple-caped clergy; judges from the Sacred Rota, canon lawyers, theologians, and minor curial officials. The Sacred College of Cardinals followed, at least the sixty-three of us who had remained in Roma after the conclave or had left but then flown back to the city. We wore gold chasubles over white surplices and, on our heads, white mitres (the tall, peaked cap bishops put on for formal ceremonies).

Behind the cardinals marched the master of ceremonies, Monsignor Dell'Aqua, the only man whom LaTorre trusted to do all things well. Immediately after Monsignor Dell'-Aqua, came the *sedia gestatoria.* Francesco wore a plain white cassock and a scarlet cape—colorful but, according to me, not a reasonable vestment for such heat. On his head was an unjeweled bishop's mitre. In his left hand, he held a plain crosier—a shepherd's crook—and was constantly using his right hand to bless the crowd. Unlike most of his predecessors, he did not wear gloves.

The throne was flanked and slightly preceded by two officials holding the *flabella,* a pair of huge fans constructed from ostrich and peacock feathers. A few paces farther out on each flank were more Swiss Guards. These men wore silver breastplates and carried highly polished swords or pikes. Immediately behind the *sedia gestatoria* marched the commander of the Noble Guard. His uniform was scarlet and gold, his eighteenth-century cavalryman's steel helmet as shiny as the tall black boots that reached his knees. At the finish of the cortege filed a *misto* of purple- and red-robed archbishops, bishops, patriarchs, and generals of religious orders. Finishing the procession was a third contingent of Swiss Guards.

It took a full fifteen minutes for the assembly to pass through the bronze portals. As the first guards reached the floor of the piazza at the foot of the stone steps, a pair of trumpeters high in the balcony of the loggia sounded their call; then two choirs, one on either side of the altar, commenced to sing *Tu es Petrus,* "Thou art Peter." As the *sedia gestatoria* entered the piazza, the master of ceremonies walked alongside the chair and three times lifted a tuft of hemp and set a match to it. Each time, as it puffed into short-lived flame and smoke, Monsignor Dell'Aqua said distinctly: *"Pater Sancte, sic transit gloria mundi."* I translate for you: "Holy Father, thus passes the glory of the world." According to me, this admonition, like the statement "Thou shalt not see the years of Peter," was a Christian adaptation of the warning of the Roman slave who would whisper into the ear of the triumphantly parading general, "You, too, are mortal." It was not a bad thing to remind a Pontiff.

Upon arriving at the foot of the temporary altar in front of the basilica, the cortege divided, and we ecclesiastical dignitaries took our places along the façade of the church. *Il Papa* himself was aided from the *sedia* and stood for a moment looking toward the basilica. (I would have preferred the backdrop to have been formed by the main altar within the church and the magnificent baldachino of Bernini. So gently do those four columns of twisted bronze support the tons of ornate and statuted canopy that one has the impression that a small breeze would send that thirty-meter-high mass of baroque art floating through the basilica. But Francesco's choice was not mine. He preferred the simplicity of a makeshift altar—and the adulation of a quarter of a million people.)

Allora, il Papa submitted to the ministrations of several deacons and subdeacons—all cardinals—who under Dell'-Aqua's watchful eye and sharp tongue assisted the Pontiff into his sacred vestments. The High Mass itself was done in thirty-five minutes. Among the omissions was the traditional ceremony in which *il Papa* was presented with a purse of twenty-five silver coins for "a Mass well sung."

When the Mass was completed, Francesco received the formal homage of the cardinals. Each of us came up to him, knelt, and kissed his ring. It was a return to an ancient ritual that Francesco himself, not LaTorre, had instituted. It was a useful reminder to curial cardinals, he told me, of where ultimate authority rested. After that ritual, *il Papa* removed the Mass vestments and, with a small group of cardinals and the assistant to the papal wardrobe, went inside the basilica and up to the loggia high above the piazza. In full view of the people and television cameras, the Pontiff sat on a carved wooden throne topped by a red velvet canopy. On his left, a Swiss Guard unfurled the papal flag over the balcony rail. (Lying on the floor of the balcony, where they could not be seen by the crowd, were two television cameramen and their portable equipment.)

The ceremony itself was brief, with a slight but pleasing change from tradition, which had stipulated that the senior deacon cardinal should crown *il Papa.* Instead, Francesco, as was his right, asked that the role be played by the eldest member of the sacred college, in this case Simon de Brion, who was ninety-one years old. The cardinal first draped *il Papa*'s shoulders with a simple woolen pallium, the symbol of his becoming the Bishop of Roma. Next, de Brion removed the triple-tiered crown from the cushion, raised it high so that the people in the piazza could view it, then placed it on Francesco's head. As he did so, the old man spoke the venerable formula in a voice that, although trembling, was loud enough for the microphones to carry to the piazza and to the radio and television networks:

> *Accipe thiarum tribus coronis ornatum et scias te esse patrem principum regum rectorem orbis in terra, Vicarium Salvatoris Nostri Jesu Christi, cui est honor et gloria in saecula saeculorum.*

> Take this triple crown and know that you are the father of princes and leader of kings of this world, the

Vicar of our Saviour, Jesus Christ, to whom are honor and glory forever and ever.

Allora, il Papa raised his right hand and imparted the blessing *"urbi et orbi"* to the city and to the world. For a few moments he accepted the tumultuous shout of *"Evviva il Papa! 'Viva il Papa! 'Viva il Papa!"* Then he placed the tiara back on the velvet cushion and walked from the throne to the battery of microphones on the railing. He raised his hands for silence.

"People of God," Francesco commenced in Italian, but the loudspeakers placed around the colonnade caused his voice to echo off the buildings, and he was obliged to speak more slowly than he had planned, making his Roman accent less obtrusive. "People of God, we exist in a world in which life often sits like vinegar on our tongues. Everywhere we are told that we do not practice the values that we profess, that our children do not respect those values, and that the world laughs at them—and at us. These are serious charges, hurtful charges. Insofar as they express truth they point to the fact that we have forgotten our purpose in this world, the central purpose that orders our lives and our values. We retain our sense of hearing, but we do not truly listen to the message, our own message. Perhaps we have retained our sense of sight but have lost our vision.

"We see a world on the brink of revolution, and we are afraid. Why? Why should the people of God be afraid of change and revolution? We are the inheritors of a revolutionary tradition. Christ our Savior was a revolutionary. He preached change, peaceful change, but still a sweeping, rapid, revolutionary moral change that could not help but bring social change as well. Because of His message he was nailed on a cross, the ancient Roman punishment reserved for sedition. Our Savior was thus a convicted seditionist. His revolutionary idea was that of love, of sharing material goods, of forgiving injury, of laying down our lives and, what is often more difficult, our fortunes, for our fellow men.

"That doctrine was subversive of the values of the pagan world. It may be subversive of the values of the modern world as well. If so, we are at fault, grievously at fault, for modern civilization is our civilization. If our civilization commands competition rather than cooperation, if it demands war rather than peace, hatred and envy rather than love, avarice rather than charity, then that civilization must be changed. It must be changed completely. It must be changed now. That change is our task, the task of all of us, not of our priests or our politicians or even our children, but of us, each of us. The change must come first within ourselves. We must reorient our values away from materialism and greed for the ephemeral things of this world and direct our hearts and minds toward simpler but more lasting goods, toward loving not outdoing our neighbor, toward social justice not personal advancement. We must return to the basic tenets of Christianity: to help everyone, to harm no one.

"Once we have reoriented our personal values, we must live lives that effect that same change in our society. We cannot as Christians use violence to impose our values on others, but we can set examples by what we do and by what we refuse to do, by practicing the virtues of justice and charity in our personal lives, by refusing to support social and political systems that conquer, attack, oppress, torture, or otherwise deliberately deny justice to any peope, whether foreigners or citizens.

"I know these counsels are hard and that following them will bring turmoil. But we must remember the words of Christ about his teaching: 'Do not believe that I have come to bring peace on earth. I have not come to bring peace but the sword.' As Christ's Vicar I come to bring that same sword, the 'terrible swift sword' of God's love to a world that wants only to revel in material prosperity. I come to preach that same revolutionary doctrine for which Christ was crucified. I call on you, the people of God, to become seditionists, to join in a crusade, a new crusade not *against* our fellow man but *for* our fellow man. I call on you, the people of God, to participate in a spiritual renewal, to reflect on our real purpose on this earth, and then to accept our lawful inheritance, that of the cross, and to become part of a worldwide revolution of love against hatred, envy, poverty, ignorance, disease, and suffering.

"Obviously, I am speaking of several kinds of crusade: first, a call to our fellow clergy throughout the world to cleanse their own minds and spirits and to join with the laity in a similar undertaking, instructing the laity where necessary, learning from the laity where appropriate. The objective of this renewal is to enable all of us to understand more fully so that we can put into practice more completely in our daily lives the principles of Christian love and of social justice.

"I do not preach any political ideology, certainly not as the world understands that term. I do not speak of any economic ideology, neither of capitalism, socialism, or communism. I shall speak out, and I hope the bishops of the Church throughout the world will speak out, against any government that preaches hatred because of race, religion, or social class, or against any government that practices or allows exploitation of one group of human beings by another.

"The second kind of crusade I am preaching is a physical crusade, an actual going forth, as commanded by the Gospels, to teach by deeds as much as by doctrine the words of Christ. At one level, we hope to organize groups of specialists—doctors, nurses, teachers, and technicians—but most of all groups of young people, men and women, to go out into the poorer areas of the world, to share with these people knowledge, understanding, and even suffering. To heed this call for revolution is to run the risk of being jeered at by fellow citizens, abandoned by families, harassed, imprisoned, and perhaps even tortured and killed by unsympathetic governments. But I ask you to join with us, your fellow men, and face these risks.

"At another level, I ask that all people who stay at home continue to practice—and urge others to practice—the doctrines of social justice and Christian charity. The main outlines of these principles are contained in papal encyclicals from Leo XIII through Paul VI—*Rerum Novarum, Quadragesimo Anno, Pacem in Terris, Populorum Progressio.* The duty of each of us is to treat his neighbor as a beloved brother, that is, with justice and charity; the right of each of us is to a fair return for his labor, a decent standard of living for himself and his family, and to be treated as a human being equal in dignity and worth to every other human. The duty of each of us is not only to practice these commands in his private life but to make sure that his society practices them.

"We do not make these appeals only to Catholics or even only to Christians. We call on all people of good will to join with us in these crusades. We are not embarking on a narrow sectarian venture to convert people from one religion to another, but to preach in the most effective way possible—by good deeds—the joyous tidings that God is love and that only by partaking of that love in helping our neighbor, by sharing with him both happiness and sadness, can we achieve the true meaning of life in this world or attain the happiness that can be our reward in the next life.

"My hope thus goes far beyond formal conversion to Catholicism or to Christianity. Much has been spoken in recent years of the quest for Christian unity, indeed of the unity of all religious creeds. Much has also been spoken about the ideas that divide men, that keep us tightly segregated in the ways we worship God and serve our fellow humans. I do not want to make people into 'rice Christians' or to win debates about theological abstractions. I want to see people practicing a gospel of decency and love.

"Can we afford to debate fine points of theology while children are unloved, the hungry unfed, the naked unclothed, the ignorant uneducated, the sick untended, and the old lonely and unwanted? Disputes about the virgin birth or papal primacy may be interesting ways of whiling away winter evenings, but the answers do not help to feed the hungry, to heal the sick, clothe the naked, or bring love and justice to mankind. And those are the things that Christ commanded us to do. I find in the Gospels no precept that we bicker among ourselves about points that cannot be definitively proved in this life. Our instructions are to go out among the nations and to preach and practice a gospel of love. If we do those things, we may find that men share more than enough to live with each other in peace, in grace, in dignity, and in diversity as well as in harmony.

"We bring you the message of the prophet Ezekiel: 'A new heart I shall give you, and a new spirit I shall put within you; and I shall take out of your flesh the heart of stone and give you a heart of flesh.'

"People of God, I have taken up the sword of Christ along with the cross of Christ. That burden is strange but it is sweet. Come, follow me. For the love of God and for the love of our children and their children, let us go forward with a new heart in peace and justice."

Il Papa again raised his right hand and made the sign

of the cross, chanting rather than speaking: *"Benedicat vos, Omnipotens Deus, Pater, et Filius, et Spiritus Sanctus."* ("May the Almighty God bless you, the Father, the Son, and the Holy Spirit.")

Allora, the crowd in the piazza stood hushed; according to me, they were confused whether to kneel, to cheer, or merely to depart in silence. Then a few shouts of the traditional *"Il Papa! Il Papa!"* rang out and were picked up around the piazza. The noise of more than 200,000 Italians clapping their hands can be deafening, but this noise was certainly not. It was quiet, sustained but subdued. I had seen no other Pontiff elicit such a response—or speak for such a short time.

Francesco replaced the tiara on his head and accepted the cheers for a few minutes, then spoke to the crowd again.

"A new heart of flesh in place of a heart of stone; eternal justice in place of transient materialism; love in place of hate. Come, follow me." This time the crowd knelt and Francesco, after once more making the sign of the cross over them, left the loggia for the palazzo.

According to me, we had just heard a prayer. More, we had witnessed the commencement of a miracle. I do not mean to be melodramatic, but I realize clearly now what then I could only dimly perceive: in trying to lead the Church, Francesco was going to lead and even transform himself.

TWELVE

THAT VERY NOON on the day after his coronation, Francesco behaved again like an American. He had instructed Dottor Twisdale to arrange a lunch for him with twenty journalists so that they might talk with him—how do you say?—off the record about the plans that he had just announced. According to me, the effort was a failure, as in fact I had predicted it would be. Pontiffs almost always dine alone; seldom do they eat with secular dignitaries and never with journalists. Taking a meal together is an intimate thing and, done with prying strangers, it can dissolve some of the mystique that must surround *il Papa.* A lunch of journalists with Dottor Twisdale would have been a thing entirely different and perhaps even desirable, but not with Francesco himself.

The journalists were not at ease. Who would be? Nor were most of them accustomed to Pontiffs making more than pious statements; thus they were not aware that the Church was perhaps on the brink of a new era. As a result, the questioning was desultory. The only advantage that I could see was that the table conversation supplied these people with a store of small nuggets that would encourage them to write more stories about the Vatican and the new Pontiff than they otherwise would.

After a brief siesta, Dottor Twisdale and I returned to *il Papa*'s studio to meet with Francesco and *Avvocato*—I am sorry, you do not, as we do, call lawyers by their title—*Mr*. Keller. I had made his acquaintance many times in Washington at the home of Declan and Kate. He was their closest friend. No, it is more precise to say that he worshipped them, and they enjoyed him in the mode that parents enjoy an impish child. (I say this even though Mr. Keller and Kate were the same age and Declan Walsh not much older. Declan would continue to mature all his life; Mr. Keller would still be an amusing youngster at age 100.) Still, it was apparent that Mr. Keller's impishness concealed a marvelously analytical intellect.

Despite his usual affectation of being "the Smart Money," Mr. Keller was uncomfortable. I sensed that he and Dottor Twisdale were not warm in their relations; much more important, his mentor's new position confused and troubled him. When we arrived, Francesco was pushing him for reactions to the call for a crusade.

"It's an exciting idea, Holiness." (Actually, he had commenced to say "Declan," but corrected himself in mid-syllable.) "It's long overdue. There's been a void since the United States retrenched the Peace Corps. But can you pull it off?"

"I can't, no. Together we all can. There are almost fifty million Catholics in the United States, another quarter of a billion supposed Catholics in Europe. If we can inspire only a small fraction of those people, if we can persuade only a tiny percentage of people of good will from other faiths to join with us, if we can arouse just a small proportion of educated and trained Latin Americans, we would have a huge army. If we succeed in Latin America, we'll be inundated with recruits for Africa and Asia. Our biggest source will be young people. This sort of idea should appeal to their idealism, and if we can harness their energy, there are few limits on what we can accomplish."

"Recruits are not the problem," Mr. Keller said soberly. "Young people will flock to you in far larger numbers than you can use. And you can probably pick up enough physicians and nurses and agricultural technicians and so forth. The big problems will be money and organization. This is a fantastically ambitious job that you have outlined. When I was working with the Peace Corps in 1962 we figured it cost us about $10,000 a year per volunteer. With inflation you would have to double that figure at the very least—maybe $25,000 would be more accurate. On top of that figure—and that means 4000 volunteers would cost you $100 million a year—you have to add the cost of the medical supplies they would distribute, the fertilizer they would use, the building materials, and so on."

"I hope that we can persuade drug companies to donate medicine and others to give what else we need," Francesco intervened. "We can cut costs by using monasteries and convents to house our people. And what money we need will come. The Vatican isn't rich, but it isn't poor either—at least not as poor as it will be, and should be. This evening at nine-thirty, after the diplomatic reception, we are having a small dinner party for six multi-multimillionaires, men who own more than $100 million each. Like every good charitable institution, we keep tabs on rich persons likely to donate money; in this case we can confine ourselves pretty much to Catholics. Tomorrow, I'll start to work on them individually."

Mr. Keller then asked about how the crusade would be organized.

"That is the first major problem," Francesco replied. "I'm going to have the Jesuits and the Franciscans run much of the spiritual renewal, but I'd like to keep them or any other order out of the crusade. They might not be able to resist the temptation to start converting people. I want a central organization here in Rome to give overall direction and provide coordination. I also want that central office to be international; it should include Latin Americans in prominent posts. I'd like to see some sub-organizations that aim not at the very poor, although they will be the main objective, but also at successful Latin American businessmen teaching smaller operators how to do simple things to improve their efficiency. I would like to see Latin American labor leaders trying to help groups in small towns and rural areas express their grievances, and so forth. In short, this can't be an instance of Yankee—or papal—imperialism."

Francesco waited a few moments; then he said very simply, "Mike, I'd like you to come here to Rome and run the crusade."

Mr. Keller was startled, visibly so, but he tried to hide it by laughing. "The Smart Money in the Vatican? Havva no. The last time these Roman pagans caught a Jewish boy on this hill they crucified him—and upside down, too. I'm not up to that."

"Seriously, Mike," Francesco persisted, "I need you. I need you because I can trust you and the world will trust you not to try to turn the crusade into a missionary effort."

Mr. Keller laughed again. "That's for sure. Converting people to the religion of the *goyim* isn't my bag." Then he paused and spoke gravely. "Since I met Declan Walsh at the University of Chicago two or three centuries ago, his 'I need you' has been the strongest sentence in my vocabulary. And it still is, I guess. I'd do anything for him, except hurt him. Look, I had difficulty staying celibate on the transatlantic flight. In two weeks you'd be knee deep in sex scandals. You don't need that."

"Don't you think I have weighed the risks?"

"You've weighed what you *think* are risks. I'm talking about a sure thing. The Smart Money chases girls and he enjoys chasing girls and he never has nor ever will keep that a secret. Actually, it attracts women so I don't have to run so hard. I just can't do what you ask. This is the first time I've ever said no. Tell you what, I'll come over any time you want advice. I'll help on any short-term project that keeps me here only a few days at a time and doesn't put me on the payroll or give me any official position. I'll help raise money, give money, borrow money, or even steal money—that's what lawyers are for."

"Mike, I—" Francesco commenced, but Mr. Keller did something unheard of in the Vatican. He interrupted *il Papa*.

"No, if I were to come here I'd be tearing down what

you're building up. You know I couldn't do that. I've never let you down."

"Only when you tried to read a map," Francesco smiled gently.

"I never said I was perfect," Mr. Keller replied. "Look, I'll even give you a new name. How about your abbot friend, Pryce? I'm as atheistic as any man who has two rabbis in his family, but if Robert Pryce said there wouldn't be any partisan missionary hanky-panky, I'd believe him and so would everybody else. He was an ecumenist when these folks in the Vatican were implying a Catholic would go straight to hell if he addressed a Protestant minister as 'Reverend.' And the fact that your lads in the Holy Office forbade him to speak in public makes him even more credible."

"I hadn't thought of him." Francesco's eyes brightened. "He has some relevant experience outside of the monastery. He was a middle-level executive for IBM before he went into the priesthood."

Four days later, Robert Pryce, former businessman, current Trappist, mystic poet, ecumenist, theological radical, and servant extraordinary, was installed in the palazzo. He was a most unusual man, efficient at his work, a quality one does not expect from an abbot who is internationally famous for his poetry—or was, before LaTorre sniffed heresy in his meters. I confess, however, that I did not find the abbot *simpatico.* I mistrusted the strange, bright fire of his eyes. Yet he was always gentle and soft-spoken in his dealings with people as individuals or, after Francesco had the Holy Office's ban lifted, when he preached a sermon.

Francesco, on the other hand, was very close to him. They were close in age if not temperament, and the abbot had been his confidant during the two years in the monastery. He knew Francesco as only I did. Perhaps in some aspects the abbot knew him better. It was a peculiar thing, as I believe I have already remarked, that Papa Francesco, the epitome of the pragmatic man of action and of practical thought, should have been so strongly attracted to mystics and mysticism. It was almost as if he was trying to construct some dimension missing from his own soul.

Allora, I did not envy the abbot his tasks. When he arrived, we had no organization at all to help him, no staff, no office, not even stationery, a typewriter, or a telephone. Worse, we had no money and no blueprint, only a general —I grant you exciting—idea. We could, however, offer him some suspicion that what he was about to attempt was, at best, tangential to the Church's true mission and, at worst, counterproductive to that mission. Out of that chaos he would have to create a mass movement which he himself described, with only slight exaggeration, according to me, as rather like the Children's Crusade 800 years earlier. I warned him to stay out of Venice, lest those merchants again sell his people to the infidel.

When the abbot arrived, Francesco said clearly, even bluntly, that he was answerable to no one but *il Papa* himself. No one from any curial office was to exercise jurisdiction or supervision over the abbot's work. That was a gallant statement, the opposite of your old saying about a sailor trying to whistle up a wind. Who can stop, merely by commanding it, bureaucrats from being jealous and expansionist where their own prerogatives are involved? Every lira that went to the crusade, everyone knew, would not always go to the missions or to efforts to promote Christian unity or to seek closer ties with our non-Christian brethren. I add this last to remind you that more than frail pettiness was at work.

THIRTEEN

A FEW DAYS after Papa Francesco named the abbot to lead the crusade, Bisset and Chelli joined LaTorre for lunch in his apartment in the Holy Office. Since I was not invited—although I later became privy to much of what was told—the menu was that of a wealthy peasant, perhaps of a Sicilian who had relatives in Roma. First came an *antipasto misto:* black olives, artichokes *alla Romana* (not *alla Giudea,* unhappily), radishes, translucent slices of prosciutto, two kinds of salami, a taste of tuna, and a bit of *cotiche e fagioli*—heavy white beans cooked and served with pieces of pork skin, an interesting but strong plate, especially when, as in this instance, there was yet some hair on the pork skin. Instead of ordinary bread, LaTorre's cook had prepared *bruschetta,* thick slices of heavy

Trastevere bread that have been toasted over an open fire, vigorously rubbed with pods of fresh garlic, then liberally sprinkled with olive oil (I would have insisted on green olive oil, but LaTorre's chef used yellow) and garnished with small pieces of red pepper. (For my taste, one also needs to add salt.) Next came a huge plate of *spaghetti alla carbonara,* a Roman specialty widely imitated in the south, made with spaghetti cooked *al dente* and smothered in a white sauce with much garlic, parsley, bacon, and cheese mixed together with raw eggs that are instantly cooked by being poured over the steaming spaghetti.

The principal plate was *coda alla vaccinara*—oxtail, *alle* Sisters of Charity, according to me. I have never been able to eat it or even smell it with good appetite. The *contorni* were green beans with mushrooms and prosciutto, and sliced tomatoes. For after, there was goat's cheese from the Abruzzi and a mound of huge Sicilian oranges. Inside, this fruit is seedless, sweet, and dark red. (I remember Kate's commenting that she always ate hers rapidly before it clotted.) The growing season is normally from late fall through the spring, but one of LaTorre's *paesani* had found some in the middle of summer. (I should tell you that the cardinal was kind enough to send me ten of them.)

When they first sat down, Chelli observed that Cardinal Greene was late, "probably saying 'God bless' for the fiftieth time."

"I doubt if His Eminence will be joining us today," Bisset laughed. "We left the palace together yesterday, and I would not be surprised if he is now suffering from 'the sickness.' Events have made him melancholy." Those references were spoken in a rather cheerful tone. I have said you that despite his strengths Cardinal Greene had the Irish problem with alcohol. That was his escape from loneliness, one not uncommon among the lonely men of the Church. Others found work a preferable, and far more functional, escape. But, according to me, for some people that path led to an even more dangerous result, one that threatened others as well as the clergyman himself; a delusion of possessing with absolute security plenary knowledge of the justice of God as well as of the moral laws regulating that justice.

"I wonder," Bisset went on merrily, "what the newly crowned bishop of Rome would say about the Irish now if he could see our brother Sean. Yesterday His Holiness was claiming that the Irish had 'that rare combination of faith and idealism that will make the crusade a success.' If that is not an exact quotation, it is very close."

"Do you really think he was the choice of the Holy Spirit?" LaTorre mused out loud.

"He must have been," Bisset answered, "for he certainly was not mine."

"Nor mine," LaTorre boomed.

"No matter whose choice he was," Chelli said, "he is now the Supreme Pontiff. The sooner we accept that fact of life, unpleasant as it may be, the more effective our own actions can become and the better will be the life of the Church."

Bisset ignored his young colleague. "Speaking of the crusade and His Holiness, I sensed a feeling of confusion in the crowd at the coronation. I don't think our Roman flock had the vaguest notion what our legitimizing layman-turned-monk was talking about."

LaTorre snorted. "No wonder, did you listen to the coronation homily? We should have been warned he would bring that heretical abbot right here to the Vatican."

"No," Bisset responded, "Roman-accented Italian grates too much on my sensibilities. One who has been brought up in Paris acquires certain standards for the spoken language. But I did read what he said, although I would not call it a lecture. I wonder if one of us here should not break the news to His Holiness that the Messiah has already come. *Alors,* Your Eminence may have been right last week. If this crusade, or whatever it is, does succeed in keeping his mind off serious problems like birth control and celibacy, we shall all be ahead. But I have my doubts there. In any case, how did our Most Reverend Brother Galeotti let him imply that doctrines like the virgin birth were trivial?"

"Ugo protested, I hear," LaTorre answered, "but *il Papa* went his own way. That is precisely the pattern that I fear. He did not ask any of us what we thought, and he did not even follow the advice of the cardinal closest to him."

Chelli, who as always only picked at his food—and today for good reason—removed one of his slender Cuban cigars, rolled it appreciatively in his fingers to warm the outer leaves, and then, muttering something about communism and the inscrutable will of God, sniffed the strong fragrance.

"I think you're wrong," Chelli responded. "He did consult us. He brought us together and asked our opinions, gave us time to talk the matter over while he was absent, returned and both answered and asked questions. Then he invited each of us to submit further thoughts both orally and in writing. We have been fully consulted; we simply did not respond as intelligently as we should have. I fear, God forgive us, we are not accustomed to such candor."

"But those requests were only charades," Bisset told. "He really didn't care what we thought."

"Perhaps," Chelli replied, "but I think not, at least not totally. I have heard that he does listen to reason—not that he always follows it. If we did not speak wisely then we should look to ourselves."

"Allora," LaTorre intervened, "last week I thought that these notions of a crusade and spiritual renewal were good things, but after hearing that address or whatever it should be called, I am afraid both ideas are only ways of outflanking us on moral issues. We—the Church—must preach first of all the kingdom of God, a kingdom that is not of this world. Our mission is to save souls for the next world, not to promote earthly happiness. Christ is our true bread of life."

LaTorre paused to chew. He was near choking, as his face reddened with anger. "That homily or whatever it was should have been our warning. I am furious that I let myself endorse his idea of a crusade. Now he brings a heretic, that half-Hindu, half-Protestant abbot who calls himself a poet into the bosom of the Vatican itself. I myself read what he calls poetry. It was my own hard conclusion that the man is a heretic. I silenced him. I was protecting the Church. Now this, this man who wears the tiara brings that heretic to the heart of the Church and says he will run the crusade. We now know what this will be, a crusade for heresy, an organized effort to wipe out holy doctrine."

" 'Vanni, 'Vanni," Chelli soothed. "The man's theological views may well be heretical. I confess I could never understand enough of what he was saying to have a firm opinion. But when you told him to write no more, he acceded—and without appealing to his friends in the Church or outside of it. And this post he now holds is one from which *il Papa* has specifically excluded discussion of dogma. From *il Papa*'s point of view it makes excellent sense. No one will believe that our good abbot would be proselytizing. Besides, as Italians, we both know that the abbot befriended *il Papa* in a time of need. Even Pontiffs must pay their just debts."

"I hope you are correct," LaTorre said. "I cannot bring myself to trust heretics or to trust those who trust heretics."

"I fear the abbot less for what he can do in his current office with this crusade than for what his appointment may mean for the spiritual renewal," Bisset interposed. "We may have precious little left of true Catholicism when *il Papa* and his friends—friends like the abbot—strip away 'nonessentials' and return us to 'fundamental principles.' The more I think about it, the more I fear this man whom the conclave accepted."

"I, too," LaTorre agreed. "Fear is not a pleasant emotion for an old man to experience."

"In this case," Bisset nodded, "it is prudent. This 'people's Pope' is not pushing celibacy or birth control or any of the important moral problems into the background; he's arranging it so that when such problems do come center stage their force will shove us in the direction he wants us to go. When we have hundreds, perhaps thousands, of young priests and nuns living and working together in Latin American fields and villages, we shall probably have much more than spiritual camaraderie; then the end of clerical celibacy may seem the easy way out."

"But," Chelli protested, "I did not understand that priests and nuns would go on that part of the crusade. He said that was strictly for laymen, and while I think it would be more doctrinally prudent to have the movement directed from here in the Curia, I can also see some political prudence in having it under the control of laymen. If it succeeds, we can take much of the credit; if it fails we can blame amateurs."

"Of course," Bisset rejoined, "he speaks of this as a lay movement. But do you think he will really get enough volunteers? I doubt it, and I suspect that His Holiness has doubts as well. Yesterday he had a two-hour audience with the 'Black Pope.' The ruler of the Jesuits is always a dangerous man—this one, who thinks himself a servant, more so than most. Mark my words, he'll soon persuade the

Pontiff to use Jesuits to flesh out lay ranks, and then other orders will have to be called on."

Chelli sipped that dreadful Sicilian white wine. "Perhaps, but I think that you are both underestimating this man. I don't believe that he would have suggested the plan if he did not think there would be more than enough volunteers. Declan Walsh sometimes appears to be precipitate, but I think that his apparently hasty actions have almost all been carefully considered and staged to look like instant judgments. For reasons probably known only to God and his psychiatrist, he likes to create a shadow image of himself."

"Speaking of shadow images," Bisset added, "I have heard he said in private that he chose the name Francesco to signify a blending of the simplicity of San Francesco of Assisi with the zeal of San Francesco Xavier."

"That would fit," Chelli nodded. " 'Zealous simplicity' is the theme of Christian virtue he would like to strike, and you have undoubtedly noted—it is no coincidence—his selection of the Franciscans and the Jesuits to lead the spiritual renewal. Again Assisi and Xavier."

LaTorre only groaned and pushed his plate away. "The two of you are spoiling my digestion."

"Incidentally," Chelli went on, "I agree that the crowd at the coronation was confused, but that was an Italian crowd, a Roman crowd. Here in the Vatican we are often more taken with pomp and spectacle than we are impressed with papal rhetoric. After all, we have written too much of that ourselves. When he leaves Rome to preach his crusade—and I am sure he will, for he loves the melodramatic touch as much as Verdi or Puccini ever did—the problems are likely to be only financial and logistical. I expect we'll face a tidal wave of volunteers who will have to be fed, clothed, housed, trained, and transported. I do not look forward to paying the bills."

"Alors," Bisset told, "if wiping out poverty rather than saving souls becomes the main aim of the Church, then artificial birth control is as inevitable as it is logical. If he converts the concern of the Church from the next world to this one, then holy purity will become redundant."

"Yet, to be fair to the man," Chelli intervened, "he said that he wanted more than a crusade to wipe out poverty. After all, as he himself said to us in private, Lyndon Johnson tried that and ended up fighting a war in Vietnam.

What he says he wants is a crusade to show man's love of God in the only way he can truly express that love, by helping his fellow man."

"Do you honestly believe," Bisset asked, "that he can go beyond a war against the physical aspects of poverty? The man has no theological training, no experience in spiritual affairs, and none in dealing with our good bishops. When he speaks of a spiritual renewal within the Church, he becomes very vague. When he speaks of the bishops and priests of Latin America preaching social justice to the laity and working as partners with the laity, he becomes very foolish. God knows my Congregation for the Clergy has had its troubles with guerrilla priests, but can you imagine trying to persuade some of those Latin American prelates even to listen to, much less preach, concern for social justice? At times even I have sympathized with the guerrilla priests when I have dealt with their bishops. They have sorely tempted me to violence at a distance of 8,000 kilometers."

"What makes you think those prelates will remain in power?" Chelli asked. "The red hats for the archbishops of Recife and San Carlos were clear signals of change. I would put credence in the rumors that our Argentine friend Martìn will be the next prefect of the Congregation for Bishops."

"Mon Dieu," Bisset moaned.

"I repeat," Chelli continued, "do not underestimate this man."

LaTorre lifted one of the huge oranges and tore the skin off with a single powerful and complex set of twists. "I sympathize with the political opinions of these new members of the sacred college, but I know nothing of their theological views. Are they sound?"

"Simple, if not sound," Chelli answered. "They speak like our Pontiff: love thy neighbor; do justice to one's fellow man; and leave theologizing to those who have nothing better to do with their time. They're pastors and, within narrow limits, good ones. I doubt they could ever become theologians, good or bad."

"Be that as it may," Bisset persisted, "I predict that this American will soon be trying to change our teaching on birth control."

Seeing that the others had finished their meal, Chelli

paused to light his cigar before answering. "I wonder," he mused, "whether that change should not have been made during the closing stages of Vatican II or thereafter when Paul VI took the matter to his own bosom."

"You speak heresy," LaTorre spoke sharply. "You know our traditional teaching."

"There is no infallible doctrine on birth control. Besides," Chelli smiled, "do you recall the draft of the encyclical *Humanae Vitae* which the Holy Office prepared? Not the draft that was published and strictly reaffirmed the ban on 'artificial' methods of birth control, but the one that the Holy Office's own theologians prepared. Remember, the Holy Office draft practically—not quite, but practically—said that while birth control raises serious moral questions, they are best resolved by prayer and consultation with one's confessor."

"Well," LaTorre sputtered, "that was before I became prefect. Sometimes a few young *monsignori* exert more influence than they should. But what counts is the final version, the one that *il Papa* issued—"

"The one that was redrafted in the secretary of state's office, where His Eminence Cardinal Bisset was, as Monsignor Bisset, working at the time," Chelli jibed.

"—the one that condemned artificial means of birth control," LaTorre continued, ignoring his younger colleague. "The magisterium of the Church does not encompass what every group of theologians says"—and here LaTorre was forced to smile—"even if they work for the Holy Office."

"True, but the point is also that the Pope's own advisory commission of clerics and laymen urged a change at least in application. You and I remember the hours we spent arguing against the majority position. Then the Holy Office prepared a draft of a softened position. But some of us—and you and I were among them—prevailed on Paul to stand fast. Sometimes I wonder if we—you and I—advised unwisely."

"We were right then and we are right today," LaTorre insisted.

"I hope so, Your Eminence," Chelli said. "I would hate to face God if I thought that we were wrong. Sometimes, however, I wonder how I would have advised His Holiness if I could have seen a logically—and theologically—defensible stopping place between artificial birth control and sexual license. Once one concedes that sexual relations may be divorced from the propagation of the human species, I do not know how one can stop short of admitting the legitimacy of couples living together outside of matrimony or even of those so-called homosexual marriages."

"Of course," Bisset agreed, "once you start down that road, there is no turn before Roman orgies and no end but total corruption and eternal damnation."

"I do not know," Chelli told, "I honestly do not know where or how to draw a line between the legitimate sexual pleasure involved in propagating the race and complete license. Yet I fear that the official position of the Church on birth control will change, if not under this Pope, then the next. We are already several Pontiffs removed from Paul and his anguish. I cannot help wondering if we might not have been more prudent to effect a change when the power to do so and to control that change was in our hands."

LaTorre was aghast. "Why do you say such a thing?" he sputtered. "Do you know something about this new Pope?"

"No, I am not thinking specifically about this Pontiff. I am simply impressed by the fact that so many of our brethren in the clergy, many theologians but far more pastors, disagree with *Humanae Vitae*. Most of those people are not radicals, but intelligent and holy men."

"I doubt that evaluation," Bisset sneered. "By definition they cannot oppose *Humanae Vitae* without being either stupid or sinful—and in many cases, they are Americans and thus both."

Chelli commenced to respond, but LaTorre spoke first. "Our task is to insure that that change and others like it do not come during our stewardship of Christ's Church. I think we must dig our heels in and fight him for every centimeter. Keep him from touching issues like birth control, celibacy, and the doctrine of the Holy Eucharist."

Bisset pursed his lips thoughtfully. "I believe, my dear 'Vanni," he said slowly, "that more subtle means are appropriate. He says he needs us. He does, if he wants to run the Church or to think he runs the Church. We should listen to him, consult with him, and then do as we in the

Vatican have done with every Pontiff—do what we think is right."

"It's not going to be that easy," Chelli riposted. "This man is a little more subtle and much more shrewd than he seems, and that easy smile—"

"That insipid American grin," Bisset interrupted.

"—that smile," Chelli continued, "unless I am badly mistaken, hides a streak of ruthlessness. He had a long career in politics before going to a monastery. If we fight him in the ways either of you suggests, he will throw us out, all together or separately, and put men like Gordenker in our places. If we ignore him, he'll soon ignore us; he's shrewd enough to find ways to run the Church without us, at least without us three. I have no doubt that under any circumstances, this man is likely to form a clique of 'dependable' advisers and make most decisions through informal consultation rather than through more formal machinery."

"*Ecco,* what do you suggest we do then? Resign and go home to become curates in Protestant parishes?" LaTorre asked bitterly.

"No, although he may dismiss us and solve that problem for us," Chelli smiled. "I suggest loyalty. I am moderately optimistic, not overly so, but moderately. I have been reading about his Supreme Court and the way he directed it. He ran it well, so he'll probably try the same approach here. He listened to others and did not ignore them. As a leader, he sought consensus, depending on reason to bring men together, to find common ground on which opponents could agree, issues on which they could compromise and so forth. He would typically try to persuade liberal judges to write opinions in cases that reached conservative results, and conservative judges to write when the result was liberal. A man like that is not apt to appoint a Curia composed only of our brothers who call themselves servants. Since the appearance of unity is important to him, most of us will keep our jobs and thus our power to protect the Church. And, if we do not openly oppose him in the beginning on the small things, if we give him our wholehearted support when he deserves it, if we oppose him to his face on matters of principle when we think he is wrong, but explain carefully why we do so, he is likely to trust us and to respect our judgment on the issues on which he does not consider himself an expert—and, of course, those areas of ignorance could include theology."

"Suppose," Bisset offered, "just suppose he did not respect our judgment on a moral issue but instead listened to the abbot or to Gordenker and his radical friends?"

"I think if we behave wisely," Chelli replied, "he will consult with us and, if we argue well, go along with us. At the very least he will respect us, cooperate with us, and compromise with us, and so minimize any damage. If he begins to issue decrees that endanger faith or morals, we have other alternatives open."

"Such as?" LaTorre asked.

"Such as a very wide range," Chelli said drily. "I suggest we consider some, just in case, of course."

"A heresy trial might be one," Bisset told. "A heresy trial for a Pope would be a terrible thing, but then it is not totally without precedent in the history of the Church. The idea has a certain appeal."

"That is a possibility," Chelli admitted, "but I would hope that we would never need to face that issue. More immediately, I suggest less traumatic tactics to avoid a direct confrontation."

"Perhaps," Bisset spoke in his most sardonic mode, "we might offer a novena that the Almighty would soon see fit to call His Holiness to His bosom."

"What I had in mind," Chelli explained, "was that we take advantage of his personality and style of operations."

"Namely?" LaTorre asked.

"Most fundamentally," Chelli explained, "he's an American politician. A few years in a monastery cannot change that. He's shrewd, even very intelligent, but he has that naive American belief that if he gives a little something to everybody, everybody will be happy and work together. He is not accustomed to dealing with immutable principles. He will be willing to compromise on most of his ideas, and we, in turn, must be willing to compromise on details. But on matters of principle we must stand firm, and not be argued, bargained, or bullied into submission. On the other hand, we can't just stubbornly dig our heels in and say no to everything. We'll have to give in where principle is not involved, and when we stand firm to give carefully reasoned explanations for our positions."

"That, of course," Bisset said, "is our life-style: cool logic and sweet reason."

"Second," Chelli continued, "he likes to make decisions himself and to feel as if he's running an organization. I recall when he was here in Rome that we always dealt directly with him, not with his two staff members. We saw a bit of that in the Spanish affair recently, and on his Court only two other chief justices personally wrote as large a proportion of the Court's opinions as he did. These two traits go together with a third: his sense of fairness requires him to consult. I'm optimistic because I see a way of slowing him down, perhaps even of controlling him. We must be prepared to reason, to argue, and to stand firm on principle while giving in on details. At the same time, we must indulge him his compulsion to make decisions."

"Aah, yes," Bisset intervened, "we in the Holy See have long been aware that an idle Pontiff's mind is the devil's workshop."

"Exactly," Chelli agreed. "I am sure that each of us can discover a whole series of knotty problems with which only *il Papa* himself can cope. For myself, I am finding it necessary to go into great detail on my budgetary review. Certainly the Pontiff must take a major part in these processes. Next week a group of central bankers from the countries of the European Common Market are meeting in Rome. I know that they will want an audience and would like to hear a message from Papa Francesco, one that he should draft himself, dealing with central banking and social justice. I am equally certain that there are many other problems concerning the clergy and the faith that demand His Holiness's personal attention. Naturally, he will first need to read lengthy and thorough reports so that he can understand these problems.

"If we do our work well," Chelli concluded, "and offer him reasoned arguments, he will soon become trusting of us. Moreover, he will have little excess energy to devote to mischief. We have a sacred duty to help this intelligent, well-meaning, but uninformed man to find the right path."

"As His Eminence Cardinal Greene would say, 'Just so.' "

"And thus will the papacy control the Pontiff?" Bisset asked.

FOURTEEN

I LOOK BACK on the next few months as the busiest of my life and the happiest since my childhood. My disease remained in a state of remission, but my energy was severely taxed as Francesco turned the palazzo into a maelstrom. It was like living in a gigantic American clothes dryer. Events and people were constantly tumbling around us, or we around them; there was a pulsing exhilaration of movement, even of progress, although never enough to be pleasing to Francesco. He was constantly frustrated by what he felt was the slowness with which the Vatican responded to his ideas. Later I shall explain you something about the mode in which Francesco labored and how in some measure he contributed to his own frustration in this regard.

He expected an old lady like the Vatican to react instantly to his commands. But as he was to be reminded almost every day, there one thinks in terms of centuries rather than minutes, as was Francesco's custom. Part of the problem was that my brethren, as we say, put on feet of lead; but, according to me, that was more of an aggravating than a causal factor. *Ecco,* it is easier to make lightning from a serene sky than, at a stroke, to create institutional machinery to operate a gigantic crusade and spiritual renewal, especially while one is trying to restaff and, to some extent, reform the fundamental institutions of the Curia itself.

My impression, unlike Francesco's, was of progress that was, by Vatican standards, swift. Now, after several years, it is difficult for me to sort out the precise chronology of those exciting days. Everything was happening simultaneously. Thus I must warn you that my recollections may be out of order, and I know that I have forgotten much that is important.

Those were the days of the creation of the first concrete plans for the crusade, for the spiritual renewal, for restaffing the Curia, and for Francesco to learn the modes of the Holy See while executing the routine but important tasks of the papacy—and for him to cope with Chelli's tactic of forwarding snowstorms of requests for personal papal attention.

It was a time of action and excitement. The abbot first presented us with new ideas, and then blueprints, and then budgets. Pritchett, Gordenker, and Martìn made several visits to discuss men to take over command of the various offices of the Curia and to plan for a coming session of the World Synod of Bishops. LaTorre, Chelli, and a bevy of other cardinals had regularly scheduled appointments, and the secretary of state's office channeled huge sheafs of paper to us. But Francesco's energy was nothing if not amazing, and so was his knowledge. His patience was sometimes short, but his humor was generally good.

The affair of Chelli's international bankers makes an excellent example of how active Francesco was. Chelli had transmitted to us a request for an audience and some remarks by *il Papa* himself, reminding us that bankers might be useful if we needed money for the crusade—which, assuredly, we did. Francesco agreed immediately. His reaction was rapid and direct. He telephoned an old friend who was a professor of economics at Yale, explained the problem, and asked for a draft allocution, with as much empirical data as could be squeezed in on the need for reform in international banking practices. "I want," he said, "to sear their consciences and show them the way to heaven—in their own language. I'll have a man from the apostolic delegate's office pick up the draft from you and put it in the diplomatic pouch so that it'll be here within a day of its completion."

Ten days later Francesco gave the bankers a thirty-minute audience. According to me, Chelli was as astounded as the bankers when they heard a learned allocution, full of economic jargon that I could not fathom and several equations that I could not even decipher. But most of all, Francesco told them of their sins in a style that they could not ignore. His talk was a *capriccioso* of economic erudition, the Sermon on the Mount, and San Giovanni's—John the Baptist's—call to repent. *Il Papa* even listed four ways in which procedures and substantive rules could be changed to protect not merely the poor nations but also the ordinary citizens of all nations. Like a good professor, he reserved ten minutes for questions. No one dared raise his hand. I have never had much hope of saving bankers' souls, but this group did not leave Roma with tranquil consciences.

That was a virtuoso performance, and it could not be repeated every day or even every week. But that sort of thing happened often enough to create a vast aura of respect. There were dozens of other, more routine, matters that demanded the attention of *il Papa*—letters to retiring cardinals and bishops, condolences to families and flocks of deceased prelates, or to countries whose heads of state died, encouragement to members of the hierarchy, congratulations to clergy and famous laymen celebrating birthdays or anniversaries, appearances at the palazzo window at noon on Sundays and holidays (of which we have a plethora in Italy), audiences for ambassadors accredited to the Holy See, for nuncios returning from missions, and for bishops making their annual or biennial visit~ to Roma (and leaving gifts as token acknowledgments of the primacy of San Pietro and his successors). Other demands on his time included occasions such as the annual blessing of the troops of the garrison of Roma, the pilgrimage of the Austrian Union of Catholic Families, the sessions of the General Chapter of the Claretian Fathers, conventions of the International Civil Aviation Organization, the International Association of the Charities of San Vincenzo de' Paoli, and on and on and on. At each of these audiences, the Holy Father was expected to give a brief homily.

At first, Francesco permitted the office of the secretary of state or the appropriate curial congregation to draft the letters, messages, and homilies, but after reading the first two or three in appalled silence, he telephoned the cardinal archbishop of Dublin and asked to borrow a young priest, Conor K. Cavanaugh, who was a lecturer in literature at University College, Dublin. *Il Papa* had met Father Cavanaugh some years earlier and had been impressed with the Irishman's wit. Francesco remembered that the young priest had a reputation for tossing off quick quips in Latin. After Monsignor—under the circumstances, how could he remain a mere priest?—Cavanaugh arrived, Francesco's letters assumed a tone that made LaTorre wince. According to me, joy is not out of place in Christ's Church, but I concede that occasionally there was more levity in Francesco's correspondence than was proper, for the psychological reasons I earlier told.

The allocutions never ceased to surprise me. Franc— asked that he be given a schedule about ten days in advance. For most audiences he rarely, to my knowledge, prepared a word. His meeting with the central bankers' association, when he thought it necessary to use specialized knowledge, was an exception. Generally he would simply walk into the room, offer his ring to be kissed, shake a few hands, then speak for five or ten minutes, linking his spiritual renewal or crusade to the labors of the particular group, and returning always to the theme of social justice.

Ecco, like everyone else who saw him leap from a conference with a cardinal and stride, without notes or visible preparation, to speak to a group, the fear of what he might inadvertently say gave me nerves. I remember LaTorre's once asking him as we all but ran down the corridors, "What will Your Holiness say to the International Theological Commission?"

"We do not yet know," Francesco replied, "but something will come to us. It always does. Don't worry, the Holy Spirit still has thirty seconds."

That *something* always did come, usually not eloquent by the rotund standards of expected papal piety, but there was often an elegant simplicity.

Because of my many duties—I frequently did not know what tasks Francesco had assigned to me until I appeared at the palazzo at eight in the morning—I could not follow all that was happening. Permit me to interrupt myself to tell that during this period I grew closely acquainted with Signora Falconi. I had met her once in Washington. It was she who often transmitted *il Papa*'s requests to me. You recall that Mr. Keller had escorted her to Roma for the coronation. (Francesco must have spoken to her earlier by telephone, for she came prepared to stay and quickly settled in an old apartment on the Via Giulia, not too distant from the Vatican.)

I found her interesting, of course, because her parents were from Trento, which is near the head of my lake here, not seventy kilometers away. Naturally, her Italian had the proper accent, and while—you say rusty?—while rusty when she first arrived, it soon became expert. In all, she was a remarkable woman, efficient as well as handsome. Outwardly she was one of those authoritarian females whom males instinctively dislike. I could smile at her ability to make *monsignori* jump. But that was only her professional mask. Once that protective cover was removed, there lived a charming person, both extremely intelligent and extremely feminine.

I had a vague recollection that Kate had disliked her, and I could understand how a wife could be jealous of her—though let me say immediately that I saw no evidence of any illicit relation between her and Francesco. In fact, Monsignor Bonetti was also quite jealous of her. *Il Papa* gave him more than enough to keep a dozen men busy, but it was not the close relationship he had enjoyed with the late Pontiff. It was now the *signora* who anticipated *il Papa*'s wants. Like Mr. Keller, she was absolutely devoted to Francesco. His work was her life, and she handled that work with skill, energy, and, unlike Francesco himself, with neatness. Soon she knew where virtually every piece of paper in the Vatican was located, while his desk remained constantly what you call a shambles.

I have seen such situations before, situations where several people will do anything for a particular person who, in return, appears to offer nothing except the chance to be helped again and again. It is, according to me, not only the magnetic personality of the taker that is important, but also the intrinsic worth of the things for which he asks help. The givers sense that they are participating in a great work and draw satisfaction from that. Surely Francesco offered little else, other than more hard work, for he drove those around him almost as relentlessly as he drove himself.

As I told, I could not follow all the meetings between *il Papa* and the abbot on the crusade, but I could view the outlines of an organization assuming shape by the way various people paraded in and out of the palazzo—several Latin American businessmen, a former Chilean minister of agriculture, a former minister of finance of the Irish government who now operated a chain of hotels, an American layman who was the president of a charter airline, a Canadian physician who was *direttore* of a large hospital in Montreal, the dean of the University of Chicago's School of Business, a retired Italian-American *monsignore* named Ligutti, who had labored for decades on agricultural problems in the American Midwest, had helped feed the hungry in Europe after World War II, and then had served as the liaison between the Vatican and the UN's Food and Agricultural Organization. (We call it FAO in Italy and pronounce those initials as a word.)

I remember well one conversation that *il Papa* conducted with the Prefecture of Economic Affairs. The members, as I have said, were LaTorre, Bisset, and Greene, with Chelli as president. The abbot and I were present. It was one of the first meetings that we held in the Pontiff's redecorated studio in the palazzo.

He and Signora Falconi had made the plans themselves. They had left the magnificent marble floors untouched, and, despite Signora Falconi's wishes, the ornate ceiling and the frescoes high on the walls. But the drapes were now a plain, heavy white, and all the paintings and oriental rugs of the former Pontiffs were gone. The only mark of the old regimes was the sixteenth-century illuminated Bible that now rested on its own stand by the wall nearer the piazza. According to me, the room was too stark, despite the ceiling and the frescoes. El Greco's small painting of the Redeemer had been placed on the wall behind *il Papa*'s desk, but Greco only emphasized the starkness.

That desk, I should explain, was a massive, horseshoe-shaped structure. In reality, it was three desks of dark Spanish wood joined together. On the inside its various drawers held a complex of telephones (American-made rather than Italian), dictating equipment, and even an electric typewriter. The chair was the same big black leather *poltrona* that *il Papa* had used when he was chief justice. From the wall facing the Pontiff's desk hung Francesco Nagni's modernistic sculpture of the crucified Christ; the cross itself was not visible, only the outstretched Savior. On a Spanish table to the right of *il Papa*'s desk, on the side away from the piazza, was Francesco Messina's sculpture of Giovanni the Baptist (removed from its holy water font). Both of these pieces had been taken from the Room of the Sculptors in the palazzo, and I found each a little strange—perhaps cold would be more precise.

I preferred the warmth of Renaissance paintings, but I confess that I could sense the raging strength of San Giovanni in Messina's work and the agony of Christ (and thus of all of us) in Nagni's sculpture. El Greco has never appealed to me, nor, in truth, has San Giovanni. Mystics do not please me. At one time I thought it peculiar that a supposed pragmatist like Declan Walsh could have argued heatedly that the greatest collection of art in the world was located in the sacristy of the cathedral in Toledo—a dozen or so small paintings by El Greco. That taste seems less incongruous from this perspective.

The remaining walls of *il Papa*'s studio were bare and white. Francesco and Signora Falconi had viewed this room as a working studio and planned to install bookshelves later, after the *casina* of Pio IV had been refurbished and they could decide what would be most useful to situate in either location. (I should also explain that despite its official designation as papal library, most Pontiffs have maintained few books in the studio, and those that have been here have usually been housed in massive, glass-enclosed cases.)

About three meters in front of *il Papa*'s desk was a heavy, dark conference table—it, too, was Spanish—that could comfortably seat ten people. The chairs were smaller models of *il Papa*'s high-backed *poltrona*. In the far corner to the left of a person sitting at the desk, near a window overlooking the piazza, were a maroon sofa and three smallish blue *poltrone* clustered around a small coffee table. Under that table was a black and grey Andalusian fur rug. The table itself was a thick sheet of curved glass resting on dark wooden feet designed by the same Spaniard who had fashioned the desks and the conference table.

Il Papa and the other six of us were seated around that table, examining copies of the document that Monsignor Bonetti had placed before us. *Ecco,* it was a single sheet of paper with several sets of figures. At the Pontiff's request, the abbot explained that the figures were a proposed budget for the first year of the crusade—a sum of $125 million.

LaTorre, Greene, and Bisset said nothing. Bisset, I believe, thought it useless to talk to a man who would at any moment be struck down by lightning. And because Bisset as well as LaTorre were yet convinced that the abbot was a heretic, neither would address him. Chelli, however, probed around the edges of the document. "Do you see this as an abnormally large budget because it covers the first year?" he asked.

"No, Your Eminence," the abbot replied. "I do not. In fact, this budget is probably abnormally low. It is based on the assumptions that we process no more than six thousand volunteers that year, that we operate in only three countries (I have recommended Panama, Peru, and Bolivia), that American and European drug companies donate almost all medical supplies and equipment that we need —FAO will give some food, seed, fertilizer, and expertise —and finally that John Carpentar's airline will fly our volunteers so that our traveling expenses can be kept down.

"We're also planning to make maximum possible use of church facilities such as convents, seminaries, and similar buildings that are not being fully utilized. How effectively we can use these will depend on negotiations with local bishops. I have dealt with some of those reverend gentlemen on other occasions, and I believe we shall have to apply some pressure from the Curia, perhaps even from the Pope himself."

Bisset smirked at this remark.

"That, Eminence," the abbot concluded, "is a long way around your question. The short answer is that when we expand our operations—and as inflation continues—our budget will go up."

"Or the operation will collapse?" Chelli asked.

"Retrench, at least," Francesco intervened. "Cardinal Chelli, how much can be raised from our own resources?"

"That depends, Holiness. If we used only our surplus —that is, money that we are not planning to allocate for other uses—very little. By using all our contingency funds, cutting back elsewhere—such as our emergency relief efforts in West Africa—and spending the money we would normally reinvest to keep ahead of inflation, we could certainly put up one-fifth of what the abbot has asked, perhaps even as high as one-fourth. Of course, we could finance everything for several years, but at the price of total bankruptcy."

"Incredible," Bisset told. "Holiness, how can we even think about throwing away the patrimony of the Holy See in such a fashion? This is not our work."

"Feeding the hungry, tending to the sick, caring for the widow and orphan—those are our tasks."

"But," Bisset persisted, "we are doing those things now, as His Holiness well knows. We are sending food and medicine to those infidel Indian ingrates who spend thousands of millions of francs on atomic weapons while weeping to us that they are too poor to cope with cholera, smallpox, and famine. Perhaps we can do better. That is always possible. But full implementation of the abbot's plan would destroy our ability to do anything to help other people, certainly for a generation, perhaps for a century."

"Not necessarily, Your Eminence," Francesco replied. "You must have more faith in God's bounty. I have said before that our task is to do what is right; supplying the money is God's concern, not ours. You may be aware, speaking of God's bounty, that I have talked with several extremely wealthy men. It is possible that I can persuade them and others to put up a large share of the cost of the crusade. Who knows what other gifts God will provide? He may soften the hearts and loosen the purses of governments. I would hope that after we start in Latin America we could persuade the United Nations to take over much of the cost. But first we'll have to prove that in fact we are conducting a nondenominational effort. Still, the Church must begin this crusade. Others lack the will, even though they have the means."

Bisset told nothing further, but his face showed scorn. LaTorre and Greene were obviously dismayed but silent. Chelli betrayed no emotion whatever.

Allora, Francesco looked around the table. I am secure that he read the faces as I did. "I would like several items from you gentlemen. I need a reasonably concise memorandum setting out ways of amassing funds along the lines that Cardinal Chelli has just outlined: full support, minimal support from surplus funds, and something in between. I need to talk in very specific terms to some of our potential donors, and the sooner the better.

"Abbot Pryce has mentioned his assumptions about our beginning in three countries in Latin America. For the moment, let us assume no more than three. The question then becomes which three. Each of you here has some expertise. I do not want snap judgments. I would appreciate it, Cardinal LaTorre, if as secretary of state you would have your office prepare a set of recommendations for us on this issue. I am particularly interested in what you four people think, but I want to have the views of all relevant curial departments. To save time, I have asked Cardinal Galeotti, who tomorrow is attending in our name a meeting of the Pontifical Commission on Latin America, to ask for opinions from the commission and to have them sent to the secretary of state's office."

LaTorre nodded solemnly. Coordination was not one of his strengths, but, as I said, it was one of the principal tasks of the secretary of state.

"Now," Francesco went on, "let me pick your brains on a related matter. As you know, the regular session of the World Synod of Bishops is scheduled to meet in late September. I have been thinking of calling, later in the fall, a special session restricted to the bishops of Latin America in addition to those prelates who by the synod's constitution have a right to attend all sessions. What I would like is to hear your ideas—and to read your thoughts—on specific topics for the bishops to discuss in that special session, in light of the spiritual renewal and the crusade. One immediate item: Should the bishops meet here in Rome or would it be more effective, and symbolic of what we are trying to accomplish, if we met in Latin America? If so, where?"

"Holiness," LaTorre spoke, "I understand that you want a spiritual renewal, but even after our first meeting before the coronation, I do not understand precisely what you have in mind. You have spoken about a reinvigoration of the hierarchy that will infect the laity, and you have talked about the laity and the clergy working together. What are the concrete steps that Your Holiness has in mind?"

"To be honest," Francesco smiled, "I am not precisely sure how I intend that we—cardinals and bishops and priests—should accomplish this goal. I have been talking to the Jesuits, as you may know, about organizing a series of retreats for bishops. I want to involve the Franciscans as well. I think the combination of the zeal and intellect of the Jesuits with the simplicity of the Franciscans would provide just the right match of elements."

Bisset could barely restrain himself from sneering. I confess that the thought of the Jesuits and Franciscans laboring together had never occurred to me—and probably had never occurred to a Franciscan. Certainly a Jesuit would never have even considered it when sober.

"What suggestions do you have?" Francesco asked LaTorre.

"I had thought, Holiness, of an encyclical that would warn the bishops about the recurring dangers of modernism that have arisen in the wake of Vatican II, an encyclical that would remind bishops of their duties to maintain the integrity of the faith and to preach the danger of carnal temptations and the necessity of avoiding occasions of sin—"

"And encourage revival of devotion to Mary, don't you think?" Greene added.

"In short," LaTorre continued, "a new *Syllabus of Errors* and, of course, as His Holiness has indicated, a restatement of what recent Pontiffs have said on matters of social justice. I see a document around which the hierarchy and all the clergy might rally as a bulwark against communism and fascism outside the Church and against modernism within our own ranks."

Francesco listened to LaTorre without changing expression. He even made a few notes on the paper in front of him, although I do not know if they related to what LaTorre was telling.

"Thank you, Eminence. Cardinal Bisset?"

"I tend to agree with His Eminence. Perhaps in a memorandum I might make some specific suggestions." (*Senta,* from experience I knew that such a memorandum was not likely to materialize. Bisset was not a man to commit himself.)

"Thank you. Please do. Cardinal Greene?"

"Just so, Holiness. I would urge that we bring Mary back to the Church. The people of Christ need her. That return would reopen old paths as well as create new ones to heaven for our people."

"Cardinal Chelli?"

Chelli placed his hands together so that the tips of his long fingers touched each other. He nervously tapped them together. "Holiness, my differences with my brethren are more a matter of emphasis than substance. While the world needs to be convicted of sin periodically, I believe that one should proceed more positively at this time. The retreats seem an excellent idea if—and the *if* is vital—they are conducted to give true spiritual nourishment. I would hope that Your Holiness might consider whether or not the Dominicans would be a more appropriate order to conduct such retreats. With due respect to the Jesuits, they have in recent years become too worldly for spiritual undertakings, and the Franciscans have never been noted for the cultivation of that intellectual power so necessary when one is dealing with trained theologians and experienced pastors."

"I agree to some extent," Francesco responded. "That is why I am arranging for the two orders, the Jesuits and the Franciscans, to work together. I believe either alone would not be fit for the task I have in mind. But if we can combine the Franciscans' simplicity of spirit with the Jesuits' prudence and zeal, we shall have the ideal instrument. Of course, as with all hybrids, we shall have to wait for the birth to see how well our genetic tampering has worked."

Chelli looked a bit perplexed—LaTorre, Bisset, and Greene seemed utterly confused—but the young cardinal went on. "Holiness, I would hope that these retreats—by whomever run—could restore faith in the traditional machinery and processes of the Church. An encyclical would, without doubt, also be a good thing, but only if it stressed the vitality of our traditional doctrine and its relevance to the modern world. I would think it wiser to emphasize the positive than to list the errors, however numerous and serious they may be."

"What would you think," Francesco asked, shifting the point slightly, "of inviting bishops to a series of regional synods on their own continents and going myself to attend and address these meetings?"

We could all see the implications. Distant from Roma and liberated from the Curia, *il Papa* would have direct contact with local bishops, able to discern what he and the local bishops—not curial officials—wanted to discuss without the mediating influence of the cardinal prefects and their staffs.

"No, Holiness," LaTorre blurted out. "Such trips would leave you too physically and emotionally exhausted to take proper care of the other affairs of the Church. There is also the danger that, fatigued after one of these journeys, the Pontiff, like any other human being, would say something that would be badly, perhaps disastrously, misinterpreted."

Greene nodded agreement. Bisset put on his bored expression, one appropriate for use on a child who has made a foolish suggestion about how to enjoy the afternoon. Francesco looked at Chelli.

"I think His Eminence is correct," Chelli told, "but for

a different reason. The Pontiff must remain aloof, above the struggle of contending factions within the Church. He must direct all of these people, allow them to debate, even to argue, but he must stand above that struggle so he can intervene at the proper moment to set the right course. If he becomes involved in the debate himself, or even if he gets too close to that debate, he may well lose his perspective.

"There is a second reason," Chelli went on, delivering a sermon in which I heartily concurred. "Papal power is basically charismatic in the classic sense of that word; the Pontiff is touched with grace. There is a mystique about his office and his person that is absolutely essential to his authority—and so to the authority of the Church. The Pontiff should not come to the bishops, but the bishops to the Pope. If a Pontiff were to travel often and extensively, he might damage his mystique through overexposure. With all deference to His Holiness, we here all know that none of us has all answers to all problems. Yet much of the authority of men like Pius XI and Pius XII was rooted in the fact that their aloofness gave the impression of wisdom. Pope John meant well, but he admitted his humanity. The reaction to Vatican II and its tendency toward theological and moral anarchy are obvious results. We cannot blame all of these events on John's lowering the veil so that all might see his human face, but that lowering played an important role in breaking the unity of the Church and lessening the power of the Pope. I fear I have talked too long."

"No, what you say interests me. You have given an excellent lecture on the *realpolitik* of the Vatican." Francesco looked at his watch. "We shall keep all your suggestions in mind. Please send us any others you have or any additional reasons for the ones that you have advanced. Now, we must adjourn this meeting so that we can have an audience with another potential benefactor."

FIFTEEN

THAT SUMMER, instead of following the papal custom of enjoying several months at Castel Gandolfo to escape the heat of Roma, we went there to live for only a few weeks toward the end of July. Francesco, the abbot, Signora Falconi, Monsignor Bonetti, and I spent long hours working in the offices overlooking the lovely lake or in the gardens during the day. (As usual, workmen had placed a sea of huge canopies over parts of the gardens so that we might have shade.)

Daylight hours in the Alban hills are warm but dry, and nights delightfully cool. The trout from the lake are exquisite, and the village of Frascati is so close that the wine does not suffer much from traveling, or whatever it is that makes it mediocre in Roma. I must confess, however, that I ordered the steward to purchase mostly Trebbiano grown at Aprilia, which is also nearby. While none of the wine from the vicinity of Roma can claim greatness, I have a slight preference for the Trebbiano grape's yield at Aprilia over Frascati, unless, of course, LaTorre were to offer some of his special stock.

In contrast to the pleasant weather of Castel Gandolfo, Roman summers are hot, noisy, and full of pollution from tour buses disgorging hundreds of thousands of people into the Piazza di San Pietro and from the exhausts of the Vespas of the *scippatori,* the motor scooter-mounted purse snatchers who descend on tourists like flies on raw meat, happy to relieve them of the burden of carrying money and passports around the Eternal City.

To move us to Castel Gandolfo and to try to keep us there, I reminded Papa Francesco of these unpleasant facts. Once we found ourselves there, I also argued that we seemed to be accomplishing a great deal of work. I even played on Francesco's sympathy by pointing out that the people in the village of Castel Gandolfo depended on heavy tourist traffic during the summer to survive the long winters; and without *il Papa* there would be no tourists. Still, Francesco would not remain. He proffered the thin excuse that he wanted to spur the renovation of the *casina* of Pio IV, which, like all else in a Roman summer except tourism and the *scippatori,* languished.

According to me, the real motive for our return was that *il Papa* was a compulsive worker. In fact, he was addicted to work. For the first time I truly understood what he had been trying to explain me at the Trappist monastery. I now understood why he had never known peace. In Italy we would say that to him a problem was not merely an intellectual challenge but a threat to his *virilità.* That is a true malady of the spirit. Certainly God did not create all the beauty of the world if He did not want us to enjoy those vistas. But Papa Francesco labored day and night and without ever stepping back to take pleasure in an accomplishment. For him, as soon as one task was done, there arose another challenge—or threat—that he felt compelled to conquer. And, there was always another such challenge, and always another behind that other.

Before I said my morning Mass I would see him walking along the side of the Castel that faced the lake, brooding; when I extinguished my light at midnight I could usually see him in the garden, framed by the four American torches that repelled insects, scribbling on a yellow notepad or dictating into a portable German register—how do you say? —tape recorder. According to me, he enjoyed Castel Gandolfo, but something in him told that he was not in fact laboring unless he was experiencing discomfort.

The work was coming more slowly than Francesco planned, but, as I have said, very rapidly for the Vatican. One phase was finished. At the Castel in very early August we had our final conferences with Cardinals Martìn, Pritchett, and Gordenker about new curial appointments. We had even talked at some length with LaTorre and Chelli. Although Francesco respected Chelli highly, he did not care, in a substantive sense, what LaTorre thought. On the other hand, *il Papa* understood the affection in which LaTorre was held by the cardinals in the Curia. I am not secure that I ever persuaded the Pontiff that LaTorre also possessed many talents that were precious—a trained intellect, a vast store of learning as well as practical knowledge about the operations of the Holy See, and, not least, a total devotion to the Church.

Allora, Francesco assured LaTorre in a private conversation that Paolo Cardinal Fieschi would be the next secretary of state, and that news delighted the Holy Mule. Francesco added a touch that could have been meant either as diplomacy or a subtle, ironic pricking. (I often did not know what was transpiring in his mind; Signora Falconi could usually tell, and I remember that when she was alive Kate could read those shades of meaning even when neither the intonation of his voice nor his facial expression changed. I could only occasionally catch a glimpse of something flickering across his grey eyes.) In this case *il Papa* had confided to LaTorre: "We share your admiration for the archbishop of Milano, and had we been in the conclave we might well have preferred him over other cardinals." It was the word "other," not "the other" as one would normally say in Italian, that raised questions in my mind; *ebbene,* LaTorre was pleased.

Francesco had given a private audience to each prefect whom he was not retaining and had offered each of them real or honorific positions that they indicated might please them. He also flattered each by asking him to remain in Roma or the vicinity for several weeks to assist his successor and also to remain a member of his congregation so that his advice might be obtained on a regular basis.

In recounting what I said Francesco about the Curia, I explained to you something about how the congregations of the Holy See, or as you would call them, departments or ministries, function. I need to speak more specifically now about the offices themselves. There are the Secretariat of State and nine congregations, somewhat equivalent to your cabinet-level departments, one each for the Doctrine of the Faith (unofficially we still call it the Holy Office), for Bishops, for the Oriental Church, for Rites and Sacraments, for the Clergy (those priests not belonging to special religious orders like the Jesuits), for the Religious (for those priests, brothers, and nuns belonging to the various orders), for Propaganda Fide (the missions, that is), for Saints (canonization), and for Catholic Education.

The names of these congregations give reasonable indications of their jurisdiction, but it is also clear that those jurisdictions overlap. For example, it is difficult for the Congregation for the Clergy to deal with a problem that does not raise questions concerning sacraments (for all priests have received the sacrament of Holy Orders) or the authority of bishops, or the performance of divine rites, or things of the Faith. To make some order from the inevitable chaos that would come of trying to separate what is essentially one unity, Papa Paolo VI gave the Secretariat of State both formal authority and the actual machinery to act—how do you say?—as a clearinghouse to assign tasks to congregations (often to several) and to coordinate actions and recommendations of congregations with those of other interested departments.

The secretary of state himself is also responsible for carrying on the relations between the Holy See and the nations of the world—the papacy's diplomatic affairs. Historically, these operations were executed within the Secretariat of State, but in 1967 Papa Paolo established a separate Council for the Public Affairs of the Church. That council, while formally outside of the Secretariat of State, is nevertheless headed by the secretary of state; and, while its second in command is not the same person as the archbishop who is second in command of the Secretariat of State, both offices are largely staffed by those of us who follow diplomatic careers. Further confusing things, the functions of the two offices have never been cleanly divided; the undersecretary of state, most especially, yet performs many diplomatic tasks. That confusion arises because the roles of the Holy See as an independent nation and as the center of the universal Church cannot in fact be separated. According to me, creating new offices only worsened the fundamental confusion.

Besides the various congregations, I have said, there are special commissions, secretariats, and committees that, depending on the particular Pontiff, may play important roles in governing the Church. The more significant of these during Francesco's papacy were the Secretariat for Christian Unity, the Secretariat for Non-Christians, the Secretariat for Nonbelievers, the Pontifical Commission for the Revision of the Code of Canon Law—more because Chelli headed it than because Francesco had any special interest in revising canon law—and, of course, the Prefecture for Economic Affairs.

There is also the Sacred Roman Rota, in effect a court. In fact, it is several courts since its judges sit in panels of three or occasionally five members rather than all together *(en banc)* as your courts tend to do. To assist in creating uniformity, the membership of the panels is overlapping, i.e., each judge sits on several panels. Most of the rota's business concerns marriage cases, particularly requests for annulments; but sometimes a case will arise in which two religious institutions are in dispute, usually over ownership of property or fulfillment of a contract.

There is another office that I would mention here, although it is technically not a part of the Curia: the Secretariat for the World Synod of Bishops. As you recall yourself, the Second Vatican Council looked to the establishment of a more or less regular form of representation in Roma for pastoral officials of the Church. In 1965 Papa Paolo published the constitution of a World Synod of Bishops that would meet in Roma every several years. It is composed of bishops, archbishops, or cardinals elected from national episcopal conferences (the exact number varies according to the number of bishops in a country), some members serving *ex officio* because of their posts in the Vatican, and some appointed by *il Papa* himself. The Secretariat for the World Synod of Bishops is the office, located in Roma just outside Vatican City, that funnels information to and from the bishops, arranges for the details of reunions, such as translators and staff assistance, solicits suggestions for items to be discussed, and, in consultation with the Pontiff himself, establishes the agenda for the next session.

The congregations, the rota, and these secretariats, commissions, committees, and so forth carry on the day-to-day affairs of operating the Church, either deciding themselves or recommending decisions to *il Papa* about such diverse things as dispensing a priest from his vows, approving a new translation of the Bible, establishing new regulations for fasting before Holy Communion, granting or denying an annulment of a marriage, cautioning a bishop who appears to be undercutting the ban against divorce and remarriage by allowing such people to return to the sacraments, warning another bishop about permitting too much experimentation with ritual, and reminding a third that the decrees of the Second Vatican Council are not entirely meaningless. Recommendations also treat questions of increasing the missionary efforts in a particular country or region, advising a theologian that he is stumbling near the brink of heresy, trying to renegotiate a treaty with West Germany to regulate the teaching of Catholicism in public schools, using diplomatic channels to negotiate the release of a missionary imprisoned in Hanoi, seeking a new archbishop for Denver, Colorado, dispensing a man from the law against marrying his brother's widow, or settling a property dispute between a bishop and an order of nuns operating within his diocese, and trying to find money and resources to send food to drought-ridden areas of Africa.

I have told that each of the congregations as well as most of the other offices is headed by a cardinal who has the title of prefect, and that directly under him is a secretary, usually a curial careerist who is a *monsignore* when appointed. If he performs ably, he is normally consecrated an archbishop after a few years, and he may even rise to higher office.

The secretary of each congregation functions as a chief of staff for the prefect, supervising what may be a rather large staff of experts. Almost all of these staff members will be priests or *monsignori,* with only an occasional nun or lay person. Secretarial services, such as typing, are often performed by brothers or nuns, sometimes by lay people, and on occasion by young priests. The custodial staff of the buildings are almost totally laymen. The language for ordinary business is Italian, largely because most of the clergy and almost all of the laymen who work in the Vatican's offices are Italians. Any curial member with ambition, however, is fluent in at least one or more foreign languages, most often English.

I believe I have already mentioned you that Papa Francesco found pleasing Papa Paolo's technique of keeping men personally loyal to him in key positions. In fact, Francesco did not consent to appointing Fieschi as secretary of state until I introduced him to Jan Zaleski, a Pole who was performing episcopal duties among his country's exiles in Roma. He had worked for eleven years in the secretary of state's office, but during the papacy of Paolo VI he had had a series of disputes with Monsignor Giovanni Benelli, the undersecretary of state, whom Papa Paolo had appointed to balance the liberal views of the Frenchman, Jean Cardinal Villot.

Ecco, it was easy to have a dispute with Monsignor Benelli. He was a very efficient, very traditional, and very tough man. In fact, before those sordid Watergate scandals in your country, someone had called Monsignor Benelli "*il*

Papa's Bob Haldeman." There were, of course, important differences not only in intelligence and professional skills, but also in moral character. Still, Monsignor Benelli was not the sort of man with whom to fight unless one had first made his peace with God and *il Papa.*

Zaleski's theological approach, closest to that of the servants, had grated on Monsignor Benelli's institutional orientation; their relations were not made easier by the fact that Zaleski was one of the members of the Curia who was as bright as Benelli and as hard working. The question of who would depart became an issue of sheer power within the Vatican's structure, and since Monsignor Benelli was both extremely valuable to the Pontiff and was an old and trusted friend—he had served as one of Paolo's secretaries when, as Monsignor Montini, Papa Paolo had been undersecretary of state during the reign of Pio XII—it was obvious who would remain. Within a year Zaleski found himself consecrated a bishop. (In the Holy See, we tend to promote enemies and incompetents out of important offices. Where else would the "Peter principle" have originated?) The bishopric, however, was in Roma as director of the spiritual welfare of the many Polish exiles in the city.

According to me, Zaleski and Francesco would appreciate one another, and in fact they did. I would call Zaleski a holy man. He was extraordinarily intelligent and wise in the ways of the world inside and outside the Vatican walls, but he remained at heart a simple priest. I have called him a servant; the press called him a liberal. But he was not a reforming zealot like Gordenker or Fournier. Rather, it was more that he possessed an open, inquiring mind—according to me, a rare thing among Polish prelates or even, I hope I do not sin against charity, Poles generally. He would not engage in intrigue himself, or pursue vendettas against traditionalists, even those who had assisted in squeezing him from the Curia. On the other hand, he would not permit excessive devotion to the cause of the traditionalist faction to go unnoticed. And the personal friendship that grew between him and Francesco would make communication easy. Thus, Fieschi could be effectively checked if he tried to use his power to hamper *il Papa*'s policies.

To operate the new Curia, Francesco retained LaTorre

in the Holy Office, Chelli as prefect of Economic Affairs, Aspaturian, the Patriarch of Armenia, in the Congregation for the Oriental Churches, and Greene in the Congregation for Sacraments and Rites. *Il Papa* shifted Bisset from the Congregation for the Clergy to the Congregation for Saints. Francesco considered Sacraments and Saints of minor importance.

All of the other prefects and presidents were new men. Cardinal Martìn became prefect of the Congregation for Bishops; that Korean, Chi Goon Su, whose mystical *misto* of an oration in the conclave I described earlier, was an old friend of Francesco from the Korean War. He became the new prefect of the Congregation for Propaganda Fide. Harold Buckley, an American who belonged to the Order of Holy Cross and was a noted educational psychologist and a wonderfully successful rector of the seminary at the University of Notre Dame during a period when most seminaries had experienced serious difficulties, became prefect of the Congregation for Catholic Education.

To head the Congregation for the Clergy, Francesco selected Peter Rauch, the archbishop of Cologne. A Spaniard, Arriba y Enrique, received the Congregation for the Religious. For the Secretariat of Christian Unity, we selected James Liu, a mainland Chinese archbishop who had remained in China for two years after Chiang fled to Formosa. Ultimately, the Communists had expelled Liu—then a very young priest—to Hong Kong, and he had remained there and in Singapore as shepherd of other Chinese exiles. For the Secretariat for Non-Christians there was the famous French scholar, Maurice DuVal, who had directed the Pontifical Biblical Institute, and for the Secretariat for Nonbelievers that Tanzanian with the unpronounceable name, Danielo Mwinjamba.

To direct the Secretariat of the World Synod of Bishops, Francesco had, after the conclave, asked Pritchett to stay in Roma. He was sixty-eight years old; that is about the average age within the sacred college, but according to me it is too advanced an age for a man to learn our Byzantine ways. But Pritchett was interested, and Francesco wanted a cardinal to head the office and give it prestige. He also wanted the cardinal to be someone with whom he was on close terms. In those days, Francesco had great plans for the World Synod of Bishops.

Ecco, it is obvious that the new prefects and presidents formed an international group. It was also a Curia that could not be neatly categorized in terms of servant or traditionalist categories. LaTorre, Bisset, and Greene, of course, were the hard core of the traditionalists and Chelli was certainly with them. On the other hand, Martìn and Rauch were identified, not altogether accurately, according to me, as servants. I would place them, rather, along with most of the rest of the new people as open-minded.

We had also given a great deal of thought to who would serve as secretaries to the various offices. There was no firm tradition, although many examples, of a prefect's being able to name his own man immediately. Francesco, however, wanted to retain plenary control here. As in selecting Zaleski, *il Papa* realized the impact that the careerist in charge of a congregation's professional staff could make on how a prefect, and perhaps *il Papa,* saw a problem. Here, however, Francesco was less successful in imparting an international character. Italians still dominate the higher levels of the curial careerists just as they controlled the college of cardinals until Papa Giovanni's reign. There are many reasons for that domination, not least of which, according to me, is the simple fact that the Vatican is an Italian institution. It is Italian in its language, in its location, in its history, and, most important, in its operating style. An American, an African, a German, or any other nationality is a foreigner here. He feels his foreignness and, God forgive us, we Italians make him feel it.

Allora, I do not think anyone is to blame for this situation. No one sat down and told, "Let us make the Vatican in the Italian image." As the seat of the bishop of Roma this development was more or less natural over the centuries. I have confessed to you that that Italian character has tended to make outsiders seem and feel strange; other, closely related factors also operated here, as I have told, to turn Francesco's efforts into an attempt to make a wedding with dry figs. First there was and is the matter of incentive. Generally, it does not please many foreign clergy to live in an alien atmosphere; in their own countries they can live comfortable and useful lives in either pastoral or administrative work, but in Italy things are different. Except in some areas of the northeast, especially the Veneto, Italy is Catholic more in name (and, I hope, faith) than in practice. This is what Francesco had in mind when he let slip that oft quoted remark that Italy may be Catholic but it is hardly Christian.

In truth, male Italians tend to be bitterly anticlerical. That anticlericalism even permeates our language. For instance our colloquial expression for "dirty trick" is *scherzo da prete*—"a priest's joke." I do not imply that Italian men do not respect priests and bishops; they certainly do, but for the wrong reasons. The respect that an Italian clergyman receives is based on his influence in the secular world, not on his spiritual authority. Pastoral work in much of Italy, unless one wishes to make a life's occupation of talking to pious old ladies and of finding jobs for shiftless young men, is hardly as interesting as it is, for example, in English-speaking countries. Moreover, life for a young priest is likely to be dull and hard, especially in the Mezzogiorno south of Roma. In fact, even for a pastor, existence in one of the towns south of Naples will be close to the bone, cold and hungry in the winter, hot and hungry in the summer, and to a great extent always frustrating. Carlo Levi's novel, *Christ Stopped at Eboli,* still retains much of its validity today. (I remember Kate's comment in 1952 when she read the book and visited the town: "If Christ stopped at Eboli, He must have stayed at a stable again; there isn't a decent hotel in the place.")

A second factor is the attitude of bishops outside of Italy and especially in English-speaking countries. I have seen—and I speak from personal experience as apostolic delegate in Washington—American bishops fight to prevent their most capable young priests from going to Roma to serve in the Curia. I have also listened to those same American bishops angrily complain that the Curia does not understand American problems. I agree that Italians who have not lived in the United States have no more idea of what an open, candid society is like than they can imagine life on Mars. But I ask you, as a fair man, are we totally to blame? *Ebbene,* I wander again; my age overtakes my mind.

The Italian bishops have by no means been overjoyed to see their brightest young priests gravitate toward the Vatican, but they have generally realized that they will receive a more responsive audience if their own people operate the Curia than if a group of foreigners govern the

Church. Because of the difference in attitude among bishops, I have seen a tendency—I would not name it an invariable rule—for Italian careerists in the Holy See to be more intelligent as well as to center their ambitions on the Vatican itself rather than treating it as a mere interlude between stages in a pastoral career. I confess, too, that some of my countrymen have tried to block the promotion of foreigners who seemed to be moving up the career ladder without first becoming "naturalized" into Italian culture.

Francesco understood these conditions, and wanted very badly to change them. I shall explain later how cleverly he acted. But at that time we had to accept reality and work with the people who were available to us.

I have spoken a great deal about LaTorre, Bisset, Greene, Chelli, Martìn, and Pritchett, and to a lesser extent about Fieschi. Let me explain a little more. *Ecco,* Pritchett I mentioned when I told you about the conclave. He was a very modest, soft-spoken American, born and reared in Iowa and Michigan. He had, however, a temper that could flare. Because of his modesty, few people realized that he once had possessed a sizable reputation as a scholar. As a young priest before World War II, he had been dispatched to the North American College. Later he earned a doctorate in canon law at the Gregorian University and published a treatise on canon law that is still used today. He loved pastoral labors, however, and he wanted to make his career there.

He looked much younger than sixty-eight, although his brownish hair was thinning noticeably and his shoulders had a definite stoop. His green eyes still had a gentle twinkle that flashed a warning of his sense of humor. It was easy to understand how he and Francesco would have made friends. In truth, Pritchett's penchant for atrocious puns was, if anything, even stronger than *il Papa*'s. His Latin was superb; indeed he could make bilingual plays on words, and occasionally even trilingual, since his Italian, although heavily accented, was still fundamentally sound.

As I have already said, Francesco chose Martìn to head the Congregation for the Bishops because local bishops would be critical elements in the larger transformation of the Church that Francesco intended. (It was curious, given Papa Francesco's desire for a crusade and a spiritual renewal, that he did not consider the Congregation for Propaganda Fide, the office that historically directed the Church's missionary efforts, as especially important. That is why he could entrust the congregation to a Korean who, *il Papa* himself conceded, was not an especially gifted man —pious, even saintly, but not a person of intellectual power or organizational skills.)

I have described Martìn before. He did not have the rapierlike mind of Chelli, the waspish sting of Bisset, or the ponderous learning and gruff candor of LaTorre. But Martìn was shrewd, in judging men perhaps shrewder than any of his colleagues. And he was certainly no less dedicated to the Church than any of us. He had a style of looking at a person—how do you say?—sideways. He would turn his head from the person to whom he was talking or listening but keep his eyes riveted on that man. It was just as well for Francesco that Martin considered himself a political liberal and wanted to reform the social performance rather than the theology of the Church, for at times his eyes burned like Torquemada's.

I also discussed Paolo Cardinal Fieschi when we talked about the conclave. Let me say a little more, because he becomes important to the rest of my story. Sixty-five years earlier he had been born in Genova of an old noble family that had produced several Pontiffs, most notably Innocenzo IV. On one of his visits to Roma, Mr. Keller, in his rough humor, noted that cardinals seemed to be either "skinny guineas," such as Chelli, Bisset, and Martìn, or "fat wops," such as LaTorre, Greene, or me. (The fact that Bisset was French, Martìn Argentine, and Greene Irish did not deter Keller's wit. As he once said, "Anyone can be accurate; all it takes is a lack of imagination.") *Ebbene,* Fieschi was definitely one of the "skinny guineas."

The cardinal was an imposing man physically. It was not his size. He was not especially tall; you would say about 5 feet 9 inches. And, of course, he was slender. It was rather his demeanor that awed people. He possessed, as I told earlier, the *gravitas* of a true Italian nobleman. Among Germans that attitude often degenerates into insolence; among Italian *arrivisti* it becomes pomposity; and among the new American rich, just plain bad manners. In fact, in the western world, only the old English and Italian aristocracy can tread that narrow line between overbearing arrogance or rudeness, on the one hand, and supreme, though still arrogant, self-confidence on the other. Francesco once told that in the jargon of the military this characteristic is called command presence. Whatever the name, Fieschi possessed it, together with a magnificent bass voice that made his most trivial remarks echo like a sermon in a well-filled cathedral.

His dark grey hair and black eyes added to the portrait of a prince of the Church. He possessed a mind that was beautifully retentive and keenly analytical, but he was, as are many ascetics, devoid of intellectual curiosity and so of imagination. He led a strange life, surrounded by the comforts that can be afforded only by those whose wealth is extraordinarily old and extraordinarily large. But he disdained all these comforts and lived among them without enjoying them or even noticing them. In fact, after his death, it was discovered that he had worn a hair shirt under his elegantly tailored cassock.

Allora, Fieschi was an enigma in another sense. He was, according to me, a man who at bottom disliked his fellow human beings and would have preferred to be a monk (or, rather, an abbot), a biblical scholar, or even *il Papa,* but who, after fifteen years in the papal diplomatic service, had decided to devote his life to pastoral work with its inevitable close contacts with people and their troubles. According to me, that choice was his spiritual hair shirt.

When Fieschi first arrived in the Curia as a young graduate of the diplomatic academy, he bought a villa off the Via Aurelia Antica, which his relatives soon furnished with splendid antiques and marvelous wines. (One night I sipped a Barolo there that had been bottled in 1912. That is not my favorite wine, as I may have said, but this bottle, which had to be opened fourteen hours before it was served so that it could breathe, was as delicious as anything I have ever drunk, far superior to the younger Barolos to which I am accustomed.) According to me, however, Fieschi never saw the antiques and, although he drank some of the wines, he never tasted them.

I had urged Fieschi on Francesco, but I had some reservations even at the time. There were many entries on the positive side of his ledger. His identification with the traditional faction among the hierarchy would help prevent an irreparable breach within our ranks and confer additional legitimacy on difficult decisions. He could also act as another conduit of information and judgments to *il Papa,* of views that might balance those of the servants to whom Francesco would be more attracted.

There was also Fieschi's very real ability. During his fifteen years in the Curia he had come to thoroughly understand the strengths and weaknesses of the system. Added to that knowledge was the factor of command presence that I explained. He would secure compliance from other curial offices as much by his patrician mode as by any formal grant of authority from *il Papa.* I said earlier that I once described him to Francesco as the closest thing we had to a marine in the Vatican. The exactness of that description still pleases me, even though I now have a finer appreciation of American misgivings about a hyperefficient organization.

Ecco, why the reservations, you might ask. There were three sets of reasons, all having to do with loyalty. The first concerned personal styles. Francesco's open, informal, easy manner was the antithesis of Fieschi's ultraformal, stiffly condescending approach to people and problems. I had fear less that Fieschi would grate on Francesco—*il Papa* told me once that he actually enjoyed dealing with such people, at least when he had the upper hand—than that Fieschi would be horrified by what he would consider improprieties, and so not give Francesco the full measure of personal loyalty that he deserved.

The question of loyalty nagged me in yet another way. I was not secure, even without conflicts in personal style, how much loyalty Fieschi would feel to a Pontiff who was a foreigner, psychologically if not canonically a layman, who had, in effect, deprived him of the tiara, and was also friendly with his other antagonists, Fournier and Gordenker.

There was also the question of change in the Church. Fieschi was a traditionalist not so much because of an articulated theology, as because he was at ease with the status quo in the Church and in economic and social life. His aristocratic—do you say haughty?—style prevented him from perceiving, much less sympathizing with, the reasons that caused people to press for change in the Church. It was blazingly evident that Papa Francesco understood much of the torment within the Church and was determined to change the institutions that posed potentially serious conflicts.

I know how much of life in the Vatican, as everywhere else, is injured by jealousy, vanity, and pettiness, but I hoped that, once Fieschi understood why Francesco was trying to restructure the Church, devotion to that institution would win out. If such were to happen, we could not obtain a more efficient secretary of state. And if it did not come to pass, we had Monsignor Zaleski.

Our most difficult search was for someone to head the Congregation for the Clergy. Here, as with the Congregation for Bishops, Francesco wanted a person who shared his views and to whom he could feel personally at ease. With the approval, although not the ringing endorsement, of Gordenker, we settled on a relatively young (fifty-seven) German, Peter Rauch, archbishop of Cologne, a man who had not yet then become a cardinal. He was a Rhinelander whose family had migrated from the region around Dresden during the Napoleonic wars. Having been vintners in the east, they bought several vineyards in the Rheingau, between Mainz and Rüdesheim. (Some of the fields there had initially been planted by Caesar's army, when the troops stood guard against the barbarians.) Naturally he and I struck up an immediate friendship. I conceded to him that no Italian white could equal the Johannisberger Kabinett that his family produced—and of which he would generously supply me a half dozen bottles from time to time—but I improved his palate by letting him taste how much better we Italians make reds than do the French.

Rauch had been a submarine officer during the Second World War, although I do not understand how a man almost two meters tall (about 6′6″ by your standards) could fit in one of those little boats. His Italian assistants called him *l'Asparago* because, despite his great height, he could not have weighed more than about 150 pounds. He was still muscular, with wispy hair that had turned from straw blond to white so easily that no one could have noticed. He was essentially a quiet, scholarly man who listened well, but, as one must in Italy, could use his baritone voice to create more decibels than his colleagues. And, although he was open-minded in discussion, once he made up his mind he clung to his opinions with classic Teutonic stubbornness, ignoring our neatly constructed avenues of gracious, Latin retreat.

Like Fieschi and Zaleski, Rauch was not a newcomer to the Curia, and, also like them, he had had ample pastoral experience. He had studied at the Gregorian and at the papal diplomatic academy and then worked for six years in the Secretariat of State before returning to Germany as an auditor in the nunciature in Bonn. After two more years, when he was about to be promoted to the senior rank of counsellor, he asked to remain in Germany and engage in pastoral duties. His elevation, less than a decade and a half later, to head the archdiocese of Cologne was an indication of his native intellectual ability and of his political skills.

Allora, these were the new people, the important ones, through whom the Church functioned. According to me, although there were weak posts as with Bisset and the Korean, it was as distinguished a group as the Church could boast, at least since Galilee. But, as I have said, Francesco took no time to sit back and enjoy his accomplishment.

SIXTEEN

Allora, as I warned you, events occurred during those months as fast as your tape spinning on this register, twisting around each other so continually that I have difficulty pulling out the actual sequence. I remember that the work of selecting and announcing the new prefects for the Curia was finished in early August. But completion of the task did not slacken our pace. For Francesco the next project, no matter what it was, was always the most crucial thing in his life—and thus in the lives of those around him.

The next critical item after appointing new curial prefects was the reunion—I am sorry . . . you say meeting?—of the World Synod of Bishops, scheduled for the first three weeks of September. Conferences of bishops in every nation of the world—or where there were only a few bishops within a single country, regional conferences

—elect a number of delegates who are of the rank of bishop, or higher. The exact number each conference selects varies from one to four, depending on the number of dioceses in the country or region. In addition to these delegates (145 of them for this particular synod), the Roman Union of Superiors General—the chiefs of the more than ninety religious orders—elects ten representatives, all of whom must be both male and themselves members of a religious order.

Two other sets of people are *ex officio* members of the synod: the sixteen cardinals who head the most important curial offices and the fifteen leading officials of the Eastern Rite: patriarchs, metropolitans, and major archbishops. In addition, *il Papa* appoints a group of prelates, as many as fifteen percent of the synod's delegates. Some he names to balance inequities in the representational formula and others to insure that views he wants expressed will have spokesmen. Before his death, the old Pontiff had already named twenty-two of the papal quota of twenty-seven for this synod, leaving us able to choose only five prelates from the entire Church. As a symbol of his interest in Latin America, Africa, and Asia, Francesco selected men from those areas. As a further indication of his concern for social justice and as an additional warning to the Brazilian regime, he included the cardinal archbishop of Recife.

The old Pontiff had formulated the agenda, or agendum as it was in this case: discussion of a draft of a fundamental law (or constitution) for the universal Church. For more than a decade, a special papal commission had been trying to prepare such a document, and in recent years Chelli had been its president. Around 1970, an earlier draft had been informally circulated, but it had been met by a barrage of criticism that labeled it an effort to return the government of the Church to the centralized power that the Second Vatican Council, in its endorsement of collegiality, had attempted to reverse. According to me, Chelli's new draft was almost equally as vulnerable to such an attack.

Papa Francesco, of course, had no fear of centralizing power in the Vatican; nevertheless, the draft was not pleasing to him. His reservation was fundamental. He believed that it was imprudent to try to freeze the relationships among *il Papa,* the Curia, the bishops, and the laity at a time when those relationships were in a state of rapid development.

Because Francesco had more experience than anyone in the Curia in interpreting a constitution, I was secure that he was correct. Not all of my brethren agreed, however, and at that time Francesco was not ready to force his views, at least not on an issue he did not consider of great importance. Discussion at the synod was, on the other hand, a different affair. I have related his naive, typically American notion that the synod might become a sort of legislature. The success of your governmental system colors the thinking of all your people, even the most intelligent and least parochial. *Ebbene,* Francesco did not want the first session of the synod during his papacy to concern itself solely with an issue he considered relatively unimportant.

I remember a hot afternoon in July, sitting in the papal gardens at Castel Gandolfo with *il Papa,* Pritchett, Monsignor Zaleski, and Archbishop Konrad Schaufele, the outgoing secretary of the World Synod of Bishops. The archbishop was saying that it was now much too late to change the agendum. The synod would meet in six weeks, and the old Pontiff had announced the agendum five months earlier. A number of episcopal conferences had already discussed the draft document and instructed their representatives to voice specific recommendations and criticisms.

"I believe," the archbishop told, "that many curial cardinals find the idea of a new constitution for the Church more appealing than do most of the pastoral bishops. They are too busy enjoying what freedom they can find under the guidance of Vatican II to want to restrict themselves by a fresh outburst of Roman authority."

"At least," Francesco nodded, "to replace the Emperor Constantine as the model for the Church with James Madison and the Constitutional Convention of 1787 is a long step forward. But I'm still not ready to have 200 bishops sitting around Rome for three weeks debating a document that we shall not approve. That is the best way to retard the development of the synod as a meaningful institution."

"What should we do then, Holiness," Schaufele asked, "cancel the session?"

"Cardinal Chelli would have a mixture of feelings about that," I intervened. "As president of the Pontifical Commission for the Revision of the Code of Canon Law, he wants his proposals debated and approved. As president of the Council of Economic Affairs, he would prefer to see the bishops keep away from Roma."

"What has money to do with it?" Francesco asked.

"The cost of the session will be considerable, Holiness," the archbishop noted, "and we—the Vatican—will pay a large share. Papa Paolo had definite ideas about money. He said that the Church must be poor and must seem to be poor. He discouraged bishops from bringing gifts on their visits to him. He abolished most of the fees that the Curia charged dioceses to process their requests. And he felt that the Holy See should pay for the administrative costs of the synod—simultaneous translations, the recording of proceedings, the printing of documents, personnel to brief the press, and, of course, costs of operating and maintaining the building. Papa Paolo went even further. He said he was willing to pay the travel and living expenses here in Rome of all those prelates who indicated that they needed financial assistance."

"What does 'all expenses' include?"

"Transportation, food, lodging, and any other costs here, such as taxis or car rentals."

"Now that is a quick way to impoverish the Church. How many bishops will we be subsidizing?"

"I don't have the exact figures, Holiness," the archbishop responded, "but the number is substantial. We shall have to pay for everything for most of the Asians and Africans and something for most of the Latin Americans. We shall pay full costs for at least thirty bishops and be fortunate to keep the cost at $2000 each. I cannot even guess how much we shall have to provide in partial subsidization."

"That money could feed a lot of hungry people," Francesco mused. He looked directly at Pritchett when he spoke.

"I am afraid we're committed, Holiness," the cardinal replied. "If we cancel now, we would damage, perhaps irreparably, the prestige of the synod."

Francesco looked first at me, then at Zaleski. We nodded. "I agree," Archbishop Schaufele added. "The cost of cancellation at this late date cannot be measured in monetary terms."

"Nor can saving human beings from starvation, Still, I cannot have it both ways," *il Papa* conceded. "If I want a strong synod, I have to pay the price. Well, it still isn't too late to modify the agenda."

"How so?" Pritchett asked.

"Let's keep the draft of the new constitution as the framework. We can say that Chelli will welcome general comments in writing on the whole document or on any part of it. Discussion in the synod, however, will center on one facet of the document: the relationships between pastoral bishops and the Vatican in light of the spiritual renewal and the crusade. 'Collegiality, the Papacy, and Social Justice' might be a good title. Among our specific discussion topics we can include financial problems, how the bishops and the Holy See can work together to use our resources to help the poor, the old, the sick, and the hungry."

"Could His Holiness show me the connections more precisely?" Archbishop Schaufele asked timidly.

"My ideas only seem disjointed, Excellency, because they are disjointed. I want these people to discuss important things, to help lead the Church to meet the needs of the twenty-first century with the gospel of the first. I have faith," the Pontiff smiled, "in your ability and in that of the others here to weave our ideas into some sort of coherent whole."

The next specific problem that we attacked was another created by the old Pontiff, though I did not then see it as a problem at all. In any event, he had appointed LaTorre president-delegate of the synod. I tried to explain to Papa Francesco that the Holy Mule was an excellent presiding officer, but he would have none of it. There was bad chemistry there. In the end, he determined to exercise his power to add another president-delegate. To soften the blow, I persuaded him to name not one but three more, one from the Eastern Rite, a black from Africa, and a Latin American. Thus we could plausibly say that the catholicity of the Church was being emphasized: presiding officers from the Old World, the New World, the

Third World, Eastern Rite, Latin Rite, pastors, and administrators. It would not deceive LaTorre, but it would protect his pride.

A few weeks later, the barbarian hordes descended on Roma. I am not disrespectful toward our pastoral bishops when I use that word, for they constituted only a small—and civilized—portion of the invaders. Some of the episcopal conferences also sent priest-observers, clerics who lacked official status as far as the Vatican was concerned, but to whom their national delegates could talk and explain what was going on. The hope of the conferences was that these priests—who, of course, would eventually meet prelates and priests from other countries as well—would convey information to their fellow clergy at home and so lend additional legitimacy to the synod's work.

Moreover, a number of North American and European bishops brought along their own staffs—sometimes a canon lawyer, a theologian, a priest-secretary, and even occasionally a press officer. Bringing canon lawyers and theologians made a great deal of sense if the synod were to function independently of the Curia. For the Holy See is densely populated with theologians and canon lawyers ready to pick at nits, and pastoral bishops, assuming they were ever trained in these fields, have long ceased to think in such intellectual terms.

There was also an army of newsmen crowding about the Vatican press office, near the Piazzo Pio XII, in front of the Piazza di San Pietro. They spent their time in the bars and restaurants nearby or in the press office itself telephoning friends or contacts within the Vatican or among the delegates, or going in and out of the small, dingy hotels in the Borgo in which various dissident groups established headquarters.

Ecco, those dissident groups! To a reporter they were probably colorful. According to me, they were mostly insane. There were the Concerned Laity clamoring for greater lay participation in Church government, as well as various groups of servants and traditionalists, each asserting that the Church was on the road to perdition, but for diametrically opposed reasons. There were black clergy—priests, brothers, and nuns—seeking to broaden the Church's cultural base; Hungarian refugees demanding beatification of the late Josef Cardinal Mindszenty to atone for Papa

Paolo's summarily removing him; Arabs urging recognition of Palestinian refugees' claims to Jerusalem and parts of Israel; Jews asking for full diplomatic relations with Israel and a condemnation of Arab terrorism; and, most amusing of all, nuns and laywomen demanding full female participation in the priesthood and even in the hierarchy of the Church. Even the most liberal of servants in the Curia enjoyed reading the ladies' demands.

One of the largest and consistently most active organizations was the ultraservant priests, the Committee of the Church in the Modern World, with headquarters in the Hotel Alicorni near the Via della Conciliazione, about two blocks from the Piazza di San Pietro. Another of the largest and most active groups was the ultra traditionalists—heavily sprinkled with laity—who held forth in the newer Hotel Michelangelo, near the Holy Office. The servants were mostly Americans and northern Europeans, while the traditionalists, who called themselves the Comitato della Chiesa Tradizionale, the "Committee for the Traditional Church," were mostly Italians, with a few Irish, Spanish, Portuguese, and Americans. Each group held regular press conferences, and one could follow their arguments along a trail of leaflets scattered around San Pietro and the posters plastered along the walls of the buildings in the Borgo. Inevitably the two groups became identified with the acronyms from their initials. The servants were called CIMM (pronounced *cheem,* in Italian); the traditionalists, COCT.

Few of these people could establish direct contact with the bishops, and that was a good thing. I am something of a pragmatist in secular politics, due to the influence of Declan Walsh when I lived in the United States. I concede that in most countries parliamentary democracy functions less badly than other forms of government, although I do not profess to understand why. Indeed, I do not understand how parliamentary democracy functions at all. With lobbying, electioneering, and so forth, it seems to be what we call a "market of cows." My reaction is perfectly natural for an Italian, since democracy here has produced only anarchy. That condition, however, is still preferable to fascism.

Even though I respect parliamentary democracy in secular affairs, it has no place in the ecclesiastical world. After all, we cannot conduct popular referenda on God's will, and public clamor might sway the thinking of some bishops. I mention one incident, extreme and unpleasant, but an example of what can happen. The outside of Cardinal Rauch's titular church here in Roma, Gesù Divin Maestro, was painted with black swastikas during the synod. I do not know who did that foul thing, but the press claimed it was ultratraditionalists or perhaps even neo-Fascists.

Ecco, someone retaliated with signs reading *il Finocchio Francese* painted along Bisset's titular church. I do not translate such vile slander, nor do I believe that it influenced the synod, other than to sicken bishops. But it can be dangerous in possibly swaying some wavering prelates to support a proposition sponsored by a slandered colleague.

I wander again. Let me speak rapidly about the synod itself. I was there throughout, at Francesco's request, although I had no voice or vote. The general sessions were held in the special chamber that had been constructed for the synod in the audience hall. There are splendid leather *poltrone* for 350 people, each with a folding desk in front and an arm rest containing a microphone—so that each delegate may speak from his own seat—and connections to five different simultaneous translations. That is important equipment, we learned at Vatican II. While Latin is still officially the universal language of the Church, it is not easily comprehended by many pastoral bishops outside of France, Spain, and Italy. Many bishops who think they can speak the language, especially Americans, do so with accents so thick that we who are fluent in the tongue can barely discern their words.

The president's bench seats nine people. Each of the four president-delegates sat there as well as *il Papa* himself, who is the overall president of the synod. Francesco gave the opening address, but he chose not to give it in the chamber. The choice was a symbol, he said, of the synod's being an institution of the pastoral bishops. Rather he spoke in the Sistine Chapel after he had concelebrated Mass with the four president-delegates. (It was one of the few times that I saw him say a Mass.) The oration was brief:

> We welcome you to this synod and join you in praying that it moves the Church and the people of God closer to the gospel of Christ's love and the salvation that gospel promises. Each of you has received a copy

of our formal address, which you may read at your leisure. It sets out, with appropriate curial circumlocutions and pomposity—

(I saw Fieschi's face redden. His office, in fact, he personally, had prepared the first draft of that address. But, I must admit, it did read like a printed book, as we Italians say about a pompous speech.)

—the reasons for our coming together. Let me speak more plainly. As I have said before, I want to return the Church to an old path; I want it to be a living embodiment of social justice. As the synod of 1971 declared, "Whoever intends to speak to men of justice, must first be just toward them." I would add that we must also *seem* to be just toward all; and, as each of us is aware, seeming to be just is often more difficult than actually being just.

He then explained that because the internal affairs of the Church were in a state of healthy change, he thought it inappropriate at that time to discuss Chelli's draft constitution as a whole; rather, he had modified the agendum to focus on the single problem of relations between the Vatican and the dioceses, especially concerning the spiritual renewal and the crusade against hunger.

"I hope," he said, "we can do so with the same charity we urge others to practice. We have no time to drag up past sins of prefects or pastors, even if the love we bear each other did not forbid such recriminations." In this context, Francesco mentioned the perennial problem of money, how both the Vatican and pastoral bishops could continue to aid one another, maintain their existing charitable works, and support the crusade.

He spoke without notes, and held in his hand the attention of men who were used to and bored by conventional sermons and exhortations. They were enjoying an experience that was unusual if not unique in recent history: being addressed by a Pontiff as if they were intelligent adults rather than children. According to me, Francesco also had a memorable experience during the next few weeks, though one could not say he enjoyed it. He sat at the president's bench next to whoever was presiding and followed the debate. At first he listened intently, then with increasing disillusionment.

The traditionalists, led by Chelli, Greene, and Bisset, deftly deflected Francesco's efforts to shift the focus of the synod. Quickly Bisset provoked the servants to respond to some of his snide remarks about pastors and collegiality.

"The only true act of collegiality recorded in scripture," Bisset told, "came in the Garden of Gethsemane: All the Apostles ran away together and abandoned Christ to the mob."

Gordenker rose to the bait and delivered a searing intervention that demanded rebuttal from the traditionalists. LaTorre presided fairly. He allowed ample time for assertion, rebuttal, and surrebuttal, all the while consuming valuable hours. *Ecco,* I concede that on this matter Francesco had been correct, but for the wrong reason. It was LaTorre's sense of fairness that caused the difficulty, not his partisanship.

Francesco endured three days of fruitless but acrid debate, then he gave curialists and pastors, traditionalists and servants alike, a sharp lesson in parliamentary politics. That evening he summoned to his studio a group of servants: Gordenker; Fournier of Belgium; the cardinal archbishop of Recife; Pritchett; a young American named Long who was bishop of Charleston; Rauch of the Congregation for the Clergy; Martìn of the Congregation for Bishops; Buckley, the American who headed the Congregation for Catholic Education; and myself, as well as Mwinjamba, the tall, heavyset, blue black Tanzanian who was president of the Secretariat for Nonbelievers and was scheduled the next day to replace LaTorre as presiding officer of the synod.

In very precise terms, Francesco explained to them that they were being—how do you say?—mousetrapped. The important thing was to focus on the points he had outlined in the Sistine. The first step would be for Cardinal Mwinjamba to rule out of order any speech not on one of those points.

Next, Papa Francesco handed each of us a Xeroxed list of the delegates and instructed Martìn to assign each of us a dozen or so sympathetic delegates whom we would visit individually to arrange support for Mwinjamba's rulings if they were appealed to the floor. Then Francesco handed us another sheaf of papers, a plan that he himself had drafted while listening, or pretending to listen, to the debates. The opening section required all rectors of seminaries throughout the world to transmit each year to the secretary of state names and biographical information on all seminarians in the upper quarter of their class. The information would be coded and filed in a computer's memory bank. Bishops would be required to provide biannual reports on the progress of these men, and the men themselves would be obligated to complete periodic questionnaires keeping their files current with information on advanced degrees and languages studied. When a vacancy occurred in a curial office, the secretary of state would obtain a list of qualified people from this memory bank.

The second section of Francesco's plan would have a more immediate effect. It required every bishop to send to the secretary of state similar information on clergy in his diocese whom he considered to be the most promising intellectually. To bolster his recommendations, the bishop would be obligated to include a transcript of the candidate's *voti*—you say grades?—from the seminary and reports from the pastors under whom he had served. Again this information would be coded and recorded.

In no case would anyone be obliged to accept a curial post, but the secretary of state would be obligated to set out a description of the requirements of the post and to consider any cleric who met those requirements.

"I do not know, Holiness," Gordenker mused. "This sounds interesting, but I do not know that I want the Curia picking off my brightest young men to work in Rome."

"You cannot have it both ways, Eminence," Francesco replied. "You cannot criticize the Curia for being unrepresentative at the same time you are holding back the most qualified of your people from working here."

"It is a problem," Fournier agreed. "*Bien,* I understand my colleague's reservation, but I agree with His Holiness. Either we try to change the Curia or we stop criticizing them."

"I bow to your logic," Gordenker replied, "although I would still rather see the Curia abolished than reformed. I shall, of course, support the proposal."

"Perhaps," Pritchett said to Mwinjamba, "the chair

might recognize one of us first in the morning, and he could move out the proposal."

"I would be honored to make the motion," Bishop Long volunteered. "I have not spoken yet, and I am not so identified with any of the various factions that my sponsorship would generate opposition." That was a deft way of excluding Gordenker and Fournier.

"Good," *il Papa* responded, "and perhaps the seconding speech should come from a member of the Curia."

"I would be honored, Holiness," Buckley said. "Seminaries come under the jurisdiction of my congregation, and I could speak about some of the practical problems and how they could be overcome."

"Fine," Francesco nodded, "but the next speech should be from an Asian or an African so this would not seem to be an American proposal."

"I shall arrange that, Holiness," Cardinal Mwinjamba spoke solemnly, but then His Eminence always spoke solemnly.

"Excellent. Now," Francesco said, "we shall need to have a big gun to rebut the attacks. Who can best undermine the traditionalists' attacks and speak also as an expert?" It was a rhetorical question. "Our secretary of state, Cardinal Fieschi, is in general charge of personnel problems for the Curia and he also is not identified as a servant. We shall talk to him ourself."

When we adjourned an hour later, each of us possessed precise marching orders: whom to contact, what to say, and what to do the following morning.

Like Mussolini's trains, it all went on schedule. The curialists were helpless. After noting his determination to keep debate relevant to *il Papa*'s agenda, Mwinjamba recognized Bishop Long, then Cardinal Buckley. Although not a wise proposal, it was difficult to attack. Who can explain to pastoral bishops why they should have little role in determining who will staff the Curia? But my brother Bisset managed to make an argument insinuating that many local bishops would use the occasion to dump their problem priests on us. (I seldom agreed with Bisset, but, according to me, there was much in his implication.) Mwinjamba next recognized Fieschi, who made a devastating intervention on behalf of the motion. I do not know what Papa Francesco said to him, but I saw my own description of him as a marine made true. His argument was lucid, but most of all his status as both curialist and traditionalist demoralized opponents.

Needless to say, the proposal triumphed by far more than the required two-thirds majority. Francesco was deeply pleased. He had started the synod moving and had also pushed a plan dear to his own foreign heart. Had he himself publicly made the proposal, local bishops would certainly have dragged their heels. Now the plan had greater legitimacy, having been proposed by a pastoral bishop and overwhelmingly endorsed by their own elected delegates.

(I have explained to you my belief that the Curia functions best as an Italian organization. We are less troubled by nationalism than other Europeans and certainly less so than North Americans. And, although there are significant exceptions, as a group Latin Americans, Africans, and Asians simply do not have the cultural maturity and intellectual education to compete with us. Alas, Francesco never understood this.)

That evening, Papa Francesco again summoned us to his studio and instructed us to gather support for a motion that the synod divide itself into individual study groups to discuss specific facets of the modified agenda, such as coordinating the work of the spiritual renewal and works of charity. Again the debate was long, but our caucus once more demonstrated that we were adept at rallying support. One traditionalist bishop from the United States moaned, "We have been flattened by a steamroller."

The results of the study groups' labors were not intellectually impressive. Our pastoral bishops spend too much time away from logical argument for their reasoning to be tight and their thinking clear. I do not wish to demean their contributions to the Church. Certainly it is essential to carry the gospel to laymen, listen to their problems, and offer Christian solutions. But that sort of labor does little to sharpen the intellect, at least as far as I can judge from performances at episcopal conferences, world synods, or even at the Second Vatican Council. In all those settings, the traditionalists in the Curia generally had the better of the debate even though they often had the weaker case. On the other hand, with Francesco's guiding strategy, the servants had the votes in that synod.

When the synod adjourned *il Papa* was a very tired

man. He had sat at the president's desk during all nineteen sessions. We had met for three weeks and had taken holidays only on Sundays. By actual count, we had listened to 127 formal interventions, 6 of which lasted more than an hour and 13 of which more than forty minutes. Francesco had worked each night, not merely "politicking" as you would call it, but taking care of the regular affairs of the papacy. He even continued to hold his normal general audiences at noon on Sundays and on Wednesday afternoons, with the time advanced to 2:30 P.M. so that he could attend the afternoon reunions. He had given the opening and closing allocutions—the latter also delivered in the Sistine Chapel—and in his own handwriting had drafted the plan to internationalize the lower ranks of the Curia.

Now he faced the task of examining in detail the final resolutions—"a flaky lot," Pritchett had called them in his amusing American dialect—and deciding how to implement their substance (if any could be found). You know, of course, that formally the synod only recommends to *il Papa.* What he does with those recommendations is solely his decision, although we in the Curia usually have a large role in shaping those decisions. But Francesco was determined to enhance the prestige of the synod by executing as fully as he could the bishops' proposals, especially those relating to recruiting staff for the Curia.

Looking back, I now see this synod as much more important than I did at the time. Its significance lay, I believe, in its failure. It convinced Papa Francesco that if the Church were to be led, he would have to do the leading. For quite different reasons, neither the Curia nor the World Synod of Bishops could provide the leadership needed. It was a message that did not discourage Francesco.

SEVENTEEN

THE BISHOPS RETURNED to their dioceses, the curialists to their congregations, the journalists to their homes, the various agitating groups to whatever lairs they infested, and Roma to peace. Or so we imagined. But another and far more serious crisis was about to afflict Papa Francesco, though, of course, none of us had advance knowledge of its shape or dread import. I come to it in a moment, in what I recall as its proper sequence.

Meanwhile, the secretary of state's office was only gradually checking the paper avalanche that threatened to bury us. Chelli's strategy to immobilize *il Papa* had been adopted by many curial offices, including some headed by cardinals whom Francesco had selected with the approval of servants like Gordenker. The cause was that senior careerists continued to operate the offices. Sometimes I could see the paper taking its toll of Francesco's energy, which though vast was still limited. Out of loyalty, I explained to him why he was seeing so many and such voluminous documents. (I did not think it necessary to explain how I knew or who was the originator of the plan.) He laughed when I told him.

"I thought something like that was going on. It's a classic bureaucratic reaction to a new boss. Well, we'll have to slow it down soon, but I'd like it to continue for a time. Our reverend prelates may not realize it, but they're giving me a wonderful education in the way this place operates."

Wisely, Francesco did not attempt to handle all these affairs personally, although he read most of the papers. Some he gave to me, some to the abbot, despite his heavy burden with the crusade, and some to Pritchett, who had little work of his own now that the synod had adjourned. Sometimes Francesco acted as his own secretary of state by returning a packet of documents to the appropriate curial department with requests for clarification or specific action. He always sent a photocopy of his handwritten note to the secretary of state's office, through which most of the paper had flowed on its way to *il Papa*. During the days when he had been acting secretary of state, LaTorre had little time to read these memoranda, and Francesco's notes had made no visible impact on the undersecretary, a taciturn and very traditional Portuguese, who used much of his time to bemoan the independence of Angola.

Ecco, once Fieschi and Zaleski commanded the office of secretary of state, the volume of paper coming to us slowed. Fieschi was himself partially responsible. I have already confessed that I had suffered some misgivings about recommending him, and a few of my fears became realities. He displayed no personal warmth toward Papa Francesco, but that was normal considering Fieschi's personality. Francesco once remarked to me that Fieschi could raise his temperature by chewing ice cubes.

More serious was the cardinal's commitment to the status quo in the Church. Neither the crusade nor the spiritual renewal received his full enthusiasm—*ebbene,* his energetic attention. I concede you I had never seen Fieschi demonstrate enthusiasm for anything, and I never expected to see it. I had, however, hoped to see him striving to execute *il Papa*'s policies. I do not imply that he tried to sabotage our plans, only that he did not provide as much assistance as he could have in—how do you say?—cracking the whip over curialists to make certain that they were efficiently expediting Papa Francesco's plans.

Il Papa handled Fieschi with a Roman touch that surprised me, although less so than it surprised Fieschi. Francesco, I have told, found Monsignor Zaleski congenial, and, after talking to Fieschi about several things and finding that little happened, Francesco rapidly—perhaps too rapidly, but that was his way—began, in the style of Papa Paolo VI and Monsignor Benelli, to telephone Zaleski, largely ignoring Fieschi except for ceremonial occasions. The *monsignore,* of course, entertained great enthusiasm for the Pontiff's plans, and he had labored in the Curia long enough to know most of the careerists' ways of diverting papal policy.

It took Fieschi several weeks to realize what was happening to him and his power; not wishing to be forced into the role of a figurehead, he anguished over resigning. He once talked briefly to me about the situation in which he found himself.

"This man," he complained, "does not understand the Church. Organizing crusades and spiritual renewals are not bad things, but we have here in Rome more than twenty offices with important work to be done, and we also have several thousand bishops around the world who have problems. They need our advice, our help, and sometimes our correction. We cannot neglect them and their flocks for dreams of a brave new world. We have only so much time and energy."

"But is it not the prerogative of *il Papa* to say how that time and energy will be distributed?" I asked gently.

Fieschi looked at me for a long time before he answered.

I thought for a moment that he might—how do you say?—let his hair down and unburden himself to me, talk about how his patrician pride had been injured in the conclave, how he could not fully accept as the Vicar of Christ a mere monk who had been a layman most of his life. Instead, he said only, "In general we agree, but when a Pope does not understand the Church and, however well-intentioned, threatens to harm that institution and its mission, then it is the duty of those of us in the Curia to protect the Church, and ultimately the Pontiff himself, from both the judgment of God and that of man."

"As our brother Jean Bisset would tell, 'We are the papacy; he is only the Pontiff.' Is that what you mean?"

Fieschi drew himself up. "We do not always approve of our brother Bisset's way of putting things or doing things. But, although we would phrase it more humbly, in essence that sums up our position in this case."

"Perhaps, then, if you cannot serve Papa Francesco with full personal loyalty, you should not serve him at all," I commented.

"Yes, that is a powerful argument. We are torn, however, by the argument that our first loyalty is not to Papa Francesco or any other Pontiff, but to God's Church."

"In either case, I do not understand your dilemma. If you think you are serving the Church, why consider leaving?"

"Because we find ourself with so little power. For a few weeks all went well, but now he consults us only on the great questions: Does God exist? Is the Church eternal? Do we have a nuncio in Brasilia? But the little questions are important. How should we handle the political conservatism of some Latin American bishops? Who should be recruited to the lower ranks of the Curia? These sorts of things he discusses with Zaleski and others. Perhaps we are not sufficiently humble—"

I resisted the almost overwhelming urge to chant a great amen.

"—perhaps we should pray more for divine guidance both for ourselves and the Pontiff."

I have fear I gave Fieschi little comfort. I have explained why I had thought him a good choice. His presence in the Vatican pleased the traditionalists and he possessed impressive managerial skills. But now I felt very serious doubts. Chelli, however, believed otherwise, and, according to me, it was Chelli who persuaded Fieschi to remain in office. (It goes without saying that Fieschi would not have consulted LaTorre; the feudal lord seldom feels need for the peasant's wisdom.)

Allora, in Fieschi's defense I must emphasize what I started to say earlier, that the cascade of paper turned into a slower flow in part because what had been transpiring offended Fieschi's sense of rational, orderly administration. Many documents went back to curial offices with curt notes asking for more information and fewer words, or with instructions to handle the problem within existing guidelines and without troubling *il Papa.*

Zaleski was even more responsible for the greater order that was emerging. He asserted himself vigorously here. After all, that was his principal task, while Fieschi, as secretary of state, had many other obligations. As a result of Zaleski's close scrutiny, secretaries of sacred congregations began receiving stern rebukes. With most of the papers that he forwarded to *il Papa,* the *monsignore* also sent along accurate but concise summaries of what the documents contained and recommendations for action. Both were of real assistance to us, and did nothing to weaken Francesco's reliance on Zaleski, or Fieschi's resentment of their relationship.

It was in early October, as the Vatican and the Borgo were basking in the sweet relief caused by the departure of the bishops, and the advent of cool, pleasant weather, that the crisis of which I just spoke stuck us. I had reached *il Papa*'s office shortly after eight in the morning, when Monsignor Candutti—you recall he in effect was *il Papa*'s foreign minister—came rushing into the studio with the news that Syrian and Egyptian forces had again invaded Israel and that long-range, Russian-built missiles were bombarding Tel Aviv. Fortunately, the rockets contained only conventional explosives; nevertheless, there was the horrible possibility of nuclear war. For some weeks we had been hearing running voices that, like the Israelis, the Egyptians now possessed the capability to construct atomic weapons. After all, you naive Americans had given the old regime under Sadat the technology to use atomic power for peaceful purposes, and it was child's play to construct devastating weapons with that knowledge and equipment.

I entered the studio a few minutes before Monsignor Candutti; shortly afterwards the abbot and Signora Falconi arrived. She brought a portable radio. *Il Papa* sat on one of the blue *poltrone* by the window. The abbot and Signora Falconi seated themselves on the sofa. Monsignor Candutti and I and later Monsignor Bonetti placed ourselves at the conference table. LaTorre, whose regular weekly audience as prefect of the Holy Office was scheduled at eight-thirty, joined us at that time.

The news was grave. There was no doubt that this was not just another "incident." Radio Cairo and Damascus, so Italian radio told, were saying that direct and indirect peace talks had failed to budge the Israelis. The only alternative left was force. The Arab leaders were calling for a *jihad*, a holy war by all Islam. They announced that their missiles would obliterate every city in Israel, sparing only towns in the areas still occupied by Israeli troops from the Six Day War of 1967.

"What do you suggest we do, Excellency," Francesco looked at Candutti. (Because the abbot was with us, we spoke English. He was learning Italian, but was not yet fluent.)

"There is not much we can do, Holiness," Candutti replied. "Our diplomacy in the Near East has not been effective. We can issue a statement calling for both sides to accept a cease-fire and plead that all nations respect the sacred character of Jerusalem. We can try to make some money available for relief activities. That is about all."

"There must be something else."

Francesco turned to LaTorre. "Eminence, from your experience as acting secretary of state, can you add anything?"

"Only that Your Holiness call on the world to pray for peace."

"There must be something more we can do."

"Problems do not always have solutions, Holiness. I do not see one here. At least," LaTorre continued, "God may be showing a kind of mercy. If the Jews are defeated—and the threat of another oil boycott will certainly force the Europeans to pressure the United States into not resupplying the Jews—fewer people may be killed and we may at last have peace in the Mideast."

"The peace of the grave for millions of Jews," the abbot intervened.

"I doubt that," LaTorre replied smoothly. "The Arabs are a very civilized people. And we must keep in mind that the Church may fare better in the Holy Land if the area is under Arab control. After another ten years of Jewish rule I doubt that a Christian would be welcome in Jerusalem."

"That is utter nonsense, Eminence," the abbot said angrily. "Jews have been persecuted too much themselves to persecute others. The slaughter of a few million Jews now doesn't worry you any more than it did during World War II." (The abbot's usual gentleness had left him, and the fire that burned in his Torquemada's eyes was matched by the heat of his words.)

"*Ecco,* that is not true," I intervened quickly. "Some people in the Vatican begged Papa Pio to speak out against the Nazis and their butchery. Cardinal LaTorre, who was then only a young *monsignore,* was among them. Papa Pacelli elected to remain silent for his own motives, which neither Cardinal LaTorre nor I understood or approved then or now. You should also know that for more than six months in 1943–44, Cardinal LaTorre hid a Jewish family in his apartment in the Borgo. Had the Gestapo caught him he would probably have been sent straight to Auschwitz with his wards."

"I apologize, Eminence," the abbot spoke, his anger not yet cooled. "I was unfair to you personally, but I smell a general odor of anti-Semitism around the Vatican."

"You must keep in mind that the Arabs are Semites, too," LaTorre told.

"That's just playing with words, Eminence. In English anti-Semitism means anti-Jewish. I know you have to remember that many Christians live in Arab countries like Lebanon; and I know you have special interests in the Holy Land. But you're thinking of dealing with the Arabs as you did when they were weak and disunited. If they win, you'll soon be crawling to them, because those Christians will be their hostages. And you'll do your crawling through Jewish blood, no matter how civilized you think the Arabs are."

"Gentlemen," Francesco spoke out, affecting a pontifical mode that he had begun to use in dealing with traditionalists, "bicker at a more opportune time. We did not know of Cardinal LaTorre's actions during World War II. That was Christ's work. Men like you saved the Church from Pius's shame. But we are still troubled about what the abbot has said. I recall in 1952 sensing anti-Semitism here in the Vatican, and I still sense it. It is an odor that offends us deeply. We shall deal with it later. For the present we have a more tangible problem. We cannot be content with prayers. We must offer to arbitrate."

"I can recall," Signora Falconi spoke for the first time, "a learned judge saying 'Blessed are the peacemakers for they shall be spat on by everyone.' Has Your Holiness forgotten?"

"No, I haven't," Francesco sighed, "but it's a price that I'm willing to pay. The Church can't take two silent Popes in the same century. Monsignor Candutti, can we have the Egyptian and Syrian ambassadors here this morning? And someone from the Israeli embassy in Rome—the ambassador if possible? I'd like to see the Arabs and the Jews separately, of course. And please brief Cardinal Fieschi. Invite him to be present if he can spare the time."

"I shall talk to His Eminence as soon as I contact the ambassadors, Holiness," Candutti replied. "I'm sure that we can have the Arabs here very quickly. I'm not certain about the Israelis. But, Holiness, I think it's a vain hope, and I do not think that the papacy should risk its prestige on vain hopes."

"Most of my hopes are vain, *Monsignore*. It gives me something to look forward to in the next world."

It seemed that Candutti was correct in his assessment of the situation. When he ushered in the Egyptian and Syrian ambassadors, they were politely, although a trifle condescendingly, adamant. Francesco had opened the meeting with a blunt offer to mediate or arbitrate.

"This time," the Syrian replied, "the war must be fought to a final solution." He spoke in English, and, according to me, the term "final solution" was not accidental. It sent a shudder through the room.

"Surely, Your Excellency," *il Papa* said to the Egyptian ambassador, "the rocket bombardment of Tel Aviv can be halted. We ask you to convey our personal request—no, our plea—that the bombardment cease. We also ask—no, we beg you—to reconsider our offer to help bring peace."

"Holiness," the Egyptian smiled, rolling his eyes, and raising his palms upward in the classic Levantine gesture of helplessness, "my government anticipated your request when I spoke to them a few minutes before this audience. I am instructed to convey their grief at not being able to grant His Holiness's slightest whim, but on this issue they must remain firm. The Jews must surrender or the Jews must die. Years of fruitless negotiations convince us there is no third course. It is a *jihad.*"

"We cannot accept that answer, Excellency," Francesco responded. "We must publicly speak against this war and condemn it before the world."

"My government understands Your Holiness's concern, and it shares your love of peace. But Zionist imperialism is a cancer in the bowels of the world, and we must perform surgery. Inevitably some healthy tissue will be cut out, but we must save the patient's life. In the long run, you will see that our action will turn out to be a kindness. We ask that His Holiness reconsider our views in this matter; we also ask that when he prepares his public statement he keep in mind how well we have treated the Christian minority within our borders. They are not living in the filthy squalor of camps as are our homeless Palestinian brothers in Israel. We would not want our Muslim majority to turn against those Christians because His Holiness did not fully understand our cause."

Francesco stood up. "We hope that you will convey two messages to your government: first, our readiness to mediate or to help find a mediator who will be concerned for the plight of the Palestinians; second, our lack of fear of martyrdom for ourselves or for our people."

Thirty minutes later, when the Israeli ambassador to Italy arrived in the studio, the odor of blackmail still sat heavily in the air. In contrast to the cool urbanity of the Arabs, the Jew was already fatigued and testy, although it was scarcely noon. He also responded less diplomatically to Francesco's offer to mediate. "Holiness, why should my government trust the papacy? We remember too well the silence of Pius XII during World War II. We remember the Vatican's friendliness toward the Arab states since World War II and its coolness—even hostility—toward

Israel. We also remember the unhappy exchange between Pope Paul and Mrs. Meir, and the insulting remarks of the Vatican spokesman after that meeting."

"We hope you remember, too, that there is now a new Pope and a chance for a new outlook."

"We do, Your Holiness. We have few friends left in the world, but then Jews have never had many friends when the road got tough. I shall convey your offer to my government, but I am not optimistic about their reply. The war seems to be going badly for us at the moment, and even if all doubts about partiality were removed, it might not be expedient for us to accept mediation now. And, of course, we could not accept it at any time without assurances of simultaneous Arab acceptance."

"Very well. Has the bombardment of Tel Aviv slackened?"

"One can't be sure from minute to minute, but as of a half an hour ago it seemed to be increasing in intensity. At least 300 people are known to be dead and probably ten times that number injured."

After the meetings with the ambassadors, Francesco commanded Dottor Twisdale to convene an emergency press conference in the Sistine Chapel. I am certain that the *dottore* was obliged to make many telephone calls, for despite the Vatican's new attitude toward the news media, unless something special like the synod was in progress, few journalists spent their free hours in our press office on the Piazzo Pio XII, especially when what you Americans call the action was obviously happening somewhere else. It was after twelve-thirty when Francesco, Dottor Twisdale, Monsignor Bonetti, Monsignor Candutti, and I entered the chapel. None of us knew what *il Papa* was going to say.

"Ladies and gentlemen," Francesco began, "we appreciate your coming at such short notice. The news from the Middle East is grave; it is shocking. Not two decades ago Pope Paul VI stood in front of the United Nations and pleaded that there be no more war. His plea has not been heard. We have repeated his plea this morning to officials of the governments of Egypt, Israel, and Syria, and we have offered our services as mediator or as arbitrator in this conflict. Neither side has yet accepted our offer, and in all candor we do not expect immediate acceptance. But the offer remains open, today, tomorrow, or any time in the future, near, intermediate, or remote.

"We call on people of good will everywhere to pray for peace, and we ourselves shall pray. But we feel compelled to do more."

Candutti looked at me quizzically. I could only return the curiosity.

"In the hope that we can lessen the war's brutality if not end its slaughter, we shall fly today to Tel Aviv and take up temporary residence in the city. We hope that respect for our own person will cause the Egyptian government to cease its rocket bombardment."

Ecco, there were no sounds from the journalists. According to me, they simply could not comprehend what they had heard.

"We can allow just a few minutes for questions, then we must join Monsignor Candutti in making arrangements to fly to Israel."

For a full minute no hand was raised. Then an Italian newsman motioned.

"*Il Tempo.* Was this decision made at the recommendation of any of the curial prefects, for example, the secretary of state?"

"No. It was our decision and ours alone. We believe that if you look at Monsignor Candutti's expression you will know that this is the first he has heard of it. And," Francesco smiled, "we shall let someone else break the news to Cardinal Fieschi and face his anger."

"*L'Unita.* Why does Your Holiness pretend to be impartial and offer to mediate, then side with Zionist warmongers?"

"We do not side with anyone. We pledge that if the Israeli government retaliates by attacking the civilian population of an Egyptian or Syrian city, we shall go to that city as well. The reason for our going to Tel Aviv is that, to our knowledge, only the civilian population of that city is under bombardment."

"*Time* magazine. How will Your Holiness live in Tel Aviv?"

"Frugally. I hear the prices are high. Sericusly, we have an old friend from America who has an apartment there. We shall move into that apartment and share the dangers with the city's residents."

"*Der Spiegel*. What if you should be killed?"

"Then we shall have another conclave, and, who knows, perhaps even another Pope in your lifetime," Francesco smiled again, then paused. "But the question is important and deserves a more serious answer. It is a probability that we have considered. Our death could be an upsetting force in world politics, but we would hope it would have more of a settling effect. On occasion, death may shock us back to a state of reason and let us see violence in all its brutal stupidity. Besides," Francesco added ironically, "is there a more fitting place for the Vicar of Christ to die than in the Holy Land?"

With that very Italian touch of melodrama, the press conference adjourned. Monsignor Bonetti went scurrying to the palazzo to pack for *il Papa*, and Monsignor Candutti almost ran to his office to begin the necessary arrangements, diplomatic and logistic. Francesco decided to take only Monsignor Bonetti and the abbot. I insisted that I, too, be permitted to go. There was no heroism on my part. I simply could not endure the cooking of another conclave, and I told him so.

Fieschi was waiting for us in the studio. He had been attending a ceremony at the Laterano earlier in the morning and had missed our meetings. His face was red. *Ecco,* it was the first time I had seen him display true emotion. Certainly I had seen Fieschi become angry, but always a carefully controlled anger that lashed out in icy sarcasm, never confused rage.

"Holiness," he began as soon as we entered the room, "please tell me that this rumor about your going to Israel is false."

"The rumor is true. Monsignor Candutti is making the arrangements right now."

"Holiness, this is madness, absolute madness." Fieschi was almost shouting. "You could be killed. You must think beyond yourself and even beyond this crisis. You are risking the prestige of the Church. If your authority is challenged here, that authority will be useless in all other situations for years, perhaps generations. You have no army with which to silence Egyptian guns."

"If we do not risk our authority then we can never use it. What good is prestige or authority that cannot be used?

We have weighed carefully the potential costs and benefits and have decided to go ahead."

"Holiness," Fieschi pleaded, "let me go in your place. Let me take several other prefects with me. That way we risk far less."

Francesco's eyes softened. "I must go, Your Eminence, but you may have to follow. Death is a free gift of God."

Fieschi bowed and marched out of the room. He had recovered some of his poise but he was still racked with anger and frustration. I was not sure how much of his frustration came from not having been consulted in advance.

At five that afternoon we departed the papal gardens by helicopter and flew to Ciampino airport, not far from Castel Gandolfo, and boarded the military jet transport that the Italian government had placed at our disposal. It was a comfortable aircraft, the same one used by the president and the prime minister for their trips. We flew at 20,000 feet, with our course, speed, and altitude set by the Israeli government and broadcast by Italian and Israeli radio stations. The three hours and fifteen minutes in the air were uneventful. Francesco slept most of the way, and I dozed a bit as well. We had all missed our siestas.

Allora, we crossed the coast after sunset. Below us were islands of blue, white, and yellow lights against the dark land. I was surprised that there was no blackout, but I suppose it would have done no good against rockets. In any case, one could see fires, several dozen of them, burning around the city. When we touched down at Ben Gurion airport, we taxied beyond the administration building and were whisked past a small knot of reporters. The police drove us rapidly—although not so rapidly as the Italian police would have—to the apartment, already ringed with armed guards. The few people in the streets, from what we could see of them at night, seemed curious but reserved. Without doubt, the missiles dominated their minds, and it would not have been uncharitable for them to have thought that it was past time a Roman Pontiff did something *for* Jews instead of *to* them.

The apartment itself was very spacious: four bedrooms, a studio, and a large living room with a terrace that provided a vista of the sea. I found the days even warmer than in Roma, and the nights welcomely cool. The food was bland, but the Jewish kitchen has never appealed to me. I have also never understood how a region that grows such magnificent grapes produces such poor wine. I was obliged to content myself with Latroun—there is both a red and a rosé—grown by Trappist monks.

The trip immediately served its announced purpose. The final missile exploded in Tel Aviv some fifteen minutes before we landed. That night we listened to Radio Cairo announce that out of respect for the safety of the Roman Pontiff, the attacks on Tel Aviv were being temporarily suspended, but that other cities might become targets. It was late after a long day, but Francesco prepared another statement for the press, pleading for peace once more and announcing his readiness to travel anywhere in the Near East and live in any town whose civilian population was being bombarded.

The threat to attack other cities was not executed, and the press gave *il Papa* great credit. In private, Francesco said that he thought the Israeli counterattack that two days later sent the Egyptians reeling once more toward surrender and the canal had far more to do with the end of the bombardment. He was always realistic about such things.

Each day the Pontiff repeated his offer to mediate. The Israelis were silent and, according to me, embarrassed; the Arabs were silent and, according to everyone, angry. When the cease-fire came, it was, as the others had been over the years, arranged between Russia and the United States and expressed in the form of a resolution adopted by the Security Council of the United Nations.

There was yet another effect from *il Papa*'s trip, and that was on Francesco himself. Earlier I told you that at the coronation we witnessed, though we did not know it at the time, the beginnings of his transformation. This new crisis provided an additional catalyst—I do not know if one can say cause. According to me, the first person whom Francesco converted in his coronation address was himself. Moreover, I truly believe that he was as surprised as anyone else when he heard himself announce that he was going to Tel Aviv.

What I am saying was that Francesco came to us from the monastery physically restored and spiritually almost healed. During his first months in the Vatican he was the shrewd American political leader, devoted to a worthy cause. He understood some of the Church's problems and he was determined to try to solve them. He knew how to organize men and ideas to effect institutional policy. Still, as my brother Chelli had correctly surmised in the conclave, he was a secular leader transported into an ecclesiastical office.

In sum, he was missing a dimension as a religious leader. He was a good human being, not always sweet-tempered and surely not without ego, but he was a man of integrity, fair, just, and morally upright. Nevertheless, he was not yet a holy man. When a person has given himself totally to God it shows. I concede you that it shows seldom because it so seldom happens. Still when it does, we know it. There is an aura that envelops such people. I do not mean they automatically become patient, loving, and wise. Quite the contrary, they may become very impatient, irritable, and, by the standards of the world, foolish. But their frustrations are not for themselves or their personal goals, but rather, as the Jesuits put it, for the greater glory of God.

Francesco was beginning to acquire that aura. I can see that now in retrospect. He was, I believe, truly mistaken when he told Fieschi that he had carefully weighed the risks in going to Tel Aviv. That was an *ex post facto* rationalization. His decision, I have faith, was made instinctively, without calculation beyond its chance of saving lives. Please understand me carefully. I am not asserting that Francesco had suddenly or even slowly been transformed into a saint. He was far from that state. Nor was he yet totally dedicated to God—toward the Church of God, yes, because it was his own. That is not quite the same thing. It still involves a great deal of human ego, and I must repeat that Francesco was not lacking in that respect. What I am telling is that he was no longer merely the manager of men and ideas in the cause of social justice. He was, without realizing it, acquiring an even higher purpose which was already showing in a certain aura of holiness.

The abbot recognized this change before I did. The three of us talked at length when we were in Tel Aviv, for we were mercifully freed from the flood of paper. Looking back, I can now see that the abbot was trying to nourish

Francesco's development. Although I never could warm to the abbot, I grew to appreciate Francesco's affectionate admiration of the man. He had a gentle mind that could lead one into interesting fields of theological speculation. I confess, however, that I often did not understand his terminology and I retained some wariness about the brightness of the fire in his eyes.

Those days were good for me. For the first time since I had flown to America to bring the conclave's message to Declan Walsh, I was enjoying a full night's sleep. And I knew the same was true for Francesco. I rose late every morning, ate a leisurely breakfast on the terrace high over the city, and read the morning papers. I could absorb the vista of the Mediterranean on one side and, on the other, the brown hills that rolled toward Jerusàlem and then down to the Jordan.

Those were not days of indolence, only of comparative repose after the pace of life in Roma and Castel Gandolfo. We continued to labor. As I have now often said, Francesco was always working. The most important thing that he accomplished there was to write a first draft of his encyclical on social justice. In its initial form, it was not pleasing to him, nor was it yet pleasing to me. But at least he had put on paper his fundamental ideas: the right of every man to share in the earth's goods to the extent of having enough to feed, clothe, house and educate himself and his family; the universal obligation of acting as a brother and helper; the more particular but more pressing obligation of the wealthy to share their material goods with the needy; the absolute necessity of peace and, thus, the necessity that nations as well as individuals share their blessings.

As yet these were general ideas, and hardly new ones, even in papal encyclicals. What Francesco was groping for was a set of specific recommendations to implement these principles. When we returned to Roma, Francesco sent a diplomatic courier to Mr. Keller, asking for assistance in redrafting. That aid immediately came, but also a more general piece of advice: "Hit all your millionaires for every cent you can before you publish this jewel. You won't get more than fishy eyes afterwards. You are denying their god, private property, and you're preaching a share-the-wealth plan that out-Hueys Huey Long."

Francesco was aware that people unfamiliar with the

social teachings of the last century of papal encyclicals would think his statements radical. Actually, however, they were no more so than what Papa Paolo VI had written in his *Popolorum Progressio* of 1967. "But few people paid attention to Paul," Francesco noted. "He was the Pope of *Humanae Vitae,* banning artificial means of birth control as effectively as King Canute held back the tide. The poor devil's social message just got drowned by the static of sex. I want to avoid that trap."

Just ten days after the first rockets had landed, Israeli and Arab representatives in Geneva signed a cease-fire agreement, and the next morning we were permitted to visit Jerusalem. It was not a triumphal entry as Papa Paolo's had been in 1964; nevertheless, it was a solemn occasion. With Israeli security agents on all sides, we walked the hilly alleys of the Via Dolorosa from the place where Pilate's palazzo had stood to where tradition places Calvary, now inside the Church of the Holy Sepulchre. We were spared the fawning and persistent requests for money by the Greek Orthodox priests who own the church. It does not please me to offend against charity, but, in their bestowal of blessings followed by demands for money, those priests come closer to simony than any God-fearing man should care to travel. Worse, they are a source of scandal both to believers and nonbelievers. *Ebbene,* they are outside of Roma's jurisdiction.

Like good tourists, we visited the Garden of Gethsemane near the base of the Mount of Olives outside the walls of the old city. In this context, *old* means sixteenth century, when Suleiman the Magnificent rebuilt the city. Almost all the shrines of Christianity are "traditional" sites rather than precisely verified locations, because in about 70 A.D. the Romans destroyed the Jerusalem that Christ knew. In any event, in a display of ecumenism, we also visited the Garden Tomb, a lovely spot controlled by the Anglicans, outside the Damascas Gate along the Nablus road, where some people believe Christ was actually buried.

Before departing, Francesco had tried to see the prime minister, but each time we received a note of appreciation for *il Papa*'s humanitarianism—the words "aid" or "assistance" were carefully avoided—and an expression of regret that, as the Holy Father would understand from his own experience, the prime minister was obligated to remain at the front. Francesco snorted something about "front of the chow line," that I did not understand at the time. (As you know the colloquial word in Italian for hello or good-bye is *ciao,* pronounced like your English "chow." In fact, it comes from the Venetian dialect and is a corruption of "your slave.") I had imagined that *il Papa* was referring to some sort of reception line.

A few hours later, Francesco's requests to meet with the prime ministers of Syria and Egypt, transmitted by the American embassy, received similar refusals.

"I recall a parable about a wedding feast," Francesco grumbled, "and guests who were too busy to attend. Well, we shall see."

He said nothing more until we were in the car returning to Tel Aviv. That road is most interesting. The Israelis have constructed an *autostrada* between Tel Aviv and Jerusalem, but they have left in place (although sometimes repainted) the trucks and tanks that were destroyed along the way to Jerusalem during the "War of Liberation" of 1947–48. There was something about Francesco and police cars, I remember thinking, as he leaned over and spoke to the security agent in the front seat. "We have changed our plans. Please take us back to the Knesset building. We shall talk to the prime minister."

"We must go to the airport, sir. My orders are very strict."

"We know what your orders were, but our plans have been changed. Let us go back."

"I can't do that, sir. I must follow my instructions."

"Then we shall jump out and break a leg—at least. That would provide a considerable embarrassment for your government. Kidnapping Popes just isn't done these days. And don't forget that the Arabs thought we were bluffing about coming to Tel Aviv."

The agent picked up the radio microphone, and with sirens blaring the convoy made a U-turn across the center island and pivoted back to Jerusalem. The drive was not easy because of heavy city traffic, but the prime minister was awaiting us at the entrance of the Knesset building. It did not please him to see us, but he was properly cordial. Francesco took him by the arm, and the two of them went into a small room. I remained with Monsignori Bonetti and Candutti, chatting with the minister of foreign affairs, who was as baffled as we by *il Papa*'s breach of diplomatic decorum and at least as curious about what was being said. Within fifteen minutes, the two men returned to us, shook hands warmly, as people often do when they respectfully and reluctantly disagree, and the foreign minister escorted us back to our cars.

Francesco was silent all the way to the airport, only perfunctorily waving to occasional groups of people along the airport road. Near the plane, he posed briefly for photographs with the chief justice of Israel and several members of the Knesset, then hurried on board the aircraft and ordered the pilot to fly to Cairo.

The pilot, an Italian colonel, looked at me, but I avoided his eyes. I had fear of what he would read in mine. "It will take several hours at a minimum to obtain clearances, Holiness, if we can get them at all."

"It will go more quickly. The Egyptians will already know we are coming. The Israeli government will have informed them. The tower here will be able to give you full instructions. Contact Cairo as soon as we're airborne."

Francesco said nothing further; he sat in one of the *poltrone* and closed his eyes. He should have at least taken Monsignor Candutti into his confidence and have asked his advice; but *il Papa* said nothing to any of us. *Ecco,* as soon as our wheels had stopped rolling at Cairo, two jeeploads of Arab security agents came bustling on board. They inspected us carefully, then radioed to the limousine carrying the president and his minister of defense. Francesco greeted them at the portal and ushered the president into the forward compartment. Once more, Monsignori Bonetti and Candutti and I were left to entertain a cabinet official. As in Jerusalem, the conference was brief, no more than a quarter of an hour. We shook hands cordially, the Arabs departed—the security agents last—and our plane taxied toward the principal runway. Francesco still said nothing.

It was the abbot who broke the silence. "What happened?"

"I don't know if anything happened," Francesco spoke sullenly.

"What did you say?"

"Obviously not enough or well enough. I tried to emphasize the useless waste of lives and resources, but neither wanted to hear any more of that. I could make only two positive suggestions and neither was new: internationalization of Jerusalem and creation of a Palestinian state along the Jordan."

"What did they say?"

"Both said flatly no, absolutely no."

"At least you tried," the abbot told and reached over and touched Francesco's shoulder.

"Trying's not good enough," Francesco snapped, "and for God's sake don't touch me."

The abbot leaped back as if he had been on a spring. I tell this in confidence. You may use it only if you place it in full context. It is true that one never touches a Pontiff, but Francesco's laxity regarding papal decorum encouraged a human response to his sorrow. For Francesco's part, one must remember the transformation that he was experiencing was no doubt painful and the frustrations that he felt that day were major. Usually he was much more tender toward us all.

Once we returned to the papal palazzo, what you Americans so well call the rat race began again. I did not fully realize how pleasing the previous ten days had been until I saw that mountain of paper on my desk. I immediately decided to go home, enjoy a decent supper, and have a full night's sleep. Papa Francesco went immediately to his desk.

EIGHTEEN

IS IT NOT STRANGE how rapidly after a voyage all the events seem never to have really happened, but to have transpired in a dream or to have been something that one has read about rather than experienced? It was so with our effort in Tel Aviv, at least for me. I did not see LaTorre or Chelli for a few days after our return, and when I did visit them the events had already receded into that state of unreality. Both were curious to know about everything that had happened, but I could tell them much less than they wanted to know, although for different reasons than they believed.

Fieschi, I heard, was still upset, badly upset. I do not know to what extent this upset was due to Francesco's having risked his life or to Fieschi's aristocratic pique at having, in effect, been snubbed. Without saying anything to Fieschi, whose pride would have disapproved of my intervention as meddling, I had a brief conversation with Francesco about the affair. According to him, Fieschi had brought his troubles upon himself. According to me, that was indeed part of the problem, but only part. Francesco was not an easy man to work for, and I told him that. I also admitted I had second thoughts about Fieschi, but I was willing to allow him more time to prove himself, and urged Papa Francesco to take that risk. I reminded him of the genuine nature of Fieschi's concern over the safety of *il Papa* and his offer to go to Tel Aviv in the Pontiff's place. At the finish, Francesco agreed to make another attempt to utilize Fieschi's talents.

Chelli was more calm about the whole Jewish affair than either LaTorre or Fieschi, but that accorded with the Neapolitan's phlegmatic personality. Chelli's comment was that he continued to underestimate *il Papa.* It was a fault of which I also was guilty. At that time, I thought the whole episode was a failure. I was wrong, of course.

Allora, the rush of business went on. The crusade created its usual share of problems. The abbot returned to find his staff having difficulties with several local bishops who were unwilling to agree that volunteers for the crusade (if and when we had any) might be housed and trained at their half-empty seminaries. As for the spiritual renewal, already the Franciscans and Jesuits were predictably, perhaps even inevitably, at each other's throats. In the United States, some priests were campaigning for an end to mandatory celibacy, and agitation for ordination of women into the priesthood continued. Missionary efforts in Africa were causing friction with the cannibal who governed Uganda. Moreover, the president of the Portuguese National Conference of Bishops flew to Roma demanding an audience. He complained that Bisset's final letter as prefect of the Congregation for the Clergy had arrogantly insulted him by making false statements about his views on birth control and abortion. The cardinal archbishop threatened resignation unless an apology was forthcoming.

At the same time, a note arrived from the apostolic delegate in Washington that a dozen or more American bishops were going to quietly defy the ruling of the Congregation for the Sacraments that required even small children to attend confession before receiving Holy Communion. Three Christian Democratic deputies from the Veneto area of northern Italy were asking for a private audience so that they might apprise the Pontiff of the chances of trying again to repeal Italy's libertine abortion law. The rota—recall that is our court—had sent *il Papa* six marriage cases involving the Pauline Privilege, the authority of the Pontiff to dissolve marriages between a baptised person and a non-Christian. The rota had recommended dissolution in four of the six cases, but because only the Holy Father himself can make such decisions, the full papers in all six cases had been transmitted with the recommendations. There were other affairs, but these were the sorts of things, along with endless requests for private audiences, that greeted us.

We also received some welcome news. The refurbishing of the *casina* of Pio IV was almost completed. It was a delightful spot on the edge of the papal gardens. Toward the Vatican museums, it presented a large exterior fountain with water piped from Tivoli. Above the fountain, still facing the museums was a large oval-shaped terrace, paved with marble. Protecting the terrace from the view of the museums was what you Americans would probably call a gazebo, a stone and marble edifice of two stories, open on all sides but roofed. In the *casina* itself the Hungarian architect whom Francesco had engaged had arranged that *il Papa*'s studio would be on the second floor (what we Italians would have called the first floor), overlooking the oval terrace. The architect had not touched the frescoed ceilings there or elsewhere in the building, but it would not have displeased me had he destroyed them. Despite the fact that they had been done by supposedly first-class artists, they are a jumble of suffering Christian martyrs and reveling pagan gods.

Signora Falconi and the architect were now involved in the task of furnishing the residence. Apparently they had decided to do so in Italian modern, which is not to my taste, although judging from the cost of such pieces, it must please many people. Cardinal Pritchett and I walked over with the *signora* one warm October afternoon and ate a small lunch served on the terrace. We could see the *sam-*

pietrini—workmen who climb around the Vatican like monkeys—painting black the windows facing on the museums.

"Privacy," the *signora* explained, "although there is not much we can do about that." She pointed to the bar—you would call it a coffee stand—that jutted out between the gallery of modern art and the principal building of the museum. It was more than a hundred meters distant, but the people sitting there could look directly into the terrace. I suggested several trees for screening, and the *signora* seemed pleased.

Francesco was the principal topic of our conversation at lunch. (It was a simple meal of a *risotto alla pescatora, calamari,* and *gamberi fritti*—fried squid and shrimp—and salad. The wine was an undistinguished Orvietto, and for after we had fruit and *caffè*.) When we were finished, we took a walk in the gardens. We had intended to remain only a few minutes but the day was so gorgeous and the gardens so inviting that we spent nearly an hour wandering from fountain to shady grove to fountain. Occasionally we sat on one of the benches while I regained my breath.

Signora Falconi talked a great deal that day, more than I had heard her previously speak. As I told earlier, I had gained great respect for her efficient and devoted service. Now she expressed deep concern that Francesco was pushing himself into illness. Cardinal Pritchett and I agreed that *il Papa* was working much too hard and promised that we would encourage him to rest, but I doubt if any of the three of us thought that we would be effective. Although neither of us mentioned it, Pritchett and I were concerned about the incident on the plane. Pontiffs are not always gentle men—I suppose at times none of us is—but that outburst was very unlike Francesco. And, I inferred from what was said and, even more, not said, that it had not been a unique incident in the last few months.

A few days later I was called in mid-afternoon to attend a conference in *il Papa*'s studio. The topic was the bishops of Latin America and the spiritual renewal. When I entered, I found Fieschi, Pritchett, Martìn, and the abbot seated around the table.

"As usual," Francesco began as soon as I had closed the portal, "we need your advice. If we are to renew the

Church spiritually, to resurrect some measure of evangelic fervor that won't die out tomorrow when the preacherman leaves town, we must have the full commitment of the bishops and priests. They will have to lead in the beginning, although we hope that quickly laymen will take over some of the responsibilities. What I saw at the synod and what reports I have received via the grapevine don't give me much encouragement."

"I am certain that most bishops are preparing to cooperate fully," Fieschi said. (It pleased me that if he did not speak intelligently on this affair, at least he spoke without any trace of resentment.)

"Most, yes," Papa Francesco agreed, "but certainly not all. Few will be openly defiant, but a sizable minority will not give us more than formal cooperation."

"That is true," Martìn intervened, "and my people are trying to predict how bishops will react and to locate possible successors."

"Obviously we'll have to use the axe," Francesco said, "but let's talk of chopping heads in a few minutes. First, we were thinking that we might follow up on the few positive aspects of the last session of the synod. Cardinal Fieschi, we would like your help in drafting an encyclical stressing the immediate priority of the spiritual renewal and a specific set of steps that local bishops should begin taking. We would like you to comb through the debates and pick up on any statements. We can surely use the final recommendations. To assist you, we shall appoint a special task force, or whatever the papal name might be."

"Commission might be appropriate," Fieschi offered.

"All right, commission, to advise us on the whole problem of the spiritual renewal. As secretary of state, you, of course, would be the president, and as members the director general of the Jesuits, the minister general of the Franciscans, Cardinal Rauch as prefect of the Congregation for the Clergy, and Cardinal Galeotti will serve as our special representative."

"Should not," Fieschi asked, "Cardinal LaTorre be asked to serve and some of the other prefects, perhaps Cardinal Arriba, as prefect of the Congregation for the Religious?"

"Perhaps, perhaps," Francesco nodded. "We shall leave any other names up to Your Eminence, but we want this to be a working committee, a rapidly working committee, not a large assembly. There is another consideration," Francesco added with a nice, Italian touch of irony. "We do not yet know each other well but Your Eminence is probably not unaware that some of our brethren in the sacred college find our ways of proceeding to be strange, if not downright wrong. We do not want differences in temperament and personality to appear to become differences about fundamentals. Many of our brethren ask 'What should we forbid?' rather than 'What should we encourage?' In short, we grate on each other. Having said that, we leave it to Your Eminence's good judgment to select the other members of the commission."

Fieschi listened impassively. He nodded and jotted a few notes.

"Next is the matter of persuasion," Francesco continued. "We have considered several alternatives here, and we think that the best means will be a series of regional conferences of Latin American bishops. Each of those bishops would be invited to one of them. We ourself would attend each conference for several days. The last session of the synod has given us some ideas about how to proceed. Essentially, we wish to meet and talk with every bishop individually or in a small group. We erred at the synod in being too distant. What we missed was feedback from the bishops. We shall not repeat that error. Cardinal Pritchett will handle the details of these conferences."

Cardinal Pritchett spoke. "I think it would be better to allow the Latin American bishops themselves to arrange the details. We can look at your schedule and give them possible dates. After that and after telling them of Your Holiness's desire to meet with them as individuals, everything should be left to their discretion."

"You're right, of course," Francesco said to Pritchett. "Now, let's return to the basic problem. Persuasion alone will not suffice. We recall a parable about some seed falling on barren ground. Cardinal Martìn, tell us about the barren ground among our Latin American bishops."

"There are about 600 dioceses in the Caribbean, Central America, and South America. We have fifteen cardinals. Two of us are here in Rome. Of the remainder, four are anxious for such a revival; indeed, they would probably carry out a similar program themselves without any urging from Rome. Most of the others can be stirred to cooperation if not enthusiasm, though that stirring may not always be easy. Two, however, will probably think ill of the ideas, one because he is an old man opposed to all change," Martìn concluded.

"Who and how old?" Francesco asked.

"The archbishop of Lima; he is seventy-eight. He is fundamentally a kind man, but he has stayed on past his time. The last Pontiff would not accept his retirement because he could not find a replacement whom he thought suitable."

"We take it you have overcome that difficulty?"

"I have several candidates in mind, Holiness. I can present their names and dossiers to you whenever you are ready."

"Very well, let us accept the archbishop's resignation, reluctantly and with appropriate thanks, of course. Now, the other cardinal?"

"The other is younger, about sixty-two, but he fears, as you North Americans say, to rock the boat. His relations with his government are now pleasant, even cordial, but only after years of antagonism, hatred, and even persecution. He will not, to be sure, disobey, but he is convinced that the Church must wait before doing anything in his country that will raise the suspicions of the government. Thus he will give minimal cooperation."

"The archbishop of Mexico City, obviously. We had thought him an able man."

"He is able, Holiness, very able and very dedicated. But he is determined to solidify the Church's position and he fears any sort of large-scale ecclesiastical activity will regenerate the old fears and antagonisms. Actually, he may be right."

"In fact, probably right," Francesco agreed. "We mean to make the Church an independent force, and every intelligent politician fears an independent, powerful force. Well, we said we would not bring peace but the sword. We must rock the boat. What do we do about the cardinal archbishop?"

Martìn was silent, but Fieschi spoke up. "I have not yet been in my post as secretary of state long enough to speak with great authority"—one of the cleverest tricks of Fieschi's arrogance was his frequent assumption of a humble pose—"but I have personally known the archbishop for many years. He is, as you both say, a man of considerable ability. I would be willing to talk to him or correspond with him via courier to ensure privacy and prepare the way. Perhaps Your Holiness could then talk to him in person. He has always been open to reason." (Fieschi's intervention pleased me. He was making an obvious effort to assist.)

"The archbishop is eminently a man of reason," Martìn said, "but I am less sure that he can be swayed on this issue. Nevertheless, because of my great respect for him, I would suggest that we follow the suggestion of the secretary of state."

"Very well," Francesco concurred, "but we would like your congregation to be giving some thought to a potential replacement if the archbishop will not move. So much for the cardinals. How about the archbishops and bishops?"

"I cannot speak so precisely, Holiness, because of the greater number of people involved," Martìn replied. "As close as I can determine, however, there are about seventy-five bishops who will go to great lengths short of open opposition to frustrate this plan. Their motives vary from those of the archbishop of Mexico City to a deep political and social conservatism that convinces them that their dioceses are already the best of all moral places in this immoral world. I have prepared a list of their names."

Martìn handed *il Papa* four typewritten sheets. Francesco scanned them. "I recognize only three names. Two we recall from the early 1970s as being very friendly to the Brazilian regime and trying to silence priests who were exposing the government's frequent use of torture against political dissidents. The other made a point of welcoming the military coup in Chile in 1973 and had himself photographed shaking hands with the local general. We do not recall his ever speaking out for social reforms or against the brutality of a police state."

"There are several others in similar categories," Martìn noted. "Four to be precise. Those are the ones whose political conservatism pervades their ecclesiastical roles."

"They must go. Are any overage?"

"Only one."

"Accept his resignation and retirement, then transfer the others to unimportant posts." Francesco related this casually as if he were moving men on a chessboard. As you can see, the change I described as developing from the coronation to Tel Aviv was not complete. Total dedication is not quite the same as ruthlessness.

Fieschi lifted his eyebrows quizzically. I am not sure he was now happy to be reincluded in the inner circle of Vatican power. "Retirement is easy, Holiness," he remarked, "but transfer poses delicate problems. There is an ancient tradition of the Church, one as old as St. Gregory Nazianzen in the fourth century, that a bishop is wedded to his see; Vatican II's emphasis on collegiality reinforces that historic independence."

"We recall," Papa Francesco mused, "that in *Inter Corporalia* our great predecessor Innocent III said that he could dissolve a bishop's marriage to his see."

Fieschi was silent, taken aback by the precise reference. I confess a similar reaction. As a canon lawyer, I knew Innocenzo's dictum, but I hardly expected one who was neither a canon lawyer nor a Church historian to toss off such arcane knowledge.

"Well," Francesco went on, "collegiality does complicate matters. Do what you can, Cardinal Martìn. Bring them to Rome, if you must; send them to monasteries in Tibet if you can. Wait, what about our appointing coadjutor bishops with authority to exercise full power?"

"That would certainly be a slap in the face of healthy men."

"Yes, it would. Cardinal Fieschi, would it be possible for our nuncios in these countries quietly to inform Their Excellencies that we are disposed to accept their resignations and transfer them to other posts, letting them know that the alternative is a coadjutor bishop with full authority?"

"It could be done, of course, Holiness, although it is, as Cardinal Martìn said, an unkind fate for those who have served the Church for many years."

"We can't keep shepherds who can't protect their flocks from being eaten. Let us plan on that course for these men. Now, Cardinal Martìn, how many of the remaining bishops are near retirement, say over seventy?"

Martìn opened a thick loose-leaf binder and riffled through the pages for some minutes. "About twenty-three, Holiness."

"Very well, let us appoint coadjutor bishops to work as

their assistants and with the right of succession. That should save some face, while indicating where the real power lies. We suspect that the others will quickly get the message, but in case they do not, we want your office to continue screening candidates to succeed them or to act as coadjutors."

"Holiness," Fieschi put in, "Cardinal Martìn's work is going to be more complicated than it seems."

"Yes, we know," Francesco interrupted. He perceived, as I did, that Fieschi, while trying to be cooperative and helpful, still had major reservations. I shared some of them. *Il Papa* looked annoyed. "That's one reason we invited you here. We are aware of the various concordats that give the local governments a veto and of traditions in other countries that amount to the same thing. Your nuncios are going to have a difficult time dealing with military dictators, but we think enough word of the Spanish affair has trickled through diplomatic circles for people to know that we are ready to push hard for what we want. Those concordats must go. Cardinal Fieschi, we would ask that you and Monsignor Candutti take that as one of your principal tasks over the next few years. We have to free ourselves of control by secular power."

Fieschi nodded. "I concur, Holiness. We shall do all we can." There at least the two men agreed completely.

"Cardinal Martìn," Francesco said, "when you have a list of candidates as successors and coadjutors ready, we would like to see their files. How long will it take to prepare their records?"

"Three weeks, possibly four, Holiness."

"That long?" Francesco asked impatiently.

"Yes, Holiness. Unfortunately, the congregation only keeps certain files active all the time. Our having to choose so many people at one time and, of course, the political problem that His Eminence just mentioned make our work more difficult."

"Va bene," Francesco spoke. "Do it as quickly as you can. And when the new appointments are made, we want them staggered so as to attract relatively little attention from the secular press. The pattern will soon become obvious, but we want it formed before it is fully perceived by the outside. It will be recognized immediately within the Church."

When the meeting was finished and the others had departed, Francesco looked at me. "Ugo, when is the last time that the Church had such a bloodletting in one morning?"

"Probably not since Diocletian," I muttered.

Francesco laughed. "I would have said Pius X and the modernists, but that slaughter wasn't done in a single day. Well, I'm sure many people, at least many bishops, will look on this as a new persecution. I think the message will get through. I don't really think that we can keep what we're doing a secret, even during the next three weeks. The Vatican is a leaky sieve, but those leaks will put the fear of God into many of Their Excellencies, and staggered announcements of change will keep that fear alive."

"I hope it will make the Church a more effective instrument. The remedy is drastic," I admonished.

"I doubt that it will do all that I want or the Church needs, but it will help. Speaking of instruments, what's your impression of the reaction of our secretary of state?"

"Senti," I responded, "he is an able man. He has learned a lesson. Give him more time."

"A little, only a little. We do not have much to give."

NINETEEN

THAT EVIL THING MONEY was a constant problem for us in the autumn after Francesco's election, and it generated several serious problems of which we already possessed a plenitude. The necessity to obtain funds to operate his programs for the Church caused *il Papa* to irritate further some traditionalists, and, far more important, it led to his fateful decision to visit the United States on his way to attend the conferences of Latin American bishops. That necessity also distracted his attention from other pressing concerns, a fact that Francesco lamented more than anyone else. Yet how could it be otherwise? *Ecco,* let me proceed in a more orderly fashion and, as best I can, also tell you of another continuing problem that threatened the Church.

Despite Chelli's reservations about the crusade, he spent long hours manfully trying to reshuffle budgets, to pare away something there, to locate a purse hidden in a congregation's files, or to refuse to allow new expenditures. All these things helped. By the third week in October, his labors had garnished $30 million for us, an accomplishment that he—and I—felt was truly Herculean.

For his part, Francesco gave private audiences to eight American multimillionaires, three Italians, two Germans, one Irishman, and the directors of at least four foundations. From the Americans we received nearly $14 million, from the Germans and the Irishman a little more than $1 million, from the directors of the foundations promises to consider the matter, and, of course, from the Italians nothing at all. As had been noted during our discussion of the Church's finances, my countrymen tend to think that they have fulfilled their obligation to support the Church when they dramatically place a hundred-lire coin in the collection basket—and that only on the infrequent occasions when they attend Mass.

Fifteen million dollars was welcome, even when added to Chelli's $30 million, but it fell far short of the $125 million that the abbot's budget demanded for the first year. We all suspected that he had inflated that budget, but we were still nowhere near even a minimal goal.

Then another disaster struck. On the very day Chelli reported his successful gleaning of funds from the budget, the last of that year's tropical storms in the Caribbean veered sharply west and struck Honduras, leaving almost a thousand people dead and destroying the coastal economy. Obviously we, that is, the Vatican, would have to give liberally to aid these poor people, initially to ward off the immediate danger of epidemic and, later, to rebuild homes and posts of work.

Francesco's reaction was to convene what he called a council of war—Pritchett as secretary of the World Synod of Bishops, Martìn as president of the Congregation of Bishops but more important as a Latin American, Chelli as president of the Prefecture of Economic Affairs, and Fieschi both as secretary of state and president of the Administration of the Patrimony of the Holy See. (That office, you remember, is responsible for investing the Vatican's resources. The secretary of state is *ex officio* its chief, thus Fieschi had replaced LaTorre in that post.)

For hours we thrashed out problems of money. Again and again we pressed the abbot for a minimum figure. He stubbornly although sweetly stuck to $125 million, claiming that the hurricane only worsened the situation because it would increase pressure to add Honduras to the list of beneficiaries. Finally, after much coaxing that seemed to annoy Francesco, the abbot admitted that for $90 million he could do much good, though any lesser amount would be more wisely used for conventional works of charity.

Our $45 million thus put us halfway to our goal, but only on the unacceptable assumption that we would not help the poor people of Honduras. Francesco then raised the possibility of a special collection in all churches of the world for a Honduràn relief fund. Cardinal Pritchett, however, was opposed on pragmatic grounds. He argued that most of the money for such a fund would come from Canada, Germany, or the United States, and all three were again caught in an economic recession. Moreover, by the time the request went out through channels, Christmas would be hard upon us and people would be spending their money for gifts.

"Could we assess each diocese?" Francesco asked. "We could tax them to spread the burden and insure enough money."

"Holiness," Martìn spoke up, "the bishops would resent that. They don't like assessments, and they really don't have a great deal of cash or liquid assets. Even the Church in the United States is largely rich in schools, convents, and cathedrals; and those are hard to turn into dollars."

"We should also recall," Chelli observed—later he admitted to me he was testing Francesco's knowledge—"what happened when Papa Bonifacio VIII tried to tax the French clergy."

"This isn't the fourteenth century," Francesco retorted. "On the other hand, I have enough troubles without encouraging a Nogaret or a Colonna." (As you can see, Chelli's test was easy for Francesco, Nogaret and Colonna were the names of the cardinals who led the revolt against Papa Bonifacio.) "But need the preparations for a special collection take so long? Could we not have a letter ready within a day or two setting aside the last Sunday in November—no, make that the first Sunday in December, right after people are paid—for a special collection? In the United States we could call our plea a form of Thanksgiving. More generally we could phrase the letter to encourage people to give spiritual Christmas gifts this year rather than squander their money on material possessions. We could have people buy hospital beds or schoolrooms to carry their names or the names of others. What we don't use in Honduras, we can use in the crusade."

"I share Cardinal Pritchett's doubts, Holiness," Chelli said, "but we can certainly try."

"Yes, do try. Perhaps you and Cardinal Pritchett could have a letter drafted for me by tomorrow afternoon. Please give it to Cardinal Fieschi so that we can have the benefit of his views. I want a strong appeal, and, Cardinal Martìn, I want *all* the pastoral bishops to support this appeal. Now," Francesco halted, then began again, "it might help if the papacy itself were to do something to dramatize this attempt to raise money. Cardinal Chelli, we have heard that you are a connoisseur of art. Would it be possible rather soon for us to sell a few paintings or sculptures from the Vatican museums for the Hondurans and later for the crusade?"

Fieschi blanched; even Chelli blinked. Those ruptures in reverend masks indicated how deeply Francesco's suggestion had sliced. Chelli took a moment to sniff one of his Cuban cigars, then shrugged his shoulders. "Liberal cardinals have been urging such a course for years, but I need not tell Your Holiness that many of us would be firmly opposed to such action. We look on the art collection not merely as part of the patrimony of St. Peter but also as something held in trust for all mankind."

"Yes, we know and we sympathize," Francesco acknowledged, "but mankind desperately needs some of its trust funds right now. Thousands of Hondurans are facing death today, and millions of Africans, Asians, and Latin Americans face a subhuman existence. As chief justice we served on the Board of Trustees of the National Gallery of Art, so we know personally the curators of several American museums who would be very interested—and very capable of offering high bids."

"Holiness," Chelli told, "under this best of circumstances a decision to sell part of our treasure will breed fiery resentment; to do so under conditions that seem to give American institutions special favor will cause even more bitterness."

"Likely. Why not an auction then?"

Fieschi and Chelli were obviously appalled. " 'And over

my vestiture they cast lots.'" Fieschi spoke softly. Francesco looked at him with a coolly questioning smile. "Holiness," the cardinal went on, "it does not seem fitting for the Church to be auctioning her treasure like a common merchant."

"Is it any less fitting for the Church to have amassed a treasure in the first place? While we're quoting scripture, we recall something about selling one's goods, giving the proceeds to the poor, following Christ, and trusting in God's providence. The only questions we see are what to sell and for how much. At one time the Church did the world a great service by encouraging art and by preserving art. But the day is long past when that civilizing burden needs to fall on us. Dozens of other institutions are encouraging and preserving art better than we ever have or could."

Francesco glanced around the table with a look that indicated the thing was settled. Neither Fieschi nor Chelli met his gaze.

"Now," *il Papa* continued, "we don't want to flood the market. Since the art treasures are part of the patrimony of St. Peter, the sale falls under your jurisdiction, Cardinal Fieschi, but perhaps you might consult Cardinal Chelli, who, after all, is the Curia's expert on such things." (I was surprised to learn that Papa Francesco had heard about Chelli's love of art. It was something he talked about only among close friends.) "We shall leave it to your judgment to pick out several pieces that you think would bring more than a million dollars apiece—but we sell nothing by El Greco. That is a personal foible. You can start making whatever arrangements you think proper for the actual sale, but do so within ten days."

Fieschi began to say something—according to me, he wanted to ask *il Papa* to reconsider—but then changed his mind. Like Chelli, he merely shrugged his shoulders in an eloquent Italian acceptance of defeat. The sale would be made.

Francesco then paused to make some calculations on his pad. "It still will not be nearly enough, Holiness," Chelli said.

"You're right, of course," *il Papa* sighed. Then his face flashed a different mood. "Cardinal Pritchett, who is the best fund raiser in the American church?"

"There is no doubt there, Holiness: James C. Heegan of New York."

"Indeed. A week after New Year's we are scheduled to leave for Latin America to attend regional conferences of bishops." (You will note that Francesco had rejected the advice of Chelli and LaTorre and had decided to travel to the bishops. He had also rejected my advice on the subject.) "Why not leave a few days early and visit His Eminence in New York? Cardinal Pritchett, could you alert Cardinal Heegan about our problem and our plans? Perhaps he could arrange audiences with some wealthy American Catholics whom we have not yet met. We'll stay at his chancery. Ask him to call Mike Keller and have him join us. There is no one in the world more adept at separating a man and his purse than a Wall Street lawyer." Although he was now speaking rapidly, Francesco was talking more to himself than to us. "By then the Honduran disaster will have been forgotten by most people, but we can keep the image of the crusade bright and push for the spiritual renewal. As long as we're in New York, we should address the United Nations. Sooner or later they must help us with the crusade. Cardinal Fieschi, can your office secure an invitation to address the General Assembly?"

"I am sure that Monsignor Candutti can, Holiness, but do you think it wise at this time to—"

"No," Francesco interrupted, "I do not think such an address is wise at this time; I only think it is necessary."

Once more Francesco gave us each precise marching orders and dismissed us. That sort of meeting with its decisive ending typified Francesco's reign: the calling together of an ad hoc group and then swift, decisive moves. During his first few months, Francesco encouraged debate; then, more and more often, discussion by others would be brief. Their contribution came to consist more in providing accurate data than broad ideas. Francesco would swiftly inform us of his decisions. In private he told me that it sometimes happened that, in preparing for discussion, he could see things very clearly and would make up his mind. The conference on such occasions would be more the catalyst of his decision than its source.

I also should add that Francesco did not encourage the monthly plenary meetings of the prefects under the chairmanship of the secretary of state. Of course, he did not yet fully trust Fieschi, but there was more to it. Francesco explained to me that he did not want to give cardinals like LaTorre and Greene—Francesco was as late in recognizing Bisset's role as he was in recognizing LaTorre's ability—a forum in which they might make speeches that would solidify traditionalists and set servants against them. Second, and much more important, he believed that he could function more effectively standing at the center of several groups, none of whom was quite certain exactly what the others were doing. I found the situation ironical: a Pontiff trying to keep the Curia in the dark.

Even when the crisis of the dissident priests came that same week, Francesco worked in his usual way. The affair had had explosive possibilities from the beginning—and the beginning went back to the days of good Papa Giovanni and Vatican II. More recently, about the time of the conclave, a small group of young priests, mostly Americans but also several Dutch and Germans, and at least one Italian, had been using an apartment in Monte Sacro, on the far side of Roma from the Vatican, as headquarters for a movement to modernize the Church. Their three immediate objectives were an end to mandatory celibacy, a revision of the teachings of *Humanae Vitae* regarding birth control, and ordination of women as priests. For a time—and, as I have said, especially during the session of the World Synod of Bishops—these people contented themselves with issuing press releases and distributing pamphlets in the Piazza di San Pietro, in the Church of Santa Susanna, an English-speaking parish not far from the Via Veneto, and in several other churches that were likely to be frequented by foreigners.

Allora, at 9:00 A.M. on 1 November, the feast of All Saints, seventy-five of these dissidents gathered in front of the Hotel Alicorni and marched to the papal palazzo. The Italian police had received no advance notice, but no incidents occurred because the route was only a few blocks long and traffic was light—all major feasts of the Church are national holidays in Italy. It was not until the demonstrators reached the Swiss Guards at the bronze portals at the foot of the scala regia leading into the palazzo, that we realized what was happening.

The noise was tremendous. The priests were shouting (mostly in English) and pushing against the guards, who had placed their pikes as barriers across the open portal. Now and then a few irate spectators, mostly Italians, would throw chunks of horse manure, which is always in plentiful supply from the dozen or more tourist carriages parked in the shade. These missiles fell largely among the ranks of the priests, although some splattered inside the portals.

As far as we could determine, the priests were demanding to see *il Papa.* Monsignor Bonetti and I—Fieschi was in Palermo that day and Zaleski had gone to Fiumicino to greet an aged Chinese bishop from Formosa—peered out the studio window, but the angle was such that we could see only the tail of the mob and the manure throwing. We also saw three Italian police cars drive to the white line that separates Vatican City from Italy. I believe I explained that, for some years before Francesco, we had had an arrangement with the Italian government whereby they helped police the piazza, but Papa Francesco had ended that agreement.

Il Papa's reaction was swift. He ordered Monsignor Bonetti to ask the Italian police to move out of sight, and to send a contingent of Vatican police to disperse—peacefully—the manure throwers. Then, with Cardinal Rauch, the prefect of the Congregation for the Clergy, Francesco descended the scala regia. I followed at a safe distance. I am willing to die for the Church, but I shrink from the thought of being martyred by fresh horse droppings.

At first, when the front ranks of the priests saw *il Papa* they howled more loudly, but as we came nearer, they quieted.

"Why do you try to break into an open house?" Francesco asked. "If any of you had asked to see me, we should have invited him in. But we shall not treat with a mob, not even a mob of priests. We shall meet with three of you in our study tomorrow at eleven and discuss whatever problems trouble you. Now you must go home—but first, let us all go into St. Peter's and pray."

With that touch of bravado, Francesco motioned to the Swiss Guards to lower their pikes and walked calmly through the group and led the way into the basilica and up to the main altar. For ten minutes he—and they—knelt in silent prayer in front of the giant baldachino and its twisted bronze columns. The tourist traffic was light, but those in the basilica enjoyed the spectacle. Then, Francesco stood up, faced the group, and while they were still kneeling, blessed them and said, "Go in peace."

The Pontiff had intended to invite only Rauch and me to attend the next day's session with the three priests, but at my urging he included Fieschi. We listened for more than an hour. At first we heard a screed, bitter outbursts against authority in the form of *il Papa,* the Curia, various national conferences of bishops, individual bishops and pastors, parents, teachers, and so forth. Then the tone slowly changed from raging anger to frustration, then to revelations of loneliness. These men, I could see, had once been among the most fervent of young priests, but their pastoral work had disillusioned them with the institutions of the Church, with their superiors, with their flocks, and perhaps, with themselves as well.

I knew the despair and the loneliness they described and so did the other two cardinals. Every priest knows it—which is why, perhaps, the Curia or the bishop's chancery attracts so many of us. There we are secure in the company of other lonely humans. Two years in a monastery could not have led Francesco to understand these emotions as we did, or so we thought. The conviction—not false pride in theological knowledge—the conviction that their loneliness is the supreme sacrifice to God is, according to me, the foundation for the sense of superiority that clerics have over laymen.

Francesco listened without saying a word until the three had talked themselves out. His first response, he said, was from the gospel according to Pogo: "We have met the enemy, and they is us." Fortunately, having lived in the United States, I understood, as did the two American priests. The Dutch priest and the two cardinals were equally confused. Francesco then admitted that although he had not experienced their particular pains and problems, he had known enough of each in his own life, especially in the loneliness of the two and a half years since Kate's death, to feel a strong chord of human sympathy.

"You want to reform the Church," he said. "So do I. We differ in our approaches and in our immediate, though probably not in our ultimate, objectives. I want to start at the roots, to return the Church to its origins and so revitalize it. I do not want to dissipate my energy on problems, however serious and however painful, that are at the periphery of the Church's basic condition. I know that, in effect, I am asking you and others to continue to suffer and perhaps unjustly. I understand what that means. I have been a soldier whose life and whose men's lives were only a single marker on the map of a general who was quite willing to see all of us killed if our deaths would buy time for the rest of his army. I am asking you to buy me time, to allow me to concentrate on the most fundamental problems now. Celibacy, birth control, ordination of women are real problems, but they are not the fundamental problems. When the Church is firmly set on its new course, when its revitalization is an actual process, then I shall give priority to the problems you raise. To attack them now would be to divide the Church before our real work had begun."

"I think we can understand," one of the Americans said, "but understanding is not enough. You are our one hope. You have an open mind on these issues, not the closed curial mentality of your predecessors—or likely successors. Help us now. We are crying out to you not only for ourselves but for men and women around the world, for lonely priests, for holy women who cannot answer God's call, and for conscience-racked lay people."

Francesco was churning inside. One could read the anguish in his face. I had fear that he might give in to cries for help where he would have repulsed a frontal assault. I sensed that at least Fieschi shared that fear.

"You are right," *il Papa* replied. "It is not good, but it will have to suffice. It is no less easy to decree than to accept. I shall make you only two promises. I will continue to do everything within my power, which is more limited than you think, to renew and revitalize the Church so that you will know that your suffering is not in vain. And I will re-examine the question of priestly celibacy now. Not the others, not yet. But I would be deceiving you if I held out any implied promise of change. In 1971, the World Synod of Bishops explored the problem and by an overwhelming majority voted to retain celibacy. Earlier Pope John had worried over the problem and later Pope Paul. Whatever criticisms you have of Pope Paul, certainly you agree that John was a man of great charity and warm human understanding. And surely all of those in the majority of the synod were not old men whose juices of life had long dried up."

Francesco paused to let his words sink in. Then he went on: "Let me also remind you what you must already know from the confessional. Marriage is not a panacea for loneliness, frustration, or sexual drive. It brings its own problems. Love can turn to indifference and even hate; illness can disrupt all plans; and even children are sometimes less than appreciative of parental sacrifices. Thus, although you did not speak of them today, you are raising questions about divorce."

Francesco stood up and, of course, we all rose.

"We wish that we could offer you more personal encouragement; we wish that we knew some formula that could help you and hundreds of thousands of others—and could help ourself as well. But we were only consecrated as infallible, not as omniscient or omnipotent. We repeat our pledge to renew the Church and to worry again over the question of celibacy. Let us pray for each other to receive God's wisdom and mercy."

As the group left the studio, Francesco turned from his desk. "Incidentally, if you wish to see us again, please telephone Monsignor Bonetti. Some of the Swiss Guards have had a difficult time removing certain brown stains from their uniforms."

TWENTY

THE CHRISTMAS SEASON, with its demands for papal participation in various rituals, added to Francesco's burdens. That should be a time of great joy in the Church, as we celebrate the birth of the Savior. I confess, however, that Francesco took scant joy. Even after his participation in the Mass at San Pietro he returned to his desk, though in the *casina* in the gardens rather than the palazzo. The most cheerful note was that the special collections for Honduran relief had netted us $16 million, half from the United States. Francesco apparently knew something about the psychology of his countrymen. We used $6 million of this money to replace what we had "borrowed" from our own accounts to aid the Hondurans in November, and put the remainder aside for the crusade. Chelli's sale of art treasures netted us another $3 million for the crusade.

Meanwhile, Cardinal Pritchett and Monsignor Candutti had been laboring to arrange not only for *il Papa*'s trip to Latin America but the complications of a visit to the United States and an address to the UN. Both of the latter turned out to be dramatic events, benchmarks in Francesco's reign and perhaps in the life of the modern Church, but everything began most inauspiciously.

Before our convoy of automobiles formed in front of San Pietro, a cold rain had almost emptied the great piazza of spectators. We moved out slowly behind the screaming sirens of police cars and flanked by the big black motorcycles of the *carabinieri,* trying to navigate the Roman traffic without injury to life. Despite the biting weather, Francesco chose to use the open Mercedes that allows *il Papa* to stand and be seen. The rain discouraged the crowds more than it did Francesco, for even along the Viale Trastevere there were only small clumps of spec-
and the *autostrada* to Fiumicino, I insisted that we stop
tators. Once we reached the junction of the Via Magliana
and that Francesco join us in one of the sedans. He did not argue. He seemed cold and his cheeks were flushed. He had wanted—and, according to me, needed—the exhilaration of a cheering crowd and was disappointed by the sparse turnout.

At the airport, the motorcade drove directly onto the runway to a 727 trijet bearing the papal crest on its nose. One of Francesco's millionaire friends from Chicago had put his personal aircraft at our disposal for the entire trip. It had been refitted with additional fuel tanks so that the transatlantic voyage would pose no difficulty. Inside, the plane differed markedly from its commercial sisters. Forward, there were three small bedrooms (more like cubicles), in the center a pleasant but narrow studio, then a small kitchen. The rear of the craft had comfortable seats for eighteen people.

The plane had arrived in Roma two days earlier and had been subjected to thorough checking by mechanics from Alitalia. Francesco said something about his having greater faith had it been gone over by Germans. "The Italians are like the Irish. They don't understand any piece of machinery more complicated than a wheelbarrow." For me, at least, it was true enough.

We had a full complement of personnel with us. In addition to Francesco and me, there were the abbot, Monsignori Bonetti, Cavanaugh, and Candutti and Cardinals Pritchett, Martìn, and Fieschi. We also carried a *misto* of others: Dottor Twisdale and Grottanelli (the latter, you recall, was Francesco's choice to edit *L'Osservatore Romano*) to deal with journalists; two security agents to help cope with crowds; and several young clerics who were secretaries to older clerics.

On board I could not follow my usual routine of a light lunch and a capsule because *il Papa* wanted the abbot and me to go over again with him his orations. Francesco recounted a remark by Adlai Stevenson that when Cicero spoke men commented on his eloquence; when Demosthenes spoke, men said, "Let us march." *Il Papa* wanted men to march. And so for at least the twentieth time we read aloud the texts of the address to the United Nations and the three interventions to the regional conferences of bishops in Latin America.

The final review of those orations was far more painstaking than usual, but the genesis was quite normal for formal addresses. Unlike his impromptu allocutions at special audiences, Francesco labored carefully on his formal speeches. Here, as usual, he had sketched an outline and dictated a rough draft to Signora Falconi. That product was given to Monsignor Cavanaugh and usually someone else, most often the abbot, Cardinal Pritchett, or me. Together they would make a second draft. At that point Francesco would re-edit the manuscript, and give it to me to check for what he called latent heresy. After that he would send a copy to the secretary of state's office for distribution to and comment by appropriate curial offices. Meanwhile, Monsignor Cavanaugh would be revising the draft. When all the comments were prepared, Francesco would himself edit the manuscript one final time. Finality, however, never seemed to arrive on this trip.

In truth, all that staff work usually gave Francesco relatively little help. He had a—how do you say?—a knack of catching the heart of a problem. Monsignor Cavanaugh helped most of all in suggesting phrases that would strike sparks, but that was hardly creative in the true sense, since the *monsignore* spent a good part of his time reading the books and opinions of Declan Walsh and inserting Declan's style into the speeches of Papa Francesco. I should note also that Francesco's knack was not always a good thing. He was so knowledgeable and so quick to focus his knowledge that even his apparently spontaneous reactions often appeared as intricate and fully developed ideas. That capacity could paralyze a staff. The interesting work of creation was done for them, and tedium does not stir the imagination.

Ecco, in this case, Bisset had provided a number of comments that, although individually carping, taken all together pointed to several weaknesses. As usual, Chelli provided an excellent critique. But the orations retained the ideas of *il Papa* and remained in the strong if—I grope for the precise word in English—earthy style of Declan Walsh. What I mean is that the talks lacked the ethereal quality (Francesco said "vagueness") that one associates with papal pronouncements or their normal shroud of sanctity (in Francesco's opinion, "lugubrious Latinese"). There were a few remarks that bordered on quips; other sentences snapped like whips rather than rolling out like soft carpets leading to salvation. *Ebbene,* as one says, all tastes are tastes.

The flight went smoothly—something I mention whenever I speak about flying because I have been on several near disasters. We departed Fiumicino just before noon and arrived in New York eight and a half hours later, about 2:30 P.M., local time. We were routed, as planned, directly into the airport at Newark, where air traffic would be relatively light. The day was sharply cold—below zero centigrade, in the twenties according to your Fahrenheit standard—and blindingly bright for those of us whose internal clocks told it was 8:30 P.M.

The cold had not, however, deterred the Americans. Hosts of government dignitaries were present, including the governor and chief justice of the state, two United States senators, three congressmen, the mayor of Newark (someone said that the Italian vote was important there despite the fact that the mayor was black), and various party leaders. Of course, there was a large clerical gathering: the archbishop of Newark and several bishops in the state; James Cardinal Heegan, the archbishop of New York; John Cardinal O'Brien, the archbishop of Chicago and president of the National Conference of Bishops of the United States; Archbishop Giuseppe Rossati, my successor as the apostolic delegate in Washington; and a gaggle of *monsignori* and priests, all, God help us, beaming smiles as bright as the day itself.

As he stepped from the plane, Francesco accepted the greetings of the governor, shook hands with the other officials, waved to the ecclesiastical dignitaries and asked Monsignor Bonetti to request them to wait inside the terminal for him. Then, to the horror of the security agents—and, I confess, to me as well—the Pontiff walked toward a crowd of people who had somehow forced their way onto the concrete apron and were being restrained by a tight cordon of state police with drawn clubs. *Il Papa* made the sign of the cross and most of the people knelt. Then, like an American presidential candidate, he came into the crowd and began touching hands. According to me, the police hated him, but the crowd loved it. There were no unpleasant incidents.

Trans World Airlines had put their Ambassadors Club at our disposal, and we walked there, twice stopping, however, for Francesco to repeat his blessing and hand touching with crowds within the terminal. *Ecco,* with the prelates and priests gathered around, we experienced another round of ring kissing and handshaking. Francesco used the occasion to make a brief allocution. He told that he had returned home to preach the simple message of the Gospels: to love God by loving one's fellow man. The world, he said, was in the throes of massive change. Christians, laity as well as clergy, had to lead in reshaping the modern world. But first we all need "to touch again the rich red earth of our fundamental commitment to love God and neighbor" and to rededicate ourselves to those purposes. Renewal, he stressed, was a continuous process, not a single event, but he wanted it to begin in a formal way to signify both to each other and to our inner selves our unyielding commitment to social justice, to sharing material goods with the poor and the hungry.

"We live in a world," he concluded, "that is begging for spiritual guidance as well as material progress. We live in one of those critical times in civilization when a few men and women can change the course of human history. Let us seize our destiny and operate in our revolutionary tradition of love, peace, and justice."

Francesco had intended to crowd Cardinals O'Brien,

Fieschi, Heegan, and Pritchett and himself into one limousine so that they could talk during the drive to the chancery of the archdiocese of New York; instead there was an open touring car for *il Papa,* with room for only one or two other people. *Ecco,* Fieschi rode with Signora Falconi and me. The rest of our group were scattered through a long motorcade.

Fieschi was happy with the shift in plans. His English was good but not fluent, and having to converse in a noisy, crowded automobile was not something that would have pleased him. On the other hand, during the past few weeks, he, Signora Falconi, and I had begun to strike what was to become as close to a warm friendship as, according to me, Fieschi had ever known. Despite his aristocratic hauteur, the Genovan had recognized at a drumbeat how effectively the American woman handled *il Papa*'s business. He did not fully approve of lay persons, especially a female, in a position of potential influence within the Vatican. (Perhaps he remembered how Sister Pasqualina had come to control access to Papa Pacelli.) Nevertheless, he respected efficiency and loyalty. For her part, Signora Falconi respected the cardinal's single-purposed mind, and, like all women, she was fascinated by his gallantry and good figure. Had he not been totally true to his vows, Fieschi might have become notorious as a Lothario. But above all else he was a man of honor and integrity. The *signora* recognized these traits and, much more rapidly than Francesco, sensed that bringing him "within the family," as she phrased it, was important to *il Papa*'s success.

Our convoy into New York was slow in starting because, as we were on the point of leaving the terminal, Francesco again wandered over to the crowds of people. It was obvious to me how much he needed their physical presence. It had never occurred to me before because in so many ways Francesco was an aloof man, one whose apparent friendliness was itself a mode of keeping people at a distance.

Ecco, the drive between Newark and New York City is obscene. You Americans have blighted your countryside even worse than we Italians. God will call us all to answer for sins of waste and ingratitude, and his laws of nature will punish our children. At least the drive came before the rush hour; even so, the streets were stuffed with people. It was all the police could do to keep a path open for us into the chancery on Madison Avenue behind St. Patrick's Cathedral. Waiting for us outside in the cold, where they could be seen by the television cameras and the crowd, was another collection of public officials, this time from New York—the governor, the mayor, more senators, and what appeared to me a sea of faces and outstretched hands. The sun had by then fallen below the mountainous buildings, and an icy wind was whipping through the deep canyons, but, despite the ugly weather, we suffered through a quarter hour's ritual of exchanging greetings and pleasant words into the microphones. After *il Papa* had blessed the crowd several times, we finally entered the more blessed warmth of the chancery.

The politicians came with us, accepted coffee—not real *caffè espresso,* but that sickeningly weak *caffè Americano*—chatted for a few awkward moments, and then made their excuses. *Il Papa* then joined Cardinal Heegan in his studio along with the Cardinals O'Brien, Pritchett, and Fieschi. I was invited to accompany them, but I was not able. (I pray you remember, even though it was only five-thirty in the afternoon in New York, it was eleven-thirty at night in Roma, and we had risen at five-thirty in the morning Roman time.) Instead I asked for a light tray to be sent to my room. There were numerous bottles of all varieties of whisky and even sherry available, but the only table wine in the cupboard was a poisonously sweet, red beverage labeled "burgundy" from New York State. I decided that a half a bottle of sherry was preferable, although I had never before practiced the Spanish custom of drinking fortified wine with a meal.

Francesco must have spent several hours with the cardinals. From what I learned later, much of the discussion centered around money since that was Cardinal Heegan's forte. Morally he was a fine man, I pray you understand that, and a fine prince of the Church. He had been, I am sure, one of those silent cardinals who had voted for Francesco in the conclave. You must also understand, however, that he was not heavily gifted intellectually. His strength lay in his integrity and in a personal style that American millionaires considered attractive. He could be what you Americans call "one of the boys," a role he played easily because, according to me, no acting was required. He was,

I heard, an excellent poker player; it pleased him t wager on horses, and he had capacity to drink a great deal of bourbon without demonstrating any ill effects. As a fair-minded administrator and as a fund raiser, his reputation was fully deserved, but he neither knew nor cared anything about theology in the formal, scholastic sense. He possessed a simple faith in God, Christ, the Church, *il Papa,* and himself that I always marvel at and sometimes envy. Of all people, Heegan could help Francesco to find money for the crusade, and he would dutifully execute every directive regarding the spiritual renewal, but without adding a single idea of his own or perhaps without understanding any of Francesco's.

Allora, about ten-thirty Heegan's special guest, Charles Patrick Randall, II—the oil speculator, financier, Las Vegas casino owner, and God knows what else other than being a fallen-away Catholic—arrived for a late supper with *il Papa.* Later, Mr. Keller estimated for us that Randall's wealth totaled about $75 million. There was a connection here to Francesco's earlier life. Signor Randall was the father of a young officer who had died of wounds when serving under Declan Walsh's command in Korea.

I had no idea when Francesco went to bed that night. Certainly it was much too late. The oration at the General Assembly of the United Nations was scheduled at noon, and we all slept until after nine; then we ate one of your marvelous American breakfasts. There, your first collation, is one place that you and the English could teach continentals about food. We are accustomed to a dry roll, perhaps with a little marmalade, and several quickly gulped cups of cappuccino. But your large glasses of fruit juice, grapefruit halves, and melons, ham, sausages, bacon—even the British fish—toast, eggs, waffles, and coffee, all eaten slowly over the morning newspaper, form one of the most attractive parts of Anglo-American culture.

We had kept the morning free, which was just as well, for Francesco suffered a bad throat and a small cough. He closeted himself in Heegan's studio to review his speech once again, although he was already too much prepared. The cardinal's Irish housekeeper brought him several cups of strong, hot tea, her folk remedy for a bad throat. Fieschi and I, with overcoats buttoned high, took a stroll and did some sightseeing, while Signora Falconi shopped on Fifth

Avenue. We all left by the posterior entrance, because there was yet a crowd—or again a crowd, I cannot say which—in front of the chancery. By eleven-thirty we returned, red cheeked and ready.

Without doubt you have read the published version of the oration. That version is more polished than what Francesco actually spoke. I have listened to the recording many times. He did not stand behind a podium with the manuscript before him, but stood before the assembly, a wireless microphone at his throat, and he spoke without manuscript, even without notes. His hands were joined together as if in prayer. He began:

> We come in the name of justice and in the name of peace. We come to beg you, the leaders of the great powers, not only to redouble your efforts toward understanding and disarmament, but also to share some of your wealth—certainly that portion which you have been spending on weapons—with the poorer peoples of the world. We come to beg the other developed nations to join in this sharing of largesse with their brothers and sisters.

Then he went on to ask the leaders of developing nations for patience and charity toward their own people, to beware lest domestic tyranny replace foreign imperialism, and also to keep in mind that economic development was not an end in itself but only a means to allow individuals to realize their potential for goodness. Further, he warned all leaders of men that "those of us" who held temporal or spiritual power held it in trust for their people and would some day have to account to God for the use of that trust.

He made a special plea for peace and justice in the Near East, repeating standard suggestions for internationalization of Jerusalem. He also urged that, whatever the final terms of peace, the Palestinian refugees be immediately allowed, according to their own choice, to resettle in lands occupied by Israel or to migrate to other Arab nations. Then he added to the prepared text a sentence that appalled Chelli: "We know such an exodus is costly, and we pledge not only the moral support of the Catholic church but also to accept our fair share of the financial burdens of such resettlement."

At that point, Francesco linked the crusade to the more general cause of peace, a means of reducing want and envy and hatred. "We lack the eloquence of St. Paul; therefore, in these matters we ask you to look to our deeds. We have tried to bring peace in the Near East, and we are about to begin a crusade in Latin America against hunger, poverty, and disease. We have sold some of our age-old treasures to finance these efforts, and we shall sell still more." He urged the United Nations to take over financial responsibility for the crusade within a year. The Church, he promised, would continue to give all it could, but its limited resources would soon be drained. If the UN would so act, he offered another pledge: to begin, as soon as the Vatican's finances permitted, similar campaigns to help the poor and the hungry in Africa and Asia.

More generally, he pleaded for nations to share their goods with each other, and labeled such a policy as not only charitable but prudent. To those in dire need, violence was often an acceptable risk; and the world had shrunk to the point that, as crises in the Near East, Africa, and southeast Asia had shown, even small wars threatened holocaust by bringing the great powers into confrontation. "So far such confrontations have stopped short of total destruction, but we have already tempted fate—and God—too often. Sooner or later one of these exercises in brinksmanship will send this planet tumbling through space as an uninhabited and uninhabitable desert."

When he came to the conclusion of his oration, Francesco deliberately shifted from the papal "we" to the more personal "I":

> As did the prophets of the Old Testament, I call on you to join us in repenting our sins. As did the evangelists of the New Testament, I call on you to love your fellow man. As do moral men of the modern world, I call on you to remember that love and justice are not merely virtues, they are necessities if humanity is to survive. In the name of God and in the name of mankind, I beg you on my knees to practice justice and love and so to bring peace.

At this point, Francesco knelt down. I could feel that the delegates were as astonished as I was. We had never discussed such a dramatic—according to me, melodramatic—gesture. The oration was to have finished with the sentence about survival.

"I beg you," Francesco repeated softly as he stood up, "in the name of God and in the name of your children." He paused and with his right hand made the sign of the cross: "May the Almighty God bless you, the Father, the Son, and the Holy Spirit." There was absolute silence in the General Assembly, as *il Papa* strode from the platform. No one moved or spoke for some minutes.

I cannot say what lasting effect the oration and the kneeling had on the delegates themselves. Cynically, perhaps realistically, one could argue it had small effect, although the promise of shifting the crusade to Africa and Asia did arouse some delegates to support our efforts in Latin America. But more generally, one certainly looks in vain for an epidemic of justice in the world. Yet I am secure that the speech made a deep effect on hundreds of thousands, perhaps millions, of individuals who saw on their televisions *il Papa* kneeling to beg justice and peace for them and their children.

The oration to the UN and the coronation address were in some modes similar; the first convert of Francesco's plea to the UN was Francesco himself. That oration marked another significant step in his transformation from secular to religious leader—*ecco,* from good man to holy man. He had convinced himself of the veracity of his vision and his mission; that conviction showed in his voice, his face, his entire manner. I saw hovering about him the aura of a man dedicating—I do not yet say "fully dedicated"—himself to God. At his election, he had been a brilliant, energetic, moral man touched with luck. Now, his coronation address, his trip to Israel to stop the rockets, and his speech to the UN showed there was more. He had been touched not with luck but by God's lightning. I could not help but recall Michelangelo's frescoes on the ceiling of the Sistine Chapel and my own vacillation during the conclave as I had pondered the finger of God reaching out toward Adam. I was still troubled by my decision, but for very different reasons.

If I needed confirmation of my perception of Francesco's process of transformation, it came in two respects that very afternoon. When we left the UN's building, the crowds were no longer merely curious; they were excited and truly moved. Even in the horribly frigid air of New York, I could feel a tingle of emotion that was far more intense than it had been for Papa Paolo or even than it had been for Papa Giovanni in Italy; it was also more subtle and more soul-piercing than the emotion that *any* recent Pontiff had generated.

The second confirmation came from Mr. Keller, who was at the chancery awaiting our return. Francesco greeted him warmly but quickly, and hurried away to rest, promising a longer visit in an hour. I could read the shock on Mr. Keller's face. We sat together in Cardinal Heegan's living room, before an open fire, pouring out in utter silence our confused hearts to each other about what was happening to our friend.

TWENTY-ONE

AS MR. KELLER and I sat in front of the fire that afternoon, we had no reason to believe that the day's real surprises had only begun. God was merciful in granting ignorance, for the fatigue of jet lag, the strain of preparing the orations again and again, Francesco's surprising pledge of aid to the Palestinians, and his dramatic kneeling gesture had left me in what medical men call a state of adrenal insufficiency.

Mr. Keller and I were both grateful that Francesco had been able to enjoy an hour's rest on our return from the UN, for that evening he was scheduled to speak at a Mass to be said in a giant *colosseo* in the Jersey Meadows across the river. Then the following morning we were to fly to Mexico City to attend the first of the regional conferences of bishops.

Francesco had joined us for only a few minutes and we had just begun what promised to be a relaxed conversation when Cardinal Heegan entered and asked us to come into his studio. I came, not out of curiosity, but to insist that the meeting be brief. As we entered the room, Signor Randall rushed to us and fell to his knees, grasping Francesco's hand. "Holiness, what can I do?"

"I think we are reenacting a scene from the Gospel according to Matthew, although there the two people were both younger," Francesco said gently as he aided the *signore* to his feet. "We both know the answer to your question."

"This time, Holiness, the rich man will not go away sad. I offer you half of everything I own—and my full allegiance as well." He had placed two large briefcases and a small envelope on the table. The briefcases, we learned afterwards, were stuffed with stocks and bonds valued at more than $30 million; the envelope contained cashier's checks on several banks, totaling $6 million. The rest, the *signore* said, would come in a few weeks.

"I gladly accept your allegiance in God's name," Francesco said, "but the goods go to the poor throughout the world, and so also to God, not to me."

Cardinal Heegan, who was a master at handling donors and donations, although never any of this size, made a rapid (and, according to me, often given) allocution, then offered sherry. Francesco, now coughing heavily, barely touched his, and at that point I insisted that he return to bed. On the way upstairs I tried without success to persuade him to cancel the Mass that evening or at least to substitute a televised address. (There was an immense screen at both ends of the *colosseo* for what you Americans call instant replay in your game of *calcio—ecco,* football.) But, as you know, he was stubborn.

Later, when it became apparent that Francesco was running a fever, Mr. Keller, who remained with me, made the same plea, but also without success. In anger, he refused to go to the *colosseo,* saying the Smart Money would have no part of suicide or martyrdom. I was severely tempted to remain in the warmth of the chancery, but I wanted to retest my perception that the address at the UN had changed the way people viewed Francesco. Obviously, it pleased me that I went.

As we had had fear, it was achingly cold in the *colosseo.* The temperature was about thirteen degrees by your reckoning, and a damp, harsh wind was blowing from the desolate marshes. Occasionally, when the wind twisted around from the south, the stench of the oil refineries was almost asphyxiating. The officials had placed a stand and an altar on the playing field which was itself crowded with seats occupied mostly by dignitaries, journalists, and television camera crews. The camera would project *il Papa*'s image on the replay screens for those spectators who wanted a closer view of his face. The only touches of comfort were a plastic windscreen that gave a small amount of shelter and heaters of electricity along the floor of the stand. They helped us remain barely above the critical point of freezing solid.

Outside the *colosseo,* thousands of people had tried to touch *il Papa* as he reached out toward them. Only a double cordon of big, blue-uniformed policemen kept us from being trampled to death. Inside, the crowd gave Francesco a thundering ovation, and knelt reverently as he blessed them. The Mass, concelebrated with the archbishops of Newark and New York, went as rapidly as we could canonically speed it. Afterwards, in his homily, Francesco repeated his fundamental theme of love and justice, but aimed at the life of each of us within the family and place of work. It was a simple homily, devoid of the usual quips and asides that spackled allocutions to journalists and small groups. It was a plain message of love, justice, and peace within ourselves. The text was from the prophet Jeremiah: "Behold, the days are coming, says the Lord, when I shall make a new covenant with the house of Israel and the house of Judah. . . . I shall put forth my law within them, and I shall write it upon their hearts." According to Papa Francesco, that new covenant had been made by Christ, and we, as Christians, were obligated to demonstrate by our good works to our families and to all whom we met that the law of love was truly written in our hearts.

It was simple but effective. The talk was also mercifully brief, about twelve minutes.

Allora, the oration finished, Francesco, with the two archbishops in the rear seat and me next to the *autista*—you say the French chauffeur?—was driven slowly around the track inside the *colosseo* in an open car so that the crowd could see *il Papa* more closely. At the far end of the field, Francesco noticed a group of old people holding up a sign —there were dozens of similar signs about—indicating that they had come from a Catholic nursing home outside of Trenton, New Jersey. I recall wondering what pious, ignorant fool had permitted old people out on a night like this. (In truth, what was I myself doing there?) The same thought must have crossed Francesco's mind, because he ordered the chauffeur to drive close to the retaining wall and stop so that he could reach up and touch these people and give them some small attention that would sustain their faith during their last dark days in one of your cruel institutions for the aged.

With a burly policeman helping him, Francesco stood on the boot of the car and touched outstretched hands. It was then, as you well know, that it happened. *Ecco*, an old woman suddenly started screaming, "I can see! Blessed Jesus! The Pope touched me and I can see!" At a blow, there developed, as you can imagine, great turmoil in the stands. Fortunately, most people could only vaguely know that something was happening; in that mass of humanity, they could not see precisely what. Francesco was embarrassed. He touched a few more hands and, with the woman still screaming that she could see, we continued our circuit around the *colosseo* and exited to the waiting convoy.

After we had changed cars and returned to the cardinal's deliciously heated limousine, Francesco regained his composure. Between paroxysms of coughing, he said he was sure that poor, hysterical old woman had been carried away by cold weather and excitement. She was probably senile anyway, Cardinal Heegan added, and I agreed, with more force than perhaps was necessary. But the affair could not be so facilely dismissed. It had, after all, happened before 80,000 people in the *colosseo*. More important, as we later discovered, television cameras with—how do you say?—zoom lenses had focused on *il Papa* during the drive around the field, and the car behind ours had been crowded with journalists.

The telephone at the chancery rang for hours with reporters calling to ask about "the miracle." Cardinal Heegan wanted to close the switchboard, but Dottor Twisdale persuaded him to keep a priest there all night, replying that neither the cardinal nor *il Papa* had any information; indeed, those who saw the event on television knew far more than either of them.

The next morning, Francesco was physically far worse. His cough was steady and hacking and his cheeks more flushed. Moreover, psychologically he was still shaken by the events of the day before, even more than the rest of us.

Nevertheless, he would not listen to our arguments that he should see a doctor and delay our trip to Mexico City.

Outside the chancery the next morning, there were ranks of reporters as well as a huge crowd of spectators. We were able to move through the newsmen by promising a brief interview at the airport. The crowd was wildly enthusiastic but orderly in a prayerful way, content with a papal blessing. At the airport, TWA again made its Ambassadors Club Lounge available to us, and we permitted journalists—but no cameras—inside. There must have been twenty-five or thirty people.

"Ladies and gentlemen," Francesco told between fits of coughing, "what we say must be off the record because we do not wish to offend a pious lady. We are certain that what happened last night was an instance of hysteria. We've all read about such occurrences at fundamentalist revivals in the South and at charismatic meetings. I do not believe there was any miracle at all, just a great deal f noise, excitement, and too much cold combining to produce an emotional reaction. Now for the record, you can report that a high Vatican source says that the Pope is delighted that the lady has regained her vision but is certain that there is a perfectly logical and perfectly natural explanation for the phenomenon."

"Holiness," a woman from *The National Catholic Weekly Reporter* asked, "will the Church investigate this event as a potential miracle?"

"Off the record again, no, absolutely not. The Church will take no action." Francesco stopped to cough again. "You can report, however, that there is a miracle this Pope intends to work: to drive out hate and greed and envy from the hearts of men, and leave room only for kindness and justice. Now, if you will forgive us, we must go to Mexico City."

TWENTY-TWO

As soon as we boarded the plane, I insisted that Francesco go to the bed. Signora Falconi and I decided that the first thing we would do in Mexico City would be to request the archbishop to summon his personal physician.

We were furious with ourselves for not having made that decision the previous evening in New York. For, as Signora Falconi put it in an unusually undiplomatic fashion, "Mexican doctors are probably no better than Italian." Fieschi harrumphed a bit, but her remark did not bother me. When I live in Italy, I fly to Switzerland for my medical treatment. Even apart from air fare the cost is large, but I have never found myself at home in the Middle Ages, either theologically or medically.

While Francesco was resting in the first bedroom, Fieschi and I sat together in the small studio and talked between ourselves. I believe that our subject of conversation was the same as that of everyone else on the plane, the "cure" of the old woman. Fieschi was disturbed. I did not then realize how truly pious a man he was, so I yet assumed that his concern was fundamentally that of the papal secretary of state, rather than that of a priest. He asked my opinion, several times, in fact, which was quite unlike him. His imagination was not overdeveloped but his analytical abilities were keen, and usually he forgot nothing. I said that I agreed with *il Papa,* that the poor woman had experienced an hysterical reaction to a great emotional experience.

"What if it was a miracle?" he finally asked. That, of course, was the question that most severely gave me nerves. "What then?"

"I don't know," I replied, "but then I doubt that we shall ever know. There is no scientific litmus paper to test the presence of a miracle."

"But what if it is the hand of God that has touched that woman through Papa Francesco?"

"At least," I smiled, "it would be an indication that the conclave had made the right choice."

Fieschi's mouth flickered in a small smile. I had not meant to be hurtful and he knew it. "It would mean that much," he agreed, "but it would mean more. It would be a sign of a mandate from heaven, an indication that what this Pontiff wants is the will of God."

"*Bene,* as far as the Church is concerned, that is always supposed to be the case."

"Supposed to be, yes, but only up to a point," Fieschi said, truthfully enough. "We give the Pope unlimited power and then bind him with invisible chains. You and I know that the Curia acts both as a screen against the outside world and as a net around the Pontiff. It keeps certain information away from him, makes sure he sees other things—and not necessarily in full perspective. It also cushions his decisions. Most of us who are cardinals—and many bishops and *monsignori*—are convinced that we know more about what's good for the Church and for men's souls than *il Papa* does. We interpret his wishes and sometimes in the process twist his words so that what we believe is right is announced not as our judgment but as that of the Pontiff. Usually we do it out of love of the Church which we equate with love of God, not personal ambition, but somehow these things sometimes get very mixed up."

"I concur," I put in. "I recall how even under Papa Paolo, who probably controlled the Curia better than any modern Pontiff, how even under his tight discipline a group of cardinals and archbishops were able to convince him that the moral and theological questioning by some of their rivals was a personal attack on Paolo himself."

"I remember well," Fieschi nodded. "I suspect their motives were good even if their means were bad. We are all complex beings—which may be why we can sometimes understand others better than we can understand ourselves. But most of us in the Curia try, subject to all the failings of our humanity, to serve the Church loyally."

"I am in accord with that. That is why I count LaTorre among my dearest friends." (I could not resist that—how do you say?—dig.) "But what is the relation of any possible miracle to the Curia, other than to try to shield *il Papa* from becoming a sort of peripatetic Lourdes pool?" (*Ecco,* I must tell you that I was not so obtuse as the question might indicate. For the first time I felt Fieschi unburdening himself; I wanted to give him every opportunity to talk.)

"Simple but critical. If this was a miracle, if it was a sign from God, then we must follow this Pontiff blindly, totally, absolutely; carrying out his smallest whim must be our constant objective." Fieschi began to become excited. "Ugo, my old friend" (That word "friend" sounded strange coming from Fieschi. He had many admirers but few friends.) "you may have been more inspired than you knew last summer. God may indeed be planning a drastic renewal for his Church, and we may have a part to play in that divine plan."

"I recall Papa Francesco making that point several times."

"Yes, he made it as a human being, as a Pontiff who stumbles like the rest of us and whom—God forgive us—many of us have looked on as a man to be penned up rather than a divine force to be unleashed on the world."

I had never viewed Fieschi so wrought up. Except for his excited anger over Francesco's sudden decision to go to Tel Aviv, utter calmness, patrician imperturbability, had always been Fieschi's dominant characteristic. At the time that excitement gave me care, but not as much as the possibility of a miracle.

Most of all, of course, I was worried about Francesco's health. I knew that the high altitude of Mexico City would contain less oxygen and mean increased difficulty in breathing. At least he slept for three full hours on the aircraft.

Again the flight went smoothly and quickly, but on the ground there was a pandemonium that made the scene at Newark seem like the inside of Francesco's Trappist monastery. We could hear the screams of *"El Papa!"* as soon as the big jets stopped. Then the crowd burst through the cordon of police and surrounded the plane. There was no way the mob could reach up to us, but neither was there a way we could safely exit from the plane.

From a nearby hangar, a fresh phalanx of police was forming to charge the crowd with drawn clubs. Francesco saw what was about to happen and grabbed a loudspeaker that was strapped to the closet above the seats and ordered the front stairs of the aircraft lowered part of the way. *Allora,* he exited just as the first rank of police were nearing the edge of the crowd, ready to introduce their clubs to bare skulls. Rapidly—although in very halting Spanish since he had no true facility in the language—he made the sign of the cross and began the blessing. Most of the crowd fell to their knees; even those pouring across the barricades hesitated.

I signaled the leader of the police to bring his men to the foot of the steps, and in a combination of Spanish, English, and Italian, we made him understand that he must instruct the crowd that it was necessary for them to remain kneeling to protect the safety of *il Papa.* (In fact, we later found out that one person had been killed and several injured seriously enough to require hospitalization when the crowd first burst through the police lines.)

Francesco then came down the stairs—he told the rest of us to remain on board the plane—and for almost a half hour walked through the kneeling and sitting crowd, touching hands and giving frequent blessings. *Allora,* as he reached the edge, an old man on crutches was standing on the other side of the wire fence that enclosed the field. He was shouting hoarsely, *"El Papa! El Papa!"* Francesco saw him and touched his fingers clasped through the wire. "Jesus! Jesus!" the man screamed. As close as I could make out—my Spanish is not fluent—he shouted, "I can walk! I can walk!" and threw his crutches in the air.

The people again went wild. Only because Francesco was at the edge of the crowd and in the vicinity of a gate in the heavy metal fencing, and because the police were alert, was he saved from what you Americans call the stampede. The police somehow conducted him into the terminal, where the official greeting party, including the cardinal archbishop, the president, and several cabinet members, had taken shelter. At one point the mob was pressing so close that the president's bodyguards unslung their automatic weapons and pointed them at the portals. Once more, however, Francesco intervened. He took another loudspeaker from one of the policemen and again asked the people to be calm. At first he made no effect, but as soon as he gave the papal blessing, people immediately began kneeling again and the stampede lost its momentum.

The rest of us from the aircraft joined the party a few minutes later. Actually, we had no trouble. Once *il Papa* had left the plane, the crowd lost all interest in us. Nevertheless, the whole party was obligated to wait another two hours until troops could be brought to form a wedge six deep to clear a path for the motorcade. It was still—how is that exact word?—bedlam, with everyone shouting, mothers holding babies high, and on the fringes, old and sick people begging to be cured.

As we were entering the cars, Francesco saw two old people on stretchers, peasants obviously, who had been transported by their Indian-looking family to a post where we would have to pass. "Touch me! Cure me!" each begged.

"I cannot cure your bodies," Francesco said, using as an interpreter an officer who spoke English. "Only God can do that. But what I have I give you. I forgive you your sins, as Christ said I might." He touched them, made the sign of the cross, and laid his hands on the forehead of each. They looked disappointed but resigned.

In the open limousine Francesco slumped in the rear seat, mentally and physically exhausted. The only thing he said to me was "God, no, no." I do not know if that was a prayer or a refusal.

As we entered the city, however, and began to see large crowds again, Francesco sat up and waved, forcing himself to smile. He knew, as now we all did, that it would not stop here. Possibly it would never stop. Once the excitement had died, it would have been possible to dismiss one cure as a case of hysteria, but two cures, whether real or imagined, would feed more hysteria and probably cause new "miracles" to multiply. Our only hope, and, according to me, it was not a promising one, was to deny emphatically that these were miracles and to keep the Pontiff far from large crowds, especially Latin crowds, for several months until memories faded.

In the terminal, I could not get close to the archbishop, and so I talked to one of the president's aides about Francesco's health. The officer paid careful note, and when we arrived at the archbishop's new palazzo, the president's personal physician and a lung specialist were waiting, together with several assistants. Francesco reluctantly submitted to an examination. I do not believe we could have ever persuaded him had not the experience at the airport so emotionally drained him.

Ecco, the diagnosis was exactly as we expected: pneumonia in one lung and possibly in the other as well. The physicians wanted X rays to confirm their findings and said that they would order a set as soon as *il Papa* entered the hospital. At this point, Francesco's resilience—it was, according to me, at that time only stubbornness—reasserted itself. He agreed to remain in bed at the palazzo for a day or two, but adamantly refused hospitalization. There was nothing to do. To argue with him was not possible. The physicians, apparently accustomed to dealing with strong-willed officials, merely shrugged their shoulders and made arrangements for antibiotics, nurses, and an oxygen tent to be brought in, by regular car rather than by ambulance, as Dottor Twisdale wisely requested. We had enough problems without rumors of *il Papa*'s illness—you say leaking?—leaking, then, before we prepared a story.

Within five minutes of the decision, Francesco was asleep, wheezing noisily and, I believe, painfully, but in a merciful state of unconsciousness. When the oxygen tent arrived, his breathing improved dramatically.

Fieschi, Pritchett, Martìn, Dottor Twisdale, and I met with the cardinal archbishop of Mexico City to decide what to do. Clearly, *il Papa*'s scheduled appearance for the next day at the opening of the regional conference of bishops in Mexico City would have to be canceled. Realistically, it did not seem that he would be able to participate at all, for four days later we were scheduled to arrive in Lima for the second regional conference.

We would be obligated soon to make some sort of public explanation. Dottor Twisdale already had drafted a bland medical bulletin that described the physicians as saying that Papa Francesco was suffering from a very bad cold that had worsened into a lung inflammation, that he was responding well to treatment, and that he expected to be up and about, although not fully recovered, within three or four days. We all agreed that would be sufficient. If there were questions, Dottor Twisdale could say that *il Papa* had taken cold in the ride through Roma in the rain, and that the frigid weather in New York had brought on complications.

"Now," Dottor Twisdale cautioned us, "we come to the difficult part. What about the new 'cure'? What do we say about that?"

I suggested that we could do no better than to repeat what Francesco had said at Newark. I added that, all things considered, it would be best for us to use the illness as an excuse to cancel the trip, return to Roma as soon as Francesco could travel, and have him keep himself in seclusion for some weeks until the excitement had died down. Cardinal Fieschi, as secretary of state, Cardinal Pritchett, as secretary of the World Synod of Bishops, and Cardinal Martìn, as prefect of the Congregation for Bishops, could continue, attending the regional conferences in *il Papa*'s name. The allocutions were already written and could be read by one of them.

Pritchett nodded agreement. "We must play down this miracles thing. It's foolishness, of course."

Fieschi cut in sharply: "I disagree strongly. We are curtly dismissing the very real possibility that we have seen the hand of God, not once but twice in two successive days. We must leave open, both in our own minds and in what we say publicly, the possibility that we have witnessed true miracles. Summarily to deny that possibility would show lack of faith in God's providence."

The cardinal archbishop of Mexico City smiled wryly. He was clearly not a man of miracles. "I am sure that Señor Twisdale can manipulate the words so that, as his countrymen say, all options will be left open. But I agree that the trip should be canceled. There will be great disappointment here as in Lima and Rio, but the Pontiff's health must come first."

I knew, as did the others, what was going on in the archbishop's mind, and I was not in sympathy with it. Yet, to me he was a welcome ally, despite his self-seeking purpose of ridding himself and his bishops of a *Papa* who threatened his carefully balanced and tediously arranged rapport with the government. The archbishop was doubly welcome as an ally because I knew even before he spoke that Cardinal Martìn would urge that the trip not be canceled, that we merely delay in Mexico City for seventy-two hours. There would be no difficulty in keeping the bishops in session that long, Martìn argued, and with a pair of telephone calls the conferences in Lima and Rio could each be postponed three or four days with only minor inconvenience. "Only the Pontiff can succeed in uniting the bishops in this task of cleansing the Church and ourselves. If we fail now, our whole effort to renew and rebuild the Church in Latin America will fail and so will similar efforts elsewhere."

"I agree most heartily with Cardinal Martìn," Fieschi told. "This renewal is close to the heart of the Pope. It must be carried out and carried out by him. God will not take him from us."

I regarded Dottor Twisdale. "You see things from a different perspective. What do you think?"

The *dottore* helped himself to one of the archbishop's

short, wide cigars, and sniffed it as caressingly as Chelli would have. "As for miracles, I usually don't believe in them, and I certainly don't think those senile old dolts were cured of anything real. But I did see one miracle in New York—old man Randall opening his wallet. I've watched that bastard operate for more than twenty-five years. He'd steal from a blind leper, even if she were his own mother; he wouldn't open his wallet for a fireman, even if it was smoking. Then he pops in, falls on his padded knees, and offers us $36 million. Now that's more than a cynical journalist can understand. I wouldn't have thought that Yahweh Himself could have pulled that one off.

"About coming or going or staying," the *dottore* went on, "I think that what we think won't make a bit of difference. If I know Declan Walsh, he'll come roaring out of that oxygen tent in about twenty-four hours and do what he well pleases—which is likely to be something along the lines of what Cardinal Martìn has suggested, only with shorter delays."

"I am afraid you're right, *Dottore,*" I told, "which is why it would please me to put him on that airplane quickly and have him locked in the papal palazzo or the *casina* before he knows he's gone from Mexico."

"But we all know that's impossible," Cardinal Martìn said.

We looked at each other. There was little more to be said, but Pritchett put our agreement into words. "Very well, let's ask the archbishop to delay the start of the conference here for three days. Cardinal Martìn and I will call our colleagues in Lima and Rio and arrange for postponements there. Then we'll see how the Pope feels tomorrow morning. Meanwhile, with the archbishop's help, Mr. Twisdale and I can work out a statement for the press."

"As secretary of state," Fieschi spoke up, "I shall have to approve that statement and be present at the press conference. I must make certain that we leave open the very real possibility that we have witnessed a pair of true miracles."

We were all surprised by the vehemence of Fieschi's voice. "Of course, Your Eminence," Pritchett responded, "your approval would be welcome, but I was afraid that, since newsmen sometimes twist words out of context, it would be better if no cardinal were present at the conference. Quite frankly," Pritchett smiled, "it will be easier to rectify any 'error' if only Mr. Twisdale is there. But if one of us, especially the secretary of state, were present, then we would run a greater risk of being misunderstood and not being able to explain."

"I insist," Fieschi spoke in his most haughty, aristocratic manner. "As secretary of state I am second in ecclesiastical authority only to the supreme Pontiff himself. I have participated in this discussion as an equal, but I am in charge until His Holiness recovers. We shall do as My Lord Cardinal Pritchett suggests, but only because I think that is the wisest course; and I shall attend the press conference."

"Of course, Eminence, as you wish," Pritchett said. He and I exchanged glances, silently agreeing that if Fieschi were to be in attendance, we would be present also.

At 5 P.M. about twenty-five reporters entered the archbishop's palazzo. Dottor Twisdale had specified that there would be no pictures and no direct quotations other than from the medical bulletin that he had prepared. The *dottore* was magnificent. He was at ease in English and French and, according to me, was also fluent in Spanish—that was surprising, because his Italian was still hesitant. Most important, he gave the impression of being candid and sincere. Listening to him I could not help recalling Declan Walsh's claim that his father had once instructed him, "Always be sincere, son, whether you mean it or not."

My mind flashed back to the present when I heard Dottor Twisdale saying, "You now have about as much information as we do on the Pope's health. His illness is potentially serious, but, with antibiotics and rest, the doctors are certain that he will recover quickly. Right now we're thinking in terms of a few days, but that's a guess more than a prediction."

"Will the Pope be able to attend the conference of bishops here?" a Mexican reporter asked.

"I honestly do not know. We hope he can. The cardinal archbishop of Mexico City and Cardinal Pritchett will ask the bishops to delay the conference for a few days in the hope that the Pope can attend. That's all I can say, other than that we're trying to delay the opening of the other conferences by a few days as well."

Having paid the courtesy of a single question to *il Papa's* health, the reporters turned to the subject that most interested them.

"Mr. Twisdale," *Time* asked, "have you a statement about the second miracle?"

"The first miracle I know; it's a reporter who asks an intelligent question. What's the second miracle, an intelligent answer?"

The reporters chuckled. According to me, Dottor Twisdale was handling the matter with the appropriate light touch. But I could see Fieschi frowning darkly.

"The two cures," *Time* said good-naturedly, "and not of alcoholic reporters or skirt-chasing lawyers."

I winced at the obvious reference to Mr. Keller's visit with us at the chancery, but Dottor Twisdale did not even blink. "I believe that a well-informed Vatican spokesman issued a statement this morning in Newark, before we left the United States. We really know nothing about what condition either person was suffering from, or anything at all about the man at the airport here. So there's nothing I can say."

"Did you know that the woman from New Jersey had been taken to the University of Pennsylvania hospital for an examination?" the Associated Press representative asked.

"No, I did not, and I doubt if anyone else in the party knew. With the excitement at the airport and the Pope's illness, we haven't had much contact—any contact—with the outside world."

"Would you, as a former newsman and one who knows the Church well, speculate about the causes of these cures?" Reuters inquired.

"No, I wouldn't. I have my own opinion, of course, and it is the same as that of the Vatican spokesman this morning; but I think only a physician who had carefully examined the people both *before* and *after* these events would be qualified to offer a scientifically reliable judgment."

"Cardinal Fieschi," *Il Tempo* called out—just as I had had concern that someone would—"what attitude will the Church take toward these cures?"

Fieschi stood up and answered in halting English. "We can have no position about events on which we have no real information. At the moment, no one can be sure whether we have seen the hand of God or merely two widely separated but similarly hysterical reactions." (So far, so good, I thought.)

"Then you would leave open the possibility of miracles?" the reporter went on.

"Without knowing something concrete about either event, it is difficult for a rational man to dismiss any possibility."

"Do you, personally," the reporter persisted, "think that these were miracles?"

I inhaled deeply as Fieschi hesitated.

"You ask what I cannot answer," he finally replied. "I must leave open all possibilities now. In all honesty I do not know anything about these cures. I can say no more."

"When," *Der Spiegel* asked, "will you have the necessary information?"

"I can't answer that either. Like Dottor Twisdale, I was not aware that the woman from New Jersey had been admitted to a hospital for an examination."

"The Church," Pritchett injected, "is always slow in making up its mind about miracles, but I'm sure that we can have a tentative answer for you in a century or two."

The reporters laughed, but Fieschi did not, and I could see that several correspondents took note of this fact.

We came out of the press conference rather well. Fieschi had told a word or two too many, but a transcript—and Pritchett had made certain that a tape register was recording the words—would show that the secretary of state had not committed the Church to any interpretation. Still, I knew that the next morning many papers would have front-page stories that PAPAL SECRETARY OF STATE REFUSES TO DISMISS POSSIBILITY OF MIRACLES. I would have much preferred a simple repetition of Francesco's statement at Newark, but, given Fieschi's near conversion to the idea of real cures, we had escaped rather nicely, not to say miraculously.

By eight that evening, after the news of *il Papa*'s illness had been broadcast on radio and television, a crowd of several thousand people gathered outside the archbishop's palazzo. It was a quiet, kneeling crowd, lips moving in muttered prayers and fingers twisting rosaries. Some of them were old women and old men, but there were also very many young people, men and women—a rare sight in Italy, and, I hear, in much of Latin America except for a fiesta. Some of them remained all night; others left after a few hours; and still others replaced them. *Ecco,* by morning, the crowd had grown, and by noon the police estimated that more than 20,000 people were clustered around the palazzo and in surrounding streets. By nature, it gives police nerves when more than two or three people congregate, but this crowd was so peaceful that not even the Mexican government thought to disperse it.

Francesco awoke at about ten-thirty, and, as Dottor Twisdale had predicted, he was in no mood to return quietly to Roma. The penicillin had not yet begun to take effect, but the oxygen had eased his breathing and his fever was down a little. He remained inside the tent, but started giving a series of orders. Begrudgingly he approved our decision to postpone the regional conferences of bishops.

After a few minutes he came around to asking me about the man at the airport. The same as in the United States, I told him, an old person, hysterical. The Mexican police had taken him to a hospital—a state hospital, not a Catholic one—where he would be examined carefully. I also told the Pontiff that the Mexican papers had given the cure what you call banner headlines and had printed long stories which, as read to me, bore little relation to what I had seen happen.

I did not give *il Papa* concern with other information that I possessed. Dottor Twisdale had telephoned a friend in New York, who had read him the stories in the *New York Times* and the *Washington Post.* As it had with the first "miracle," the *Post* gave the story more news space than did the *Times,* but on its—what is that strange phrase?—op ed page the *Times* printed two analyses by physicians offering a natural, that is to say an hysterical, explanation for the supposed cure in New Jersey. Both papers printed Francesco's statement issued at Newark, properly attributing it to a high Vatican spokesman, but both also noted that after the second "cure" the papal secretary of state refused to rule out the possibility of miracles. *Va bene,* we were stuck to that, but on the whole the accounts in these two papers were factual and fair. It would have pleased me had they been more cynical.

I could see that Francesco wanted to talk about the two affairs, but I could also sense that he feared to talk about them. I suppose that is a normal reaction. Most of us have fantasized about making a miracle, and it must be flattering to the ego to think that it is just possible that one has in reality done so. *Ecco,* at the same time, that thought must also be horribly frightening.

Whatever the status of his lungs, Francesco's mind was clear. In fact, as he was sitting up in the oxygen tent listening to various reports, he suddenly intervened and asked that we invite the president of Mexico to visit him in the palazzo. With that crowd outside, the visit would do no political harm, I agreed. I should not have mentioned the crowd, for at noon Francesco insisted on being aided onto the balcony. As you can imagine, the crowd went wild with glee. Francesco waved and made the sign of the cross and then came back to the tent. He seemed glad to return.

The president—a short, stocky man, balding but with flashing black eyes—entered just before dark and sat near *il Papa*'s bed. The archbishop, Fieschi, Monsignor Candutti, and I joined them, along with two presidential assistants.

"Excellency," *il Papa* said softly, "I need to explain to you how I see the Church's place in the world changing. That change may frighten many secular rulers—and for good reason, since it threatens some of them. You know that we've sometimes been a kept institution—kept by the government, by conservative economic interests, and also kept by our own concern for preserving our material goods. Sometimes, too, the Church has been kept by force. But I do not try to assess blame. I prefer to concentrate on making a new set of rules."

The president listened. His face was expressionless, but his bright eyes darted. One could almost see his mind weighing the implications of each sentence.

"The Church must be independent. We have to operate in the world, but we cannot be a part of the world. We cannot have a material stake in the status quo or in revolution or in any of the other possible political events in between. We must be free to preach justice and to do justice. We must be witnesses for the truth of Christ. We must be free to criticize ideas, practices, politics, anything, anybody."

"You speak of an independent force, Holiness," the president intervened, "but that could itself become—almost inevitably would become—a major political force, competing with government and the would-be government."

Francesco thought for a moment. "You're right. Moral ideas make for political force. The Church would be a rival to government in many areas, yes; it has to be. The Romans understood that. Their persecution of Christianity made a good deal of short-range political sense—although the Latin American habit of capturing the Church has been more politically prudent in the long run."

The two men smiled at each other. "You may remember that when you were a lawyer and I wanted to become a judge," Francesco reminded him, "I said that church and state should be separate but that no one could separate morality from politics. I am trying to say that same thing now, although in a broader context. Just as we cannot have government officials telling us what we shall preach or who shall do the preaching in the name of Christ, so we cannot have the Church and churchmen tied to the government—or to the opposition—by current privileges or anticipated rewards—or, what is more likely, by internalizing the norms of the prevailing system. We must be ready to speak out against all forms of injustice. I want a Church whose sole concern is with the souls of men and women."

"As Your Holiness undoubtedly knows," the president said, "I do not believe that men, or even women, have souls, but if they do, I am perfectly willing to leave them to your care. It is what my people do with their minds and bodies, with their actions and their plans for action, that interests me. I will not surrender control over their actions to anyone."

"Unhappily, soul and body are not so neatly separate. Thought and action go together. You remember Oliver Wendell Holmes's saying 'every idea is an incitement.' And, as you know, our Church believes that salvation is dependent on both faith and good works. To take an extraordinary case, the Church should not condone genocide any more than you should. We cannot stop with telling our people what is right and wrong in the abstract. We must urge them to do right in concrete cases and chide them when they do wrong. We would have to tell them not to obey laws requiring them to commit evil acts; we might, if the situation warranted it, even instruct them to withdraw allegiance from a totally immoral regime—as Pius should have done during World War II."

"What are the limits on such a power? I see none," the president told.

"There are critical limits on what we should say, how far we should go. We have no right, for instance, to tell people which political party to support, or which candidate is more moral than the other—under normal circumstances. It is only when a regime is committing or is about to commit serious crimes that we can justify direct intervention. Our usual course of action must be to speak clearly and unequivocally about the necessity of social justice and to point to actual and potential injustices."

The president remained impassive, although obviously unconvinced. "And, of course, Holiness, you must encourage your people to become involved in public affairs to put their ideas into practice?"

"If you mean am I aiming for a revival of Catholic Action, the answer is no. If you mean am I aiming for a strengthening of Church-backed Christian Democratic parties, the answer is again no. If you mean do I want Catholics to be deeply concerned with problems of social justice in their private lives and in their public lives the answer is yes. I say this knowing full well that one form such public concern might take would be Catholic Action and another might be Christian Democracy. But I do not urge these specific forms, nor do I want individual bishops to urge them. Our tasks are more to provide moral direction; specific leadership must come from the laity."

Allora, the president arose, walked to the window, and pushed the curtains back far enough so that he could see the people kneeling in the street. Then he turned. "Holiness," he told slowly, "with all respect, you speak like a naive American idealist. You're transposing the image of American politics to the rest of the world. It does not fit. In the United States you have two parties, very close together, and both agreeing to compete within certain peaceful, constitutional bounds. There is no problem for a Catholic who is a daily communicant to be a Democrat or a Republican, or even to join one of the minor parties. Both parties live well within the moral framework of Christianity—except, perhaps," he smiled, "when they deal with us. But here in Latin America, we have Fascist dictators, nonideological dictators, a Communist dictator, a welter of oligarchies, and sporadic but serious efforts at constitutional democracy. All of these governments face strong and sometimes violent opposition. By violent I mean terrorist, literally murderous, and from both the left and the right.

"We, too, often have a two-party system," the president told sardonically, "one in power and willing to use every conceivable means, including terror and assassination, to stay in power, and a second party out of office, equally willing to use any available means to seize and retain power. More often we have an unscrupulous and unideological clique in power and a series of similar cliques waiting to strike. When Marxists and Fascists clash with each other or with a military clique, or when two cliques confront each other, there can be no neutrals. Innocent victims, perhaps, but not neutrals.

"In those kinds of situations," the president continued, "the Church that speaks out cannot any more be politically neutral by your general standards of social justice than it can by older standards of self-interest. A Church that truly preaches social justice cannot keep silent when a government allows corporations to keep miners—or the government itself keeps them—in virtual slavery. Nor can the Church keep silent about opposition plans to slaughter the bourgeoisie. We do not have here two differing parties trying to compromise competing interests. Rather we tend to have only committed friends and implacable foes, ready to fight to the death, at least to the death of the poor devils caught in between. At the very least the Church will have to build a middle political ground. In fact that is what I would like to see you do."

"But," Francesco responded, "if the Church undertook that task, it would be a prime political mover. Those who do not want such a power would try to stop the Church; to survive, we would have to seek political allies. Once again we would be part of the opposition or the status quo."

"Absolutely true, Holiness, absolutely. You are inevitably a political force, as you yourself said."

"Of course, but what if we refuse the alternatives and choose to stay with the poor devils caught in the middle?"

"That means perishing."

"At least persecution."

"At the very, very least."

"It is a risk that we must take."

"There is no risk. It is what you North Americans call a sure thing."

"But can you understand what I am saying between ourselves, here in Mexico, regardless of the situation elsewhere in the world? If you are trying to practice social justice you need not fear us. We must preach justice between men, between men and their governments, and between governments."

"Holiness, I understand what you are saying and what you want. I think that your ideas would work in the United States, England, and Canada. I believe you want good for my people. I do not know enough about the rest of the world to pass judgment. But in Latin America your good intentions would bring evil results. I have tried to explain that some of my fellow rulers would not let your solution work. But there is more. Some of your bishops will not be able to withstand the temptations of power. With due respect, Holiness, for all their talk of the next world, Catholic bishops seem to be extraordinarily ambitious for power in this life."

"There is much in what you say, Excellency. It will be our task to select men whose ambitions are restricted to the next world. We both know that we shall not always be successful, and that problems will arise from within the Church. Watch us and make sure that we do not per- other secular force. I do not want bishops to be feudal lords. I want them to be seekers after justice who are willing to face martydom, although not to court it."

The president smiled again. "I have tired you, Holiness. I shall let you rest."

"You have counseled me, not tired me," Francesco said. "I appreciate your candor. Let's go to the balcony together." Francesco swung himself out of bed and put on a robe. Then with one arm on the shoulder of the archbishop and the other on the president's he went out on the balcony. The cheering was tumultuous, but I suspect that the president noticed, as I did, that *"Viva el Papa!"* drowned out the more scattered *"Viva el Presidente!"*

TWENTY-THREE

FRANCESCO'S RECOVERY was rapid if not plenary. Within twenty-four hours the penicillin began to take hold, and his improvement became obvious. After a week in bed, he would probably have experienced no more problems. But after only forty-eight hours, he got up and addressed the opening session of the regional conference. The oration was short but sharp. The bishops' agendum had only one item: implementation of the spiritual renewal in Latin America. And *il Papa* candidly explained that Latin America was serving as an experiment. The Church had centuries of experience with spiritual retreats for individuals and for small groups, but not for a worldwide effort. Inevitably mistakes would be made, but that was a price that had to be paid. The problems of Latin America and the rest of the world were too acute to permit delay. The Pontiff then outlined once more his ideas of what new roles the Church should play in society.

Most specifically in Latin America, Francesco stressed, social justice demanded that the Church separate itself from various regimes and from dissident political movements as well. He traveled the same ground as with the president: the necessity of independence, of courage, and of wisdom, and the risk of suffering, even of martyrdom for clergy and laity.

"We know," he said at the finish, "that the road we have charted is narrow and twisting and that along its edges there are deep cliffs. We know, too, that this road may be mined with political bombs, and that following it may produce bloody casualties. The Church has known persecution before. Martyrdom is not a fate that a sane man seeks, but neither is it a fate from which a loyal Christian may shrink when he knows he walks in truth. We cannot surrender to threats of imprisonment, torture, and death any more than we can to their reality. We have no more right to surrender than had the original Apostles. For us. Christ conquered death. Our humanity fears it, but the divine spark that God has kindled in each of us cannot allow us to dread it. We follow in the footsteps of Christ and his Apostles. Suffering and death can have no power over us."

After the Holy Father's allocution, business began immediately. Pritchett—operating largely through Martìn and his friends so as to avoid the spectre of what Francesco called "the Roman Gringo"—had organized the affair beautifully. The 140 bishops divided themselves into ten committees to discuss and report on five specific problems. Then, the conference reassembled to hear reports. There was much discussion, for two separate groups reported on each facet.

Va bene, I do not know how to judge how much good these committees accomplished. We were obligated to leave before the end of the meetings. I do not think that Francesco was primarily interested in specific solutions. It was enough that the bishops were meeting together and trying earnestly to work them out. In addition, Francesco wanted the opportunity to talk with the bishops in small groups. During the next three days he somehow managed to spend an hour or more with each committee, and in each instance quickly turned the meeting into what you Americans call a seminar rather than a lecture.

In that context Francesco was magnificent. I have sometimes spoken critically about his style of oratory, but in the less formal setting of a small group—once he was able to put the bishops at ease—he asked provocative questions and, in turn, responded with disarming candor to questions put to him. In these meetings he was always *il Papa,* but he was also *il professore,* with a finely honed mind and a vast store of knowledge. His intellectual power and integrity, and even a certain kind of humility, emerged in an engaging way. As you have no doubt learned and I have probably already said several times, Italians live in dread of making a *brutta figura,* doing something to lose face. Thus Italian intellectuals tend to use pompous verbiage to discourage honest exchange of ideas. In contrast to this penchant for long circumlocutions as ponderous as they are dreary, Francesco quickly came to the point in sharply etched sentences. Often he would respond with a simple statement, such as "I hadn't thought of it that way before," or "That's interesting; let's follow it and see where it leads."

In those small groups, Francesco's aura of holiness was even more apparent. His mind was, as usual, a probing instrument, but one could sense the operation of a power far beyond intellectual strength; perhaps that sense was made more acute by the absence of what you Americans view as the heavy pomposity associated with the papacy.

Most of the Latin Americans were both awed and moved by Francesco's performance. I believe that, when we were finished, he could have ordered mass suicide and some of the bishops would have cheerfully slit their throats—unhappily, the wrong ones. Persuading them to part with the Church's property was going to be more difficult, however. Of course, not all of the bishops were favorably impressed. In fact a few were appalled rather than pleased that *il Papa* would sit down around a table with them and discuss their problems.

In sum, the first of the regional conferences went very well. Pritchett and Martìn were even more enthusiastic than I. We left the bishops hard at work mapping out retreats and formulating procedures to coordinate with the Jesuits and Franciscans. The bishops also had before them an outline of a joint statement on political neutrality that national conferences would complete, and even an outline of a declaration encouraging dioceses to dispose of certain ecclesiastical properties. Martin was especially encouraged by the last, although I found what the bishops were saying to be very vague. They had no need to encourage themselves to give their goods to the poor; they could have simply done the deed, as had Signor Randall, if they had serious intentions of doing it.

To Fieschi's delight, there was overwhelming support for a resolution calling for a renegotiation of the Vatican's concordats with secular governments. That was exactly the sort of "pressure" that Monsignor Candutti could use most effectively in discussions with secular governments.

I must confess also that Francesco's success was not due solely to his intellectual power or personal aura or even to the inherent attractiveness of his ideas. A number of the new bishops whom Martìn had chosen were present, and so were the new coadjutor bishops. Not present were many of the "retired" and transferred bishops. What Roma wanted was clear, as was Roma's determination to get it. In that milieu, it was relatively easy to resolve intellectual doubts in the Pontiff's favor. (Let me add that I met several of the men whom Martin had recommended, and they were an intelligent, young, and energetic group. They reinforced my admiration for the cardinal.)

I had only two reservations. First and foremost was Francesco's health. Each evening he returned to his room exhausted. If it had not been for the Mexicans' civilized observance of the siesta—the holy hour, Signora Falconi called it—*il Papa* would not have survived. The physicians were unperturbed. They merely stated quite firmly that the Pontiff needed a week in bed and that without such rest he would undoubtedly experience a serious relapse. He laughed. They shrugged their shoulders and did not laugh. The archbishop and I, however, had no difficulty in persuading them to leave the oxygen tent in the palazzo and to continue the penicillin by tablet for another ten days. I know that at least once during the period Francesco went back inside the tent during the night.

Allora, the second problem, that of the "cures," was chronic. Because of the way the archbishop's palace was constructed, it was possible for Francesco to meet with the bishops without going outside the gates. His public appearances were frequent, but they were made from a balcony, where he was safe from the press of the crowds. According to me, as is usually the case in hysterical cures, there would have to be actual physical contact. Without that touching, we would be spared more embarrassment; but one can keep a man like Francesco isolated for only so long. Besides, I believe I have said that he had once told that living in a bunker had made him claustrophobic.

Francesco knew at least as much about hysterical cures as I did; I suspect he knew more. I knew that he was curious about his power, for it *was* a power to be able to excite people to hysteria merely by one's physical presence and touch, even if it fell far short of the miraculous. And although he had fear of it, Francesco wanted to test that power. On the morning that we left for Lima he insisted that we ride in an open car and he frequently leaned over the shoulders of the police to touch the hands of those reaching toward him.

Predictably there were more cures. But you know all about them. They are now jumbled in my mind. I think I am correct in recalling that on the way to the airport in Mexico City a teenage girl was instantly cured of acne. That, according to American television commercials, was an everyday affair if one used the right soap. But the girl —and the press—hailed it as another cure, although a minor one. There was another. I remember the man who had been deafened as a result of an automobile accident, but I cannot say whether that was in Mexico City or Lima. I recall only that there were two on the way to the airport. I would recommend you read the *Irish Times*. They carried what, at the time, I thought was a coldly factual set of reports.

With those two new "cures" behind us, the scene when we landed at Lima was even wilder than that at Mexico City. There was another "miracle" there. Another man who had been injured in an automobile accident and claimed to have been paralyzed from the waist down suddenly said that he could now walk. Even if true, it was small return for the fact that three people were killed and dozens injured in stampedes to get close to *il Papa*. It was Francesco himself who suggested at Lima that we must travel by helicopter to and from airports.

His reaction to the events in Mexico City had been one of deep depression rather than elation. He experienced similar periods of emotional despondency after each of the other supposed cures. The hysteria he generated in others apparently drained his own emotional reservoir. *Allora*, after Mexico City and even before Lima, he had to accept the fact that he held a power over people. Perhaps it was no more divine than the power of a hypnotizer or of an eloquent salesman, but there now could be no doubt that his power was real. I sympathized with him. He had acquired a truly terrible gift. God alone could know what it would do to the man—or to the Church.

He would not speak about it. Perhaps he could not. I joined him for a time in the forward bedroom of the airplane. He and the abbot were sitting quietly in the two lounge chairs, and for once Francesco was not examining documents or listening to Spanish lessons on his tape register. I sat on the bed and looked at the two of them.

"He doesn't want to talk about it," the abbot told.

"We must," I replied.

"I can't, not and make sense," Francesco muttered. "All I can think of is, why me?"

I inhaled deeply. We had had this conversation in America in June. I suspected we would have it again and again as long as we both lived.

"Because you are *il Papa.* You have done some dramatic things, deeply holy things. Against the advice of most of us in the Curia, you are going into the world preaching social justice and selling some of the Vatican's treasure to finance that justice. You are trying to bring peace; you've stopped the bombardment of a city by risking your own life; you've gotten down on your knees to beg secular rulers to give peace and justice to their people. You're traveling to Latin America to encourage bishops to return to a simple life, so that all men can find the kingdom of God within themselves. These are exciting actions, and they have captured the imagination of the world."

"I have done nothing that a Pope should not do."

"*Ecco,* that may be true. But, God have mercy on their souls, your predecessors did not do them. Certainly not Papa Pio; certainly not Papa Giovanni for all his charisma; certainly not Papa Paolo, who saw the same opportunities that you have seen but was too knotted up within himself—and, I have to speak it, too parochially Italian—to take advantage of them. And certainly not his successors, whose reigns were so short. You have touched people's hearts and minds. And you yourself have changed. It has given you a great power. The price of that power is in part—only in part, I fear—these hysterical cures."

"Hysterical cures? I believe that. You believe that. But read this." He handed me a crumpled message that the plane's radio operator had given him. It was the preliminary report of the physicians of the University of Pennsylvania hospital. It was guardedly worded and prefaced with a statement that the physicians had not examined the patient before her sudden recovery and had depended solely on an incomplete medical history supplied by an ophthalmologist in Trenton, New Jersey.

Nevertheless, the sum of the report was clear: the patient's vision and ocular organs were normal for a person her age. There was no evidence whatever of glaucoma, advanced or incipient, even though the ophthalmologist in

Trenton had listed that disease (untreated for years, he said) as the cause of blindness. Four days of tests had yielded no provable explanation for a sudden reversal of the patient's condition, assuming glaucoma had ever been present. The report also stated that the patient had no known history of mental illness and despite her "advanced age" of seventy-three—I found that an unintelligent observation; many of us are at our intellectual peak at that age or even older—showed no signs of pathological impairment of intellectual faculties.

The radio message reported also that an unidentified physician at the university had told newsmen, "Whatever the original disease—and I doubt that we shall ever really know—the woman underwent an astonishingly rapid recovery."

I placed the message in my pocket and promised to give it to Dottor Twisdale so that he could prepare a draft of a statement for the press.

"There will be no statement," Francesco spoke without turning his head away from the window. "Nothing at all, not even 'no comment.' "

"But," I protested, "the questions will be asked. Dottor Twisdale cannot pretend to be deaf, at least not without causing wild speculation. He must say something."

"All right," Francesco snapped. "Just say that the matter is under study, and we see no reason at this time to change the statement that we issued at Newark last week. Have Pritchett laugh it up a bit again. But I do not want any reporter asking *me* anything about this."

Francesco's eyes were steely hard. "And tell Fieschi that I want as thorough an investigation of these cases as he can possibly conduct—in secrecy, of course."

I went to the rear of the plane and motioned to Fieschi to join me in the second bedroom. "I expected as much," he said as he read the report. His eyes were glowing brightly, but he did not have happiness or excitement in the usual sense; rather he found himself in a state much like what young people describe as high when one is using drugs. There was something almost trancelike in his expression. "Those two new cures on the way to the airport, and now this report. God forgive us all for doubting. He has reached out and touched us. Ugo, have you ever had a vision?"

"Not while I was sober." My effort at humor was faint. I was feeling very ill.

"This is no time for levity, Ugo. God has shown Himself in the world, among us. Not since the days of the Apostles has such a thing occurred."

"Eminence, we can't be certain that anything at all happened, except that a few people have become hysterical when *il Papa* touched them."

I may as well have not spoken, for Fieschi went on without hearing me. After all, he was Italian.

"I did once."

"Did what?"

"Had a vision."

"Of what?" I confess he was giving me care. I have spent much of my life praying and in the company of others who pray a great deal. *Allora,* when I was young, I prayed for a vision or at least a sign. I still do on occasion. As a youngster I would spend hours in prayer looking up at the clouds from the Alps dancing down toward our lake, hoping for some evidence of divine recognition—really approval, I suppose, or even gratitude—that Ugo Galeotti was going to devote his life to the Church. Later, in the seminary, I prayed harder, but God never deigned to show Himself to me in this way. As a mature adult, I have generally been glad of His reticence, even relieved by His mercy, although, as I said you, on occasion I still have need to seek a sign.

I have known several people who have claimed to have had visions. In a subjective way, each was speaking the truth. But each was also a person lacking in emotional stability. Fieschi, on the other hand, had always seemed like a rock to me. Dottor Twisdale once described Fieschi as unflappable. That is too slangy for my tastes, but it is accurate.

"It was more a vision of vision," Fieschi was saying. "It came to me in a dream. I dreamt that I awoke on a white marble floor. It was winter, but the floor was warm. I was looking up at the ceiling—also white marble—and was exhausted. Then someone told me that I had been asleep for three days. I explained to him why: I had seen the face of God. I awoke shortly after that and had a feeling both of exhilaration and deep peace. But my secretary was worried. He said that I had been asleep for almost seventeen hours. It was five o'clock in the afternoon. You know I never sleep more than six or seven hours at night."

"An interesting experience," I remarked guardedly.

"It was more than interesting, Ugo. I am convinced that my exhaustion was caused by the fact that I had had a supernatural experience."

"Do you remember it?"

"No, I recall only waking in my dream with a sense of reality that is more vivid than one usually has in this sensible world. I know I had a vision, but I could never understand the form it took—my inability to recollect anything. Now I understand its meaning. The dream meant that the vision of the face of God was not to be mine, but I would see and feel its effects."

I did not know what to say; I do not now remember what if anything I spoke immediately. Eventually, however, I changed the subject to how we would handle the inevitable questions, and, at a blow, Fieschi switched roles and became the hardheaded administrator. He listened while I explained how Francesco wanted the matter handled, and Fieschi agreed without question. "Let us confer with Dottor Twisdale and prepare ourselves for the reporters and their questions."

Allora, the regional conference at Lima was larger and thus much more physically taxing. At least *il Papa*'s opening oration was only a variation of his talk to the bishops at Mexico City. That spared some energy, but the sheer labor of meeting more than 200 bishops, of sitting with the meetings of twenty different study groups, and of listening and talking to each session would have drained the energy of the healthiest man. Francesco withstood the strain, but his cough lingered and he looked very, very pale as we boarded the helicopter to take us to the aircraft. Cardinal Pritchett and I had cheated on him just a little. We had arranged for the helicopter to put us on board the airplane a full two hours before we were scheduled to take off for Rio. Once on board we had no difficulty in persuading Francesco that he should go to bed and sleep.

The helicopters at Lima and Rio spared us the crush of crowds, and for once Francesco seemed to be glad to be away from the people. The welcoming party at the airport included two generals of the Brazilian junta. They were cordial enough, although they could not have interpreted the conferring of the red hat on the archbishop of Recife as anything other than a slap in the face, especially since just before his elevation the archbishop had publicly accused the junta of conducting systematic campaigns of torture and murder against its own citizens. (Indeed, Martìn said that the generals had already decided to arrest the archbishop when they learned of Francesco's decision to make him cardinal.) Francesco took the two generals completely by surprise by inviting them—within earshot of the reporters—and the president to a private audience that evening in the palazzo of the cardinal archbishop of Rio.

The generals were—how do you say?—flustered, and could only stammer something about appreciating the honor but not being sure about the president's plans. Francesco smiled genially. "We are certain that, if the honor is as great as you describe, His Excellency will have no difficulty in arranging his schedule. We shall expect him at six."

The generals were sweating profusely. Even though Rio in January is like Roma in July, they were nonetheless losing an inordinate amount of water. *Il Papa* closed the meeting with a wave of his hand: "My sons, may the Almighty God bless you and fill you with love toward your fellow man." ("My sons" was a phrase that I had never heard him use before.)

At the audience with the president and his two cabinet members, conversation flowed too rapidly for me to give an accurate verbatim account. I can tell you only the sum of what was said. (Incidentally, within a few days the *New York Times* published a remarkably exact account; I have always suspected that Francesco had Dottor Twisdale leak the story.)

I was present as were the abbot, Dottor Twisdale, Fieschi, Martìn, Candutti, the cardinal archbishop of Rio, the new cardinal archbishop of Recife, and our nuncio in Brasilia. We had no need for a translator; the generals were fluent in English. (They would have to be. Who can speak Portuguese? Only a Genovan who knows Spanish, or a Spaniard who knows the Genovan dialect.)

Francesco was gentle but firm. "With a troubled heart," he described for the junta the reports that he had received about systematic torture and murder. The generals derided our information as coming from Communists, anarchists, and social malcontents.

"We know it to be true, my sons," Francesco insisted. "Our secretary of state has irrefutable documentary evidence, including Xeroxed copies of orders signed by the president himself."

"Forgeries, no doubt," the president scoffed. "Those things are easily manufactured."

"We have checked out that possibility, my son. The signature is yours. No one could doubt it. Now we do not wish to publish these documents, but unless we receive immediate assurances that conditions will radically improve within the next few weeks—followed by hard evidence that they have changed and permanently changed—we shall be obliged to let the world know what we know."

The tone of the meeting immediately became less formally polite. One of the generals said something to the effect that priests could never understand politics and that a North American could never understand Latin America.

"Stern measures are often necessary," the general added, "when one is dealing with people who have no respect for law and no conception of justice and order—in short, when one is dealing with anarchists, terrorists, and Communists."

Francesco replied that terror and oppression by government usually destroyed respect for law and helped convert decent men into anarchists and Communists.

I cannot recall his precise words, but the president said that his government would rule Brazil as it thought best and that if churchmen did not like it they could leave the country, or be driven out. "Or perhaps," the president said with a sneer—these words I remember clearly because they burned fear into my heart—"we might keep some of these churchmen in our special apartments so they might see whether there is torture there or not."

"Then we might also see, my sons," Francesco shot back, "if you can rule Brazil without the love of God. As the moon only reflects the light of the sun, so you reflect only the authority that God has allowed you. And we are His Vicar. We may remove that authority."

The president smiled unpleasantly.

"Do you believe," Francesco asked rhetorically, "that we could not start a revolution here tomorrow? Think of the crowds that wait outside this place just for a glimpse of our person."

The generals were shocked, and so was Monsignor Candutti. But one of the junta had the presence of mind to ask quietly whether such a threat was consonant with *il Papa*'s supposed policy of disengagement of church and state.

"Of course," Francesco told smoothly, "if one also recalls that we have stressed that morality and moral choice cannot be taken out of politics. You have claimed we do not understand your politics. Perhaps that is so. But you do not understand either the necessity of goodness nor the nature of our charity. Because we want to save your souls as well as to protect your people, we have tried to persuade you in private to take the way of decency. But do not mistake concern for your souls for weakness. We now privately call on you to repent. The next time our call will be public. It may then be too late for you to do anything more virtuous than to die bravely, however stupidly."

"Do not forget, as you are threatening and blackmailing," one of the generals retorted, "that we hold thousands of priests and bishops hostage against the Vatican."

"We cannot forget that. But our people, yours and mine, will remember, if they face martyrdom, the words of the hymn: 'Joy is dying with Him; nailed is to be free.' And you cannot forget that eight out of nine of your people profess the Catholic faith. Your creating martyrs will strengthen the Church in the hearts of those people. You would be inviting a struggle in which you would lose your power, your lives, and worst of all, your souls. Listen to us, not defensively, not in anger, but in prudence if not repentance. We preach the separation of church and state but also the unity of the necessity of social justice and the duty to speak out and fight against social injustice. We accept the risk of martyrdom for our clergy, for our people, and for ourself. Those are not empty words."

Allora, we adjourned in anger. I had no optimism that there would be improvement. In fact, Francesco had worsened the situation, first of all, by meeting with these gangsters and, then, if he had to meet with them, by not letting Candutti talk so that the Pontiff might remain above the struggle. Fieschi, on the other hand, was sure that Francesco had done precisely the right thing. Monsignor Candutti was gloomily silent. I think *il Papa* agreed with me because in his conversations with the nuncio and the Brazilian prelates he seemed to be preparing them for persecution. That prospect did not seem to depress *il Papa.* In fact, if anything, he seemed elated. Perhaps I exaggerate, but certainly he accepted the possibility calmly, just as one might accept fog in Bologna during the winter or a traffic jam in Roma at any time.

I must confess that in this instance Fieschi's judgment was somewhat more accurate than mine. Perhaps his total faith in Francesco was not altogether misplaced. After we left Brazil, there was no sudden, public change in policy, but our sources—mostly local priests and nuns—told that conditions began to improve in a small but real sense.

At the regional conference, Francesco adhered to the same approach of a general address, followed by meetings with smaller study groups. It was another grueling experience, because the conference at Rio was by far the largest of the three. Brazil has almost 200 bishops, Argentina 55, Uruguay 10, and even the Falkland Islands have one. We had to cancel several evening sessions that we had planned, and even the cardinal archbishop's physician pleaded with Papa Francesco to rest. By and large Francesco gave that advice a merchant's ear, although he did agree to limit himself to two public appearances, one in Rio and the other—planned after our audience with the leaders of the junta—in Brasilia itself.

His appearance in Brasilia came first. We went there by helicopter to a soccer *colosseo* for an afternoon Mass and homily. The government had done its best to prevent our visit by raising all sorts of problems, but Fieschi and Candutti were at their best negotiating. Fieschi was like a bulldog, patiently tenacious, refusing to be deterred. He used Francesco's trick of speaking in the presence of reporters, effectively coupling it with his own aristocratic manner of making his opponent feel clumsy in his presence. We also heard that the government had tried to discourage attendance, but if that news were true it could hardly have been a successful effort. Newsmen estimated that inside and around the *colosseo* had gathered more than a quarter of a million persons.

With some misgivings on our part and against the prudent advice of the chief of police, *il Papa* drove around the outside of the *colosseo.* Only with great difficulty were the police able to prevent the crowds from crushing us. Twice Francesco tried to reprimand the officers for using excessive force, but I doubt if anyone heard him speak. I was next to him and could hardly hear him above the shouts of the crowd.

Inside, there was no trouble until we sought to leave. The main exit was blocked by beggars, sick people, and their friends and relatives. The police reacted in typical style by drawing their clubs and preparing to charge into the suffering mass of humanity to clear a path. The cardinal archbishop of Rio used the loudspeaker to beg people to stand absolutely still lest *il Papa* be injured, and Francesco walked up to the group. As in Mexico City, he denied that he had power to cure, only to bring the Gospel of Christ's love and the forgiveness of sins. It was a memorable scene, the Roman Pontiff going from beggar to beggar and from stretcher to stretcher smiling, touching, blessing. His translator, a Brazilian *monsignore,* was visibly shaken.

It had to happen again. How no? The scene was too filled with emotion not to tip an unstable person. A woman on a stretcher suddenly leaped up and claimed that she had been cured; I do not now remember of what ailment. Two minutes later a young boy who had been dumb since his parents' death four years earlier began to speak as Papa Francesco touched his lips. It had not been a deliberate gesture, Francesco later told me. He had no idea why he touched the boy on the lips instead of the head or shoulders. He had only reached out to touch the appealing face of a child.

As the news of the cures rippled through the *colosseo,* I could feel unrest moving like the sweeping second hand on a time bomb. The police acted swiftly, and, despite my general impression of these people, I must say wisely. They radioed for the helicopter to take off and hover above the stage in the center of the *colosseo* where Mass had been said. Then they rushed *il Papa* to that post and helped him up the ladder into the aircraft. As the helicopter circled slowly above the stadium, Francesco stood in the entranceway, making the sign of the cross.

That appearance was, as Francesco had intended it to be, an important demonstration of power in the very teeth of the junta. The generals might sneer at Francesco's pleas to do justice, but they could not help but be impressed by his capacity to mass and to move a crowd. The affair of the "cures" probably impressed the generals as well. Although they would have had no faith in the supernatural, they could appreciate the miracle of a magnetic human person's hypnotic effect. We never received a report from the Brazilian doctors on either case, and I do not recall ever seeing a reliable report on the nature of the woman's malady. The child, of course, fitted the classic model of an affliction caused by hysteria and cured by a similar process.

Il Papa's appearance in Rio provoked an even grander demonstration of popularity. With difficulty we persuaded the police to clear one of the central piazzas and to allow *il Papa* to address the crowd from a balcony so that there would be no physical contact. I have no idea of the size of that crowd. The piazza was packed solid, as were all the streets leading to it. The cardinal archbishop had ensured that loudspeakers were placed every fifty meters for a full block in each direction. Some newspapers said that a half million people were present; some told three-quarters of a million, and one even claimed a million. In truth, I have no idea.

TWENTY-FOUR

On the return trip to Roma, events continued to surprise us, but events of a very different kind. Signor Randall's gift had been a cause for joy, and I do not know how to characterize the phenomena of the "cures" other than as a terrible gift. The next occurrences brought us death and a threat of death. I speak of that part of the trip with great pain—one of your psychiatrists would probably say with great guilt. He would probably be right.

We had planned to fly from Brazil to Dakar to refuel and then on to Barcelona to visit the new archbishop. According to me—Monsignor Candutti agreed—it was imprudent for *il Papa* to visit Spain until several years had passed. In fact, in Mexico City I had decided that it was dangerous for Papa Francesco to go anywhere until this thing of the "miracles" had run its course.

Monsignor Candutti had cabled the police in Dakar and Barcelona about the gravity of the problem of crowds. I knew that the officials at Dakar would cooperate, and our stop of only an hour would ease problems. Francesco would remain on the aircraft, greet the archbishop, a French-speaking black man, and various political dignitaries, and from the steps of the plane bless any group of people in attendance. It was all to be very quick and simple.

Barcelona was another matter. We were scheduled to leave the aircraft and travel by helicopter to the port, then by motor to the chancery. I did not like it. Many of the streets were very narrow, and the Catalans were excitable. I was not certain that the Spanish government might not take it as sweet revenge to see their antagonist trampled to death by the people whom he had fought to protect.

We took off shortly after nine, and Francesco, Fieschi, the abbot, and I met in the plane's forward conference room. *Il Papa* was obviously feeling somewhat better and was outlining his plans to reform the lower ranks of the Curia, the plans that the World Synod of Bishops had approved. First, he wanted some astute public relations done to create a favorable image of the Curia as an interesting post in which non-Italians could do useful work. Second, in canvassing pastoral bishops, asking them to recommend promising young and middle-aged men for work in Roma, the Secretariat of State would need to stress the benefits to be gained by the Church at large and by individual countries in having knowledgeable officials in the Vatican.

Third, the secretary of state's office would need to establish a computerized system for—how do you say?—keeping track of these clerics and also the young students whose names directors of seminaries would send us each year. I was born too early to find electronics comprehensible, but Fieschi was far more flexible than I. He was also younger. It was Francesco, however, who was the most knowledgeable. He quickly explained how easily such a system could be established. Fieschi listened avidly and took notes on his pad. I used the time of the discourse for prayer.

When they seemed finished, I asked if they thought the idea—not the electronic system but the fundamental idea—would be successful. I wanted—how do you say?—to nibble at the edges and lead them to the core. Could the Vatican function, I inquired, if its officials were not in effect volunteers, men who wanted to work there?

"We must make it clear," Francesco conceded, "that we understand that not everyone who would seem to be qualified would want to come or should come. We want only to be able to learn who is qualified. After that we can find out if he would like to come. What worries us is that at best we now have a system of rather broadly based nepotism in the sense that personal knowledge and recommendations of friends play the critical roles in deciding who works at the Vatican. That's a very Italian system"—according to me, it is the essence of the Italian social system—"but it's a very inefficient system."

"Unless," I pointed out, "the objective of the system is to continue the system. Then it is a most efficient means. Besides, even in the achievement-oriented society of the United States you depend heavily on recommendations from people you know."

"Yes," Francesco admitted, "but the difference is we depend on recommendations from people whose judgment we trust—not, of course, that nepotism is totally absent from any society. Besides, we do not want to eliminate the personal element entirely. We want to broaden the base of selection from the acquaintances of a relatively few people—mostly Italians and frequently Vatican careerists themselves—to anyone in the universal Church who has talent and wants to serve."

"I do not know," I told. "It would be an intelligent plan in an America. Whether it will work with us is another thing. Besides, there is also a different problem." I repeated, in more diplomatic terms, Bisset's contention (echoed by Gordenker) at the synod that local bishops would not cooperate. Francesco agreed that would be a problem, but thought that once the system was operating, pastoral bishops would see its advantages. Besides, he said, he planned to set a limit of five to eight years of service within the Curia before a cleric returned to his diocese. Thus a bishop would not permanently lose any priest.

"But we," I objected further, "would lose the benefit of experienced staff."

"Experience of longer than five years more often leads to boredom and arrogant behavior than to efficiency," Fieschi put in. I kept silent; I was not about to quarrel with his expert knowledge of arrogance. "Our most difficult task," Fieschi continued, "will be to convince pastoral bishops that it is in their interests to cooperate. We can do that. Cardinal Martìn can help. We must, as His Holiness says, exploit the role of the World Synod of Bishops here. Pastoral bishops have always been critical of the Curia. We shall make it clear in many subtle ways that this is the synod's plan to bring the Curia closer to the real shepherds. Holiness, my office can have a set of detailed plans on your desk within a week."

If I had not talked to Fieschi so often during the past ten days and heard his reaction to the "miracles," I would have been astounded. At the synod I had viewed such a scheme—as I know Fieschi then also had despite his present intervention on its behalf—merely as a tactic to start the synod in motion. As a practical plan, it was not just what you call a pipe dream but a dangerous pipe dream that threatened the continuity of the Vatican. The Church *must* remain in many ways a stagnant society.

Ecco, I know I have spoken of the necessity of change to make our teaching relevant; I do not recant it. But just as a bureaucracy can be wedded to the status quo, so also it can become enamored of change for the sake of change. That, after all, makes the bureaucracy, insofar as it directs the change, more important. A few weeks earlier, Fieschi would have grasped this point, and, because he had then believed in stability even more strongly than I, would have argued eloquently against what he now accepted without question or even internal doubt. At that moment, however, he saw his only task as executing every scintilla of Papa Francesco's wishes. Once again I had doubts whether I had done Francesco a service in recommending Fieschi, but for the very opposite reasons that underlay my earlier doubts. An adviser should not uncritically accept his leader's ideas.

Francesco seemed relieved by Fieschi's promise. "We can turn our attention to the spiritual renewal and the crusade again, thanks to the gift from our friend Mr. Randall. By the way, Cardinal Fieschi, have you had any reactions to our request that the UN take over the direction and funding of the work in Latin America?"

"Monsignor Candutti has been in close touch, Holiness. The poorer nations are all in favor, of course. They see the UN as an instrument to redistribute wealth, and your ideas fit nicely with theirs. The developed nations fear just that sort of use of the UN and see your request as a step in the wrong direction. However, you have put them in an awkward position. They can't fight you openly, but they may just sit on their hands—"

"Or their wallets," I observed.

"Yes, their wallets. In sum, Holiness, we have had talk but no action. Monsignor Candutti will maintain pressure at the UN. I thought it might be a good idea for him to fly back to New York after a few days of review in Rome."

"Good. We, too, are ready to go back to New York and prod them again when you and Monsignor Candutti think it would be wise."

Allora, at that point, the radio operator knocked at the door and brought in a cable. Francesco read it quickly. His face, which had been pale, now grew ashen. He dropped the message on the table. It was dated noon, Roman time. Two Dutch priests and a Belgian nun had chained themselves to one of the concrete posts at the base of the obelisk in the middle of the Piazza di San Pietro, poured gasoline on each other, and immolated themselves, in the fashion of the Buddhist monks in Vietnam, to protest against "a Pope who works miracles but cannot abolish the cruelty of clerical celibacy or allow the ordination of women."

Francesco held both hands tightly against his temples. The abbot leaned over and asked, "Are you all right?"

"Yes, just leave me alone for a while, all of you, please."

We left immediately, but that was a mistake. With hindsight we are all omniscient. I later came to understand that Francesco had probably suffered a minor stroke. I do not know precisely what we could have done had we recognized the nature of his ailment. Perhaps we could have reversed our course and flown to Argentina; we certainly could not have returned to Brazil. *Ebbene,* knowing nothing, we did nothing.

When I returned more than an hour later, I found Francesco half-conscious. He was able to talk only with great difficulty. Had I viewed any sign of paralysis, I might have suspected a stroke, but as it was I thought only that he had suffered the relapse that the Mexican physicians had so confidently predicted. Naturally we radioed Dakar to cancel any reception and to have a doctor awaiting us. As soon as we landed, the physician—a Frenchman whom I would not have selected for myself or my friends—came aboard and examined *il Papa.* When he heard about the pneumonia and the prediction of a relapse, his diagnosis was made. He prescribed oxygen, which we easily obtained from the portable bottles on the plane, continuation of antibiotics—we had a sufficient supply on board—and complete rest.

Fieschi shared my opinion of the Frenchman and ordered that we take off for Italy as soon as the plane was refueled.

Even though we had planned only a brief stop at Dakar with few ceremonies, there was a crowd at the airport which journalists estimated at 25,000 people. They were disappointed, of course, as was the official reception committee. Fieschi, speaking flawless Parisian French, explained that *il Papa*'s health had worsened and, before suggesting they return to the city, led them in prayer for his rapid recovery.

We chose to come down at Ciampino airport outside of Roma to avoid the possibility of crowds at Fiumicino. The Vatican's—I call it ours even though it was a loan from Italy—helicopter's blades were already idling. Attendants carried Francesco out on a stretcher; twenty minutes after the wheels of the 727 had first touched the ground, Francesco was in bed in the papal apartments. I suggested, and Fieschi agreed, that there would be more privacy within the palazzo itself than in the *casina.* Once we were within the Vatican, my first act was to make certain that the carnage had been cleaned from the piazza. I did not want Francesco to suffer unnecessarily. *Ecco,* I discovered a jagged and still charred patch on the stones in front of the obelisk, but no other evidence.

When we were secure that *il Papa* was settled in bed and had been seen by our own physicians, Monsignor Alessandro (my secretary, you recall) and I walked two steps to the Via delle Fornaci and ate a pleasant supper at the Trattoria Vittoria. We ate inside, of course, but Roma seemed doubly cold after the heat of Brazil and Dakar. It was mostly a psychological reaction, since we were enjoying a very mild winter. Tomorrow, I promised myself, when I had less fatigue, I would eat at a good *ristorante,* perhaps Il Galeone or Da Gino; but tonight the simple food of the trattoria was what I needed.

When I returned to my apartment in the Palazzo di San

Calisto, LaTorre and Chelli were awaiting me in my sitting room. The prospect of a long talk was not pleasing. Almost three weeks of travel had left me exhausted, drained of all energy. However, I offered LaTorre a Grappa and Chelli a Courvoisier. (I sipped a bit of that delightful Irish Mist that Cardinal Greene had given me.) They told me of their shock at the immolation and how such human sacrifice indicated fanaticism. I told them, briefly, very briefly, what I knew of Papa Francesco's health. Although it was plainly in their minds, they did not ask about the "miracles." Instead, after one drink, I invited them to dine with me the next night. They accepted and were enough gracious to leave me to my sleep.

The following morning I rose late and was slow in celebrating my Mass; I did not arrive at the palazzo until shortly after nine. I went directly to Cardinal Pritchett's office, and felt some comfort in seeing him as uncoordinated as I. Both of us went to *il Papa*'s apartment and found him sitting inside the oxygen tent, reading morning papers from Roma and Milano. I did notice a slight slur in his voice but attributed it to his having been given a sedative the night before. Monsignor Bonetti came in and out several times with news summaries and the international edition of *Newsweek*. Signora Falconi brought in a large *practica*—an Italian file— from Fieschi. It contained a draft of a *motu proprio* to reform the Curia along the lines that the synod had approved and we had discussed on the airplane. Fieschi must have had a white night—I mean that he could not have slept and produced such a document.

I walked Signora Falconi to the door and asked her if in reality she thought that Francesco should be seeing such things. I had acquired fondness for the *signora,* as I have said, and had come to depend on her judgment.

"No, of course not," she told, "but we don't have much choice. He was awake at seven this morning and my telephone rang ten minutes later. You know how much good it will do to argue with him. But don't worry, he won't see anything that will tax him or upset him. I'll stop anything like that and send it on to you or Cardinal Fieschi."

The physician who had attended the last two Pontiffs arrived, but was able to do little good. Francesco placed little faith in Italian medicine (which put in my mind that it was time for me to go to Switzerland and my own medicine men). Rest, oxygen, aspirin, and continued antibiotics were the physician's instructions. Although Francesco had not permitted him to complete a thorough examination, the physician said that he thought there was still a trace of pneumonia in the right lung. He also told that Francesco was physically exhausted. The ache in my own bones said that that part of the diagnosis was correct. The other part of the diagnosis was more tentative and gave me concern: the possibility of a stroke, a small one but a stroke nevertheless. The physician wanted many tests, but because Francesco would not even discuss entering a hospital we could only perform some of these in the palazzo. The physician explained that many physicians would prescribe anticoagulants under the circumstances, but he preferred to rely on rest and aspirin, while oxygen and antibiotics cleared the other symptoms. If Francesco's speech again became slurred or he showed any signs of paralysis, we would have to take drastic action.

I visited several times during the day to make certain that all was going well. Signora Falconi assured me that everything was going as well as one could expect when the patient was a fool, and she said it so that Francesco could hear her. Probably the *signora* pleased me because, although she was normally very tactful, when irate she possessed something of Kate's frankness and sharp tongue. Your American women tend to display independence without meanness or hardness; that is a pleasant trait.

In the evening I took LaTorre and Chelli to Il Galeone, to a small private dining room above. Elio, my usual waiter, outdid himself. He had ready three chilled bottles of white Frecciarossa (that is a delightfully light wine from Pavia), and an antipasto of mixed *frutti di mare*. How do you translate fruits of the sea? *Ecco,* shellfish. My opening plate was a *risotto* stuffed with more *frutti*—clams, shrimp, and squid. My principal plate was a whole grilled bass, which Elio filleted at the table with the skill of a surgeon, using only a large spoon and a fork. For *contorni* we had cold spinach with lemon and a mixed salad. For health, I restricted myself to some cheese for after. Chelli contented himself with the *zuppa di pesce*—the spicy soup with shellfish from the Tyrrhenian Sea. The French imitate it and try but fail to improve it by adding saffron and calling it bouillabaisse. LaTorre had the Roman *spaghetti carbonara*, and a huge *bistecca alla Fiorentina*, the proportions of which he himself marked from the slab of beef that Elio wheeled in.

I had assured my brethren that we could talk safely in the private room. The woman who operated the *ristorante* respected my need for privacy; and, besides, the sound of the middle-aged minstrels singing folksongs from the Trastevere made conversation difficult to hear more than a meter distant. Still, it was not until we had almost finished our principal plate that we went beyond my recounting some of the details of the trip, and their describing an atmosphere of high confusion in the Vatican over recent events. The Pontiff's illness had further disturbed life. Even the stenographers do not type, LaTorre told, but spend their hours speculating about martyrs, miracles, and the death and election of a Pontiff.

Finally, LaTorre and I nodded to Chelli, who for ten minutes had been hungrily fingering and sniffing his Cuban cigar, and he lit the ugly thing. *"Senti,"* he said as he graciously blew a big black ring of putrid tobacco smoke away from the table, "what do you think of these so-called miracles?"

"Have you talked with the secretary of state?" I parried.

"We have," LaTorre snorted. "That man has either had too much tropical sun or too much New York cold. He left Rome a sensible Italian cardinal; he has come back a mystic as wild-eyed as that Trappist abbot. He is convinced that God is in our midst."

"Is he not?" I asked.

"Of course," LaTorre told, "but you know what I mean. The man has lost his judgment on this issue. What have you given us as secretary of state?"

"The man," I chortled, "whom you would have given us as *il Papa*."

"Touché," Chelli smiled. *"Nostra culpa.* We have all misjudged our noble Genovan."

"Agreed," I said, "perhaps we are doing so at this moment. I do not know if he is right or wrong. I shall try to hold an open mind because, even though my intellect says that I saw only hysteria, in all candor the array of 'cures' was dazzling. The more so because after the first I think

Francesco knew that they were going to happen even if he did not know precisely when and where."

"Well, are they real or hysterical?" Chelli asked.

"They could be a plot, either by the Communists or the Fascists, to trap us into saying something affirmative," LaTorre added, "and then they would reveal the whole hoax."

To avoid the basic question, I treated LaTorre's comment seriously. "I doubt that. The affairs were too complex. How many people would you have to place in a crowd of more than 100,000 to have a chance of touching *il Papa?* As for hysteria, that is what Papa Francesco believed. It is the theory to which I lean. As I said, intellectually I am secure that that is the explanation."

"And His Holiness?" Chelli inquired. "Has he changed his original view?"

"I do not know. At first, in Newark, it gave him concern, but he stated unequivocally that it was a case of hysteria. The affair in Mexico City shook his confidence. The others may have shattered it. But the last time he spoke to me about it, he insisted the cause was hysteria. I know he is praying that the evidence will prove that to be the case."

"That is fortunate," LaTorre muttered. "The Church could not survive another Messiah."

"*Allora,* we must face up to the fact, however," I tried to stress, "that many people are going to look on *il Papa* as a man of miracles; physical movement will be difficult always, and sometimes impossible. For Francesco th.. will be horrendous, because he is somewhat claustrophobic.

"There will be other problems as well, and more serious ones," I continued. "As you have viewed, our brother Fieschi has taken an attitude toward Papa Francesco that may become typical—absolute reverence, almost adoration."

"We saw," LaTorre snapped.

"That would be bad for *il Papa* and it will be worse for the Church," Chelli noted. "A cardinal does not serve either well by not having opinions of his own or by suppressing advice when he sees a Pontiff about to act unwisely."

"Certainly," I smiled, "neither of you will have to answer to his Creator for being slavishly obedient to the

Pontiff, at least to this *Papa.*" LaTorre grinned boyishly and Chelli actually blushed a little. "*Ecco,* you both know that despite our close friendship, I see this world—and possibly the next—differently from you."

"That is true, but—," LaTorre started to say.

"But we've always thought of you as educable rather than as invincibly ignorant," Chelli intervened.

"*Allora,*" LaTorre went on, "we share the same love for the Church. That is why, dear Ugo, we wanted to talk to you, to ask you to join us."

"But I am already a member of the Church and have been for many years."

"This is not a time for levity, please," LaTorre said.

"I am not making a joke. I merely fear what you might be asking."

"We ask only that you join us."

"For what purpose?"

"To put a brake on *il Papa* and those like Fieschi who would unthinkingly obey him."

"I am still not precisely certain what you are asking. *Senti,* if you want me to offer *il Papa* my best judgment and try to see that he hears the two bells before making a decision"—You say that? *Ecco,* he hears all sides—"then I can only say I have tried to do those things all my life, as you have tried. What other do you want?" I fear that my voice betrayed my suspicions.

"We are not speaking a cabal or a conspiracy or anything like that," Chelli told reassuringly. "We simply want you to know that we three—and Cardinals Bisset and Greene—share a common set of concerns. We realize that the rest of us have never experienced your enthusiasm for the new Pontiff and that our orientation toward the teaching of the Church is different from yours. Some would say we are more rigid, others that you are too flexible. Let us not quarrel over words. We do not want you to betray friendship or to be disloyal to Papa Francesco either as Pontiff or as friend. We merely wish to be able to consult freely with you, to exchange information and opinions about the wisdom and propriety of certain courses that he may take.

"We ask this," Chelli went on, "because, in all candor, we do not think that Fieschi in his present state of mind can offer critical advice. And the undersecretary of state—"

"That Pole, whom Monsignor Bonelli sent packing years ago—what's his name?" LaTorre asked.

"Monsignor Zaleski," Chelli said us, "a man who is very sympathetic with what the popular press calls the liberal elements in the Vatican. He might be a brake on Fieschi if Fieschi were behaving more as one would have expected from a man of his class, but as things now exist Zaleski will only reinforce any momentum for change."

"We fear," LaTorre broke in, "that in the midst of adulation Papa Francesco will close his ears to people like us and our ideas. But he will listen to you, and we want you, if we cannot be heard directly, to have the Pontiff consider our point of view."

"I seem to recall," I responded, "our covering this ground before. Now, as earlier, you have made several erroneous assumptions. *Il Papa* often consults me, but he consults many people, anyone whose ideas he believes may be relevant. But he makes up his own mind. Also, I think you underestimate his ability to cope with adulation. I know that Papa Francesco is no longer the same person as Declan Walsh was, but the surest way to have alienated Declan Walsh was by flattery. He possessed—probably yet possesses—much vanity; but he knows the difference between just praise and false flattery."

"Perhaps," Chelli agreed, "but the power of the secretary of state, when he is not checked within his own office by a man with the skill of a Bonelli, is immense, And, from what we have seen of Fieschi yesterday and today, his admiration—adulation or even adoration—of Papa Francesco is genuine. Fieschi is above all, as we three know, a man of absolute integrity. He would not know how to use false flattery. Oh, no, Ugo, he is a true believer, and even a prudent Pontiff would find it difficult to cope with a true believer with Fieschi's ability and power. In coordinating activities and recommendations and in assigning problems, he can subtly squeeze out those whose views he wishes to exclude from the Pope's attention."

"But each prefect has regular audiences with *il Papa;* each of you sees him once a week."

"True," Chelli responded, "but we discuss what Papa Francesco wants us to discuss. Besides, by the time we bring up a problem, the matter may have already been decided."

"I believe—hope—you have undue fear of Fieschi's conversion. Have faith in his prudence, of which you spoke so eloquently not long since."

Chelli smiled. "It may well be that we are only reacting like Italians. We always suspect the worst, and generally we are right, perhaps because we are usually dealing with other Italians. But you have lived in America too long, Ugo. You should have come back to your culture. No man is to be trusted with power, especially not one who shows signs of fanaticism. We know the Vatican is an Italian institution, and that we must operate by devious ways."

"Even when you could attain the same result openly?"

"But that would take so much of the joy out of accomplishment."

"Perhaps. Let me be un-Italian and state my position clearly. If, according to me, your ideas are not being heard and if, again according to me, they have merit, I shall see that they are presented to Papa Francesco, if not through regular channels then through personal intervention. I say this even though I might not personally believe in your ideas. But in our 'exchanges' of information I cannot discuss with you matters that *il Papa* has said in confidence."

LaTorre shrugged his shoulders, raised the palms of his hands upwards, rolled his eyes toward the ceiling, and pursed his lips in the classic Sicilian gesture of incredulity. (You should understand that the southern Italian assumes a more flexible view of secrecy than do people from the north. A man from Sicily or the Mezzogiorno thinks that he is keeping a confidence if he only says it to family and friends or trades it for something of equal or greater value. After all, if you cannot use what you know, why bother to know it? Besides, since no one else keeps secrets, why should you, especially if there is profit to be gained from revelation? That attitude is the fundamental reason we experience such problems with security in the Vatican. Except for the seal of the confessional—that is absolute—a southern Italian and even, I concede, many northern Italians simply do not think of secrets in the way an American of Englishman or German would.)

"Of course," Chelli quickly told. Being less parochial than LaTorre, he was better able to understand and even sympathize with strange cultural traits. "We would not want you to betray a confidence. But some matters may, on occasion"—daily, I thought—"become common knowledge even before the secretary of state or His Holiness has discussed them with the prefects concerned. It is only then that we would want to talk to you."

"Exactly," LaTorre told, quickly stilling the motion of his hands and shoulders.

"We can talk at any time," I assured them. "We have done so often in the past and are doing so now in a most candid fashion. I have also tried to say what I know about things like Papa Francesco's health, where I might at the moment have more information than you. We are old friends and we share, as you say, a deep love for the Church. But let me repeat that I have deep faith in Francesco's judgment and his fairness."

"Let us pray that you are correct," LaTorre told. "Let us pray. Just so that you do not think us paranoid, I ask you to read this." He gave me a document written in English. I recognized the style, but not the machine, the typewriter. It was Francesco's style, without doubt. The document was a three-page letter to the bishops of the world, encouraging them to establish programs within their dioceses to return to the Church people who had divorced and remarried—even to help them return to the sacraments.

I assume you know that the policy—I should sa, *recent* policy, for it was not always so in the early Church—has been that divorced Catholics who remarry during the lifetime of their original spouses are excommunicated. Until they abandon their new spouses and confess their sins, those Catholics are barred from the sacraments. In reality, only Holy Communion is withheld. That is, nevertheless, harsh punishment. The justification is that the persons involved are committing adultery while living together and, since their cohabitation is widely known, are a source of scandal to others.

Allora, this document—Francesco's document—would have lifted this barrier against reception of the sacraments. It did not, however, recant the Church's historic—in fact, Christ's explicit—condemnation of divorce and remarriage. It repeated, although without using the words "condemn" or "condemnation," the Church's basic teaching that marriage vows were sacred promises before God that bound husband and wife until death.

"I had not seen this," I told as I returned the documents to LaTorre.

"Nor had I, as prefect of the Congregation for the Sacred Doctrine of the Faith," LaTorre responded. "Indeed, I have not yet officially received it."

"Nor has Cardinal Greene," Chelli put in, "our most eminent prefect of the Congregation for Rites and Sacraments."

"You see here," LaTorre said, "one piece of the pattern: a document that touches our faith—one that could shatter it—and we in the Curia who are most intimately involved and informed are ignored."

"It is late in the evening to discuss the merits of this document," I told. I did not add anything about discussing the ethics of how they had obtained it. "The procedural aspects are serious. They also underline for you what I earlier told about *il Papa*'s not always consulting me. *Allora,* my promise stands."

The night was not a total loss. Chelli and LaTorre may have thought that I had become too American in my thinking, but I was yet enough Italian to suspect that, if they had taken me this far into their confidence, there was much more going on. I would not say that I suspected a conspiracy in the sense of a group of people plotting a coup d'état, but someone close to *il Papa* was enough out of sympathy with him to steal documents. My earlier information about the traditionalists' loose cooperation with Papa Francesco was probably out of date. While we were in the New World, these people had probably decided on a new strategy. I decided that it would be expedient to discover more. That is one reason why I told that I would cooperate. But in all candor I must add that I did have concern about the document—less about its merits than the lack of consultation.

There was a second positive result from the evening. At 2 A.M. I returned to the *ristorante* with my machine and chauffeur and conducted Elio and his friend Massimo, the chef—a heavyset man with huge jowls who obviously enjoyed the fruits of his labor—to their homes in Ostia. It was a long ride, and there was much negotiation, even haggling. But at the finish they agreed that they would staff Papa Francesco's kitchen. It displeased me that I would be barred from one of the best restaurants in Roma, but greater love hath no gourmet than that he offer his chef to another. Since coming to Roma (probably since Kate's death), Francesco never ate properly. Now that his health was suffering, we had need to tempt him to take care of himself.

TWENTY-FIVE

THE NEXT MORNING I telephoned Fieschi and arranged an immediate appointment to discuss the draft of *il Papa*'s letter to the bishops about the return of divorced people to the sacraments. Fieschi demonstrated serious concern about the theft, but he was surprised that anyone would object to the substance. He also thought that lack of consultation was blameless. The document was an early draft that *il Papa* himself had written. It had not been circulated because his thoughts were still in the formative stage. If, however, many cardinals knew about the draft, it might as well be discussed at our second meeting scheduled for that afternoon.

Ecco, I had allowed myself the luxury of forgetting those two meetings. The first was at four, the second immediately following. The double thought was not pleasing to me. I had not returned from Ostia until three in the morning, and was yet feeling the effects of our voyage. I was down a rope—you say that in English? Well, I was very tired and had been looking forward to a long siesta. Under the circumstances, I thought the sage thing would be to enjoy a light lunch and take as much of a nap as possible. Signora Falconi agreed. She said only routine affairs were on my desk, although their number was legion.

I believe I have told that Francesco avoided calling meetings of all the heads of congregations, preferring to deal with the cardinals individually rather than together where they might have a more accurate sense of how others felt. Fieschi apparently assumed that the reason was *il Papa*'s lack of time. Now, with Francesco indisposed, responsibility for running the Vatican's machinery fell on Fieschi, and he had called such a meeting for that afternoon.

As we entered, he was already seated at the head of the long conference table in his office. He was flanked by his two chief assistants, Monsignor Zaleski, the under-secretary responsible for internal coordination, and Monsignor Candutti, the undersecretary responsible for foreign relations. The green felt cover of the table was littered with ashtrays, pads, pencils, glasses, and bottles of mineral water—the water was Appia, another indication of Fieschi's utter indifference to things of the palate.

Under his crisp direction we moved rapidly along. He opened with a statement about *il Papa's* health and offered a masterfully concise but accurate summary of our trip to the UN and Latin America. Then we disposed of our substantive business in less than an hour. Before we adjourned, Fieschi gave us an oration.

"Most Reverend Brothers," he said, switching his tone from the flat voice of the administrator to that which a spiritual adviser would use in addressing first-year seminarians, "the Church must wait until all the evidence has been sifted by competent medical authorities and by theologians before we can be sure what has happened. But it is my personal belief that, even if the cures were due to emotional causes, we have been touched by the finger of God. This visitation has a momentous meaning for all people of our time. Through our Papa Francesco, God is making manifest His grace by giving us outward signs that His Vicar must be heard.

"We have read," Fieschi continued, "that in calling the Second Vatican Council Papa Giovanni counted on a wave of inspiration from the Holy Spirit. We have also read that he gambled and lost, that it was the spirit of Babel and not of God that descended on the Church. There was some evidence for this view, but it was a false interpretation, another example of man's lack of faith. We sometimes look to God to answer our prayers as if He were a waiter who takes our order and swiftly returns with steaming plates of what we asked for. That is not God's way, as we at this table well know. He hears our prayers, but He responds in His way and in His time. God heard Papa Giovanni's prayer for inspiration. He answered that prayer, not in Giovanni's lifetime, but during the last conclave when He spoke through our most reverend brother, Cardinal Galeotti. Papa Francesco is God's answer, His way of renewing our faith, of allowing us to rededicate ourselves. We hear the word of God in Papa Francesco's preaching the gospel of love; we see the actions of God in his generous giving to the needy; we see the approval of God in these miracles.

"For us in the Curia, this visitation has glorious significance. We are to be integral parts in the renewal of Christianity. We have no higher duty than to act with all our hearts, minds, and souls to bring about within ourselves, within the Church, and throughout the world the transformations that Papa Francesco—and through these signs, Christ Himself—wants. In the past, all of us have sometimes seen it as our duty to protect a Pontiff from himself and the Church from a Pontiff. We have not always fully carried out *his* decisions in *his* way. That day is no longer with us. Our task is certainly not to obstruct, but to act wholeheartedly to carry out the will of God.

"The Secretariat of State is charged with the duty of directing and coordinating the activities of the Curia. We in the secretariat will follow to the letter the course just outlined.

"We urge you as sons of God, brothers in Christ, and princes of the Church to join with us in this endeavor. We deliver a suggestion, in all charity and in all humility"—in all candor, Fieschi possessed many virtues, but humility was never one of them—"that anyone who does not honestly believe that he can serve Papa Francesco according to the ancient imagery of St. Ignatius Loyola, with 'corpselike obedience,' that is, by yielding his entire will to that of the Pontiff, such a person should resign his prefecture immediately. Our office will not tolerate any of the stratagems that have been employed in the past to restrain a Pontiff. More important, God Himself will severely punish anyone who willfully obstructs His divine plan."

Fieschi looked around the room, letting the full impact of his heavy words press into our minds. Then he concluded: "Let us end this meeting with a prayer for the speedy recovery of Papa Francesco and for our own total dedication to his work." He led us in the Our Father.

It had been a tactless oration. One does not talk to powerful princes of the Church as if they were adolescents. He had, as we say in Italian, made the fly jump at our nose—not a good thing. As Fieschi had been delivering his sermon, I had watched the choler creep up LaTorre's neck to his cheeks and even shine pink under his white mane. Greene's clenched fists had threatened to mangle the arms of his chair, and several times he had run his hand through his hair until it stood nearly on end. Bisset's eyes had shot out black, contemptuous fire. Pritchett had appeared embarrassed, Rauch and others incredulous. Chelli was the only cardinal present who seemed unperturbed. He listened intently, but his only motion was occasionally to twist one of his cigars under his nose to savor the aroma of its dry leaves. From the expression on his face, he could have been listening to a weather prediction or a suggestion to issue different-colored library cards.

The second meeting began ten minutes later. Present were only LaTorre for the Holy Office, Greene for Rites and Sacraments, Rauch for Clergy, Martìn for Bishops, Buckley for Education, Arriba y Enrique for the Religious, Pritchett and I because Francesco—and thus, now, Fieschi—wanted us there, and, of course, Zaleski and Fieschi. Copies of two documents were distributed to us.

The first item on the agenda was a draft of the *motu proprio* to broaden recruitment for the Curia. Fieschi asked for comments within the week. "Not on the merits of the idea itself," he said. "That is settled. The Pontiff would like to know how the draft could be changed to carry out the synod's decision more effectively."

"This is a charade, Eminence," LaTorre snorted angrily. "Why should we bother to speak at such a late stage in such a limited way?" I have told that LaTorre silently endured Fieschi's slights for many years, when the thing had been merely personal. But now LaTorre saw the welfare of the Church at stake and he would fight with all his power.

The secretary of state removed his steel-rimmed glasses and spoke with a smoothness that oiled the path of condescension. "At earlier stages, we all had opportunity to comment on the merits. At this stage we shall read it and offer more restricted comments because His Holiness, Papa Francesco I, the Vicar of Christ, has asked. If he had asked us to paste it on the walls of the museum while wearing our sacred vestments, we would do so. His function is to command, ours to obey. It is that simple, My Lord Cardinal, that simple."

Treating that issue as closed, Fieschi moved us briskly to the document regarding readmission to the sacraments of the divorced and remarried. He explained that the matter was yet at a very early stage. "We had no desire to trouble Your Eminences at this time, but since someone has stolen and circulated the document to friends, we thought it wise to have Your Eminences see the actual draft and to offer comments. Here you are free to touch on the merits, though His Holiness believes that only questions of charity toward these people are involved, not issues of faith, morals, or sacraments in any basic way."

Enraged, LaTorre slammed his heavy fist into—of truth, nearly through—the table. *"Ecco!"* he shouted. "To allow public sinners to take Communion with those in the state of grace does not involve the faith or the sacraments?"

At the same moment, Greene, his left hand running back and forth through his hair and his trembling right hand shaking a volume of canon law like a weapon, was trying to inform us of various papal decretals on the point as well as the teaching of San Agostino. It was of no use, however. LaTorre shouted louder.

"Scandal! If nothing else, scandal! We shall seem to be condoning adultery, tolerating defiance of Christ's explicit words, opening the door to hedonism and paganism. Scandal, man, scandal!"

Fieschi's voice remained calm, though the tone was icy. "Perhaps to *deny* these people the sacraments is the scandal, Your Eminence. As sinners—a condition to which we, of course, are immune—they need God's grace even more than do the just. Your Eminence undoubtedly recalls that it was sinners whom Christ claimed He came to save."

"And He provided a way of salvation," LaTorre stormed. "They can abandon their adulterous beds, confess their sins, and return to the bosom of the Church. But they must first give up their sin, renounce it—in the privacy of the confessional and of their own hearts, to be sure—but they must renounce it. They cannot continue to enjoy their adultery and at the same time ask to be forgiven their enjoyment."

"I am not a scriptural scholar," Pritchett intervened, "but as I recall, the Church's historic position is based on the accounts in the synoptic Gospels of Christ's explicitly forbidding divorce."

"Of course," LaTorre half snarled. "It is in Mark, Matthew, and Luke, and in terms that are crystal clear. There is no room for doubt as to Christ's teaching."

"On the issue of divorce and remarriage, no doubt at all," Pritchett conceded. "But I also recall that St. John relates the meeting at Jacob's well between Christ and a much-divorced and remarried Samaritan woman."

"The fourth chapter, verses 4–30," Greene advised.

"Probably. As I recall, Christ offered that adultress the water of eternal life—an image, we believe, of the grace bestowed by His sacraments—and Christ did so without imposing the condition that she first leave her current husband or lover."

"But that was before He instituted the sacrament of penance to cleanse her soul of sin," Greene noted.

"Perhaps," Pritchett riposted, "but I also recall that Christ frequently said that he forgave sins, so penance—and in a form more marvelous than we know it—did exist. It is strange that if Christ wished us to impose a condition on the reception of His grace He did not impose that condition Himself."

"Scandal," LaTorre blurted out. "The problem is scandal. We cannot seem—"

"Such an approach," Greene told simultaneously, "is based solely on an interpretation of an incomplete scriptural text. That approach ignores the critical institutional role of the Church as mediator between God and man. It—"

Fieschi cut them both off. "The Holy Father will weigh these issues. He will decide them. He seeks our advice. Please submit your views in writing to my office.

"Now," Fieschi continued, "we have a third matter. As you know, *il Papa* promised the dissident priests that he would re-examine the problem of celibacy."

Fieschi then informed us that *il Papa* had no preformed opinions. He wanted advice from a special committee composed of the cardinals present, with Rauch as chairman. The report should be submitted within thirty days and should include the principal arguments for and against celibacy as well as a recommendation regarding its continuance. A minority report was in order if the committee were not unanimous. Fieschi added that the Pontiff wanted the committee to consider psychiatric evidence and would ask Cardinal Pritchett to arrange for testimony from two American doctors who had treated priests in Detroit. Cardinal Rauch would contact the German analyst who had worked with priests in Cologne.

"You are reminded," the secretary of state again spoke sternly to his children, "of your special oath of secrecy. There must be complete confidentiality in this matter. None of you is to work with or inform anyone else in any way. We shall have to take special pains with the physicians."

He halted to make sure that we had understood his words. "Very well, this meeting is adjourned."

Allora, with that sentence our meeting abruptly ended. Perhaps I should say the spiritual adviser dismissed his seminarians. LaTorre, still full of rage, almost ran out of the room. He could talk to no one. The rest of us left quickly and quietly; none of us was anxious to discuss what had just taken place.

According to me, we had just witnessed some of the worst results of an adviser's uncritically following his superior's wishes. The problem was not merely or even mostly Fieschi's arrogance. In the Vatican we all had often been offended by others and probably would be again. The major fault lay in the substance. During the autumn, Papa Francesco had explained to the dissident priests an intelligent strategy of concentrating on the principal issues. Out of concern for their suffering, however, he had agreed to re-examine the volatile issue of clerical celibacy. That had been a grave mistake. We have a saying in Italian: "A compassionate doctor makes for a gangrenous sore." Because Papa Francesco, however, had committed himself, did not mean that we had to move as Fieschi had outlined. In the weeks that had intervened between our trip to the western hemisphere and the meeting with the dissidents, I had not once brought up with him the subject of celibacy. The papacy works slowly. Without any breach in propriety or ethics, we could have delayed a year before beginning serious reflection, and surely such a process would consume many months. By the end of that period, the spiritual renewal would have become a reality, and the crusade would have been in full operation. In sum, the reorientation of the Church that Papa Francesco wanted could have been well underway.

Then, as he himself had explained, the time would arrive to discuss peripheral issues.

The immolation of the priests and nun had been shocking, of course. Nothing like it had occurred in modern Church history, if, indeed, ever. With Francesco so emotionally moved by that event and in fact not physically well, a wise adviser would have delayed discussion of the issue of celibacy for some weeks, certainly until *il Papa* were completely recovered and able to make a more detached decision.

The unfortunate matter of the stolen document regarding the divorced should have further alerted Fieschi to the depth of feeling about such issues. That theft only underlined the wisdom of Francesco's initial strategy and the proper function of his adviser in adhering to that strategy. The letter itself would have been far less controversial at a later time. After all, it reaffirmed the Church's historic teaching that Christ had forbade divorce and remarriage. The document's emphasis was on charity. It reasoned that we should show mercy and understanding to those who were less than perfect even as we hoped to receive mercy and understanding for our own failures. But, before the meeting we cardinals all knew that celibacy was on the agenda just as we knew the *motu proprio* regarding recruitment for the Curia was scheduled for discussion—though we did not know how restricted that discussion would be.

In that general context, the attention of the leading members of the Curia—and so of their staffs and so also, as news trickled down, of many pastoral clergy—was diverted from Francesco's principal target, the revitalization of the Church and creation of a burning concern for social justice. That *il Papa,* during his illness, would temporarily lose sight of his goal and forget his strategy was understandable. It had been Fieschi's duty to explain to the Pontiff his errors in judgment or at least to have temporized until *il Papa* had fully recovered. I determined that, as soon as I thought Francesco was sufficiently himself, I would speak plainly to him about the matter.

During the succeeding few days, Francesco seemed to recover rapidly. The physician expressed amazement at *il Papa*'s resilience. I think Fieschi interpreted the rapid recovery as another sign from heaven.

Within four days Francesco was able to sit on the terrace of the *casina* during the late morning and enjoy the sun. It had been the mildest Roman winter that I could remember. It did not snow a single time, and our ugliest weather had come just before we left in January. Now in early February several of the restaurants in Trastevere were serving lunch out of doors. I did not wear an overcoat after our return from Latin America. We even had several electrical storms in February, with lightning illuminating the great dome of San Pietro, and on one occasion striking the rod on top of the cupola. I avoided Fieschi for several days thereafter, lest I be tempted to say something blasphemous in response to what I imagined would be his explanation of the lightning.

Ecco, I also noticed more change in Francesco's personality, but I did not have time to think much about it. I knew that, although improving, he was still ill and was harassed by work. Moreover, the "miracles" were eating at him. I assumed that his new personality traits would vanish as soon as he had fully regained his strength. But they did not vanish. I refer to frequent irritation and impatience as well as what was arrogance, though not of Fieschi's brand.

Now, Francesco had never been the most patient of men; and while I have referred to his occasional display of intellectual humility, it was a humility that grew out of grand self-confidence. He knew he was right most of the time; thus, he could afford to listen to and profit from criticism, and even on occasion to confess error or ignorance. He had also generally been sensitive to the feelings of others. Now, however, he was often black-black (you say that, yes?) and permitted his temper to flash—not explode, but flash with sharp sarcasm against Fieschi, Greene, Chelli, Monsignor Candutti, Monsignor Bonetti, and even with Signora Falconi. Monsignor Zaleski and I were the only ones who seemed immune from his impatience, I probably because of my age and health, and Zaleski because his crisply efficient reports and taut control of the Curia left little room for complaint—although even he was not always able to keep my brothers—how do you say it?—in line.

Monsignori Bonetti and Candutti reacted as Italian bureaucrats, subservient and submissive in the face of superior power. Bonetti, in fact, had expected worse treatment and might have received it from Francesco's predecessor. Fieschi took the rebukes as just punishment for his sins and drove himself, and us, even harder. Greene sulked like a child. Such an outburst once precipitated an attack of the cardinal's illness, his melancholia. Signora Falconi managed to laugh off at least some of Francesco's barbs, but I could see that they stung her sharply because they were so unexpected and so unjust.

In retrospect, what I believe we were seeing was the incompleteness of Francesco's transformation from secular man to religious man. He had always been the typical American in a hurry, and without doubt, the slow, plodding, and patient institutions of the Vatican frustrated him. At the same time as he suffered frustration in effecting his ideas for the Church, he was aware, at least subconsciously, of the change going on within himself. And, of course, he realized that others almost worshipped him. He lived in the twin worlds of those who would, as you say, hog-tie him and those whose adulation made them obedient slaves. The latter made it easier for him to look with contempt on the former.

In speaking of Papa Francesco, I must describe something that at first may seem paradoxical but is really only complex. By prayer and self-sacrifice he had earned part of the aura of holiness that now surrounded his personality. No man earns it all, of course—perhaps in an exact sense no one earns any of it, for grace is a free gift from God. What I mean to say is that Francesco had not yet "earned" enough of his special grace nor possessed it long enough to wear it easily. He was still at a stage in which he was conscious of his unique spirituality, enjoyed its novelty, and even exploited its visibility to gratify his ego. In my experience, this stage is relatively short and very dangerous. The people whom I had known in this stage of development either rapidly deteriorated into charlatans prostituting their aura, or they painfully progressed to the next higher level toward perfection. Few remained long on this plateau of conceit. I prayed that my decision in the conclave had not condemned both Francesco and the Church.

This may be the time to say something about the strange relationship among Francesco, Signora Falconi, and the abbot. Francesco always had a marvelous ability to instill loyalty in those who worked with him. *Ecco* the Cardinal Galeotti. What more can I say than that I felt God had touched him? Fieschi's worship was of a different sort. His was a sudden religious conversion, something I have always viewed as perilous. And then there was Signora Falconi. Like Mr. Keller, who would drop all his law practice and instantly appear in Roma at Francesco's whim, Signora Falconi loved *il Papa*. Obviously I am not speaking of romantic love, but of a devotion that goes far beyond. If one wishes to speak of romance, I believe that Mr. Keller was in love with the *signora*. I have not an inkling —you say that?—if she returned that feeling. There had been, I also believe, something of that emotion in Mr. Keller's relation to Kate. I imply no scandal. The presence of Declan Walsh excluded all other men from Kate's life, and Papa Francesco left no time in the *signora*'s day for other than work.

The relation between the abbot and Francesco was even more complex. It had begun with Francesco as the student, the abbot the *professore*. Their roles had shifted, but not completely. Francesco, harboring a fondness for mysticism, looked up to the abbot, though it was the abbot's practical side that he depended on. According to me, despite the proximity of their ages, the abbot saw Francesco as his son, his master, and—I know how strange it sounds—himself. That complex of roles created powerful bonds, but it also created powerful tensions. Journalists liked to refer to me as the *éminence grise* of the Vatican, but I often felt that if there were a shadowy figure behind the throne it was the abbot.

For his part, Francesco loved them both, just as he loved Mr. Keller and, I do not think I speak boastfully, as he loved me. But, and I pray this does not sound too harsh, he loved us less for ourselves—though he did love us as people—than for our usefulness to him. And Francesco used us all. I do not mean that he consciously exploited us in a cynical way, only that he was unthinkingly selfish, even ruthless, in accepting, no, monopolizing, our devotion. In a sense, I could understand the abbot's identification with Francesco, for he absorbed each of us into himself. We became other sets of hands and minds that would do his bidding as readily as his own body and mind.

Allora, these may not be exactly the sorts of things you want to learn, but you must understand the people around Francesco if you are to understand him. In truth, not even the Supreme Pontiff may escape, for better or worse, the influence of those who surround him.

TWENTY-SIX

As each day passed, I experienced mixed emotions about how much better Francesco was looking. I knew that soon we would have to face a public appearance. There were still several hundred people praying daily in the piazza. As soon as the news spread that *il Papa* was to make an appearance, the crowd would grow a thousandfold. If Francesco tried to leave Vatican City, we would run serious risks of death or injury to himself and, more likely, to others.

We all knew that in a large crowd of Italians, at least one and perhaps a dozen hysterical cures would occur. Those "miracles" had almost unbalanced Fieschi, and they were interfering with the Church's work. They were a constant source of gossip and discussion in curial offices, and the Italian newspapers were still printing all sorts of stories, none of which seemed even remotely plausible to me. The most astonishing was that Papa Francesco's illness had been caused by the damaging effect on his body of his wielding supernatural powers. I wanted a full month or even more of papal confinement so that reporters could find other sources of amusement.

Allora, I had no control over these affairs, and I thought it best to immerse myself in things on which I could have some effect. With the exception of a four-day visit to my physicians in Switzerland, most of my time during the succeeding few weeks was spent with the special committee on celibacy. It was the most difficult assignment that Francesco had given me. Fieschi had sensed, as had I, that a recommendation for change would have been pleasing to Francesco; but his three most recent predecessors had considered the problem, as had the World Synod of Bishops in 1971. Each had opted to continue the Church's historic rule, which Papa Paolo had described as "a brilliant jewel" and a "golden law," and Papa Giovanni had named one of "the purest and noblest glories" of the priesthood. On the other hand, many priests called it "the cross of the Church but not of Christ."

The testimony of the three psychiatrists was fascinating, but incomplete. They spoke of injuries to personalities of priests, of their incomplete development as human beings, and each physician provided details of actual cases to substantiate his points. But each also admitted having solely talked to priests with serious emotional problems, not priests in general. That is, they had seen only the pathological cases, and relatively few of those. In fact, the three physicians together had treated less than forty-five priests and only two bishops.

Chelli, for his part, invited a French psychiatrist—LaTorre had preferred an Italian but Chelli thought it wiser to rely on a well-trained man—who testified that in the eighteen priests he had treated, he had been unable to link neurotic symptoms to celibacy. He conceded that the neuroses may have been worsened by the strains of celibacy, but added that a weak personality could also easily break under the strains of marriage and of raising a family.

The only *medico* to offer solid information was a man Fieschi discovered, an Austrian psychiatrist, a Jew who had treated many priests, more than seventy, during the years. He was adamant in placing much of the blame on celibacy, but he, too, admitted that these same persons, if they had been in other situations of great stress, might also have developed serious neuroses or even psychoses. Also, I found his connection between celibacy and neurosis required a leap of faith rather than resulting from a weighing of evidence and application of logic.

In sum, the testimony threw us upon our own experiences and intuitions—what Francesco called our biases. Predictably discussions were acrimonious. Chelli was ill much of the time, and without the support of his cold logic and political sensitivity, LaTorre's erudition sometimes became pompous dogma and his bluntness at times degenerated into ill temper. Fieschi's scorn for LaTorre—in charity to Fieschi, he was probably not conscious of how badly he sometimes treated the Holy Mule—coupled with Fieschi's newly found divine mission and LaTorre's fear for the Church, made angry exchanges both inevitable and frequent.

At least Francesco's selection of Rauch to preside over the committee was brilliant. It was a natural choice in that the question of celibacy intimately touched the Congregation for the Clergy, but one could have made an equally strong case for the Holy Office or for the Secretariat of State. But Francesco knew that LaTorre and Fieschi would fight with each other, and he wanted neither in the chair.

Rauch was a marvel of even temper and fairness, never black-black; but then he is essentially a very gentle man. He possessed what you call the backbone, but also patience and a willingness to listen. He was always tactful yet firm; in fact, when pushed—and he was often pushed beyond the point that I could have endured—he could become as stubborn as LaTorre. But those meetings strained even Rauch's talents. I tried to help as best I could, as did Cardinal Martìn, but sometimes I felt, to use one of Mr. Keller's expressions, as if I were a small piece of meat thrown into a cage with a pair of tigers.

For two weeks we made no real progress. I had expected little but I had hoped the events in th› New World at least had made it reasonable to hope for the miracle of a fresh thought or even a new phrase. I was disappointed on both counts. Then Francesco decided to attend a late afternoon session himself. I do not know how he found the time between his meetings with the abbot, with Chelli's secretary for Economic Affairs, with the Jesuits and the Franciscans on the spiritual renewal, with Monsignor Candutti on the UN and continued efforts to locate a peaceful settlement in the Near East, with Martìn on new bishops, with Pritchett and me on the preparation of a new encyclical on social justice, as well as with a bevy of special audiences with diplomats, bishops, and potential donors. (At least there were as yet no general audiences, but that would come.)

Because there were only eight of us on the special committee, and, lacking Chelli we were only seven, we held the meeting in the *casina,* in the studio overlooking the oval terrace. It was a strange room. The view of the terrace, of the back of the fountains, and of a bit of the gardens was pleasing. It was the chamber itself that was disquieting. I have already described the vaulted ceilings covered with a mass of frescoes depicting a curious assortment of suffering Christian saints along with pagan nymphs and minor gods. At one point, the Hungarian architect and Signora Falconi had wanted to paint over the frescoes, but they had been dissuaded—unhappily. As you know, I am an admirer of the rococo, but that mélange has always been too much for me. Yet there are some who think the *casina*'s collection of sixteenth-century art is a treasure.

As long as one did not look up, the room was pleasant. The walls were lined with bookcases filled with Francesco's personal volumes. He had donated all his library to the Supreme Court when he had retired to the monastery. In a generous gesture, the new chief justice had returned them to Roma after the conclave. The volumes were mostly about secular law: reports of the U.S. Supreme Court and all sorts of big blue, red, black, and green tomes. (I did not see a single biography of a saint.)

There was a smaller horseshoe-shaped desk much like that in the studio in the palazzo but this one was strikingly different, and not merely in size. The sides consisted of bookcases and the top was made of three thick slabs of reddish marble with thin grey veins running through them. The gross weight must have put a heavy strain on the flooring—which, of course, was also marble, but of a medium grey with white striations. As in the palazzo, *il Papa*'s *poltrona* was of highbacked leather, but this one was dark red, almost perfectly matching the marble of the desk top.

The room was too small for a conference table but there were eight small but commodious red leather chairs, clustered around a large, circular tea table the top of which had been cut from the same vein of marble as the desk top. Italy abounds in leather and marble, but I had never seen the two more interestingly—not to say beautifully—combined.

I was glad that we were not meeting in the palazzo. The effects of the immolation had not yet left the curial offices I visited, and I knew that it was preying on Francesco's mind. From his studio in the palazzo, he could have, had he followed his usual practice of staring out the window when trying to concentrate, seen the spot where the deaths occurred. Workmen had scrubbed with harsh chemicals, but the small ugly scar was still burned into the floor of the piazza. *Ecco,* a glance at that reminder of death might have colored Francesco's judgment.

His Holiness insisted that Rauch should preside at the session. The cardinal began by summarizing our progress to date. His remarks were appropriately brief. Francesco intervened to ask that the discussion be confined to spiritual arguments. The administrative and financial advantages of celibacy were obvious enough. (In fact, his request sounded more innocent than it was. I had seen the books by Görres, Greely, and O'Neil he had been reading as well as the thick files of his predecessors he had been going through.)

Rauch looked at LaTorre, "Perhaps Your Eminence could begin."

"Holiness," he began, "as St. Paul wrote, we are 'made captive by Christ Jesus.' Celibacy was not commanded by Christ, nor was it ever demanded by the Church from any but the willing. In the West, it has been accepted as a sacrifice given by those wishing to pursue a particular kind of religious ministry. Celibacy is a free gift that priests make to God. It can be an immense sacrifice—as we in this room understand—but it is an offering freely and knowingly made by intelligent, educated, and mature adults. A priest cannot be ordained until he is twenty-three—usually he is older—and has completed many years of study and moral discipline; if he is not mature then, it is not likely he ever will be. In any case, puberty is hardly likely to occur after twenty-three.

"Celibacy is a symbol of the priest's total consecration to God and his renunciation of the things of this world. It says to God that my love and devotion are such that I renounce the highest of earthly joys, those of a woman's love and companionship and of siring and rearing children. I seek my immortality only in my Savior, not in my children.

"Celibacy also symbolizes Christ's virginal love of the Church. It is, as Pope Paul VI said, a 'heavy and a sweet burden.' It brings pains of loneliness and frustration, but it also brings comfort in the knowledge that we have given something, a little thing perhaps but still something, to God in return for His countless blessings.

"Furthermore, in an age of licentiousness, celibacy stands out like a beacon of purity, not only an ideal to adults but living proof to young people that the spirit is not slave to the flesh and that the things of the spirit are both more important and more enduring.

"We hear much from these dissident priests about the emptiness of their lives. All of us—as have all humans—have felt loneliness and emptiness and even at times despair. These afflict us because of the darkness of our intellects and the weaknesses of our wills, not because of celibacy. Christ Himself felt those temptations. He asked in the garden that the chalice pass from Him, and again on the cross He asked His Father why He had deserted Him. But He also said 'I am not alone for the Father is with me.' None of us, especially not a priest with his training in prayer and meditation, is ever alone, no matter how lonely he may sometimes feel.

"The answer to a priest's suffering—and I know it sounds cold and even harsh—is prayer, learning how to unite himself closer and closer to Christ and remembering that his goal is not happiness in the ephemeral sense of this world but in the eternal sense of the next. I concede the burden becomes too heavy for some men to bear. Until a few decades ago we were harsh with such people, marking them as cowards and failures. Now we allow them to leave the priesthood after ensuring only that they are not pursuing a whim but following a deeply felt need. We hope that these men can live good, decent, and productive lives in other fields. But we continue to demand that those who practice the religious vocation not reclaim the gift that they so freely gave."

LaTorre stopped. He had spoken quietly, and the impact of his words was visible on the face of each person in the room. He had talked in the positive terms that Francesco preferred. I found the reasoning utterly convincing, as I know some others present did. Out of respect for LaTorre's simple but direct rhetoric, Rauch paused a few moments before asking Cardinal Pritchett to state his views.

"I look on celibacy," the cardinal said, "not as a theologian but as a pastor. I agree many priests can carry out *in joy* their sacrifice of marriage and family, but many cannot. I do not know how many, but if we stress the words *in joy,* I would say a majority are not able. Among those who are not, some fall and occasionally become a source of public scandal. Their number is relatively small. Even smaller is the number of womanizing priests, men who take advantage of their clerical privileges to obtain sexual gratification. They exist, but they are very rare animals. Yet by causing scandal far beyond their numbers, those who occasionally fall—leaving aside the womanizers as sick people—undo much of celibacy's symbolism regarding the superiority of the spiritual over the physical.

"Most priests keep their holy vows. The cost, however, is high to their own personalities and the efficiency with which they are able to practice the gospel. All too often our priests—and our bishops, and our cardinals—who successfully adapt to the celibate life do so by becoming cold, selfish persons, unable to help their flocks not because they do not understand people's problems but, worse, because they do not really want to understand.

"In sum, Holiness, celibacy is a 'sweet obligation' for a large minority of priests. But for many others it is counterproductive, occasionally resulting in scandal and more often a drain on one's capacity to serve others through loving sacrifice."

"Are we not," Francesco intervened to ask a question typical of him, "faced with essentially an empirical question? Are celibate clergy, in fact, more holy, more loving, more useful to God and His people than married clergy? The Greek experience may be helpful. Certainly none of us questions the viability of the Greek Orthodox Church or the personal sanctity of the Greek clergy. Yet their priests may be married men." (*Ecco,* from my experience with the near simony of the Greek clergy in the Holy Land, I would not hold those men up as models.)

"I do not think it is an empirical question at all, Holiness," LaTorre told. "And if it were, we would lack calipers to measure holiness and love."

"But does not your whole argument rest," Fieschi put in, "on the supposition that such calipers exist and also on the supposition that you, if not the rest of us, can read them correctly?"

"Nonsense," LaTorre riposted testily. But before he could finish the sentence, Rauch had gently asked if any of the others on the committee wished to speak. We shook our heads.

"Then I would," Rauch told. "Holiness, you have heard

the opposing views neatly outlined. I believe from our discussions that if the committee were asked to vote, we would divide either 5–2 or 4–3 against a resolution to abolish mandatory celibacy in the priesthood. Some of the majority, however, might be willing to modify the existing rules in some fashion. Would you like us to pursue that possibility?"

"Yes," Francesco responded. "We have thought of several possibilities here. For example: requiring, with appropriate exceptions for developing countries where resources are simply not available, all candidates for the priesthood to have attended a minimum of two years at a secular university; and/or requiring a probationary period for young graduates of seminaries. During that time they would work as assistants in parishes and would take only temporary vows. After the probationary period they would be free to remain or leave, assuming their performance had been of such a calibre that the Church would want them to continue in the ministry. Only then would they take permanent vows. We might also make greater use of married deacons, many of whom could be former priests who had gone through the canonical process of laicization—not those who had simply left the Church."

LaTorre looked horrified. "To have former priests, now married, on the altar of God would be a source of great scandal."

"Now that truly is an empirical question, Eminence," Francesco told, "and we—you as well as ourself—lack data. Probably many people would be scandalized, but are not as many or more now scandalized when they see a Church, based on Christ's understanding love, treating former priests as pariahs?"

"Justice demands that they be punished, Holiness, and our punishment is light. If they go through the canonical processes of laicization, they remain full members of the Church, but they may not continue to practice the religious vocation they have renounced."

"Justice makes no demand for punishment of a person who has fully complied with the law. Humans may make such demands, but not in the name of justice or in the name of a God of love." I could see the anger welling in Francesco's eyes, but he was speaking with great self-control. "You yourself spoke of our treatment in the past having been too harsh. We would be better off if we left the question of punishment to God on the reasonable assumption that He knows more than we do. We suggest the committee take that much as decided. We shall look forward to hearing your specific recommendations soon."

I remained behind. I knew that Francesco had been deeply impressed by LaTorre's argument—which, according to me, is the reason why he had baited the Holy Mule at the end. I wanted to use that favorable atmosphere to emphasize not only my substantive agreement with LaTorre but also to reason along the strategic lines that I earlier sketched for you.

Francesco listened pensively. "On the merits," he said, "I cannot see that celibacy makes priests more holy. Certainly it does not make them work harder. Few priests work such long or hard hours as the average American doctor, lawyer, or even professor. But," he sighed, "as a matter of strategy, you're right. I've been tired and upset and not thinking carefully. You can have my basic decision now but for your ears only: no fundamental change in celibacy. That doesn't mean, however, that we shouldn't make some changes in the rules along the lines I mentioned at the end. And, most assuredly, it doesn't mean that some time in the future we won't abolish the whole requirement."

It was not a complete victory, but it would have to do. As I started to leave, Francesco called my name. "Ugo, I know the ordination of women as priests would bitterly divide the Church, but would making them cardinals be all right?"

I smiled, less from his attempt at humor than from the realization that his effort indicated he had yet retained a sense of perspective.

He went on. "I see many senseless things in the Church—anti-Semitism, sexism, national chauvinism, bureaucratic arrogance, all mixed with medieval notions about man's duty to punish his fellow sinner. My intellect tells me to be quiet, to wait, to change the basic mood first, then mop up the specific wrongs. Another part of me cries out against these injustices."

He smiled again and, as was his custom, walked to the window and looked out. He spoke with his back to me. "Old friend, you have an odd role to play for me; you are the priest who keeps my strategic conscience and helps me still the voice of my moral conscience."

He was right, of course, which was one reason for his frustration at what he considered the slow pace of change within the Vatican. Knowing that his sense of justice was a cause for his frustration comforted me when I thought of what might happen to Papa Francesco the man and to His Church.

TWENTY-SEVEN

DURING FEBRUARY, we—that is, Dottor Twisdale, the abbot, Signora Falconi, and I, for Fieschi was no help in this regard—managed to keep Francesco from close touch with crowds or even with journalists. When he insisted on public audiences we persuaded him to restrict himself to appearances at the window of the palazzo at Sunday noon and to substitute a similar appearance for the normal Wednesday afternoon audience in the auditorium. As for the reporters, our official explanation was *il Papa*'s health. It did not fully lack truth.

Allora, changing public appearances caused less difficulty than our decreased scheduling of press conferences and our preventing journalists from seeing *il Papa;* they knew he was granting private audiences to many lesser as well as more important dignitaries. Dottor Twisdale bore their wrath almost alone. According to me, Francesco had been too free with reporters, and as a result they bitterly resented his isolation that spring. We who were close to him were frequently referred to in the press as "the papal *mafiosi*" or "the papal jailers." It was unpleasant, the more so because it had some truth. But we—at least some of us—preferred resentment to the questions that would inevitably be asked and the wild stories that might be written if journalists were allowed to intrude.

During that time, Francesco continued to be—how do you say?—edgy. But it was a period of great creativity within the Vatican. That is not an easy state to bring about in the apostolic palazzo, for as I have related, we pride ourselves on knowing the precedents and never doing anything for the first time. Despite his health, Francesco drove us hard, and Fieschi drove us even harder. Monsignor Zaleski found himself in the unexpected position of soothing feelings frayed by Fieschi's pushing and scolding rather than himself acting as the goad. Needless to say, no one any longer looked on the secretary of state as a figurehead. He had become a powerful force. Some of my brethren bestowed on him—in private, of course—the title previously reserved for Attila the Hun: the Scourge of God.

Fieschi's attitude toward LaTorre did not make the Holy Mule's life—or mine—easier. I had frequent visits from 'Vanni, sometimes several times a day. Alternately he complained about not being consulted and about being overworked. To his credit, he never mentioned the haughty, imperious fashion in which Fieschi addressed him. For all his faults, 'Vanni was too large a man for that. There was little I could do to smooth his life, but I did listen and, according to him, that helped. I also noted that for a man who claimed to have been ignored, he knew a great deal about what went on in *il Papa*'s studio. But, as I have said, the Vatican is not a place where secrets are well-preserved.

There were two historical patterns of Vatican operations that Francesco either did not understand (which I doubt) or chose to ignore. As I said earlier, the real labor is done by our staffs, especially the archbishop-secretaries and senior *monsignori*. The cardinal prefects are responsible for their congregations, but they are usually too old and certainly too busy to be active, energetic researchers, initiators of ideas, and careful supervisors of day-to-day operations. Nevertheless, Francesco insisted on seeing the prefects at a moment's notice and also insisted that they personally, with little or no staff support, serve on his special committees.

Despite Fieschi's blunt warning to his brothers in the Curia, some of what you call foot-dragging continued, but Fieschi and Francesco exaggerated the degree. The simple fact was that the cardinals were accustomed to receiving fully researched reports from their staffs and found it difficult to create such reports and recommendations themselves. I do not claim that all my princely brothers blindly followed Fieschi and so Francesco, but, as I had originally hoped, Fieschi's loyal support meant much in encouraging cooperation, especially among traditionalists who were professional members of various staffs. Fieschi's driving assertiveness, however, also alienated several cardinals. But they were his peers; subordinates in the Curia were accustomed to strange behavior by cardinals and were more apt to consider obedience the course prescribed by self-interest as well as by virtue.

According to Francesco, the benefit of his direct use of cardinals was that he received at first hand the perceptions and judgments of experienced and supposedly wise counsellors rather than their reactions to reports prepared by others. The price, however, was twofold: first, papal frustration because of the cardinals' inefficiency in their new roles, and second, a certain loosening of prefects' control over their congregations. I need not stress that a seventy-year-old man who has just endured three gruelling hours in a committee meeting and another hour being—how do you say?—cross-examined by *il Papa* is not apt still to possess energy enough to closely supervise the work of his staff. On the other hand, it is also true that after a session with Fieschi more than one prefect came roaring into his own office and made life miserable for the archbishop-secretary who had been deviating from papal policy.

Francesco continued to amaze me with what he knew about what was going on within the Vatican. Some people thought he knew little but guessed much. In truth, he guessed often. But he read or at least looked at every piece of paper that crossed his desk. He thought nothing of lifting the telephone at ten-thirty at night and calling the prefect of a congregation if he was troubled by a document. In fact, he maintained a special list of the home telephone numbers of all the curial officials of whom he might have need. More important, he asked questions of everyone. Any visitor—a priest escorting a dignitary, a *monsignore* delivering a report, a bishop making his annual visit to Roma, or a diplomat presenting his credentials—was likely to be bombarded by *il Papa* with unexpected and seemingly unrelated questions.

Papa Paolo had been criticized for using too much time in learning every detail of what transpired within the Holy See. Without doubt, Francesco was not as minutely informed as Papa Paolo had been, but he may well have been more accurately informed because he could take a few scattered pieces of information and at a blow fit them into a pattern.

For example, within a few days of the dinner that I had with LaTorre and Chelli at Il Galeone, Francesco asked me to tell him why LaTorre had come to me for help. I explained as best I could; and even though *il Papa* was highly irritable, he accepted it in rather good stead. In fact, his mood was sufficiently pleasant that I asked him how he had known about the conversation.

"Twice yesterday when I began to push our friend from the Holy Office, he looked to you for understanding and help. Last week, when he looked at you under similar circumstances, he was reproachful, blaming you for inflicting me on the Church and on him personally." We both chuckled a bit; but the incident revealed how Francesco's restless mind was always accumulating, assorting, and analyzing tiny pieces of information. At times it was frightening to know that he was often piecing together trivial fragments of information about one's behavior.

Ecco, I wander once more. I said that Francesco violated two historical patterns of decision making in the Vatican. His use of cardinals was one. His second was related. Traditionally, *il Papa* blesses rather than creates policy. Just as cardinal prefects have tended to receive completed staff work to bolster specific recommendations, so Pontiffs have usually responded to problems as outlined by curial officials. *Professori* in the Gregorian or Lateran universities often write encyclicals; when they do not, most of the work is done in the various curial offices rather than in the personal studio of *il Papa.*

There have been notable exceptions, without doubt. Papa Giovanni's calling of the Second Vatican Council provides a dramatic example. On the whole, however, the rule was general. And, according to me, it has usually been a good practice. For, like his cardinals, a Pontiff is apt to be an old man, heavily burdened with ceremonial duties. He is also likely to lack the energy necessary for intellectual creativity. That, according to me, is properly a task for the young and the middle-aged. Older men, looking at problems and alternative solutions from the vantage point of decades of experience, function better as wise judges.

Francesco, however, was the dynamic force in the Vatican. The rest of us spent our time responding to *his* ideas. I do not mean that he never accepted others' ideas, but when he took them, he converted them so that they became totally his. Sometimes, as with the question of celibacy, the problem was not of his choosing, but his method of attacking the problem was peculiarly his own. The point is that he was trying to govern the Church and was doing so in a way that upset established curial procedures and annoyed curial officials whose jobs became less interesting. And that kind of upset further slowed work and also further frustrated Francesco. He was a man conscious even of seconds of time. That is not a typical Italian trait. Foreigners often complain that there is no phrase in Italian signifying "to be early." Technically that is not correct. We have several such phrases. It is the concept we lack.

Allora, Francesco would allot so many minutes to a conference, so many to a private audience, so many to read a report—indeed, he often did two things at the same time. But, despite his hoarding of minutes, spring was now upon us and he had begun talking about the spiritual renewal and the crusade in June. Neither was yet a reality. That slowness of pace ate at him. But it also drove him harder, and thus it drove us as well.

Those three weeks of semiconfinement were not easy ones for us around the Pontiff. The frustrations were many, and his temper quick. At the end of February, the abbot brought the good news that he could begin recruiting and training volunteers at almost any time. He had completed arrangements for feeding, housing, and transporting 1500 people and would need only two weeks' notice to put the process into operation.

Our bad news was that Chelli was only slowly recovering from what physicians diagnosed as a severe case of influenza, complicated by a kidney infection. Unlike the typical cardinal I have described, Chelli himself ran the economic affairs office. In fact, since his entire staff consisted of only one *monsignore* as secretary, three accountants, one *avvocato*—I mean lawyer—an investment counsellor, and three stenographers, he made most of the decisions himself. His secretary was intelligent and ambitious, but Chelli, who shared many of Francesco's working habits, carried much of the information in his head. Thus, we had to postpone final action until Chelli's recovery.

I thought the delay was a good thing because Francesco wanted to open the call for volunteers himself. I tried to argue that the longer we waited the more likely we were to be able to focus attention on the crusade and away from any additional "miraculous cures." I pointed out that since our return we had read hardly a single news item or columnist's story about *il Papa*'s plea at the United Nations. That message, marvelously effective for a day or two, had been lost in the headier melodrama of "miracles." The world was moving on, and interest in the "miracles" was fading. There was a new crisis in the Near East which Francesco again attempted, again unsuccessfully, to mediate; re-evaluations of currency that sent the lire tottering to 1100 to the dollar, and the dollar to near parity with the Swiss franc; another economic recession in Japan; collapse of the military dictatorship in Thailand in the face of populist demands for land reform and pressures from indigenous Communist guerrillas equipped with Chinese matériel; trials of new dissidents in Moscow, and, more recently, coincidental "accidental" deaths of two writers the Russians had expelled in the 1970s, one in Vienna, the other in Princeton, New Jersey. These were all sad events, but their march left the "miracles" further receded in the wake of time. And each passing day made our task easier.

The spiritual renewal was still experiencing troubles. These were organizational rather than financial. As I explained, Francesco wanted the Jesuits and the Franciscans to carry the message and to assist local bishops in conducting retreats and instruction for the clergy. *Il Papa* had asked Cardinal Chi Goon Su, prefect of Propaganda Fide, to coordinate the activities of the two orders with each other and with the needs, if not always the desires, of local bishops. Now here, according to me, Francesco did *not* understand what he was doing. He said he wanted, as with the choice of his own name as Pontiff, to combine the simplicity of the Franciscans with the zeal of the Jesuits. That is a noble ideal, and at times I think that Francesco achieved it in his own personality. But to impose that ideal on others is much more difficult.

As we say, the defect was in the handle; it was wrong from the start. The root of the problem was that Franciscans and Jesuits are usually very different sorts of people. The Franciscan tends to be warm, friendly, somewhat lazy, to have a comfortable paunch, and to be careless about cleaning bread crumbs from his coarse robe of brown wool. When the weather is good, one sees the Franciscan padding around in the web-footed walk he affects because of his sandals, the skirts of his robe hitched up in his rope belt, so that he can play ball with youngsters. The typical Franciscan is a simple, loving person, who would suffer no cultural shock were he to be transported back into the thirteenth century. (What you have heard of Franciscans persecuting Jews in Yugoslavia during World War II is largely true, but a horrible exception to their usual docility.)

The typical Jesuit, on the other hand, is always a man of his own time. He is highly trained, awesomely educated, nimble-witted, and ambitious for the papacy and the Church, if not for himself. The enemies of the order have always used terms like cunning and ruthless and scheming. These are accurate, although incomplete. The Jesuit's reliance on logic and learning rather than love does not help him make a more Christian figure. His forte is instant diagnosis and immediate solution. His milieu is never the playground with children but either the university library or the salon of the rich and the powerful. Not that he is the captive of the establishment. The Jesuit speaks out, lashes out indiscriminately against real enemies, potential enemies, and even friends who arouse his suspicions. And he can express himself with such grace and charm as well as fervor that even his targets sometimes take intellectual delight in his attacks.

Anyone who knew anything about the two orders should have realized that the simplicity of the Franciscans and the Jesuits' penchant for sophisticated machinations would be more likely to yield fission than fusion. I tried to tell Francesco this, but at times he listened to no one.

Francesco compounded his initial error by, for once in his papacy, assigning responsibility where it organizationally belonged. The spiritual renewal seemed to fall under the jurisdiction of Propaganda Fide or the Holy Office. With LaTorre as prefect, the Holy Office was, as you say, out. But Francesco should have considered whom he had appointed to the Congregation of Propaganda Fide and, as he often did, have stretched logical administrative allocations to give Catholic Education control. Chi Goon Su of Propaganda Fide was a very pious man, but, as I remarked during the conclave, he was a mystic Oriental who accepted Marxist economic theory and spoke either in Buddhist terms or in the arcane theological-anthropological concepts of Teilhard de Chardin. If such a person tries to coordinate Franciscans and Jesuits while working with the vagaries of local bishops, one can confidently predict disaster absolute.

And disaster was precisely what we obtained. There was a circus of audiences with Cardinal Su, representatives of the Jesuits, and representatives of the Franciscans. From the Jesuits we heard inevitable complaints about the simpleminded stupidity of the Franciscans; from the Franciscans we heard the equally inevitable complaints about the logic-chopping of the Jesuits. Cardinal Su would then deliver an oration about the spirit of peace, using such words as "otherness," "complexification," "convergent integration," and the "noosphere." Francesco's attraction to mysticism had certain practical limits, and I could see that at times he was barely restraining himself from shouting at the people he saw. I confess that I had a preference for throwing spoiled fruit at them.

Eventually, Francesco asked Cardinal Buckley of Catholic Education, Pritchett, and me to straighten matters out. With the help of two young theologians whom LaTorre generously loaned us, we did prepare the basic documents for the renewal, but by then it was early March. Still, we had taken another step. I could see the blood in my footprint.

After Francesco approved them, Fieschi took the documents and swiftly distributed them to pastoral bishops around the world, together with the names and locations of Franciscans and Jesuits who could help the bishops conduct retreats for their clergy. Here Fieschi was a true miracle worker. With help from Martìn's Congregation for Bishops and Rauch's Congregation for the Clergy as well as through our own system of nuncios in most countries, Fieschi commanded, checked on, cajoled, whipped, and cooperated with more than 2000 pastoral bishops. Exactly seventeen days after Francesco had approved our work, the spiritual renewal for the clergy had begun in almost half the dioceses in the world. We were sure that it would soon begin in the other half, for Fieschi's wrath was as severe as it was disciplined.

TWENTY-EIGHT

Our accomplishments with the spiritual renewal left me content to sit back and enjoy the warmth of success. Francesco was of a different mind. He exploded his next bomb on us almost immediately. Indeed, the very morning that Fieschi called to report that the renewal had begun in more than a thousand dioceses, Francesco invited him to bring Monsignori Candutti and Zaleski and join us for lunch at the *casina.* (The "us" were, besides *il Papa,* the abbot and I.)

We sat on the oval terrace enjoying a glass of chilled Pavian Riesling and the promise of spring in the midday warmth. I recall Francesco's holding his crystal goblet up to catch the rays of the sun, asking Monsignor Candutti how arrangements were proceeding for his visits to Dublin and Warsaw where he planned to open the drive to recruit volunteers for the crusade. Candutti's reply was interesting. The Irish government was reluctant. They feared that the Pontiff's presence in the republic would exacerbate religious problems in Ulster by fueling Presbyterian hatred of all things Catholic. Only after being assured that *il Papa* planned to meet with prominent Anglican and Presbyterian clergymen from the republic and the area under British military occupation did the Irish government give accord. Even then they did not evidence enthusiasm.

The Poles had also reacted negatively, but, unlike the Irish, they had not changed that initial reaction. Negotiations had been difficult because of the absence of officially accredited representatives, but Monsignor Candutti had himself twice flown to Warsaw. The answer, however, remained a polite but very firm no, no less firm for being couched in language that left open the possibility of a papal visit in the indefinite future.

"Why this sudden cooling?" Francesco asked.

"It is not a cooling, Holiness," Monsignor Candutti responded. "We have never been that warm, except in newspaper reports. The government is still neurotically suspicious of the Church. We must remember that the Poles would not let Papa Paolo visit Warsaw. Our detente there has been uneasy. It is a three-sided affair. We in the Vatican have been far more eager to compromise differences with the regime than have many local bishops. That attitude complicates an already delicate situation. Our bringing Cardinal Grodzins here to live his last days in peace eased tensions a bit with the government but not with some bishops. And, frankly, what the government has read of your Holiness's remarks in Latin America about keeping the Church an independent force has worried them. They simply do not like the idea of your coming to Warsaw to urge their best young men and women to leave Poland and join a crusade that the government inevitably views as part of a capitalist canard. I think the matter is hopeless, Holiness, absolutely hopeless."

Francesco glanced sharply at Monsignor Candutti. No one told anything for a few moments. Then Candutti again spoke.

"I have been candid, Holiness. I had assumed that you preferred the hard truth over soft but false hopes. If you wish I shall continue to press the government even though I am convinced that we are doomed to failure. Perhaps I can fly to Warsaw again."

"That won't be necessary," Francesco snapped. "We want no further discussion of the visit to Poland to go through diplomatic channels." *Il Papa* held up his glass again to catch the sun. He looked at the beauty of the crystal and the shimmering wine for a full minute, then said, "But we *are* going to Poland and we shall do so immediately after our visit to Dublin. We shall announce our plans at the appropriate time."

Candutti was stunned. Such conduct was unheard of. Papa Francesco plainly saw the *monsignore*'s face, but, before Candutti could voice his protest, abruptly changed the subject.

"Cardinal Fieschi, you have received comments from the various congregations on the draft of our encyclical on social justice?"

Fieschi looked at Monsignor Zaleski, who patted his heavy briefcase. "We have them here, Holiness. We have read them all and are now collating them. The remarks are not significant in any substantive way. We can have something to you by this evening."

Francesco only nodded, but I knew he was pleased. He had hoped to publish the encyclical before the spiritual renewal had begun, but his health and the other demands on his time—especially the crusade—had slowed his writing. As I explained, he himself wrote the first draft and would also write the final version.

Francesco leaped to yet another topic. "We are deeply troubled, by a report in *Le Monde* last week that so far not a single Latin American bishop had followed the example of the cardinal archbishop of Recife and distributed ecclesiastical lands or other property to the poor. Cardinal Martìn is making some discreet inquiries."

"Perhaps the time has been too short, Holiness," Fieschi offered.

"Perhaps, but the longer one holds material goods, the more precious they seem. We would like your office to make inquiries and to be prepared to use nuncios to prod our holy shepherds into being more generous in feeding their flocks. The Church cannot afford princes in a world over-populated with paupers. And we do not want tokenism. We want to see a large-scale distribution of goods, especially of land."

It displeased me, but there was no further hope of avoiding a press conference, and toward the end of the third week in March, reporters assembled in the Sistine for their first meeting with *il Papa* since the impromptu affair in Newark. I had wanted to delay even longer, but Dottor Twisdale said that it was important to proceed at that time. It was common knowledge that for some weeks *il Papa* had been working a full schedule, and further postponement might cause speculation that Papa Francesco was in hiding. (He was. Most Pontiffs spent most of their lives in hiding. It was an advantage that Francesco's openness with the news media had surrendered.)

We came prepared to announce that *il Papa* was going to Dublin and to Warsaw. (At Monsignor Candutti's request, I had prevailed on Francesco to allow the *monsignore* to notify the Polish ambassador to Italy so that at least the regime would not have to read the news in the morning papers. *Ecco,* it seemed such a small thing when one is about to violate protocol long sacred to diplomats.) The reporters accepted the news calmly, but it soon became apparent that most of them had missed the point. The man from the Italian communist daily, *L'Unita,* apparently miffed because the Slavs had once more ignored the Italians, asked: "Holiness, when did the Polish government consent to this visit?"

"We are sorry," the Pontiff fenced, "we do not understand your question."

"I asked, Holiness," the reporter switched to English, "when the Polish government consented to your visit."

"We understand your words," Francesco said in Italian, "but we do not comprehend your question. We do not understand that the Vicar of Christ needs the consent of any government to visit his people. We are sure that the government of Poland would insist that they do not wish to interfere in any way with legitimate religious exercises. Are you implying that we should have a visa or something of the sort?"

"Yes, Holiness. Have you applied for one?"

Francesco seemed playfully perplexed. "No, we have not; but, of course, you're correct. We must. We shall ask the secretary of state to comb the archives and use the same form as Peter when he applied to come to Rome. That should be precedent enough to satisfy the bureaucrats both here and in Warsaw."

The reporters laughed a bit, more in embarrassment at having missed the point of the first announcement than at *il Papa*'s teasing of *L'Unita.*

"What does Your Holiness think these visits will accomplish?" the *London Tablet* asked.

"Our primary aim is to make an appeal to the young people of Poland and Ireland to join our crusade in Latin America. We do not want the crusade to be staffed by people from one region or from one political ideology. It would be good to involve Marxists as well as capitalists in an enterprise for which neither could take credit. All the people might truly benefit. In the past both the Poles and the Irish have generously given their lives to the service of God. We go to ask them once again to serve God."

"Does Your Holiness believe the Polish government will let you come in?" the *Washington Post* asked.

"Because we can see no reason why a government that

professes to defend freedom of belief and freedom of non-belief could object to a pastor visiting his flock, we can see no reason why the government would not receive us as we would receive them: with open hearts."

(There was a Polish newsman present, but he kept his silence. Without doubt, he was a man of prudence.)

Der Spiegel brought up the touchy subject: "Has the Church come to any conclusions, even tentative hypotheses, about the alleged miracles in the United States and Latin America?"

Papa Francesco hesitated. It was the first time I had seen him do that at a press conference. "No"—the word was extended to at least four syllables. "We have seen only the preliminary report from the doctors at the University of Pennsylvania. That report is inconclusive. We understand that scientists in Mexico and Brazil are examining the other cases. Under the circumstances it is difficult to know what to say beyond what was said at Newark."

Der Spiegel persevered: "Does His Holiness himself feel that these incidents, or at least one or more of them, were miracles?"

Francesco looked beyond the group of reporters for a full thirty seconds, then told: "Every time a sperm and an ovum unite and a new human being is formed, we have a miracle. Every time torn human tissues or broken human bones heal, we witness a miracle. Specifically, you want to know if there was some divine force transmitted between ourself and those people? We do not know, and we do not think that the answer is important except as another example of God's mercy, and surely we already have millions of these.

"Let us," Francesco mused, "consider the Evangelists' account of the multiplication of the loaves and fishes. You remember that Christ had pity on the crowds that had been following Him. He wanted to feed them. The Apostles, however, reported that they had only a few loaves of bread and a couple of fish. Nevertheless, Christ ordered the crowds to sit on the grass and told the Apostles to distribute what food they had. There was enough not only for everyone to eat but the remains filled several baskets.

"That was a true miracle," Francesco continued. "But what was the miracle? Was it merely some kind of divine trick multiplying bread and fish? Surely for a divinity that would hardly amount to much. Perhaps there was something more that we literalists of the twentieth century miss. Then there was no public transportation and few restaurants. Their own two feet moved most peasants from place to place and beneath their robes they usually carried food, some fruit, bread, dried fish, perhaps even a small skin of wine. I believe the actual miracle there was that Christ's message of love caused the crowds to open their hearts to one another and share their food. And that would have been a far grander miracle. It is the miracle that I want to perform: to convince the people of our own time to share with each other."

It was a masterful effort to silence questions about miracles. At least it temporarily brought silence to the Sistine.

Finally a journalist whose affiliation I missed asked: "There now have been more than thirty-five resignations, retirements, or transfers of Latin American bishops since Your Holiness was elected. Would Your Holiness comment?"

"Yes."

After thirty seconds of silence, the reporter asked again: "Holiness?"

"We said yes. Your figure is more or less accurate. The exact number is thirty-seven." Francesco nodded to the man from *Il Tempo*.

"We have noted that Your Holiness has kept away from the public and has been giving only private audiences and blessings from the palace window. Does Your Holiness expect more miracles?"

"Signor Gaspari, we never know what to expect here in Rome. We may even witness the miracle of the Italian Socialist parties uniting." (At least the reporters laughed at that neat turn. You may not know it, but Socialists in Italy are divided into one party—and occasionally even two—for each Socialist.)

The sparring went on for another twenty minutes, with Francesco, on the one hand, trying to guide the discussion toward the spiritual renewal, the crusade, and his forthcoming encyclical on social justice, and the reporters, on the other hand, trying, as you say, to pin him down on the question of miracles. Only a few seemed fully aware of the possibility of a confrontation between the papacy and the Polish government. *Ebbene,* I can understand that miracles sell more newspapers than does social justice, but one still wishes for a greater sense of responsibility by those who claim such sweeping privileges as do journalists. As I expected, several papers printed stories on their front pages entitled, for example, VATICAN SPOKESMAN REFUSES TO DENY POSSIBILITY OF MIRACLES. This was pleasing to Fieschi, at least—the more so, according to me, because he did not have time to read the transcript and learn what the Pontiff had actually told.

There is no need for me to give you much detail about the voyage to Ireland. *The Irish Times* and the *New York Times* printed long and accurate reports. Our most serious problem during the trip to Dublin was the management of crowds. Just before we departed, *il Papa* spoke from the palazzo window to a large general audience in the piazza. Then we flew by helicopter to Ciampino, and immediately boarded the 727. Monsignor Candutti had stressed to the Irish the absolute necessity of similar arrangements at Dublin, but when we landed we found security lax.

The first error came with the ground control's order to our aircraft to park in front of the main terminal. The second error was one of timing. We were ordered to disembark only moments after a 747 from New York had begun to disgorge its passengers. As soon as these people saw the papal crest on our plane, they crowded around the steps. The Irish police, the *garda,* had set up their lines to meet incursions from the terminal or from the road leading to the runway. To cope with this unexpected problem, the *garda* commander pulled out a contingent of his police from the terminal; and he did so precisely as the people being restrained near the terminal became angered at the sight of tourists swarming around our aircraft.

There was much pushing and shoving, and within a few seconds the police lines wavered and rapidly broke. Then, suddenly, our plane was surrounded by several thousand people, some wildly cheering *il Papa,* others equally wildly cursing the police as they nursed bruises, and others simply caught up in the confusion of the mob. For their part, the *garda* were reforming their ranks to disperse the crowd with a hasty assault. That seems to be an international reflex of police.

In sum, it was almost a repetition of the scene in Mexico

City, and Francesco handled the affair in the same way, using the loudspeaker to call the people to order and to bless them. Predictably, the miracle was also reproduced, although this one should have caused no one a second thought. A young tinker—or gypsy, as the Irish call their professional beggars—screamed that she had been cured of deafness by the touch of *il Papa.* Even Fieschi was unconvinced when he read about the girl's background the next morning. But the injury had been done.

After the near tragedy at the airport, the *garda* were more alert, but I cannot say that they were particularly efficient. Francesco made his talk—televised in Ireland and Great Britain by Television Eireann and BBC and relayed by satellite around the world—in the big *colosseo* in the area called Ballsbridge, near the American embassy. The crowd was immense, and when only a fraction of them could be accommodated in the *colosseo,* the rest threatened to turn ugly.

We had been resting at the president's palazzo in Phoenix Park on the far side of Dublin, and Monsignor Candutti had persuaded the government to use one of its helicopters to transport us directly into the *colosseo.* The streets outside the *colosseo* were a pitiful sight. Every hospital bed in Ireland must have been emptied. There were literally thousands of sick, crippled, infirm, and retarded people gathered along the streets, most of them on litters carried by friends and relatives. Traffic—it flows only slightly more easily in downtown Dublin than in Roma, even though the streets are wider—was a massive, honking snarl of polluting machines and cursing drivers.

On our way to the *colosseo,* the helicopter flew low enough that at one place we could see a clump of about fifty people on stretchers lying in the street blocking traffic. When Francesco saw what was happening he insisted that we land for a moment. It was not an easy task for the pilot, but fortunately the street was very wide and the cars ahead of the sprawl of sick people had moved on. Francesco rapidly walked among the litters, offering a few words of consolation. When others saw the helicopter and a figure in white, they came rushing over—I do not know how many, but surely more than a thousand. Tragically, one person lying on a stretcher was trampled to death.

You can read all that in the newspaper archives. I have

little to add in the way of personal recollections, except that it was clear in my mind that Francesco was seeking the opportunity for more "miracles." One part of him rejected the whole notion and recognized the cures for what, according to me, they were: hysterical reactions. Another part of him, however, was less secure. I do not know whether Francesco was testing his power or his faith. In either case, he was successful, if one discounts the fate of the poor devil on the stretcher. Two more people whom he touched claimed to be cured. I cannot now even remember their alleged ailments, but I can recall that at the time I was not impressed.

In two other respects, one must count the visit to Dublin a success. First, the abbot reported that as soon as his recruiters opened their offices in Ireland they were swamped with volunteers. While many eventually changed their minds, the crusade had more volunteers than our people could process.

Second, Papa Francesco had cordial talks with a group of Anglican and Presbyterian clergymen from both the free part of Ireland and the area occupied by the British Army, as he had promised he would. Together we issued a joint statement asking for an end to violence: "Whatever the political differences among the people of Ireland, they can never be as important as their shared heritage as children of God and brothers and sisters in Christ. Terrorists may like to think of themselves as Catholic or Protestant, but they cannot be Christians if they continue their violence."

I do not know what effect the statement had on the terrorists—little, I would infer from the fact that the murders continue even today—or on extremist agitators and sympathizers—again little, if the fiery denunciations issued the next day by that evil old man so full of hate and devoid of love, Ian Paisley, are any indication. But I am sure in my heart that the common people of Ulster were comforted.

Francesco's meetings with public officials in the republic were brief and almost totally ceremonial. We stayed in the president's palazzo for reasons of security. *Il Papa* had suggested a visit with leaders from the North, but Monsignor Candutti and the Irish *taoiseach* (the prime minister) had agreed that it would be unwise since it would make the Protestant moderates more vulnerable to th vile demogoguery of Paisley and others of his ilk.

I must mention one thing about the trip that showed Papa Francesco at his diplomatic best. He managed to spend a half an hour with two rabbis. It had never occurred to me that there were Jews in Ireland, but having lived there for a time as a youngster Francesco knew better. Later I remembered reading years ago about a Jewish lord mayor of Dublin. *Ebbene,* his son, a distinguished member of parliament whom Francesco had known when he was chief justice, escorted the rabbis to the president's palazzo.

We left Dublin on a bleak, rainy morning. The crew were quite nervous because we had flight clearances only as far as Berlin. Neither the East Germans nor the Poles had responded to the pilot's requests for instructions. Francesco was unperturbed. He simply directed the captain to monitor the Berlin and Warsaw frequencies and to transmit our course and altitude every five minutes.

The Poles, of course, were furious at *il Papa* for ignoring accepted rules of international diplomacy and coming to Warsaw without their permission. (Candutti was also less than happy; after all, he was a professional diplomat who took the rules of that game very seriously.) Other than a terse announcement that *il Papa* would be received as the head of Vatican City State, the Poles said to the world nothing at all.

Not only were we lacking a flight clearance but we also had no indication as to who would meet us, where we would stay in Poland, and where, if at all, we would be allowed to speak to the people. We knew that the abbot had been curtly refused permission to establish any sort of office in the country. We had tried to prod the government, directly through conversations between Monsignor Candutti and the Polish ambassador to Italy and indirectly through leaks to the press, but the government would not budge. "We are a proud people," Monsignor Zaleski told, "not always intelligent, but always very stubborn." It was difficult to argue with that statement.

From the Polish clergy, we learned that police planned to speed us from and to the airport and send us packing within three hours of landing, allowing us only to shake hands with the prime minister and other members of the politburo. The government news agency had also made no announcement to the Polish people that *il Papa* was visiting Warsaw, an omission that the priests and bishops quickly but quietly rectified. In addition, we later discovered, on the morning of our visit several hundred thousand leaflets were scattered about the city giving our estimated time of arrival and our planned route from the airport through the city.

It was clear as our aircraft arrived at the terminal that the government's efforts at secrecy were a total failure. I am not skilled at estimating crowds, but the area was filled with people. Reporters guessed that there were at least a quarter of a million people present. They were sealed from us by a six-deep phalanx of troops with fixed bayonets, backed by several dozen tanks and armored cars.

Ecco, Francesco could not ignore such an opportunity. The—how do you call it, the bullhorn?—came down again, and with Monsignori Bonetti and Zaleski at his side, he quickly shook the outstretched hands of the minor governmental officials at the foot of the stairs. Then, with Monsignor Bonetti carrying the loudspeaker and Zaleski trailing behind, Francesco strode toward the crowd, climbed on top of a tank, and began to talk in English. He paused every two or three minutes and handed the bullhorn to Monsignor Zaleski so that he could translate into Polish. The soldiers were aghast, but there was little they could do. Under no circumstances would they have wanted to use physical violence against the person of *il Papa,* and certainly they would not dare to do so in front of 250,000 devout Catholics.

Francesco's message was, as usual, simple. He had come to preach the gospel of love to the people of Poland, a people who for centuries had cherished and spread that gospel even to Roma itself. He was there to ask them to renew their faith and rededicate their lives to God through the love of their fellow man, even in the face of grave difficulties. At that point he gestured toward the troops and the tanks. Then he asked those who could to join in the crusade and everyone to participate actively in the spiritual renewal. In all, the allocution consumed ten minutes—double that with Zaleski's translation.

When he was finished, Francesco did not return to the officials near our plane. Instead he ordered the tank driver to go to the left edge of the crowd. The driver appeared helplessly confused, but he obeyed. There Francesco repeated the same talk he had given the group in the center.

Then, holding to the turret of the tank he directed the driver to the other end of the crowd, where he once more repeated his message. It was a scene that was typical of Francesco's dramatic, or melodramatic touch—a bright, cold day, a Roman Pontiff clothed in a white cassock and red cape riding a Russian-made tank. Puccini would have loved him; Verdi would have worshipped him.

The Polish officials were livid with rage, and became more livid each time they heard the wild shouts of approval from the crowd. None of them spoke a single word to us as we drove into town, although Francesco, enjoying himself like a mischievous child, thanked them for the opportunity to speak to the people and promised that he would mention their courtesy to the prime minister. The car was closed and the windows heavily curtained. *Il Papa,* however, simply pulled the curtains apart, rolled down the glass —almost killing us with the bitter cold—and waved to the crowds who lined the streets.

At one intersection we had to stop because of construction and a stalled bus. Francesco swiftly opened the portal and stood, arms outstretched, to be embraced and kissed by a crowd of twenty or thirty laborers. His white cassock had been stained by grease from the tank and now his cape showed the dirty handprints of the laborers. As our convoy started off again, the vice-minister of foreign affairs leaned over and locked Francesco's door. The driver did not decelerate below eighty kilometers until we halted inside the government building.

That meeting went quickly and poorly. Our reports had been accurate. We were expected to leave as soon as we had been formally presented to the president, the prime minister, and other members of the politburo. The cardinal archbishop of Warsaw was pointedly uninvited. Francesco, however, was adamant in pretending not to understand. Finally, after being informed in very crisp Oxford English that the convoy was waiting to return us to the airport so that our aircraft could depart immediately, *il Papa* answered that he was anticipating preaching the next Sunday in the restored cathedral of Warsaw. The prime minister then explained in halting English that the Pontiff had been received as the head of state of Vatican City State and not as a religious leader.

"Absurd, my dear fellow," was Francesco's reply. "You

are talking nonsense." I saw Monsignor Candutti wince. "We are the Vicar of Christ, and we have come to Warsaw to preach the word of God."

" 'The word of God,' if there is such a thing," the minister of security said in his Oxford accent, "is preached here daily by Polish clergy. We have no need of foreigners."

"No man is a foreigner in Christ," Francesco told smoothly. "We are all brothers in Christ." He then walked to the window and looked down on the square where a huge crowd—again kept back by a thick cordon of soldiers with fixed bayonets—was gathered. "Excellency," Francesco spoke to the prime minister, looking straight past the minister of security. "We see our people, yours and ours, so we each think; but actually they are God's people, not yours, not mine. You must have loudspeaking equipment in this building. You wish us out of Poland. We wish to preach in the cathedral. Let us be two reasonable men. We shall preach from here to that crowd and then leave, but in an open car"—I shuddered at the thought of the cold and the recollection of Francesco's recent pneumonia—"from which we can see and be seen to bring God's blessing to His people."

"No. It is not possible."

"Very well. We shall stay here until we are allowed to preach in the cathedral."

"You will leave now, Holiness. Please let us not argue."

"You can make us leave only by violence against our person. We doubt if you wish to undo all the work that you and your predecessor accomplished in easing tensions between church and state. We have no doubt that your regime would survive our anathemas, but it might not survive the anger of those people outside. Ask your officials who were at the airport or those who saw the people along the way, ask them to whom those people give their primary allegiance, to Caesar or to God?"

Allora, poor Monsignor Candutti was visibly shaking. Francesco did not remove his eyes from the prime minister. "You see, Excellency, you have three alternatives—to let us preach here now, to let us use the cathedral, or to use violence against us and so incite riots and perhaps even revolution. We recall that certain elements within your own party might not be unhappy at the last possibility."

The prime minister ignored the barb. "Many innocent

people would be killed if there were riots." His voice was flat.

"Martyrdom is a saint's death, one that the people of God have often gladly accepted, as the history of Poland shows."

As you know, Francesco had his way, as he usually did. He always had cool blood, but in Warsaw I felt an icy chill in his words. According to me, the prime minister recognized that Francesco would accept death for himself and his people and do so willingly, almost cheerfully. That attitude frightened the prime minister. What I am trying to say is that the Pole, who was a much more political animal than I, sensed something awesome in Francesco, either a fanatical ruthlessness, a readiness to pull down the temple on himself, his enemies, and his people, or, on the other hand, a selflessness. The first was the attitude of a man of politics, the second—the selflessness—of a man of God. Francesco's personality was still changing. That much I could see. It was the direction of change that was unclear to me at that moment, though I soon formed an opinion.

I do not know how much in immediate terms the trip to Warsaw was worth. Our clerical sources told that thousands of Polish young people tried to obtain visas to join the crusade, but the government granted only a token quota of several hundred. More generally, the visit set back the long and delicate negotiations involving the Communist government, the Vatican, and the local bishops. Francesco's brashness undid several years of Monsignor Candutti's work, and the *monsignore* was almost in tears. On the other hand, for the first time in history, a Pontiff had come to Poland, had directly reached perhaps a half million Polish people, and had also impressed the government with his determination and his power inside that troubled country.

The effect of the trip on me was one of depression. It marked, I realized after our return to Roma, the opening of a triumphal phase of Francesco's papacy. Much of his easy style of openness, personal gentleness, and displays of intellectual strength began to ebb after the trip to Poland. I came to realize he had taken a long step backward in his journey from political to religious leader. He had actually enjoyed pitting his moral power against the physical force of the Polish regime; I do not think that had been true when he threatened the junta in Brazil. There he had been fighting for his people. In Poland, he had been wrestling with another leader; winning the game had been critically important to his pride.

I move ahead of my narrative, but let me say that after Warsaw *il Papa*'s manner became more overbearing. Rather than overpowering us intellectually as he often had earlier, he relied on his institutional authority and his personal charisma much more than he had previously. As the head of the Church, the maker and unmaker of bishops, the worker of miracles, the man whose moral power made dictators on two continents tremble, the father of the crusade and spiritual renewal, and God's special apostle for social justice, he had no need to convince us, only to command us. Your English word *pontificate* connotes precisely the style he would use in speaking to us, even to me.

I am referring not merely to personal irritability, though there was much of that. Holiness and a sweet temper are not synonymous. Christ Himself is evidence of that. The Gospels record His human side. His forceful eviction of the moneychangers from the temple provides an excellent example of a flaring temper, and his curse of the fig tree illustrates a trivializing of divine power in a fit of pique. What I am describing goes beyond displays of temper and frustration to a general mood of arrogant assumption: instant possession of truth coupled with scorn for those who failed to recognize that light. *Ecco,* there was still an aura of holiness there, though, according to me, it was fainter than it had been in New York or Latin America. But far more evident than before was the huge ego—no, I must use the word again, *hubris.*

To say that I was concerned is too weak a statement. I was appalled at what was happening to my friend and I was frightened by the spectre of a shepherd who so freely gambled with his own life and those of his flock.

TWENTY-NINE

We returned to Italy on the night of the fourth day after leaving for Dublin and Warsaw. Before we landed at Ciampino, Francesco changed our procedure and insisted that we drive back to the Vatican rather than take the helicopter. It would be almost ten-thirty, he said, and there would be little traffic. Besides, the weather forecasts stated that Roma was enjoying one of its many stretches of clear, balmy spring days with the temperature in the mid-fifties on your scale. According to me, Francesco was deceiving himself more than he was others, but I, too, was deceiving myself, refusing to read the signposts pointing to the direction of change in his life.

The drive from the airport to the Vatican was not a secret, nor could one have expected it to be. Francesco had asked to be met by his open Mercedes, and a car of that size and design—I believe it is unique in the world—cannot be sneaked across Roma, especially with dozens of journalists willing to wait all night just to take a picture of *il Papa*. Still, the crowd at the airport numbered no more than several thousand, and there were only scattered clumps of people along the way. The Piazza di San Pietro, however, was crowded for that time of night. The newspapers estimated 25,000 people. While that is only a small portion of what the piazza can contain, it is, nevertheless, a sizable number of humans. And being Italian, the crowd pushed and elbowed and swore as they went about their Christian duties.

Fortunately there were no incidents. God was good and the motorcycle escort ruthless in closing around the open car and refusing to slow for anything, neither traffic lights, pedestrians, nor well-wishers who were blocking the road. We had several near misses with some of the latter who were reluctant to move from our path, but no one was hit or hurt beyond the bruises one always receives from being in a Roman crowd.

The next morning, Francesco was still annoyed at not having experienced closer contact with the crowd, but even Fieschi agreed that closer contact might have been fatal to someone. Francesco was—you say grumpy?—grumpy, yes, at a breakfast meeting with the abbot until it became clear that the abbot had good news for us. In three days the crusade's organization in Ireland had screened more than 250 volunteers and found that 150 of them met mental and physical qualifications. Within the week they would be joining several hundred Germans and Americans for two months of intensive training in Mexico. More people, of course, would be screened out during that time, but the important thing was that the machinery had begun to function.

The abbot also noted that he had received a telephone call that morning from Cardinal Martìn, who had been traveling in Argentina, Chile, and Mexico formally inaugurating there a call for volunteers (and informally checking on the progress of the spiritual renewal). He reported relatively few responses—less than 750—but almost all were being accepted. They, too, would soon fly to the training camp in Mexico. God knows, the crusade was yet filled with problems, as I shall explain later, but for the moment we had two pieces of much-needed good news.

During the weeks of early spring, Francesco further intensified his work. His desks, both in the palazzo and the *casina,* became his life. Occasionally, if he was working in the *casina,* we would take a walk in the garden together, but only if I insisted. At other times I persuaded him to join me on the walk that Papa Paolo had constructed on the roof of the palazzo. Still, he obtained very little exercise, and that worried me.

His day gradually lengthened, stretching at both ends. During the first months of his papacy, Papa Francesco had begun work shortly before eight and continued until twelve-thirty, with a halt of a half hour for walking through the gardens before a light lunch and a brief siesta (usually after reading the *International Herald Tribune,* which arrived in Roma about one-thirty). Then he would return to his desk between three-thirty and four and would work until nine.

I can remember many of the dinners we had those late evenings. To eat at the Pontiff's table is an extraordinary thing in itself, and before Papa Francesco, very rare. But these dinners were often marvelous events in their own right, even though—before I seduced Elio and Massimo from Ristorante Il Galeone—the food was barely palatable. (In contrast, the wine, which I insisted on choosing, and often provided, was generally excellent.) It was the evenings themselves that were delightful. Pritchett, the abbot, and I were regular participants; Monsignor Cavanaugh, the Irish priest who helped write allocutions for Francesco, was also often with us. When he was in Roma, Mr. Keller would invariably join us and on those occasions he would escort Signora Falconi. (As a woman, she could never come in the company of clerics; it raised enough hairs that a layman escorted her to the papal table.)

I have already told you of my fondness for that extraordinarily efficient woman, but perhaps I did not mention that she was a person of wide reading. Francesco once joked that she had read and rewritten all of his opinions for the Supreme Court. She certainly well understood most of what transpired in the palazzo and in the curial offices—and much that did not happen. I had learned to trust her judgment as soon as I saw that she regarded LaTorre with a kind of affectionate wariness and Bisset with utter contempt. Between her and Francesco there was a strange, warm relationship. I imply nothing scandalous, of course. She understood him and anticipated his wants. He exploited her talents to the fullest, which seemed to please her. I understood her reaction, at least in part, for surely Francesco exploited me just as much—but that is the Pontiff's job.

An occasional cardinal, sometimes Chelli but more often someone like Martin, Pritchett, or Rauch, with whom Francesco felt more *simpatico,* would join us. And from time to time there was a whole range of other guests—a bishop who had come to Roma to make his formal visit to the Pontiff, a vacationing judge, or a diplomat passing through, a journalist, a marine general assigned to NATO, a secretary of one of the curial congregations, or a simple priest.

These were seldom large gatherings. On the contrary, rarely were more than six guests present, and usually only four. We talked and talked and argued and argued—of theology, politics, art, literature, and drama. (Signora Falconi knew far more about Irish playwrights than did Monsignor Cavanaugh, and she delighted—how do you say?--to rub that in. Cavanaugh's responses were always learnedly philistine.) Only two subjects were prohibited: things of business settled, or likely to be scheduled. That left us a wide field in which to canonize and anathematize over bottles of soft wine.

Initially, certainly during his first summer, Francesco was at his best during those evenings; he was urbane, charming, witty, and absolutely unpretentious, willing to argue anything, accepting intellectual contradiction as a felicitous challenge instead of as an affront and usually able to give much better than he received. I remember the evening when two of your seminarians from the North American College were pompously discussing the great theological difference between the Greek Orthodox and Roma on the nature of the Holy Trinity. As you know, the Greeks assert that the Holy Spirit proceeds directly from the Father, while we know that He proceeds from both the Father and the Son. For ten minutes Francesco listened intently to the discussion, then asked his usual kind of question: "What are the data?"

"Holiness?" the older seminarian inquired.

"I asked: What are the data?"

"I do not understand, Holiness."

"You have been talking about a factual problem, not one of logical relationships. Either the Holy Spirit proceeds one way or He proceeds the other. Either is perfectly justifiable in logic. What are the data on which we can determine which is correct?"

That sort of hardheaded indifference to 2000 years of theological debate, but gentle tolerance for those whom it pleased to engage in such activities—provided they kept themselves fully detached from the real world—was typical of the Francesco who had been Declan Walsh.

Those evenings served all of us well. The guests came to know *il Papa* and often had an opportunity for a private discussion of a special problem with him, or, in the case of a journalist, to file a guardedly worded but authoritative and revealing story. Papa Francesco often used these occasions to infect his guests with his own ideas and enthusiasm. I can still recall how, when a reporter would be present, he sometimes carefully planned to tell something that would sound just a little indiscreet, so that the story would be quickly spread.

Most important for Francesco, those evenings provided sources of information about the outside world and even the world of the Vatican from which he was shielded. He received two press briefings per day from the secretary of state's office, a summary of diplomatic dispatches, and stacks of official reports from various curial congregations, secretaries, committees, and commissions. But these were all transmitted through official channels and had been prepared by career curialists. Of course, Francesco also read three or four newspapers each day, but these evenings gave him firsthand information from other sources. A visiting bishop's account of problems in his and neighboring dioceses might vary greatly from the dispatch sent by a nuncio; the impressions of a journalist might differ from both; and a fledgling priest in a curial office might provide yet another perspective. In sum, Papa Francesco could make up his own mind without depending on the predigested reports that careerists often tried to feed him.

By fall, Francesco's participation was less fluid and more aloof. He became less and less a debater in our discussions and more a questioner and still more a solemn listener. His withdrawal from active to passive participation was due not only to his growing acquaintance with papal pomp, but also to the inner transformation that I have described. He gradually yet noticeably lost, even in private, some of his spontaneity and open-minded curiosity.

Furthermore, Francesco's workday intruded more and more into the hours that could be used to relax. By the time we returned from Warsaw he was at his desk before seven in the morning, with breakfast always, lunch often, and even occasionally dinner served to him on a tray—a terrible abuse of Massimo's and Elio's talents. After Warsaw—in fact, after Latin America, but that was perhaps because of his illness—I remember very few of the wonderful evenings we had earlier enjoyed. When Francesco did invite guests, the affairs tended to be large and formal, and conversation rather stilted.

Il Papa did continue one practice regarding those evenings that I thought marvelous. One night a week he invited for dinner in the *casina* ten or twelve seminarians from the Ethiopian seminary or the North American College, and later from other seminaries as well. These gatherings were more like small audiences than the freely flowing exchanges of summer, but at least the youngsters could spend an evening with *il Papa*, something they would remember and recount all their lonely lives.

There was another habit that Francesco developed, namely, daily general audiences. After our return from Dublin and Warsaw he began appearing every noon at the studio window overlooking the piazza, and there was always a fair-sized crowd on hand. After about a month the Secretariat of State announced that whenever *il Papa* was in the city, he would give a daily general audience at noon to the people in the piazza. Soon even this practice would not sufficiently satisfy the public's demands or Francesco's needs.

THIRTY

EARLIER I MENTIONED Francesco's irritability. At times it might have been more accurately called irascibility. One example involved LaTorre and the encyclical on social justice.

Shortly after our return from Warsaw, Francesco completed the final draft of the document, from its opening words in Latin, *Justitia et Pax*, "Justice and Peace." As was his custom, he put it aside for some days before issuing it. It was during that period, fortunately, that the leak occurred. But I am moving ahead of myself again, like a talkative old man who wants to tell two tales at once. Let me begin again.

The document's social and political messages hardly seemed radical to anyone familiar with pronouncements on the same subject by Leo XIII, Pio XI, Giovanni XXIII, and Paolo VI. It was somewhat more socialist in economic and political outlook than the others, but not glaringly so. Certainly Papa Paolo had been almost a Fabian Socialist and—although many Catholics forget it—the Church has historically condemned laissez-faire capitalism as being no less destructive of human values than atheistic communism.

The draft told nothing novel when it spoke of the evils of the profit motive and the dehumanizing effects of the concentration of wealth either by a few people within a single nation or by a few nations in the world. Nor was it a new departure to severely criticize the arms race and its drain of resources needed to feed, clothe, and educate the poor. The draft spoke little that was fresh, although it added emphases missing in earlier documents, when it condemned racism of any shade as well as notions of ethnic or national superiority. In sum, *Justitia et Pax* stressed the duty of each person, and thus of each nation, to care for his neighbor. It was an old message. As Francesco himself scribbled in the margin: "We can ask Cain's ancient question of God, but the answer remains unchanged. We are our brothers' keepers, bound by that brotherhood to share all things with our fellows."

There was, however, one thing that was startlingly new. After the draft had been circulated to the appropriate curial offices, and their comments made, collated, and to some extent included, Francesco added two substantive sentences absent from earlier versions. They were cumbersome but critical:

> While we unreservedly condemn compulsory sterilization and abortion as an immoral means to control the growth of population, it remains an important duty of all persons to exercise prudence in the number of children that they conceive. Governments have a positive obligation toward their people, especially the poorer groups on whom the burdens of parenthood fall especially heavily and on whose children conditions of life are especially hard, to instruct them so as to prevent increases in population that diminish not only material prosperity but, far more importantly, the possibility of a spiritually fruitful life.

The Holy See is a Byzantine world, one that shares much with the regime in Moscow and Peking in that momentous changes in policy are often announced by small adjectives or adverbs that are added to or omitted from conventional phraseology. In that world of deft innuendo, these two sentences would seem as subtle as one of those taped conversations between President Nixon and his assistants with the expletives *not* deleted. All knowledgeable persons—like Roman reporters—would see in these two sentences a screaming repudiation of Papa Paolo's encyclical, *Humanae Vitae,* which in 1968 had reaffirmed, although not as a matter of binding dogma, the traditional teaching that artificial means of birth control were prohibited by the moral law.

Under normal conditions, Fieschi would have resigned rather than allow such words to go out across his desk. Now, however, he was so enveloped in blind faith in Francesco's charisma that he exercised no independent judgment. *Il Papa* had commanded; Fieschi would see that the world heard and obeyed. I need not repeat that that attitude did *il Papa* a disservice. He was coming perilously close to stirring revolt among the traditionalists. I could not be sure of the extent to which Francesco appreciated this danger, but it was apparent that Fieschi did nothing to apprise him of it. I could not offer counsel, nor could Pritchett nor the abbot, because at the time none of us had even seen the final draft.

In fact, Bisset, LaTorre, Greene, and Chelli learned from their special source about what Francesco had added before the rest of us did. Fieschi did not alert me until he had received a wrathful visit of protest from the four traditionalists. When they appeared in his office, he permitted them—LaTorre was their spokesman—to present oral objections, then placidly informed them that His Holiness had considered all such matters and had still decided to write the sentences in question. Fieschi gave not the slightest indication that either he or Papa Francesco would be interested in further discussion or even in reading a statement. He did, however, accede to their request for a special audience with *il Papa.*

It was at that point that LaTorre telephoned and explained that the four wanted to discuss "an urgent matter" with me. I had no need to ask questions and suggested they join me that evening for dinner in my apartment in the San Calisto. They arrived together, which I interpreted as a bad omen since it indicated a united front. I had hoped that Chelli might temper LaTorre's bullheadedness and Greene's stubbornness, and cut them loose from Bisset's waspish tongue, leaving him to oppose or whatever was pleasing to him.

I had planned a simple meal. We would have Campari as an *aperitivo,* then a first plate of hot *lumache,* those lovely snails, and some cold, raw mussels with lemon juice. (I had, as subtly as I could, suggested to Vergilio, my chef, that he dispatch our chauffeur to walk to Il

Ristorante Da Gino and obtain the *lumache* there; Da Gino's chef always made them much better than Vergilio.) With these *frutti di mare,* we would drink chilled Verdicchio.

For the second plate, Vergilio, who had been reared in the Abruzzi, made *frascarelli,* a regional pasta which, because of the spinach with which it is prepared, is green in color. In shape it resembles what you call string beans and, served with a light sauce of meat and tomatoes and with a Chiaretto rosé to drink, makes an excellent transition to the principal plate. For that, I had chosen some tender cuts of *bistecca Fiorentina* (reasonably close to what you call T-bone steak), fried zucchini, and a mixed salad. I had selected three bottles of a potable Turkish red, Yakut, that some friends in the embassy in Roma had been kind enough to send me. For after, we would have a good Danish blue cheese and some American cheddar, with a bottle or two of that superb but dreadfully expensive claret from your Mondavi vineyards in California. For a *dolce,* I planned some of LaTorre's huge Sicilian oranges, and a bottle of moderately chilled Korbel champagne—the vintners had sent Francesco a dozen cases and he had given one of them to me. For a *digestivo* after espresso, I had some Grappa for LaTorre and Courvoisier for the rest of us.

As you can see, I had planned the meal to be a simple but soothing experience. Although the food was delicious, the effect was not what I wanted. Bisset, Greene, and Chelli savored the *lumache* and mussels. This was unusual for Chelli; as a Neapolitan, he said, he knew too much about what went into the Gulf of Naples to enjoy what came out. LaTorre gulped them down, too, and then began a heated discussion that diverted attention from the food and wine, and gave me horrible indigestion, a malady from which I rarely suffer.

Chelli managed to calm LaTorre by insisting that we not attack the merits of the encyclical but explore ways of persuading *il Papa* when they met with him the next afternoon. "The first point to settle," Chelli said, "is whether His Holiness fully understands the significance of his words in *Justitia et Pax.*"

"I cannot be absolutely sure," I replied, "but I am reasonably certain that he does. He wrote them himself."

"What did he say to you about it?" LaTorre asked.

"As long as I am the Pontiff's counsellor I cannot repeat conversations with him." (It was easy to be virtuous for Francesco had told me nothing. I learned of the affair from Fieschi, as I mentioned earlier.) "But because I share your concern in this matter—although not necessarily your objective of maintaining the teachings of *Humanae Vitae*—I would suggest an approach that might be effective."

"Namely?" Bisset asked. One could not tell if his superciliousness was caused by pretentious Parisian disdain for the *frascarelli* or by a conviction that I could not possibly offer intelligent advice.

"Namely to stress that, even if *il Papa* has reservations about *Humanae Vitae,* this is not the proper way to express them."

Nodding toward Chelli, LaTorre told, "Mario has been urging the same course; according to me, however, we must get to the substance. The point is not how *Humanae Vitae* is changed but that it must not be changed at all, unless it is strengthened."

"I fear that what you want is impossible," I intervened. "*Il Papa* looks on *Humanae Vitae* as a misguided document. He has respect for Paolo—indeed he has tried to carry through much of Paolo's effort to reform the Curia, to the pain of some cardinals." I could not resist this tweaking of Bisset. "But Francesco thinks that Paolo committed a grave error in judgment in issuing *Humanae Vitae*. At least," I aimed a small barb at LaTorre, "he should have followed the Holy Office's earlier draft." Neither cardinal responded to my thrusts, so I continued: "The finish of *Humanae Vitae* is inevitable. It has been attacked by eminent theologians as well as by conscientious bishops, and largely ignored by confessors and laity around the world. Francesco thinks that the basic error of *Humanae Vitae* is that it looks on sex as an evil thing that can only be justified by the possibility of conception."

"That is God's truth, not error," Greene burst out. "Just so. Sex can be justified only by the purpose that you mention. Its sole legitimate objective is continuation of the human species, not the immediate gratification of two sweaty bodies."

"And what about love?"

"Love is not the same as lust," LaTorre put in. "One

of the most tragic errors of the modern world is to confuse the two. Love is dedication to the welfare of another, to his or her protection, most of all to his or her spiritual welfare, not the exploitation of sexual facilities. Satiation of lust is not the fulfillment of real love."

"Just so," Greene added.

I had hoped to avoid this argument. It had spoiled the *frascarelli* and was making the Chiaretto sharp and bitter. But I could not totally abandon the field lest LaTorre decide to fight there the next day with Francesco.

"I think that you have misunderstood and so misphrased the argument, just as you have falsely assumed that the only legitimate purpose of sex is procreation. But we did not come together to change each other's minds."

"I agree," Chelli spoke for the first time. "If a man as moderate as Cardinal Galeotti thinks as he speaks, then the Pontiff is apt to be further to the theological left. I think the idea of postponement is a prudent one. If we force the issue now, we shall surely lose; if we delay we may win, although in the future."

Bisset turned quickly: "How can we temporize with evil? 'If you are lukewarm, I shall vomit you out of my mouth.' "

Chelli remained tranquil. "First of all, I am not totally convinced that the basic premise about sex and procreation is correct. I incline that way, but I have doubts, as I have said before. Certainly the proposition cannot be proved by logic or by evidence or by Scripture, unless one includes someone like Augustine as divinely inspired."

"I do," Bisset injected.

"But the Church does not," Chelli went on. "Learned, yet not divinely inspired in the same way as the writers of the Gospels. But let us not choose sides among saints and theologians. The vital point is that the Pontiff will reject such an argument."

"Is he really the Pope?" Bisset asked sarcastically. "And if he is, do we have to allow him to remain so?"

I intervened. "I have told you before: Francesco was elected by a conclave at which we were all present. We were all satisfied that the vote was the canonical two-thirds plus one. Let us not, as the Americans say, whip a dead horse."

"Allora," Chelli spoke again, "we must choose between certain defeat and postponement."

"I disagree," LaTorre cut in. "We met the issue of celibacy head-on with the Pope and we won."

"I am less certain of that," Chelli replied. "I think that we won a postponement, nothing more. Papa Francesco listened to us because we—really you, 'Vanni—had an excellent argument, and he temporized because we shook his confidence."

"Fair enough," Greene said, "that's fair enough; but we also have excellent arguments here. Why can we not shake his confidence again?"

"Because," Chelli answered, "our arguments are based on a premise that is not even shared within this room and is thought to be eccentric if not absurd in most parts of the world—by many dedicated bishops and priests who have care of souls, not merely by wild-eyed Dutchmen trying to solve their country's political problems by posing as theologians. *And* because we are dealing with a different man from the one we knew a few months ago. I do not believe that the Pontiff's confidence can now be shaken by reason or evidence."

(I listened intently, for Chelli was speaking my own mind.)

"But it was you who argued last summer that we could bring him around," LaTorre began angrily.

"I know, I know, and I think I was right about *that* man. But we are facing a different man now. Something has changed him."

"Perhaps His Holiness believes himself to be a miracle worker," Bisset observed sarcastically.

"Whatever he believes about himself," Chelli continued, "he is not now a man to tolerate open disagreement with his ideas. That situation may change in a few weeks or months. He may only be suffering from fatigue. He has been seriously ill, we should remember. Despite antibiotics, pneumonia is not a minor malady. It severely weakens a man, especially one who continues to work at a pace that is almost frenzied. I have only recently had a similar bout of serious illness and I can understand how that drains energy and patience."

"What your counsel comes to, then," LaTorre remarked, "is to pray that God will open His Holiness's eyes."

"Or perhaps close them," Bisset injected.

I started to intervene angrily, but Chelli was swifter. "Rather let us pray that God gives us all wisdom, especially the wisdom not to confuse ourselves with God. But in all seriousness," Chelli nodded toward Bisset, "Your Eminence has touched a matter we should consider. Francesco will not be Pope forever."

"It will only seem that long," Greene sighed.

"It may," Chelli agreed, "but only to us, not to God and not to His Church. If we can postpone decisions, we may win with the next Pope. I suspect that the next conclave will be more careful about choosing unproven monks—"

Chelli looked at me as he realized what he had said. "I am sorry, Your Eminence. I did not mean to scratch old sores."

I smiled. There was no denying the truth of Chelli's words. The Church is inherently a conservative institution. After all, to preserve the Faith is one of its missions. One can argue, as I have, that the best way to conserve is to grow and to take risks in order to grow, and that Christ Himself instructed us to do so. But the Vatican tends to follow the example of the servant who wrapped his talent in a napkin and buried it, rather than the example of the two servants in the same parable who invested their master's money. *Ebbene,* even though I agreed with Chelli that the next Pontiff was likely to be a more traditional, plodding man—which is one, but only one reason I was willing to work so hard for Papa Francesco—I nevertheless thought that the time was ripe for a brief sermon to this group.

"You do not scratch old sores, Eminence, at least not harshly. We have never agreed about the conclave's wisdom and probably never shall. It is a waste of time to continue that ancient argument. But, I agree that we have a different person in the papacy than we had a few months ago. We face a contradiction, a man who is more holy but also less open to reason, less calm, and less kind. Each of us must examine his own conscience to determine how much responsibility we share for these changes. The papacy is a heavy cross under the best of circumstances. To attempt to add to those burdens, as some members of the Curia have, is worse than personal disloyalty; it is worse than a sin against charity. It is a sin against the Holy Spirit in attempting to hamper His work in governing the Church. We are paying for those sins now, My Reverend Brothers. A Pontiff who tried to lead the Church has found himself deluged with urgent trivia and beset by foot-dragging subordinates. He has been physically exhausted by that experience."

I looked around the table and saw that my remarks had hit home for LaTorre and Chelli. With Greene I was not sure; he smiled as happily as usual as he finished his *bistecca.* Bisset was obviously untouched. I could read the defiance in his eyes over the red of the wine glass.

I went on: "Forgive me. I sound like our brother Fieschi." I smiled at the group. "I speak in generalities. I am sure that all of us here have clear consciences." I lifted my glass. "Here is to cardinals with clear consciences and Pontiffs with good health."

My counsel would not have had effect had Chelli not agreed with me. But the two of us, one supposedly close to *il Papa,* the other a respected member of the traditionalists, brought the others into line, at least for a time. I should also explain my position. At the time *Humanae Vitae* was in preparation, I was not consulted about its contents, but I thought the final version was neither wise pastorally nor correct morally. I was therefore reconciled to its demise. But, I wanted Francesco to adhere to his original strategy: first to change the mood of the Church, then to attack such problems by a gradual, subtle technique of erosion—a typical Vatican treatment of an error—that would not shake faith in the magisterium, the teaching authority, of the Church. Thus, for motives quite different from those of my guests, I wanted to postpone the death of *Humanae Vitae.*

The following week, the traditionalists' audience with *il Papa* began with mixed omens. Francesco was in his library in the palazzo, a much more formal and austere room than his studio in the *casina.* Moreover, Fieschi was present, alert to play Arcangelo Michele to Francesco's Jehovah. On the other hand, Francesco had also invited Pritchett and me, and we might be able to exercise some soothing effect. Furthermore, Francesco seemed in a rather cheerful mood, although he was distracted and kept walking about the room, pausing every few minutes to observe the people in the huge piazza.

LaTorre's opening statement was modest. He told, as was true, that while he spoke only on the specific behalf of the four cardinals who had requested the audience, he was certain that many other prelates in the Curia, and in the Church generally, shared his views. Then he explained how the two sentences in the encyclical would be interpreted, and calmly—and for LaTorre, gently—pressed the argument that *Humanae Vitae,* as a long and deeply considered pronouncement of a respected Pontiff, deserved a different fate, lest the magisterium of the Church suffer grievous injury. As an affair closely connected with faith and morals, any revision should at least be preceded by a thorough study by theologians of the Holy Office (LaTorre used the newer title: the Sacred Congregation for the Doctrine of the Faith) and, if *il Papa* thought it advisable, by other theologians as well. In all, LaTorre gave a concise fifteen-minute presentation that, like his argument on celibacy, showed him at his best—learned, thoughtful, a bit ponderous, perhaps, but as totally dedicated to the Church as he was in command of his thinking.

When LaTorre finished, Fieschi started to say something, but Francesco, still pacing around the room, put his hand on Fieschi's shoulder and walked to the window again. "I think the fundamental point, My Lord Cardinal, is that you believe that *Humanae Vitae* was correctly decided."

"That is true, Holiness, but we do not base our reservations about the encyclical on that ground."

I glanced at Chelli. His eyes gave a bare flicker of response, but I could read that he had as much concern as I that LaTorre would be goaded into a tactical blunder. I also noticed that Fieschi and Pritchett had moved forward so that they were occupying only a small fraction of their chairs at the conference table.

"Still," Francesco went on, "that is the essence of your position, and we must be as candid as you, Lord Cardinal. We believe that *Humanae Vitae* was based on a false view of the nature and functions of sex. One of its objectives is procreation, but that is not its sole objective. Love is important in this world and, if we read the New Testament rightly, in the next as well. Sex can be a sublime expression of love. You theologians are fond of quoting St. Paul that the love of Christ for the Church is like that of a groom for his bride. If that analogy symbolizes the closeness and the sanctity of the bond between Christ and the Church, it provides the same symbol for the bond between man and woman in marriage and for the expression of their love.

"Sex has another function, one less elevated: the simple relief of tensions that all humans experience and the necessity to feel cherished, wanted, or even useful.

"Never to want to have children," Francesco continued, "is wrong under most, although not necessarily all, circumstances. We can no more ignore the procreative purpose of sex than we can its other functions. But whether a married couple should have one or two or three or four or even no children depends on a host of psychological, economic, and ecological factors. We can save souls neither by oversimplifying reality nor by imposing on the people of God the conclusions of a syllogism that reasons from false premises."

"Theologically, Holiness—" LaTorre commenced.

Francesco cut in: "We have written a pastoral document, not a theological one. You theologians may spin your spidery webs but our task is to lead souls to Christ. *Humanae Vitae* was wrong. It must be discarded."

"But surely Your Holiness would not want to act until he had weighed the opinions of his theologians."

"We have responded to that objection, My Lord Cardinal. This is a pastoral not a theological document."

"Yet it will have theological repercussions," LaTorre persisted.

Francesco had been staring out the window during most of the exchange. Now he turned quickly, but before he could say anything I spoke: "*Allora,* perhaps, Holiness, an American lawyer would phrase His Eminence's statement as a plea for due process of law."

Francesco hesitated a moment then smiled, but it was not a warm smile or even a pleasant one. "The sentences stay. We know the Roman Curia's concept of due process. From Galileo to *Humanae Vitae* it has been to *insabbiare* the good without a fair trial." (Do you know this word, *insabbiare?* It means "to bury in sand" and is much used in Italian politics.)

"That is not true, Holiness," LaTorre sputtered. "*Humanae Vitae* was not issued until theologians, pastors, and laymen had had ample opportunity to speak."

If LaTorre had stopped there, much evil might have been avoided. In fact, Chelli and I had both started to stand as a signal that the audience was finished, but LaTorre, red-faced and angry, took no notice of us. "I would be remiss in my duties as Prefect of the Sacred Congregation for the Doctrine of the Faith if I did not warn His Holiness that as presently phrased this document comes near to condoning heresy, if in reality it does not condone heresy."

The room became very still. I could see Fieschi's color change from olive to bronze, and I imagined I could hear Chelli's heart beating. Probably it was my own.

"Say that again, please." Francesco's voice had an icy calm. LaTorre, now himself standing, repeated his statement.

"The Pontiff cannot be a heretic!" Fieschi burst out. "The papacy is infallible!"

"He is the Pontiff. We, *noantri*"—meaning "ourselves alone," sounds so much stronger in the *romanaccio*—"we ourselves alone are the papacy."

"You, Cardinal LaTorre," Papa Francesco told stonily, "are a part of that papacy only as long as it pleases us to have you. You are dismissed. When we desire your presence or your views, we shall summon you. Now leave!" Francesco turned his back and stared out the window.

LaTorre nodded. He was neither contrite nor defiant, merely determined.

Fieschi rose and all the other cardinals, still in shock, filed out. I remained behind and walked over to the collection of *poltrone* and sat down. I knew that I was presuming on Papa Francesco, although Declan Walsh would have welcomed my company. "I recall an old friend who used to say about occasions like this that he was annoyed at pipe smokers because he envied their ability to gain time to think by seeming to concentrate on lighting their pipes."

Francesco turned and smiled again, this time more warmly. "That was in another incarnation." Then he switched: "Why do they fight me, Ugo? I've listened to them, given in to them, and for nine months they have fought me, sometimes with bricks, usually with pillows."

"Holy Father, they fight you because they're convinced that they are right and you are wrong—in this case, perilously wrong. They love the Church with their whole hearts, and they are certain that no one who has not spent at least thirty years as a priest can really love the Church the way that they do—and certainly not a man whose total years in a monastery and in this palazzo are less than three. I fear that I am culpable for bringing you into this situation."

Francesco slumped into the chair next to mine and patted my arm. It was our first intimacy in some weeks. I also noted he was saying "I."

"It's not your fault, Ugo. I knew the basic problem, or thought I did. I just get so tired and so frustrated. I want to lead the Church out of the sixteenth century, but it's a difficult business. Did Christ know that His sheep have mindless wills of their own? I remember old Harry Truman saying that he spent most of his time in the White House trying to persuade people to do what they should have done without his asking. I understand now. I should have fired LaTorre right off. Now I have to find another place for him and soon. He cannot stay in the Curia after this incident."

"Let me suggest the headship of the biblical institute in Jerusalem. He was once a fine scholar."

"I feel like sending him to Lapland as our emissary to the Eskimos. Enough of him. What do you think of those two sentences?"

"I think they should go. This is neither the time nor the place."

"You too?" His eyes narrowed, but I was determined to—how do you say?—see it through.

"No. You know I think *Humanae Vitae* was wrong, but LaTorre's argument for due process is a good one, as far as it goes. I accept it, but I have another reason. You may have forgotten asking me to serve as keeper of your strategic conscience. My strategic advice must be to wait, Holiness. Focus on the spiritual renewal, the crusade, the concern for peace and justice in the world. In that context *Hu-*

manae Vitae is a secondary objective, as your marine friends would say. It is a small thing strategically."

Francesco got up and walked back to the window. "I see another small thing down there: that black scar in front of the obelisk. It reminds me of injustice within the Church." His voice became soft. I had to strain to hear him. "Do you know, Ugo, that at night I hear them calling to me for help: young priests drowning in lonely despair; women, whose devotion to God is probably far greater than my own, being denied the opportunity to heed their calling solely because they are female; millions of husbands and wives who no longer practice their religion and are losing—if it is not already lost—their faith because Paul told them it was a sin to love each other fully unless they were willing to have a baby every year; millions more men and women forbidden to practice their religion fully because after an unhappy marriage they found it possible to love again. They call out to me at night. During the day their agents call out to me—bishops with their official visits, reporters with the articles they write, keepers of statistics with their counts of church attendance, scholars with their data on sexual practices, priests who cannot pass on Paul's command. These people are not asking us for charity, Ugo. They are asking for justice—and within their own lifetimes."

He threw himself into a *poltrona*. I saw fatigue oozing from the pores of his skin. "Forgive me, old friend. The mixture of adulation and resistance I encounter leaves me exhausted."

"I know it is a grinding ordeal, Holiness. But over the years you will achieve more and more."

Francesco looked at me, then gazed at the modernistic statue of a wild Giovanni the Baptist. "But will we have years? You, or I, or our people?"

Ecco, for the first time I saw that Papa Francesco had become an old man. We learn to accept our own mortality easier than that of those we love.

I believe I reached Francesco that afternoon. He made changes, in his own clear handwriting, in the margins of the manuscript. He removed the sentence about governments' having a positive obligation to restrict births and left in his condemnations of compulsory sterilization and abortion *as policies.* I stress those final two words because

Francesco stressed them. He did not mention birth control at all. Here there was only silence, very fruitful silence. You can see for yourself how *Justitia et Pax* reads:

> While we unreservedly condemn abortion and compulsory sterilization as immoral policies to control the growth of population, we remind the people of God that they have an obligation not to conceive children for whom they cannot provide the necessities basic to physical and, more importantly, spiritual life.

As for LaTorre, my dear old one, Francesco did not see fit to accord him the post in Jerusalem, even though it was vacant. Instead, Francesco named him archpriest of the Basilica of San Pietro—Cardinal Monteferro had turned eighty and had expressed a wish to retire. Francesco also accepted LaTorre's "resignation" not only as dean of the Sacred College of Cardinals, but also from membership in all the curial congregations except our court, the Supremo Tribunale della Segnatura Apostolica. He was even required to move out of his spacious apartment in the palazzo of the Holy Office and into a smaller one at the rear of the building. It was not a gentle thing.

The Holy Mule accepted his defeat with both humility and dignity. Even Fieschi was impressed when, after he delivered the news of *il Papa*'s sentence to LaTorre—Fieschi had the courtesy to bring the news in person—he heard him respond: "We thank Your Eminence. We shall now have much time to pray for Holy Mother Church and ourself that we may all be forgiven our trespasses."

I told LaTorre that he should return to his beloved but long-deserted biblical studies. In fact, he did so, though not, of course, with the enthusiasm or energy of youth. We kept our friendship and had a meal together once a week at least. On the outside he was cheerful, but I know the hurt he felt. For the first time in many decades he had no real part in governing Christ's Church and he deeply believed that that Church was in peril. My brothers Greene and Chelli were frequent companions, but to LaTorre's sorrow, our good Frenchman Bisset never called on him after his fall from grace. At least my digestion was spared that evil, but I ached for 'Vanni.

THIRTY-ONE

FRANCESCO TALKED to me and several others about a successor to LaTorre in the Holy Office. His choice of Rauch was wise. For a German, Rauch had shown considerable gentleness and intelligence as well as good judgment in conducting the Congregation for the Clergy during a time when the issue of celibacy was threatening to tear the Church apart. He possessed the diplomatic touch and firmness of will needed to restrain that mass of theologians and would-be theologians in the Holy Office from engaging in their favorite activity—cannibalism.

Francesco's choice of a new prefect for the Congregation for the Clergy was less wise; in fact, it was a serious error. I had urged that he choose the young French cardinal, Stephan DuPrè. He would have given us an unusual geographical bonus in that he had been born in Quebec but his family—his father was the famous novelist—had emigrated to Paris when Stephan was eleven. Thus DuPrè combined the culture of the Old and New Worlds in a mind that I always found brilliantly encyclopedic. (I also freely confess that the presence of a second Frenchman among our prefects would have made it easier to dismiss Bisset.)

Francesco instead chose Gordenker, that contentious and liberal Dutchman. According to me, it was an invitation to trouble. As a close examination of Gordenker's own archdiocese would have demonstrated, he was not an effective administrator. He was intelligent and could swiftly perceive problems, but he was a—how do you say?—gadfly, lacking the patience to execute carefully even his own ideas. Also, he sympathized totally with the demands for an end to clerical celibacy (as well as a half dozen other radical schemes). Thus he would immediately be opposed to one of Francesco's official, however tentative, policies and to the view of most of us in the Curia. Finally, Gordenker was as tactlessly candid in his servant mentality as LaTorre had been from the traditionalist perspective. But, while LaTorre had the capacity to generate a great deal of affection along with exasperation, Gordenker created only cold anger among opponents.

There was another troublesome dimension to this appointment. I have mentioned that even though they are in divine service, cardinals and other curial officials are very human, subject to all sorts of petty jealousies and rivalries. I do not imply they are worse than the rest of men; in fact, they are probably better. But, despite Christ's warning that the last shall be first and the first last, bickering and concern for prerogative are no more lacking in the Holy See than they were among the original Apostles. Francesco used more of his time than he should have soothing princely anxieties. Some Pontiffs have refused to acknowledge the existence of such problems and have permitted conditions to fester; others have delegated the function of peacemaking to the secretary of state or some elderly cardinal. Papa Francesco, on the other hand, felt that he should be personally involved in such matters so that he could know what was happening within the Curia and also so that the resolution of the conflict would be his own.

At best—and I say only what you must already know—easing personal frictions among vain old men is unpleasant and time-consuming labor. The volume of such problems increased by a leap after Gordenker's arrival. Having no regard for the Curia as an institution and lacking the tenacity to adhere to a problem until it was resolved, Gordenker did not hesitate to become involved in any matter that titillated his knight-errant instincts; in his typical style, he rarely remained with a single problem longer than to encourage one of the participants to fight and to enrage the other. Thus, the burdens on Francesco were augmented at the very time when he needed more aid, not more worry.

Allora, the period from winter to Easter rapidly slipped by. My memories of those days are not as happy as those of the autumn. There was now more tension than excitement in the palazzo. I found myself often working in a room in the *casina* to escape the strains, and was not surprised to find that the abbot and even Pritchett sometimes joined me there. It was a period of bickering, very unlike the discussions that surround creativity. Those are often angry, but they are positive. These were petty and typically personal.

We also had problems with local bishops. The spiritual renewal remained a cause of frustration. I have already spoken of the difficulties of coordination within the Vatican and the friction between the Jesuits and the Franciscans. A number of bishops, as you would expect, were not in sympathy with the idea of a spiritual renewal, at least not with Francesco's idea of such a renewal; even many bishops who were basically sympathetic were suspicious of, if not actually hostile to, an influx of outsiders within their dioceses. The reports that we were receiving were very mixed. Many bishops—especially in North America, northern Europe, the developing countries, and in those Latin American dioceses to which Martìn had nominated new men—cooperated fully, even magnificently. Priests and nuns had gone on a series of retreats led by the Franciscans and the Jesuits and were, in turn, now leading laymen through a similar series of spiritual exercises stressing the simple gospel of love.

I must also tell that a few bishops dragged their heels in almost outright defiance, finding all sorts of excuses to deny use of diocesan facilities for the retreats, and using various pretexts of "urgent Church business" to obstruct clergy in their sees from attending retreats that were being conducted. These bishops were easier to deal with—Papa Francesco summarily removed six of them in Latin America alone—than were those who merely showed no enthusiasm. Ostensibly the latter cooperated, but only ostensibly. They rapidly communicated to their clergy and their laity their belief that the renewal was an eccentric wish of the new Pontiff, and that it would do no harm to humor him as long as the business was not taken too seriously.

The evidence against such prelates was inevitably less than clear, but I suspect that the number involved was quite substantial, perhaps as high as one-fifth. In most instances, Francesco could only fume impotently, but in three cases in the United States, one in Ireland, and several in Italy, he appointed coadjutor bishops with right of succession. The sting of the rebuke was sharpened by the fact that in no instance was the offending bishop within a decade of the canonical retirement age of seventy-five.

I mention these things not to criticize our pastoral bishops, for most of them, especially in the poorer countries, agreed with the basic idea behind Francesco's policy and threw themselves and their resources wholeheartedly into the project. We saw, however, no rush among any national group of prelates to divest their dioceses of the land holdings and other forms of wealth that the Church had amassed over the centuries.

Martìn, Pritchett, Chelli, the abbot, and I, as the special task force to conduct what Chelli called a war for poverty, took careful note of what was not happening. For the time being, we decided—actually it was Pritchett who made the suggestion—not to pass the information along to *il Papa,* but follow a triple-headed course: first, to communicate informally through the Council of the World Synod of Bishops papal concern about inaction; second, to talk quietly with those members of national hierarchies with whom we could speak in confidence and friendship; and third, to prepare a draft of an encyclical that Francesco might issue on the implications of ecclesiastical charity.

Chelli had reservations about the whole policy of liquidating much of the Church's wealth, but he did not attempt to obstruct our work. Even when Francesco ordered us to sell more of the Vatican's art as an example to our pastoral bishops, he quickly arranged an auction. Chelli functioned, in fact, as an effective devil's advocate, posing difficult but real questions, and his interventions clarified our thinking. On one point there could be no question: each time a bishop made a major donation of land or money, we received much favorable publicity. In fact, the diplomatic pouches would bulge with clippings from newspapers and magazines. Even Chelli conceded that such notoriety was a good thing, although he warned that, since our wealth was small, our giving could not continue indefinitely.

As Easter approached we began to grow more concerned about security and the problem of the "miracles." The daily audiences from the window of the palazzo had provided more distant contact than Francesco wanted, but at least that distance had prevented him or the crowds—and there were still huge crowds—from doing anything foolish or dangerous. I thought perhaps a press conference might be used effectively here. It might provide a good indication of how—you say, hot?—how hot the issue of miracles still was. I did not phrase the suggestion in those terms when I talked to Francesco, but merely mentioned that many weeks had passed since his last press conference and that it would be inappropriate to schedule such affairs during Holy Week. It turned out to have been one of my least wise suggestions.

Dottor Twisdale made the arrangements, but the day before the press conference he flew off to Mexico on what he cryptically described as urgent business. The *dottore* had decided the conference should take place on the oval terrace of the *casina* if the weather changed for the better. It did. The morning was bright and warm, putting us in good spirits after four days of steady rain.

The first questions from the journalists were concerned with the "miracles," but they were not especially pointed; instead they took the form of polite inquiries about whether the Church's investigations were leading to any definite conclusions. The answer, Francesco replied, had to be no; the Church was always slow to affirm or deny the occurrence of a miracle. "Who knows the mind of the Lord?" He quoted Scripture or perhaps me. "Who has been his counsellor?" It was not as negative a response as we had heard in Newark, but it was, as we Italians would say, *abbastanza*—it would serve.

The next line of questions touched on the new encyclical, *Justitia et Pax,* but the reporters were much more concerned about the omission of any mention of birth control than about the positive aspects of the message concerning social justice and Christian duty. Francesco parried the questions on birth control and delivered a ten-minute lecture on the problem of social justice. He was at his best in that context—lucid, succinct, witty, and exactingly precise in explaining the theme of the encyclical but still good-naturedly chiding the reporters for their concern with the drama of sex rather than the more important aspects of human love.

It would have been a very successful conference had it finished there. In fact, I remember having pangs of conscience for having opposed the idea of allowing *il Papa* to respond to reporters' questions. I nudged the *monsignore* from *L'Osservatore Romano,* but that moron misconstrued my elbow as a signal to ask one of his more banal questions, and he blurted out in English: "Has Your Holiness any news to give us about the progress of the canonization of Pope Pius XII, of blessed memory?"

Francesco's face filled with contempt. If he had not been exhausted he would have simply said something laconically flippant. Instead, his riposte was clear, too clear. "*Monsignore,* let us assure you that as long as we are Pope, Pacelli's canonization would be a true miracle. We do not question the plenitude of God's mercy, but if ever a modern Pontiff needed the full scope of that mercy it was Pius. It will take the Church another century, at least, to live down his silence over the fate of the Jews during World War II."

"But surely, Holiness," the *monsignore,* courageously mustering both digits of his I.Q., persisted, "there would have been danger to the Pontiff's own person had he dared to speak out."

"Indeed. Pacelli changed 'Greater love hath no man than that he lay down his life for another' so that it read: 'Greater prudence has no man than that he save his own skin by letting six million burn.' Who should be prepared to accept martyrdom if not the Vicar of Christ? Certainly the first Pope had his problems with courage, although he came back to Rome and accepted his fate. We are all human and we can forgive. But, even if we can understand as a normal, human reaction Pacelli's refusal to risk his own life, we need not canonize him and elevate cowardice or stupidity to the status of virtues."

That unexpected outburst left the group very quiet. We desperately needed Dottor Twisdale. I feared to nudge the *monsignore* from *L'Osservatore Romano* again lest he ask another idiotic question. The moment for an ending was once more lost as *Der Spiegel* asked: "Has His Holiness any comments on the scandals that have occurred in the Mexican training camps of the crusade?"

I remind you that in those first few weeks of the crusade we had knowledge of only one rather small incident: a Chilean assistant director of a camp had absconded with about $12,000 in cash. That sort of thing is to be expected in any large-scale enterprise. But the question was a joltingly curious one, for $12,000 seemed too small a matter for the attention of *Der Spiegel.* According to me, both Francesco and I realized at the same instant why Dottor

Twisdale had flown off in such a rush the previous afternoon. I also understood why the *dottore* had said nothing to Francesco—after all, I, too, was now keeping secrets from *il Papa*—but I could not help wishing that the *dottore* had confided in someone.

"Scandals?" Papa Francesco responded suspiciously. "We have no knowledge of any scandals."

The man from *Der Spiegel* passed up to *il Papa* a small packet of photographs of young men and women, photographs which can best be described as lewd. "Holiness, these were taken at the training camp in the Yucatan. I do not wish to offend, but these pictures will be appearing in newspapers and magazines during the next few days." (We could all guess which magazine would publish them first.)

Francesco glanced at the pictures, then threw them onto the marble floor of the terrace. His face had flushed very red and his voice was almost shrill. "We do not look at such filth, Mein Herr. Nor shall we be a part of any scandal that you and your editors may manufacture to sell magazines. Your camera is as filthy as your mind."

Il Papa's voice became even louder. "You would like to bring down these reforms into the stink of the outhouse where you belong. We shall not give in. We have an assurance that the gates of hell shall not prevail against us. We have nothing to fear from lascivious journalism."

Trembling with rage, Francesco marched off the terrace into the *casina*. The reporters waited respectfully for a few moments, then most of them broke into a trot to return to the press office in the Piazza Pio XII and telephone in their stories.

By the time I overtook *il Papa* he was in his studio in the *casina,* having what can only be described as a temper tantrum. Signora Falconi wisely called the papal physician before joining me in attempting to calm Francesco. It was difficult, for he wanted immediate information, and we learned that the abbot had preceded Dottor Twisdale to Mexico.

It took our switchboard a full hour to contact Martìn in Mexico City, and that gave the physician enough time to give Francesco a mild sedative. The cardinal had just returned from the Yucatan and was able to give us the complete story. We are all subject to temptation and on occasion we all fall—which is why the Church stresses the importance of the sacrament of penance. When one collects together several hundred physically healthy young men and women, inevitably there will be some illicit sex play. It seems that in this instance about six young men and women in the Yucatan camp thought that an orgy provided a proper way to celebrate a Sabbath afternoon, and, as fortune would have it, one of the participants had a Polaroid camera. The pictures fell into the wrong hands and were swiftly sold. *Der Spiegel* played up the story as did communist newspapers such as *L'Unita* and *Il Manifesto* in Italy, but on the whole we received rather sympathetic coverage. Dottor Twisdale's being in Mexico to talk to reporters undoubtedly helped.

Our second brush with scandal was far more painful. It came only a few days later, on the Saturday before Holy Week. Dottor Twisdale stopped at my apartment in the San Calisto shortly before seven-thirty in the morning. I have found early morning visits to be bad omens, and this augury quickly became reality. It was the abbot, the *dottore* haltingly explained. A friendly Italian journalist had passed on information that *Der Spiegel* was going to publish an article to the effect that, before becoming a priest, the abbot had had a lengthy homosexual relationship with an English businessman.

I scoffed, of course, but the *dottore* said that the magazine had interviewed the Englishman, now living in New York and a member of one of those "gay rights" groups. He confirmed the story, claimed that the abbot was still a homosexual, and urged him to "come out of the closet."

"They seem to have the real goods, Eminence," the *dottore* said. "I heard about this yesterday and I've spent hours on the phone with people I trust in New York, Paris, and Frankfurt. The worst part is that *Der Spiegel* will claim that the abbot recently had a homosexual liaison with a young Italian actor in Trastevere, and they'll imply that was only one out of many."

I was aghast. In retrospect I realize that I should have been more concerned about the abbot's soul, but it was Francesco who monopolized my mind. This news would crush him; it might even kill him. As I have told, he and the abbot had built a very close relationship based on mutual trust, understanding, admiration, and even affection. I was never on especially warm terms with the abbot, but I could readily comprehend why Francesco was attracted to his genius. I greatly respected his ability as a practical administrator and I had grown more understanding of his efforts to find God through oriental mysticism.

There was nothing to do but confront *il Papa* with the news. I sent the *dottore* ahead to make arrangements with Signora Falconi for an immediate interview and also to allow me a few moments to collect my thoughts and, as you say, order my priorities. Francesco listened to Dottor Twisdale tell his story. (I was a coward, I confess it; I let the *dottore* break the evil tidings.) Francesco said nothing, but what little color he had, drained from his cheeks, and his eyes narrowed to mere slits.

When the *dottore* finished, we sat in silence for several minutes. When Papa Francesco first spoke, it was in an attempt to find an escape. "You know," he said, "in American politics no decent reporter would write a story about a public official's sexual irregularities unless they were carried on in public, became a matter of public record through an arrest or law suit, or were directly relevant to some problem of public policy. And if any reporter did write such a story, no self-respecting editor would publish it."

"This is Europe, Holiness," I replied. "Neither the intellectual nor ethical standards of journalism are as high as in the United States. What can we do to protect the abbot?"

"We have to protect the Church first." He said it heavily, almost sighed it.

"The Church has survived scandals since Judas," I argued. "She does not need the same protection as a vulnerable human being. Besides, whatever his weakness—and we should not prejudge the facts—the abbot is a force for great good within the Church. I have some friends in Paris and perhaps Dottor Twisdale has more. . . ."

"If word of an effort to bury a story leaked out, we would look even worse."

"But it need not leak out, Holiness. Still, if you fear that, let us talk to Chelli or Pritchett; they are all men of experience and wisdom. They may have some good advice for us."

"No, the decision is mine alone. I brought the abbot here. I knew what the risks were. He is a man of honor; he told me about the Englishman before agreeing to run the crusade."

Francesco pushed a button on his desk and spoke into the telephone. "Elena, please ask the abbot to join us."

Within five minutes he stood before us, probably wearing the same plain, woolen habit as the night we first met. He had only two. As he accepted *il Papa*'s invitation to sit, I thought I could read in his eyes some premonition of what was to come. If my face was as contorted as Francesco's, we had supplied him with generous clues. The abbot listened wearily—he had returned from the Yucatan only the preceding morning—as Dottor Twisdale again recounted his story.

The abbot's first move was toward survival. He spoke quickly, nervously, the fire in his eyes burning brightly. "Perhaps, Holiness, we can start a counteraction. Some of our journalist friends might publish an article about how scandal-mongering magazines are hiring private detectives to spy on papal aides and bribing witnesses to create lurid stories. It might scare *Der Spiegel* off."

"We do not think so," Francesco replied quietly. "We have only one question, Robert." I had forgotten the abbot's Christian name; in the Vatican he was always called the abbot, or *l'abbate* by Italians. "You do not have to answer, but we must ask the question. Have you had any homosexual liaisons since coming to the Vatican?" I could sense the strength it took *il Papa* to force those words from his mouth.

The abbot paused, then said almost indistinctly, "Yes, Holiness. Like you, I seek God; like you, I fall."

Pain etched even deeper lines into Francesco's face. "Robert, you must be on the next plane back to the United States."

The abbot visibly flinched. He stood up, his eyes flashing their brightest, his voice strident with self-pity. "Have you no compassion, not just on me, but on those like me?"

Francesco sat in silence. The palms of his hands remained flat and steady on the top of his desk.

The abbot spoke again, more softly. His personal survival was receding in importance, and he began to return to his accustomed role of spiritual leader of monks. "You and I have fully confessed our faults to each other. Do you remember when you first came to us at the monastery? You were a broken man then, broken by your own failings, not those of others. You told me about a friend named Kasten and a hill in Korea; you also told me about your wife. Their deaths haunted you. Intellectually, you understood your feelings of guilt, but on an emotional level you did not understand, just as you do not understand now. For the sake of your own sanity—for the sake of your own soul—stop and 'feel' as well as think before you do this thing to us both."

Il Papa spoke heavily. "Then you were right, Robert; now you are wrong. I understand too much. Please go."

A mixture of anger, pity, and despair flashed across the abbot's face. His voice dropped still lower. " 'Taking the objective,' like a good marine cannot be the most important thing in your life. You have to sacrifice for real, live, individual people, not for abstract goals like honor or justice. Declan, Declan," he was whispering now, "because you love no one, you think you love God."

With that, the abbot turned on his heel and left. I believe he was crying, but I could not be certain. I was fighting my own tears too hard. They were welling up in me for the soul of *il Papa*—and, I admit it, for what I had done to him.

THIRTY-TWO

AS WAS ITS HABIT, Easter came and went that year. We were well prepared for the great feast itself but hardly for what happened after. *Ecco,* we persuaded Francesco to limit himself to two ceremonies outside of Vatican City. The most effective argument for this had been our reminder to him that people had been killed trying to touch him and that extreme care was still needed. He agreed reluctantly, and, he said, for the last time.

The first ceremonies took place on Holy Thursday evening at the Regina Coeli jail. To commemorate Christ's washing of his Apostles' feet before the Last Supper, *il Papa* washed the feet of a dozen prisoners. The jail itself was only a few steps from San Pietro, and security there and along the way was tight. No hysterical cure would have been taken seriously in that place.

The second ceremony was on Good Friday evening outside the *Colosseo*, where so many early Christians met violent deaths for their faith. Tradition gave us safety there, for the ritual is usually held on the Palatine Hill, near the ancient site of the Temple of Venus. The crowd was kept well back and most of them were slightly below *il Papa* as he carried a large wooden cross on his back and recited the Stations of the Cross. Our coming to and from the hill by helicopter further reduced danger of disorder. In sum, all went well, not a common outcome in Italy.

Francesco, however, took scarce comfort in that. The abbot's departure had torn away a large piece of *il Papa*'s soul; the wound ached even more because of the bitterly cruel, though perhaps not inaccurate, words at the end. It was not a thing that Francesco wanted to talk about—perhaps he could not. Not knowing what to say, I said nothing. But I could and did worry, for his mood was truly depressed. Even the warmth of the bright sun of the opening days of April did not cheer him. (He was usually a creature whose spirit flourished in bright sunshine, and flagged when the weather was dreary.)

His desk, usually a shambles, was now piled high with masses of unread papers and unfinished directives and memoranda. His ability to concentrate on work obviously weakened dramatically, and Signora Falconi shunted more and more things to me. She, too, had come to fear Fieschi's uncritical adulation.

One thing had changed, and I believe it was connected to the abbot's dismissal. A Pontiff, like the rest of us, can always turn to prayer when the world (or those of us in it) fail him. And Francesco began to spend much of his time in prayer. He prayed before, but how much I do not know; his schedule allowed him precious little time even to sleep. Now, however, while the papers were stacking up on his desk, he would often spend several hours kneeling in the private chapel in his apartment in the palazzo. Prayer was, of course, good, though I wished its cause were one of joy or hope rather than of grief.

Allora, the practical problem of finding a new director

of the crusade Francesco supposedly delegated to me. I began by soliciting much advice. By my standards, though not by Francesco's, I was moving rapidly. Yet he apparently took no interest in my search. It was a difficult task to find someone with the skill to manage, without the aid of an organized, experienced staff, such far-flung operations. It was even more difficult to find a Catholic who would not act in a sectarian fashion.

The solution to many problems began to appear on the morning of 6 April. Signora Falconi was smiling when I arrived at the palazzo. Before I went into *il Papa*'s studio, she whispered that she thought he was feeling much better. I could perceive that immediately. There was no joy on his face, but amid the pain was more tranquility than I had seen in many weeks.

Cardinal Pritchett, Monsignor Bonetti, and Dottor Twisdale were already with him. As soon as I entered the room, Francesco began to speak in a tone that was almost as brisk as that of his old self. He began by telling me that he had solved the problem of a director for the crusade. (He did not say a successor for the abbot.) It was a lady, Signora Maria Arrigada y Padilla, the wife of the Chilean senator who, after being incarcerated for more than a year by the Chilean junta, had died in jail in 1975. The *signora,* a distinguished economist, was living in exile in the United States, teaching at Stanford University. I did not know her, nor did Francesco, but she had the reputation of combining intellectual power and iron will. More important to *il Papa,* she would be a double symbol —a woman playing a leading role in the Church and a firm opponent of military dictators.

Next, Francesco asked me what day it was. I replied that it was Friday, the sixth of April.

"Which is two weeks after what day?" he asked.

I paused to calculate. "The twenty-fourth of March, the feast of the vigil of the Annunciation."

"And what else?"

"I do not know." I was genuinely perplexed.

"You are not a good Roman, Ugo," he said gently.

"You are right, Holiness. I am not a Roman at all, but an Italian. There is a difference."

"I am learning many things," he replied with a tinge of self-pity in his voice. Then he added: "It's also the anniversary of the Massacre. The celebration was postponed two weeks because it fell on Good Friday this year."

Then I recalled. On 23 March 1944, a group of partisans exploded a bomb alongside a contingent of SS troops marching along the Via Rasella, near the Piazza Barberini, killing 32 of the Germans. In retaliation, that night and the next day the Nazis gathered 335 people from Roman jails—criminals, suspected partisans, Italian soldiers, and Jews awaiting transportation to death camps. The Nazis put these people onto trucks, drove them to the Ardeantine area of caves and quarries southwest of the city, tied their hands behind their backs, and marched them into a cave to be executed a few at a time. Afterwards, the Huns poured lime over their bodies and tried to cover the site of the mass grave by collapsing the cave with explosives.

The Fosse, graves, are Roma's principal monument to the Resistance, although there is no evidence that more than a handful of the 335 victims were connected to the Resistance movement. You may remember that an American historian published a book on the Massacre and that Richard Burton starred in the movie made from it. The book and the movie charged that Papa Pio XII had had advance knowledge of the slaughter but had declined to intervene with the Germans to prevent it. According to me, that part of the story is not true. I am not at all certain that, *had* Papa Pacelli known, he would have intervened. He was not a man of courage. But, I believe that events ran too rapidly for him to have obtained what Francesco would have called hard intelligence about the Nazis' plans until the executions had been finished.

In any case, the Communists have always made much political capital out of their leadership of the Resistance —which, except in some parts of the north, was seldom much until after the Americans, British, or, at Bologna, the Poles had liberated an area. Then hundreds of men and even women would claim to have been heroically fighting the Nazis and Fascists. The Fascists, as Italians, understood, but I am sure that the Germans and the Allies must have been equally confused by these claims. We Italians have always been better at theater than at real life. It is no accident that we have written all the truly great operas.

What was my point? *Ecco,* I had to concede Francesco

that his appearance at the Fosse would make a nice touch. Privately the Communists and many other Italian political leaders knew of his attitude toward Papa Pacelli, although neither *L'Unita* nor *Il Manifesto* had published his uncharitable remarks at his press conference about Papa Pio. As a man himself wounded in wars against fascism and communism, Francesco's placing a wreath on the monument would symbolize for many Italians the "new Church." And, while there would be many reporters and full television coverage, there would not be large crowds present. In sum, I was delighted with the idea as were Cardinal Pritchett and Dottor Twisdale; Monsignor Bonetti lacked an opinion of his own.

In fact, all went well at the monument, very well. The day remained cloudless and cool. Monsignor Bonetti, Dottor Twisdale, and I rode in the closed limousine while Francesco stood in the open Mercedes. Our timing was excellent. With the morning rush hour finished, the streets were relatively free of machines—which means "crowded" by the standards of other cities—but there were still many people along the way to cheer and wave. Our escort of ten motorcycles experienced no difficulties.

At the monument itself, there were less than a hundred people if one does not count the newsmen, and most of those present were government officials. With the help of the ministers of defense and justice (the latter a solid Marxian socialist whose fifteen-year-old brother lay buried there), Francesco placed a wreath at the entrance to the monument, then led the people present in an Our Father and a Hail Mary for the repose of the souls of all the victims. Calling the people closer to him, Francesco gave them a short but eloquent plea that we all work and pray that never again would brothers murder each other. (The entire allocution took less than five minutes and was played in its entirety that night on our RAI television and in other countries as well.)

Francesco gave his blessing to the group and walked around touching hands with the people. Then we made a brief tour of the caves where the shootings had occurred and walked slowly through the monument itself—a man-made cave containing 335 tombs, each with the victim's name, birth date, and picture. Some of the tombs were empty because families had preferred that their loved ones be buried nearer to their homes. But most of the bodies, or what was left of them, were there—Jews, Catholics, atheists, agnostics, private soldiers, colonels, even generals, old men in their seventies, a fourteen-year-old boy, a priest, merchants, farm workers, lawyers, professors, students, artists, criminals, and possibly even a few saints. If ever there was a monument that eloquently cries out against war and slaughter, it is this simple collection of graves. There were no infelicitous incidents, no hysterics. This is the one place in Roma where people always conduct themselves with dignity.

We returned to the palazzo in time for a luncheon meeting with Fieschi, Gordenker, Pritchett, and Martìn to discuss the spiritual renewal. Before we were finished, Gordenker raised again the question of celibacy. (I knew he would and had dreaded the moment.) For his benefit, Fieschi rapidly recounted the recent history of developments within the Vatican. When he was finished, Francesco riffled through a *pratica*—I said that was an Italian file, did I not?—and produced a manuscript of about ten pages. "This is the outline of an encyclical that we once prepared," he commenced.

At that instant, however, Monsignor Candutti burst into the chamber with urgent news. There had been an attempted coup d'état in Spain. An apparently rather liberal group of army officers were trying to seize power in Madrid, and there were reports that the Basques were in full revolt and that Catalans in Barcelona were attacking the police. Everything was unclear at that point, but it seemed that Spain was on the brink of another bloody civil war. The one report that *was* clear was a list of policies promulgated by the liberal junta. It included "thorough revision" of the concordat with the Vatican as well as recognition of the necessity for "autonomous regions" within a single Spanish nation.

You can imagine that *il Papa*'s attention for the next few weeks was focused on Spain. The new junta gradually extended their authority over most of the country. While violence was seldom lacking, it slowly receded in intensity. This, as you recall, was also the moment when the Brazilian government announced that it was barring entry into the country by crusade members whom it labeled as "subversives paid by the rich to help rob the poor" and "sexual libertines preaching the dogma of Marxian socialism and Freudian hedonism." Francesco fumed in anger, but for the moment he told nothing in public.

April—March really, but *il Papa*'s demands and Chelli's health pushed back the schedule—was also the month for the audit of the Vatican's budget for the previous year. Despite the millions of dollars that *il Papa* had received from Signor Randall and other wealthy Americans and Germans, from the sale of Vatican art treasures, from the special Christmas collections around the world, and from that year's Peter's Pence, our accounts were not balanced. The costs of operating the Curia, our missionary efforts, and our normal charitable undertakings—not to mention reserves in case anyone took seriously Francesco's offer to help resettle the Palestinians—were eating our assets. Inflation in Italy had been rampant over the past decade—at first five percent, then ten, then for a few years fifteen, then twenty-four, and finally last year it had been running at more than thirty percent. Without doubt, we had to provide large salary increases for our staffs and to allocate much more money for everything—heat, light, gasoline, even writing paper.

Despite much stroking by Monsignor Candutti and our "observer" in New York, the United Nations had not yet supplied a single lira or responded in any official way to Francesco's request that it assume the financial burden of the crusade in Latin America. FAO, the Food and Agricultural Organization, was supplying technical assistance and even donating seed and fertilizer, although in small amounts.

For almost three weeks after the audience at the Fosse, life in the Vatican gradually returned to its normal level of chaos. Francesco slowly regained his ability to concentrate on work, though I believe his praying continued. His face bore the unmistakable lines of sorrow, but also, as I said, evidence of more inner peace, perhaps of acceptance.

Then, without warning, television and newspapers carried reports of yet another "miracle." Paolo Corsetti, the Socialist minister of defense and a noted antireligious Marxist, claimed that *il Papa* had miraculously cured him of cancer a month earlier at the Fosse. It seems that Corsetti had been suffering from Hodgkins Disease—cancer of the lymph glands—and after months of unsuccessful chemical and radiotherapy had been told by his physicians that his case was hopeless. The best thing to do was to suspend all treatment, which was itself painful for him to undergo, and prepare in peace for death. He could expect at most a few months, probably less. His placing the wreath at the Fosse was to be his last official act. His resignation was already drafted, though not yet submitted, because his colleagues in the party, being good Italian Socialists, had been unable to agree on a successor.

His story was that after being touched by Francesco at the Fosse, he had suddenly felt dramatically better. A few days later he visited his physician at the *policlinico* at the University of Roma for a thorough examination. After five days of tests, the physician informed him that there was absolutely no evidence of cancer. Unbelieving, the minister had flown to Zurich for a week at a Swiss clinic. The diagnosis remained the same: high blood pressure, a slightly enlarged heart, seven kilos overweight; all other tests, including those for Hodgkins Disease, were negative. The physician in charge informed the minister that had he not held in his hand the *pratica* containing months of laboratory reports from the *policlinico,* reports showing progressive victory by the disease, he would not have believed such a diagnosis had ever been made. Spontaneous remissions, he explained, were rare at his stage of the malady.

Even the intellectual *Corriere della Sera* treated the affair seriously. A spontaneous remission, the editors conceded, could have occurred, but why at that very moment? Could it not be argued that the coincidence was itself significant? Further, the minister was hardly an hysterical peasant. A former professor of jurisprudence, a noted anticlerical politician, a man accustomed to deal with presidents and prime ministers, he was not, at age fifty-seven, apt to be awed by *il Papa*'s charisma or to be swept away by religious fervor.

By 10 A.M., the piazza was filling with people. Television cameramen were swarming over the roof of San Pietro, with a satellite system ready to relay to the world Francesco's daily appearance at the window. Again *il Papa* was the center of international attention.

Fieschi was—you say beside himself?—beside himself

with elation. Even I found it difficult not to become emotional. Signora Falconi was the only one in our immediate group who remained cynical. Francesco himself was strangely tranquil. I do not know quite how to describe him. He was not only very different from the Declan Walsh of old, but also from the irascible, petulant Pontiff of previous weeks.

Only once did Francesco discuss this new "miracle" with me. I cannot recall the exact time—it was some weeks later—but I remember his precise words. "That was my sign. The frustrations, the obstacles, your good friends, all those problems were my temptations. What I felt I had to do to the abbot almost toppled me over the brink of despair. I prayed, Ugo, as I prayed only during my first weeks at the monastery. That gave me some strength, first enough to keep alive, then enough to keep functioning, but not yet enough to move ahead. Corsetti was my sign that we would prevail. It has given me the strength to continue to try to move this Holy Church."

I asked him if he believed, truly believed, that it was a miracle.

"Whether I have actually saved Corsetti's life, for however short a time, I do not know. I hope so. Each of us would like to be able to work an occasional miracle. That's a sign of our pride rather than our holiness. But there was a miracle there, of that I am certain. I was at the end of my strength," he explained. "I was fighting thoughts of suicide. Johnny Kasten—whom you don't know—Kate, and the abbot were crying out to me, and so were those tortured souls to whom the Church has been so unjust. I was able to get to sleep at night only by pretending that I was back in the monastery again. Then God spared Corsetti. He brought a man teetering on the edge of death back to life. Like the rest of us, that poor devil will have to walk over that edge some day. But I do not believe that it was an accident that he was spared at the moment that I was with him and at a time when my own faith—it had never been robust, as you know, Ugo—had almost completely ebbed. I was not the miracle worker, but the one on whom the miracle was worked. Now I can go on."

And, of course, Francesco did go on. With his vigor and his faith restored, he was now living on four hours' sleep at night with a siesta of only thirty minutes. He was in his chapel before five in the morning, at his desk before six. Only occasionally would he walk in the gardens to meditate, formulate new ideas, read reports, and meditate again. Only Papa Paolo VI ever maintained such a regimen, and like Papa Paolo, Francesco became enmeshed in every detail of the life of the Church.

Let me give you one example, that of an Australian Jesuit who was "the person responsible for" the English-language edition of *L'Osservatore Romano*. It seems that there had been a death in the Jesuit's family and he had asked the editor-in-chief's permission to return to Australia for two weeks. Signor Bobbio had referred the request to the palazzo, with the notation that the Jesuit was the editor of the English-language edition. Francesco approved the request but struck through, with a fine black pen, Bobbio's description of the Jesuit and added in the margin: "person responsible for," followed by his own initials. (I assume that you are of accord that such things were a criminal waste of *il Papa*'s time and energy, but that is not the point of my story.)

In sum, Francesco, even more than Paolo VI, was translating the Church into the province of one man. Papa Paolo, at least, had shared power with his assistant Giovanni Benelli. He was a tough, independent man on whom Papa Paolo could rely totally. Nevertheless, he was not Papa Paolo's unquestioning slave, his corpse, in the sense that Fieschi now was for Francesco. Francesco still consulted with me, and with Cardinals Pritchett, Martìn, and Rauch—seldom, it pleases me to say, with Gordenker and never with Bisset—but all decisions were completely his. Rarely did a paper clip move in a curial department without Francesco's knowledge—*ecco,* or even, it seemed, without his consent. That was something that my brother Bisset did not realize.

I must recount something else of which you are partly aware. Earlier I mentioned Francesco's daily audiences from the window in the palazzo. Now he complicated affairs by insisting that the weekly audiences be held in the center of the area in front of the basilica, in the piazza itself. Erecting the equipment posed no problem, for many ceremonies are held there. The problem was the crowds. Now, after this newest and greatest "miracle," we were inundated by people. We needed several hundred police to prevent the crowds from touching *il Papa.* It was most difficult and it was most expensive. Francesco knew, but he insisted.

I have told you that he had needed the reassurance of popular acclaim. To some extent, he still did, but with the revival of his spirit and the strengthening of his aura of holiness, another important need arose: to share his gift with others. His blessing, even his look, was significant to people. Despite his constant labor, he was developing a visible serenity that strengthened the faith of others, and he realized that fact. He radiated not the secular confidence that Declan Walsh had possessed, but faith that his mission was endowed with divine grace and a calm acceptance of God's will in the fate of that mission.

From the start, LaTorre and the traditionalists had interpreted Francesco's concern for social justice as basically secular in that it had been, despite his rationalizations to himself and others, actually an end in itself. At the time, I fought that interpretation, but, as I await death, I am sufficiently removed to admit that LaTorre had been more correct than I. At the time of which I now speak, however, Francesco's concern for justice and peace, while no less passionate, was truly becoming a means toward a divine end. Once again Francesco had been touched by God's finger.

Even then I could see some of this, and I rejoiced in it. But I was still troubled by long-range spiritual concerns as well as by more practical and immediate worries. All my efforts at shielding Francesco had been wasted. Fieschi might be pleased that the world was finally recognizing the charisma of *il Papa,* but I lived in dread that a new "miracle" would convert a crowd into a stampeding mob.

THIRTY-THREE

IT WAS IN MAY, on another of those gorgeous days that Romans race to enjoy before the oppressive summer heat attacks the city—but why does a cold, old man think of the warmth of a spring day? I wander.

I began to describe that lovely day during the new

phase of Francesco's papacy. It is difficult to put a name to that chapter; if we christen the stage that started after our return from Latin America or Warsaw as triumphant, I would describe this third phase as apocalyptic. Francesco was sometimes now, all in one, Giovanni the Baptist, San Giovanni of the Book of Revelations, and even, on occasion, Savonarola. He was no longer the shrewd but moral political manipulator using a charismatic—that word does not please me, but here it is good—personality to move people. Rather his was the strident voice of repentance as well as the soft call for love and social justice. His message was clear and consistent. Yet there was a contradiction in that he retained the inner tranquility of which I spoke. He could easily stir emotions in others—and his voice could shout and his eyes flash—but within he remained, according to me, calm, accepting. What I saw, more and more, was outward fire, inward serenity.

Allora, Francesco had invited me that morning to walk the gardens with him before lunch, and we were both enjoying the sun. "We do not see how we can let them do it," he suddenly said aloud, even though neither of us had spoken a word for the previous five minutes. "We simply cannot."

"Cannot do what?" I asked.

Francesco looked at me as if I were a cretin. "Fight another war. The error came in the early Church when its fathers made a false peace with Rome and allowed Christians to serve in the legions. The only way not to have war is not to have armed forces. The Quakers have been right all along on this. The Church must make pacifism an integral part of its moral teaching."

I said nothing, but I must have looked dumbfounded because Francesco patted my shoulder and told, "But it's really the only way when you stop and think about it. Human life is sacred. How can it be moral for mass armies to kill each other as well as innocent civilians? Or for Christians to join those armies? Christ was a pacifist. He preached pacifism, and he practiced it in the Garden of Gethsemane and on Calvary. There is simply no way you can love your neighbor and then go about preparing to murder him."

"But what about our ancient Catholic moral and philosophic tradition of 'just war'?" I was groping for ideas to slow him down.

"How can there be 'just murder'? But don't worry; we need not shake the magisterium of the Church—not any more than we have already. It will be sufficient for us to say that modern weapons, conventional, nuclear, and biological, require a whole new way of looking at the moral problems of war. We must not only condemn war but categorically forbid all Catholics—yes, all humans—to participate." *Il Papa* placed both hands on my shoulders and held me not a half meter from his face. "Ugo, we must do this thing. We must."

Francesco's eyes were wide apart, staring straight through me, aimed at me but focusing through my skull on an imaginary object behind me. I confess it gave me an eerie feeling. I needed time to think.

"But what would happen, Holiness, if only Catholics or Christians refused military service? Within a decade the world would be ruled by atheists, Communists, and Fascists."

"That is not the important thing. The inner life of faith and morality can remain, while the outer political order changes. What matters is that we love one another and practice that love."

"But would not an oppressive government violate the sanctity of human life by murder and torture? And might it not force Christians into military service?"

"Why do you assume that good will be conquered by evil? Why do you assume that the teachings of the Gospel will always fall on barren ground? By putting into practice the word of God we can change the world. And we must change that world or it will perish, and our children along with it."

I said nothing. There was a certain truth in his words, although the full truth was more complex. The early fathers of the Church had come to understand that pacificism was an ideal, but that it could be only an ideal in the real world. Performing one of the great historic functions of the Church, to mediate between God and man, they sowed the seeds for what became in the hands of more systematic theologians the doctrine of just war. That is, it is morally legitimate for Christians to wage war when their cause is just, and thus for Christians to serve in the armed forces, even in times of peace, so that a nation might have the means to protect or foster its just aims. That two Christians from opposing nations might each view his own country's cause as just was a fact, created by human fallibility, with which we would have to live.

Now, my dilemma was whether to unravel the long theological and philosophical defenses of this doctrine of selective pacificism or to wait. I had learned that usually the most effective way to guide Francesco was not to interrupt when he was first expressing enthusiasm for an idea, but to listen, indicate some skepticism, think about the problems, and then, when he himself brought it up again, to try to rebut his arguments. Lacking more positive thoughts on how to cope with the situation, I followed a temporary tactic of silent listening.

"Ugo, we want this to be our first encyclical from the new—no, the old Holy See."

"Holiness?" I was rapidly returning to my original state of shock.

"We are now convinced that the only way to reform the Church is to return to the simplicity of Christ and His Apostles. We must abolish the Curia, sell our treasury, allow our buildings to be used as museums and these gardens as a public park for the people of Rome. We shall live simply and in poverty, but in Jerusalem. That move will symbolize our return to the spiritual values of the Gospels and our renunciation of the material values that both ancient and modern Rome signify."

Again I kept silence. I could think of nothing to tell. But Francesco could read my thoughts. "We are not mad, old friend. We are beginning to see things clearly for the first time. We cannot live here in a palace or even a villa, sit on a throne, wear a jeweled crown, drink your marvelous wine, and preach from the largest, gaudiest cathedral in the world and still convince mankind to abandon the values of mammon.

"A few weeks ago," he went on, "when we were wallowing in self-pity over our failure to lead the people of God effectively, we remembered the two words that the Marine Corp- uses to summarize all of its precepts of leadership: Follow me. That is also what Christ said: 'Come, follow me.' How can we live like a Roman emperor while asking the people of God to take up the cross?"

"But think of the good that the Church has done over the centuries," I protested, "and with its wealth and organization intact can continue to do—the crusade, for example."

"The Church does good, Ugo, less often than we would like to believe but more often than we are given credit for in this world. At the same time, however, we take the pressure off others to do more good than we ourselves can. The world suffers a net loss, at least in modern times, because of our organization and wealth and charity. We grant you that we may again have to accept the role of the voice crying out in the wilderness, but no one has seriously listened to us on questions of justice and peace for some centuries. We do not risk a great deal except as measured in material terms."

I could only shake my head in disbelief. A thousand objections arrived at once, but I could not find the words in English or Italian to express them. *Allora,* I also doubted that even the most eloquently phrased arguments would have been heard that day. Thus I followed my strategy of passivity and silence.

Francesco did give some warnings before he struck. During the next few weeks he talked privately with diplomats from most of the western world, the Soviet Union, and even China. I was present on several occasions; Monsignor Candutti bravely endured them all. *Il Papa* pleaded with each of them for an end to the armaments race and begged for diversion of more resources from the developed to the developing countries, especially to those that were suffering most from the worldwide drought. He reminded the diplomats of the basic immorality of modern war, but, according to me, none of them perceived the admonition as more than the broad and general piety that everyone had been preaching since the finish of World War II. Certainly in later discussions with Candutti none of them seemed aware of Francesco's conversion to pacifism.

In sum, the discussions had no apparent effect on the foreign policies of the great powers. Despite his newly found serenity, Francesco was not yet able to take defeat easily. To be ready to accept the will of God, after all, is not quite the same as readiness to bow to the will of man.

In several of his homilies at daily general audiences, he posed the question of whether, given the inevitable mass slaughter that would accompany a modern war, a Christian could in good conscience participate in such a conflict. He offered no direct answer, but in the shadowy world within the Vatican walls, the mere fact that he would pose the question in public was of great moment. No one in the Curia who talked to me had serious doubts about how Francesco would himself respond, but most of us thought that the question would remain rhetorical.

A number of newsmen who were close—how do you say?—"Pope-watchers?"—dimly understood what was happening. Their writings should also have given fair warning to the nations of the world, but their reports were so hedged with saving clauses that they were easy to disregard. We received no official responses beyond the usual polite diplomatic nothings, not even indications of strong interest in pursuing what *il Papa* had in mind. Francesco was being ignored, and that served as a goad.

I was with *il Papa* when, two weeks after the completion of the diplomatic talks, Candutti presented his negative report. It was late afternoon, and we were seated on a bench deep in the gardens, enjoying espresso in the cool shade.

"Very well," Francesco snapped, "many have been called and none has chosen. We shall soon hear weeping and wailing and gnashing of teeth." Declan Walsh would have told that as a mildly sacrilegious joke. Papa Francesco meant it literally.

At Francesco's request, Cardinal Pritchett dropped hints to some of his friends that the Pontiff would welcome an opportunity to return to the United States to present an important discourse. Within a few weeks, Cardinal Heegan, the archbishop of New York, flew to Roma as the emissary of two institutions, Catholic University in Washington and Princeton University, which is located fifty miles from New York City in that horrible sludge pot called New Jersey. The two universities wished to honor His Holiness with special awards for his efforts to preserve peace and promote justice. Francesco accepted both invitations, and I accompanied Heegan to Fiumicino to impress on him the necessity for stringent security measures to protect the Pontiff from thrill-seekers, religious fanatics, and those unfortunate beings who wanted cures for real and imagined illnesses.

I shall not bore you with the details of the voyage. Going by helicopter from Vatican City to the airport would have been the intelligent thing to do, but we could not persuade Francesco. Several times before arriving at the *autostrada* on the outskirts of Roma we were in peril of killing some of the cheering Romans who tried to run out to touch *il Papa.*

I used the hours crossing the Atlantic to try to convince Francesco that, as with birth control, celibacy, and all the other specific problems, it would be wisest for him to move very slowly on the issue of pacificism, if for no other reason than its enormous complexity and its potential impact on every nation in the world. I used the analogy of the gradual, case-by-case development of the common law of England and the United States, but at that he only smiled. Indeed, that smile was the most positive reaction I received. Candutti, who was with us much of the time, also pleaded with *il Papa,* but to no avail. The most we, together, could wring was a promise to weigh our views. When we returned to our seats just prior to landing, Candutti was near tears.

We arrived in New York before noon on a day in early June. The cardinal archbishop had delivered my message well, for we were smothered with a blanket of security as thick as Bologna's winter fog. Our plane parked in a United Air Lines hangar. After greetings from assorted civil and clerical officials, we were whisked off by helicopter—much to Francesco's annoyance—to Princeton, landing in an orchard behind the president's house. We went inside for a light lunch with the boyish president—he was very intelligent but also very nervous—his family, and several university officials. Then we were again taken by helicopter to a giant, domed auditorium on the edge of the campus. It comfortably seats, I was told, 12,000 people, but today at least 25,000 were crowded inside and more than that number stood outside, hoping for a glimpse of *il Papa.* Francesco would have pleased them, but the cordons of state police—there must have been several hundred—took us quickly inside.

When the presentation had been made and appropriate speeches delivered—they were succinct and to the point, a talent you Americans display that Italians find amazing—Papa Francesco launched into the heart of his allocution. I did not know what he was going to say, although I had my fears. He had written the oration himself; not even Monsignor Cavanaugh had been consulted. I am certain that Monsignor Candutti knew nothing of its content. Here, I read you:

> We have all heard too many speeches against war. Every decent person appears to be appalled at the prospect of the use of modern weapons. But their use is as likely today as in any time in the past. The time is long gone for general condemnation of mass slaughter. We must be more specific. We must return to the teachings of Christ in this regard as well as in others. We must return to pacifism as the moral stance of the true Christian; we must reject violence, especially mass violence, and embrace love and trust. The injunctions to love our neighbor and to turn the other cheek are not compatible with red telephones that can trigger hydrogen-tipped missiles or germ warfare.
>
> In the past, before the horrors of modern weapons were known, some theologians differentiated between just and unjust wars. We concede that some wars may be more immoral than others. But the least immoral war fought with modern weapons remains an abomination before God and before man. We do not understand how anyone professing the Christian faith—and though we know less about them, the other great religions of the world that join us in respecting the sanctity of human life—we do not know how any moral man or woman can participate in modern war without damning his or her immortal soul. Further, we do not understand how such a person can take part in preparations for holocaust by serving in the armed forces even in time of peace.
>
> We call out for peace now just as we have called out for peace before the United Nations, before the Arabs and the Israelis, and, privately, before the diplomats of every major nation on this planet. We call out for peace again. But now we call out not only to governments; we call out directly to you, to the peo-

ple, especially to the young men whose souls as well as bodies war would most searingly condemn. We call for a return to Christ's pacifism. Without armies, governments have no alternatives to peace. We can be certain that old men will not risk their own lives or property.

My message to you is old: Love thy neighbor. Do not kill him; do not make ready to kill him. Love, trust in God's mercy. Let us pray as did St. Francis:

> Make me a channel of Your peace, O Lord.
> Where there is hatred let me sow love,
> Where there is injury, pardon,
> And where there is doubt, faith. . . .
> For it is in giving that we receive;
> It is in pardoning that we are pardoned;
> And it is in dying that we are born to eternal life.

There was silence when Francesco stopped. He gave his blessing and walked down from the podium. As at the United Nations, people hesitated to applaud a prayer. Besides, according to me, most of the people there were in a state of shock. The young president could barely say a word as he ushered us through the lines of police to the helicopter.

The next day, diplomatic sources around the world would insist that the Pontiff had been misquoted. The fact that the allocution had been broadcast on television, taped, and rebroadcast would, for the purposes of this explanation, be irrelevant. The actual diplomatic reaction was much more plainspoken. The messages that Candutti began to receive within hours of the address were a mixture of enraged protests and incredulous anger.

Nor was that sort of response forthcoming only from government officials. On the way back to New York, Cardinal Heegan expressed grave misgivings to Candutti; on the flight to Washington, the cardinal and two of his bishops cornered Candutti in the rear of the aircraft and angrily insisted that he persuade *il Papa* to speak more softly of the big stick. At the residence of the cardinal archbishop of Washington, while Francesco endured the usual rituals of ring-kissing and hand-shaking with hundreds of clergy and governmental officials, several bishops and two senators attempted to closet Candutti, speaking, if anything, in even stronger terms than had Heegan. Interestingly, while I was present, no one directly broached the matter with Francesco.

I was, however, not present the entire time. The cardinal archbishop of Washington had arranged a dinner with several other American cardinals and archbishops; I excused myself from attendance. We had been traveling or standing for more than twenty consecutive hours. Bed was an absolute necessity. Before retiring, however, I saw Francesco talk briefly with a strange looking young layman with long hair. Francesco was obviously giving the young man detailed instructions about something, and the cardinal archbishop, who was listening, was just as obviously frowning disapproval. I had some fear about what might be in Francesco's mind; he had said nothing to me nor, as far I knew, to anyone else in the papal party. But, I was too exhausted to do anything except leave it in the hands of God with a brief prayer.

Allora, the celebration at Catholic University began the next morning. Because of the huge crowds that were expected, the university used that mammoth but unfinished Shrine of the Immaculate Conception on the outskirts of the city. It is not an attractive edifice, but some 25,000 people could be accommodated within. There Francesco continued to press his attack. I know you remember those crowds and the millions who heard him on television—perhaps hundreds of millions, when you consider how his allocution was relayed and replayed around the world. He stood there sounding like Giovanni the Baptist, telling the world and especially his own nation to repent. It was a long oration for Francesco, and it stung an unprepared audience expecting sweet nostalgia from a returned exile.

"Yesterday," Francesco began softly, "we spoke of peace. We questioned the possibility of reconciling Christianity not only with use of the horrible instruments of modern war, but also with military service itself, with the training necessary to use such weapons. We repeat those questions. We ask you to repeat them time and again to yourselves. But if we spoke mostly of peace yesterday, today we speak mostly of justice."

His voice became more strident as he urged his people to abandon material values, to reverse their unjust consumption of the earth's riches. Americans, he pointed out, make up only five percent of the world's population but each year they consume almost half the world's production of natural resources. The wealth of individual groups of Americans was incredible to most of the people of the world. While most people in developing countries were poor, and millions thought themselves fortunate to have shacks to shelter them from the weather, millions of Americans enjoyed lavish luxuries—*several* automobiles and *several* homes. While millions of people in Asia and Africa teetered on the brink of starvation, Americans ate grain-fed beef and each year threw to their pets enough food to feed whole nations.

"What shall you say," he asked, "when you face your Creator and hear that dread question: Did you allow your fellow man to go hungry? What will you answer? You, as a nation, have helped others, probably more than any other country. But you have given from enormous wealth and offered only a pittance of that treasure. In the last ten years you have given less to combat hunger than you have spent in any one of those years for bombs and missiles. You know," he said harshly, "what Christ has promised to those who deny bread to their brothers and sisters."

Francesco then outlined several small but practical steps that each person and each family might take: to forego one meal out of the twenty-one each week and to donate the money saved to a special fund that the National Conference of Catholic Bishops would soon establish. If every Catholic family in the United States and Canada were to offer such small weekly sacrifices, the fund would collect almost $3 billion annually. Half that money would remain in the country to help the poor at home; the other half would go to the crusade to aid the poor and starving around the world. Francesco further explained that the bishops would help their people in this campaign against hunger by weaving the fast into the liturgy, perhaps by having special Masses at noon or in the evening to replace the normal meal with the Eucharistic meal.

These were small steps, he continued, a start not a finish. No one should think that doing these things fulfilled his obligation to love God with his whole heart and his neighbor as himself for the love of God. Much more had to be done.

"We bring a clear message," he summed up:

> "Dives, love your brother Lazarus. Share with him your plenty." Repent! Change your ways before it is too late. Share your wealth. God gave that wealth to all men in common. His word demands that you share it and that you stop consuming that wealth at a rate that prevents others from having their fair share of the goods we all need to survive. The word of God demands that you reorder your values, your entire system of values. The word of God demands that you stop making your principal objective the purchase of material goods. The word of God demands, instead, that you devote yourself to the pursuit of spiritual values, most especially to the love and welfare of your fellow man.
>
> The day of judgment is coming for each of us; for most of us sooner than we would like. Prepare yourselves. Before you go to sleep each night, ask yourselves what you have done this day for the least of these, Christ's brethren and your brothers and sisters in life and in death. As you mull over your account, recall Christ's warning that a little is not enough: "If you are lukewarm I shall vomit you out of my mouth."
>
> We call on you to repent, to reform, to recast your values, to give up the hollow trappings of materialism and accept in their place the true riches of the spirit. We call on you to make this change completely and to begin to make it now.
>
> It is not the Pope who asks these things of you. It is not the Catholic church. It is the demand of the holy justice of God himself. Remember the teaching of St. Ambrose: "You are not making a gift to the poor man . . . you are returning what is his. . . . The earth belongs to all, not to the rich." Share, I tell you. Share! Practice God's justice now, that you may obtain His mercy later.

These words were pure fire and brimstone mixed with a brand of modern Christian socialism, perhaps even communism, and delivered in a haranguing voice that was very unlike the quiet, almost mocking tone that Declan Walsh or even the earlier Papa Francesco had habitually used in private.

The three archbishops and two bishops whose faces I could see were struck with amazement at Francesco's specific requests—and, according to me, at his arithmetic. *Il Papa* was supposed to speak in abstract generalities about love and duty, but not to outline specific plans, set timetables, and discuss exact numbers of dollars. If I knew my brother Fieschi, he would soon be riding the backs of the bishops, first demanding money for *il Papa,* then demanding a strict accounting of how they had helped the hungry of Canada and the United States. Francesco had found the jugular of money for the crusade—more than a billion U.S. dollars a year would satisfy even Chelli of our solvency.

Ecco, Francesco was not yet finished. He continued to speak, but in softer tones:

> I tell you to repent, to reform, but not to do so with sadness. You are not casting away the better for the worse. Share with joy, for you are throwing away the least for the best. "Come to me. My burden is sweet; my yoke is light," the Lord told us. Come to Him in joy. Spread his Gospel by your deeds, by your love. Let the world know that we are Christians by our love.

Francesco motioned to the long-haired young man whom I had seen the previous evening at the archbishop's residence. He was sitting among the hierarchy inside the altar rail, a guitar on his lap and a microphone a meter or two in front of him. He stood up rapidly and began to sound his guitar and sing—how do you call it?—a folk hymn popular with young people in your American Church. Liturgy with guitar and folk music is not pleasing to me; I prefer Gregorian chant. *Ebbene,* all tastes are tastes. But I wander. Despite his hair, this young man sang in a beautiful tenor voice.

> When Christ came to call did you hear? did you hear?

When Christ came to call did you hear?
The creed and the color and the name don't matter.
Do you hear? Do you hear?

I was hungry and thirsty, were you there? were you there?
I was hungry and thirsty, were you there?
And the creed and the color and the name don't matter.
Do you hear? Do you hear?

I was cold, I was naked, were you there? were you there?
I was cold, I was naked, were you there?
And the creed and the color and the name don't matter.
Do you hear? Do you hear?

The chant continued with more verses of the same theme. By the second stanza the students in the audience and even the younger priests and nuns were singing. By the end, practically everyone, including our solemn bishops, archbishops, and cardinals had joined. At the last strums of the guitar, Francesco spread his arms and gave his benediction: "Repent your sins. Reject material values. Go in peace, and in love, and in joy to serve the Lord by serving His children, your brothers and sisters." Then, he made the sign of the cross over the audience: "May the Almighty God bless you, the Father, the Son, and the Holy Spirit."

We were fortunate to leave the shrine alive. The audience, an American audience heavily flavored with priests and nuns, became as wild as any crowd that I have seen in Latin America and even Italy. To touch Papa Francesco was all they wanted. It was a stampede to rival any in a cinema western. The guards and police were completely taken by surprise—I noted that some of them had been singing as fervently as the audience. A tragedy might have happened had not our good bishops possessed the presence of mind to join hands behind the altar rail and form a line between the mob and *il Papa.* (I pray I do not offend against charity, but that was the only time that I ever saw our bishops act unanimously for the good of

Holy Mother Church.) Even their ample girths—I am not unique among the hierarchy—were wavering when, after a hurried whisper from Francesco, the rector of the university announced over the shrine's loudspeaker that *il Papa* would bless each person individually, if only the people would form orderly lines leading to the altar rail.

It went well, reasonably so, at least at the start. Francesco stood for a time—then someone brought him a chair—at the altar rail and touched the head of each person who came and knelt before him. I say it went well only at the start because within two hours the line was longer than when he had begun. Now the people were no longer students, clergy, faculty, and their guests, but the old and the sick, mostly black ones. We had not thought about the whole affair's being telecast; now thousands of people were descending on the shrine. One of the archbishop's assistants reported that police were halting cars a mile away, but people were abandoning their machines and walking, limping, or carrying their sick. Other thousands sat congealed in traffic, shouting and sounding horns in helpless frustration. It was a pitiful sight inside the shrine: the old, the crippled, the blind, the disfigured, the terminally ill. Francesco openly wept. I have seen the poor of India, but I had to wipe tears from my cheeks more than once, for only those hysterically ill could be hysterically cured.

Of course, I was greatly worried for *il Papa,* not only about what might happen were another "miracle" to occur, but about the possibility that the intense and prolonged emotional strain might cause another stroke. It was now two in the afternoon. He had neither eaten nor drunk anything since nine that morning when we left the archbishop's residence to go to the shrine. I knew he was still weary from the flight from Roma. Then it happened, as we all knew it would. Like an explosion, as Papa Francesco touched him, a young black man, a former soldier blinded in the Vietnam War, leaped up and shouted: "I can see! My God! I can see!"

Cardinal Heegan motioned toward the sacristy; twenty uniformed police came rushing out, and propelled Francesco quickly out of the rear of the shrine. They had moved in the proper time, for the crowd had again turned into a screaming mob, this time uncontrollable, shoving, pushing, and kicking each other, demanding to be next to touch *il Papa.* Had we not parked the helicopter close to the exit, Papa Francesco would have been crushed. As in the other instances, there were deaths. Two old people were trampled by the crazed mob.

Those of us in the helicopter were all shaking from our own close escape from death—all but Francesco, that is. At first he had been annoyed that the police had rushed him out of the shrine; then, once he understood the alternative risk to our safety, he sat in seeming calmness.

THIRTY-FOUR

We were very late for our state visit to your White House. At the planning for that meeting, no one had anticipated problems. Declan Walsh and your President Lawrence Fletcher, a staunch Methodist from Michigan, had been friendly for some years, though never close friends, starting when President Fletcher had been a senator and Declan Walsh had shown some interest in a political career. Both sides had looked forward to a pleasant talk, smiling photographs, and a bland joint statement of mutual desires to achieve justice and peace. Francesco's allocution at Princeton destroyed many of those anticipations.

Even during the official greeting and photographs on the White House lawn one could sense tension. When we followed the president—we being *il Papa,* Candutti, the American secretary of state, and I—into his oval studio, hostility replaced tension. Your president made an opening effort to avoid confrontation.

"I heard your talk on television this morning, Holiness. I'm glad you're out of politics." He laughed a bit more than necessary to underscore his attempt at wit.

"We spoke only the word of God," Papa Francesco responded stonily. "Our people must abandon the materialism that dominates their lives."

"Materialism? I don't know," President Fletcher mused. "What other people have given so generously to others? What other country has ever had a foreign aid program like ours in the forties and fifties? In what other nation have private citizens given so much to others? And what other country has been spat on so much by those who were helped?"

"No other nation in the world," Papa Francesco agreed. "But that is not our point. As a nation, Americans have been generous, but generosity is not enough. The acquisitive drive of western society has created many of the problems that American generosity soothes but cannot solve. Western nations are buying up the very food that poorer nations need, and we are doing so at prices that effectively deny poorer people a chance to eat. Almost as bad, the ideology of western society turns conspicuous consumption from a sin into a deity who commands his subjects both to deprive the poor of a chance to live and to ignore the cause of their plight."

"Without that acquisitiveness here and elsewhere in the western world," the president retorted, "we would not be in a position to help the starving in Africa."

"But without that acquisitiveness, Africa might not need so much help."

"Well, we never had any colonies in Africa. You should talk to the British, French, and Germans. Besides, acquisitiveness has no effect on climate," the president told, "and it is climate not materialism that causes shortages of food there today."

"Only in part," Papa Francesco answered. "Drought has reduced food supplies, but America still produces more than enough food to feed itself *and* Africa, if Americans did not insist on eating so luxuriously and wastefully."

"Perhaps," the secretary of state smoothly intervened, "His Holiness would be pleased to learn that we are about to negotiate a $100 million loan to West African countries so that they can buy grain."

Candutti played his role neatly by responding: "That is indeed good news, Mr. Secretary. His Holiness has also decided to use the first $50 million from the special fund he outlined this morning to purchase food as a gift to the people of Africa."

"That is most generous. I hope that you and I can confer closely and coordinate our actions, Your Excellency, so that we do not compete with each other and drive the price of food up."

"With pleasure, Mr. Secretary. I had planned to make the same request of you. That would be most helpful."

(I recount this conversation because it shows how two professional diplomats could make huge advances in a half dozen sentences, while two amateurs had succeeded only in antagonizing one another. The professionals had dealt not on an ideological level but on a practical one. They had attacked the problem of how we could act together, not how we could or could not agree on fundamentals of philosophy or theology.)

"Holiness," the president intervened again, even more ill at ease, "we have another immediate problem, one more permanent than a drought. I cannot tell you how seriously, how perilously, our government views the implications of your speech yesterday at Princeton."

Papa Francesco spoke quietly, too quietly for my nerves: "Again we spoke only Christ's message. We do not know how military service in the context of modern weaponry can be reconciled with the commands of the Gospel."

"But you've been a soldier in two wars, yourself. You know the Russians would occupy Western Europe in a couple of days if our armies folded up their tents and went to prayer meetings. Pretty soon, there'd be a foreigner of some sort sitting at this desk."

"We do not 'know' these things, Mr. President; we have more faith in God's goodness than to presume that disaster would strike us for obeying His word. But even if it should, Christ did not promise happiness in this world. It is the next world that is critical for a Christian. This world is only a testing ground. As for your point about our personal history, it is true that we have sinned; sinned, we like to believe, through thoughtlessness and ignorance, but sinned nevertheless. We have sought and are still seeking God's forgiveness. Our personal failures cannot serve as an excuse for condoning the sins of others."

The president appeared *stufato; ecco,* you say "exasperated"? I kept silence but I felt sympathy. Fortunately your secretary of state, who is a very shrewd man, made a new intervention.

"As I understand it, His Holiness has not issued any decree or formal statement that morally binds Catholics not to engage in military service."

"That is correct," Candutti put in. "His Holiness has not defined an article of faith or morals that completely binds all Catholics. He has only asked some serious questions. All Catholics—and one would hope, all men of good will—must ask themselves those same questions. On the basis of mature reflection and a rightly formed conscience, a Catholic may disagree with the answers His Holiness has suggested and pursue different courses of action, such as those permitted by the traditional distinctions between just and unjust wars. But no Catholic can merely ignore what he has said. More than that, barring some compelling command of conscience, a Catholic must follow the Pontiff's teaching."

"As of now," Papa Francesco added, "that is a correct statement of the binding force of our remarks. But that does not preclude our issuing a definitive decree that would bind all Catholics."

"What are you trying to do to us?" the president asked, his voice betraying both annoyance and incredulity.

"We are trying to preach the word of God. That is our mission. For this we came into the world." Then his voice softened. "Mr. President, we are neither so naive nor so arrogant as to think that we alone can change the world. Only God can do that. Still, we have a mission that you, because of our common religious heritage, can understand. We must preach the word of God, and on the subject of violence that word is clear, turn the other cheek, walk the extra mile, love your enemy. If you honestly believe that you cannot practice those commandments at this instant, can't you at least make a start? Adapt William Lloyd Garrison's policy toward emancipation and apply it here: Not immediate pacifism but pacifism immediately begun."

The president seemed confused, but the secretary of state swiftly took over. "That is a most interesting suggestion, Holiness. Perhaps Monsignor Candutti and I can explore it further in a less formal setting. If I may return to Africa for just a moment," the secretary said as he deftly moved us away from a perilous impasse, "I was hoping, Mr. President, although we did not have time to talk about it yesterday, that you might approve our doubling the sum we had agreed upon as a loan to the Africans, but disbursing part of it in Latin America in conjunction with the Pope's crusade in order to stimulate agricultural production there. That would have a long-range rather than an immediate effect on the Africans. A surplus in Latin America would both ease the Africans'

—and our—financial problems and, of course, make it easier in a few years for grain to be diverted to any needy part of the world."

"It would also help," Candutti added, "if the United States could prod the United Nations to consider the Pontiff's request to assume funding of the crusade in Latin America. Then we could devote more of our resources to Africa and ultimately to Asia, as well."

"I think we might be able to do both things," President Fletcher said.

I was not certain whether the secretary and the president had rehearsed this display, or whether it had spontaneously occurred to the secretary. One could see little by looking into the president's eyes, scrunched up as they were beneath his eyebrows. But if the two men had not rehearsed the dialogue, the president had a quicker mind than many reporters credited him, for he had swiftly pushed the king's pawn before the bishop.

It was a tempting gambit, offered with a gracious shrewdness: one gift to help the crusade, another to save the lives of millions on the verge of starvation. The price, because it was unspoken, even unhinted, could not trigger moral repudiation, but that price was nonetheless clear to all of us in the room: Papa Francesco's muting of his pacifist message and acceptance of a token move by the United States.

Francesco hesitated for a moment then responded with a certain cunning. He pretended not to understand the proffered bargain. "Mr. President, we are sure that God will remember this gift, although the people of this world may not. We ask, however, that you go further, that you consider our words and use your magnificent office to help us in persuading mankind to reject materialism and accept Christ's teaching against violence."

Candutti quickly stood up and reminded us that the helicopter was waiting and that our aircraft was scheduled to return to Roma that evening. His timing was superb.

On the trip back to Roma, Francesco said that he had suddenly realized why the crusade had been in such financial difficulty. Our vision had been cramped because our faith had been weak. Underestimating God's mercy and man's sense of justice, we had thought in terms of millions rather than of billions. Fieschi took up the refrain, assuring

Francesco that the Secretariat of State would begin co-ordinating efforts with the North American bishops moments after our tires touched the tarmac at Fiumicino. He was bubbling with ideas about how to integrate fasting into the liturgy.

After a few minutes' discussion, *il Papa* turned to Candutti. "In your discussions with the Americans be very careful. They will try to equate renewed efforts toward disarmament talks with the Russians with pacifism. We want to encourage those talks, but we cannot stop there. In fact," Francesco paused, "on second thought, it may be better for you to postpone talking to the Americans at all until we have visited more countries and preached our message. It may seem unfair to Americans to be the only country in the world we ask to accept pacifism."

Following that conversation, Candutti and I retired to the rear of the aircraft, he, I am sure, to pray at great length, I to sleep after a short prayer.

When we landed at Fiumicino outside of Roma the next morning, a group of reporters were standing in the Alitalia hangar near our waiting helicopter. A double line of police kept them away from us; several newsmen called out, and despite Candutti's pleas, Francesco walked to them and offered to answer a few questions.

"Is Your Holiness concerned about the new 'miracle' on this excursion?" *L'Unita* asked. It was not meant to be a pleasant question.

The Pontiff looked steadily at the reporter. "True miracles are worked in the hearts of men. Thus we seldom know when, or if, they occur. Even your dialectic is of little help."

"Is Your Holiness ordering Catholics to become conscientious objectors?" *Die Welt* asked.

"We are preaching God's word: Turn the other cheek; love thy enemy. 'Let him who has ears to hear, hear.' "

"But what about Catholics who are already in the armed forces?" *Il Tempo* asked.

"We do not see how, as a matter of morality, a promise to participate in fratricide can be binding."

"What specifically did Your Holiness have in mind when you talked in Washington about changing the American way of life?" the *Washington Post* inquired.

"We spoke in the United States, and used American

examples, although we included Canada in our statements. We were speaking generally, however, of modern society, American, European, Asian, communist and socialist as well as capitalist. Within the materialistic context of our planet, North Americans have been the most generous of all peoples. But we ask first for justice, then for generosity. We want to change the world's idea of justice and so to reorder its values. Conspicuous care must replace conspicuous consumption."

"Holiness, isn't that a tall order?" *Newsweek* intervened.

"We are aware of the immensity of the problem, but we have faith in God. Surely if that faith can move mountains, it can move men. We can point to several small but immediate gains. A weekly fast by more than fifty million Catholics in the United States and Canada will make more food available for the hungry. A billion dollars in additional annual contributions will allow us to save hundreds of thousands, perhaps millions, of lives each year. We intend to preach this same message all across Europe, in Japan, and in all the so-called developed countries, freeing additional food and additional money for the hungry. No man has a *moral right* to two slices of bread when his neighbor has none."

"You said there were several pieces of good news, Holiness," *Le Figaro* intervened.

"Yes, the second is that the President of the United States yesterday gave us his solemn promise to arrange a large loan for the drought-stricken nations of Africa and another loan or set of loans to stimulate agricultural production in Latin America, in cooperation with the crusade already in operation there. The latter will help prevent a reoccurrence of famine."

"How large would the loans be?" *Le Figaro* persisted.

"The president spoke of a total of $200 million, a pittance in terms of the total wealth of the United States, but another indication of the generosity of the American people and their universal concern for fellow humans."

Candutti looked at me in horror. Francesco had violated one of the cardinal rules of diplomacy by stealing the stage from a donor and one who would have to, as you say, mend some political fences before he could make good on his promises. On the other hand, according to me, Francesco had also neatly pinned the president to his part of the tacit bargain while he himself completely avoided making any commitment on pacifism. He had captured the king's pawn without moving the bishop. Candutti, however, remained unimpressed. As I have explained, he took the rules of conventional diplomacy very seriously.

Returning to the Vatican by car was impossible, according to the police. Even Francesco was by then too tired to argue, and we were taken by helicopter to the gardens. Francesco went on to his studio in the palazzo, but I collapsed in one of the bedrooms in the *casina,* exhausted and confused by Francesco's torrent of ideas and by God, Who seemed content to let His Vicar have his way.

The next day's general audience in the piazza listened to a blistering attack on pornography, "another symbol of modern man's worship of the flesh of the materialism of his culture." In particular *il Papa* lashed out against Italians and against Romans. "There is scarcely a newsstand in this supposedly Holy City which does not degrade women by prominently displaying magazines whose covers show naked lesbians or nude men and women engaged in indecent sexual acts. Adults stop to leer at these pieces of filth. Worse, young men are encouraged to look on women not as their equals before God but as objects to sate their lust. And, worst of all, little children cannot help but be influenced in their immediate actions and their moral values by such vulgar and lewd displays. Remember well Christ's warning against scandalizing children: 'It were better for that man that a millstone be tied around his neck and he be thrown into the sea.' "

That night, several groups of "Christian women" moved through the city overturning more than twenty news kiosks, burning six of them. A small but angry crowd of women in Padova stopped a truck delivering magazines, assaulted the driver, and burned his cargo, neglecting to remove them from the truck. The machine was a complete loss, and the driver was not much better off. There were similar incidents in Brescia and Bolzano.

The following day the Piazza di San Pietro was thronged with perhaps 150,000 people for the general audience. I suspect that the spectacle of a miracle-working, fire-spout-ing Pontiff had brought out more of the curious than the pious. Whatever their motivation, the audience heard Francesco denounce in very clear and very specific terms the "inhuman conduct of the military junta in Brazil. They have imprisoned then tortured men and women whose only crime has been to speak out against oppression. We join in spirit with those suffering from cruel denials of their rights as human beings. As a first step toward acceptance of its duty toward its citizens, we call on the government of Brazil to release immediately all of its political prisoners. We further ask that it schedule free elections in the very near future so that the people of that wounded country may express their legitimate preferences."

It would have been difficult for a civilized man to have quarreled with the substance of the message—except, perhaps, for the call for free elections. It was the tone of that message that disturbed me. His voice rang out above the piazza, offering a double quotation—Christ quoting the prophet Isaiah: " 'The Spirit of the Lord is upon me, because the Lord has anointed me; He has sent me to bring glad tidings to the lowly, to heal the brokenhearted, to proclaim liberty to the captives, and release to the prisoners. . . .' The cries of suffering from the torture chambers reach our ears. The stench of the jails clogs our nostrils. In the name of the God of justice, we can stay silent no longer."

Within twenty-four hours we received news of civil war in Brazil. Francesco listened to the reports without changing his expression. Immediately, however, he began to draft the text of his allocution for the next day's general audience. He condemned the violence and repeated his call for free elections.

Fieschi was with us when the first reports of the revolt came. Instantly he offered us his ponderously triumphant views. "This is the will of God, Holiness. You have used your power to raise up and pull down nations. This is the vengeance of God working His justice. We are His instruments."

Monsignor Candutti was clearly appalled. He walked out of the room and motioned for me to join him. I suggested we take a walk in the gardens.

"Eminence," he commenced, "I feel as if I have been living in a nightmare for the past weeks. I fear for my sanity. I cannot go on. *Il Papa* does not listen to me, and Cardinal Fieschi merely echoes his every word. Either they are not behaving like rational human beings or I am not."

I muttered something appropriately encouraging and Candutti went on: "The Pontiff leaps from topic to topic. Sometimes he speaks like the last chapters of the Gospel of St. John, or like John the Baptist would have, if the wild honey had been fermented. He can be both mystically vague and ominously threatening. You should listen to the screams that my office has been receiving from every western country about the speech on pacifism. The Americans are in a turmoil. They're not sure how many Catholics will stay in their armed forces. God knows the Italians and French need little encouragement to desert. Even the Communists are upset. We've had reports of desertions among Polish and Rumanian troops. This is sheer madness, Eminence, sheer madness!"

"A holy man often appears irrational," I told, "but that does not mean he is insane. Remember that rationality has to do with the most efficient way of achieving a certain set of goals. A pagan Roman would have thought the Christian martyrs irrational, but if their goal was happiness in the next life they were behaving rationally. I fear the problem is that you and Papa Francesco may not share precisely the same goals." Then I added, although the words came with great difficulty: "Nor, I fear, do I. He thinks he can bring the kingdom of God into this world within his lifetime."

"Then you do not think him insane?" Candutti asked.

"Unfortunately, *Eccellenza,* I do not know whether he is sane or not. I can only be sure of my own confusion. At one time," I said lightly, "I prayed that God would help him take on the attitudes of a religious leader and discard those of a secular statesman. I fear that I may have overdone it. Now my concern, like yours, is that he can walk on the safe side of that invisible line between religious leader and religious fanatic. He believes—perhaps 'accepts' better describes his own perception—that he has some sort of divine mission. I do not know if that is insanity or sainthood. Perhaps it is a bit of each. Insanity may be a necessary element of sainthood. For, according to me, saints do not make nice people. They are always too certain of themselves and of God."

It was plain that my own self-examination was not helping Candutti. "You may be right, Eminence, but there is no hope for it. I must resign."

"You have good reason," I conceded, "but have you considered who might replace you? Probably another man like Fieschi who would serve *il Papa* without doubt, without question, and without benefit to him or the Church."

Candutti was near tears. "Eminence, you do not know the cross you offer me—my own sanity."

I squeezed his arm. "God will give you strength, *Monsignore*. He is with us all days, and He knows our limitations. Remember that San Paolo promised that we shall not be tempted beyond our strength."

Candutti forced a smile, one of the few I had ever seen from him. "I wish St. Paul were here now."

"That," I told, "is precisely the problem. He may be."

THIRTY-FIVE

IT WAS IN LATE MAY that we had one of the dinners at the palazzo I earlier described. It was an evening I remember well; that night, for the first time in months, Francesco actively participated in the discussion. It was also memorable because his words would deeply disturb several traditionalists in the Curia. I was there as were Monsignori Cavanaugh, Zaleski, and—it was not unusual—Bonetti. Also present were a bright, young Irish bishop who was in Roma to pay his biennial homage to *il Papa*, several seminarians from the Ethiopian College, and two from the North American College.

I explained before, I believe, what a shattering of tradition these dinners represented. One who has not been inside the Vatican cannot understand the awful—I use that word in its proper sense; you do not say "full of awe," do you?—respect with which we treat the person of *il Papa*. To have even thought of dining with Papa Pio XI or Papa Pio XII would have been so full of exaggerated self-importance as to merit discussion with one's confessor.

That night, Francesco as usual ate very little and barely touched the wine. To accompany the principal plate -e had a magnificent Cabernet Sauvignon from your Mondavi vineyards. (Cardinal Heegan had brought us a case when he had come with invitations to Princeton and Catholic University.) The conversation flowed easily enough after the first hesitations. Monsignor Cavanaugh and I had learned from experience how to draw guests into conversation. Massimo's kitchen, Elio's serving, and the wine—we all helped. At dessert, one of the North American seminarians, a bit *prepotente*—you say "show off"?—of his learning in ecclesiastical history was giving us a lecture on Arianism. (You recall the troubles during the early Church over the mystery of the nature of Christ and the Trinity. In sum, Arian, a contemporary of Constantine in the fourth century, argued that Christ was not truly divine in the sense of being of the same substance as God the Father. The Council of Nicea condemned that view in 325 A.D., but the heresy lingered for many decades.)

After listening to the oration for at least ten minutes, Francesco interrupted: "We wonder what the young man Christ would have said about Arian."

"Holiness?" The seminarian gasped in shock.

"Would He have understood the basic questions?" Francesco asked.

"As God, He certainly understood everything," the seminarian riposted.

"As God, of course; but as man?"

"But we cannot separate Christ's human and divine natures and talk of Him as two persons. He was one person. The Council of Chalcedon settled that in 451."

"Two natures in one person, yes. But why not speak of Him as only gradually becoming aware—and not fully until after the Resurrection—of the divine part? Indeed, must we not? If we cannot, then doesn't the whole pattern of what we call Redemption become only playacting? Divine playacting, but still a farce?"

"Holiness?" Now it was the good Irish bishop who intervened.

"We know," Francesco nodded, "that the teaching of most—but not all—Catholic theologians is that Christ always knew what He was and that He always enjoyed the Beatific Vision, fully knew Himself as God. But that argument, while it maintains an internally consistent defense against Arianism, does so at the cost of making Good Friday a cruel charade."

"I do not understand, Holiness," our good bishop told.

"All right. A person who knew he was immortal, omnipotent, and so forth would also know that he could wipe out by a simple act of his will all pain or suffering, including his own. To an eternal, perfect being—one who knew himself to be such—giving up our kind of flawed human existence would be a minuscule sacrifice. In fact, it's hard to see how it would be a sacrifice at all if he could get it back anytime he wanted it—if he wanted it again. Besides, he could simply will not to suffer any pain at all."

"But we believe that he did not will to avoid the pain of a horrible death," the bishop insisted.

"Perhaps Christ did, perhaps he didn't. Certainly we would have to believe that He accepted the pain if we accept that He knew His divine as well as His human nature. But if He did know, He would also know that He was eternal; and three hours on a cross or thirty-three years on this earth would be less than a trillionth of a second to one who is eternal. Our point is that if Christ fully understood that He was God, His suffering was trivial in comparison to the pain that mere humans who are tortured feel, to what the Jews underwent at Auschwitz, or what a wounded soldier experiences when he fights on to help his comrades. The pain that one who knew He was God suffered on Calvary would be nothing to what a woman undergoes to bring her child into the world. Besides, if He fully knew He was God, Christ risked nothing."

"Risked nothing? I do not understand," the bishop muttered.

"Yes, risked nothing," Francesco said impatiently. "Look at it this way. When a man persuades himself to lay down his life for another or to risk his life for another, he is risking more than his life. He is risking *not* only being killed but worse, being horribly maimed—being blinded or terribly disfigured or being paralyzed, being doomed not to die immediately but to live on for many years, perhaps forty or fifty, in pain and loneliness, longing for the comfort of death. One who knows He is perfect and eternal need have no such fears. We can assure you from personal experience those fears are far worse than those of death itself."

"I admit I have never had such experiences," the bishop said.

"There's another risk, even more serious," Francesco continued.

"What is that, Holiness?"

"Every intelligent human has some doubts about an afterlife. We may believe. We may hope. And we surely may pray. But we cannot be absolutely certain that there is anything beyond the grave but cold blackness. If Christ knew Himself to be God He ran no risk whatever that there was nothing after death."

"Holiness, do you speak seriously?" the young seminarian asked. "Is that not heresy?"

"If *we* say it, it cannot be heresy," Papa Francesco answered. (Declan Walsh or an earlier Papa Francesco would have said that with a twinkle in his eye. This Papa Francesco spoke solemnly; yet he also spoke it in a gentle, thoughtful way, as if, all things considered, that power was a burden.)

The young seminarian seemed scandalized.

Francesco saw this reaction and softened his tone. "Look at St. Matthew. Granted it's an episodic, not a complete, account, but Christ is certainly not consistent over the years. Either He develops a different sense of His mission as time goes on—which means He did not fully understand that mission in the beginning—or He is schizophrenic. At one moment He's the fiery prophet of repentance, threatening the vengeance of God; then suddenly He's the tender prophet of God's love and mercy. At one point He comes to bring the sword, at another He says he who picks up the sword shall perish by the sword. I rather prefer His human side as confused; He was a pious young Jew driven by a divine force that He did not completely understand before His death—and in that ignorant human capacity He suffered as each of us would have suffered and subjectively risked as much as any one of us would have risked."

"Your Holiness seems to accept the views of certain modern theologians over those who are more traditional," our pious Irish bishop intervened. There was more than a hint of disapproval in his tone.

"Accept? No, we think not," Francesco said. "At least we are not sure. We faced this problem many years before we knew there were any theologians whose ideas fitted our own. Perhaps we now find this interpretation more comfortable than the older statements because if one accepts the traditional—which is not to say it is the orthodox or even the most reasonable—interpretation, then Christ and so His Vicar must speak with the clarity and the force of lightning. We—the institutional 'we' of the teaching authority of the Church—must always speak with absolute authority and absolute certainty and absolute finality. There is no room left for development, only application of predetermined rules to meet new circumstances. If, on the other hand, one accepts the kind of interpretation of which I have been speaking—that, as St. Paul wrote to the Philippians, 'Christ emptied Himself' of His right to Godness while He was on earth—then the Church may stumble and grope toward the truth, not fully comprehending the fire of ultimate truth that burns within it. It can err in the sense of failing to achieve ultimate truth."

"Although," I rapidly added, "without ever embracing error or evil."

"Of course," *il Papa* agreed; then he went on. "Perhaps we see ourself, in a much less exalted way than Christ, as stumbling down a road, burdened with the cross of humanity on our back, yet pushed by a divine energy the meaning of which we do not totally comprehend and the power of which we do not even know how to use efficiently."

According to me, there was much wisdom, as well as peril, in what Francesco told that evening. Perhaps even beauty. Doctrinally, it was not completely orthodox. In truth, a large majority of Catholic theologians who have written about the topic would disagree, in part because it could easily lead, as our brash young seminarian pointed out, to Arianism and acceptance of Christ as merely human. But not a few, and perhaps even a majority of recent theologians, especially those identified as servants, would agree with Francesco. But because this interpretation went against the grain—you say that?—of the Church's historic teaching, it was scandalous to some of the guests present that evening. Worse, when news of what *il Papa* had said circulated around the Curia, many traditionalists were severely concerned about doctrinal purity. That evening's discussion provided a catalyst for intrigue in the Vatican.

Actually, I found the evening both comforting and informative. I had never before heard Francesco speak so openly about what he conceived to be his mission; perhaps it was the discussion of Arianism that clarified his notions of himself. But his explanation, brief as it was, gave me strength and comfort. To see oneself as stumbling and groping is a symptom of spiritual as well as mental health.

The next few days went well enough. Fieschi was pleased with his staff's work in preparing guidelines for the North American bishops. He was most cheerful because he was most busy: instructing the pro-nuncio in Ottawa and the apostolic delegate in Washington; talking to people in the Sacred Congregation for Bishops; arranging coordination between, on the one hand, the Sacred Congregation for Sacraments and Divine Worship, and, on the other, the Holy Office to try to integrate fastings into the liturgy; and learning from Chelli about financial matters.

Late one morning I talked to Chelli by telephone. He was amused by what he had heard was the rueful astonishment of the North American bishops at having invited *il Papa* to their university only to provide him the occasion to force them to produce $3 billion. As the one whose office would handle our half of that money, Chelli could afford amusement.

On the other hand, he voiced real concern about the pacifism in Francesco's oration at Princeton and warned me that, according to running voices, Francesco had gone mad—*pazzo* was the good Italian word he used. While there were people within the Vatican who might encourage such stories, Chelli suspected the source may have been the American CIA. As an Italian, I could not be sure that Chelli was speaking the full truth. That the CIA or a similar agency of any nation would spread such gossip, I had no doubt. But I was wary that Chelli might be trying to lead me away from a source within the Vatican.

Who began the story disturbed me less than the likelihood of its enjoying some popularity among a few curialists and many governmental officials who were not intimately acquainted with Papa Francesco. I have confided in you that from time to time I myself had had certain fears about him. And despite the real assurance of his fascinating discussion a few evenings earlier, I was still troubled by his penchant for making decisions without consultation, by his utter confidence in his own judgment.

I also still had a fear, though of a very different nature, about the weekly audiences in the piazza. The auditorium or even the basilica itself offered greater security from the pushing crowds. On Wednesdays we were forced to keep all Swiss Guards on duty and even to borrow several hundred police from Italy. (We did not explain this latter fact to *il Papa,* though perhaps it might have helped make him more careful, because he continued to object to the presence of "foreign" police on Vatican territory.) But even then our ability to control the crowds was tenuous.

I prayed for guidance for Francesco as well as for myself, but, as usual, the Holy Spirit kept His own counsel. I did not have time to reproach the Almighty for His silence, for shortly thereafter we received the tragic news of Archbishop Candutti's death. I know you have heard the stories that he took away his own life. It displeases me much, but they are true. His physician announced that the *monsignore* had died of a coronary. That may have been the effect; I do not know about such medical things. But the proximate cause was an overdose of sleeping capsules. I pray you to use this information with discretion. I would not wish to dishonor the memory of a gentle man.

I felt deep guilt as well as great sorrow. According to me, Francesco felt both these emotions also, as I believe he should have. He took the original news well, but later, when he returned from prayers in his private chapel, I saw evidence of tears in his eyes.

Candutti was a person of talent and piety. He loved God and the Church and served them both with skill and devotion. Had I been less concerned with my own fears for Francesco, I might have given more care to Candutti's mental health. But Francesco monopolized the attention and energy of those around him. I pray that God judged the *monsignore* with mercy and took account of the strain under which he suffered.

THIRTY-SIX

THE DAY AFTER Monsignor Candutti's funeral, I received a curt note from Bisset asking if I would call on him that afternoon at his apartment in the Borgo, just outside the Vatican walls near the Gate of Sant'Anna. As you may have inferred from what I have said, I did not number His Eminence among my closer friends. In fact, this was the first time I had been invited to his home. I considered that an ominous omen as indeed it turned out to be.

When I arrived there, I found not only Bisset but also Chelli and Greene, as well as Giovanni Cardinal Lanzoni, archbishop of Palermo, and Bernardo Cardinal Freddi, long retired and almost blind, but still at eighty-two as acute, and theologically reactionary, as he had been during the fourteen years in which his iron fist had guided the Sacred Congregation for Bishops. Archbishop Kevin Moriarity, an Irishman who, as secretary of the Congregation for Sacraments and Divine Worship, was Bisset's chief assistant, ushered me in and took part in the discussion.

LaTorre was also in attendance. Officially, of course, he was, as archpriest of the basilica of San Pietro, still in the Vatican, but he was without much formal authority nor, as far as Francesco was concerned, did he exercise anything beyond a ceremonial function. The other person in that room was Monsignor Bonetti, *il Papa*'s official secretary. His presence solved the mystery of leaks of information from the Pontiff's office. He was the anonymous one whom Cardinal Pritchett had christened Holy Throat.

I did not like the face of this group. Chelli and LaTorre were the only two in whom I had ever seen even the barest flicker of an inquiring mind—which is not to say the others did not have intelligence, only that their minds were shut tight like the jaws of giant turtles. Bisset, for example, had a flashing intellect; he could instantly divide a problem into thirty-two parts and brilliantly analyze the nature of each. As a critical machine his mind was superb. But, as Mr. Keller had rather vulgarly although very precisely phrased it on one of his visits to Roma, His Eminence was an intellectual virgin: no original idea had ever penetrated his skull.

Bisset's opening statement—in a fashion typical of French hospitality, he did not offer us refreshment of any sort—gave me more disturbance. "My Lord Cardinals Galeotti and Chelli have not been privy to our earlier exchanges of views. We thought that the time had come to invite them here to listen to our discourse. The tragedy of Monsignor Candutti's death presents us with a situation of crisis proportions. If we intend to act, we must do so soon, before more damage is done, before more holy men of God are driven to the depths of despair."

"Act?" I intervened.

"Before proceeding," Bisset responded—or did not respond—"we must ask our two brothers to make the same pledge that each of us has already agreed to: nothing said here or even the fact of our meeting will be divulged outside of this room except with our unanimous approval."

Chelli took out one of his Cuban cigars and admired it. Bisset was not a smoker—according to me, one of his few virtues. "His Eminence has us at a disadvantage," the young cardinal told. "It is difficult to pledge secrecy when we do not know whether we are being asked to be secretive about sedition, heresy, or a birthday party."

"We can assure My Lord Cardinal Chelli that we shall not discuss heresy or sedition or even birthdays, only the good of the Church."

"In that case—and as long as we discuss *only* the good of the Church," Chelli told, "I can give that pledge, although I do so with a certain unease."

"I, too," I added, "can give only such a limited pledge. I share my most reverend brother's unease, and if at any point I find the topic changing, then I shall terminate the pledge."

"That is fair," Bisset agreed, "providing that you give us warning." Then he began to speak softly, mustering all the sincerity that he could find in his heart. I thought of the speeches of your former President Richard Nixon telling the American people how earnestly he had pressed for a full investigation of the Watergate affair. "Some of us have argued that the time has come for united action. The Holy Father is either becoming mentally ill or is nearing the brink of heresy—indeed, he may already have tumbled over that edge into the black pit. Without doubt, he has been a source of scandal within the Church. He is even considering abolishing the central institutions of the Church."

"Wait, wait," I intervened.

Bisset held up his hand. "May we ask His Eminence to hear us out? We promised to speak of the good of the Church. We must be allowed to develop our argument in our own way. When we have done, we shall grant My Lord Cardinal Galeotti ample opportunity to present his views."

I thought it prudent to acquiesce, and Bisset continued: "Taken together the evidence is overwhelming, although perhaps only one piece is conclusive by itself. We have a general picture of an emphasis on improving the condition of mankind. That is a laudable goal, but our primary mission is to convict the world of sin and preach the good news of how salvation may be obtained. We cannot legitimately offer a promise of earthly happiness, for Christ's kingdom is not of this world. And His direct command to us was to preach *first* the kingdom of God.

"*Alors,* let me sum up the specific points. First is the implicit repudiation of *Humanae Vitae* and, what we all know is impending, the explicit repudiation of a moral tradition that goes back to Christ through the Apostles and finds its roots solidly in the Old Testament, one that popes and the universal Church alike have accepted as part of unchanging and unchangeable natural law, the necessary linkage between legitimate sexual congress and the possibility of conception."

I started to intervene to correct this gross misstatement of moral doctrine, but then thought it better to wait.

"Second," Bisset went on, "he is preparing an encyclical now, so rumor has it, that will not only end holy celibacy within the priesthood, but will also admit females to holy orders."

I confess you that I laughed out loud.

Bisset regarded me angrily. "We do not jest, My Lord Cardinal, nor should anyone who loves Holy Mother Church take our words as less than dire. The very thought of the end of clerical celibacy is shocking. The ordination of females would be disastrous. They do not possess Christ's nature. Moreover, their admission to holy orders would be an invitation to turn the rectory into a carnal house. That goes far beyond even the intentions of the Dutch to pervert the Church."

I intervened: "However accurate your wild predictions, they have nothing to do with Papa Francesco. He has made no plan to ordain women or abolish celibacy."

Bisset waved me to silence. "Once again we ask our brother's patience. His turn to speak will come. *Alors,* we have reason to believe that this man Walsh *does* have such plans, if not for today, then for tomorrow. The third pair of items in our long list is the dismissal from the Holy Office of our esteemed and saintly brother LaTorre, when he warned the Pontiff that he was treading on the edge of heresy, and the appointment to the Congregation for the Clergy of that red Dutchman Gordenker, whose words and writings are heretical by any acceptable Catholic standards."

Chelli could tolerate immobility no longer. He used his pen knife to cut the tail from his cigar and then fumbled noisily in his pockets for matches.

Bisset ignored the distraction. "Fourth, the Pope brought into the Holy See as a close personal aide—and only recently dismissed him and then only because of severe pressure—an abbot well known as a heretic who while here added sins of a different sort. Fifth, there have been scandals within the so-called crusade involving illicit sexual conduct. Sixth, and part of the same general picture, the Pope has also brought into the Holy See as his personal secretary a divorced woman."

"Let us be precise, My Lord Cardinal," Chelli intervened sharply. "Signora Falconi is a woman who obtained a civil divorce on grounds that decisions of the Sacred Roman Rota have held may be a valid basis for an ecclesiastical decree of annulment. In any case, Signora Falconi has not remarried; and it is not civil divorce that the Church condemns, but remarriage after a civil divorce. Her husband has been dead some years; thus God Himself has dissolved her marriage."

"That is true, My Lord Cardinal," Bisset smiled, "and that brings us to our seventh point, one that we mention not because we personally believe it, but because we must consider it as an additional source of scandal. There have been rumors, and more frequently pointed hints in news stories, about a romantic liaison between the Pontiff and his divorced American assistant."

"Merda," I said—in truth, I almost shouted. I confess it was a crude intervention, one not fit for a conversation among princes of the Church, but I had been sorely tempted.

"As a question of fact," Bisset told most agreeably, "Your Eminence may be correct, albeit intemperate in language. Yet the rumor persists. It was given credibility by the difficulties of the crusade, and will be given more credibility with the invitation to libertinism implied in repudiating *Humanae Vitae,* ending celibacy, and ordaining women.

"In a more general fashion but related to these last points, this Pope is about to order bishops throughout the world to begin programs that would allow Catholics who were divorced and remarried to return to the sacraments. Insofar as such an order weakens the Church's—and Christ's—teaching against divorce and remarriage, it abets heresy. Insofar as it scandalizes practicing Christians, it is sinful on a further count."

"Has Your Eminence finished his recitation?" I asked.

"Only partly, My Lord Cardinal. I leave until the end the most telling point regarding heresy and turn now to matters that, while still occasions for scandal, may indicate mental derangement. Consider these 'miracles,' especially the last incident involving that atheistic government minister. We are certain that there are natural causes for each of these events. Some are ludicrously trivial, and all fit classic descriptions of hysterically induced ailments being cured by a countervailing bout of hysteria—with the exception of the last. There we see fraud. We do not say that the Pontiff himself was party to fraud, only that his state of mind has allowed him to be the victim of a clever effort to discredit the Faith. We believe that the Pope thinks there was a miracle; certainly his secretary of state is openly saying that he himself is sure the Pontiff worked a miracle there and in other instances. As soon as the Church moves to acknowledge these supposed miracles, the Socialists will reveal their trick and make us the laughing stock of the world.

"At the very least," Bisset continued, "it is a dangerous sign when any man, much less a Pope, thinks that he can cause miraculous cures. We see signs of the growth of a kind of megalomania, fertilized no doubt by public adulation. One may also interpret as indicia of megalomania his daily public audiences from the window of the palace, his insistence on being carried on his throne, whenever the weather permits, across the piazza to hold his weekly general audiences on the steps of San Pietro. Clearly the man is intoxicated by the sound of cheering crowds."

"Like Pius XII, of sainted memory," Chelli told, half to himself.

Bisset smiled coldly but did not reply. "We also see signs of megalomania in these outbursts of temper. Only you, My Lord Cardinal Freddi, have been spared the sharp and unfair bite of His Holiness's tongue—and you have escaped through the mercy of your retirement, not through his sense of justice."

Despite his usual courtesy to nonsmokers, Chelli lit his cigar and blew out a thick ring of smoke that danced in Bisset's general direction. His Eminence paused to cough a bit testily. Chelli used the pause to say, "Forgive me, Eminence. I have worked with four Popes. Despite their public images as saints, I do not recall one who was always sweet-tempered. Nor would I care to argue that we in the Curia did not deserve even more stringent correction than we received."

"My Lord Cardinal Chelli may be generalizing from his own conscience," Bisset snorted. "We have seen with this Pontiff childish outbursts of temper in private and public. His tirade against Pope Pius XII and against *Der Spiegel* —however much the latter may have been deserved— hardly set models of decent, not even to say papal, behavior. His public adulation adds another danger. We have just witnessed a mob's physical violence triggered by his verbal attack on Italian magazines. A similar outburst has precipitated bloody civil war in Brazil."

"Fortunately for your argument," I intervened, "the magazines were selling wholesome fare for families and the Brazilian government was a shining example of Christian charity."

"We shall be done shortly," Bisset replied, "and would appreciate Your Eminence's courtesy until that time. We add three additional points that indicate mental derangement. The Pontiff has sold some of our historic treasure, the patrimony of St. Peter, and is talking of selling more. Further, he is calling for pacificism by all Christians, repudiating almost 2000 years of Catholic moral teaching on the distinction between just and unjust wars.

"Besides these things, he has been talking of abolishing the Curia—the lynchpin of the very institution of the Church itself—and taking up residence as a simple monk in Jerusalem. To call that plan evidence of mental derangement is to err on the side of charity. More realistically, one might look upon it as a deliberate effort to destroy the Church, for surely that would be its inevitable—and quick—effect."

(Francesco must have spoken to others, for when he talked to me of Jerusalem, there had been no one else present, and I had buried his remark deep in my heart.)

Bisset smiled grandly at me—no, I would say triumphantly. "These together are telling arguments against our incumbent. But they pale before my final charge. His Holiness has been speaking in private and may be preparing a document—I would not honor it with the term encyclical—that revives the heresy of Arianism. He is questioning the divinity of Christ."

I inferred from the absence of shock within the group that Bisset's speech, at least this part, had been rehearsed. Only Chelli and LaTorre seemed surprised; the others maintained their grim faces.

"That is not true," I intervened heatedly, but once more Bisset waved me to silence.

"In a moment, My Lord Cardinal, just a few more seconds."

"I insist," I exclaimed, "to be allowed to make a brief intervention. You have falsely stated His Holiness's position. He no more denies the divinity of Christ than anyone in this room."

"To anticipate your response," Bisset continued, "I see no use in making fine distinctions between saying Christ was not divine and saying that He did not realize that He was divine. If that distinction had any validity—and I would rest my reputation as a theologian and my Christian soul that it does not—it would still unloose Arianism to prey once more on innocent souls. His sainted Holiness Pius X condemned as part of the general heresy of modernism the belief that Christ was not always fully aware of His divine, messianic mission. As recently as 1966, the Holy Office," Bisset nodded graciously to LaTorre, "gravely warned all bishops of the Church against 'christological humanism that would reduce Christ to the condition of a mere man, who gradually became conscious of his divine Sonship.' Coupled with Walsh's emphasis on good works to the exclusion of the sacraments, a statement that Christ was a mere human would complete the Church's transformation from traditional Roman Catholicism to Unitarianism."

Chelli exhaled another thick, pungent ring of smoke and told, "Some of us obviously know something about these secret plans for Arianism, but I do not. I can make no sense out of this discussion. I would like Cardinal Galeotti to tell me his understanding of what is in the Pope's mind. I might then be better able to evaluate Cardinal Bisset's charges of heresy."

Bisset nodded in a bored, condescending mode. I then explained as best I could Francesco's thinking, his effort to cope with the mystery of Christ's redemption of mankind. I tried to stress that, as far as I knew, it was a personal solution. He had said nothing of an encyclical, although that remained a possibility.

Chelli and LaTorre were listening closely, but I had doubts about some of the others. I could not discover if my words were convincing, for all faces maintained impassiveness. When I had finished, there was more silence. LaTorre told only, *"Ecco,"* while Chelli started to put a question, then thought better of it.

Bisset continued. "I find My Lord Cardinal's statement a teacher's admirable defense of a pupil, but my own judgment stands unshaken. This is Arianism or it is modernism or it is both. And Arianism and modernism are each heresies. *Alors,* we must now take steps to save our beloved Church from heresy, scandal, and madness. If we, some of the senior and most skilled members of the Curia —without Fieschi, of course, since he is hopelessly mad himself—present a united front and face the Pope with our evidence we might persuade him to resign."

"Only," the aged Cardinal Freddi intervened, "if His Eminence Cardinal Galeotti would join with us in talking with others in the Holy See and in confronting the Pontiff himself."

"Exactly," the cardinal archbishop of Palermo agreed.

Everyone except Chelli was looking directly at me. Chelli seemed to be fascinated by the wispy course of yet another of his thick smoke rings. "If I am not in accord?" I asked.

"We do not know, Eminence. We do not yet know. Perhaps we would have to force the Pontiff's resignation."

"And how, pray tell," Chelli asked without taking his eyes off the smoke ring, "would you do that? He is getting on in years but I would not like to challenge him to a wrestling contest."

"We appreciate our young colleague's wit," Bisset said, "but we had rather thought a heresy trial might be more in keeping with ecclesiastical dignity."

"Leaving aside for the moment the question of whether you have stated a convincing case, what tribunal would have jurisdiction?" Chelli inquired.

"We have given only cursory study to the problem as of yet," Archbishop Moriarity put in. "Some think that the entire college of cardinals might be the appropriate body. For my part, I find it a bit large, don't you know? I would prefer the *Segnatura Apostolica*. It is a smaller institution of only ten cardinals, and it is our 'supreme' court—a nice touch of irony there, you know. Moreover, since Cardinals Bisset, Greene, and LaTorre are among its members, its behavior would, let us say, be likely to be less erratic than that of the full college."

(According to me, Moriarity's words lacked elementary shrewdness. In fact, Bisset, Greene, and LaTorre were members of the *Segnatura,* but so were five cardinals who were supremely loyal to Francesco.)

"Come now, Mario," Greene added, "surely you must have given some thought to the problem yourself. It was you yourself who first suggested it last summer."

"Was it? If so, it was an unthinking remark, Sean," Chelli said. "What you propose could tear the Church apart."

"No more," Greene responded vehemently, running his hand through his hair, "than what this man is doing, and far less than what he is threatening to do. Sacred Heart, Mario, have you gone over to the enemy?"

"I do not think in terms of friends and enemies where only members of the Church are involved. If you mean to ask if I have changed my mind about Papa Francesco, the answer is yes and often, as some of you know. He has also changed some of my views of myself and of the Church and of the world—in fact of God Himself. I am troubled by most of the things that you mention. I wish the Pontiff's temper were less volatile. I wish that he had a more realistic appreciation of the sinful nature of man and thus of the ultimate ineffectiveness of reforms, renewals, and crusades. I wish that he would discharge Fieschi and put this thing of the miracles behind us. I would have preferred to avoid the question of whether those who are divorced and remarried should remain excommunicated; I am not sure of the proper answer, but Papa Francesco's, if it is wrong, is wrong because it is too charitable. And, if a Christian must err, that seems to me to be the more fitting direction.

"I also wish," Chelli continued, "he had not brought up the question, fascinating though it is, of how much Christ the man was aware of His having both a human and a divine nature. His is not a novel theory, nor is it *necessarily* heretical. The issue of pacifism also troubles me deeply. The Church's historic solution has been pragmatic. His response, as naive as it seems in the modern world, is much closer to Christ's—and I say that with trepidation. In sum, I see much here that I do not like, but I see neither madness nor heresy, and I am not aware of any scandal that Papa Francesco himself has caused."

Everyone was looking at me. "I associate myself with Cardinal Chelli's words. *I* do not know that *il Papa* is planning to end clerical celibacy." (I stressed the first person singular. It is easier to do in Italian because *io* has two syllables and is a much stronger word than your "I.") "I hope he is not. But it is within his power to do so. It is a law created by man, not by God. As for *Humanae Vitae* —and we have thrashed this out before—neither Papa Paolo nor the Second Vatican Council nor the two together ever decreed that, as a matter of faith and morals, artificial means of birth control violate God's law. Change —and we cannot be sure that it will come—thus remains within *il Papa*'s power. One can say the same about barring divorced and remarried people from the sacraments. Nowhere in Scripture or in our tradition is that commanded by God; it is only a policy of the Church—and not one followed in all periods of history. According to me, lack of charity, rather than fear of scandal, has provided the motive for our current punishment of the divorced. We punish the murderer only once, but the divorced and remarried daily."

I paused to be certain that my audience was awake. I could see that they were attentive, but I was less convinced that all were hearing my thoughts as well as my words. I continued: "My Lord Cardinal Bisset speaks of the ordination of women. I laughed when he told that; I laugh now. That Papa Francesco is troubled by the anguish women of piety feel when they realize they cannot become priests is a credit to his compassion, which, I recall, is a noble Christian virtue. But it is false to say he now has any plans to allow ordination of women and foolish to fear he might in the future."

I again examined my audience, but I could yet read nothing in their faces. I continued once more: "As for the abbot, he was never even charged with heresy. The Holy Office, at one point, was worried about the direction in which his mysticism led and forbade him to publish more. He obeyed, and without protest. None of us here can claim to be a stranger to sin, no matter how earnestly we strive and how steadfastly we pray. His sins may be different from our sins—our pride and our lack of charity are not secrets—but that does not make him worse than we are.

"You speak of Jerusalem. What Pontiff, frustrated by the sins and slowness of the world and of his own supposed assistants, has not dreamed of starting fresh in the Holy Land? Even Papa Paolo talked to friends of such a dream. It was not madness then, nor is it so now.

"Next, we come to pacifism. How can any of us preach that all men are brothers and human life is a sacred gift of God and yet not do all we can to prevent war? *Il Papa* feels he must speak out in the name of humanity. To say that nations as well as individuals should turn the other cheek may be madness, but it is a madness shared with Christ."

"Why not," Bisset sneered, "persuade Walsh that the slaughter of war is only retroactive birth control? That should change him into a veritable hawk."

I stood up. "I shall not demean myself or my office by

responding to such a monstrous calumny. I remain here no longer. I shall honor my pledge not to talk of this meeting, not even to Papa Francesco. Unless, that is, I receive evidence from another source about what transpired here. In that case, I shall give the Pontiff a full and immediate report."

Bisset nodded stiffly. *Ecco,* first Chelli then somewhat slowly LaTorre came to their feet with me. Bonetti commenced to rise, then slid again into the *divano.* Bisset dismissed Chelli with a Gallic shrug, but 'Vanni's action disturbed him.

"Do you leave us, My Lord Cardinal LaTorre? Do you leave us for that mad heretic who used you and threw you away a broken old man?"

In Italian, the Holy Mule told quietly the words of Job: *"Il Signore ha dato, e il Signore ha tolto. Sia benedetto il nome del Signore."* ("The Lord giveth and the Lord taketh away. Blessed be the name of the Lord.") "I have served God through His Holy Church with all my love and all my life. The Pope is the Vicar of Christ, the symbol of the universal Church. To whom could I now turn in my old age?"

We three said nothing until we were back in the piazza. "Let us go into the basilica," LaTorre suggested. We joined the throngs of tourists walking up the stone steps into the giant cathedral with its brass markers in the pavement humbly noting how every other cathedral in the world could easily be contained within its walls. Inside that marble universe the air was cool, almost chilly after the warmth of the piazza. We walked up the center aisle, around the papal altar with Bernini's magnificent, twisted columns of bronze supporting the thousands of kilos of baldachino, and went to the rear of the basilica, to the symbolic chair of San Pietro set high in the wall. Above it, the later afternoon sun was streaming through the stained-glass window, turning to a bright gold the panels surrounding the white dove representing the Holy Spirit. With those two symbols before us, we each prayed silently.

THIRTY-SEVEN

CRITICISM OF *il Papa* from within the Church is usually indirect, muted. We who accept Catholicism accept his intrinsic authority as coming from God Himself. Those of us in the Curia are aware, usually far more than other clergy, of the delicate nature of papal power and the necessity of symbolism and ritual in preserving that power in this world. Thus I had prayed that the group who remained at Bisset's would retreat when they realized what they might do to the Church in attempting to remove a Pontiff.

It turned out, however, to have been a vain prayer. By the very next morning, Bisset's cabal had broadened the arena of conflict. The dispute exploded across Roma itself. Someone had acted late in the night after our meeting, for in the morning visitors to San Pietro would be greeted by large posters on the buildings along the Via della Conciliazione. These signs, supplemented by leaflets scattered about the streets and the piazza, demanded in four languages either the resignation of *il Papa* or a heresy trial for him. The charges, more succinctly put, were essentially those that Bisset had described us the previous afternoon. Copies had gone to all the Roman newspapers and, for once, *L'Unita* and *Il Manifesto* roared out in defense of a Pontiff. In truth, the world had turned upside down. The morning news broadcasts carried reports that, to dramatize the situation still further, a demonstration of Catholic students would form at noon in the Piazza Venezia—a traditional site for Roman political rallies—and march to the Vatican to demand the resignation of Papa Francesco.

I entered *il Papa*'s studio that morning with considerable dread. But, instead of a raging bull pawing the ground as he prepared to attack his torturers, I found a tranquil Pontiff studying the penultimate draft of his encyclical on clerical celibacy. It was a lengthy document and I shall explain it now, because it was not at all what Bisset had alleged.

The encyclical was reformist rather than revolutionary and for that reason would have been disappointing to the dissident priests. (Gordenker would have suffered a crushing defeat.) Moreover, it contained not a single word about the ordination of women. Essentially Papa Francesco created a series of new regulations for those entering the priesthood in the future. The most important paragraph stipulated that young men would be ordained as deacons rather than as priests upon completion of their seminary education and would take only temporary vows of three years' duration. After working satisfactorily in a parish during that period, they would be eligible for ordination to the priesthood, but again would take only temporary vows, this time for five years. At the end of those years—assuming, once more, satisfactory performance—they could either leave the ministry in good standing or take permanent vows.

There was much more, but I do not want to wander from the path of my story. Papa Francesco gave me the draft and asked that I go over it quickly in his office at that moment and then later with much more care. I read it as rapidly as I could and told him that in general it struck the right note, retaining celibacy but surrounding it with longer periods of probation to stress the significance—and the holiness—of that choice. I did not think it necessary to express my relief that it said nothing about ordaining women.

"By the way, Ugo," he shifted abruptly, "have you read our good Roman newspapers this morning or driven down the Via della Conciliazione?"

He spoke softly, but I had care. I had seen the panther spring. "No, Holiness, but I have heard the radio and have also seen a few of the leaflets that are scattered around the piazza."

"It is an interesting spectacle, and not without a touch of irony." *Il Papa* was mimicking Monsignor Moriarity's lilting speech, but at that moment I did not understand. I noticed only that he was smiling and it was with his old, gentle appreciation of humor—a characteristic I found lacking in the situation. I confess that I was having a difficult struggle within my conscience. I wanted to tell him about the meeting at Bisset's apartment, but I had—foolishly, I now thought—pledged my word. Could I serve God by breaking my word? On the other hand, could I serve Him by honoring my word?

Francesco must have noticed that I was suffering mental

anguish, for he said: "Relax, old friend. We have some visitors coming. They will arrive momentarily. I would like you to meet them with us. Incidentally," and here his voice was perfectly sincere, "I now appreciate your old friend LaTorre. He is a mule, but he is also holy."

I thought it prudent to remain silent, but I thought I understood. A few minutes later Bisset, Greene, Lanzoni, Moriarity, Bonetti, and Fieschi came in. Each was attired in full clerical regalia, red-piped black cassocks, scarlet capes, pectoral crosses, and, except for Moriarity and Bonetti, red hats. All seemed anxious except Fieschi; he was consumed by cold rage. They genuflected as they came into the room, and Papa Francesco extended his hand so that each could kneel and kiss his ring. Then he sat behind his desk, but gave no indication that any of the rest of us should also sit.

"My Lord Cardinal," Francesco looked at Bisset, "we understand that you are more skilled in matters scriptural and theological than we. Thus we ask your aid. We have a recollection that Christ was criticized for eating with sinners and even for having a prostitute and a publican among his followers. Is our recollection basically correct?"

"It is correct, Holiness," Bisset told nervously.

"We thought so," Francesco remarked, "but as one grows old one's memory sometimes plays tricks. Madness often creeps on us slowly. Now, perhaps you would be so kind as to refresh our failing memory on another point. What were Christ's exact words to Peter when He made him chief of the Apostles and head of the Church?"

Bisset glared at me. I kept my expression as blank as I could. I had not betrayed him, although clearly someone had. Still glaring, Bisset quoted from San Matteo. Actually, Bisset spoke in Latin, offering the Vulgate of San Jerome, but I give it in English.

> Thou art Peter, and upon this rock I shall build my Church, and the gates of hell shall not prevail against it.

"Interesting, Eminence. We admire your memory and your diction. Your Latin is most melodious. It reminds us of the church of our youth. Please, go on."

Bisset hesitated. He knew he was spinning his own trap, but he saw no escape.

And I shall give thee the keys of the kingdom of heaven; and whatsoever thou shalt bind on earth shall be bound in heaven, and whatsoever thou shalt loose on earth shall be loosed in heaven.

"*Whatsoever* we loose and bind? Do we translate properly? Yes, we thought as much. No restrictions at all, just the word 'whatsoever.' " Francesco paused and rubbed his beard. "Then much indeed seems to fall within the arc of our covenant. If we choose to loose the people of God from oppressive rule by laymen or churchmen, we are acting within our jurisdiction. Also within our jurisdiction, Eminence, is our appointment and continuation in office of bishops and cardinals, is that not so?"

"Some would argue it is so, Holiness," Bisset responded.

"Yes, some would." Francesco picked up a set of photostated papers from his desk. "Here, in fact, published in *Civiltà Cattolica* is an article by a noted French theologian. He argues strongly against the collegiality of bishops because the bishop of Rome is the Vicar of Christ; all other prelates have only such authority as he chooses to give them. They—the other bishops—may be equal to each other, but they cannot be equal to the one on whose discretion their own authority depends. Do you recall that article, Eminence?"

"Of course, I recall it. I wrote it."

"Indeed." Francesco turned to Greene. "Eminence, we have here a summary of remarks delivered at the Second Vatican Council on this very same point. The address was by a learned Irish archbishop, now a cardinal. Would you recall the speech in question?"

"I would, Holiness, precisely," Greene said sadly. I knew his melancholia would soon be upon him.

Papa Francesco looked at Lanzoni. "Eminence, our notes say that at Vatican II you associated yourself with the Irish archbishop's remarks. Are they correct?"

Lanzoni nodded. I had fear he was going to burst into tears.

"*Giusto,*" Francesco snapped. "Before these witnesses, Cardinals Fieschi and Galeotti, we the bishop of Rome and the Supreme Pontiff of the universal Church, the successor of St. Peter, the prince of the Apostles—we, the Vicar of Christ, accept all your resignations from all ecclesiastical office. We even dispense you from all priestly vows and grant you complete laicization without any formalities other than your own request. If you choose to remain in clerical service, it will be as simple priests assigned to monasteries that we shall designate. Each of you has an hour in which to make up his mind on that point. But as of this instant, each of you is without high office in the Church and totally without office in the Holy See. . . ."

"Holiness," Bisset intervened, "it is not at all clear that you may strip us of the permanent rank and privileges bestowed on us when we were ordained bishops. We, too, are successors of the Apostles."

Francesco's expression remained gentle, as if he were lecturing a little boy. "My son, since your soul is dear to us, we tell you that the precedents may be unclear on this point, but we think our action on this day will yield charity as well as justice—and even mercy. Christ's grant of 'whatsoever' surely covers you, Father Bisset."

Then to the group: "As a symbol of your new status, each of you will lay his bishop's ring and pectoral cross here on the table. You, Cardinals Bisset, Lanzoni, and Greene, will place your reds hats alongside." (Bisset's ring and cross were heavily encrusted with jewels, despite the strong admonitions of Papa Giovanni and his successors that such emblems of office be of the plainest design and least expensive material.) "Perhaps," Francesco mused, "we might sell them and give the proceeds to the poor as a large gesture of your love for Holy Mother Church and her shepherd."

Ecco, "executions" have never been pleasing to me, and the memory of that grim morning still haunts me, although not so much as having witnessed LaTorre's fate. I know that the sentences were just—as LaTorre's was not—but, according to me, they were also harsh. Lanzoni, Bonetti, and the two Irishmen elected to remain in the clergy. Francesco sent Bonetti to a Franciscan monastery near Milano, Moriarity to a Benedictine monastery in Sicily, and Greene to a Trappist monastery in Israel. Of the cabal, only the aged Cardinal Freddi escaped punishment—whether because Francesco had pity on his age and blindness, or Francesco's informant had omitted his name, or for another reason, I do not know.

Bisset stalked out of the palazzo. Later he would return

to France, not to Paris but to the south, joining a community of dissident, ultratraditional Catholics, remnants of *Action Française,* who oppose all the reforms of Vatican II—and, in fact, condemn most as heresies. His interests have broadened. He continues to write learned theological treatises, but he is also now a political pundit, publishing brilliantly vindictive tracts against communism, socialism, Dutch Catholicism, international Zionism, and American imperialism, all of which, he tells, fused in the Vatican during the reign of Papa Francesco.

Allora, in Roma at that time there was also the demonstration of the students against Francesco and their march from the Piazza Venezia to the Piazza di San Pietro. I must relate another sadness. We Italians are not so tender toward freedom of expression as you Anglo-Saxons. The students were not able to move two hundred yards down the Corso before they were attacked by another and far larger mob, soundly thrashed, and dispersed into the narrow alleys around the Pantheon to nurse their broken heads. I heard that the police tried to intervene, but were simply overwhelmed. This news saddened Papa Francesco. In his heart he probably did not love all of his enemies or even all of his friends, but he did tolerate them if they did not get too close to him.

Who told Francesco about what happened at Bisset's apartment is a question that I cannot answer, even now. LaTorre is the most obvious person, given *il Papa*'s remark to me just before the "executions." I know him too well, however, to take that comment at face value. Declan Walsh loved to—how do you say?—put people on, and even Papa Francesco was not at times above doing that to old friends. Chelli, of course, is the other prime suspect. He could have told. His shrewd Neapolitan mind, skilled in the casuistry of canon law, might have found a loophole in our pledge. (LaTorre would have been more direct; he would simply have tried to stamp out sin without calculating the niceties.) Chelli could have, but did he? I do not know. Age and blindness would have made it difficult for Cardinal Freddi to have warned Francesco, but not impossible. And he did escape punishment. Moreover, I would not eliminate any of the others merely because they were punished. Machiavelli warned us centuries ago that conspirators have an incentive to betray their colleagues, and one of Bisset's friends might have thought he could save himself—perhaps profit—by condemning the others. If so, he made a grave error. *Ecco,* the question is truly fascinating, but I doubt if we shall ever learn the answer.

THIRTY-EIGHT

THE "EXECUTIONS" were only one of many items on *il Papa*'s agenda that day. An hour later, he, Fieschi, Pritchett, Dottor Twisdale, and I met with Monsignor Ernesto Parisella, who had been Candutti's undersecretary, to sketch preliminary plans for coming trips to Western and Eastern Europe. The *monsignore* had some initial reports that to me were completely expected: no country seemed interested in receiving a papal visit. The qualifying diplomatic phrase was always "at this time." We all knew that meant any time the Pontiff endorsed pacifism. Francesco, of course, was not deterred by a lack of welcome. Our planning continued.

I was away from Roma during the first four days of the following week. It was time to visit my doctors in Switzerland, and Francesco insisted that I keep my appointment despite the work that lay ahead. We had not yet given serious thought to who would replace Bisset and Greene in the Curia. I had intended to suggest LaTorre's name for one of the posts, but, perhaps anticipating me, Francesco had asked whether I thought LaTorre would accept appointment as master of the papal palazzo. (That, if you do not know, is the misleading title for the Pontiff's personal theologian; it is usually held by a Dominican but had been vacant during Francesco's reign.) I said I thought he would be delighted, but I could not help asking Francesco if this arrangement would be tolerable for him. He smiled and said he thought it would; he felt the need of a little, but not too much, traditionalist theology. "He will prick our conscience," Francesco said. I agreed on that score.

For the next and fateful period you will have to talk to others. Dottor Twisdale was close at hand to *il Papa* through it all. He knows more than any one. Rather than tell you of events secondhand, let me make some general remarks.

We have been conversing for many weeks. I did not think it would be, at the beginning, but it has been a good thing for me—and not only for my English. I see many events and many questions starkly outlined, now that I have had to describe them to you. It has forced me to try to understand why I first proposed Declan Walsh's name to the conclave. Choosing a Pontiff is an awesome business; being a Pontiff is far worse. Was I so frightened by the responsibility of the first that I was terrified by the second? I pray not, for I have truly tried to serve God. Still, cowardice may be among my sins.

As we have been talking, I have often wondered—only sometimes out loud—what I would have done had I, not Declan Walsh, walked in the footsteps of the Big Fisherman. I have said enough to make it clear that I would have done many things differently, but—except that I would have never dismissed LaTorre—I am not at all sure that I would have done them better or nearly as well. In fact, I confess that my prevailing emotion in reliving those magnificent days has been one of relief that I do not have to answer to Almighty God for what I might have done.

The Church, existing as we believe it does in the next world as well as in this one, remains a mystery. I mean in the religious sense, something that human understanding, however deep and accurate, never fully grasps. I was born into a Church ruled by Papa Pio X. Fortunately I was too young to know of his war against what he called modernism—a "heresy" that can be roughly defined by the positive notions that the Second Vatican Council endorsed more than a half century later as the bishops obliquely repudiated a long-dead Pontiff. Like all Catholics, however, I felt the effect of Papa Pio's war, all the more because I had never known a different Church. If he was not the father of traditionalism, he was its great nourisher. Thus you might understand better why Vatican II and, more so, Papa Francesco upset traditionalists so badly.

I grew to maturity under the sad but generous reign of Papa Benedetto XV; I became a priest and a curialist under a tough martinet, Papa Pio XI. I agonized through Pio XII, rejoiced under Papa Giovanni, suffered with poor Papa Paolo, and hoped under his short-lived successors. What did I do under Papa Francesco? I suffered, endured, agonized, hoped, and rejoiced—all of them. But why had I thought that he, open, direct, practical, American pragmatist, would sit comfortably in a chair warmed by those convoluted, indirect, and very professionally religious prelates? I do not know. I believe—but then I want very badly to believe—that it was the Holy Spirit. But I cannot be sure. That is part of what I mean when I say the Church remains a mystery. How does one recognize the wishes of the invisible Church and then reconcile them with the human needs of the visible Church, the one here on earth?

Sometimes I was not certain whether I had helped unloose the Holy Spirit or the wrath of God upon the visible Church. In this regard, I was reading this past week some Jung—one has need of occasional respite from the piety of saints—something about irritability, black moods, and outbursts of temper being classic symptoms of habitual virtuousness. Papa Francesco, except in the last few weeks I described to you, clearly met those standards.

Seriously, I repeat what I have voiced on several occasions: he changed the Church, but even more he changed himself. The office, its rituals and trappings, brought a new self-image for Francesco, forced him into a new role. According to me, however, far more important in his development were his own reasoning and later his prayer. The logic of the gospel of love converted him, and God's grace sustained him. I remember he said years ago at the hearings in your Senate for his appointment as chief justice that he lacked faith. He repeated those words to me on that hot, stormy night at the monastery in South Carolina. He found faith, though, through his own reasoning and, according to me, through his prayer; he found it because he sought it. Faith is always a free gift of God, but if any man can be said to have worked for that gift, it was Francesco.

Translation from secular statesman to religious leader is not easy. Francesco provides ample proof of that truism. As he himself said that night to the young seminarians, he groped, stumbled, and fell. But he got up to walk, to stagger, and to fall again, only to get up once more. He knew guilt and despair, but always an inner core of courage drove him, even when his faith flagged. At times he succumbed to pride and arrogance. He strove always for *arete,* the word the Greeks ascribed to the manly virtue of doing all things well; but, as I have already implied, the result was sometimes only a demonstration of *hubris.* On other occasions the results were more successful, if one sees success as preaching Christ's gospel of love to a world that does not want to hear, and achieving a holiness partly based on a selfless acceptance of God's word and will.

Even when I say all these things, I still do not know whether I listened to my God or to my own fear or love that day in the conclave. At my age it is hard to tell the difference. *Ebbene,* I enjoy some comfort. The blind saw; the lame walked; and the poor had the Gospel preached to them. As I read the evangelists, these are good omens, and, as a true Italian, I have always placed great store by omens.

I do know that when I left for Switzerland, Francesco had found peace. It is not a ready combination, power and peace. Yet he found the two. He was leading the Church as it had not been led for centuries. I cannot, in truth, say that he was leading it in the path that God had chosen; only Francesco and Fieschi were sure of that. Whether I had been cowardly, prudent, or inspired in the conclave, my task was to follow, to assist, not to lead. As I told at the very beginning of your tapes, I have been the shepherd's dog. That is enough if the shepherd loves his flock, and this one did, or at least he came to.

When I say Francesco found peace and love I do not mean that he had learned to love like the rest of us. That flaw—I name it so, though others would not—of sacrificing friends, family, and self for an abstract ideal was one that he never conquered. He only came to recognize it, to accept it, and to try to atone for it—all without allowing self-reproach to disrupt his sense of mission. No, that is not exact; at first it was his sense of mission; later it became his vision.

He pursued that vision relentlessly, even ruthlessly. Without our asking, sometimes against our will, he seared this vision into our souls. That burning brought pain to many individuals, at times to the whole Church. The scars will remain with us, perhaps forever, but so also will that vision. *Ecco,* I say this with the sureness of a man who feels death tugging at his elbow.

ONE

I'M GLAD to help you. It'll be useful to me to get my thoughts in order. I'm going to write a book about him, too. But not until I've put a few years between us. For now, I'm going to enjoy Paris. Then back to work.

For the tape: My name is Robert Twisdale. I first met him during the Korean War in 1951. He was a battalion commander then. I was a young reporter. Now I'm an aging reporter. I'm not that much different. He's the one who changed. I met him when he was a warrior-leader. I knew him when he headed the Court. I worked for him when he was the greatest religious figure of his time. For all I know he was a saint. From fierce courage to righteous justice to personal holiness I saw those transformations. That doesn't mean I understand them, any more than I understand why people always followed him.

You want to know about that June, I guess. For us it was a time of great excitement. The American trip had been a huge success. For him it was a time of peace. Decisive actions but without temper. He cleaned house on the Curia, really put the fear of God in them, but he did it without anger. The old power was still pumping, but so was an inner peace that I'd never even glimpsed until a few weeks before. He still needed the crowds—Cardinal Galeotti used to say he needed to share with them. That may have been true, but he still needed them, and that worried us. We didn't have many security people who could handle crowds that might turn into mobs like the one in Washington had. That didn't bother him. He knew the dangers. But he still held the Wednesday audiences in the piazza itself.

More important to him were the plans for the next trip. Austria, then Germany—West Germany for sure, East if there was any way. We'd rest back in Rome, then try the Balkans. We missed Monsignor Candutti's smooth diplomatic touch. Monsignor Parisella worked hard, but he wasn't a Candutti. We were having trouble. Tito's people would probably let us in; the Rumanians were a good bet. It was unlikely the others would allow us to come. Afterwards, or if the whole Balkan thing fell through, we'd go on to Holland, Belgium, and even France, though none of them really wanted us either. Spain and Portugal would come later, when the climate was calmer. He was even talking in private about Japan and maybe China. Poor Parisella just shook his head at those two.

The message was going to be the same simple one: Love thy neighbor. Love by joining the crusade, or by sacrificing for it, or by taking care of one's fellow man at home. He was going to repeat his pacifist questions. Just as he had at Princeton, he was going to ask again and again whether military service was compatible with Christianity. And he was going to suggest the answer. Actually, he hadn't stopped raising the question. He asked it during the first Wednesday audience after our return. The reference was oblique, but several newsmen caught it. So did all the diplomats.

He was already working on a major encyclical. *Monstrum Bellum* ("The Horror Called War") he decided to label it. He got three or four Jesuits from the Gregorian University to start compiling what previous Popes and important theologians had said about "just war." He was especially interested in the early Church. That's where the error began, he said.

The Vatican has enough leaks to sink the *Queen Elizabeth.* Within ten days two different reporters had asked me what the new encyclical was going to be on. I fenced with them, but they wouldn't quit. I had to stop trying to answer their questions. It didn't help. Soon the story was in print that the Pope was writing an encyclical forbidding Christians to serve in the military.

He only smiled when I told him about it. There was just a faint grimace when I confessed that it was *Der Spiegel* that had broken the story. He refused to issue a denial or allow me to comment in any way. He added that I could truthfully deny any knowledge of the substantive content of any new encyclical because he himself hadn't decided what if anything he'd say. He knew the question, but he only thought he knew the answer.

That leak bothered me a great deal. It bothered a lot of others, too, but for very different reasons. An Italian reporter whose uncle was an aide to the minister of justice tipped me that the *carabinieri,* the elite Italian police, had recognized agents from at least seven countries plus two well-known free-lancers in the piazza at the last audience. (I didn't ask what the hell the *carabinieri* were doing in the Vatican.) I talked to Cardinal Fieschi about it. He was as concerned as I was. He took personal charge of security. That was comforting. He was the closest thing I'd ever seen to a human machine. Still, he didn't have much to work with in the way of personnel or organization. The Swiss Guards would make pretty conspicuous counterintelligence agents. We didn't have many other police.

The people Fieschi had (and maybe borrowed) followed up at the next audience. They confirmed the report. In fact, they found even more suspicious characters. It was frightening. The crowds at the audiences would run as high as a hundred thousand. An agent could pick his cover from a wide spectrum. He could be an American tourist in a bizarre sportshirt, a German in smelly *lederhosen,* an Irish bourgeois in his woolen suit sweating through the 90° heat like Mrs. Murphy's pig, a ragged hippie from God knows where, a neat American sailor, an Italian soldier in an unpressed uniform cut for a man a hundred pounds heavier and two inches shorter, a fat nun with enough room under her black petticoats to hide a machine gun, or even a saintly priest with a pistol in his breviary. Anything or anyone could fit into that kaleidoscope of human shapes and colors.

I felt the need of advice from a pro. I went down to the Via Veneto and had coffee at Doney's with an old friend in the CIA. He owed me. He was brutally frank.

"What the hell do you expect? Your man goes around the world interfering with wars, flouting rules about passports and national sovereignty, running crusades for peace, staging phony miracles, and preaching love and social justice. That's upsetting, but at least it's all within tolerable limits, if just barely—as long as he doesn't stay too long in one country. People like us don't know much about love. We make love but that's not like living love. Hate's our bag. You can measure it, predict it, use it, and most of all you can depend on it. But love? Who the hell knows what stupid things a man might do if he loved his neighbor? Now, if he loved his neighbor's wife, we could understand it, predict the results, and probably use them to our own advantage. But his neighbor? Unless he's queer, we're up a tree."

"So," I asked, "what then?"

"So we stay uncomfortable. We can live with discomfort. We're used to it. We just list your man as a bad guy. But now he threatens the whole system of power politics. He starts going over governments' heads and talking directly to the people, and a lot of them listen to him. He criticizes pornography and that night a batch of porn dealers feel the hot end of riots. He criticizes the Brazilian junta and twenty-four hours later we get a revolution. He asks questions—and suggests the 'right' answers—that stack the deck in favor of pacifism, and in Catholic countries the enlistment rate falls off and the desertion rat~ goes up. Even the Communists get troubles with that one. And it's the kind of trouble that strikes panic.

"What your man is doing is tickling jugulars, jugulars of big boys who are very powerful and very, very nervous. He says all he has is a feather in his hand; they think he's got a fistful of razors. These guys whose throats he's tickling have a lot of hang-ups. They want to be on top in their own country and they want their own country to be on top in relations with other countries. And they're scared as hell about a lot of other things, like Communists or capitalists, whites or blacks, Prods or papists, Zionists or Palestinian terrorists. Anybody who has power or wants power can find it awful easy to get very paranoid about your boy. I don't know what's happening, but I can speculate. I'd bet my company's got a couple of people poking around in Peter's pocket, and so does every other company in the business including the Russkies, the Israeli, and the PLO. My best guess is that right now they're watching each other more than planning a caper themselves. You've got two things to worry about. The first concerns that planned encyclical. If it forbids people to go into military service and one of those countries finds out about it in advance—well, I can't say exactly but I'll bet my pension against a ten-lire coin it never gets published."

"That sounds pretty drastic," I said.

"So does starting civil wars or taking away armies from a good chunk of the world. And you're messing with drastic people. Hell," he smiled, "what would the world be like if we couldn't have us a nice little mass bloodletting every decade or so?"

"What's the second danger?" I asked. I had no time for black humor.

"A free-lancer, of course. Somebody who hopes to strike now and collect his honorarium later from the grateful—or the gratefuls."

"What can we do?"

My friend leaned back in his chair. "I'd say pray, but your boys know all about that. I'd say try a little power politics, but your boys know that one, too. Your hierarchy took the Good Book's advice and made friends with mammon a passel of centuries ago."

"Don't joke. You know I'm a believer."

"Yeah. We've all got our hang-ups. Okay. First, your Vatican diplomats in the countries you think are snooping around let each of those governments know that you know what's going on. And your boys let them know that if there's any hanky-panky you're going to blow the whistle—or the trumpet, or whatever you Holy Joes blow. Second, and more important, you persuade your man not to forbid people to serve in the military. Third, your diplomats assure all the countries involved that they're safe. Your man can salve his conscience by circumlocuting just as mincingly as old Pius did when he condemned the slaughter of Jews in statements that only a friendly Jesuit biographer can decode."

"Can we take any security precautions?" I asked.

My friend arched his eyebrows. His tone was condescending. "Bob, baby cat, these people are tigers, real tigers. And they're professional tigers. Sure you can do a few things. The safest way for an agent to get him is by using a rifle with a sniperscope; so when your man is at his window or in the piazza you put people on all the roofs and windows that overlook the area."

"We can do that," I said. "The Vatican or various religious organizations own most of the tall buildings in the vicinity. The owners of the others will cooperate. We can have them sealed off during audiences and use seminarians as guards. It won't be perfect, but it'll be good."

"Fine. And don't let him come out from the palace through the crowd. Have him come out from the church."

"That we can't do."

"Well, I'm not sure any precaution will make much difference," my friend said drily. "You can scare off the amateurs with a show of competence, but that sort of thing only makes a pro's work a little more difficult—and might make the pro a little meaner. And he's awful mean to start with. When you get right down to it, there's too many ways to get him—a bomb, a knife, a sniperscope, a pistol with a silencer, even poison, like Mussolini's supposed to have done to old Pius XI."

"You don't really believe that story?" I asked.

"No, but I don't disbelieve it either. What I believe is that Benito was ready to kill Pius XI just like Uncle Adolf was ready to kidnap Pius XII during World War II, and both those Fascist swine had a hell of a lot less reason than a dozen or two countries have right now to eliminate your man. By the way, he knows, doesn't he?"

"We haven't discussed it with him, but yes, I think he knows."

"He was a marine," my friend said. "He knows, but remind him. It can help if you make him nervous. Now look, let's get back to basics. You've got one real hope: get rid of their incentive to play dirty. Have your man stop asking those silly questions and squash that encyclical. Honest Injun, it's your only real hope."

There was nothing more to say. I paid the outrageous bill—but stiffed the rude waiter—and left.

The diplomatic warning was easy. I had no doubt that Fieschi had already done it. But that precaution would mean little without the second and third steps. There were simply too many ways in which a country could act without fear of detection. I talked to Cardinal Fieschi about my conversation. He agreed with my assessment. So did Cardinal Galeotti. But they also agreed that the three of us should visit him, explain the situation, and try to persuade him to take the second step and let us take the third.

The appointment was for 10 A.M. I came fifteen minutes early. Like most people around him, I hadn't seen much of him since we came back from New York; and I had some other important business. Elena had promised to slip me in before the others arrived. When I got there, a monsignor whom I didn't know ushered me into the library. Elena was inside, sitting at the conference table next to him. Her hand was on the table, covered by his. He didn't move it or look embarrassed when the monsignor opened the door and I came in. (I admit it. For a moment I thought the worst. I'd read too much about Renaissance Popes.) He didn't offer his ring to me. He seldom did. "Sit down, Bob. Elena and I have been talking. I should be saying some of the same things to you and to Mike Keller."

I sat down. He went on. "For years, I've exploited Elena. I've kept her for myself and used her. At first I rationalized it as being for the Court, later for the Church. There's enough truth there to satisfy, especially if one doesn't want to discover much about oneself. I've used Elena's talents for those purposes, but also to serve my ambition. And I've never offered her anything in return, not even the right to share in my accomplishments—accomplishments that were really partly hers, too. I've told her—in fact, I've ordered her—to go back to the States to ease my conscience. She's entitled to a life of her own. Mike's been in love with her since he first saw her. She's to bring him my petition for his forgiveness. Over the years I've abused his love almost as much as hers. I've also abused yours."

"But you've repaid me with the sort of stuff that makes reporters' dreams." It was the truth.

"I know. That's why I don't order you to go. Elena must. You can choose."

"I'll stay."

Pritchett and Fieschi arrived then, and Elena left hurriedly. I don't know what she was thinking or feeling. She hadn't said a word during the conversation. I have seldom seen her since then and never to talk to alone. She's taken up with Keller. I never cared for him or his life-style.

As Pritchett, Fieschi, and I had feared, he wouldn't listen to us about the encyclical or about how serious the problem of security had become. Pritchett took it more philosophically than Fieschi. He came as close to losing his temper as an iceberg can. I never understood that cold fish. I appreciated his dedication. I admired his intelligence. And he was easy to work with if his superciliousness didn't bother you. I got used to it. But what went on inside him was always a mystery to me.

He brushed aside Fieschi's arguments, although with thanks. "The Holy Spirit cannot be silenced by secular pressures. It is we who prevail against the gates of hell," he said, "not the gates against us." And that was that.

That afternoon at the general audience in the piazza, he repeated his questions about Christianity, war, and military service in sharp, clear terms that nobody could miss.

TWO

IT'S STILL HARD for me to talk about that Wednesday. I'll start with Willie Adams. I know him better than I know myself. I've read his police record in Newark a dozen times. I've memorized his dossier from the CIA and his *pratica* from the *carabinieri.* I own a Xerox of the Vatican's file on him. I've talked to his sister, his mother, his parole officer, to two public defenders who represented him on different occasions, to four detectives who arrested him at various times, to the judge who first sent him to reform school, even to a couple of real Mau-Mau who shared a cell with him in the maximum security prison in Trenton. I've grilled taxi drivers, waiters, and beggars in Rome. I can tell you most things that happened in his life. And I can tell you every step he took that Wednesday. I know him from the inside out.

It was late in a Roman June, full of sunshine and rapid voices, honking cars, hawking vendors, and rattling dishes. Willie sat at an outdoor table of a small trattoria on the Piazza di Risorgimento. You can be sure he was enjoying the sunshine more than the warm beer and cold cannelloni that he had been served.

A crippled beggar had been playing—badly—a violin. He was now passing around the tables accepting donations for his concert. Willie reached in his pocket, pulled out a few strange coins, and dropped them into the proffered hat.

"Grazie, signore, grazie," the man murmured.

Willie noticed that, like the beggar, no one stared at him. Few people even gave him a second glance. That was good. It would make both his work and the aftermath easier. During the morning he had seen a number of black seminarians dressed in red-piped cassocks walking around the Borgo outside the Vatican. Two black soldiers, and at least a dozen black tourists, complete with maps and cameras, had been strolling in the piazza.

Willie looked at his watch; it read two-thirty. He still had an hour and a half to kill before his appointment at the Vatican. He ordered another beer to wash down the greasy lamb of the second course. He had spent part of the morning carefully walking around the piazza in front of St. Peter's, familiarizing himself with every detail. He had looked at maps and photographs. His suitcase had been full of them. But he was a pro. And a pro always eyeballs the area before an operation. Executing the contract would present no technical problems. After, things might be difficult.

Over the babbling conversation—the locals' rapid Romanaccio mixed with squeals from American tourists—and the traffic roaring around the shaded park toward the Via Crescenzio, Willie heard music again. This time a shabbily dressed man in his early thirties was playing an accordion. Ahead of him, a dark-eyed little girl of seven or eight walked sadly along. She was rattling a tambourine more or less in time to the music. Occasionally her attention wandered to the food on the tables, and the man would nudge her. It was not a gentle tap but neither was it an unkind shove. It was more like the nudge one gives a trained animal to jog his memory. After that she would shake the tambourine again.

The child's eyes touched Willie. She had the same vacant stare that his younger sister had had. He knew that expression. It was the look of those who expected nothing from life and got nothing. She was a white girl but damned no less than his own black sister in Newark. He motioned to the waiter and asked him to give the child a Coca-Cola. The girl's eyes danced with pleasure when she was handed the cold bottle. There was no gratitude in her smile, only anticipation. I think Willie immediately regretted his act. The lack of gratitude would not have affected him; he would have expected none. It was the happiness that flashed for a second across her face. He knew that the life of people like her was more bearable without the pain of dashed hopes. He would have cursed himself for having done something to make the child think that her life might include joy.

When the music was over, the little girl passed her

tambourine around. Again Willie reached into his pocket, but the man grabbed the child roughly and pushed her toward another table.

"Scusi, signore, scusi," he said obsequiously. *"La bambina . . ."* he pointed to his head, indicating she was too stupid to understand the code of Roman beggars: never hit the same mark twice in one day.

Willie was angry, but he controlled himself from striking the man. Then he did something he came to regret even more than the Coca-Cola. As the girl passed back by his table—the man was now looking the other way—Willie pressed a 1000-lire note into her hand. As soon as the two of them disappeared around the corner, he no doubt realized that for the second time that day he had done a cruel thing. He always rationalized that, although he was in a cruel business, he was not a cruel man. He was only an efficient man in the harsh world that whitey had created. In that jungle, he simply performed a service for one set of big white cats against another. Yet twice today he had been cruel to a child for his own pleasure.

He would be glad to finish his afternoon appointment and go back to America. This country bothered him, with its white beggars and white cripples. In his world those roles were reserved for blacks and Puerto Ricans.

Willie sipped his beer slowly, then paid the check. He had been charged the equivalent of seventy-five cents for the Coca-Cola. He got up and walked inside the trattoria and found the men's room. It was small, dirty, and smelly, but it served. He opened the plastic shopping bag he had been carrying and slipped a red-piped black cassock over his light summer suit. Then he put a biretta on his head. Now he looked like any of the black seminarians around Vatican City. He was older, but to whitey all black men looked alike. He folded the plastic bag and carried it with him. It would be useful at the appointment.

Walking the few blocks back to St. Peter's in what shade the Leonine Walls offered probably left Willie perspiring. The sun was warm, and the cassock over his suit would have made him uncomfortable. It was a little after three o'clock, still siesta time for the Italians. Nevertheless, the piazza was beginning to fill with people. A crowd of perhaps 20,000, mostly German and American tourists, was milling around near the colonnade, trying to keep out of the sun while waiting for the audience.

The practice of holding general audiences on the steps of the basilica had enormously simplified the task. He would be carried on his throne from the bronze doors leading to the palace, straight through to the center of the piazza. There, the throne bearers would make a right turn to the foot of the basilica's steps. At the center of the steps that ran the width of the building was a narrower, semicircular incline that rose to the level on which a wooden stand had been placed. This slope allowed the throne bearers to climb without having to negotiate the individual steps. Circling around the foot of the incline were eighteen concrete pillars, about three feet high, arranged so that the incline itself could be chained off. But today, as usual, there were no chains in place. There was, however, a corridor through the piazza, marked by wooden barricades, indicating the path that the throne bearers would take.

Twice during the morning he had walked off the distances. It was fifty-four paces from the edge of the colonnade to the middle of the piazza, and forty-one paces from that spot to the corridor between the two center posts. He intended to execute the contract when the throne bearers had covered about thirty-eight paces from the middle of the piazza.

There was nothing left for Willie to do now but stand and wait and make certain that no fat nun elbowed him out of his place. He undoubtedly wished that he could smoke a little pot to steady his nerves but that would have to be postponed until he was back in New York. At least the sun was slipping below the top of the church and cool shadows were creeping nearer to him. The appointment was at 4:05 P.M. There would be a car waiting for him at 4:18 by the open-air market along the southwest wall of Vatican City. He would be driven, neither so fast nor so slow as to attract attention, to Florence. He would spend two nights there at the Hotel Lungarno. Then he would take a train to Milan and fly to London. After several more days, he would fly to Toronto and cross into the United States by car or bus. In leaving Milan, he would use a neatly forged diplomatic passport from Nigeria. In London, he would probably receive another passport. Instinctively he must have patted the left breast pocket of his jacket to feel the comforting bulk of the envelope that contained the first passport and the tickets from Florence to Milan, London, and Toronto.

Somewhere in the crowd, Willie knew, was a collaborator. There was no point in looking for him. Willie would not recognize him; nor was the man—or woman—supposed to know Willie. That way neither could betray the other if one were caught. Willie didn't care who the person was as long as he or she was a pro. The task was simple but critical: cause a diversion that would direct everyone's attention to another part of the piazza long enough to give Willie a few seconds. Willie did not know what the diversion would be.

A few minutes after 4 P.M. a pair of trumpets sounded inside the bronze doors, and a small procession got under way. Willie could make out flashes of color within the barricaded corridor. He could see a figure in white being carried on a throne. In less than a minute the cortege reached the middle of the piazza. Willie's view became clearer. He slowly reached inside his cassock and jacket and gingerly removed the 38 from his shoulder holster. The silencer made it awkward to handle the weapon secretively in the jostling crowd. On the other hand, the crowd's pushing and shoving also made his movements less obvious. He deftly slid the pistol inside the shopping bag.

Now the figure on the throne was less than twenty paces away. He was a tall man, handsome by whitey's standards. He was still muscular, with clipped grey hair, a short but full grizzled beard, bright, hard eyes, and a long scar that ran from his left eye back along the temple. Willie had never seen the man before and must have been impressed by his obvious toughness. The excited screams of *"il Papa! il Papa!"* were deafening. The Swiss Guards alongside him were alert to keep the crowd from overturning the barricades protecting the corridor.

As the man on the throne turned toward Willie and lifted his hand to make the sign of the cross, there was a sudden explosion in the fountain nearer the palace. Two thick trails of green smoke rose up—a small bomb plus two smoke grenades. It was simple, but enough to send a number of people in the emotional crowd into screaming panic. The throne bearers stopped. Then they lowered their load, lest the passenger be injured if they themselves were thrown off balance. Willie carefully rested his arm against the concrete pillar, pointed the bag, and gently squeezed the trigger twice. Both bullets struck home, and the man toppled backwards off the throne.

"Il Negro! Il Negro!" a shrill voice screamed in Willie's ear. A heavy hand slammed his wrist against the concrete post, knocking the bag and pistol out of his grasp. A shout of *"Assassino!"* and the sight of the pistol focused the hysterical crowd's attention on Willie. He might not have glimpsed the calm, cold eyes of his assailant, but he must have realized that his discovery had not been accidental. He never felt the fists and kicks of the angry mob. The burning, twisting thrust of steel between his ribs came first.

On the right side of the throne, the Swiss Guards were still unaware of the shooting, but they were desperately fighting to keep the suddenly surging crowd away from the Sedia Gestatoria. On the left side, they were trying vainly to separate the raging mob from their victim. I was walking in the barricaded corridor about ten steps behind the throne. For a few moments I was the only one who both knew what had happened and paid any attention to him, but I couldn't get to him because too many of the mob were running across the corridor between us.

The impact of the bullets had knocked him off the throne onto the cobblestones of the piazza. He struggled to his knees and began climbing up the incline toward St. Peter's. He must have been bewildered by the noise. His head had to be spinning. Now the fog began to clear. He could have been wandering through the twisting streets of the Trastevere looking for his father. Or was it the surf and beach of Iwo Jima? No, the floor would have felt more like rocks. There had only been soft, black volcanic ash on Iwo. He must be on Caspar. That was it, Caspar. Silk Hat Six. He was Silk Hat Six, leading the counter-attack on Hill 915 where Johnny Kasten was still holding out. I saw him rise up a bit and cock his head to listen. A machine gun was probably tapping out "shave and a haircut," then SOS. He might have heard the roar of the planes diving and have seen the bright orange flashes of napalm. "Silk Hat, Silk Hat," his radio must have crackled. I tried to reach him, but I couldn't quite make it. Somebody knocked me down, but I was close enough to hear him answer, "This is Silk Hat Six. Over," enunciating the words clearly, as one must for a radio transmission. He had to get to the top, but it was difficult to move, not painful, just difficult. His legs would only feebly respond. "Johnny! Johnny!" he called out. Where was Johnny Kasten? There was a babble of other voices, of screams and curses. He probably thought it was the wounded.

With a tremendous effort he pulled himself to his feet. He looked at the thick spouts of crimson blotching the white of his cassock. "Good God, I've been hit again," he said as he fell forward and once again began crawling toward the top of Caspar. It must have been getting dark quickly for him. I could hear him distinctly say the same words he had spoken to Guicciardini on Caspar before the counterattack: *Introibo ad altare Dei, ad Deum qui laetificat juventutem meam.* "I shall go unto the altar of God, to God who giveth joy to my youth."

His hand reached out to pull himself farther up the mountain. I grabbed his shoulders to help him. Then he relaxed. He was at the top now. Johnny Kasten must be there. He would be smiling a smile of peace, not the grotesque grin of the violently murdered. Once more he pulled himself erect and opened his arms. "Johnny!" he shouted. Then, before I could tighten my grip, the lifeless body of the bishop of Rome rolled back down the incline, leaving a bloody trail that ran onto the cobblestoned floor of the piazza.

THREE

THE CHURCH OBSERVED only three rather than the traditional nine days of mourning for a dead Pope. But the funeral was no less ostentatious than that of his predecessors. His will specified that his body should lie in state in St. Peter's itself rather than in the Lateran, and only for a period of seventy-two hours. After that he was not to be buried in either basilica but in the floor of the piazza at the foot of the small obelisk. In death as in life, Paolo Cardinal Fieschi carried out the slightest papal whim.

The short period of official mourning encouraged crowds in Rome. People lined up in double files stretching all the way through the piazza, down the Via della Conciliazione almost to the Tiber. The basilica had to be kept open for the entire seventy-two hours to allow a portion of the crowds to pass by the body.

Not even the miracles ceased. No less than seven people claimed cures from touching the plain cypress coffin. Once the news spread, the huge crowds were quickly swollen by the old, the ill, and the pitiful of southern Italy. Fights for places in line were frequent. Verbal disputes sometimes flashed into violence. Three people were stabbed, one fatally. The police made no effort to count the number of fights from which casualties were not hospitalized.

There were several other stipulations in his will regarding the funeral rites. An emotionally crushed Fieschi carried them out to the letter. At ten on the morning of the burial, the entire eighty-two members of the sacred college who were present in Rome marched in slow, solemn procession from the Sistine Chapel within the papal palace to the makeshift altar in front of the basilica. There High Mass was sung in Latin. It was concelebrated by Cardinals Martìn, Mwinjamba, Su, Tascherau, and Fieschi. Throughout the ceremony, the huge bells of St. Peter's tolled in heavy mourning. Elena Falconi, Sidney Michael Keller, and I had seats in the first row. Next to us were heads of state and very senior diplomats. As the Mass began, Cardinal Galeotti left the altar and sat with us.

The Church ineffectively forbids preaching a eulogy over a dead body. Priests have always been able to eulogize under the guise of a homily. At the conclusion of the Mass, Cardinal Galeotti left us and walked to the front of the altar.

"I read you two documents," he said in English then in Italian. "First are the opening paragraphs of the message that Papa Francesco would have delivered to the general audience on the day he was killed:

> We have a vision of the kingdom of God with us and within us, of mankind fired by love rather than hate, moved by justice rather than greed. That vision can only become reality when every one of us rejects nationalism and racism and materialism and all other

political and economic "isms," and in their place accepts the fundamental notion that we are, each of us, brothers and sisters, children of the same Father. That vision can only become reality when each of us admits that all men and women have an equal right, if not to all things, at least to those necessary to feed, clothe, house, educate, and protect themselves and their families.

That vision can only become reality when each of us also accepts the hard fact that true happiness cannot be found in the transitory pleasures of this world. Thus we must realize that amassing material goods is not merely useless but dangerous. "Remember," Christ said, "where your treasure is, there your heart is also." We must also realize that we cannot love our brother if we kill him *en masse* in the name of that pagan idol, the nation state. "Thou shalt not have false gods before me" includes nations as well as graven images. We cannot render unto Caesar the supreme obedience that is due only unto God. "Thou shalt not kill" admits of no exception to please Caesar.

We urge you not to be distracted by personal or national ambitions from your true goals: to achieve here on earth, in our exile, that full development as human beings that can only be attained by giving ourselves totally to God and to His other children; and, by achieving our full humanity to win eternal happiness in the next world."

Galeotti paused and looked around the great piazza. "Only God can now judge Papa Francesco, but I say in truth that this vision is neither more nor less than that of the gospel of Christ. To preach that gospel is the duty of His Church, of His clergy, and of all His people. Papa Francesco wanted us to preach that gospel as he did: by deeds, not merely by words; by deeds of peace, not of war."

Again Galeotti gave us a few moments to digest his words, and then he read the second document, a small variation on the burial prayer of the Essenes, as recorded by Nikos Kazantzakis. The will directed that it be read over the body:

> Once you were dust; to dust return. The soul that fed you has fled. Depart, for your work is now done. You helped this weak man to walk, to pray, and to get up and walk again when he stumbled and fell. You helped him when he knew pain and despair, joy and hope, even glimpses of faith. Those needs are ended; flesh, dissolve.

Galeotti rejoined us; then two honor guards formed at the head of the procession. One was a platoon of Swiss Guards in their full Renaissance regalia. The second was a platoon of blue and scarlet-uniformed United States Marines. Both formations were unarmed. Next came the Sacred College of Cardinals, each prince clad in a gold chasuble and white mitre. Immediately behind the catafalque marched the U.S. Marine Band. As the procession organized near the altar, the papal choir began chanting "The Battle Hymn of the Republic." It was not a display of ecumenism, but another specific order in his will that that hymn be played. As soon as the procession began to move, the marine band took up the music, shifting the soft chant of the choir into the powerful mood of the marching song of a victorious army. The words were picked up and sung by the seminarians from the North American College. An Irish journalist caught the scene perfectly. Let me read you what he wrote:

> The pageantry was an exotic medley of ritual Romana and martial Americana: cardinals trying to march to the beat of the marines' drums while the voices of the choir and seminarians echoed from the façade of the great basilica and the colonnades of the piazza. The chorus was taken up by some of the prelates who knew English, then by those in the vast crowd who had any knowledge—and by thousands who had no knowledge—of the language. The words of the Civil War battle song rolled ponderously around the piazza: "Mine eyes have seen the glory of the coming of the Lord. He is trampling out the vintage where the grapes of wrath were sown. . . . His truth is marching

on. Glory, Glory, Hallelujah, His truth is marching on."

Perhaps the crowd, moved by sorrow as deep and genuine as one ever sees in this city of cynical playacting, was stirred by the thunder in the beat of the hymn's martial cadence; perhaps some who understood English appreciated the appropriateness of the reference to the "terrible swift sword"; or perhaps some even thought that God's truth was marching on. In Rome one cannot say. Even Romans find it difficult to tell when their playacting ends and their real emotions begin. In any case, the tears, as always, were genuine.

Once the catafalque had been gently pushed down the incline from the basilica to the floor of the piazza, his throne bearers, sweating under his weight for the final time, picked up the casket and carried it to the dark hole at the base of the obelisk. The sacred college formed a hollow square around the grave. Eight *sampietrini* swiftly filled the hole with red Roman clay, like that on the dead Palatine Hill. They then replaced the cobblestones. The cardinals chanted a few more prayers and afterward strode to the bronze doors while the band retreated to the basilica, the drums now beating at quick time. The Swiss Guards positioned themselves around the grave. The dead had been buried. Still, most of the crowd lingered. Some for a few minutes, many for a few hours, kneeling and praying at the grave.

Several days later the *sampietrini* returned and reopened the hole. They replaced the red clay with cement, to prevent vandals from stealing the body. Then they embedded a small bronze plaque in the piazza floor to mark the grave.

I don't know who was responsible for the assassination, who paid the bill. Willie was a pro; he killed only for money. I've told you that I spent months investigating. So did a lot of people better at it than I. If they know, they aren't saying. It could have been a plot engineered by a lunatic, by our CIA, the Soviet KGB, the British M16, the PLO, or even the IRA. It could have been a wild hope of a free-lancer or the Brazilian junta's revenge. They all had reasons. So did a dozen other countries, including the Egyptians and the Spanish. But what difference does it make? He was a seditionist. My friend from the CIA was absolutely right. His doctrine was subversive of the world's ways. What he was preaching inevitably led to a demand for a total revolution in values and behavior in the West, in the East, and in all the Third World that I know. Sooner or later one of the defenders of a political system would find that threat too menacing to live with. I guess we all—he, certainly—knew that.

The life cycle of the Church went on. Following the *motu proprio* he had issued in response to Cardinal Galeotti's suggestion, the conclave opened three days after the funeral. Many reporters saw Cardinal Fieschi, as *camerlengo* and secretary of state, as more *papabile* than ever. The more sophisticated were betting on Rauch. The more cynical predicted temporizing compromise and picked Galeotti.

Eight days later, a few moments before noon on a warm and brilliant Roman day, I was standing in the piazza when the senior cardinal-deacon appeared on the loggia of St. Peter's. He repeated the ancient formula: "I announce you a great joy. We have a Pope. He is My Eminent and Revered Lord, Mario Cardinal Chelli. He has chosen to reign under the name of Boniface."

The crowd in the piazza went wild. The new Pope spent almost an hour responding to ecstatic cheers of *"Evviva il Papa! 'Viva il Papa! 'Viva il Papa!"* As the noise reverberated around the giant piazza, I walked to the foot of the obelisk and read the small bronze marker:

HIC JACET FRANCISCUS I
VICARIUS CHRISTI

Here lies Francesco I, the Vicar of Christ.